TEN REALMS: BOOK 7

The Seventh Realm

Part 1

MICHAEL CHATFIELD

Cover Art by Jan Becerikli Garrido
Jacket Design by Caitlin Greer
Interior Design by Caitlin Greer

eBook ISBN: 978-1-989377-88-8
Paperback ISBN: 978-1-989377-87-1

Prologue

Commander Stassov of the Frigate *Eternus* sat at her desk reading through reports. Her cabin was sectioned off into a large office with equally large windows, private quarters, and a seating area, all richly appointed with Expert-grade furniture from across the seventh realm. Red, green, and white lines danced across her features, emphasizing her beauty rather than overwhelming it. Her eyes glowed with power, but they weren't washed out, showing reds, greens, blacks, and blues. To complete the ensemble, she wore a black cloak with red thread that made powerful, yet beautiful formations.

She looked up at the knock on her cabin door. "Come in."

Gregor, her second in command and leader of her personal dungeon hunters, stepped into the room. He was a brawny man with wild hair and beard, and rarely looked anything but serious in his red-and-black armor. A green ink tattoo trailed out of his hairline to under his left eye and down his cheek, tracing down his neck, drawn in formation.

He ushered in a young man with tanned skin, chestnut brown hair, and low cultivation for the seventh realm. A simple-looking man, but there was intelligence in his eyes.

The guards closed the doors behind them as they bowed.

"Rise."

"Commander Stassov, this is Petros, one of our eyes and ears. He has some rather interesting but troubling information." He indicated for the man to step forward.

Stassov activated her sound canceling formation, cutting them off from the rest of the world. "Continue."

Petros's eyes studied the flooring, keeping his head half-bowed. "I was tasked with following one of the marshal's attendants, his niece Esther. While she doesn't have much pull in the military, she is effectively his ambassador. W-we lost track of her for some time."

"Where did she go?"

"The Fourth Realm."

Stassov frowned. The battlefield realm had little to interest forces from the Seventh Realm. "The Sha clans extend all the way down into the lower realms, but they are little threat to us."

"She didn't go to the Sha. I checked. I think she met with someone else."

The ambassador for the Sha wasn't going to go on a trip for her own interest at a time of war. She must have gone to the Fourth Realm for a reason. "Very well, Petros, head to the Fourth Realm and find out where she went and what she was doing."

"Yes, Commander." Petros bowed, hiding his grimace, and left the room.

Gregor shut the door behind him. "Do you want me to inform the rest of the clan?"

"Not at this time; it could just be a rumor. Petros will find out more for us. No one likes going to the lower realms with all that sparse mana."

"Yes, commander." Gregor bowed and left the room.

Stassov turned her chair and stood, moving to the windows and looking out upon the sky above and the land far below.

1 Queens and Sect Heads

Lord Salyn marched across the polished floors. Armored knights opened the grand door of the Shikoshi Kingdom's throne room ahead of him. He lowered his gaze to the red carpet fringed with silver. His pace didn't slow as he felt her knights' sharp eyes on his body.

He stopped himself from gritting his teeth, conscious of his muddied riding leathers and boots. He hadn't dared to delay her summons.

"Queen Ikku." He dropped to one knee and bowed before her throne. Her fine silk gown of blacks, reds, and golds with detailed needlework depicting dragons and tigers fighting one another spread out before her.

"I am told the group you returned with is much smaller than you promised it would be, Lord Salyn." Queen Ikku sounded regal, far older than her thirty-year-old appearance, but she had been born and trained in her position and all its subtleties.

The hairs on the back of his neck rose; his life teetering on the edge as sweat trickled down his back. "Your Majesty, the conspirators fled into the Beast Mountain Range to a place called King's Hill. They recruited the help of a group called the Alva Healing House to make good on their escape."

Queen Ikku was silent. Salyn kept his head bowed, despite wishing he could see her expression. If he could deflect her ire, he could destroy the Alva Healing House in one move and remain clear of any blame.

"This Alva Healing House, are they independent?" Queen Ikku asked.

"They have close ties to the leadership of King's Hill. I do not know if they are connected to others. I request your permission to return to investigate the Alva Healing House and track down the conspirators." Salyn's nerves drained into his words. He half-raised his head before ducking back down and swallowing hard.

Silence dragged on as Queen Ikku tapped her finger on the armrest of her throne. "King's Hill is the new outpost in the middle of the Beast Mountain Range? The heart of the outpost leader's alliance?"

Advisor Vesair cleared his throat. "Yes, my queen. The outpost leaders created two alliances. One wanted to control the Beast Mountain Range as a kingdom and harvest the beasts within to increase their power. The other group wanted to stabilize the area and increase trade with one another and the outside world. The trading alliance won."

"Do you think they were behind this?"

"I dare not make any conclusions," Vesair stated.

"If I was to ask you to guess?" There was a cold playfulness in Ikku's voice.

"As the queen commands." He cleared his throat to collect his thoughts. "The trading alliance, while focused on creating connections with the surrounding nations, are not simple traders. They make use of spies and use tactics to strike at their enemy without employing their complete military. They are newly formed; a small disturbance and it could all come apart. They are just outpost leaders, after all. They have not run a nation. Their military is divided, though they do live in an area of powerful beasts. While they might not have many soldiers, they have to be strong to deal with the number of mercenaries in the area."

"A healing house is not a small power to be annoyed. Are they linked to the major healing houses?"

Salyn felt Queen Ikku's gaze on him. "They are only located in Vermire and King's Hill. The leader of the alliance, Aditya, was the leader of Vermire first."

His leg cramped as the tension in his neck built in the silence that answered him. His upbringing as a lord didn't allow his expression to change. *Does she know?*

"Raise your head, Lord Salyn," Queen Ikku's voice settled his nerves as he hid his micro-stretches. She had a graceful beauty and a stillness about her that came with a lifetime of practice. Her lips gave out death sentences just as easily as they gave praise. Her eyes were unreadable as she snapped her fan together, tapping it against her chin. "Vesair, you will craft a letter, in my name, demanding that this Aditya hand over the members of the healing house, or he will force us to act. Lord Salyn, you will find these conspirators and bring them to me or bring me their bodies. I will not accept anything less."

"Yes, my queen." Salyn bowed his head deeply again.

"This alliance of outpost leaders grows too bold if they think they can step over my head and steal from me. They should remember who the true leaders of the land are." There was heat in her words as she tilted her head to the side. "Tell this Aditya to submit to me and I will think about not pursuing the connection between him and this healing house. Suggest that if the conspirators were to reappear, it would make things easier. Also, send word to people in the alliance. Tell them that if they are willing to remove Aditya from power, then we would be interested in trading with them."

"Yes, Majesty." Vesair bowed his head.

Such actions would destabilize the alliance, pull them into chaos, and could take down everything they had worked for. Even if he couldn't find the conspirators, bringing her a reason to take over a new territory should be enough.

"Lord Salyn, you will leave tomorrow. I will send a group of Red Falcons with you."

Her knights had the best training and gear, and were completely loyal to Queen Ikku. She often sent them to remote locations across her kingdom to assert her rule. They acted in her name and there was no power greater than them. But, if they figured out who the Alvan people were, they would find out about the village he had created in secret.

The chill on his neck returned before it had truly faded. "Y-yes, my queen, I will make preparations right away."

High Elder Cai Bo's face was emotionless as she marched into the Willful Institute's headquarters, her head raised high as her guards flanked her. She had returned directly from Vuzgal, reeling from the knowledge that war was coming, and yet the people within the institute were *still* attacking one another for position. They were Idiots! All of them. Their enemy would take that as a sign of weakness, leaving them open to even more attacks.

People moved out of their path, whispering to one another in her wake.

She let out a long breath through her nose. Her group dispersed as they got closer to a pair of doors protected by guards wearing the Institute's Head's personal seal. The room inside was filled with low murmurs, promises of security, confirmation of support, and furtive glances to opposition they had never seen eye to eye with. It was more like a dark swamp with concealed dangers than the sect's high table.

She stopped herself from showing her derision at their little games and took her seat at the table as representative of the Cai Family. It was one of the weakest groups, and rumors of how she had gained the position were whispered in dark corners. She sat straight, but back in her chair, not wanting to draw attention to herself as she glanced at several powerful figures who lowered their eyes. *If they only knew.*

Asadi sat at the top of the table, a telltale vein on his neck pulsing. When he shifted in his seat, the High Elders quietened. He opened his mouth as his sound transmission device buzzed. He answered the call, his words whisked away by the formations. His expression turned from annoyance into calm.

Cai Bo's hairs rose. Dealing with someone who freely showed their emotions was much easier than someone who covered up everything.

He finished the call. "Meokar City has fallen."

Shocked silence created a vacuum in the room.

"They were attacking a Grey Peak Sect City who, somehow, gained support from the higher realms."

For years she had maneuvered and schemed, getting stronger groups under her banner. Many didn't even know they were allied through her. Now, it seemed that something or someone was trying to destabilize *her* Institute. Asadi thought he had power, but she commanded the hearts and minds of the leadership through contract and blood.

She didn't have to fake her anger.

The Head snorted and lowered himself back into his seat. His every action was a warning. "Our forces in the Third and Fourth Realms are mobilizing. Those in the Fourth who have bases in the Third are the first. Our enemies are drawing together a lot quicker than I was expecting. There are three armies moving on three of our cities in the Third Realm. They all have the backing of level fifty members. Their numbers are swelling as they hire on the Adventurer's Guild members. High Elder Cai Bo, were you able to get more information on this guild?"

Cai Bo bowed her head before she looked around the table. "I ran into the Adventurer's Guild in Vuzgal. They are one of the largest guilds in the city, if not the largest. They seem closely connected to the leadership. Through my sources, I found that they have early level forty fighters, though their cultivation appears higher than most people in the Fifth Realm. They purchased a massive number of weapons, armor, concoctions, training aids, and more from Vuzgal, and transported them into the lower realms. Their people are loyal and they have solid connections with the Fighter's Association and loose ones to the other associations."

"They have a lot of powerful experts too. They fielded an army of thousands at Meokar. Now they are sending out groups of five to fifty thousand to support the different battlefields against us," the Head concluded. "Cai Bo, do you think that if we asked for peace, paid them off, that they would take it?"

Cai Bo shook her head. "I don't think so. They're a new group, but they are determined and vicious. If we ask them to back off, they will double their attacks. I think their end goal is to wipe us out."

A high elder scoffed. "Some upstart guild thinks that they can eliminate us!"

"An upstart guild with members numbering in the hundreds of thousands. They are merely working as a support to these other groups, bolstering their numbers. Though it is enough to make other armies join in." The Head flicked his eyes to the high elder, silencing him before he studied the table in front of him. "Consolidate our locations in the Third Realm. Call all of our people back."

"Other groups will see us as weak and attack," Petrunas said.

"The enemy is coming at us from every direction. If we overextend, we will lose much more. We must hold on to the cities with the greatest value so that once this ends, we can recover quickly. Communicate with our allies, see what their stances are. Find where we can get more support."

"Our supplies and resources are low; it will hold back our development," another Elder argued.

"The factions will work together to share their resources," Asadi insisted.

There was a shift in the room as the high elders looked displeased and nervous.

"Are you refusing to carry out my orders, *again*?"

"It is not that, Head Asadi. My faction's resources are lower than ever.

We have been dealing with a number of price fluctuations, and there are issues with our contracts," Tolentino said.

"You as well? Bandit attacks weakened our trade routes and allowed new groups to take over protection." Petrunas glared at Ramus.

"I didn't order anything of the kind," Ramus growled. "I'll have the heads delivered to you from those that dared to create their own orders!"

"How convenient, seeing as how the dead can't say anything." Petrunas sneered.

They grunted, planting their feet, straining under an unseen weight. Their eyes washed over the room, turning pale at the Head's gaze.

"The factions will work *together!* Anyone found attacking or working against their fellow Institute members will have their cultivations, and their family's cultivation destroyed!"

2 Trouble in the First Realm

"What the hell was that!" Aditya rose from his seat and looked in the direction of where a wave of mana had come from.

Old Quan stood as well. "Is that—"

Pan Kun barged in through the door, his sword out and ready.

"Where's Evernight?" Aditya asked.

"Right here. I was coming to see you." Evernight walked into the room and kicked the door closed. She pulled out her sound transmission device, working it.

Pan Kun moved to the windows. "Doesn't seem to be any damage."

"What the hell was that? It felt like a massive pulse of mana," Aditya asked Evernight as she finished with her sound transmission device. *Did someone find us? Are we under attack?*

"Something happened in Alva. All the floors connected, and the power that was being stored is now being directed below. Don't know why or what is going on, yet. Orders are to mobilize, make sure that no one takes the opportunity to attack. Cover it up, say it was an anomaly," Evernight's answer stopped Aditya's spiraling thoughts.

"How did that much power get out? That will change things in the Beast Mountain Range. People will ask questions. They could find Alva, or if not, attack us thinking we have some great power or tool," Old Quan said.

"What kind of anomaly should we say?" Aditya asked.

"We're investigating," Evernight said.

"Tell the council to come up with a good explanation for why this happened. We need to distract the people." Aditya used his sound transmission device to send a message out to the other outpost leaders.

"I'll ready the army," Pan Kun said.

"I hope it didn't go beyond the Beast Mountain Range. Check the readiness of everyone. There are plenty of people with connections to the different powers surrounding King's Hill. Evernight, pass on any information you get on the surrounding forces moving."

"What?" Erik and Rugrat asked at the same time. Erik's brain fought to catch up. He already felt like there was a cannonball sitting on his chest, and he couldn't believe what he was hearing. Rugrat turned from his drawings.

They were in the Vuzgal City Lord's office, *their* office. Behind them, the window showed Vuzgal's growing sprawl between the distant mountain ranges. Modern apartment buildings mixed with massive estates, towering Sky Reaching Restaurants, and opulent Wandering Inns. Closer, one could see Association Circle where the Ten Realm's associations had settled down.

"Egbert collapsed, and the power of the linked dungeon floors reversed. Instead of going into the mana-storing formation, it shot through all the floors," Gong Jin, Captain of Special Team Three said with a dark expression.

"What the hell for?" Rugrat asked.

"Unknown. It seems structurally sound. People are ready to evacuate as we speak. Those that can have already left. Delilah reported that there has been a series of notifications from the dungeon itself."

Erik walked toward the door. "We're heading to Alva. Now."

Rugrat followed him. Gong Jin quickly talked into his sound transmission device.

Han Wu and a new member of Special Team Four were waiting outside. They followed Erik and the group as they strode out of their office.

People cleared a path as the group grew in size as they passed through offices and hallways. Gong Jin's team, which had been deployed at different points or resting, rushed to meet them.

Erik reached the main door of the castle and put his fingers in his mouth, letting out a piercing whistle.

"Protective detail to the totem. Get mounted!" Gong Jin ordered. They summoned their mounts from their storage crates, climbing onto their backs.

There was a growl from above as George flapped his wings, as large as two grown men. He halted his speed as he landed next to Rugrat, who swung his leg over George's back.

Gilly appeared through a side entrance, turning and sliding to a stop. Erik grabbed her harness and pulled himself up with practiced ease.

"Sirs, I suggest wearing masks," Gong Jin said.

Erik and Rugrat pulled out their masks as Gong Jin cast an illusion spell, covering everyone and altering the appearance of their weapons and armor. The masks shifted. One couldn't tell they were fakes unless they had a strong detection spell or touched their faces.

"Move out!" Gong Jin yelled.

The group snapped their reins. They picked up speed as Gong Jin guided them away from the main entrance into Vuzgal Castle and toward the academy. There was more traffic there, making it easier for them to blend in along the roads to the Vuzgal totem.

"Move it!" The leading special team members released some of their aura, clearing a path. The rest of the group's faces were emotionless, on edge, ready for anything.

The Ten Realms' totem, which connected all the different realms and cities across them, came into sight as they increased their pace. Defense gates around the totem opened, providing a clear path forward. Gilly pulled back, trying to slow her momentum as Gong Jin worked the totem controls.

Vuzgal disappeared; Alva and status screens appeared as a flood of experience hit Erik and Rugrat.

Quest Complete: Restoring Beast Mountains Dungeon Part 1
Congratulations! You have taken control of the Beast Mountains Dungeon. Its condition isn't the best, and it will require work to repair. I hope you brought a hammer! Or crafters.
Requirements:
Repair the main Mana Gathering formation Repair the secondary Mana Gathering formations (10/10) Repair the Metal Beast controlling formations (3/3) Repair the containment formation Repair containment formation sub-arrays (12/12)

Repair the Metal Floor's Main Control formation Repair Metal Floor's Secondary control formations (12/12)
Rewards: Up to 200 ore per day +100 Sky Mana stones per day +1,200,000 EXP

Quest Complete: Restoring Beast Mountains Dungeon Part 2
Congratulations! You have taken control of the Beast Mountains Dungeon. Its condition isn't the best, and it will require work to repair. I hope you brought a hammer! Or crafters.
Requirements: Repair the main Mana Gathering formation Repair the secondary Mana Gathering formations (10/10) Repair the Earth Beast controlling formations (3/3) Repair the containment formation Repair containment formation sub-arrays (12/12) Repair the Earth Floor's Main Control formation Repair Earth Floor's Secondary control formations (12/12)
Rewards: +1,200,000 EXP

Quest Complete: Restoring Beast Mountains Dungeon Part 3
Congratulations! You have taken control of the Beast Mountains Dungeon. Its condition isn't the best, and it will require work to repair. I hope you brought a hammer! Or crafters.
Requirements: Repair the main Mana Gathering formation Repair the secondary Mana Gathering formations (10/10) Repair the Fire Beast controlling formations (3/3) Repair the containment formation Repair containment formation sub-arrays (12/12) Repair the Fire Floor's Main Control formation Repair Fire Floor's Secondary control formations (12/12)
Rewards: +1,200,000 EXP

Quest Complete: Restoring Beast Mountains Dungeon Part 4
Congratulations! You have taken control of the Beast Mountains Dungeon. Its condition isn't the best, and it will require work to repair. I hope you brought a hammer! Or crafters.
Requirements: Repair the main Mana Gathering formation Repair the secondary Mana Gathering formations (10/10) Repair the Wood Beast controlling formations (3/3) Repair the containment formation Repair containment formation sub-arrays (12/12) Repair the Wood Floor's Main Control formation Repair Wood Floor's Secondary control formations (12/12)
Rewards: +1,200,000 EXP

Quest Complete: Restoring Beast Mountains Dungeon Part 5
Congratulations! You have taken control of the Beast Mountains Dungeon. Its condition isn't the best, and it will require work to repair. I hope you brought a hammer! Or crafters.
Requirements: Repair the main Mana Gathering formation Repair the secondary Mana Gathering formations (10/10) Repair the Water Beast controlling formations (3/3) Repair the containment formation Repair containment formation sub-arrays (12/12) Repair the Water Floor's Main Control formation Repair Water Floor's Secondary control formations (16/16)
Rewards: +1,200,000 EXP

Quest Complete: Restoring Beast Mountains Dungeon Part 6
Congratulations! You have taken control of the Beast Mountains Dungeon. Its condition isn't the best, and it will require work to repair. I hope you brought a hammer! Or crafters.
Requirements: Repair and Control the Metal floor Repair and Control the Earth floor

Repair and Control the Fire floor
Repair and Control the Wood floor
Repair and Control the Water floor
Repair and Control the Living floor

Rewards:

+1,200,000 EXP

Quest Completed: Dungeon Master

As the Master, you have returned your dungeon to its former glory. Advancement quests are unlocked. Grow your dungeon's power!

Requirements:

Increase your dungeon core's grade to Sky Grand

Rewards

60,000,000 EXP
Dungeon Master Title V

Quest: Upgrade the First Realm

Well, it looks like you went the hammer route! For the greatness of the Ten Realms, you are forging ahead! With your contributions, we will all become stronger!

Requirements:

Continue drilling into the depths of the First Realm.

Rewards:

Ten Realms Dukedom

Receive a Four-Star Hero Emblem; must be collected from the Tenth Imperium's Quartermaster

+400,000,000 EXP

Quest: Dungeon Master II

As Master, you have returned your dungeon to its former glory. Advancement quests are unlocked. Grow your dungeon's power!

Requirements:

Increase your dungeon core's grade to Celestial Common Grade

Rewards

100,000,000 EXP
Dungeon Master Title VI

You have reached Level 62

When you sleep next, you will be able to increase your attributes by: 5 points.

26,219,539/172,300,000 EXP till you reach Level 63

Erik glanced at the screens quickly, then flicked them away.

"Well, that's not supposed to happen," Rugrat said in a gruff voice.

"Let's hurry up." Erik pushed Rugrat toward the inner dungeon.

The illusion-breaking formation spells forcefully removed their disguises, revealing the masks as well as the Special Team members' gear. The Alva soldiers standing watch at the defensive structure around the totem lowered their weapons, standing at ease.

Erik gritted his teeth, waiting as they were cleared one by one by the guards and their scanning formations.

"The council is at the military command center. With the changes in the dungeon core, they had to evacuate the dungeon headquarters," Gong Jin reported as the last member was checked.

"Lead on, Captain," Erik ordered.

Gong Jin led them through the thick walls of the totem castle.

"Fuck me!" Rugrat stared at the dungeon headquarters.

Snow fell from above, but they could both feel the *pull* from the sheer power being channeled below.

"Shit," Erik agreed, glancing up at the mana stones above. He held out a hand, rubbing the shiny white snow between his fingers "This is dust from depleted mana stones."

Alva cast a beautiful sight: a land of stone and wooden houses intermixed with parks, small streams, and comfortable inns and bars. In the middle of it a pillar of light, five meters in diameter, connected the glowing ceiling, covered in mana stones, through the cylindrical Alva Dungeon Headquarters down below.

The pure, refined mana moved at such speeds and with so much volume that the very air shimmered around it. The plants —even those seen as weeds—were stronger than common ingredients in the second realm.

They rode toward the barracks and the command center underneath it.

What the hell did you do, Egbert? And what the hell is the Tenth Realm Imperium?

They arrived at the barracks. Word had made it ahead of them. Half the gate was opened for them to squeeze through. Soldiers wearing their complete body armor, with sealed helmets and their rifles at the ready, were watching over Alva. Their presence was ominous, though Erik couldn't help but look at them with pride, feeling reassured.

Erik and Rugrat dismounted before George and Gilly came to a complete stop in one of the parade squares. The barracks had been expanded, and a second barracks was being built adjacent to the teleportation pads.

The barracks were arranged like a nine-digit number pad. The outside squares were training areas, ringed by walls, sleeping quarters, cafeterias, and all the things the troops might need day-to-day. Walls separated it from the rest of the base. The interior square was its own world made up of classrooms, advanced training areas, medical facilities, as well as the command center of the Alva Military. It was the beating heart of Alva's military.

The special team members pulled on their helmets and drew their weapons, making sure they were loaded.

Gong Jin guided them through the stairwells and corridors as if the confusing maze underneath the barracks was his second home.

Erik and Rugrat wore their regular clothes: boots, hiking pants, long-sleeve insulated sweaters, t-shirts, and an expression that told one that they would go through whatever stood in their way.

Soldiers cleared a path. Doors of metal beeped, recognizing their identification medallions, and allowing them access.

Another scan and the special team members took positions outside of a doorway.

Erik opened the door.

"Wh—" Jia Feng's words died in her throat as everyone in the room glanced over.

Glosil, Yui, and their aides stood up. Glosil snapped off a salute.

"At ease." Erik snapped off a replying salute as Rugrat closed the door.

Glosil indicated two empty seats on either side of Delilah.

The young woman looked like she had aged overnight. Her expression was grim as she nodded at Erik, then Rugrat.

Egbert's skull lay behind Delilah on a table with formations carved into it. Roska and her people watched his bones with rifles drawn.

Erik nodded to them, took one of the rolling chairs, and pulled himself forward. "So, what the hell is going on? The dungeon was functioning perfectly before we left," Erik said, trying to inject some levity into the tense situation.

Their lips shifted slightly in the attempt, but there was little more.

Erik looked along the right side of the table. Jia Feng was head of Alva's Academies, the new Consortium in Beast Mountain Range, Kanesh Academy in Alva, and Vuzgal Academy that Erik and Rugrat had ridden through. Elise led the Trader's Guild, a powerhouse of a woman with the ability to move each of the lower realms with just a few orders. Thousands were under her direct command. It wasn't wrong to say that she was the reason that the Beast Mountain Range and Vuzgal had grown to their current power and remained stable. Blaze, the old leader of Alva Village and the Adventurer's Guild leader, a guild he had grown to hundreds of thousands of members across four realms and was looking to advance into the Fifth Realm.

Erik's eyes moved to the left side where he found Glosil the commander of Alva's forces, Alva Village's old guard captain and subordinate to Blaze, Colonel Yui Silaz—who led one of the two regiments of Alvan Soldiers—and, finally, Elan Silaz, Yui's father and Director of the Alva Intelligence Department, the spy leader of Alva.

His eyes tracked to Delilah beside him, who cleared her throat. Council Leader of Alva, and an expert alchemist, she was the true manager and ruler of all Alva. She was also his student, even though she had beaten him to the expert level of alchemy.

"Something that we weren't anticipating, and it seems the real purpose of the dungeon," Delilah said, taking charge. "Formation masters have been looking at everything. The formations that activated were buried in the old formations running through the dungeon. Simply put, we thought that all the power was going in one direction—up. Though it was all supposed to be going down."

"How did we not see this?" Rugrat asked, sitting down on her other side.

"When repairing the dungeon, we reverted everything back to the plans made by the gnomes, and then built on top of that. It was easier, at the time, to take someone else's plans and modify them instead of starting from scratch. It would have taken years to come up with our own formations and implement them," Jia Feng informed the table.

"This was the gnomes' real goal?" Erik asked.

Jia Feng shrugged.

"It must have been. They built the entire dungeon with this formation at the core," Delilah said.

"So, what the hell happened to Egbert?" Rugrat asked.

Mana drifted toward the skull. Lines and patterns appeared as parts looked like polished jade.

Glosil cleared his throat. "It didn't kill him. He's asleep. At least, we think he is. New runes that were not previously activated have now been activated and repaired. Davin grabbed him from the Water Floor. I stored the rest of him to make sure the runes don't continue to progress."

"I was the last person to talk to Egbert. He seemed as surprised as I was," Delilah said.

Erik raised an eyebrow at Glosil.

"He was a big driving force behind recovering the dungeon," Glosil explained. "The blast of mana that shot out has put a target on the Beast Mountain Range. He's also, conveniently, asleep. I trust Egbert, but with these new runes and changes, I'm not sure that we can trust whatever wakes up. He controls all the power in the dungeon and can use it in his spell casting."

Erik nodded. He would have done the same with limited information.

"It probably has something to do with the First Realm quest." Erik sat back, lacing his fingers behind his head, thinking.

"I saw that somewhere." Rugrat opened his screens and went through the recent deluge of screens.

"Quest?" Erik asked.

"Tap into the ley lines and make a mana well. Shit, those Gnomes had *cojones*," Rugrat hissed, interrupting Erik. His eyes raced through the description and started again.

"What are we dealing with?" Elan asked.

"Mana, shit tons of it." Rugrat was still reading. "Ley lines come in two categories, according to Tanya's research: pure and attribute. Usually, they're not that far down. They get too pressured, and they release their stored mana back into the Ten Realms, or create gems, mana stones, dungeon cores, and so on."

"In the First Realm, there have been very few instances of Ley Lines. They're rare as hell down here. Well, it looks like we found one. Though it is buried deep. I guess it makes sense, though. Mana isn't that dense, but as it goes down, the density increases and the pressure of the world would increase. So then… Shit. It's possible that it is stronger than any amount of mana we've seen before, denser, purer. Depends on how long it has been down there. Over time, it could have made massive mines, could have dungeon cores all over the damn place." Rugrat said.

"How do you know this?" Erik asked.

"The best smithies are located on or near Ley Lines to channel that power into the forge or into the weapons. I *do* read."

"When it comes to making pointy things," Erik muttered.

Glosil cleared his throat, stifling a grin. "So, what happens when we tap into this ley line?"

Rugrat opened his fist. "Bang? I'm not sure. There is no knowing how pressurized it is, or how much mana we're dealing with. Anything like that. We should get Tanya and some of her people looking at it. Easy way to think of it? Ley lines are to the realms what mana channels are to us humans."

Silence fell on the room; it was a lot to take in.

"We closed off mana storing formations where we could. We have teams removing the cornerstones. That is slowing it down, but any excess mana is being funneled through *all* the floors into the drill," Delilah explained. "Before you ask, we have no idea how long until it reaches these ley lines. Without knowing the current depth of the ley lines, we have no accurate way to guess. That is up to the experts to figure out. We have our own worries. When the mana changed direction, the massive influx of mana smashed into the ground and created two ripples; one was dense and short-lived, and the other lasted much longer and went further out."

"How exposed are we in the First Realm?" Erik asked.

"If every leader in the First Realm doesn't know about the mana wave coming from the Beast Mountain Range by now, they either have no friends or are on the other side of the planet," Elan answered.

Erik's body tensed, hot blood pumping through his chest.

"Have they taken action?"

"We haven't seen anything on the surface. People are talking to one another. Secret meetings are going on. We need to come up with an excuse and quick," Elan said.

"Aditya wants to change how people view this. Use it as an opportunity to promote the Consortium and get the interested parties to fight one another rather than the people of the Beast Mountain Range," Elise quickly interjected. "We need to get ahead of this."

Erik nodded, his head still resting on his hands as his eyes flicked to Glosil.

"All units have been activated and are on high alert. All reserve force members have been placed on notice."

"If we need to evacuate everyone from the mountain range?" Rugrat asked.

"We can evacuate them within fourteen hours, less if we move more people out now." Delilah sighed.

Elise shook her head. "Most of our people in the mountain range are traders. If we evacuate them, the whole economy will collapse. People will panic. We'd kill the Beast Mountain Range."

"We'll only do it if there is no other option," Erik agreed.

He took in a deep breath and let it out through his nose. They were already fighting one war across the realms. They didn't another one on their doorstep. His eyes fell on Blaze.

"For now, we cover it up, increase the trade, increase the number of mercenaries allowed into the area. Send out patrols to 'discover' what happened. What am I not thinking of?"

"We should keep the outpost leaders in the dark," Elan said. "It will make sure that people don't see through them. Have the Consortium step up. We need them to show their power. Have more people with powerful backgrounds join the school. I know some people in the First Realm whose children would increase the school's popularity."

"If the Trader's Guild puts out a message that joining the school will be harder than becoming a nation's King?" Elise gave a shadow of a smile.

"We can send more Adventurer's Guild members, have them back up what Aditya and his people are saying," Blaze added.

"We need something for them to discover," Yui said. "Something that will interest them, but not crave it so much that they are willing to take it at any cost. This is still the Ten Realms."

"Okay, what can we do?" Erik asked.

Delilah tapped her finger on the desk, thinking. "Release some of the weaker beasts we raised into the surrounding area without contracts. That way, other forces will think about the losses they will take if they want to exploit the range. Second, release a small dungeon. This will gain interest, but admittance is low. So even if one power was to take it over, while they would get some benefits, it wouldn't be massive."

Erik nodded. The plan was risky, but it gave just enough benefits and hindrances that it should work.

"If we release all those beasts, more people are going to die," Delilah said.

"The routes to and from the different cities and towns are heavily protected, and there is little chance of any beasts entering. The mercenaries and guilds have increased in strength enough that there's little to threaten them. This will allow the beast mountain range to increase their stock in beasts, and there are always people willing to take some risks for money. It is the way of the ten realms," Glosil said.

"When we tap that ley line there is no knowing what will happen," Rugrat said.

"Does anyone have any ideas?" Erik asked.

Jia Feng raised her hand.

"Go on."

"Prepare a story now for the people in the Beast Mountain Range. Have the formation masters work on creating mana-focusing formations. There are mana-storing formations on every level of the dungeon. We need to repair them, put in earth or sky mana cornerstones if we can. They should weaken the release of mana. The dungeon was created for this a few hundred years ago. We need to expand as fast as possible. The dungeon cores are growing faster than before. Increase the floors, upgrade them. I can direct the schools to help. Alva school will do the practical, the other schools the theoretical. With everyone working on the problem, we can figure it out."

"This is Alva, after all. We don't need to do everything ourselves," Rugrat grinned.

"Elan, your people will have their work cut out for them."

Erik smiled, seeing Delilah take charge. She didn't even look to him for confirmation. She'd truly grown into her role.

"Yes, Council Leader," Elan smiled.

"Seems to me that there is nothing that we can do in the short term, so we might as well deal with the second matter. The Willful Institute," Erik said, changing the subject.

Elan cleared his throat. "Head Asadi of the Willful Institute has made it clear that he's not happy about the inner strife inside his group. He might be the Head, but he is just one person, and the Institute is made up of thousands of people, which works well for us. The Willful Institute's factions are still fighting one another. With their focus internal, it has allowed us to make external advances." Elan opened his hand to Glosil. The two men worked closely together, operating as a single unit.

"Meokar was the opening we needed," Elan continued. "As soon as the Third Realm city collapsed, groups that were on the fence realized that the Willful Institute isn't as strong as it once was. With the work of the different teams, the Adventurer's Guild, crafters, the traders, and intelligence department, we've been gutting their bottom line, creating tensions and breaks in their alliances."

"With war upon them, they're isolated with few friends or lines of support. I think it is now time for phase two, as Captain Kanoa calls it: Operation Doomsday. A crippling strike against any Institute vulnerabilities, our final attack before the Institute has the time to put up their defenses."

Delilah glanced at Erik and then looked away with a pale expression.

"How extended are we?" Erik asked.

"We have two battalions deployed under Colonel Domonos, a battalion of the Air Force, and seven Army battalions in reserve. That doesn't include the reserve forces, which number forty thousand strong—traders, teachers, healers, farmers, and people in the Adventurer's Guild. The Adventurer's Guild has grown and matured. Those that operated in Meokar will reinforce the new units that are heading out to fight the Institute," Glosil explained.

"Have some veterans among them to stiffen them up," Rugrat recommended.

"Creates better command and control. So we're not just relying on the Alva Military members. I reduced the hiring costs for the Adventurer's Guild. That should allow us access to more battlefields," Blaze said.

"How are things within the Guild?" Erik asked

"Do I dare say, excited?" Blaze sighed and sat forward, resting his bulk on the table. "They were angry for a long time. All of them knew the story. Knew what the Institute did to us. Now, they want to get their own back. Want to fight for one another. Want to show that we won't be stepped on. Recruiting is through the damn roof. A guild taking on a sect? People love an underdog story."

"What do you think?" Rugrat asked.

"I think that we'll need those veterans. We'll need to introduce them slowly. War isn't something to rush into. If we take in green units, they'll collapse. As you said, the veterans will know what to expect somewhat. Give them a spine and make sure they don't go do something stupid." Blaze shrugged.

"How many people can you call on?"

"A hundred and fifty thousand fighters across the lower realms. We can get another two hundred and fifty thousand fighting in a couple of weeks," Blaze answered.

"Fuck, man! Really?" Rugrat sat forward, raising an eyebrow.

"Everyone is a fighter in the lower realms. No other path. Death is cheap and everywhere, unlike the higher realms. Eighty percent of our members come from the first two realms. Given resources and training, they're more loyal than the higher realm members. You give the order and they'll do what needs to be done." Blaze looked Rugrat dead in the eyes.

"Near thirty-five thousand are sworn to Alva, many of them are reservists."

The weight of command and the power that came with it settled on Erik. Glosil, Yui, Elan, Elise, Jia Feng, Delilah… Everyone in that room would follow Erik and Rugrat wherever and carry out their orders to their last breath.

It was a heavy burden and was never easy to shoulder.

"We need to decide what to do if the guild is attacked directly," Erik said.

"The Intelligence Department, the traders, and the military have come up with a plan for the people connected to the Adventurer's Guild," Glosil said.

"What do you mean?"

"The Willful Institute might be wounded, but they are not broken. If they want to, they could attack the guild members or their loved ones to influence you. We have picked out cities and locations for the Adventurer's Guild dependents to move to, away from the Willful Institute's eyes. Those sworn to Alva can use our network of locations, but those who are not, we have a plan to protect them as well."

Blaze nodded. "Makes sense, sects only have so much honor that you can see on the surface. If my people are worrying about their loved ones all the time, they won't be effective."

"We'll get together afterward and go over the details." Glosil and Blaze nodded to one another and looked back at the rest of the table.

"Very well, then. The next thing to talk about is recruits," Erik said, looking at Colonel Yui. He had taken command of all training since his brother was leading operations against the Willful Institute with Kanoa and his Air Force in support.

"At the end of the month, we will have nearly four thousand recruits turned into soldiers and a thousand into Air Force members. Every three months, we should have the same amount of people graduating. We are also secretly training the people of the Beast Mountain Range Military. We're teaching them similar to how we train the Adventurer's Guild; working on smaller unit tactics and with class abilities. So, ranged and melee units," Yui said.

Erik's eyes slid to Glosil and Elan. "What do you need to begin phase two?"

"Permission." Glosil seemed unaffected but there was a hunger, a cold determination, in his eyes.

Erik looked at Rugrat.

"Fuck 'em. We give them more time they're going to pull together. Operation Doomsday needs to be carried out sooner rather than later," Rugrat said.

"If we get discovered?"

"Tracing it back to us is going to be fucking hard. They might know that there is someone in the shadows, but when they have someone beating down their front gate, they can't care about the person stealing their apples from behind. We hit them now while they're trying to find their balance, and we open up a new hole in their defenses."

Erik grinned without an ounce of joy in his frigid blue eyes. "You have permission, Commander Glosil. Gut them."

"Sir." Glosil nodded.

"Rugrat and I will take care of our resident skeleton—"

"Erik—" Delilah started.

"We don't have a special team to waste on watching over him. We also have a binding contract with the sack of bones. We need him to recover as soon as possible."

"But—"

"Trust in us old men. We might not look like much, and our skills might have fallen behind, but there isn't anyone in Alva stronger than us," Rugrat reassured her.

"When did I say you were old?" Delilah muttered and blushed.

"You mean devious." Elise snorted with a smile.

"Stubborn more like," Blaze muttered.

"Like bulls." Glosil sighed and shook his head.

"Somewhat smart, at times." Elan's passive expression split into a smile.

"Did you hire this lot?" Erik said behind his hand to Rugrat.

"I thought you hired them?" Rugrat hissed back.

Delilah let out a breath through her nose, but there was a smile on her face.

"Look, Rugrat has wanted to kidnap Egbert for years. Made a belt and everything."

"Don't tell them about the belt!" Rugrat glared at Erik.

"Well, we only need his skull."

"All right." Rugrat pulled out a loop of chain with a formation on it with a meek smile.

"Go grab it," Erik closed his eyes. *How in the hell did I get lumped with this idiot?*

Rugrat pulled Egbert's skull off. As soon as it was off the table, the mana entering it increased. The speed that the new runes were created on his face increased. Rugrat activated the formation on the chain and stuck it to the back of Egbert's skull. He looped the chain around his belt, like a redneck barbarian with a magical skull on his hip. *Just need some furs and a club.*

"And on the plus side, he can't wear his short shorts because they don't have a belt loop," Erik added.

"Done. You can have Egbert's skull!" Jia Feng smacked the table. There was a semi-serious nodding of heads.

Delilah raised her eyebrow. "Very well. So, what will the two of you be doing?"

Rugrat adjusted Egbert's head, pushing his shocked jaw closed. He kept doing it, and it kept opening until his jaw fell off. He looked around in a panic, holding Egbert's jaw.

Erik cleared his throat. "I need to finish my metal tempering. I'm useless until that's done. Rugrat is combat-ready and capable. If you need him, Glosil, he's a motivated and powerful individual."

Rugrat pulled out some Alva rip tape and with a loud noise he tore off a long strip. Everyone looked over at his awkward smile and back to Glosil.

Rugrat Duct-taped the jaw back in place.

"You might both be too powerful. If you show up on the battlefield, you might be too strong. You are our trump card. We don't want to show you off right at the start."

"Our people are fighting for us. We're not going to sit in the rear," Erik's said resolutely.

Glosil closed his mouth, grimacing.

"The people need to see their leaders," Blaze said, helping out.

"All right, there are a number of non-combat missions, back up for different operations. You're right, you two are the strongest people we have right now, which is also why I would like to invite you to help out training people who are taking on new courses to get their qualifications. Medic, sharpshooter, tempering the body and their mana," Glosil finally agreed.

"Let us know where we can be the most use." Erik didn't want to push too much. It was putting Glosil in an awkward position and giving him more to worry about. "Just know, if you need us or this turns on us, then Rugrat and I will back up you and our people with everything we can muster."

Rugrat grunted in agreement as he secured his duct-taped skull and took the rest of Egbert's bones into his storage ring.

"Speaking of covering for people, we need to talk about Vuzgal, about Hiao Xen and Chonglu. I think it is time we made Chonglu the new acting city lord. If the Willful Institute comes for us and Hiao Xen is in power, it will make things look bad on him and the Blue Lotus. I don't want to piss off an association over this."

"Rugrat is right. The last thing we need is an association that needs to be angry with us to uphold their honor," Elise agreed.

"Delilah?" Erik asked.

"Get it done. Elan, make sure that he has the most up-to-date information. Elise, make sure that the merchants don't get bold with the new leader. Commander Glosil, can you increase security just in case? Erik, if you talk to Hiao Xen and Head Lu of the Blue Lotus, that could go a long way in making sure Hiao Xen and the Blue Lotus look good and keep them clear of us if there are any issues."

People jotted down notes. Delilah waited until they finished before patting the desk. "Anything else?" A glance told her all she needed to know. "We have a lot to do, and the Ten Realms doesn't wait on anyone. Operation Doomsday will commence. Chonglu will be promoted, and we'll settle everything in the Beast Mountain Range. Let's just hope there are no other surprises in the near future."

After the meeting, Erik quickly headed home and took a sleeping potion.

You have 5 attribute points to use.

Erik put two points into mana and three into mana regeneration, checking his stat sheet.

Name: Erik West	
Level: 62	Race: Human
Titles:	

From the Grave II *Blessed by Mana* *Dungeon Master IV* *Reverse Alchemist* *Poison Body* *Fire Body* *City Lord III* *Earth Soul* *Mana Reborn* *Wandering Hero*	
Strength: (Base 54) +51	1050
Agility: (Base 47) +75	682
Stamina: (Base 57) +35	1380
Mana: (Base 27) +79	1060
Mana Regeneration: (Base 30) +61	55.60/s
Stamina Regeneration: (Base 72) +59	27.20/s

3 Meokar

Colonel Domonos Silaz looked at Meokar. His hand was never far from his weapon. His rough complexion seemed to suit the sweat and dirt from several weeks of hard fighting and limited sleep. The wind from the mountains ran through the gaps in his armor as he stood on the wall of Meokar, looking over the once-proud city. Smoke rose from where different fires were burning out. Buildings had been smashed apart by attacks. The Willful Institute's castle was in a state of ruin. Those that had been left behind as the rear guard were turning into motes of light, their tombstones already looted.

Lieutenant Colonel Zukal cleared his throat as he walked up. "Seems that the Grey Peak Sect are eager to get us to move along with all the pleasantries."

"I think they might have figured out there was something else going on here. But they're polite enough to not say anything, and they hate the Willful Institute." Domonos looped his fingers under his breastplate.

"So, are we at war now?" Zukal asked.

"That's what Commander Glosil told me."

"Well, then." They stood there looking at Meokar without seeing it.

"Well, best get moving. Time waits for no man, and no Commander waits for a Colonel." Domonos grinned and stretched his shoulders in his armor. "Get our people ready to move. We head out in two hours. Have everyone ready to move out in thirty."

"Yes, sir. Where are we headed?"

"Several forces have recently hired the Adventurer's Guild. We will be linking up with reinforcements, adding in new blood, and then breaking up to go to the different battlefields. The veterans of Meokar will support and stiffen the other campaigns." Domonos pulled his fingers from his vest and turned to Zukal.

"What about the Regiment?" The close protection details, select veteran squads, and most of the command from the Dragon Regiment under Colonel Domonos had been part of the fight for Meokar. Any that hadn't been in the battle had operated secretly behind Willful Institute's lines, inside their cities. Only a few key members of the Adventurer's Guild knew about the Alva Military's involvement.

Others thought that they were veteran members of the Adventurer's Guild.

"Ours is not to question where we go, it is to go and do as we're told."

"Sir, yes, sir." Zukal mimicked a brand new private. The two officers broke into grins.

"We're breaking into three units. One will support Jasper, another Blaze. The third will stay with us. We're heading to another city in the Third Realm. We'll get more information once we meet up with our reinforcements."

"Yes, sir. I'll make sure they're ready to move."

"Good man."

Zukal headed off.

Domonos shifted his sweaty armor some more. Around him, people rested where they were. Organized in an all-around defense, they sat where they could, talking to one another in hushed tones.

Closing his eyes, he recalled the flashes of light from the impacts of the penetrators, the rumble of thunder, the dust storm that was thrown up. Everything from leaving Reynir to arriving at this moment. If someone were to ask him about it, it would be a blur of actions followed by reactions, plans falling apart, and being thrown back together again.

Now, as he stood there, it all came back to him in startling clarity. Like a student before a grandmaster, he studied everything he had done. He had fought in competitions before, against small groups, one-on-one… But had never participated in a battle on such a scale. He'd trained and trained and trained. His first battle had gone off without any major fuck-ups, but instead of relief, he felt that he had much further to go. A moment of indecision had allowed the enemy to get ahead of them, and he felt a great pressure to perform better next time.

4 Uproar Within Alva

Erik crossed his arms as the close protection details marched toward the totem. They had dressed in civilian clothing, and some were acting as guards for traders.

"Feels wrong," Rugrat said, standing beside him at the window.

"We're used to being the people deployed, not the ones sitting back and watching it all going on," Erik agreed.

The silence stretched.

"Fuck. I feel like a fucking... I don't know, something useless." Rugrat went back to his desk and dropped into his seat. His desk was covered in blueprints of his new railguns. Egbert's skull, still showing faint lines, sat in a corner of the room in a restrictive formation.

"It's not some small village facing a horde of beasts anymore." Erik turned from the window.

Rugrat raised a palm. "I know, but we're always at the rear of this shit now. Grates on me. We should be out with the special teams at least."

"I get that, but if we show too much power too soon, then everything could come the hell apart. Until we're needed, we train. We get stronger so that if we are needed, we can destroy anything and everything in our way. That doesn't mean that we shouldn't *ever* be used." Erik's voice turned cold.

Instead of shivering, Rugrat's mouth lifted slightly, and he nodded.

"Sure, but it feels like we're always being held back. Erik, that isn't us."

Erik uncrossed his arms, shrugging. "Well, what the hell do you want to do?"

"Hell if I know!" Rugrat smashed his hands into his desk, breaking it. "Mother fucker!" He barked and kicked away from the desk, standing up from his chair.

Erik didn't say anything, waiting. Rugrat was a powder keg right now.

"Fuck! There's nothing to do but train more, make more weapons! Shit, I'm a marine, first and foremost."

"And sometimes we have to do the shitty things, waiting for the right time to strike. It's harder because we can see everything that's going on."

Rugrat grunted, seeming to calm down somewhat. He took a deep breath, letting out his anger. "So, more training."

"More training." Erik flexed his arm. The cracked coal-like skin and silver mercury veins had spread into his hands now. The spread had moved through his entire body. Only a necklace at the base of his neck was stopping the progression to his head.

He looked up from his broken body. He needed to work through his metal tempering—and fast. He could barely call forward forty percent of his strength.

Erik took a quick glance at his body cultivation quest.

Quest: Body Cultivation 4
The path cultivating one's body is not easy. To stand at the top, one must forge their own path forward.
Requirements: Reach Body like Diamond
Rewards: +24 to Strength +24 to Agility +24 to Stamina +40 to Stamina Regeneration +100,000,000 EXP

If Egbert was awake, he could ask his advice. He had looked in the library but hadn't found anything useful. Not many had made it to this high a cultivation in the lower realms. There would be more information in the higher realms.

"How is your Mana cultivation?" Erik asked as he looked at those quests as well.

Quest: Mana Cultivation 2
The path cultivating one's mana is not easy. To stand at the top, one must forge their own path forward.
Requirements: Reach Vapor Mana Core
Rewards: +20 to Mana +20 to Mana Regeneration +50,000,000 EXP

"I formed my liquid core and I'm working toward my solid core," Rugrat said

"We didn't get much time in the last couple of months to increase our cultivation. Just think of this time like consolidating our gains."

"I fucking hate when you say consolidating our gains. We increased in levels. Isn't that enough?"

"You know it's not. Levels were great when we were weak. Now the biggest changes come from cultivation and from our gear. Increasing our levels adds, certainly, but not nearly as fast."

"Maybe we can absorb enough mana to calm down that fricking drill," Rugrat suggested, finally getting into it.

"Way of the Ten Realms, right? On one hand, we'll tap right into the Ten Realms. On the other, it could turn the entire First Realm against us."

"Dancing on the blade's edge: exciting as hell, boring as hell, and fucking scary all at the same damn time."

There was a knock at the door. It opened to reveal Gong Jin. "Are you ready to head to Alva?"

"Time we accelerated things there," Rugrat said, clearing his desk. "I'll check in on the weapons development afterward."

"I've got an appointment with Bouchard about my metal tempering." Erik grunted as he stood up. Now, just moving took a lot out of him.

"You good?" Rugrat asked.

"Never better. Let's make sure the Beast Mountain Range is still standing."

Erik and Rugrat appeared in Alva. Nervous energy filled the living floor of the dungeon. People glanced at the open space in the middle of the floor. The pillar of mana no longer shot up into the mana storing formation. For the first time since the dungeon core had been activated, the air above the dungeon core was empty.

If one looked at the dungeon core itself, it was still gathering mana, compressing and turning it into a spiraling drill of power, directed below. The city was darker as the mana storing formation weakened, supplying the city with power and burning up in the process. As the mana stones burned up, powder like ash or snow occasionally fell to the ground to be swept away.

Formations along the walls carried power into the city now.

There were fewer people in the streets. Many had headed off to secure locations, though it wasn't quite a ghost town.

"I'm going to head to supply depot two. Good luck with your cultivation," Rugrat said.

"All right, have fun with your factory lines."

Rugrat gave him a wave and headed to the outer reaches of the dungeon. The floor had expanded so much that the teleportation pads along the outer edge of the living floor were now only a third of the way out to the center of the city.

George jumped off Rugrat's shoulders and dropped to the ground.

"You can go off and play. Don't get into trouble."

George barked. He expanded in size and went back to the teleportation pad, probably to head to the fire floor again. *Give him and Davin something to do.*

Rugrat glanced at the members of Special Team Three that had been assigned to protect him. They were scanning for threats even now.

People might be scared of the changes occurring in the dungeon, but they were focused. Alva had given them everything. Most of them had little more than the clothes on their backs when they arrived. Now they were powerful crafters, rich merchants, happy shop owners, and strong soldiers.

Alva was much more than their origin; it was the place where they had recreated themselves. Soldiers marched through the floor, helping fellow citizens, happy to assist as needed. Merchants reported to the supply depots, adding ammunition, armor, and medical supplies to their loads to pass on to the units preparing for battle against the Willful Institute.

Two thousand people applied to join the Vuzgal military a month, four hundred a month in the Beast Mountain Range, and even more joined the Adventurer's Guild.

Rugrat didn't know what to think of it all. He took out some plans and studied them as he walked. It was something that he understood.

He passed through a guarded checkpoint, entering the supply depot. Inside, the warehouses were just iron beams with machinery functioning within. Crafters walked up and down the lines, making sure that they were operating as required. Ammunition for rifles, grenade launchers, mortars, railguns, and repeaters were produced. Thousands of rounds of ammunition were made per hour on assembly lines across Alva and Vuzgal.

The people working the lines were recognized as crafters by the Ten Realms, but they'd only been introduced to the career path a few days or weeks ago. They were part of a new cohort of quality testers and factory workers. Their task was to take crafters' specialized knowledge and crank it out *en masse.*

Armor, pants, shirts, MRE's, and medical supplies, potions, IV setups, and gauze... The infrastructure was massive, and it had been operating without pause.

Rugrat headed for one of the newest assembly lines.

"Fancy seeing you here," Rugrat said to Taran, holding his fist out to his old friend and fellow Expert Smith.

Taran bumped his fist back. "I was making friggin' nails when you showed up in Alva. Now I'm working on railguns."

"Change of pace. How is the secondary barrel assembly line?"

"Slow. It was the first assembly line built, after all. Not armor or rounds. Those things are much easier to produce. We've got all kinds of parts and formations. Not as complicated as the semi and full auto rifles, thankfully. Our production is already higher than the rifle assembly lines."

Rugrat looked around. There were several groupings of machines that fed into assembly areas. "I heard there was an issue with the magazines?"

"Yeah, had some feeding issues. We've been working on the magazines. The linked feeder units are doing better." Taran pointed to an assembly area where people were working at benches where ammunition belts were laid out. "Adapted off the belt-fed guns from the ships Yui and his people used to capture the Water Floor. Uses small rotation formations to feed ammunition right into the weapon system. It means you have a larger capacity overall, but if you run out of ammunition, it takes longer to unhook the bottom of the belt and hook in a new box."

Rugrat grunted. "Not perfect, but it will work; gives our people a massive ammunition capacity. Might be best to operate them as sharpshooter or machine gun teams. One on the gun and another working on the ammunition."

"That should work. Hate not giving them the best product, though."

"Who knows? It might be more effective that way," Rugrat said, looking at the different areas. There were people putting barrel blanks into machines that milled them down into barrels. Others added threading, then boring. Each was scanned and tested by a smith for quality control. It was then fitted with heat dispersing formations that linked to the heat dissipation block rails that ran down the sides of the barrel.

Without the need for moving parts, the rear of the weapon from the chamber to the stock was lined with a series of inserts that were secured to one another with bolts.

The metal was milled down into shape. Then formations were carved into the metal. Everything was bathed in the formation medium, then cooled and milled down again so that there was no medium over the rest of the metal. Formation masters checked every rune. Everything was tumbled to remove metal burrs. The finished parts were then slotted into position, assembling a rifle.

"With the new assembly line for machine gun barrels, we can match the production rate of the body assembly line. It's much faster to make the body of the weapon compared to the barrel," Taran said.

"The mounted barrel's extra length will mean greater heat dissipation. With more heat exchanging blocks, the weapon's fire will be more accurate. Machine guns back on Earth were designed to create a cone of fire. This thing will be more like a buzz saw in a straight line. Here in the Ten Realms, where people can react nearly instantly by putting a ton of rounds *on* target, not just in their general vicinity, that will be much more effective."

"Sure would suck to be on the other end of one of these." Taran shook his head.

"Yeah. Anyway, I just wanted to come in and check everything."

"No worries. I know you're going stir crazy being here and not out there doing something."

"Yeah." Rugrat shrugged.

"Look, the stronger you get, the stronger we all are. You're close to a mana breakthrough. Take that step; increase your body cultivation. Get stronger. The stronger you are, the safer people are going to be. Work on any projects you have. Train people. At the least, you can do something, and you won't drive everyone insane." Taran grinned and scratched his beard.

"All right. I'll stop bugging you. You got those notes on the magazines and the faults?"

"Yeah, let me know if you find anything." He pulled out a magazine and a pile of notes.

"More homework." Rugrat shook his head.

"Something to keep you out of trouble!"

5
To the Next Stage

Erik appeared on the Metal Floor. He got onto Gilly's back slowly. His entire body ached deep into his bones. He opened his collar. His chest looked like crumbling charcoal. Mercury seeped from the open wounds between his cracked skin.

Metal mana was drawn into his body, making his breath catch. He coughed, his entire body shaking as the first cough pulled him in for more, and he broke out into a coughing fit. He felt a hand on his back, holding him up.

It took a few moments to pull himself together.

"Water?" Gong Jin held out a canteen.

Erik took the water and poured it down his parched throat. He wheezed and passed the canteen back. "Thanks." Erik sighed.

He closed his eyes, using his Medical Scan to look through his body. The metal mana had sunk into his entire body, through the skin, muscles, and most of his internal organs and bones. He was so close. Once he tempered the last of his internal organs, he'd have to let the tempering pass his neck and reach his brain. *Not saying I'm not a little scared about tempering my brain.* He was starting to wish there was someone else to be the leading body tempering member of Alva.

Erik pulled himself together.

"Let's go." He nudged Gilly forward. The rest of the special team had mounted up and moved around him as they headed for the body tempering facility at the center of the floor, underneath the lightning pool.

Simple Heal gave Erik some relief. *Just need more time, rarest resource in the entire universe.*

"What's up, Doc?" Erik said, half-limping into the room.

"You Americans and your cartoons." Melissa looked up from her desk, her French accent making it somehow regal.

Erik grinned. Her eyebrows pinched together in worry.

Melissa Bouchard had moved her office to the Metal floor for one reason: to watch and record Erik's progress. She was the head of the Body Cultivation Training Department. Also being from Earth, she had come in like a storm, revolutionizing the body cultivation training systems. She worked with her mana cultivation opposite Hou Jun, a Ten Realms native. With their corroborative work, Alvans' speed at increasing their mana and body cultivation shot up by fifty percent, and it was no longer a mysterious process. As long as someone could pay for the treatments, they could rapidly increase their cultivation.

"Council Leader Delilah just made it cheaper for stone and iron body level cultivation again," Melissa said, using Medical Scans on Erik.

"The potions get cheaper every day, and the stronger our people are, the better."

"Yes, though we have started to run into issues with people who have high cultivation and low levels. Creates an instability. We're calling it level sickness."

"Too much, helpful or harmful can be bad." She pulled out Erik's file, making notes. "Rugrat has started to form his Liquid Core already?

"He spent so much time on the weapon systems. It was making it hard for him to sit and cultivate his mana for a long time. Now he's got the free time." Erik shrugged.

Melissa ran another scan through his body. "How are you feeling?"

"Like a bag of smashed ass. My entire body aches to the core. I can barely call on forty percent of my power. After ten minutes of just conversing on an involved topic, I run out of energy. Lethargic for sure. Though I've drilled the metal mana into the majority of my organs."

Melissa jotted down more notes. "Thankfully, we took this slow. Your organs are operating at less than five percent capacity, but you long ago left behind human bounds. If you didn't have the stats, a strong body, and resources to help you heal, you'd be wiped out. Hell, if this was anyone else, I would have them stuck on twenty-four-seven bed rest with a stamina drip and healing formations. In fact, that is exactly what I want to do."

Erik's fatigue seemed to fade as he looked at Melissa. "I've got work to do, people to train. I can make pills and concoctions."

"Erik, here are your options." She looked him dead in the eye. "One, you can operate at ten percent or less and slowly temper your body for weeks or months. Two, we set you up in a bed, hook you up to stamina concoctions, healing formations and we blast you through this tempering. We temper right through your organs, completely temper your body, then remove your necklace and allow the changes to spread through your neck and head."

Erik closed his eyes, taking a few breaths, gathering his strength.

Gilly, who was in her small form, nudged his arm.

Erik opened his eyes and smiled, rubbing her head. His eyes thinned. "All right I'll do the blast version, but I have a question. If humans can temper their bodies, can beasts?"

"Yes." Melissa moved her head from side to side. "I have talked to the beast masters that raise the different creatures. Beasts are basically the opposite of humans. Humans are best suited to increase their mana cultivation first and then body cultivation, a distant second. Beasts are better at increasing their body cultivation, tempering with the elements. Then, once they reach a certain level of evolution, like Fred and his people whom you met in the Vuzgal dungeon, they become sentient and able to cultivate other elements and mana." Melissa shrugged.

"I focus on the human side," she continued, "but beasts consume the flesh and cores of their opponents. That increases their cultivation and gets them some more experience. Though most beasts only cultivate one kind of body cultivation. They don't cultivate water, fire, metal, and so on like humans, at least to start. They only cultivate a fire body, or an earth body, or a metal body. Dual body cultivations are rare. When they consume aligned monster cores, ones with the same attributes as their body cultivation, then their cultivation will have a greater jump as compared to neutral monster cores, and much more than monster cores that are of the opposite attribute. Cultivating a single attribute is easier to tend toward. But the capacity required to temper their body is *much* higher than a human. How much fire it took to temper your body is much lower than it would take George to temper his body."

Erik's eyes were shining.

"I only know the basics, talk to the beast trainers if you want to learn more."

Quest: Beast Cultivation
One's power is great, but the power of two united in a single cause is greater than the sum of its parts.
Requirements: Temper the bones for your beast companion.
Rewards: Beast will advance in power

"Looks like the Ten Realms agrees with you." Erik coughed and closed the status screen. "All right, yeah. Let's do this. I fucking hate being sick."

"It won't be an overnight thing. It could take weeks to complete."

"Better to get it done now than later." Erik paused, catching his breath. "Did you find out anything about the bloodline part?"

Melissa held her clipboard against her chest as she shook her head.

"Unfortunately, no. We ran into a wall information wise. Through Jia Feng, I have requested more information from the intelligence department. Seems like any information might be in the Seventh Realm and higher."

"And getting anything from sects in the higher realms is a pain in the ass," Erik added.

"All of our knowledge past the Body Like Stone stage is based on what we have learned through you and the other people tempering their bodies. You're the cutting edge for Alva. So we have no idea." Melissa shrugged her shoulders, moving her clipboard as well.

"Any ideas, theories?"

"Well, these things happen in series. We know more about mana cultivation. With mana cultivation, one goes through a mana rebirth. I think the bloodline is something similar, a point where the body goes through huge changes because of the built-up temperings. Again, this is all conjecture."

"It makes sense. The Ten Realms systems, while different, follow a certain set of rules. Tempering the foundations is like forming the mana core. Just that with mana cultivation, that is a lot more power. Well, whatever happens, happens. When can you fit me into your schedule?" Erik grinned.

"Luckily for you, I'm free. Give me three hours and I can have everything ready. Though you should let people know you'll be away for a number of days."

"They'll be happy to get the break. I'll send the messages."

After getting a message from Erik, Rugrat found himself walking toward the mana cultivation facility.

"Lord Rodriguez," the lady at the counter greeted him.

"One mana cultivation room. Open it right up to the dungeon core."

"Uhh." The lady seemed hesitant, gave a half-shrug, and pulled out a key. "Room one A."

"Thanks." Rugrat took the key. He and his protection detail walked through the honeycomb-structured training rooms. People were leaving and entering. No one was hanging around. All the rooms had a red light next to the door showing that they were occupied.

Rugrat reached the room in the center of the training facility.

A deep feeling of relaxation ran through his body as his pores and mana gates opened, drawing in the ambient mana. He had reached the point where he was almost subconsciously circulating his mana all the time.

He used the key and stepped into the training room, leaving his detail in the outer room.

The dungeon might be in chaos, turning into a massive drill digging through the ground. They'd altered the mana-storing formations, so they can only accept power coming in. The power runes on the different floors were thankfully built into the system, so the rest of the dungeon wouldn't stop running. Still, there were six massive dungeon cores drawing in and purifying mana across six floors, and then shooting it down into the ground. They were burning through a considerable amount of material every second.

Rugrat patted the taped-up skull on his knee. "Looks like that extra mana is good for you. Your carvings are coming in faster. Now, I can't let Erik get ahead of me. I've been holding back too much. I won't leave until I reach the liquid core."

His tour of Alva had made him realize everything was in capable hands. The only thing he *had* to do was classes in a week's time.

Rugrat took the health monitoring formation from the wall and stuck it to his chest, swiping a pillow to the ground, and pulled out a box of different pills and concoctions.

He parked his ass on the pillow and pulled his legs together to cross them.

"All right, let's see what you've got." He used mana manipulation to create a mana hand and reached out to pull the lever on the wall. Formations pulled into place, diverting pure mana from the dungeon core into the room.

Rugrat grunted. It was like he had turned on a waterfall that was shooting at him from every direction. "Hah! Nice!"

He released his control over his aura. His mana domain stretched around the room, hemmed in by the surrounding mana. It extended about a foot from his body.

Using his domain, he compressed the mana and drew it into his mana gates. Fifteen cyclones of mana appeared around his body. White circles appeared under his skin, shining as the cyclones drove through the center of the circles.

The compressed mana fought against his mana veins, creating a turbulent atmosphere like there were raging rapids inside Rugrat's body.

He circulated the mana, compressing and drawing it further. The different streams of mana combined, passing through larger mana veins, illuminating him from the inside.

Rugrat removed anything other than cultivation from his mind, becoming solely focused on what was happening within his body.

The mana traveling through his veins reached Rugrat's core. Like a black hole, it drank in the mana. Seconds passed as drops started to appear around the edges of his mana core.

Slowly, ever so slowly, the drops from the edges of his core released from the wall and gathered in the middle, adding to the liquid sphere resting there.

Rugrat was covered in sweat, but his face was pulled back in a chilling grin.

With a laugh, Rugrat pulled down on the lever more. The mana density in the room doubled again. Rugrat's back bent with a grunt. His nose flared as he pushed against the new pressure on his body. He sat back upright, drawing in more mana.

On his hip, the once yellowed skull was rapidly turning pearl white, without the slightest blemish. Blue and golden runes appeared on the pearl-white bone. The blue and gold runes seemed to shift and move in their carved lines as if they were liquid gold and the most brilliant blue waters.

It had taken four hours for Erik to get everything cleared. At the same time, medics were called in from across the Ten Realms to assist.

He missed Gilly, but she was off training with her elements.

A close protection detail was set up outside of Erik's room, while Roska's Special Team Two had switched with Gong Jin's team to take over protecting Erik. Each of the lords had five special team members with them as guards at all times.

Erik walked in from a side room wearing a robe and boxers, showing his withered and frail body. Several tempering nails had been driven into his body: two on each of his upper arms, others on his legs, and four into his stomach. Healing formations adhered to his skin were glowing constantly.

He was gaunt. The necklace around Erik's neck protected the healthy skin and appearance of his head.

"Jen, aren't you supposed to be in King's Hill?"

"Well, as the Head of Health Studies, I should get to know more about body tempering, right?" Jen said.

"Doesn't look the most appealing." Erik smiled weakly as he walked to the bed in the middle of the room.

"I've seen worse." Jen shrugged.

"Not the young impressionable lady running around with notes falling all over the place and studying everywhere she can find room anymore." Erik remembered the first time he had met Jen, filled with her questions.

"Had to grow up a little. Still have plenty of questions." She smiled and helped Erik take off the white robe.

Melissa finished talking to another healer and walked over. "Ready?"

"As I'll ever be." Erik laid down on the bed, grimacing as his broken skin pressed against the bedsheets.

Medics moved in. They used Iodine Touch, numbing him and cleaning the area, as they used their fingers to place IO bands. The bands adhered to the skin and the drill head dug through the skin, muscle, and into the bone.

The caps on the back of the drilled-in needles were connected to drip lines.

Sensing bands were put on Erik's right arm.

"These are new formations. They will detect your overall stamina and health," Jen explained, pointing to what looked like an EKG machine. It showed two bars: red for health and green for stamina. The red was at around seventy percent and the green around thirty percent.

The IV lines hung from surrounding stands as a ring of light shone down on Erik. All around the bed, amplification formations were activated. Medics stepped up on the platforms.

"Increase stamina flow," Jen called out as she cleaned her hands and gowned up.

Energy coursed through his body and he sighed, more alert than he'd felt in days.

The bar on the screen reached fifty percent as Jen once again stepped near the bed.

"Connect the spikes."

She and the other medics took out mana channeling lines and hooked them onto the end of the metal attribute spikes, trying to be as gentle as possible.

"Okay, Erik, this is the part when you take a nap," Jen said.

"See you in a bit." Erik smiled.

An alchemist put an oxygen mask on Erik's face.

"Breathe deep and count down from ten."

"Ten." Erik breathed in deeply twice, getting to six as he blinked twice. He closed his eyelids for longer. As he tried to count down, his head was in a swamp.

Erik got to three and slumped. Jen looked at the alchemist, who put the mask's straps around Erik's head and adjusted the out-flow of powder through the oxygen into Erik's face.

"He's asleep," the alchemist confirmed.

"Very well. Let's not fuck this up." Erik was their leader and their benefactor. She wouldn't tolerate any mistakes. "Let's get his stamina up. I don't want it to drop below seventy percent. He has a high ability to heal himself as long as he has the right resources. Turn up the healing formation to forty percent."

Jen waited for things to stabilize. Melissa Bouchard was great on the theoretical side of things, turning information into procedures, though she didn't have the training or time in the Ten Realms. All of Jen's healers worked day and night, healing and fixing all kinds of issues, taking courses from Erik and fellow medics.

They were a young organization but quick learners.

"Okay. We're ready, Miss Bouchard."

"Increase the power of the spikes. That will introduce more of the metal element into his body. Once he can handle that, we'll inject the metal element water from the lightning pool above through the spikes."

"Increase power by five percent," Jen said.

She watched as Erik's stamina, which had reached eighty-three percent, slumped.

"Increase stamina. Up the healing formation by five percent."

Erik's stamina continued to fall at a decreased rate.

"Ten percent on healing formation."

The stamina bleed slowed, came to a halt, then started to rise again. It had reached sixty-five percent at its lowest.

Jen used a Medical Scan on Erik, looking through his body.

"Healing formation up ten percent. Five percent increase on the spikes," Jen said after a few minutes.

She watched the metal attribute poisoning, destroying Erik's body, the healing power fighting back, recovering some of it.

Time passed slowly. The further they went, the less it mattered what Erik's body did. Only the formations, the concoctions, and healing spells were supporting Erik.

Jen frowned and closed her eyes, recalling what she had read on inoculations and vaccines.

"Dial down the spike's power. Do we have blood repairing formations?"

"Yes," one of the medics said, moving to a row of medical equipment.

"What are you doing?" Melissa Bouchard asked, confused. She was the leading expert on tempering in Alva, but Jen was their leading healer.

"We're supporting his life right now on our abilities and gear. I'm thinking of tempering one part of Erik's body. Say, take out his blood, purify it and circulate it back into his body. At the same time, we'll heal his bones specifically. It should teach Erik's body to fight it in a concentrated way. Not temper his entire body with metal, just his blood. Then let it teach the rest of his body. We can do it ourselves, but there is a huge risk to Erik's life," Jen said as the medics gathered the right formations.

Melissa looked at Jen and then Erik, biting her lower lip. "That should work."

"I'll need an IV kit to loop into the blood purification and repairing unit and then back through another IV. Get me bone healing focused healing formations," Jen called out.

They quickly assembled the gear. Jen watched the medics insert two new IV lines into Erik's arm.

His blood was drawn out, red and mercury, routed through the new machine where the blood was blasted with healing spells. The cells repaired and, because it wasn't in Erik's body, the stamina draw on him was minimal. The blood was then circulated back into Erik's body.

Bone healing formations were activated on Erik's body. The formations hummed with power as Jen watched the stamina levels and the color of the blood.

The mercury blood started to run redder, looking coppery.

"Increase the power of the bone healing formations. Keep up with his stamina," Jen directed her team.

Erik was starting to recover his stamina quicker; his body required less of it to sustain his life.

It went on for hours, but the results were clear.

"Well, Jen, your method is showing results," Melissa Bouchard said.

"I wouldn't have thought about it if I didn't have the information from Earth. I'm taking the process you planned out, breaking it down into a step-by-step process."

"It's brilliant. Well done!" Melissa smiled.

Jen bowed her head, inwardly relieved.

All right, Erik. We'll give you a helping hand, but this is on you. Jen looked at the coppery blood. It was becoming more viscous, filled with dense energy.

6 House of Cards

Blaze sat on his mount, observing Split Peak City in the distance. The stone mountain looked like it had been split in two. Between the two sides, there were residences, hanging walkways, and buildings that rested in between. The sound of marching boots advancing in the mud around the base of the bill marred the building's chaotic and crazy charm.

The city was massive and sprawling. Millions filled it, stacked upon one another. It was one of the largest cities controlled by the Willful Institute. Located in the Second Realm, it boasted one of the largest populations of the realms.

Fifteen-foot walls stood between the city and the outside world.

"Guild Leader." Domonos rode his beast over. Both wore the gear of the Adventurer's Guild and its guild crest.

"How are things looking?" Blaze asked. He had spent most of his younger years on campaigns and thought he had left that life behind. Certainly, he never thought that he would be bringing fifty thousand men and women under his command to attack another city.

"People are nervous. They're not sure what to expect. I made sure to impress upon everyone that looting and attacking innocents will not be tolerated."

"I heard you took some of the branch heads with you to press that point." Blaze looked at the young man-turned-commander.

"The strong make the rules. Isn't that the Ten Realms way?" Domonos was calm under his gaze.

"In the Second Realm, the Willful Institute's greatest strength is their numbers. If they can surrender, then we won't be facing a city of hundreds of thousands, just the Willful Institute's basic trainers and lowest recruits."

"They don't even have a proper mana barrier," Domonos said.

"Would cost more than the city makes to make it and power it. It's the second realm," Blaze said.

Domonos nodded. Blaze clasped his hands behind his back, surveying the sect and guild banners arrayed around Split-Peak city.

"What do you think of our employers?"

"They're bold, but they're not idiots," Domonos said. "They're using us as a cover, drawing the Institute's ire onto us instead of themselves. They're angered by the Willful Institute, so they're willing to overlook a few things. This is just an exploratory campaign to see how strong the Willful Institute is. Depending on the outcome, they could commit more to the fight, or back out of it."

After hearing what the Adventurer's Guild had done in Meokar, everyone going up against the Institute was looking to hire them.

"Isn't that what everyone is doing? Watching everyone poke the tiger and see if it really is a tiger or a pig in tiger's clothing."

Domonos shrugged. "What do you expect? Rewards govern everything."

"So, Colonel, how do you think things will go?"

"Operation Doomsday is in full swing. None of the Institute's factions trust one another. The nearby forces are different factions to the people in Split Peak. They're not going to come and help. As long as the leading families of Split Peak are given good terms, then it is possible they'll turn on the Institute. They don't care about dying for honor."

Domonos gave a savage smile. "Both our allies and the loyal families think they are talking to one another's representatives, but it is our intelligence officers going between them, three of them in fact. Surprising what three people with the right information in the right place can do."

A messenger passed through their guards and stopped in front of Blaze and Domonos. "Our allies have sent word. We will lead the vanguard in ten minutes to take down the outer wall. They want an answer."

Domonos looked at the walls. Willful Institute soldiers were preparing their defenses. The farmer's huts and slums between the armies and the walls had been vacated, the lucky ones reaching the city. The unlucky ones ran along the walls to flee into the distant forests.

"We will be ready to attack in ten minutes. If needed?" Domonos turned his question to Blaze.

"Armies are ready across the realms to attack. If we can secure victory, it should embolden those against the Willful Institute. You have command. I'm better suited for paperwork these days." Blaze grinned.

"I don't know about that, Guild Leader." Domonos smiled. "In thirty minutes, I'll open up the walls for our allies."

"Yes, sirs." The messenger bowed his head and ran off.

Once again, a meeting of the High Elders was called. What was once a yearly meeting had turned weekly. The whole mess was screwing up Cai Bo's schedule.

Their expressions didn't reveal anything as they took their seats.

Asadi walked in, leaning on the desk between them all, his eyebrows pinched together in anger.

"Two hours. *Two* hours!" He slammed his fist into the table, denting it. "Split Peak City, the largest city under our command, our largest by population, fell in just *two hours*!"

Elders' eyes flicked to the Elder whose faction had controlled the city.

"Don't look at him, you idiots! Are you so ingrained in your factions that you don't see what is happening? Are you so focused on attacking one another that you haven't noticed our supply convoys being hit across the realms? The blades both hidden and out in the open pointing at our throats?"

Cai Bo, who wasn't in the habit of bowing her head in front of anyone, dipped her eyes, not wanting to meet the Institute Head's eyes. Not from shame, but in anger. She had spent years building her power base and had been biding her time for the final blow—a move that would place one of her people in Asadi's seat. Now her plans had fallen apart. Changing the sect head would only lead to more problems.

"It seems everyone and their dog wants a piece of us. Information that should have been secret is nothing more than gossip. If I wanted a detailed plan of our supply convoy's movements or our troop deployments, I just need to go talk to the local farmhand!" Asadi yelled, the pressure of his cultivation making the High Elders sweat and strain.

"At the same time, you idiots are incapable of controlling your own people. Internally, we're in more of a mess than ever before. Are you all blind?" He fell silent and sat down in his chair. "After Split Peak fell, eight other cities—*eight*—are under attack: three in the Second Realm, two in the Third Realm, and three in the Fourth Realm! Other armies are forming up and preparing to attack us."

"We need to make an example! Cut down our enemies and show the others that we will not go peacefully!" High Elder Saddan said.

"Who the hell do we attack? Twenty-three different sects are working together, forty-seven different mercenary groups," Head Asadi sneered.

"What about the Adventurer's Guild?" Cai Bo asked. "They have been a key part in this war, fighting against Meokar, and in Split Peak City. They're offering discounted prices to join the armies attacking us."

"Many mercenary companies are reducing their prices. They want more of the loot from the captured cities, though they have been a leading part of this attack. What are you thinking?" Head Asadi thought aloud.

Cai Bo swallowed quickly under his gaze. It was like standing in the face of a rhino, not knowing if it was peaceful or would charge the next moment. She hid her smirk as the other heads hid their shame and looked away. "They're spread across the lower realms, but in the higher realms, they have a clear headquarters in Vuzgal. We should apply pressure on Vuzgal, force out the Guild, then cut them down. Put a bounty on their leaders' heads."

"Vuzgal is a place I've heard of. Do you think they will give in? There are a lot of interests."

"I think there is more to Vuzgal than meets the eye." Mistress Mercy remembered Colonel Domonos, and records of someone of the same name joining the Wilful Institute who was supposed to be dead. It was possible to survive, but to gain such a position of power was alarming.

"What do you mean?"

"I do not have anything definitive right now, but I think that the Vuzgal leadership is linked to the Adventurer's Guild."

Cai Bo waited, holding steady under the Head's gaze.

"Very well. High Elder Cai Bo, you've impressed me with your ability to put down your own conflicts and reveal information that isn't confirmed but is possible. Go and rattle the Adventurer's Guild and Vuzgal, see what you can find out. As for the rest of you..." He scanned the room. "I am calling martial law! Pull everyone back! You will create mixed units of all your factions. They'll be pissed off, having to watch one another, so it should reduce the in-fighting and reveal who is giving out our information.

"Some group must be leading this. It is too smooth, the events too close together. I am not saying that it is just one group. But there is an alliance among our enemies, moving against us. They might not have even shown their teeth. Even this Adventurer's Guild is joining in on the fight! Our old enemies are growing bold and working together. Once one attack happened, the others started coming in one after another. High Elder Caros, I expect your clan can repay the losses that will be taken with your mercenary guild's exposure?" Head Asadi's voice was deceptively calm.

Caros bit down on his words and bowed his head. "Of course, Head Asadi."

"Good. High Elder Cai Bo, find out who the real enemy is. In the meantime, we'll make an example of this Adventurer's Guild. This is a list of cities that must not fall! If the others are under attack, pull back our resources and people. We cannot defend them all. We must cut off the rot to maintain our strength!"

Cai Bo and the Elders looked at the scroll Head Asadi put on the table. It was a death sentence to the city and the leadership who were sure to lose their position.

While he did that, Cai Bo was determined to pull on the thread that was Domonos Silaz.

7

Good or Bad, in the End, All is Revealed

Elan Silaz shuddered awake as his carriage came to a stop. He rubbed the sleep from his eyes, moving a curtain to look out at the darkness all around him.

"Vuzgal's under city," Elan muttered as he saw people waiting for him outside the carriage.

He opened the door of his carriage and stepped out. The guards were all elite Close Protection Detail members. All the council leadership had similar guards to make sure they were safe at all times.

"What do you have for me?" he asked the group as he walked toward the under-castle behind them. It was the heart of the intelligence department in Vuzgal. It housed several answering statues they had been bought through Elise.

"Reports on everything happening in the Fourth Realm," Detrick, the manager of Vuzgal's intelligence networks, passed Elan a storage ring that was stuffed with information books. "I'm meeting with Chonglu tomorrow to talk about what's happening in the Fourth Realm."

"How are things with the foreign traders?"

"They're getting bolder. Based on the snippets of information we got from the answering statues, they're coordinated. If they're working with one another or another power, we don't know at this time."

"Suspects?"

"Other trading conglomerates. I think it's the Stone Fist Sect."

"They're not going to let go of Chonglu and Mira, are they?"

"They must have made the connection with Erik showing up and Mira leaving their clan. They can't go against her, but they can attack her husband and weaken him," Detrick said.

"So they think," Elan muttered as the doors to the castle opened and he walked in.

"Sir! There is something you need to see!" Dang, head scribe in charge of the answering statues, saw Elan and walked up.

"What is it?" Elan asked.

"This." Dang pulled out a piece of scroll and held it open.

"Domonos Silaz, from the First Realm. Recruited by Elder H—" The document ended abruptly. "Talk to me, Dang."

"I had the answering statue tell me where this information was recorded. I checked it against our Wandering Inn records. It was Mercy Luo, known as Mistress Mercy. She had a direct connection to Colonel Silaz before he joined Alva."

"When was this information recovered?"

"The last day of the competition."

"Why is it only getting to me now?" Elan demanded, his mind working fast. He could have her killed. No, that would draw unwanted attention. Perhaps they could cut off the information. Thankfully, the new leader of Chonglu City had changed its name to Zahir, although if the Willful Institute went there and dug deep enough, they were sure to find that out.

"We went through the information that was gathered on the most important people and filtered it down to the least important. Mercy is a hanger-on, so her information was the last thing we looked at."

"We need to take control of the narrative, send information into the city that Erik and Rugrat found Domonos. Show him getting the attention of a mercenary. He gets healed, becomes stronger, joins the Vuzgal military. Send word to Evernight. Have her cover up things there. Make sure their attention isn't drawn to the Beast Mountain Range or to Zahir City. Control the ceremony with Chonglu. We need to limit his name being used."

Sleep was forgotten as Elan's mind buzzed. "And send word to the Alvan higher-ups in the field. Have them use illusion masks or wear their headgear to keep their identity hidden. Shit, I'll have to send a report to the Council Leader."

Elan could see several paths, but he had a sinking feeling that covering up everything would lead to more questions, not fewer. If they chose to follow the thread of information, it could pull everything apart.

Elan pulled out a piece of paper. "Turn around," he said to Detrick.

Detrick did as he was ordered, and Elan used his back as a desk, writing out a hurried message. He turned to one of his Close Protection Detail people. "Take this to Alva. Make sure the Council Leader and Glosil see it." He put it in the woman's hands.

She looked at him and then at her leader.

"Go! We don't have time!"

She turned and ran out of the castle.

"Get those other messages out pronto." He looked to the assistants who had been jotting down what he had been saying. "Detrick, call up the realm Deputy Directors, get them into motion. Where the hell is Mistress Mercy? Is she doing this on her own or do others know about this? Look at discrediting her. Make it look like she is trying to get attention with outlandish theories. Dang, good find! I just hope we can get in front of this."

Elan walked toward his Vuzgal office, trying to come up with plans and contingencies.

"Push back the meeting with Chonglu, but make sure he gets the latest information books on our current intelligence."

"This is the third damn *military exercise* that the Vrunad Empire has done in the last month. Is their military so rusty that they've started to walk in circles? Maybe we should send a few of our people out there to help the feeble spinsters home!" Aditya threw the papers on the desk, causing the candle to flicker against the darkness that cloaked King's Hill.

Even with candles across the town, alone, in the middle of the Beast Mountain Range, it *felt* darker.

Evernight watched and waited as Aditya breathed deeply and rubbed his tired face. "Sorry, just.... You know."

"Indeed, I do, and so does the rest of Alva. They are hoping you can pull this off."

"I wish I had the confidence that you do," Aditya muttered.

"Don't worry. Soon enough, people won't be jealous of your Beast Mountain Range. They'll want to get the hell away from it."

"I feel so much better." Aditya looked at her from under hooded eyes.

Evernight smiled. "What do you expect with Alva releasing so many powerful beasts? Already, mercenary groups are pulling from King's Hill back to the outposts, increasing the number of people in their hunting parties. It's spread everyone out more. While some people are scared, others are eager! With greater rewards and greater challenges, people are sure to get stronger, though the possibility of getting hurt increases as well."

"Something that the other nations' leaders have to think about. Rewards and losses come on a knife-edge. Nice if they can claim it all, but to fight us just to fight beasts? Few leaders would be willing to make such a foolish decision."

"Fewer of them now that we have so many esteemed students," Evernight added as she leafed through reports.

"The Beast Mountain Range Consortium is holding weekly recruiting events now. Hundreds have joined so far. Some are coming from other academies, hoping to get a better position now that the entrance bar is lower."

There was a knock at the door. Evernight put the reports away and worked at her desk like a committed secretary.

"Come in!"

Pan Kun opened the door, dominating the entrance. "The representatives have arrived."

"Good. Well, we should give them the good news." Aditya pulled his jacket tight.

"Everyone wants an education these days," Evernight murmured into the desk as she worked.

Aditya snorted and followed Pan Kun out of the room. "Old Quan?"

"He's still in training. He sent word that he will return in three weeks." Pan Kun said.

A week had passed since the mana wave and the world hadn't collapsed. Yet. If Aditya were to reveal Old Quan now and then again in a month so much stronger, people were sure to be curious instead of surprised. Having the Alvan teaching staff should be enough.

They reached a large hall where envoys from different nations were gathered. Drinks and food were served by waiters as the envoys waited with their allies.

It was like looking at the political distribution of the entire surrounding area. Aditya pasted a meek smile on his face, greeting, smiling, and stopping just shy of groveling before the different envoys.

It took him some time to go around the room and make it to the front where there was a raised dais. There were people in simple clothes standing behind the dais, talking to one another in low voices. They didn't seem to pay attention to the others in the room that were sending them curious glances.

Each of them wore the symbol of a teacher of the Beast Mountain Consortium.

The room grew silent. Not due to Aditya's presence, but the demand of interest by the attendees.

"Thank you all for visiting King's Hill. I will not waste your time. We, the outpost leaders around Beast Mountain Range, were as stunned as you by the mana wave that spread through the area. In the last week, there has been a surge in the number of powerful beasts. Mercenary groups have reported finding beasts up to level fifteen wandering the Beast Mountain Range."

A wave of uneasy whispers and mutters passed through the crowd.

"We have increased the number of guards patrolling the trading routes. We expect that beast waves and attacks will become more frequent in the coming days. Though with all risks, there are rewards. We believe a small dungeon was the reason for the mana wave."

The room seemed to close in on Aditya.

"The dungeon is small. The group that found it reported several Earth-type monsters inside. The weakest were level seven, and the strongest they saw before fleeing were level eleven."

The noise rose, but Aditya's voice carried over.

"We are not greedy here at King's Hill. Our motto has always been to trade fairly with anyone. With this in mind, we will give each of the surrounding twenty kingdoms five open spots to the Beast Mountain Range Consortium. The five people you submit to join the school will get the highest level of education. They will be trained and tested with the new dungeon and the roaming beasts."

The room settled down as the envoys drank in every word.

"This way, everyone can get a share of the bounty. We will accept any student that passes our entrance exam as long as we have a place for them, ensuring that the best among the surrounding kingdoms will get access to the dungeon."

"Why do you think that your Consortium should hold the dungeon? The Westwood Academy's teachers are the best in the realm!" one envoy asked.

“For that, I would like to introduce some of the teachers for the Consortium,” Aditya said, cutting off the envoys before they could get into a boasting match about their academies. He turned to the people behind the dais.

They stepped forward calmly.

“These are the teachers that will be working in the Consortium. Each of them has reached at least the peak of Apprentice in their given craft.” Aditya turned back to the envoys.

Their eyes were shining. Information, powerful crafters, fighting ability, tools, and gear… It was a nation’s foundation.

“All of them are contractually bound to the Consortium to give their students the best education.”

The envoys’ eyes thinned for a half-second at Aditya’s careful words, latching back onto him.

“I hope that this can put everyone at ease and we can work together fairly to use this boon to help us all. With the new materials, I am sure the best crafters of the area are sure to come up with some great items. The future generation will only grow stronger!”

Aditya smiled as the envoys copied him and clapped. If it worked, they could stop a war from happening and leave the fighting to the training halls of the Consortium.

“Please, if you have any questions about the courses for the teachers, they are here to talk with you.”

Aditya smiled at the envoys’ expressions. Were they hoping to take his teachers from him? They might be able to steal them from him, but they would never leave Alva behind. After all, what did teachers want more than anything? *To learn more themselves.*

8
Compressing a Solid Mana Core

Rugrat felt the power in his mana veins and his core rumbling. The mana around him was shaking.

His domain now reached out two feet from his body, compressed by the mana density. The lever on the wall had reached seventy percent, while the boxes of cultivation supplies looked like they had been raided by a starved bear.

Rugrat's veins stuck out on his skin, moving like snakes, lit up by the mana driving through his body. Each breath created a vortex of mana. With each exhale, the light within his body increased. His Journeyman-level clothes had been torn to shreds, revealing his sweat-soaked body as his ribs and abdomen expanded and then contracted. The core at his center had gone from the size of a die to a softball.

He didn't pay any attention to the outside world. His eyes remained closed as he focused solely on the happenings within his body.

Just a few more. He watched more drops form around his core. He felt the pressure of his core wanting to expand and the draw of the mana wanting to compress.

He pushed on; he was so close.

Drops rained one after another into the core. It grew wider, stretching the walls of his dantain.

Rugrat felt like he'd gone all out on Momma's Thanksgiving Day meal. *You're not giving up now. Hold on!*

He made another push. A single drop reached his core, and the fight for expansion and contraction had a winner. The shimmering liquid core, which had been rotating slowly, started to speed up. The spinning sphere of liquid pulled in more drops.

The liquid started to contract, pulling more mana inward.

Like a planet forming from the dust of space, the core compressed from a softball to a grapefruit and smaller. As it compressed, his domain increased; two feet became three feet, then four feet, then raced to ten feet.

Rugrat continued to draw in mana, compressing it through his domain, through his mana veins, and feeding his transforming mana core. The natural suction from the core removed the pressure that had been resting on Rugrat's body.

His domain covered the entire room. With just a thought, mana congealed into a hand manipulating the lever, increasing the mana density by five percent.

Rugrat's domain shrank slightly, but it soon expanded again, fighting against the increased mana pressure in the room. It reached out two meters in every direction.

The room looked peaceful as it fell under Rugrat's complete control.

Rugrat inspected the changes in his body. His mana density had increased, and the core would naturally draw in mana even if he wasn't doing anything. His mana veins had become stronger, though there were some tears. No, not tears. Smaller veins had spread through his body.

Rugrat's new core looked like a shining purple gem with streaks of blue and white. Red glitter seemed to flash deep within its depths. Mana drops entered the area around the mana core, falling like rain; they nourished the core, becoming part of it.

He'd held back his cultivation for a long time and felt that he could cultivate for several weeks. Unfortunately, he had other things to do.

Rugrat created a mana hand and decreased the density of mana in the room. As he did, his domain expanded without the pressure.

"Da--" Rugrat devolved into coughing as his body cracked and ached. He collapsed backward. He used healing spells and pulled out a high Journeyman stamina potion. He chugged it, gasping afterward. "Shit, whole new level of dry mouth." Rugrat moved on the ground, his body enjoying the movement as healing spells coursed through his body.

He cracked his back and stood up.

His domain was nearly ten times larger than before. Everything within twenty meters was in his range. It felt more solid, too, like he was using a hand made of mist before. Now, the mana was like an extension of himself. Rugrat reached out, using mana manipulation instantly and easily.

He created three flames at the same time. With just a thought, three flames turned into five. Then they changed their appearances from red to yellow to blue.

He set them spinning around him, dividing and creating more. He added in mana blades, spears, and arrows. Chains made of the elements appeared. It looked like pure chaos, but none of the spells touched anything in the room. They never bounced into one another. It was a complicated and complex dance.

Rugrat raised his hand, and everything froze.

He closed his hand. The spells unraveled and disappeared. The last two chains presented him with the box of supplies he had brought and disappeared into his storage ring with a wave.

Rugrat picked at his shredded clothes. His pants ripped, dropping Egbert's head on the ground. He winced, taking a sharp inhale as he looked at the skull with a half-open eye. Other than new runes, nothing about the skull seemed to have changed.

"Looking good, Egbert."

After a shower and a new change of clothes, Rugrat stepped out of the room.

"So, what happened while I was in there?" Rugrat asked the protection detail as he rested one hand on his new skull adornment.

Either they were blinded by the sight of Rugrat in his cowboy boots, backward hat, stringer undershirt, and oh-so-famous American short shorts complete with his duct-taped skull chain sash, or just having a mental breakdown. It took a few moments for the protection detail to throw their neurons back together as brain cells.

The leader of the protection detail passed Rugrat several information books. Rugrat opened them and took in all the information within.

"Hmm, that could be a problem with Mercy, though Elan is doing everything he can to cover for it. Erik's still getting tempered. So it's been what, a week working on cultivation? Shit! Time disappears when you focus on one thing."

Rugrat tapped Egbert's skull in thought. The Willful Institute was starting to pull back and consolidate even with sabotage and assassination among their ranks, with only some of it orchestrated by Alva. Chonglu was due to take command of Vuzgal in two weeks while kingdoms and nations banded together to attack the Beast Mountain Range.

Cai Bo's people had been spotted in Vuzgal, looking at the Adventurer's Guild.

There wasn't anything Rugrat could do, and that was the worst part.

"Well, I guess I should go to school. I promised to teach some people. Everything is running fine. Okay, so guess I need a new project to work on with smithing. Let's get going!"

"So, this is King's Hill?"

Lord Knight Ikeda sat straight on his mount as they approached the gates to the city.

No, it is a random village I wanted to go sightseeing in! Lord Salyn bowed his head to the Lord Knight. "Yes, Lord Knight Ikeda."

"Such a simple place gave you trouble." The leader of the Red Falcon Knights snorted, flicking his red cape. The other Red Falcon knights with him snickered, sending derisive looks in Salyn's direction.

When he was last there, they had just one layer of defenses. They had doubled in size, adding a fifteen-foot wall. Only the major cities in the Ikku Kingdom had such walls.

Salyn held back any comments as the group of three hundred approached the gates.

Lord Knight Ikeda kicked his horse forward. The rest of his knights flanked him as they pushed through the traders and groups in their way.

People stirred in anger as the group forced their way forward.

"Who dares to butt in ahead?" a voice called from a carriage.

Lord Salyn felt a wave of déjà vu.

The carriage opened, revealing a young woman. She held up her dress as she looked out of the carriage in a huff. "Do you think that you are so important?" She stomped her foot at the passing knights and her eyes pinched together as she seemed to recall something.

"You best be aware of who you insult, little miss. Do you really want to stand in the way of the Red Falcon Knights of the Ikku Kingdom?"

"Who is raising trouble in my line?" A group of guards wearing simple but well-maintained and repaired armor walked up. Their leader, a skinny man, had a sword handle sticking up over his shoulder. He and the other guards wore bored expressions as they looked over the Red Falcon Knights.

"You want to step in our way as well?" Ikeda grinned as he slowly slid some of his blade out.

The young mistress retreated into her carriage. Her guards positioned themselves between her and Ikeda's group.

Salyn faded back, shooting Ikeda a questioning look.

With a few hand gestures, Ikeda held the rest of the force back, watching the approaching guards.

People around the two groups quickly moved aside, not wanting to be part of it.

"Cute sword," the King's Hill guard snorted. The others grinned slightly. The atmosphere became sharp in an instant. "Threatening a member of the King's Hill guards. Well, we'd be well within our rights to maintain order cleaning up this little mess." The guard looked over the group of knights with bored disinterest. "Doubt any of you would increase my level even. What are our rules, Rook?" The man rested his hands on his hips.

"S-sir!"

"I ain't a sir." The guard leader turned back as the others shot a look at the younger member. Another cuffed him on the back of the head.

"You stand in our way. In the way of our Queen's will!" A Red Falcon Knight yelled.

"Rook!"

The new guard stood tall. "King's Hill guards will enforce the peace. If you are discovered hurting or attacking people within the Beast Mountain Range or attacking an alliance member, then the guards will in turn hunt you down. If you cause unrest or rob others, you will have to atone for your actions with repayment or service."

There was a flash of reflected light. The guard leader snatched a throwing blade from the air, inches in front of the young man.

The young man stepped back as the sneer on the face of the Red Falcon Knight who had thrown it faded.

"Shit blade." The guard leader examined the blade as if he were checking out vegetables on a street stall.

Salyn felt the tang of metal and blood in the air and shivered.

The guard leader threw the blade backward. Salyn felt the rush of wind as it hit the Red Falcon Knight, tossing him out of his saddle and startling his horse. Others moved to calm the beast as a tombstone appeared.

The Knight's stirrups kept him attached as blood dripped down his red and silver carved armor and onto the ground.

The Red Falcon Knights drew their weapons, their eyes flicking to the corpse.

"Didn't Rook say, 'we'll hunt down anyone that attacks alliance members?' Guards are alliance members. I don't like people attacking my rook," the guard leader said.

Salyn cleared his throat and rode up to Lord Knight Ikeda, stepping between the weapons. "Lord Knight, we have a mission to carry out according to the Queen's will." Salyn's voice was just loud enough to be heard by the people who had hurriedly moved away from the two groups.

Ikeda glared at Salyn as if this was all his fault.

"We have a letter for Aditya from Queen Ikku of the Shikoshi Kingdom," Ikeda announced.

"*Lord* Aditya gets letters from across the First Realm. Back of the line and wait your turn. No more than ten fighters are allowed into King's Hill unless you are a registered mercenary or guard, though I'll allow three."

Ikeda gripped his sword tighter.

"Or none of you can enter and I add some more tombstones at the entrance?"

"You're always making friends." A woman laughed as another group of guards appeared.

"Back of the line and only three of you allowed in, or as my friend said, we deal with you out here."

Ikeda gritted his teeth as Salyn checked the best way to retreat. If Ikeda got himself killed, it wouldn't be a problem. He could pass the message to Lord Aditya himself. Then Queen Ikku would have to fight for nothing else than honor.

Ikeda put his sword in his scabbard. "We can endure anything for our Queen." Ikeda seemed to be addressing his fellow knights, but he was staring at the first guard leader.

"Back of the line. Three of you allowed in. The rest of you can wait out here. Don't worry; you should have plenty of fun at night."

Lord Knight Ikeda turned and led the group to the rear of the line. People moved to allow them back.

"If you give up your spot, you'll lose it till tomorrow!" The second guard leader had followed with her group. People shifted even further back, smelling the blood in the air.

The Red Falcons stored their comrade's body. They talked in low tones about the revenge they were plotting out.

"Salyn, Hiraga, you two will come with me. The rest of you find a place to stay for the night," Ikeda said after some time.

Ikeda seemed unruffled by the incident as if it had never happened, but that didn't mean the information wouldn't get back to the Queen. As her Red Falcons leader, he was her authority.

Salyn bowed his head in understanding and waited.

The rest of the group moved out of the line.

Salyn studied Hiraga, one of the few female Red Falcon Knights. She sat as straight as a spear, her eyes roving between people. She barely talked and had a simple appearance, making her easy to miss.

He turned his attention forward. Guards from King's Hill patrolled up and down the lines, making sure that no one was causing trouble. Some people were turned away or sent to the back of the line. Few others dared to get into conflict with the guards.

"You might be wondering why I didn't do anything more after confronting the King's Hill guards." Ikeda's mouth didn't move, but through a spell, Salyn could hear his voice. "You can just nod. Don't try talking back. I was testing their ability. Fernard didn't have any family connections, no one to come and avenge him. A good tool to test the guards. They had the one guard unit patrolling. The second guard unit was back up. They also had people on the walls, ready to defend or move out as needed. The first guard leader must be about as strong as Hiraga. Though none of the others revealed anything about how strong they are, which makes me think that they are weaker than they appear. This King's Hill and outpost alliance is stronger than I thought, and those in power are always looking for more. Keep your wits about you."

Lord Salyn nodded, inwardly shocked. His evaluation of Ikeda rose rapidly. Using his own people's lives to gain information on other's strengths was all an act? As was guiding people to talk to Salyn. With the attention focused on him, Hiraga would be hard to notice, and the best kind of person to gather information.

They reached the wall quickly. Deep scratches and grooves had been gouged in the wall from beasts.

"Gets a little lively out here at night," the guard waiting to take their money said with one hand resting on his blade.

"No violence or crime inside the walls. Forty coppers, each."

"Each?" Ikeda's voice rose.

"It's what everyone pays. Makes sure only the strong and capable enter the city. If you're weak, you'll turn into beast fodder."

Ikeda dug out the one silver and twenty coppers and passed it to the guard. He put it into a box and waved them forward.

They passed through the large gate and into the city.

It rested on a hill well above the treetops, with the original city at the crown and the second extension reaching a third of the way down the hill. In the distance, one could see the mountains that created the Beast Mountain Range. Roads traveled through valleys, over rivers, mountains, and forests to connect the outposts.

All the buildings in the second extension of King's Hill were a mix of stone and wood. Most cities just used wood because it is so much easier and cheaper to use.

"The guards are pulled from the military units," Ikeda said, talking freely now there were no people all around them. "Originally, they were guards at the different outposts. It made them a neutral force. Every guard watching the gates will take a little something for themselves. We raised trouble, and they didn't charge us more. Even when I was trying to annoy him."

"You sound impressed."

"Our cities are guarded by the personal guards of the ruling family or families. The Army is made up of people that have a sworn oath to the queen and bring their personal guards and some of their people to support her. Few have training, and all of them come to get part of the loot from the fighting." Ikeda turned his head, looking Salyn up and down.

Salyn tried to look as non threatening as possible. Why was he telling him all of this? Ikeda didn't trust him. Was he putting the fear into him? A warning that he would know if Salyn didn't tell him everything?

Lord Salyn stewed over his thoughts as Ikeda looked toward the road that led to the inner city.

Traveling through the city, they passed the Consortium's gates. People were lined up, wearing the crests of powerful families, awaiting entrance.

It took them a half hour to make it into the inner city and to the administration buildings under the watchful eyes of several guards.

"Do you have an appointment?" a guard asked.

"We are on official business from the Shikoshi Kingdom under Queen

Ikku's orders!" Ikeda's voice was low and threatening.

"We have many people on official business. Who do you wish to talk to?" The guard was unfazed.

"Aditya should do."

The guard raised his eyebrow. "I will pass your information on to the administrators."

"You wish to stand in my way?" Ikeda demanded.

There was movement on the top of the wall as guards looked down between the crenellations.

"You might kill us, but you won't make it out of here alive." The guards both held their weapons.

Ikeda clicked his tongue. "Salyn, the letter!"

Salyn had a meek and sorrowful look on his face as he played his part, walking his horse forward and holding out the letter.

"Stop there," the guard growled.

Salyn pulled up his horse.

"Throw it," the guard ordered.

Salyn threw the letter, but it turned in the air and dropped on the ground.

"Scan it," the guard said to his partner. He grunted and pulled out a spell scroll.

Salyn and the others watched as the guard tore the spell scroll apart. Spell scrolls were rare, but this guard used it frivolously.

A light shot out from the spell scroll and landed on the letter. The letter illuminated from within before a green light appeared.

The second guard grabbed the letter and walked backward.

"Please go and wait at the side," the first guard said.

Ikeda clicked his tongue and pulled on his reins. The group moved over to the side, unable to see completely into the tunnel and past the gate that led to the inner city.

Time passed as they waited. Ten minutes or so later, a man in colorful clothes came out. The four guards at his side carried curved swords, iron armor embedded into beast leather.

The man invited conversation while the guards scanned the area, as well as the Shikoshi Kingdom delegation.

"My name is Emmanuel Fayad. I deal mostly with trade and exterior relations. My Lord Aditya does not have time to deal with your excuses to try to place pressure on our alliance. A messenger was dispatched to your nation with an invitation for five of your youth to join the Beast Mountain Range Consortium. That invitation will be recalled. We will not tolerate these childish games. Your tax rate will increase by fifteen percent when dealing with any trader of the outpost alliance. If you want to threaten us again with some made-up excuse of fleeing traitors, and that one of our longest-standing supporters is somehow hiding them—" Fayad's eyes were as cold and flat as his words. "—we will cut off all trade to the Shikoshi Empire and ban others from reselling products bought from the alliance to your nation. Good day."

"You!" Ikeda nudged his horse forward. Three arrows pierced the ground around him and made his horse rear.

"Do not take our outpost alliance's patience as weakness, Lord Knight Ikeda. I would ask you to leave King's Hill within the next three days. The guards are rather *interested* in testing how well your people outside the walls can handle our new beast issue." Fayad looked at Lord Salyn. "I'd hope you'd have learned better manners since your last visit, Lord Salyn."

Salyn saw an opportunity to push things further to his advantage and took it. "If you don't hand over the traitors, the Shikoshi Kingdom will—"

"Lord Salyn!" Ikeda glared at Salyn.

Salyn put on a surprised expression. *Shit.* He could feel his plan falling away. He gripped his reins. He needed to deal with Alva, and quickly.

"If you're interested in making trouble for King's Hill, I hope that you would talk to your neighbors. They will not be happy to have you attacking their children."

With that, Emmanuel Fayad turned and left.

Salyn made to speak, but Ikeda silenced him with a look.

"Let's get a room to stay. I have a feeling there is much more to learn."

"What do you think they will do?" Evernight asked, looking in the direction of the main gate.

Aditya glanced up from the map on a large table in the middle of the room. It showed the Beast Mountain Range with King's Hill in the middle. Floating reds, purples, whites, greens, and blues showed the position of most forces within the Beast Mountain Range.

"Emmanuel knows nearly everything that is happening in the Beast Mountain Range. Since he knows nothing of Alva, if someone uses spells or a contract on him, he won't be lying. He just doesn't know the truth.

"He has the power to deal with an envoy from another land and the position to do so. Also, he really hates people who come and push their weight around to get more benefits.

"Those life detect formations are incredible. With linked medallions and the ability to recognize a person's mana signature, it's almost scary. Soon, it will be hard for anyone to move in the Beast Mountain Range without us knowing."

"You didn't answer my question," Evernight said.

"Lord Salyn must have been tipped off. The Alva Healing House must have reminded him about the village he betrayed. Or he simply thinks that we have a connection with the Earthers. Queen Ikku certainly must to send her Red Falcon Knights."

"You think she will try something?"

Aditya looked over the outpost in silence for a few moments.

"If it was a few weeks ago, she might have been able to wage war and get people to join her. Now? With the Consortium's rise, the new resources, and the dungeon, our surrounding friends are being extra friendly... Their future generations are trying to join the school. All of them are looking to impress us to secure more positions in the Consortium."

"No wonder you're so calm."

"Well, even if Lord Salyn knew for sure that Alva Healing House was a group of people from Alva village—Hell, if we told the entire Ten Realms, not many people would care. Wait, why don't we do that? Say that the Alva Healing House is from the Shikoshi Kingdom, a group of escaped villagers that happened to get some healing knowledge?"

"It would look badly on Salyn if people were to come out and reveal the truth. Queen Ikku would be forced to deal with Salyn, and it would look like he was trying to use her to hide his mistakes." Evernight rubbed her chin in thought. "We would have to send the information to her directly. We wouldn't want to broadcast it. It would have a greater impact on her standing, though it would spread across the First Realm. We don't need people to talk about Alva, Chonglu, or too much about the Silaz family. I'll send it higher and see what they say."

9

Body Like Diamond, Mysteries of Bloodline

Jen and the rest of the body-tempering team had been working in shifts for the last three weeks.

"The last of his organs appears to have tempered at ninety percent," one of the assisting medics said.

"Your tempering by system has worked incredibly well," Melissa Bouchard complimented.

"Thank you," Jen said as she studied Erik's body. They had tempered his blood first, then his bones, his muscles, his lungs, heart, and the rest of his organs as well as his skin.

Erik's cracked and blackened skin had flaked off, revealing his natural skin, but it seemed gray, duller than before, but much stronger.

His bones had turned gray, adding silver runes to the brown ones, taking on the attributes of metal and greatly increasing his bones' natural strength. His blood was thicker, and his heartbeat was slow, a deep bass sound that one could feel with their fingers.

Erik's body had been torn apart as the harsh, inorganic metal attribute clashed with his constitution. There had been multiple times he'd been close to death.

"Okay, let's remove the necklace." Jen finished checking the different healers' formations, medical machines, and alchemy concoctions being fed into Erik's body.

A medic unscrewed the heavy necklace.

The formations turned off.

Silver flooded Erik's neck, racing under his skin and into his head. The lower half of his body remained the same. Like shattered ice, the cracked black skin raced up his neck and across his face.

Erik's hair started to fall out as he bled on the table.

"Healing!" It had been less than a second, and already Erik was being torn apart.

Healing formations, healing spells, and healing concoctions poured into Erik's body.

A rumbling noise came from within his body as ambient mana from the surrounding area surged toward him.

"Stamina?" Jen yelled.

"It's good!"

Erik's body was fighting as well. The cracked skin flaked off as the silver lines under his skin returned to blue.

What a monstrous body to supply so much stamina to.

"It appears to be working. His bones, blood, and skin are repairing at advanced rates!"

"Brain?"

"The metal attribute is combining with the brain. The healing seems to be fusing them together."

Jen used a scan to look at the brain.

"We thought the brain would be the hardest and most dangerous part," Bouchard said. "I wonder if the mana gates at the top of the head, the third eye, and base of his skull mean that he has passively tempered his brain?"

"I'll take it," Jen said as the medics continued to pour in their healing spells. The rumbling noise grew louder as energy from the Ten Realms flowed into Erik's body, through his mana gates, through his very skin. The energy was drawn into his bones and blood, spreading through his body and reaching his brain.

Even now there were so many mysteries, so many things they didn't understand—yet.

"He's coming to. His body is burning through the concoctions keeping him unconscious!"

Pain.

Erik gritted his teeth as he forced his way through the pain spreading throughout his being.

He circulated his mana, feeling the familiar flow even as his breathing labored. It felt like his skull was expanding and contracting on his brain. Erik smacked his lips and moved his tongue. He tasted something awfully similar to a concoction gone wrong. It reminded him of the cheap beer he drank end of the month because payday was so far away. It changed to sweet and then sour before it disappeared.

Erik tried to open his eyes but couldn't. There was just darkness with faint light peeking in.

Come on body, pull it together! He increased his mana circulation and healing spells, fighting the weakness pervading his body. He felt full of energy, but as if there were weights across his body.

Panic started to set in a little.

Pull it together. Your body is just heavy. You're tired. Come on, work on the problem! Erik felt his body becoming alive. The weights weakened and then disappeared like a band snapping. Power flowed into his body. Erik roared in triumph, feeling like he had put up a new record in the gym. His body, down to his very cells, rejoiced.

Sound snapped into existence.

Noise flooded in painfully.

"Check the restraints!"

"Erik, calm down!"

"Sixty percent of his brain has been tempered, and it's accelerating!"

"Quiet, please, stop screaming," Erik forced out. He could hear *everything*—people picking up IV bags, the trickle of potions in the tubes, his own heartbeat, and those of the others in the room. He could even hear the elevated breathing of his protection detail outside the room.

Smells bloomed. Metal in the air, the sweat of those in the room.

Damn, is this the no-shower club? Not so much as a bar of soap or bottle of perfume between them!

Erik kept circulating mana and healing himself. Energy flooded through his being as if another band had released. It felt as if he had just woken up from a revitalizing sleep that had washed away all his fatigue.

The light coming in through his eyelids brightened and faded colors appeared. He moved his hand toward his face.

"Erik, you're still hooked up! Don't move!" Jen shouted, a medic restraining his hand.

Erik barely felt the medic on his arm. He nodded and lowered his arm, but was tempted to lift it to see how strong he had become.

Erik grinned. His body rumbled. His blood started to speed up. His heartbeat sounded out. He felt it through the table.

His senses had been heightened massively to a painful degree, but he could tell what was going on within his body with his medical knowledge. He could reach out to thirty meters. A regular human could focus up to ten meters reliably, though most of them had a highly defined area of sensing of two meters, passive up to five. Beyond that, they needed to scan, relying on their eyes to study things in the distance.

Erik moved his face, forcing his eyelids open and closed. He still couldn't see.

A ripple coursed through his body as if he was being coated with armor. It was like wearing a favorite, thick, close-skin sweater. It was comfortable and flexible, barely noticeable, though it also felt like he had just donned body armor; he felt like a human tank.

Erik pinched his thigh. It was supple but thick.

He moved his shoulders, opening his chest and breathing in. Mana *flooded* in from the surrounding area.

"Erik, you crazy bastard!" Jen hissed.

"Seventy perce—seventy-five!" a panicked watcher yelled.

He had been feeble and weak for too long. *Time to wake this body up!*

Erik circulated the surrounding mana, but didn't refine it. The mana was heavy with the metal attribute. He drew it deep into his body. The fire and earth mana separated, nourishing his cells. Some of the metal strengthened his body and mind. The rest of it tempered his body. Unlike before, his body fought back. Just what would be consumed and used as fuel for the other was no longer definite. Erik's body forced the metal attribute into submission.

With the power of the attributes, Erik's body wasn't just surviving anymore. His thin, emaciated frame expanded. Stamina concoctions and mana supplied the energy. The healing spells and his tempered body converted those energies into repairing power. Erik's muscles recovered at a visible rate.

Erik stopped paying attention to the other medics, silently apologizing.

He opened his eyes as more power was released from his body. He felt his eyes tearing up. It was like different systems were coming back online, injecting new life and power into the whole. Colors and shapes came in from his surroundings, tuned and sharpened. Erik focused on one thing: feeling nauseous. The sharpness of the colors softened, and Erik saw the tops of heads and the ceiling above. Lines filled with concoctions were hooked into his body. He traced one with his head.

He grunted as a wave of pain ran through his skull.

Focus. Still tempering.

Erik, secure in knowing he could see again, turned his attention back to his body. His mana circulation was stronger. *I guess it is because the container is stronger.*

"I'm ready," Erik said.

"All right," Jen said. He felt a shift as formations were refocused.

Erik felt a disconnect. He kept feeling oddities, flashes of things in his brain. Not memories, but pain, anger, love. The world would be beautiful, then green, then turning, then still. And then sounds changed or fell silent or he picked up a different wavelength he'd never paid attention to before.

These kinds of flashes were less than seconds long, creating a background noise to his being. Focusing on his mana circulation gave him something to hold on to.

Erik finished with his neck down, continuing to circulate his mana, waiting.

Then it was like the pressure popped at the top of his skull. In a rush of energy, he experienced an electric shock that started at the base of the neck, then raced down his spine, radiating out through his nerves, reaching out through his entire being.

My nervous system?

Erik felt the air on his skin, the hairs moving up and down as the skin contracted against the chilly breeze in the room.

He felt every muscle, every organ. It was like he had merely existed in his body before. Now, it was *his* body, completely under his control. He twitched the individual muscles in his hand. The sensation was incredibly strange. They had always worked in concert together without his conscious thought.

A feeling of *rightness* filled his body like it was powering up.

Holy shit! It's like I just powered up my reactor. He had so much energy, he felt like a battle mech instead of a person!

A notification rang in his head. Erik opened his eyes, looking at the ceiling. "I think I'm all tempered."

He turned his head to the side, watching the exhausted medics checking on him and their gear, just in case.

The room brightened, slowly at first, followed by a sudden rush as the world turned gold. Ten Realms energy and experience seeped through the walls, down through the ceiling, and up from the floor.

Erik laughed as it nourished his body. A wave of relaxation filled him. He breathed in, drawing in power, and relaxing his body on the exhale.

It took a few moments for everything to calm down. Erik opened his eyes and looked around. "Thank you, everyone. Could someone unplug me, please?" He smiled at the medics.

They seemed to collapse in on themselves, proud, relieved, and satisfied. It looked like things hadn't been that easy. *And I just slept through everything.*

Jen chuckled and pulled out his IV. Another medic turned and pulled the IO in a clockwise motion from his opposite shoulder.

"I feel like a marionette. IO's in my shins as well?"

"You were a bit of a problem case." Jen shrugged. It didn't take long to remove the six tubes that had been inserted into his body. Jen and the other medics took stamina potions, examining Erik thoroughly. Melissa Bouchard was there, alongside her team of body cultivation specialists, jotting down information and data.

Erik opened his notifications.

Quest Completed: Body Cultivation 4
The path to cultivating one's body is not easy. To stand at the top, one must forge their own path forward.
Requirements: Reach Body like Diamond
Rewards: +24 to Strength +24 to Agility +24 to Stamina +40 to Stamina Regeneration +100,000,000 EXP

Your personal efforts have increased your base stats!
Stamina +12 Agility +12 Strength +12 Stamina Regeneration +30 Mana Pool +10 Mana Regeneration +10

Title: Metal Mind, Metal Body
You have tempered your body with metal. Metal has become a part of you, making your body take on some of its characteristics. You have gained:
Legendary metal resistance Increased control over metal mana Physical attacks contain metal attribute Can completely purify the metal attribute in mana Physical Domain

Quest: Body Cultivation 5
The path cultivating one's body is not easy. To stand at the top, one must forge their own path forward.
Requirements: Reach Body like Divine Iron
Rewards: +48 to Strength +48 to Agility +48 to Stamina +80 to Stamina Regeneration +1,000,000,000 EXP

"Physical domain, that must be because of the enhanced senses."

Erik frowned.

"Is there something wrong?" Jen asked.

"I feel hot. My blood seems to be boiling. My entire body seems to be excited," Erik said. feeling a heat deep in his bones. It was feral. It was powerful. He reached out his hands. They were balled into fists. The tension in his muscles gave him a feeling of pleasure as if proof of his inner strength.

His veins became more vascular. They rose from the skin, as heat spread throughout his body. Energy, from deep within, begged to be used. He released control, trusting his body's transformations.

He groaned. It felt like his whole body was stretching. His internal organs shook as his heart pounded, slowly and rhythmically. A ripple started at Erik's stomach, all his muscles turned on, twitching involuntarily. It spread like a wave. Erik pushed forward, standing on his toes, and reaching his hands up above.

It was comforting, as if something that had always been resting beneath the surface had been released.

Erik was hit with a flood of experience. He rode the energy high. The warm energy from his body seemed to gather at his sternum. It was the same sensation as when he had first formed his mana core.

The heat within his body gathered in his chest. He felt something *there* and was about to use his Medical Scan when he was bombarded with notifications.

Title: Mortal grade bloodline
You have unlocked your bloodline by cultivating 1 element to the Mortal grade in your Elemental core.
You have formed a lesser mortal elemental core.

Quest: Bloodline Cultivation 1
The power of the body comes from the purity of the bloodline.
Requirements: Form an Earth Grade Elemental Core with 2 elements
Rewards: Earth Grade Bloodline +100,000,000 EXP

136,219,539/172,300,000 EXP till you reach Level 63

"What the fuck? A monster core?" Erik shifted, nearly falling over from the massive power difference within his body. "Holy shit, that is a lot of power."

He lowered himself carefully. "Don't get too close. I need to adjust to this."

He held out a finger and waved it. The air shifted each time he batted it. "That's a scary amount of power."

Name: Erik West	
Level: 62	Race: Human-?
Titles: *From the Grave II* *Blessed by Mana* *Dungeon Master V* *Reverse Alchemist* *Poison Body* *Fire Body* *City Lord III* *Earth Soul* *Mana Reborn* *Wandering Hero* *Metal Mind, Metal Body* *Mortal Grade Bloodline*	
Strength: (Base 90) +51	1410
Agility: (Base 83) +77	880
Stamina: (Base 93) +35	1920
Mana: (Base 37) +79	1160
Mana Regeneration (Base 40) +61	61.60/s
Stamina Regeneration: (Base 142) +59	41.20/s

"Okay, let's put this physical domain to use. Sorry, just adjusting to the new body, folks," Erik said. His mind was spinning with all the changes and questions.

"Well, you've done it a few times. We'll let you get to it." Jen waved him on.

She was right. Erik took a few steps. Gingerly at first, so he didn't go crashing into the ceiling or across the room, then with more confidence.

Then it was push-ups, squats, and crunches.

"Talk us through what you're going through," Bouchard asked.

"I know these exercises and how they're supposed to feel. How I should move in them. It takes me some time to adjust how much strength I should apply to them. It's like putting on the Conqueror Armor. When you do for the first time, you get a little screwed up because you have so much power really quickly. With the metal tempering, my senses are much better: eyesight, smell, hearing. My control over my body has skyrocketed as well. I didn't just get dumped with the metal body tempering, but the bloodline as well."

Erik looked at his chest and used Medical Scan. There, under his sternum was a small lesser elemental core. "Oh, and I formed a monster core in my chest. It's hooked into my circulatory system."

"What!" Bouchard and several others yelled at the same time. Jen had hungry eyes, looking at Erik's chest. She took a step forward.

"Let me get used to my power. I nearly doubled my damn stats. I'm liable to break bones accidentally if I'm not careful," Erik warned.

"Walk us through everything," Bouchard requested.

Erik relayed his notification information and what he was experiencing. By the end of that, he was pretty adjusted to his body. The medics flooded around him, scanning and checking what was happening inside.

"So, it looks like this bloodline is connected to what beasts in the Ten Realms go through. With that title, you can consume monster cores. If humans have too many of them, it can lead to massive problems. And after you have a monster core at a certain level, then having a second monster core at that same level, you won't get the massive experience boost anymore. I have no idea about the berserker and evolved form."

"They must be new abilities, but how are they activated?" Jen shrugged.

"I don't have any ideas," Erik said.

"It looks like there is a change in systems, closer to the method used by beasts," Bouchard said, writing down notes.

"We'll have to get some samples. For future metal temperings, tempering the blood with the method you came up with will be best, Jen."

"That will start to temper everything else a little too. I would suggest doing the bones first, though. They're mostly isolated and blood is produced in the marrow. Then the blood, then the organs. We saw a huge spike in stamina once the organs were complete. Even at that point, if we enhanced them medically, it would be much easier. Then on to muscle and skin."

"So, reproduce the foundation tempering stages, just flip the blood and bones and remove the mana?" Erik asked. He raised his arm as medics swarmed around him, noting all kinds of information.

"At the later stages, when you circulated the surrounding mana, it sped up the tempering process and supplied the body with more energy. It might be a good idea to have the patient circulate metal attribute mana," Jen said.

It took hours before Erik was released from the medic's custody.

An intelligence officer was waiting with information books.

The dust had barely settled on the ground as Erik frowned, taking books and reading the updates.

"Thank you. Seems it has been a busy three weeks." Erik's mind worked quickly. "Looks like everything is taken care of. There isn't really anything for me to do. In that case, I have something to talk to Rugrat about."

"He'll be at the school," Storbon said. The special teams had rotated in and out. There were plenty of missions that required their attention.

"Kanesh Academy it is," Erik said. They left the cultivation training center. Erik smiled as he sensed someone rapidly approaching.

Gilly raced up the side of the metal mountain. She was bigger than before, her markings more vibrant. She half came to a stop. Her momentum and weight would have staggered Erik before. He took her full weight with a laugh.

"Are you a small lizardling? Damn lap monster." Erik laughed as Gilly licked him eagerly, resizing herself and clambering all over him as if she was a small baby lizard.

She calmed down as Erik gave her scratches and belly rubs.

"Come on, we're going to find Rugrat, then George. Then we're going to put you and George into monster tempering school. I guess I should join you in it as well."

Erik's hand reached for his chest unconsciously. Gilly lowered her head, poking his chest with her snout before sniffing. She pulled back her head, looking at him with her large eyes. He patted her side and climbed over her back. She expanded to her full size. Her rear and front legs had developed more, but she had leathery frills and extended elbows.

"Sure looks like a dragonling to me," Tian Cui said.

"Can you fly?" Erik asked. Gilly turned her neck back to look sideways at him. She shook her head, though Erik could understand enough through their connection.

"She's tried a few times with limited results. She keeps sneaking off to the fire floor to try it out. The heat gives her more lift, probably. George makes fun of her, but he and Davin make sure she's safe."

"A water-breathing and earth-altering dragon. I thought they were all fire-related." Storbon shrugged.

"Well, she might not be a true dragon. Or the simple fact that fire looks badass might make people only talk about the fire dragons." Erik patted Gilly's side.

She set off at a sprint.

"Shit! Wait for us!" Tian Cui yelled as the four-person special team ran after the duo.

Erik threw himself forward, grabbing onto his handle. He had nearly been thrown off. He sent a reproachful thought at Gilly. She looked back with a dragon's grin and he laughed. He couldn't very well stay angry at that, could he?

"Yeah, that is weird." Rugrat nodded as Erik finished telling him about his tempering. Rugrat had already told Erik about his experience.

"So, are you still at the starting stage? What do you have to do now?" Erik asked.

"The solid core is drawing in mana on its own. I passed the low stage, and I'm at the middle stage. I really held my mana cultivation back. Now that I'm here, with all this gear and training supplies, my level's been shooting up."

"Calm down there, rocket man."

"Anyway, the next stage is mana heart. Been looking at the information we have. Mana heart basically transforms the mana veins. Instead of storing mana in the core, it spreads out. Goes through the mana veins again and enters the rest of the body. The mana heart is the center of it all, just like our regular heart. But instead of oxygen, it's mana that moves through the body. The gates are the mouth and lungs, pulling in mana. The heart core sends it through the secondary, less used, mana channels and into the body."

"The elemental core and the mana core… The two cultivation systems are linked and share a lot of similarities. Pure mana increases mana cultivation, while the elemental attributes increase body cultivation," Erik pointed out.

"It must be possible to do them both. But that would take a ton of resources. Slow and steady working on one, and then the other is the easiest," Rugrat said.

"What do you think about the fighting and what's going on?" Erik changed the subject.

Rugrat sighed, rubbed his face, and stood up. They were in the manor, one of the last remaining buildings built by the gnomes. It was officially Erik and Rugrat's home, but they'd spent little time there. A secondary council building had been built since Erik had jumped in to complete his metal tempering.

Nobody wanted to return to the dungeon headquarters where the mana pillar, while reduced, was still shooting down into the ground day and night.

"I had no idea what we were stepping into when we left Earth, that's for sure. It's all so complicated." Rugrat put his hand beside the window, looking out at the dungeon headquarters. "What happens if people figure out the truth? If they find out we're behind the Institute attacks, that we run the Beast Mountain Range, and that Vuzgal is owned by the people who call the First Realm home?"

They had kept Alva secret to protect everyone. Elise had created a trading guild that spread across five realms. Jia Feng operated three academies filled with crafters. They operated two massive dungeons—Alva and under Vuzgal — along with many smaller dungeons, and owned a city in the Fourth Realm with control over a growing regional power in the First Realm. An army of twenty thousand strong. Population in the hundreds of thousands. Blaze and Jasper had built up the Adventurer's Guild to have hundreds of thousands of members spread across several realms. What about the Wandering Inns, and the Sky Reaching Restaurants and all their friends, their people?

"We've got two options: One: we don't care. We take them all on, show our might, and put the fear into our enemies. Two: we hold back, we ready ourselves, keep the secret as long as possible," Erik said.

"Glosil has spoken about this before, and his answer made the most sense." Rugrat snorted and looked at Erik.

"If we reveal the secret, we lose the element of surprise. The longer we hold it, the more room we have to maneuver. I have a feeling that at some point, they'll figure out at least some of the connections. Shit, it might scare the hell out of them."

"Why?" Erik asked.

"Dude, man, brother, we're not just two dudes running for the Beast Mountain Range Trial to get away from Second Realm sect students anymore."

"They have the numbers, the cities. It's a massive sect," Erik argued.

"Yeah, a sect. People have their own cares and alliances. Look at how Elan has had them dancing in his hand with just a few moves! They don't even have a standing army. Our people are *stronger* on average. We opened things to everyone while they close them off to conserve resources. Free access to information, classes to the novice level are free. Apprentice classes with support and prices that won't destroy a person's future."

"You know, sometimes you make sense."

"Well, it's a Friday!"

"Is it?"

"Hell if I know."

"How's Egbert doing?" Erik nodded his chin to the skull in a box on Rugrats' belt.

"When I was cultivating, Egbert repaired or upgraded faster. I got some help from Tan Xue and Qin and made an Egbert head-charging box! It's metal and charged with mana stones. A mini mana cultivation training room."

"Why the window? And why didn't you take the duct tape off his face?"

Rugrat unclipped the box. "Didn't want to just put him in a metal box, be inconsiderate. I've been meaning to take it off, but I forgot. The box is fused together. I'd have to cut it open with a mana knife, re-carve the formations."

"Summarized, you think it will be funny and you want to scare people with the skull on your belt?"

Rugrat held up a finger to refute Erik. His eyes moved back and forth. "Yeah, pretty much."

Erik rolled his eyes. "All right. Well, lend me George for a bit. I got a quest from the Ten Realms. We know beasts can increase their ability by consuming powerful ingredients and monster cores. I think they can increase their power in a way similar to tempering their bodies. Gilly got stronger being with me on the Earth floor. George is always hanging out on the fire floor. I want to talk to Davin, then the beast trainers to see if we can't start training our mounts in the body cultivation training centers."

"Sure, worth a shot. What are you going to do with your elemental core thing?"

Erik's face crumpled as he let out a pained sigh. "Melissa and the other body cultivation experts want to run tests, feed me different ingredients, then different meats. They want me to consume a monster core normally and then try to eat one."

"You can *eat* a monster core? Wait, ingredients? Like the ingredients we feed the beast mounts?"

"Good talk. I'll see you later. Lots to do!" Erik slapped his legs and stood.

Rugrat laughed.

"They want to feed you beast kibble! Oh, come on! Maybe it will help with the hair!"

Erik touched his head. With the metal tempering, all his hair had fallen out. It was nothing more than a shiny cue ball. "Shut up!"

Rugrat's laughter grew as Erik marched out of the room.

"Asshole."

"Ask Delilah if she can make you a concoction, miracle hair grower! Maybe Zhou Heng can make you a wig!" Rugrat yelled at his retreating back, snorting and chuckling.

Erik signaled his goodbye with a middle finger. He could still hear Rugrat down the corridor laughing. With the other hand, he pulled out his sound transmission device.

"Umm, Delilah, I was just wondering…"

"So what do you think?" Erik asked.

Rex Tallahassee finished examining Gilly who preened at the praise. "Hmm, in good health, been eating well. Good activity. No abnormal injuries," He tossed her a hunk of meat. She snapped it out of the air as George looked over at Gilly and then pouted at Rex, who pretended to not see.

He had worked on ranches most of his life, and brought modern Earth practices to the beast trainers in Alva, adjusting diets, exercise and training.

When Rex had first got the Two-Week Curse, he'd drank himself into a stupor. His girlfriend left him because he had no future. It had been a mean joke and the beginning of a country song.

Arriving in the Ten Realms had been a big adjustment. Fortunately, he'd been close to a town. He learned about the Ten Realms and helped farmers with their trained livestock.

Someone must have talked, and Knights appeared one day. He was captured and taken to a city in the Shikoshi Kingdom.

There he'd met the other Earthers. The rest was common history after that.

"Well, I'm always looking for new ways to train beasts. Right now, we're focused on raising as many beasts for the military as possible. We're taming wild beasts, breeding others, and then raising the youngest. We have seven different breeds of panthers for just the regular army. Then dozens of other beasts for artillery squads, mage squads, and close protection gets whatever they want. We're still growing out our aerial beast species. Basically, we're just trying to meet the current needs. While we've got ideas on pushing beasts further, we haven't tested them out. Right now, it's healing spells, food with medicinal ingredients that speed up maturation and build strength, and monster cores are the shit." Rex put his thumbs through his belt loops. He wore a simple long sleeve shirt rolled up, jeans, boots, and a ball cap. He was perpetually chewing on a piece of straw.

"Not even the special teams?"

"They get the best of the best! The beasts that have reached the highest level and have useful abilities. We're just starting to get into selective breeding. I'm not saying that I wouldn't be interested, though. Hell, it might be a new way to raise beasts! I kind of wondered if they have an affinity toward a specific mana attribute, or if it's due to environmental factors or whatever they consume." Rex chewed on his straw in thought.

"I'm not sure about that, but when I was tempering my body with the earth attribute, Gilly was training with me. She grew bigger and was stronger. I want to learn more about how beasts cultivate."

"Well, hell, I'll give anything a shot once, though I ain't going to push anything."

"Glad to hear it. Davin!" Erik yelled into the air.

A head popped out from among the buildings of the Earth Floor's beast training compound.

"Come here."

Davin muttered to himself and flew over like a pouty kid being called to chores. He slumped down as he hung in mid-air near Erik and Rex.

"Davin is an Imp, so he has a beast core and the whole ten yards. He might be a useful resource for you."

"Hey, little guy." Rex pulled out some meat and tossed it over.

Davin's eyes went wide as his jaw seemed to unhinge, opening as wide as his head, clamping down around the meat.

"Okay, well I'll leave them with you," Erik said.

10
Vuzgal's Weight

Hiao Xen let out a satisfied sigh as he savoured a mouthful of delicious pork and rice. Chonglu sat opposite him and took some vegetables, put them in his rice bowl, added some tangy sauce, and dug in.

The dishes had been rapidly reduced between the duo in the last few minutes.

Hiao Xen looked out of the tower at the city below. He couldn't help but feel pride, seeing it all. The work was equal to the speed that Vuzgal had grown.

The twin doors to the room opened. A man walked in, the doors closing behind him as he took his hood down.

Hiao Xen and Chonglu made to stand.

"Please, enjoy your lunch." Erik smiled and sat down.

"You sure know how to make an entrance. Does anyone even know that you're in Vuzgal?" Hiao Xen asked.

"Hopefully, not if everyone has done their job correctly," Erik said as a side door opened.

The serving lady bowed, her eyes constricting in surprise before widening in excitement. "Your tea," she said.

"Please." Erik waved for her to serve the others first.

She moved close to the trio, placed the tea table down, and settled on her knees.

"How is the family?" Erik asked.

"Qiang has done well. He qualified to join a guard unit in the Fifth Realm, though the little troublemaker took a promotion in the Fourth Realm." Hiao Xen shook his head.

"The Fourth Realm is more dangerous. Won't his promotion speed be faster?" Chonglu asked.

"Yes, it should, and there are more resources for people that are willing to stay in the Fourth Realm. I feel that he craves more." Hiao Xen sighed.

"He has the training and the ability and wants to put them to use," Erik said.

"I know. At his age I was the same way, though I wanted to be part of massive deals, not join in combat."

"He has the best gear and training. The Blue Lotus is not a group to get into meaningless conflicts," Erik said as the server finished checking the tea and poured it into the three cups with reverent care. Each move was exact and careful, while also flowing from one movement and action into another.

It calmed Hiao Xen, seeing it. The smell of summer berries offset with citrus grasses made him take a deeper breath. "Nuo Xen is worried, so I get to carry twice the worries."

"Isn't that the truth?" Chonglu smiled.

"Mira and the kiddos doing well?" Erik asked.

"Mira is still doing her mission. I spend most of my days stuffing information books in my brain and my kids have a nanny, thankfully. Going to be happy when this transition stuff's over with!"

"You wouldn't want to go back to being an adventurer, at all?" Hiao Xen asked as the server finished pouring the tea and placed it in front of him. He tilted his head in thanks.

"I might have a few years ago. I might in a few decades. Right now, my children are growing up and I want to be here for them. I nearly lost them twice." Chonglu nodded to the server as she served him, and then moved to Erik. "Don't get me wrong. I love adventuring, living on the edge, the thrill of seeing new sights, and making it through terrifying ordeals. Then getting a beer after it all. Though, I guess, I kind of grew up. There are thousands of people coming through our doors, looking to get stronger in the Battle Arena. Training them, helping you with running Vuzgal... It is a different kind of thrill. A safer one for sure, but that doesn't make it any less exciting."

"Well, here is to family, to the different paths that have brought us here, and chasing that thrill." Erik held up his teacup to the other two. They raised their cups as well.

Hiao Xen inhaled the scent of his tea before taking a sip. He relaxed as the inviting sweetness and the palette-clearing sour flavors mixed on his tongue.

"Good tea," Erik said, and smiled at the server, bowing his head. "And I wasn't here." Erik winked.

The server grinned. "Yes, Lord West." She bowed to remove the tea table.

Hiao Xen looked out of the large windows as if looking away would keep the secret hidden. In his position, he had come to know certain information like how the Adventurer's Guild, the Trader's Guild, the Vuzgal Healing House, the teachers of the Vuzgal Academy, Wandering Inn, Sky Reaching Restaurant, the Vuzgal Defense Force had all known Erik and Rugrat before. He had very carefully not looked into their history, so if he was ever questioned by the Blue Lotus he could deny his *ruminations.*

The server left the room as the trio enjoyed their tea.

Erik cleared his throat and put the tea down on the table.

Hiao Xen looked over to find Erik watching him.

"Hiao Xen, thank you." Erik bowed.

"Lord." Hiao Xen was surprised, shocked even, as he made to place his cup down and return the bow.

Erik rose, halting Hiao Xen with a gesture.

"What you have done for me, for the people of Vuzgal… Honestly, we are all in your debt. If it were not for you, Vuzgal would not be where it is."

"Thank you," Hiao Xen said.

"I will not lie to you. Things have changed recently. You might have noticed some of it. It is part of the reason for Rugrat and I making the decision to move up when Chonlgu ascends to your position. I want to be clear. We are not doing this because we do not appreciate you, or don't wish we could work with you for longer. Certain things are shifting, and we do not want the blowback to fall on you or the Blue Lotus. It is fine if my name is stepped on. But I will not let them step on the Blue Lotus and your honor because we haven't told you everything."

Hiao Xen felt heavy in his heart, but it was coming from a good place. "I understand. This is an opportunity that I was not expecting to get in my lifetime. You honor me, placing so much trust in me."

"You earned it and more. Honestly, I wish that we didn't have to rush all this."

"How long do we have?" Chonglu asked.

"Two weeks, tops. To the outside world, I want it to appear like this was our plan the entire time. It secures Chonglu in his position, makes sure that the Blue Lotus isn't slighted, and then you can return with a large recommendation." Erik looked at Hiao Xen.

Hiao Xen nodded. "I will need to contact the Blue Lotus and check with them. Will there be a ceremony?"

"A small one if possible."

"Okay. I can get everything ready on the Blue Lotus side."

"Thank you, Hiao Xen," Erik said.

"Well, I'm still your acting city lord until you release me." Hiao Xen smiled.

High Elder Cai Bo marched through the halls before reaching two large doors. The guards standing in front of them knocked as she arrived.

"Send her in," Head Asadi's voice called out.

The guards opened it for her.

Head Asadi sat in the middle of the training room. He was sitting on a formation that purified and concentrated his mana. Cai Bo shuddered under its weight and slowed her steps for a half-second.

The door closed behind her as the head of the Willful Institute opened his eyes.

She bowed deeply, recovering from the massive amount of mana all around her. "Head Asadi, the group in Vuzgal led by Low Elder Kostic have had some interesting results. It looks like the Adventurer's Guild has deep ties with Vuzgal. Their primary business—"

"Just tell me their weaknesses!"

"They are a mercenary company protecting traders and people. We can use bandits to wear them down and promote their competitors. There are groups of traders within Vuzgal that want to gain more power. We back them. Get them to snub the Adventurer's Guild."

"Is the Adventurer's Guild part of Vuzgal?" Head Asadi interrupted.

"It is possible. Their members and the Vuzgal defenders talk to one another more than the guards talk with other groups. There are rumors that their guild hall was given to them by Vuzgal."

"Prepare a plan to attack Vuzgal. We will take out the headquarters of this guild and show that we do not care about our opponent."

"That will be hard with all the associations there."

"Yes, they're not pleased with us right now. They care about money more than they care about face. See what the associations want to get them back on our side."

Cai Bo nodded.

"This connection to the leader of the Vuzgal fighting force?"

"I sent a group to the Second Realm with a junior, Mercy. She knew him. They are looking into our past records in the Second Realm. Then they will work lower."

"It is odd, but not a focus. What have you found about the Adventurer's Guild locations?"

"They have hundreds of locations across the lower realms. I believe that we have all their known locations. They do not own cities, but, instead, have guild halls in cities with totems. It creates a vast network."

"Strength in these cities?"

"Not high. They are extended in the fighting."

"They have participated in three of the last eight attacks," Head Asadi growled.

Cai Bo remained silent, waiting.

There was a knock at the main door.

"Good, he is on time. Come in," Head Asadi said.

The doors opened to reveal a young man with deep black eyes, wearing fine battle armor. He moved naturally with the sword strapped on his hip as if he had been born as an armored knight.

Nico Tolentino. He was one of the top five candidates to get accepted into a fighting academy. Talented with combat techniques and smithing ability, he had formed his liquid core according to her sources and was preparing to temper his Body Like Iron.

Nico Tolentino was of the newest generation, unlike Cai Bo, who had practically reached the end of her path and was innately linked to the Institute. As it rose or fell, then she would as well.

There were plenty of opportunities for Nico to increase his strength. If he was able to enter a Sixth Realm academy, then it was possible he could reach the Seventh Realm.

Head Asadi actually paused his cultivation.

Cai Bo could only bite her cheek at the different treatment.

"Nico, you will lead the Fourth Army to attack the Adventurer's Guild.

You can use those captured as ingredients for human core pills for your training."

So opulent! Refining their entire being down into a pill. Even if they only drew out seventy percent of their overall strength, there were tons of fighters with strong bodies and some training in mana cultivation. Truly, it was the best way to cultivate.

"Head Asadi, you are too kind." Nico smiled, barely holding back a sneer, looking Cai Bo up and down as Head Asadi turned around.

She thought about smacking the look off his face. After all, his clan's leader was another of her puppets. But no, he would serve a higher purpose, a sacrifice for the greater gain. What was one more dead uppity brat?

"High Elder Cai Bo has information on the different locations. Cai Bo, guide Nico well. Crush the Adventurer's Guild halls."

"Yes, Head Asadi," Cai Bo bowed, a cold glimmer in her eye. She had the perfect target to turn this war in their favor.

11 Forward

The Willful Institute riders were thrown off balance as their charge was met with the Adventurer's guilds spells and ranged attacks, shattering barriers, beasts, and bodies.

"Brace!" Branch leader Derrick yelled. The remaining forces crashed into the impromptu wall of fused stone, carts, and anything else Derrick's force had been able to string up in the face of the massed counterattack.

There were only a few beasts of the horse kind among the mounts rushing the wall. Most of them could climb. Their momentum slowed to a grinding halt as melee fighters rebuffed them. Swords, claws, teeth, spears, and hammers opened beast and man alike.

"Spell scrolls!"

They blasted out in front of the melee fighters. The mounted forces had nowhere to go as spells carved through their ranks, removing the pressure on the front line.

"Ranged!" The melee fighters crouched. Healers pulled out wounded and healed anyone hurt. Armored ranged forces released their prepared spells, the bodies of their fellow mounted forces and the broken walls of the surrounding buildings pinned in the Willful Institute's charge.

They broke under the slaughter and ran back the way they had come.

"Have mages switch to buffing and healing. Push any reinforcements to the flanks." Derrick looked back to see the wall of a once-grand structure rent in several places, bleeding his guild mates and their allies pushing into the city.

The world exploded as he was thrown backward. He hit the ground and rolled. Stone and dirt rained on him as he pushed himself up, feeling worse than those combat training days with Blaze.

Gaping holes had opened in his impromptu defenses, turning it into no more than a rough patch of ground.

Horror ran through Derrick at seeing dead and wounded, *his* dead and wounded. His training forced him to focus, and he pulled out his map. Markers moved ahead of the wall. He couldn't hear it, but he could feel the mounted forces coming *again*.

He opened his mouth only to start coughing. He covered his mouth and activated his sound projecting necklace. "Regroup between the stables and the wall!" Derrick used his necklace to reach everyone.

Those able to move the wounded and began running or hobbling back.

Derrick tore out spell scrolls, layering traps over the area.

"Sir!" A man pulled Derrick, spinning him around. "We need to go."

His people were running for the rear as tiles slipped free of roofs and rubble crunched. The Willful Institute Riders howled as they rode through the street, across the broken buildings, and charged through the breaches in small groups.

Derrick and his small group started running.

Beasts leapt from roofs, dragging guild members to the ground, their riders lashing out with weapons and cutting down guild members who tried to get up.

Derrick's group retaliated with spells and weapons, but his guild members were broken and scattered.

A spell formation appeared in the sky. A pillar of light dropped on a breach, leaving behind a crater of tombstones and a dust wave.

One of Derrick's blades slid across the ground. He used a healing spell on himself and started toward the breach, pulling a spare blade from his storage ring. Around him, other people were getting up from the ground.

"Move to the rally point between the stables and the breach! Gather your guild members as you go!" Derrick ordered.

A rider charged Derrick and his people through a side road, his yells drawing four other Institute riders.

Derrick accelerated, drawing in mana, and reinforcing his body with elements faster than any normal human. The Fifth Realm fighters shot out spells, hitting the ground around him as he skidded from side to side.

He cast out an ice spell ahead of his charge, dropping to the ground as spells flew over him. He slid forward, hitting the ground, then launched himself up.

The world crackled around him as he landed on his feet, stumbling before he found his footing right before the riders. A spear nearly hit him in the chest as he broke his ankle. He hit the ground and rolled, careful to not stab or slice himself with his blades. The riders passed him.

He got to his knee, breathing heavily as the group of five were charging his watchers. "Lightning!" Silver lightning shot from his hand, dancing between the iron and sweat-covered riders and their beasts.

They stiffened and rolled, tombstones appearing as they flopped.

"Shit." Derrick pushed his foot into place and blasted it with a healing spell. "That'll work."

He hobbled toward the fallback position. wincing.

A rider took notice of him and charged.

Derrick cast an ice spear ahead of the beast. The beast impaled itself, launching the rider forward, his stirrups arresting his moveent and reversing his momentum.

His eyes widened at Derrick, the confusion and pain turning to realization.

Derrick used the Blade Rush technique. His sword cut a line of light, taking off both the rider's and beast's heads as he appeared on the other side of them. A rush of dust passed him as two tombstones appeared behind him.

"Ah shit, shit, shit, shit." Derrick hobbled at the speed he'd just used, straining his not-so-good leg.

He wrapped it in ice, immobilizing it, and used another small healing spell. His gaze darted around. The smoke from fires and dust from fighting cut up the battlefield.

He ran toward the stables they'd passed upon entering the city. The newly erected wall—much stronger than the first—had appeared between the different stables and surrounding homes.

Wounded were lifted back over the new wall. Others jumped and climbed the cargo nets upwards.

Derrick stored his blades. Running and jumping, he used the wall to gain height. Guild members grabbed him. They grunted, pulling him over the wall.

"Ranged, get up on the taller buildings. Mages, clear the surrounding area. Flatten everything fifty meters out! Wounded over by the well!" Derrick cracked out commands, bringing order.

"They're coming!"

"Repeaters, melee!"

He pulled out a heavy repeater.

A friendly mage used wind spells, forcing the smoke and dust away. Derrick's eyes burned, but he fought against blinking and kept his sight on the enemy.

The guild scout cast fireball. Enemy riders surged out of the smoke at where the spell landed.

The heavy repeater kicked as hard as a horse, but Derrick's aim remained flat and controlled, directing the fire right into the line of charging riders.

Dozens of others joined in, shredding weak imitations of barriers.

"Cease fire! Cease fire!" Derrick's words were passed on as he looked at the pile of tombstones.

A wind, tens times stronger than the one before cleared the area, revealing hundreds of Institute fighters. They seemed to be in every street, with many riding across rooftops. They paused as the smoke cleared.

The Guild and their allies attacked. the Institute riders yelled and charged.

Spells and attacks flashed between them. Riders died. Sections of stable and defenses crumbled to the ground.

"Brace! Melee!"

Derrick stored his repeater and took out his blades. Blades of ice and lightning cut down jumping mounts and their riders.

"Get up! Back in formation!" The armored woman's voice snapped through the air as the guild members reeled from the attacks.

He looked into her eyes as she nodded, using shield and sword, trained as all Alvans were. She took the impact off some wolf-beast, and *bashed* beast and rider back in the direction they had come from.

Derrick saw others along the defensive. Two or three people at most. They looked simple, but their movements were deadly.

CPD teams.

His ally ran toward the beast and jumped off a piece of rubble, her sword cutting through the rider's neck before she landed again. A mage shot a green bolt past her. Striking the ground, it turned into roots and thorns, ensnaring a group of riders.

The guild members pulled together, reinforcing the front wall, buffing and healing, regaining their footing.

They were using everything they had to create a stalemate and turn the balance. Derrick could feel it.

Derrick heard a roar to the right flank. *Fuck, more mounted.*

He yelled out his own frustration as his attacks came faster and stronger. He didn't care to save his stamina in his anger. They had fought so *hard.* They'd taken the walls and entered the city, but they were barely holding on against this mounted force. With reinforcements, it was a death knell.

Derrick's swords parried a spear and stabbed through a climbing beast, sending rider and beast backward, clearing his vision.

It was as if a giant had grabbed him and squeezed. The fire running through his veins turned to ice.

"Adventurer's Guild!" Kim Cheol roared as the mounted force lowered their spears and secured them.

"Hoah!" The Willful Institute riders didn't have time to form up as the force streamed through the smoke. Kim Cheol and Joan led from the front as they *tore* into the Willful Institute's counterattacking force.

Derrick dodged out of reaction as an Institute fighter ran up the bodies piling against the wall. Derrick roared, filled with energy that came from deep in his soul, and attacked using magic and blade alike.

He stood as others went down around him and took hits, trying his best to cover others. Everyone was fighting to hold on in the press around them. Willful Institute riders started to turn and leave, rushing back toward the center of the city.

The Guild riders spread out to harass the fleeing Institute members, cutting them down with spells.

Derrick coughed, feeling tired and relieved. They'd made it. His eyes dropped to the bodies across the streets wearing Adventurer's guild clothes, his relief turning to guilt.

He turned away to look at the remaining Guild members on the wall with him. There were only a few still standing from the original group.

"Care for the wounded. Use your stamina and healing potions," Derrick ordered.

He pulled out a purple and green flecked potion. He scanned the area for the worst wounded and poured some of the potion on their open wounds, and then the rest down their throats.

Derrick looked up at the sounds of arriving beasts.

They wore the Guild's emblem, fanning around the group. Healers jumped down from their mounts, moving among the wounded to assist.

"Echo's breach is secured," Lieutenant Colonel Dominik Zukal said to Colonel Domonos Silaz, who was bent over the table map of the city of Craghorn.

"The breaching force?"

"They're out of the fight. They lost too many people," Zukal said.

"Push up Reserve Unit Echo One," Domonos ordered.

The room shook, but no one reacted.

"Looks like the enemy hasn't given up on the spells," Domonos muttered. "Get Bravo to hold their position. I want Alpha and Charlie nearer to them. Don't want to get drawn into an ambush."

"Street by street?" Zukal asked.

"Street by street, and use Life Detect scrolls. They must be using secret passages to move their forces. Echo only found the rider force in the last few minutes."

"Yes, sir." Zukal turned to the messenger aides. Map aides were altering their map according to new information and sending it to the larger map, updating it overall. Linked maps updated the maps of commanders in the field, so they knew exactly where the enemy had been spotted and reported, and where their allies were.

Markets were turned into courtyards, the surrounding houses turned into walls and defenses with a little magic. Unfortunately, Third Realm fighters had more than enough power to reduce a house to rubble in a few minutes.

Domonos moved to the corner of the room. A periscope rested there. He put his eyes to it, flinching as a fireball hit the mana barrier just meters from the periscope's lens, shaking the entire building.

The mana barriers held as Domonos waited for the smoke to clear.

On either side of the Adventurer's Guild camp, there were other sect camps.

Groups with mana barriers marched across the farmers' fields, pockmarked with spell impacts, and littered with the bodies of those whose mana barriers had failed.

The city wall was like broken teeth. The groups passed through and into the large city beyond.

The Craghorn rested on the banks of a once crystal-clear river. Waterfalls from upstream spread out to create a wet plains underneath. The rich waters turned it into an area teeming with life. Even in the Alchemist's Realm, it was a jewel.

The city was filled with towers covered in gardens, catering to the massive resources required to support the Willful Institute. Many had wished to control the city, but none were bold enough to try before.

Now it was but a shell. Domonos watched a spell strike one of the towering buildings, shattering the gardens and sending the stone crashing below. He glanced at the waters. Smugglers and merchants were doing a bustling business, carrying away those willing to pay their high prices to the other bank or down the river. Those that didn't have the means, but were desperate, tried to pull together rafts, or even swim.

The clear waters were muddied with the constantly moving ships, and the blood of those that tried to climb onto other's ships only to meet the owner's blades.

Artillery spells rose and fell, raining on marked positions within the city.

The other sects dragged their feet when they could. As soon as it looked like a win, they jumped at the opportunity to advance. It was a good thing that all the spies they had were his father's intelligence officers. He didn't trust the sects; they cared too much about personal gain over the mission.

His orders could deliver the men and women under his command to death. He also knew that if he didn't command, if he didn't give them the orders to hold, then he would lose many more.

If Echo hadn't held, Delta would have been wiped out. Derrick had done a hard job, but he'd stopped the Institute's counterattack dead.

Domonos pulled his eyes from the periscope as the building shook once again.

Zukal stood nearby, holding his sound transmission device. "Do you want me to report the Fifth Realm Institute fighters to the sects?"

Domonos paused. "Leak that we ran into some powerful forces; use it to make them bolder and show their ability. Don't say their actual levels. Have the spies report that we are looking to hunt them down to make them pay."

"Make them double their efforts to hunt them down to try to look better than us." Zukal nodded.

"Out here, we have to deceive the enemy and those who hire us. Once we cut out Craghorn, the Willful Institute will only have four remaining cities that can supply their training resources."

"With how hard the Willful Institute is fighting, there isn't going to be much left." Zukal rubbed his face.

Domonos clapped him on the shoulder. "Well, it's a good thing that we don't need the city. The other sects can fight over it. We just need to get paid and move onto the next fight. Find out if the Institute is sending out their riders to attack the other sects."

"Yes, sir."

"I have a feeling they're starting to target us."

Zukal grimaced at Domonos' words. "We knew that it was a possibility."

12
Vuzgal's New Acting City Lord

Title: Acting Vuzgal City Lord
Ability to control the Vuzgal City Interface
Ability to banish others from the city's domain
Cannot create new city lord
Cannot alter the rights of the city lord(s)

Chonglu dismissed the screen and bowed from the hip to Erik and Rugrat. He turned and repeated the motion to Hiao Xen.

He rose to applause. Tan Xue, Qin Silaz, Julilah, and other teachers from the school were there with the leaders of the Vuzgal Defense force.

Domonos was still commanding the battle at Craghorn. Officially, he was training.

There were some select traders, people from the battle arena Chonglu had worked with, and others from the Vuzgal Administration.

Branch heads from Vuzgal's different associations were all in attendance: the Fighter's Association, Crafter's Association, Alchemist's Association, and Blue Lotus. Even Elder Lu Ru of the Fourth Realm Blue Lotus headquarters had come.

Chonglu smiled, but his mind kept wandering to the information he had been given by Deputy Director Detrick, Hiao Xen, and what he had figured out on his own. His eyes drifted to Mira, who was holding up their two young ones in either arm. They were clapping and wore wide smiles.

Chonglu winked at them and looked at Erik and Rugrat. He felt his throat closing as they grinned at him. He owed them a debt he would never be able to repay. Until the end of his days, he would support them in whatever way he could.

Oskar Elsi's dull blue eyes drifted across the game of Go, watching his great-grandson ponder his next move as he held the black stone in his hand.

His robe softened his large shoulders and hid his tempered body underneath. His back was as straight as a spear while his head had been shaved clean.

On his chest, he wore the emblem of a Stone Fist Sect Elder.

His smile made one think that everything happening was as he intended.

"You know, Eduard, if you hold that stone any tighter you might crush it."

Eduard released his grip and coughed. "Sorry, Great-grandfather." Eduard bowed.

A loyal child, unlike that other disappointment. Oskar's eyes chilled for a second.

Eduard placed down his stone, taking two prisoners.

"Decisive when you act, but you aren't paying attention to the long game." Oskar looked at the board and picked up a white stone without looking. He placed it on the opposite side of the board.

Oskar debated his move. Eduard swallowed, his eyes flicking across the table as Oskar's hand paused above different pieces.

There was a light knock at the door. Oskar frowned, looking up and lowering his hand. "Come in." The door swung out as attendant Ilsa walked in with her head bowed.

Oskar glanced at her before he cleared his throat. "Shall we take a break for now? We can continue after your practice tomorrow."

"Yes, Great-Grandfather." Edurad raised his hands and bowed to Oskar. He quickly got up from where he was sitting.

He closed the doors with a bow, reactivating the formations in the room.

Oskar indicated for Ilsa to speak.

"Chonglu has become the Acting Lord of Vuzgal. It was a quiet ceremony, but all of Vuzgal knows. Lords West and Rodriguez were in attendance. Hiao Xen has been awarded a position as a branch manager in the Sixth Realm."

"Rats, nothing more than rats." Oskar's face twisted into a sneer. "Did West not think we'd link him to Mira leaving the clan and the sect? Did he think we'd forget the shame? That Lord Chonglu and his bastard seed, dirtying one of our own!"

Oskar smashed the game across the floor, sending pieces everywhere. He stood, flexing and relaxing his arms as he breathed, focusing his mind.

"Without the Blue Lotus' manager as the acting city lord now, any action taken against them is on their honor, not on the Blue Lotus. What about the traders we support?"

"They have been testing their boundaries vigorously. A few have been captured by the Vuzgal police and are on trial. They don't know enough, and the police will only ban them from Vuzgal."

"There are plenty of others to take their place. What about the Vuzgal warehousing district?"

"Through different subsidiaries, we now control seventy-two percent of the warehouse district."

"Once we reach eighty percent, increase the warehousing fees, double them for traders with close ties to Vuzgal. Apply pressure to the other warehouse owners to sell off or follow what we're doing. Have the Black Hawks pay a visit to anyone that doesn't."

"We should control the majority of the warehouses within two weeks." Ilsa bowed her head.

"Seems that Vuzgal and its lords forgot about our Elsi clan. At the end, we'll have them on their knees begging forgiveness, offering to give Mira back to us." Oskar sniffed.

"Have you been working on your alchemy or healing skills?" Rugrat asked.

"Not much." Erik glanced at his skill level.

Skill: Healer *Level: 84 (Expert)*
You are an expert on the human body and the arts of repairing it. Healing spells now cost 10% less Mana and Stamina. Patient's stamina is used an additional 15% less.

Skill: Alchemy *Level: 81 (Expert)*
Able to identify 1 effect of the ingredient. Ingredients are 5% more potent. When creating concoctions, mana regeneration increases by 20%

"I've been working on mass-producing pills for tempering the body and making the revival concoctions."

Erik pulled out a needle, sharing the stat screen with Rugrat.

Revival Needle *Grade: Low Expert*
Inject directly into the patient's heart. Increases natural regeneration by 200% for 30 seconds. Increases Stamina regeneration by 400%. Heals blood vessels. Heals respiratory system.

"Enough to get the patient stabilized, tossed into a medical cage, and pushed to the rear," Erik said.

"How many can we produce?" Rugrat asked.

"Currently, about seventy per day. We've been stockpiling them. Only ten percent make it to the deployed medics."

"I've never worried as much about the supplies we have at the rear going into a fight." Rugrat passed the needle back to Erik.

"We were always at the front, wondering where the damn ammo and water was. Armies move on their supply trains. Thankfully, we have the Trading Guild to support our forces and factories to mass-produce our weapons, gear, and most consumables." Erik stored the needle away and put his hands behind his back. The duo looked out over Vuzgal. "So, have you been working on your crafting?"

Rugrat shook his head. "Distracted, still getting used to this new power. I want to work on a Gatling gun-style weapon system. though it would take time and resources away from other projects we really need. Not worth it. Was thinking about getting on the training program."

"Which one?"

"The undead one," Rugrat grinned.

"The Blood Demon Sect undead that we have grinding through dungeons to increase their power?"

"Yeah, Egbert was thinking ahead. We have multiple training dungeons, our personal crafter's dungeons. The Beast Range trial now creates random creatures from our stock of known dungeon beasts according to different levels. Endless dungeons. Same mechanism, more creatures, not as powerful."

"Wait, explain the Beast Range Trial." Erik held out a hand to slow Rugrat.

"The dungeon spawns a random powerful beastie. You have to fight and defeat it to get dungeon points and choose to move on to the next fight or exit. Still has the medallion, so if you break it, you get returned to where you started. While we were gone, Egbert worked on making the dungeons better. He took gaming knowledge and planning from Matt and Tanya. Created dungeons more in the style of games back on Earth. They were meant to be as challenging as possible, pit people against real odds. Worked out well." Rugrat tapped the box on his hip.

"They've been the best training aide we have. The crafter dungeons allow people to work with real pressure and a sense of competition. The fighting dungeons give people combat experience, solo and with a group. It's the only way we could have grown our army and our people's levels without them fighting across the realms. So, good ole dungeon grind?"

"Hell, yeah, man, and don't discount the undead. The old Vuzgal guards are hella strong now. Can't send them into the dungeons anymore on account that in fights they drain the dungeon of all its built-up affinities to create the different beasts. Some of the new guards have reached that stage and others will shortly. When they were alive, they were powerful already."

"Kind of fucked up when you think that we're using our enemies' bodies as a fighting force."

"Well, it was that, or let them disappear. We have a serious lack of people. This makes up for it. Our units are trained on how to operate with undead support. They're basically simple automatons with additional armor and gear. They're a constant hidden weapon in our back pocket."

"You keep a blade in your back pocket?" Erik asked.

"No! What idiot would put a blade in his back pocket?"

There was a knock at the door, interrupting their talk.

"Come in," Rugrat said.

A messenger walked in, looking nervous. "Sirs!" He bowed suddenly.

"Well, do you have something for us?"

"*I-am-really-sorry-lords, but-there-is-a-lady-called-Momma-Rodriguez-that-has-been-harassing-the-Sky-Reaching-Restaurant-and-asking-about-you-both*!" He gulped down air after spitting out the words rapid-fire.

Rugrat and Erik turned from the window. Erik felt his stomach tighten and Rugrat's mouth was twitching in an attempt to form words.

"What did she say her name was?" Erik demanded.

"Maria Josefina Rodriguez."

Erik's entire body shook. Rugrat stared back at him in a similar state of shock.

Is it really her?

Erik and Rugrat set their jaws.

"Which location is she at?" Rugrat said as they walked forward.

"The fifth location!"

"Stand up, boy. You're coming with us," Rugrat said, grabbing him by the shoulder, raising him, and forcing him to walk with them.

Erik used his sound transmission device. "Roska, we're heading to the fifth Sky Reaching Restaurant location. Send word ahead to bring the person calling herself Momma Rodriguez into a private room. We'll move through the under-city."

"Understood. Meet you down there in five."

Erik and Rugrat walked out of the room. Their guards moved around them. Rugrat handed the messenger to two of them. They checked the boy's medallion and his identity several times, asking him questions to verify he was who he said he was.

Erik and Rugrat kept grim expressions, ready to be let down, still hoping they were wrong, but everything checked out.

Momma Rodriguez sipped her tea. She was so focused on other things, the flavors seemed dull with her heart.

She stood up as the doors to the room opened. A man and a woman walked into the room. Both wore comfortable and loose shirts and pants with boots, but there was a hardness to them she had often seen in Rugrat and his friends' eyes.

They scanned the room before one went back out and the other moved to the side.

Maria's hands shook as time seemed to slow. Two men pulled back their hoods as they entered the room. They looked like contractors from their rugged cargo pants and shirts. The one on the right was a bit taller than the one on the left. Their broad shoulders crowded the doorway as they stepped inside. One had brown-almost-black hair and wet brown eyes with that same goofy grin, and beside him, the man had blond hair and sharp blue eyes.

Maria let out a shuddering breath. Her legs trembled as tears blurred her view. She stumbled, and the two men rushed forward to support her.

"My boys," she whispered. Tears trickled down her cheeks as she hooked her arms around both of their necks, hugging them both and covering their cheeks in tear-stained kisses.

"Momma," Jimmy choked out.

They knelt on either side of her, patting her back.

She squeezed them tight again, letting out a shuddering breath as she released them. She laughed and looked at them as they all wiped away their tears. The others in the room looked away. The door had closed at some point.

"I told you there was no getting away from me. Had to chase you across this Ten Realms!"

"How did you?" Erik asked.

"Found a lady on the internet that had the curse. With all of your experiments and posting about them on the internet we figured out what we needed to do, and I went with her," Momma Rodriguez said.

"Momma." Rugrat's words were filled with feeling and admonishment.

"I lost your brother to war and your sister to drugs. You two are all I have left. Do you really think I would just sit at home, Jimmy Enrique Rodriguez?" She waved a finger as if it were a weapon with her hand on her hip as her accent became heavier.

Rugrat bowed down, stepping back.

"You're all I have left. I might not go fight with you, but I will always be there when you come home!" Her voice softened as she lowered her finger, putting it on her other hip. "And did you think I wouldn't notice you selling all my recipes?"

Rugrat laughed weakly and tried to make himself small, looking anywhere but at Momma. "I was hungry."

"Bottomless damn pit," growled, but there was no heat in her voice. "You know how hard it is going to be to set up my own restaurant having to compete with everyone on fried chicken? What did you even use as a chicken?"

"Well, you see..."

Erik coughed, trying to hide his smile, fighting his face's attempts to betray him.

Erik laughed, shaking his head. His heart filled to bursting while his stomach churned, thinking that this was all some dream.

Rugrat scratched the back of his head awkwardly.

"Momma Rodriguez, it's great to see you." Erik smiled. "Need someone around that can keep him in line."

"Hey!" Rugrat said, glaring at Erik.

Momma Rodriguez laughed and walked up to Rugrat, pulling his cloak in, fixing it, and then patting his chest. "We made our promise long ago, you and me, didn't we?" she said to Erik.

Rugrat frowned and looked between them.

"Stick together and we'll make it through anything." Erik looked down, pressing his lips together and closing his eyes. "And know that no matter what, there will always be a home to return to." His last words came out raspy as he choked up.

Momma Rodriguez moved over and pulled Erik's cloak tight. "And home is where we are," she said softly, and wiped Erik's face.

He nodded and cleared his throat forcefully. He looked into her deep brown eyes. She was short, but as fierce as ever. Her wrinkles and easy smile comforted others.

"Lords…" She shook her head. "Seems that someone around here has *no* idea about you two."

There was a cough from the side.

Erik looked at Roska.

"I'm sorry, but we need to verify you are who you say you are."

Rugrat made to say something, but Momma Rodriguez put her hand out. "It's good that you have someone around here with common sense! A strong young lady like yourself. Do you have a significant other in your life?"

"I'm going to have you agree to this contract on the Ten Realms." Roska held out a piece of paper and a small blade.

"You didn't answer the question, and I agree to this contract on the Ten Realms." Momma Rodriguez cut her thumb and pressed it to the paper.

"Momma," Rugrat tried to hint.

"What? She's a pretty young girl, strong and determined. She's following you two around, so she's smart. I just want to know the kind of people you two have been hanging around with. So, any significant other? What's your name?"

The glow of the Ten Realms contract covered Momma Rodriguez.

Roska looked at Erik and Rugrat, who gave her no help.

"Uhh, no ma'am, and Roska."

"That won't do! Fighting isn't everything, as I keep telling these two!"

"I have to ask you some questions," Roska said timidly.

"Ask away, dear." Momma Rodriguez smiled, standing there.

She had intimidated a captain of a special team with just a few questions. *If that's not Momma Rodriguez, then the universe is out of balance. There can't be two!*

Roska went through a series of questions, then took samples of blood from Rugrat and Momma Rodriguez and tested them.

"It appears she is who she says she is." Roska put the gear away.

"Try saying that ten times fast," Erik muttered.

"All right, come on. I want to know everything you two have been up to?" Momma Rodriguez moved back to the table and sat down, waving for Rugrat and Erik to join her.

She pulled glasses out of her storage ring and poured out iced tea for the others.

Erik and Rugrat knew better than to try and take it from her.

Roska coughed and held out another contract. "I'm sorry, but this contract makes sure that you cannot reveal any information you are told by Lord West and Rodriguez to any other person without their permission. It also secures that you will not pass on certain secrets." Roska put down the contract.

Momma Rodriguez read the contract before she cut her finger and placed it on the contract. "I agree to the contract as outlined here."

Power of the Ten Realms wrapped around her, binding her to the proscribed contract.

"Do you want some tea now, dear?"

"No, thank you. I can't while working." Roska stepped backward.

"Ah, you military types. Always something holding you back." Momma Rodriguez clicked her tongue. "So, from the beginning you two."

"Well, Erik and I dropped out of the sky with those capsules I made."

"I heard that you put it all on your credit cards, so it all reverted back to your family. Nicely done." Momma Rodriguez looked at Erik and chuckled.

"Wanted to leave them a final thank you."

"So, after you landed with the capsules…?"

Momma Rodriguez, Roska, and Davos listened with rapt attention as Erik and Rugrat told their tale of entering the Ten Realms.

13
Lions, Tigers, and Momma Bears

Elder Kostic entered Lord Chonglu's office and took the seat offered "Thank you, Acting Lord Chonglu." Kostic sat down calmly as Chonglu sat opposite.

"I received your letter regarding the Adventurer's Guild," Chonglu said, interlacing his fingers together on his desk. "I'm sorry to say that right now we can't evict them from the city. They have placed well in the last two fighters' competitions. They are well connected to the traders and crafters, and have not broken any laws." Chonglu opened his hands.

"What if they were to lose their current position?" Kostic asked.

"How do you mean?" Chonglu raised an eyebrow.

"Well, there are many cities that they hold halls in. Some of the city lords have certain complaints. Having an obnoxious and arrogant guild in your city can lead to… *problems.*" Kostic seemed to search for the word.

"Depending on the situation, we might be more amenable." Chonglu opened his thumbs, keeping his fingers interlaced.

"Well, thank you for your time." Kostic half tilted his head, standing up.

"Let me see you out. I hope that you can come to me if you require any assistance," Lord Chonglu said.

"Thank you, and I will keep that in mind."

Kostic exited Chonglu's office. He gathered his guards and continued out to his carriage. It was only inside that his blank face took on a pensive look.

Chonglu wasn't as simple as he looked. If Vuzgal was connected to the Adventurer's Guild, he would warn them about the impending attacks on their guild halls. If he didn't, then they won't show any large changes. Most impressive was Chonglu's lack of a reaction.

It would also wrap up the Nico problem. Kostic sneered. Foolish boy, thinking he could slander Elder Cai Bo.

Chonglu related everything to Elan, Erik, and Rugrat. Elan had spent his time in the under-city, as Vuzgal was the main hub for the Intelligence Department. He had been working to alter the story around the Silaz family, basing it off the truth.

Erik and Rugrat had remained a few extra days, talking to Momma Rodriguez and finding out all she had been through.

Now there was no laughter and smiles.

"And there's nothing we can do unless we want to play right into their hand," Elan said.

"What do you mean?" Chonglu asked.

"He means that if we pass on that the Willful Institute is trying to get the Adventurer's Guild evicted from the different cities, then they'll know for sure that we're working with the Guild." Erik's voice was acidic as he looked at Elan with dark eyes.

Elan bowed his head, pressing his lips together.

Chonglu let his hands fall powerlessly into his lap.

"So, we don't tell them to cover our asses from the Institute?" Erik asked.

"That is your decision."

"Shouldn't this be a decision for the council?" Rugrat asked.

"If we go to the council, Blaze will have to know," Chonglu said.

Erik looked at Rugrat.

"I say we tell them," Rugrat said.

"Send word to Blaze right away. Get plans moved up to relocate Guild dependents to a secure location where the Institute can't find them." Erik sighed. It was no small undertaking with how large the Adventurer's Guild had become.

"Make sure that all guilds and groups that are associated with us are prepared to evacuate at the slightest hint of trouble. I don't like how close to the truth the Institute is getting."

14
Alvan War Machine

The lights faded as Erik and Rugrat pulled their hoods down. Their special team guards opened a gap for them as they walked through the totem gates and into Alva proper.

"*Dios Mio*," Momma Rodriguez whispered as she clutched the cross on her chain.

"Welcome to Alva, Momma," Rugrat said.

Units marched down the roads in-step. Buses running on rune-engines ran down the street with beast-pulled carts. Crews of mages and builders worked together assembling new factories and buildings.

Alvans walked on the sidewalks, off somewhere, talking to stall owners or their friends, walking into stores and restaurants or newly minted offices.

Delilah and Glosil broke off from their conversation as Erik and Rugrat left the defensive structure around the totem, surrounded by their own guards.

"Every time we come back it seems busier." Rugrat grunted as Momma Rodriguez elbowed him. "Right, uh, Commander Glosil of the Alva Military and Council Leader Delilah Ryan. This is my momma."

Delilah messed with her hands, bowing her head jerkily and turning red as she pushed some errant hair behind her ear.

Momma Rodriguez smiled. "Please just call me Momma Rodriguez. It is good to meet you both. I have heard a lot about you. You found a fine teacher, Delilah, and you have stepped into your position well. Commander Glosil, you carry a lot of weight on your shoulders, but you have accomplished so much."

"Thank you, ma'am." Glosil pressed his lips together in a smile.

"It is good to meet you, Momma Rodriguez. I have heard much about you." Delilah smiled and reached out her hand.

The little woman scoffed and hugged her, stunning Delilah before she returned the embrace.

Momma released her, a gleam in her eye as they started back to her boys. "You four clearly have work to talk about. I'll head off."

"Roska, could you…?" Rugrat asked.

Roska stepped forward and smiled. In just a few short days Momma Rodriguez had made an impression already. "I'll have someone escort you to the Lords' residence, or take you around Alva. There is no place safer in the Ten Realms. Everyone here is an Alvan."

"Best to see what state they left the house in," Momma muttered as she walked with one of the special team members.

"You said it was urgent," Glosil said to Erik. Delilah was still recovering.

Erik took out a sound canceling formation as they started to walk, their guards creating a cordon around them. "We have been stepping around it this entire time. Starting today, the Alva military will be completely activated. The Willful Institute is looking in places we don't like. We need to pull their attention away and put all the pressure on them that we can."

"I would suggest retaining a battalion in Alva," Glosil said, "and two battalions in Vuzgal. That would dedicate close to ten thousand troops to the front lines. In two weeks, another group of soldiers will complete basic training. I suggest waiting three more months before they are put into action. They'll be green and they still need to take their advanced courses."

"Do it." Erik nodded.

"What about trading and other activities?" Delilah asked.

"We will enact the wartime guidelines set down in everyone's contracts. Secondary fighting forces will be recalled. Increase their training, including the Adventurer's Guild members."

"That will tear apart the economy."

"We are prepared for that. Unlike wars back on Earth, when we conquer a city, we can loot it of all its valuables and gain. Already, the

Adventurer's Guild has made a fortune," Erik said.

"Are the backup sites ready?" Rugrat asked.

"The secondary dungeons have been set up. If need be, we can evacuate Vuzgal and Alva to them within four hours," Glosil confirmed.

"Secondary sites?" Delilah asked.

"A backup plan in case everything goes to shit," Erik told her.

"If we're attacked, the totem won't work."

"But the teleportation formations will. We have a network of them across the realms. We'll ferry Alvans across the first four realms to dungeon locations we've altered to suit our needs," Erik said.

Their guards moved around them. Passers-by cleared a path as they bowed their heads to the quartet as they passed.

The third barracks closer to the totem came into view.

"How are things in Vuzgal?" Delilah asked.

"Bandits have been causing problems and some of the traders are pushing their boundaries. Chonglu and Elan are looking into it. It was bound to happen. People have been trying to take advantage of us since the beginning. This is just in a different way," Erik said.

"Institute?" Glosil asked.

"Doesn't seem like it. Elan didn't hear anything in their back channels," Rugrat added.

"You have a plan?" Delilah asked.

"Just like hog trapping. Bait them in. Then, before they know it, drop the damn gates around them." Rugrat smiled. "With the extensive formations planted around Vuzgal, from Aberdeen in the West to the Chaotic Lands in the East, we have everything covered. They're attacking in the Chaotic Lands, which is to be expected. If they push in closer to Vuzgal, we'll see it all."

"I wondered what all those formations requested from the academies and formation masters were for," Delilah admitted.

"Anything moves on that road and we'll know. We won't even need spotters. We can hit them with mortars and artillery spells from kilometers away. Same with Vermire and the Beast Mountain Range," Glosil said.

"Have things changed on that front?" Erik asked as they neared the barracks.

"The surrounding nations are focused on fighting for spots in the Consortium now. It's grown in power rapidly. King's Hill's third expansion is already planned. The outer outposts are all expanding, as are the interconnecting roads. Things are stable for now," Delilah said.

Erik slowed his steps and turned to face Glosil. "The other thing we need to talk about is our role in all of this." Erik tilted his head to Rugrat.

"Training and support for now. If the shit hits the fan, we'll need every person we can get fighting, including both of you. The Special Teams have always been by themselves. There are few people they would be willing to take orders from. Would you want the position?"

"You lead, I follow," Rugrat told Erik.

"Understood. Commander, if you need us, we'll be there." Erik nodded.

"Morning!" Rugrat said as he looked at the men and women filling the crafter's arena. People from all different squads, from pure mages to formation masters and everything in between filled the seats.

Rugrat picked out the teachers in the front row with the Close Protection Detail members. They were revered throughout the Alva Military as the best the army had to offer, trained and now tried across many battlefields against the Willful Institute.

Qin Silaz led the formation masters of Vuzgal academy, while Julilah led the formation masters of Kanesh Academy. Tanya was head of the pure mages; Roska was the strongest war mage among the Alvan military, and Tan Xue was headmaster of the Vuzgal Academy and highest-ranked smith among all Alvans.

"In the past few weeks, you have all attended classes focused on turning your skills into tools of battle, destruction, and war. You have learned how to use composite formations to create rapid defenses and rapid attacks. You've studied defensive spells, offensive spells, and learned how to cast them faster, stronger, and with less mana draw, based on the teachings of pure magic. How to get the most out of your gear and weapons. You have learned fighting techniques. You have transformed your thoughts. You have taken the mundane and simple and turned them into weapons."

Rugrat paused, looking among the Earthers; he had expected a reaction from them, but they, like the Ten Realms natives, had blank expressions. They had all seen and understood the reality of the Ten Realms. *If you cannot rely on yourself, you cannot rely on others.*

"Simply put, you've learned what humans have been doing since the beginning of recorded time. Take the tools that you have and use them in different ways to increase your own abilities. A formation master of only level ten can command the power of spells that a level forty mage could not call down. A pure mage can cast magic *fast,* even faster than someone who has studied the spell for several years. They only have their motions and their words to stimulate a response, tricking their mind into creating spells. Pure mages are working with the elements themselves, the very building blocks. Add in the same tools as spell mages, and pure mages will be stronger and faster."

Rugrat paused, looking around, picking out people with his eyes.

"*None* of this would have been possible if you hadn't worked together." Rugrat shook his finger and looked up into the back of the stands. "That, right there, is our strongest ability."

Rugrat pulled out his railgun rifle.

"This weapon would not have been possible without smiths, formation masters, mages, alchemists, or the people of Alva. Without the factories, once this weapon broke, we would have to craft it anew. We wouldn't be able to take it apart and replace it. We wouldn't be able to produce them in the hundreds. Listen to what your teachers have to say. It could save your life, and it could give you a new idea to do something that could save another's life in the coming days.

"Three tips with this rifle: you can make it shoot faster, longer, and harder. There is a conductive filler built into the handguard that connects to the propulsion system. Increasing the flow of fire and water mana will increase the overall speed of the round exiting the barrel. If you increase the fire and metal mana, then you can increase the weapon's rate of fire. Both will increase the heat of the weapon faster. The foregrip is connected by a filler to the barrel. Increasing the water and earth attribute mana will decrease the heat, meaning you can shoot longer. If you want to add spells to your rounds, cast it on the magazine and it will be transmitted to *all* rounds. If you cast a new spell, then it will wipe the previous spell and add the new one. If I were you, I would pick either increased blunt damage or piercing. Whenever you reload, cast a new spell."

Rugrat lowered the rifle. "Let me highlight this for you. You have many tools at your disposal. Pick a situation for them. Do not get wrapped up in indecision. If it works, it is the right tool for the job."

Rugrat walked back to his seat as Qin walked out onto the stage.

"Formations, up until now, have been created and used in the rear. Setting up a formation in the middle of battle has been a monumentally stupid idea." Qin tossed a formation plate to the ground. "With this one formation plate, I can increase the power of my spells four times their initial power. More if you are a lower level. If you can cast only a level one fireball, this formation will allow you to cast at level with no extra mana or effort on your part."

Qin threw out another formation. It snapped to the larger formation plate and lit up.

"Magnetic linking formation plates. Pre-made and ready. All you need to do is throw them out, connect them and you create a new formation. I've added in a mana barrier so I will be protected while I am casting my spells." Another formation plate connected.

"Now my fire spells will be stronger." Another formation plate. "Now the power of the spells will increase." Another formation plate.

Wind and dirt whirled together, creating a golem.

"Now I have a defender to protect me." Qin threw out more formation plates, more golems rose up.

"True golems are materials that have been refined and engraved to turn into fighting machines. They cost a lot of time and resources to build, more to keep them maintained. They burn through power in no time. And if their formations are damaged, they'll be torn apart, though they're incredibly powerful and strong." Qin raised her hand to the floating dirt and stones that resembled a headless humanoid figure. The white air shimmered between the moving rocks.

"Summoned golems can be destroyed faster, but their power is reliant on the power supplied to them. Increase the amount of mana you give them, the longer you can keep them summoned for, the stronger their attacks are. Unlike pure golems, they can destroy their form and recreate it."

A golem ran to the end of the stage, the power in its body dimmed and it collapsed into dust and dirt. Back at the formation, another golem was already forming.

"Redeployment, shift your forces and the battle in moments. Some of you might ask about the range issues." Qin threw out two more formation plates. "I just doubled their range, going from four hundred meters to eight hundred meters. The range is your biggest limiting factor, which is why we need formation combat masters to get into the middle of the fight and call in the reinforcements needed. Bolster the squads on the front line whether that means close-range high-level spells, defensive spells, healing spells, summoning golems, buffing your allies, and debuffing the enemy." Qin took out another formation plate and tossed it down.

The golems grew stronger.

"I just increased the power of Earth spells, which work with the Earth golems to increase their overall power."

She threw out another formation plate. It locked into place, passing light back into the dimming formations.

The golems grew once again, the winds and dirt shifting around them as runes appeared on their bodies that took on a more refined look.

"The first rule of formations: keep them powered. If you run out of power, everything comes apart. Dump in mana stones, add in secondary power formations to distribute the load. Having them all focused on one main formation will burn it out, drain it of power, and collapse."

Qin pressed a button on the main formations with her foot. "Releases on the formations will disconnect them so you can rapidly store and re-deploy them. You can deploy them in groups if needed, though it would be better to create a formation stack and use it as required. Interlocking formations are used in fluid situations. Stacks are best prepared, pre-planned, and used for specific missions. Julilah will talk on that more."

Qin deactivated the formation and stepped away, giving the floor to Julilah. She pulled out the formation stacks. It looked like an accordion made of metal.

"Stacks. Pre-made, ready-to-use, complex formations. My friend Qin's interlocking formations are great, but they are much larger. Stacks have been optimized to be compact while giving the same power as larger-scale traditional flat formations."

Julilah turned and locked the top formation in the stack. A mana barrier covered her, and the surrounding mana stirred as the runes on the stack glowed powerfully.

"With interlocking formations, there are many factors. They're great in stable applications, just not in military ones. Stacks are better. Just charge them up, lock them in and you're good to go. With this stack, I have just created a double-skinned mana barrier, activated a clean spell within the space, as well as stamina recovery and a healing spell. Right now, it is a mobile casualty collection point.

Julilah turned it off and put it into her storage ring, pulling out a formation plate and another stack.

Qin sighed and shifted in her seat. "Show off," she muttered.

Julilah turned on the formation. Ten summoned golems appeared.

"My golems are weaker than my friend Qin's, though I have two more. This is an enhancing formation plate." Julilah held up the formation plate and put it on the ground. "It is very similar to the formation plate that Miss Qin put down." Julilah put the stack into the recess in the middle of the formation plate.

The formation plate's glow increased as runes along the sides of the stack lit up.

The golems doubled in size, each as strong as the golems Qin's formations had created.

"As Miss Qin said, the stacks are built for a situation. In this situation, we needed golem back up. Though with Miss Qin, she needed to increase her own spell attack power, created a defensive barrier, and she summoned golems."

Julilah returned to her seat and Tan Xue went up to talk about the melee weapons they were using, spells that would enhance the weapons, ones that would give them greater power at the cost of weakening the weapon, or ones to increase the durability. She talked about the conqueror's armor that was being issued to everyone, as well as the arm and leg armor.

A CPD leader went up. He had been on the training staff for a long time and spent his time talking about the benefits of using the different repeaters, bows, and firearms. He went over the new belt-fed ammunition system versus the magazines. He explained how bows, if the user was strong enough, could be stronger than the railgun.

Roska went up next, talking about small spells that could be of use: clean spell on your eyes if you got dirt in them, using dirt or sand spells to blast the enemy in the face and get an opening, how to use time debuffing on the enemy *moments* before they clashed so they had no time to get used to their new state. She advised them to train with the different settings on the conqueror's armor, and if possible, train with that power in flux so they could be ready for the chaos.

"A simple ice spell under a powerful opponent's foot could make all the difference. If they go down, they're at your mercy. Metal conducts cold and lightning, while leathers are susceptible to heat. In close range fighting, it is the small quick spells that will have the greatest effect, so listen to Tanya. With her pure magic, your larger spells and smaller spells will be stronger and not cost nearly as much mana."

Tanya stepped on stage next.

"Pure magic takes mana and its attributes and uses them together directly. Spells are a way to control the immense power of mana and the attributes easily, though spells are not formations. Formations outline specific instructions, taking in mana and releasing a result. We are adding in the attributes of our own mana and the environment. All the factors change. A formation burns out, you replace it. If a spell burns out, then the caster will have a violent backlash. While you can use less mana and get better results, remember you're taking off the training wheels. The risk of spell backlash is immense. That is why pure magic is best suited for small effects."

Tanya shrugged and looked at Rugrat.

"Unless you have advanced your mana gathering cultivations and have an incredible mana sense. With a higher mana sense, you can understand the elements around you and within your body more. Most pure magic only reaches the first three stages of spells: power, function, and direction. With a strong mana sense, you can tap into the elements and enhance your spell with the external mana surrounding you. How?"

Tanya cleared her throat.

"Mana sense. Mana sense is an understanding of the world of magic. You can sense the densities of different attributes around you, notice pockets where there is more or less mana. You could reduce the amount of Earth attribute mana you are using in your casting because you notice that the area has a greater ambient Earth attribute, thus using less mana for the same spell effect."

Tanya saw people raising their hands.

"Please wait until the end for questions, though I can think of what one of them might be. Will I run out of the attributes to cast with? The short version is *possibly.*" Tanya shrugged. "If you are, say, on the water floor and are casting fire spells all the time. In an environment without the fire attribute, you will need to use more mana to make up for the lack of fire attribute in your surroundings and from within your body. We all know how, in different environments, spells can be weaker. There is always *some* of every attribute around us, or within us, but at different levels. There are ways to counteract this, like using more mana in your cast or tempering your body. As you temper your body, your body naturally refines and holds different attributes. It means that your spells won't be as weak. It also means that your sense and control over the attribute you tempered your body with will be *much* higher."

After all the presentations were complete and questions answered, some people left, but most headed to the different arenas. Rugrat split off from everyone, walking with Julilah to their assigned arena.

"Do you think these public lectures are helping?" Rugrat asked.

"I think so. A lot of the people who want to join the military are taking this time to get some skills. We have people from all stages joining in. Most want to learn more so they can defend themselves. The majority are military. They come down here to test out what they've learned."

"How have things been for you?" Rugrat asked.

"Good. I only do this three times a week now. The rest of the time I'm in the classroom or working on the factories."

"I meant how have you been personally?" Rugrat asked.

They reached the entrance to the arena grounds. People had arrived ahead of them and were setting up. Military members and medics were spread around to supervise.

Julilah sighed and leaned against the wall. "Tired. There is so much to do, and only so much time to do it in. I only see Qin at these training sessions. Same with Tan Xue.

"Everyone is driven to improve themselves as much as possible. I just formed my mana core and I'm looking to start tempering my body. I-I'm not suited to joining the military; I'm not a fighter." Julilah dropped her head in defeat.

Rugrat put his hands on her shoulders. "And there is no need for you to be."

"But so many people are signing up!"

"We need fighters, yes, but we can't fight a war if there aren't people keeping things running here. If we don't have you here keeping everything going, then what are we fighting for? We need your stacks. We need formations. We need armor, food, all of it, and more. The military is a ravenous beast. Just being a fighter is not everything. If we were in a sect, it might be!"

Julilah nodded. Rugrat squeezed her small shoulders. She wasn't even twenty and had all these worries on her shoulders, but she had come a long way since he had first met her.

Rugrat let go as he felt the box on his hip shift. "Well, let's get this class started."

A beep came from the box, informing him that it was out of mana stones. "I swore I charged that," Rugrat muttered as he grabbed a mana stone and turned the box.

"Ahh!" Rugrat's scream was a mixture of surprise and terror, rising into a final screeching in oh-my-god-kill-it fashion. Fumbling with the box, he smacked it so hard it came free of his belt and hit the wall, coming apart.

Julilah yelled and jumped back in surprise.

Rugrat held his fist out, clenching a mana stone in it.

The duct tape-covered skull moved. It looked like a pure pearl with blue runes running through its surface, wisps of blue smoke drifting from the runes.

A grunting noise came from the skull that was face-first on the ground. Using its jaw, the head rolled to the side. Two bright blue flaming eyes glared at Rugrat before it fell on its cheek.

"*FRUECK!*" the muffled voice came from the duct tape.

"Egbert?" Julilah asked. Rugrat had a mana bolt ready to go as the skull jostled around, maintaining eye contact with Rugrat as he sheepishly released the spell and pocketed the mana stone.

Another muffled yell came from the skull.

Julilah looked at Rugrat.

Rugrat let out a dry and nervous laugh, pulling out a blade. He moved to the skull and removed the duct tape.

"What did you do with my body, you muscle-headed, tattoo-covered, cowboy hat-wearing, nudist redneck?"

"Umm, well, it-it's around." Rugrat felt his stomach turning. He backed away, a smile tugging at the corner of his lips. "S-somewhere safe!" Rugrat quickly amended under Egbert's glare.

Egbert growled, his eyes dimming as he connected to the dungeon. "Oh, that's not good. Ah, the gnome's drill. I think I need to talk to everyone."

Rugrat nodded, slowly edging toward the door. *If I can just get to the Earth floor before he checks it.*

"Egbert, what happened?" Julilah asked.

"Bit of a complex question." Egbert drew out the last word, opening his jaw wide. "So, the dungeon may or may not be one massive drill that the Gnomes were making to tap into the ley lines of the First Realm. They discovered that the First Realm had a complete set of ley lines that are interconnected and ran through the entire realm, unlike the higher realms where the mana is all over the place. When I went into standby mode, a *bunch* of my memories were blocked off. At one time, I might or might not have been well, uhh, a powerful wizard. *Yeah,* long history. The guy who ran this place, he was my brosef. We studied together. I died, he brought me back.

Kind of. Dungeon magic. I got linked up to the dungeon core and helped out. Had a soft spot for others. That human boy I told you about turned against him and betrayed him."

Egbert sighed. "Area used to be nice a few hundred years ago. I had to make sure the dungeon didn't fall apart after he stole part of the core. In the first battles, I focused on the dungeon core, keeping everything together. I shut down floors, cannibalized what I could. The Kanesh clan wasn't a clan of fighters. They were crafters." Sorrow lay heavy within Egbert's words, his eyes distant, recalling a past long ago. "I… I tried to defend them. I used everything I had. The ground of the Beast Mountain Range was changed. Rivers that lead out to the ocean were diverted underground. Towns were destroyed, hills turned into mountains and plains into valleys. Not one of the people that attacked Kanesh survived, though the cost was high. So high."

"What about the Gnomes?" Julilah asked.

Rugrat continued to listen, taking silent and slow steps. *Just a few meters more.*

"The Dungeon was broken, disconnected from the other floors, formations broken, burnt out in the fighting. Some stayed, tried to rebuild. The area was quiet and desolate. Nature took its course. Creatures became powerful, and we had to seal the dungeon. They left if they could. Some of them remained, and we worked to create the Beast Mountain Trial. It was their last act. They sent excursions to the lower floors, but there was little that they could do. In the end, there was just me to carry on with the work. With time, like the dungeon, I came into disrepair. I cut off memories, sealed my power so that the dungeon might last longer." Egbert's eyes shone.

"Though now I know what is happening and why. Rugrat, the council will need to hear…" He frowned as if recalling something. "Wha-he, why did you use my skeleton as a *scarecrow*?!"

Rugrat's eyes widened as he hurled open the door and started running, yelling as he went. "I agree. You round up the council! Have some important business!"

"Rug-*rat*!" Egbert's runes flared with power as he rocketed across the room and through the opening in the door.

"What? Ah shit! Why is your skull flying?"

"All of me flies!"

"That's cheating! Move!" Rugrat yelled.

People turned to see Rugrat sprinting through the halls with a glowing skull berating him.

"George!" Rugrat ran out into a courtyard. George swept down from where he had been circling the academy.

Rugrat jumped up. Egbert's skull charged across the courtyard.

Rugrat's stomach twisted as George saw Egbert and flapped his wings rapidly, rising into the air, making Rugrat miss his handhold.

George gave him a meek glance and rocketed away as Rugrat landed on the ground, leaving him to his fate.

"Ah!" Rugrat screamed at the rapidly closing skull.

"There aren't any birds on the Earth floor, you jackass!" Egbert yelled.

"This is all a misunderstanding! I just thought it might be a good idea to air out your skeleton!"

Rugrat ran into the other side of the courtyard.

"*Air* out my skeleton! Did you think I was your dirty underwear?"

"Move it! Skeleton head coming through!" Rugrat yelled, sprinting through the corridors. That day, the story of the lord and the flying skull was born.

Erik glanced over as Glosil entered the council office, the refined power of the dungeon channeling down below just meters away.

"Elise and Blaze will take too long to arrive," Delilah said.

"Very well." Egbert's body was transforming as his skull had. He wore a robe, hiding most of the changes.

"The Kanesh clan was a bold one—a crazy one, some might say. They were lovers of formations and creations. When we escaped to the First Realm, we just survived at first. We found an underground cavern filled with water. Using the dungeon core, we created a floor to live on. It is part of the reason why the water floor is so large, though it didn't have as much water at the time. We built it up, creating a multi-layered city. It was brilliant with the power of the dungeon core. Then, we started to build out that first floor. Druvan had this idea to separate out the affinities, a floor for each one. It gave the gnomes a goal. We rose through the mountain, creating floors. It was incredible. There were lots of trials and failures. We had to switch some floors around. Wood and earth were around the other way when we planned things out first. With the floors started, we put in formations to move the mana upward, have them support one another, creating an interlinked system. The dungeon core was essential to maintain the balance between them all. While we created the living floor, most of the Gnomes lived between floors. Only the water floor connected to the outside world. It was how the boy got in." Egbert's runes flared, distorting the air around him and making his robe flicker. The power was contained, not reaching anyone else.

Complete control over his domain, Erik noted.

"Druvan took him in, cared for him. The boy took the kindness. He said he wanted to be the bridge between their people. He went to his family, which he had been chased away from. Wanting their acceptance, he sold out the Gnomes and everything they had built. The family was fairly powerful. They convinced the boy to prove what he said was true. He took them a piece of the dungeon core. I fought to keep the dungeon operating. With only one dungeon core and so much attributed mana built up, I needed to drain it. So, I came up with an idea. Use that mana to power a drill. I built a massive energy-consuming drill before the attribute mana poisoned us all. We didn't know about the coming army."

"So, you reversed the direction of the attribute mana and drilled into the ground," Rugrat said.

"Yes, biggest drill in the Ten Realms. We got the notification from the Ten Realms, though we were just fighting to survive. Then the armies came. They used magic to attack the dungeon. The Gnomes fought back. In the last part of the war, I had them carve runes into my body to contain the power. Then I stopped the drill and used the power of the dungeon. I killed off the plants, the creatures, nearly everything on the other floors. I consumed it in the battle against the attackers, altering the Beast Mountain range into what it is today."

"What about the drill? Why is it drilling?" Delilah asked.

"Well, that is more of a technical glitch than anything. We repaired everything according to the plans during the war, not the peacetime. Once everything was done, then it was like a switch was flipped and drill powered up."

"Can you turn it off?" Erik asked.

"Yes, I can." Egbert held up a hand to stop everyone. "Though I don't think we should remove the option. If there is a time when Alva is in need, the drill can help us. Possibly save us. It was the hypothesis of myself and the other gnomes that there is an interconnected system of ley lines in the First Realm. If we can truly tap into them, then that is a massive amount of power under our command. Few, if any, people would be able to challenge Alva, even if we don't hit a ley line but strike magma. Then the attribute power alone, purified by the different floors and by our dungeon cores, will massively increase our power stores."

Erik looked at Colonel Yui and Commander Glosil.

"Egbert, shut it off for now. We need to show people that we have this under control."

"Very well." Egbert's eyes dimmed as the runes around the dungeon core powered down. Mana stopped flowing through floors. Erik saw formations in rings down the channel reaching through floors switched and altered into a new alignment.

The mana density increased on the floor, bottling up like pressure.

"What else can the formations in this dungeon do?"

"Defensive spells and offensive ones." Egbert's eyes lit up as the pressure was released. Mana was once again directed upwards, each floor connecting to the one above before they reached the massive mana storing formation on the living floor. The runes to each of the mana cornerstones lit up, gathering and converting the power into mana stones.

"When the gnomes were dying, we prepared this place to survive for a long time. One preparation was that once the dungeon was restored, there should be enough power for me to recover to my peak." Egbert pointed at his rune-carved skull. "And two, we made sure if the descendants of the dungeon were attacked, they could defend themselves. But only if they completed the dungeon and showed me that they were worthy of the Gnomes' heritage. And I guess you all are." Egbert smiled.

"What if you didn't like us?" Rugrat asked carefully.

"Then the defensive and weaponized formations would have been quietly destroyed and I would have destroyed my memories, effectively killing me and making sure I could never pass on my knowledge or the knowledge of the gnomes. What books and items I gave you, are just a fraction of the information in my brain. I was a pretty good wizard, if you don't mind me saying."

"Well, that is at least one problem dealt with." Delilah rubbed the side of her face. "It's good to have you back, Egbert, and overall, it could be a benefit with the power of the Consortium growing to new heights."

15 Thorns

Lord Salyn rose from his bow as Lord Knight Ikeda addressed Queen Ikku.

"The situation in the Beast Mountain Range is nothing like we predicted. We have heard reports of everything that is happening there, but it is far away, and we have paid little attention. For that, you have my apologies, My Queen." Ikeda bowed again.

"It is done. Now, we must learn from it. Why is it that I got a message informing me that I will not get slots within this Beast Mountain Range Consortium? What is it?"

"It is the greatest academy in the First Realm," Ikeda said in a grave voice.

Salyn held his tongue, frowning.

"They have teachers that have touched the Journeyman level. People that have tempered their foundations. With the beasts in the area and the small dungeon they located, it has turned into a training paradise. Even the mana in the Beast Mountain Range has increased compared to the surrounding areas. They are the epicenter of trade within the continent now." Ikeda took in a breath, looking Queen Ikku in the eye.

"My Queen, they are the strongest nation in the First Realm."

"What?" She frowned, leaning forward slightly.

"On the outside, it is a group of outposts working together to stave off attacks from outsiders. Inside, it is a nation operated by Lord Aditya, with King's Hill as their capital. The outpost leaders have largely retired, giving over management rights to Lord Aditya. They have created a noble class, while some outpost leaders have taken up positions of power within the Beast Mountain Range administration. Considering the rough terrain that they inhabit, other nations are not as willing to attack. Add in the trade that they provide and the consortium that trains up the younger generation, they have gained position and power without others realizing it."

"Surely, the other nations knew what was happening?" Ikku asked.

"Yes, but the time to attack the Beast Mountain Range has come and gone. A network of well-maintained roads, complete with watchtowers and armed patrols, march along the borders and between King's Hill and the exterior outposts. In hours, they can mobilize and move their forces to any outpost. The exterior outposts have swelled in size. Mercenaries flocked to the area to seek riches and strength. All the mercenary groups that reside within the cities have come to agreements with the outpost leaders, which are one and the same as the Beast Mountain Range Nation."

"A unified front agreement?" Queen Ikku said through her teeth.

"Yes, My Queen. The mercenaries get favorable prices on what they buy and sell. In return, they will defend the outposts if they come under attack. A reserve force for their army."

"Army? They have outpost guards."

"That was when the outposts fought one another. To maintain neutrality and make sure that the outposts wouldn't attack one another after the battles, guards were sent to King's Hill and camps within the Beast Mountain Range. They might call themselves guards, but they created an army, neutral within the conflicts of the outpost leaders. A true army, as well. One with training, weapons, and armor. Not a peasant army thrown together under the command of knights and lords looking to loot one another's lands."

"So, it was this Lord Aditya that hid and is using the traitors?" Queen Ikku tapped against her armrest, her eyes filled with plans.

"Quite possibly." Lord Knight Ikeda nodded.

"If we were to launch a campaign, we would open ourselves up for attack," Queen Ikku muttered. "Other nations looking to get on their good side would plot against us. The supply train for our armies would be overextended and vulnerable."

She was silent for a few moments.

"Advisor Vesair, prepare to send an envoy to King's Hill with gifts and an apology. Ikeda, Salyn, report on everything that you observed."

Lord Salyn bowed as he inwardly ground his teeth. Even Queen Ikku knew when to bow her head if the odds weren't in her favor.

Darkness blanketed the Shikoshi Kingdom as Lord Knight Ikeda entered the queen's private office. She was sitting in front of the fireplace, holding a drink in one hand as she watched the flames within the hearth.

Ikeda moved to the side and bowed.

"Take a seat," Ikku said, taking a sip from her cup. Flames danced in her eyes, her mind moving constantly.

Ikeda waited calmly.

"What if we attack them quietly, find the Earthers, and capture or kill them?"

"Their guard leaders were as strong as my knights. Even if we called upon those training demons, I doubt we would be able to complete the mission."

Ikku wrung her hands, inwardly seething.

"They're powerful, and we don't know where they came from." She drank from her glass and snarled. "Gather more information. Let's see what the other nations really think."

She stood still before yelling and throwing her glass into the fireplace, making the flames roar brighter before they calmed. "Damn them. They think they can steal those Earthers from me? They have them; they must."

She stared at the flames as they started to settle. "We need to get the other nations on our side. With the lure of their trading and the Consortium, we have to act quickly before the others are enthralled by them. Let them fight over the resources. If we can get those Earthers, we can raise the Kingdom to be the strongest kingdom in the first realm."

16 Institute's Purge

High Elder Cai Bo entered the area around Chensin totem, a city in the Fourth Realm controlled by the Willful Institute. It had been sealed off from outside transportation. Sect members dotted around the area had been pulled into groups. They were all over level fifty-five. Each wore at least one piece of Expert level gear, with no gear below the mid-journeyman mark. There were nearly a hundred and fifty people present, broken into groups of ten.

She quietly surveyed them, all from different groups, all young and *connected.* She hid her smile. If things went how she planned, a war with Vuzgal would be a matter of time. While threats from the Head might not get people moving, anger from the different groups in the sects could definitely get them moving.

Nico Tolentino walked into the area leading five groups. Each of them was wearing at least three pieces of Expert grade gear. As they stepped up to the totem, they pulled their cloaks tight, hiding their weapons and gear.

"For the Willful Institute! We will destroy the Adventurer's Guild halls! We will tear out their homes! Kill all that support them and whatever you find, you keep!"

Cai Bo raised an eyebrow. Nico shot her a sneer and raised his nose, his group following onto a totem's pad. One of the members in the group acted as the guide and they disappeared in a flash of light.

Others followed afterward, disappearing by rank and seniority, be it personal, or their family connections.

Cai Bo thought back to the meeting a week ago.

"You will be at great risk. Vuzgal is an unknown. We do not know the true extent of their people's power," Cai Bo argued.

Head Asadi shot her a look and quietened her with a gesture. She quieted. He had been a quick man. Using rumors and her low position among the other elders, he'd diminished her support—on the surface. If she had not buried her real connections, then she'd be completely reliant on him for support.

The only person one could rely on were those under a contract or those that needed the other. She would have applauded him if he hadn't tried to do it to her. Now, she had to play the weak-willed and devoted supporter, which had pushed her own plans ahead by decades.

"I will send word to the other families. If you are able to take the guild hall in Vuzgal, then it will be a great show of strength," Asadi told Nico.

He gave some more praise, bolstering Nico's ego. As Nico left, he leered at her as he passed. "Your time has passed, old woman."

The doors closed, and Asadi gave Cai Bo a pitiful look. "The younger generation is so confident to step over the older one. Don't worry; I won't leave those that help me behind."

Cai Bo let out a breath, returning to the present as the last team disappeared. She turned, leaving the area around the totem with Lower Elder Kostic when a man in a hood walked toward the deserted totem.

Cai Bo caught a glimpse of his face. She bowed her head as he snorted and disappeared in a flash of light. It was so good when her plans came together. Sho Tolentino had been in her way for far too long. Without him, the rest of the Tolentino clan would come into the fold nicely.

A sound-canceling formation separated them from the rest of the realm.

"What do you think of their chances?" Her sharp eyes watched Kostic.

"Oh, I would think they are rather low, my lady."

They shared a nasty smile as she started walking again.

"And your preparations?"

"I communicated with the other nations around Vuzgal. Many of them voiced their displeasure. I am sure they would be willing to support us for the right incentives."

"Good. Vuzgal will be a turning point. If nothing else, that arrogant child will let us know what we are walking into."

Nico blinked away the totem light and entered the busy entrance area into Vuzgal. He pulled his cloak tight, joining the line that would allow them into the city.

There were all kinds of people present, trade caravans and opulent carriages lined up on one side. Snaking lines were filled by people passing between cubicles with police officers checking everyone before allowing them entrance.

Nico gritted his teeth at the wait. They would regret allowing him to enter their city. He wondered what would happen to the guard that let him into the city. would they be turned into a public example?

He took solace in his dark thoughts. Scanning the area, he saw other members of his fifty-person group arriving in Vuzgal and lining up. They'd teleported to other locations first to not raise suspicion.

"Next!" Nico walked up to the cubicle, stepping onto a sensing formation.

The guard read some information on a formation away from Nico's sight.

"What is the purpose of your visit?"

"Meeting with some friends to watch the Battle Arena," Nico said.

The guard scanned Nico, then tapped on the sign next to the serving window that listed Vuzgal's main laws. "Make sure you don't cause any trouble. Even if you're from an association, we will arrest you if you break the law."

Nico's lip half lifted before he nodded. "I understand."

"Good. Entrance fee?" The guard tapped another list.

Nico took out the mana stones and put them onto the serving tray.

The guard pulled them onto his side and then put them into a storage crate at the rear of the cubicle. "Have a good day!"

Nico turned and walked on.

Others in his group trailed after him.

They passed through the defenses around the totem, moving with the streaming people. The area opened ahead of them, a large square filled with people waiting for those that were teleporting in. Large roads led to different areas of the city. Caravans of trade goods headed toward the warehouses to store their goods or drop them off.

People dispersed in every direction while carriages carried powerful people off toward their destinations.

Eastern culture mixed with western medieval design, with wood and stone creating the many two and four-story buildings that butted up against the street.

In the distance, the inner defensive wall with the mana barrier towers reached up into the sky. At the center was Vuzgal's main mana barrier tower, extending proudly into the sky. Between the pillars, Sky Reaching Restaurants pierced through the sky, glass shining like a sharpened blade.

Nico led his people through the streets, following the map Kostic had provided.

They reached a quiet street. It was darker now that the buildings were closer together. The businesses were closed, preparing for the night. Strings of mana lights lined the road, looking like used vines. The street was well-traveled and showed the signs of nightly revelry.

Nico headed down an alleyway between taverns. It opened to reveal a large service area between businesses. It was deserted, with no deliveries today.

The rest of the group appeared, one after the other.

"Let's go." Nico led them down another alleyway toward the Guild District.

The others loosened their cloaks, resting their hands on their weapons underneath or on storage devices, ready to draw.

Seeing the group, people hurried on their way. The group spread out as they reached the main road. The inns and taverns gave way to trading stalls, smithies, and workshops, selling gear for fighters and resources for crafters.

As the road widened, there were small planters dotted around, along with stalls selling food and drink. People wandered the area easily, wearing their guild emblems.

Guildhalls lined the sides of the boulevard. Their crests adorned their walls and gates. Crafter and mercenary guilds stood next to one another. Guild members flowed through the area, beasts, and carriages carrying important members to and from the halls.

A group of mounted mercenaries rode out of their hall and down the boulevard to carry out some mission.

The guildhalls were located in the inner city. Two Vuzgal Defense force barracks and four command towers lie around the district.

Guild members stood at every gate, checking people's identification before they entered.

"There it is," Nico said, his eyes locking onto the Adventurer's Guild guildhall.

Nico sent a signal to the others who dispersed, closing in from different directions.

Four guards were standing by the gate, checking identification as people entered and left.

Nico could see the courtyard beyond the gate and the hall beyond that, its doors wide open as people entered and exited.

A mounted group exited the guildhall, riding off.

Nico felt a rush as he gripped his sword hilt. A shiver ran through his body, tapping into the power that had laid dormant, unused, and untested.

"See you later, Tollin!" an Adventurer's Guild guard said to a young man. He wore a simple shirt and pants, his hair grown long with an easy smile on his face.

"I'll be back later. I just need to get my sister from school!"

Nico stepped in front of Tollin, holding out an arm to stop him.

"Sorry about that!" Nico laughed easily.

"I wasn't watching where I was going." Tollin tousled his hair, blushing.

"Are you a member of the Adventurer's Guild?" Nico looked at the guild hall.

"I'm not. I'm just a healer. I wanted to join as a fighter, but I had some skill in healing. This lets me be in the same city as my sister. They've done so much for me. I hope I can join them on the front lines in the future."

"Ah, good!" Nico drew his sword and stabbed it up through Tollin's stomach.

"I was so excited I could barely hold myself back!" Nico laughed. His smile never shifted.

Tollin groped at the blade, at his stomach, and the spreading red through his shirt. His mouth opened and closed, unable to connect what he was seeing with what was happening.

"Not even worth any experience. Let's see how good your healing is." Nico lifted Tollin off the ground, making him scream in pain before he tossed him effortlessly to the side.

"You're fucking dead!" a gate guard yelled, drawing her sword.

Nico parried her attack. His strength was so high she stumbled backward. With seemingly lazy ease, his sword sliced through the air, cutting her neck.

She went down, clawing at her neck.

The Institute warriors charged past Nico, their cloaks falling off to reveal their powerful armor and weapons.

Nico pulled off his cloak, letting it drop as he walked forward. One guard was left. The back of his leg sprayed red as he tipped forward. A spear rammed through his chest plate.

"Fucking dead weight! Get off of my spear!" Montes said, kicking the man from her spear and spitting on him.

"People from the Montes clan are always hotheads," Nico said as he walked by.

Montes glared at him. "Just cause the Head is interested in you now, Tolentino, doesn't mean he will be always."

Nico scoffed at the building, heading through the gates. Fighting had broken out everywhere. Those in the guild hall were rushing outside at the noise. Nico pulled out a spell scroll and tore it apart.

Lines of black traced through the sky above the guild hall, creating a spell formation that crackled with blood-red lightning. Mana was drawn into the spell formation. The wind picked up, quickly creating a vortex centered on the formation above.

Nico tossed the burnt-out spell scroll to the side and walked toward the guild hall. His people were slowed by the press of guild members pushing out of the main door.

Others rushed out of side buildings, around the courtyard, and around the main hall.

Five Institute fighters led the slaughter at the door's steps.

Another guild member dropped to the ground. A kick sent them to the side, their lifeblood pouring out.

Nico walked across the courtyard, passing bodies and tombstones. He reached the four stairs that flattened out to a wide veranda in front of the doorway.

The vortex picked at Nico's clothes as he gathered mana, waking up his entire body. He tapped into his power, drawing the power of the earth through his body and then into his sword.

He stabbed forward. The green light was covered with wood, green runes glowing throughout. It passed through the fighters, cutting through a guild member, and shooting inward.

Nico circulated his power, ready to enter the fray when he frowned.

There was a roar from deep within the guild hall. A large man covered in armor held a shield with a fresh scar on its face.

"Looks like you're not all useless. You'll be a fine ingredient for my human core pill!" Nico charged into the guild hall.

He slashed out. Wooden blades appeared in the green light left behind by his attack. The blades cut out, critically wounding or killing several, and throwing the others back.

The armored man blocked the hit with his shield, only slightly slowing down. Stone jumped from the ground as the big man struck it with his small hammer.

The stone crumbled under the hits.

Nico's sword flashed, taking out two of the five stones the man had not only compressed, but sharpened.

Nico didn't spare a glance for the scream behind him, but he saw the victorious grin on the armored man's face. Nico's blade met his hammer. The man's full strength wasn't behind it as he slammed his shield forward, aiming for Nico's feet.

He dodged, stepping backward. His sword flashed to meet stone spears coming from every direction. The man yelled and charged with the spears. Nico twisted, his sword flashing like a fencer's, destroying the spears. He twisted out the way of the hammer. His kick met the man's shield.

The shield rang out like a bell. The man's feet left grooves in the ground for three meters.

He actually remained standing as he shook his shield with a grimace.

This could be interesting. Roots grew under Nico's feet, drawing in mana as his eyes focused on his opponent.

Nico released his power, letting it flow through his limbs. The muscles in his legs compressed as he shot forward.

His steps left dents in the ground as the armored man smashed his hammer into the ground.

Nico jumped over the rippling floor. Formations appeared under his feet, balancing on air.

The ground erupted. Stone shot out at Nico from the torn ground below.

Nico pushed out his hand, a spell formation appearing on it as he forced himself out of the way of the first attacks.

He interposed his sword, fighting off the stone spears shooting at him, cutting through them as he dodged in the air.

The armored man swung his hammer and stone spikes congealed upon the head of the hammer, causing the very air to crack. Nico twisted, avoiding a spear from the ground, cutting down two more.

"Thorn Rain!"

Tens of thorns shot out from a spell formation on his hand, creating a tunnel through the spears and spikes.

The armored man threw up his shield. "Stone Armor!"

The shield frosted over with stone. The thorns struck the stone covering, shattering it, and driving the armored man backward.

"Forest's blade!"

He cut out with his blade, killing two guild members, and cutting a path out of the floor. It hit a wall, tearing it apart.

"Fire Breath!" A wave of fire shot out from the shield as the temperature in the room soared. It burnt through the thorns, pushing them backward until they were only a quarter of the distance from Nico's hand.

Nico turned his head. The ground smoked and cracked under the armored man's feet. Steam rose from his body. Veins cracked the skin, filled with what appeared to be magma.

A Fireball spell hit the armored man. The very air burnt around him. Nico felt something deep in his stomach, something he had forgotten for the last thirty years.

That acid bit in the bottom of his stomach, burning through his being.

Fear.

The armored man's body drew in the fireball spell. It spiraled and turned around him, drawn into his body.

Body Like Iron? How did a guild member from the Fourth Realm reach this level?

The man opened his eyes. It took a massive amount to control such a transformation and release of power.

An Institute member appeared out of the shadows with his blades.

Fire appeared around the armored man. Using the explosive force, he turned into the oncoming blades. Fire explosions crackled like fireworks around the man's arm, going from stationary to swinging.

Fire pooled around the hammer, doubling its size.

Time returned. The institute member was struck in the chest, sending him into the air before he landed. A ripple of fire arrived. The armored man's shield shot out, smashing into the man.

Nico canceled his thorn spell. Unleashing his mana cultivation, the runes on his armor glowed green as he ran forward, his blade directed at the armored man's back.

Nico saw movement. He slowed and turned to miss the attack. The wind rushed past him as a woman with a crazed look in her eyes passed him, the wind of her passing hurting his eyes.

Body Like Stone? Like you'll get away.

One of Nico's medallions flared to life, creating a personal mana barrier.

He was pushed back by a Tracking Force spell.

Nico waved his sword, cutting through the dissipating mana. He raised his hand. The wood under the caster started to change.

Nico's eyes widened as the armored man stepped out from the dissipating mana, his shield braced with both arms.

"Power of Earth!"

Nico braced. His personal barrier medallion activated again. A second defense medallion activated.

A wave of force blasted out from Nico.

The armored man was thrown backward. He rode the force, stabbing his raised leg into the ground, halting his progress.

"My Adventurer's Guild isn't some easy target! Unlike your Institute's cities!" the man yelled.

The guild members yelled in agreement as they clashed with Nico's people.

An Institute fighter hacked at a guild member. They grabbed onto the sword arm and dragged the fighter to the ground. Two more guild members grabbed their shield arm. A fourth stabbed with her spear, crashing into their barrier.

The fighter struggled as the guild members held them firm. The spear made it through the barrier and armor. The Institute member looked at their wound in shock.

The spear wielder tore her weapon out, covering her armor in blood. Buffs rained down on her as she and her group moved to assist others.

Nico felt the air in the room change as cultivations were ignited; Body like Stone, half step Body Like Iron, powerful mana cultivations reaching the Vapor stage, a few ready to form their cores.

Buffing spells landed on the guild members, mages in the rear watching over them, guiding them.

Nico yelled and rushed the armored man. They clashed, sword meeting shield. Nico called up roots to tangle the man's feet. The man stomped the ground, sending waves of stone under Nico's feet.

Nico altered his positioning as he hacked at the man. With the man's higher cultivation and buffs, Nico was only slightly stronger. *Damn this ground!* The man was casting nearly instantly and without chanting.

The stone softened and then hardened, trying to capture Nico's feet.

The armored man swung his hammer. A stone spike whistled past Nico's ear. He sent a cross slash at the shield, leaving a new scar.

"Thorn Rain!" Nico cast behind the armored man as the ground dropped. Nico stepped off the ground, backing up as the thorn rain hit the man in the side. He threw up a stone wall, but his right side showed dents and thorns lodged in the armor.

Nico backed off as the mana above came together. The spell formation in the sky had finally activated.

The Institute members backed up to the hall entrance.

A bloody scent filled the air. A sphere of darkness covered in red lighting formed in the middle of the formation, growing to the size of a basketball. The colors changed, turning murky and then brighter, revealing a humanoid creature. He opened his eyes, revealing red-rimmed green eyes.

It let out a scream that shook the guild hall. Parts of the ceiling collapsed. Walls, half-broken from the fighting, shuddered and gave way.

The armored man roared, using stone spikes and projecting stone shields to divert the falling debris.

The guild members grouped together, attacking the falling ceiling. The beast on the other side of the sphere reached out with its claw. The elements of wind and fire were torn away from the casters and from the world, gathering before the tear hanging in mid-air.

The beast swiped out with a claw of flame and wind tore through the hall.

The hall collapsed under the attack. Four lines continued through the guild hall, the hand evaporating. The guild hall and surrounding buildings turned to rubble.

The tear collapsed, and the beast disappeared from view.

Survivors pushed up from under rock and wood debris, some covering one another with their bodies.

The armored man's shield had been torn apart. His helmet had come apart and there were rents in his armor.

The spell formation dissipated.

"Kill!" The Institute fighters charged across the rubble with Nico.

"Healers!" the armored man yelled. He had a nasty cut on his right brow, blood running into his eyes.

Mages forced out healing spells.

The Institute members killed those on the ground and charged into the depths of the Guild's shambling fighters.

Nico sent out slashes. The armored man defended, but he was slower and breathing heavily.

Nico laughed. "You ignited your cultivation, pushing past your body's limits, but now your strength is failing and you're weakening!"

The battles were once again changing as the guild members were weakening, without the endurance to keep going.

"Sir, we have guards approaching from every direction!" One of the Institute members Nico had left outside said through his sound transmission device.

The man smirked despite his injuries. "My job was to just defend." He laughed as Nico glanced toward the beasts flying toward their location.

We should've had fifteen minutes before they responded. It has only been a few minutes!

Spells appeared on the ground, more appearing by the second.

Tentacles reached out from the spells and attacked the Institute members while the Guild members' injuries healed before their eyes.

Nico attacked the armored man wildly. He broke what remained of the man's shield, pushing him back.

"Earth blade!" Nico's sword released another blade that cut under the armored man's guard, slicing across his lower ribs. It dented the armor, cracking ribs, but didn't penetrate.

"Earth's blessing!"

Nico's speed increased. He dodged the man's stone spikes, launched from his hammer.

"I'll have your head!" Nico cut down the next two spikes. He slid to the side, raising dust and kicking out.

The armored man bent with the kick, grunting as more bones were broken with his dented armor, but he wasn't shifted.

"Earth's entrapment!" Vines rose from the ground to wrap around the man's legs.

"Fire body!" The man opened his arms wide, bringing them together as the surrounding area heated up, his dulled magma veins pulsing with power. "Lance!"

Nico only raised his sword barely, unable to get it between him and the man in time.

The spell hit Nico hard in the chest. Protective medallions activated and cracked as he skittered across the ground before stumbling back up. He coughed with the force that had transmitted into his body by the attack. If it hadn't been for his protective medallions, he would be dead.

Nico got to his feet.

The man collapsed to his knees, his arms shaking to stay up. He was covered in wounds. Blood covered his eye, stained the provocative smile on his face, dripping onto his dented and broken armor.

Nico moved forward.

"Lord Tolentino, we need to go!" an Institute member from his clan said. "The guards are nearly here!"

Guild members lay dying across the ground, a few Institute fighters seeded among them.

Still, they were fighting in the rubble of their guild hall. They were broken and battered, but they worked in groups against single Institute fighters.

Nico felt danger, ducking out of trained response.

An arrow nailed the man before him to the ground.

Mana was gathering from the surroundings in dangerous quantities.

"Run!" an Institute member yelled. The group fled through the guild's gates.

Nico heard a laugh that came from the depths of hell.

The armored man coughed up blood, his eyes locked onto Nico. "I was just the delaying tactic. You don't realize just who you've pissed off."

Nico dodged a spell that shot out of the sky and hit the ground. He could see them now, the aerial undead with soldiers riding on their backs. "Go!"

He turned and started running, pulling out his mount and jumping on its back. The members that had been waiting jumped onto their mounts and rushed after him.

They left the guildhall. The other guilds guarded their entrances, watching them.

Nico led them toward the gates, using illusion spells to hide their appearance.

The party arrived in different groups. People were checked entering the city, but only cursorily as they left.

Nico let out a breath as they left the city's short walls behind, pushing the traders entering and leaving the city off the road.

How do they expect their city to remain standing with such a small wall and these odd boxy buildings?

Nico was jittery from the adrenaline. His eyes darted around as they moved past the boxy buildings. "How many are left?"

"We lost eighteen," one of his supporters, a bearded man, said.

That was acceptable. "And our people?"

"Only three were from our clan."

"Good, we'll do our duty and get out of here."

"Those aerial beasts were much faster and stronger." Nico heard the fear in the coward's voice. He felt it deep in his own chest, too strong to make a remark.

Nico started to calm down. His breathing becoming even. They would escape the city and go to the nearest totem to leave. No one in this city would be stupid enough to stop someone from the Willful Institute.

"Found you." The land resounded with the two words. Nico felt his beast shaking. He nudged it to pick up speed, but it hunched its shoulders, taking the spurs that dug into its flesh.

All of the tamed beasts stopped and lowered themselves to the ground.

Nico turned slowly toward the voice.

Traders groaned and complained, fleeing.

Standing on an approaching bird was a demon with blue eyes. Nico's blood chilled as he recognized the callous, professional killer behind those eyes. Worse. He saw the anger.

"Thorn Rain Reckoning!" Nico raised his hand. Thorns the size of arrows cut through the sky at the man.

Traders and travelers rushed away from the road.

"Burn."

Water blades condensed from the air shredded the surrounding arrows. The blue-eyed demon *stepped off his mount.* Dropping toward the ground.

Nico's attacks were devoured as he targeted the falling man, who hit the ground like a cannonball, sending up dust, crushing the ground beneath him, and leaving a crater.

Demon! He's as strong as those old demons in the Institute! He only bent his legs slightly!

Nico and the others jumped off their now useless mounts, sending out waves of attacks at the man.

The man climbed out of the crater. He seemed to disregard the attacks; his flames burnt them apart, overpowering them. It was like the flames were taking on beast forms. Tigers, lions, dragons, and bears circled him, waiting for the command, defending their master.

"Who are you?" Nico yelled out in frustration, backing up.

"You come into my city and attack a guild residing here and don't think there will be consequences. Do you think that I will forget this, Nico Tolentino?!"

Nico shuddered under those cold eyes.

The blue-eyed demon pulled out hammers from his storage rings.

"City lord," one of the Institute members shuddered out.

Mana tore from the surrounding area, condensing as the man threw his arms forward. "Chains of Fire! Enhanced reaction, Titan's Roar! Poison Breath! Iron Skin!" Spells and attacks flowed one after another as the man struck the fighter's lines like a tsunami.

Chains of flames shot out of a formation on the ground.

"Earth Pillar!" A pillar of earth shot up under Nico's feet, throwing him backward.

Those that weren't as fast screamed as the spikes on the end of the chains stabbed into their bodies, burning them.

Nico slashed out at the chains following him. He looked for the blue-eyed demon.

The blue-eyed demon's hammer smashed into an immobile fighter's head, denting their helmet. "Flame Burst!"

He was already covered in buffing spells. Pockets of fire exploded around him, using them for movement.

Nico tracked him by the dying screams.

No, this isn't supposed to happen! I am Nico Tolentino! Cold fear reached up his spine. He stumbled backward and then staggered to the side.

"Earth Speed!" He started running through the hundreds of carriages and carts that lay along the road to Vuzgal. Their riders had run to either side of the road, most lying down on the grass there.

Nico made to run out from between the carts. Another Institute fighter was running down the side. Nico wanted to slap him. He heard the sound of crossbow bolts from within the boxy buildings.

The fighter brought up a mana barrier. Tens of bolts stabbed into it, taking it out in a matter of seconds. His medallions lasted a bit longer before they tore through his armor and into his body.

Nico windmilled his feet and ducked back into the cover of the carts. Bolts appeared where he would have exited.

Nico pedaled his feet, kicking up dirt to return to the cover of carts.

He kept running, hearing people screaming before sudden silence.

Chains appeared under his feet.

"Earth Pillar!"

Another spell formation appeared where he landed.

"Earth Shield!" The earth formed a barrier around him. He was rocked from side to side, draining his mana as he pushed forward. The trees were still seven hundred meters away. The carts were spreading out more as people weren't lining up to enter the city.

"That is enough."

Uncle Sho?

A spell formed under Nico.

A spike of ice dropped from the sky, breaking the spell formation before it started. Nico dodged around it before a mana barrier enveloped and protected him.

His body felt limp, watching his Uncle Sho walking toward him.

There was no way even that freak could defeat him! Nico managed a weak smile. His uncle was one of the strongest people in all the clan. Even the clan head respected him. Nico only had a quarter of his uncle's strength. Uncle Sho was the true power of the Tolentino Clan!

Tolentino was too weak in his current state and started to move away, cursing his weakness.

Rage bubbled beneath Erik's skin. The Institute had attacked faster than he or the others had expected. He ground his teeth, looking for the origin of the ice spike and spell.

A man wearing a simple cloak and with a hood to cover his face walked from the sidelines as people shivered on the ground. The air distorted around him with the sheer power he commanded. He had a mysterious appearance but resonated with the mana surrounding him with just three words. The man's hands were wrinkled and old showing signs of callouses borne from a lifetime of fighting.

"Do you have him targeted?" Erik asked through his sound transmission device.

"He's still too close to the civilians. Should have him in ten meters," the major in charge of local defenses repeated.

"Fire when you have a clear shot."

The man removed his hood, revealing a regal man with long gray-and-white hair pulled back in a bun. The hand-stitched runes on his robes glowed with mana.

Five meters.

"City Lord West, I presume. I am Elder Sho Tolentino from the Willful Institute. This is something between the younger generations. It is not something for us older generations to interfere in. The Adventurer's Guild attacked us. We are repaying them."

Three meters.

Erik's overall strength was still low. He couldn't use even half his strength or agility.

"You think I care what a declining sect elder has to say? You attack in my city, attack those who have my protection, you pay the price."

"Seems the Associations are not so confident in you. They were willing to take the price we offered." Sho snorted and shook his head as he gathered his mana. He acted like a teacher dealing with a student that didn't know the way of the world yet.

One meter.

"Fuck you and fuck your Institute!" Erik reached out, feeling the strain through his body, channeling mana through the ground as he formed a claw with his hand. Sweat covered his face. Chains tore free of the ground in the shape of his hand. The sound of whistling bolts filled the air as Alvans fired on Sho.

Sho waved his hand. The bolts hit his barrier, darkening it with impacts. Erik's chains made him stumble, and he looked at Erik in surprise. "You!" The repeater bolts drowned out what he was trying to say, exploding on his barrier and breaking through one layer before striking a second.

Erik fed more power into the chaotic mana chains. Links broke, but they surrounded the barrier and squeezed.

"Tracking Water! Water Waves!" Sho attacked.

Erik didn't have the mana to defend and attack. He pulled out a spell scroll and ripped it. A barrier snapped around him, and the water attack impacts made the barrier shudder.

Sho Tolentino was out of time. The bolts and chains broke the last of his mana reserves.

The chains, made of elements forced into form, struck Sho. He screamed before the energies rebounded inside his body and *exploded.*

A tombstone appeared where Sho had been.

Erik turned. Flame shot out from his hand, burning through Nico's stomach.

There was a look of loss on Nico's face as all the mana in his body left him. He coughed, blood running down his mouth as he fell backward, leaving another tombstone.

"Roska, hunt down the runners." Erik didn't look up at the approaching flying beasts as he walked toward the dead Elder Sho.

Two of the air force birds remained, circling Erik. The other two sped off toward the runners.

Erik collected Elder Sho's tombstone and stored his body in his storage ring. He would make a powerful undead. *What a fucking idiot.* Elder Sho was stronger than most people in the Fourth Realm. Though Erik couldn't have fought him head-on, that would have revealed all his trump cards.

Erik repeated the process with Nico. He glanced at the Alvan Air Force beasts as they dove. Their spells spat out, cutting down any runners.

He covered his eyes against the wind as one of the circling kestrels landed.

"Sir!" Davos slid down the back of the kestrel's ramp.

Erik jogged to the ramp, past Davos. Yang Zan was covering the area with the bay door gunner. They followed Erik inside, grabbing onto the vines along the walls and ceiling.

"Make sure they collect the bodies," Erik yelled into Davos's ear as the kestrel flapped its wings, forcing them back into the air.

Davos nodded, talking into his sound transmission device.

Erik contacted Chonglu. "It was the Willful Institute. Have the guards make sure that none of them make it out alive. Organize with Elan. Cut off the Institute where we can. Declare that we will no longer trade with the Willful Institute. Have the military on fifty percent readiness. All leave is canceled. Others will learn that the Associations are willing to cut a deal. They could try to make use of it. Have all the Adventurer's Guild halls notified. Collapse the ones that can't defend themselves. Work according to the list."

"Yes, sir." Chonglu's voice was heavy as he ended the sound transmission.

"How bad is it?" Erik used his sound transmission device to talk to Davos.

"It ain't pretty. The medics are putting them back together. They were burning their cultivations to fight. Even if they recover, it will take time for them to heal their internal injuries. Their bodies are broken. The mana systems are shattered or strained to the point of collapse."

"As long as they're alive, we can fix the rest." Erik felt the wind on his face, looking through the door gunner's position as they scanned the city with their repeaters.

"Casualties?"

"Hundred and fifty-seven at last count. It'll climb. We're still recovering bodies from the guild hall. Two hundred and thirty-four wounded."

"I'll head there and lend my skills."

"I can't let you do that, sir. You're the city lord. The guilds, traders, and others will want to talk to you. The army needs to be reassured. If there's another attack, we can't have you in the middle of it. Trust in the medics you trained, sir."

Erik let out a hot breath. Holding back from venting his frustration at Davos.

He stared at the claw marks that cut through Adventurer's Guildhall. Guards patrolled the area on the ground and in the sky. Healers had broken up the guild hall into sections, working on the people there.

Blaze took off his helmet and rubbed the back of his neck, tilting his head from side to side.

"They're stuck in like damn ticks," he sighed.

"Well, they can't let every city go." Joan checked her bow before putting it down.

"Some of the sects are rethinking the battle due to losses."

"They desire rewards. As soon as it comes to dying, they get scared."

"Just want someone else to die for them."

The flap of Blaze's tent was thrown to the side, the messenger face-to-face with Joan's loaded bow and Blaze's ready sword.

"Guild Leader! The halls were attacked!"

Joan lowered her bow.

"Which ones?"

"Several, across different realms. We don't know how bad it is. They attacked Vuzgal, and we were torn apart. We've lost contact with other guild halls. Erik sent out orders to the other guild halls. Some were able to hide or flee before they were attacked."

"Fuckers!" Blaze kicked a desk over, sending papers across the room. "That's why they've been fighting so hard here. They wanted us to dedicate more people, draw us in and attack our rear. Shit."

17 Wavering Faith

Marco Tolentino's expression didn't change as the messenger related the news of his younger cousin and uncle.

"Cowards! How dare they use all their weapons against Elder Sho!" His father and the Clan head, Andrew Tolentino, slapped his hand on his chair, cracking an armrest.

It was his own fault for being so arrogant as to think that there was no one as powerful as him. If Marco were weaker, he would use everything he had to defeat a stronger enemy. What did it matter if he won?

Marco snorted mentally, but kept it hidden.

"What does the sect head intend to do?" Andrew demanded.

"He has not promised anything at this time."

"We have lost a genius of the younger generation and a venerated elder and we won't do anything? They are but one independent city!"

The room was set up in a square, elders and clan leaders along one wall, opposite up and coming or powerful families, while anyone else could sit behind them in the rows going back.

Marco cleared his throat, making the room look at him. Among the elders and leaders of his clan, he didn't show the slightest anxiety. "The sect reached an agreement with the Associations. There is an opportunity for us. We are fighting across many fronts. The sect has to prioritize."

The sooner he got away from this sect, the better. It was crumbling, and the battle had barely begun. Not that it concerned him. His future was secure. He had been scouted by the Black Phoenix Clan in the Seventh Realm.

"Tell the sect head that the Tolentino Clan will not let this go." Andrew's words came through his teeth.

The clan had to show their strength—and now. If they made it through this calamity, they would gain greater power and open a path for them to lead the attack on Vuzgal. *Well done, little cousin! Your death will come in useful. It is good that we lost such a useless elder before we had to go into battle.*

"We ask that Marco be given the honor of leading the army."

Putting forward a powerful figure to show their dedication was a good play. They could get a commanding position over the other clans and gain more benefits. Vuzgal only had short walls with odd square buildings facing outward and a mana barrier. They were a trading and crafting city. As long as the crafters were allowed to flee, there would be no backlash to face.

Marco stood and bowed to the Clan head. "I am honored to be graced with the responsibility. I will make sure that the deaths of Elder Sho and cousin Nico are paid in full!" His voice was hot and heavy, gritting his teeth together so hard they strained.

That should be enough to secure his position. It would look good to his teachers in the Seventh Realm as well.

"What the hell happened at Vuzgal?" Head Asadi demanded as the doors closed behind Cai Bo. Several of the high elders turned, flanking him after having their discussion interrupted.

"The Guild members were stronger than we thought, and the city lord was there."

"Strong enough to kill an elder of the Sixth Realm?"

"They used everything they had on him," Cai Bo said, keeping her features suitably downcast. Elder Sho had been one of Head Asadi's supporters. Not just anyone could go in the face of their own family leader. "The guards reacted faster and were stronger than we thought."

"Stronger than you thought? The Adventurer's Guild has redoubled their attacks and revealed more experts than ever before! Your information was severely lacking! How did you not know that they had people who had formed their mana cores and attained Body Like Iron? Body Like Stone is not a rarity for them. It has backfired on us badly. People in our sect doubt our competence and other sects are forming armies to work against us."

"Vuzgal's reputation has also been harmed, and there are other sects that are undoubtedly interested in taking the city. The city will fall with time." She tried to affect some nervousness into her calm. She needed to seem weak for him to feel in control.

"We *cannot* let another sect win Vuzgal." Asadi's eyes sharpened.

Cai Bo cupped her fists to Head Asadi. "What are your orders, Sect Head?" Oh, she would have smiled if decades of plotting, backstabbing, and training had given her complete control over her expressions.

"Prepare our army in secret. Support Marco. You will go take Vuzgal and draw in support from the other sects. Then we can use them to attack the sects allied against us."

"I will see to it."

"What about that girl you sent to look for information on Vuzgal's people? Have you heard anything?"

"She has sent me updates."

"Anything of use?"

"We haven't found any weaknesses yet, but we will."

"Good. Leave me." Asadi waved his sleeves. She didn't miss the sneers or looks of derision in most of the high elders with him.

Four of the seven simply turned around. It wouldn't do to mock the lady who owned you.

Blaze waited calmly as the guards for the Alvan command center checked his identity and medallion.

"Thank you, sir." They passed back his Alvan medallion and moved to the side. The doors opened.

He nodded and walked past them, surrounded in a grim silence.

The command center was quiet as he moved to the conference room. He could feel it, *taste* it as officers watched him walk by. It was like the smell of smoke upon the air. They all knew that these were the opening shots for something much bigger.

He opened the door. Elan stood talking about the report in everyone's hands. Delilah, Erik, Rugrat, Glosil, and Yui sat at the table.

Blaze closed the door behind him. He nodded to Elan and moved to a vacant seat.

"After killing Nico Tolentino, the Tolentino Clan will need to respond, which means the Willful Institute will have to respond. They cleared out many of the Adventurer's guild locations. Other cities not part of the fighting are putting pressure on the Adventurer's guild to move."

Elan finished and sat down.

"Blaze?" Erik asked.

Blaze looked over.

"How are your people?"

Blaze's gut twisted, but he talked numbly. "The Guild has been shaken. Command and discipline have been hampered. They're angry, and anger leads to more mistakes than it helps. We got overconfident. I have ordered all of our locations to be sold and to bring everything we have back to Vuzgal and to cities we can be sure won't sell out to the Willful Institute. Different sects are pushing to renegotiate their contracts now that we can be seen on the back foot."

Erik's eyes chilled as Blaze shifted his tight shoulders, not averting his gaze.

"Glosil, is there something more we can do to assist the Adventurer's Guild? They might not all be full Alvans, but they fight for us," Erik said.

"I can think of a few ideas. Blaze, if you want to talk options afterward?"

"Certainly."

Mistress Mercy's carriage continued into Zahir City. She sniffed the air, her face screwing into a grimace. The mana in this realm was so thin it was slowing down the amount she could gather. She looked outside of the window. People moved to the side, shaking at the powerful presence of the beasts pulling her carriage. If just one of them went on a rampage, there would be nothing the city lord could do.

The carriage stopped at the city lord's manor. A muscular man wearing mid-Apprentice-level armor with a silver chain stood ready to receive her. His guards lined up on either side in formation. They had low Apprentice and even Novice level gear.

She had been searching for information for months. Everything led to Zahir City.

Her guards opened the door to her carriage. Mercy walked down the steps and looked over the assembled men. The city lord and his guards bowed deeply. The wind drifted through the courtyard.

"Rise." She looked the man up and down. "You are the lord of this city?"

"Yes, Mistress. I am Abdul Zahir." He cupped his fists and bowed again, his body shaking.

"Good. Let's talk inside."

He led her and her guards into his manor. He took them to a private room with two couches and refreshments. Mercy grimaced at the food and moved to a couch, sitting down. The mana was so thin in the food it was useless.

Zahir paled at her reaction. She waved for him to sit opposite.

As he did so, two of her guards stood behind Mistress Mercy, a third behind Zahir. Two others moved about the room.

Mistress felt a little pleasure seeing the anxiousness written on Zahir's features. "What can you tell me about the Silaz Trading house?"

"It is a large trading house with a major location in Zahir. It used to be the headquarters, but that was shifted to King's Hill. They have several locations in the Beast Mountain Range outposts and different kingdom capitals. They deal in many trade goods, but they are best known for trading in monster cores and mana stones. They also trade in beast par—" Zahir shut his mouth as Mercy raised a hand.

"Who leads the trading house?"

"Wren Silaz."

"What about his family?"

"His father was a great driving force. He took the whole house to a new level. Wren expanded into the outposts and has built on his father's past achievements. Do you know of Domonos Silaz? He had the honor to join your venerated Willful Institute."

Mercy's gaze chilled, making the mana shift.

"Where are Wren and his father now?"

"His father retired from the business. It's said that he is exploring trading in the higher realms with his last son and cultivation-crippled daughter. Wren lives at the headquarters in the King's Hill Outpost."

Mercy frowned. "What about this King's Hill Outpost and Beast Mountain Range?"

"All the outposts in the Beast Mountain Range banded together, created an alliance. The city in the middle of the outposts is called King's Hill. They trade with everyone, and created a consortium that trains talent from across the First Realm," Zahir said hurriedly, catching his breath after.

"When did this happen?"

"Years ago, before I was the city lord." Zahir grimaced.

Mercy clicked her tongue. "Where is the old city lord?"

"He abdicated and disappeared with his children. There was an attack on him that nearly killed him." Zahir shrugged. "He might have actually been killed. I'm not sure."

"We'll head to King's Hill." Mercy rose from her seat.

She made it to the doorway, her guards opening it and walking ahead.

Mercy turned to Zahir with a frown. "What was the name of the last lord?"

"Uhh, Chonglu something," Zahir said.

"What?" Mercy snapped.

"Lord Chonglu." Zahir's shoulders rose.

"The two children, were they twins? One boy and one girl?" Mercy's mouth was moving as fast as her brain.

"Yes!"

"Feng and Felicity? Were those their names?"

"I think so?"

"Do you know?"

"I-I'm pretty sure it was!"

"What happened when he was attacked?" Mercy's lips rapid fired.

"There were two assassins. They nearly killed him. I heard two people saved him from the brink. Then a strong fighter appeared. They disappeared with some of the guards and the old lord's people."

Could those two people be from Vuzgal?

"The two that saved him; were they men, women? What did they look like?"

"Two men, I think, and they were strong."

Mercy's brows furrowed. She held her head, looking at the ground and pulling her thoughts together.

Chonglu, Silaz, and the Vuzgal city lords were all connected somehow. Then there were the massive changes in the Beast Mountain Range. There was something more here. She needed to report this to Elder Cai Bo.

Yui Silaz checked the mission board in the Vuzgal command center. The door opened and Domonos walked in, gathering silence from everyone in the room.

"You need a shower." Yui's face split into a smile. Domonos' flat expression brightened as the brothers hugged.

"Ahh, smells like you need one too." Yui laughed as he patted Domonos on the back. "Come on, the others won't be here for a bit."

"Attacked Vuzgal directly. Bold of them." Domonos' tone was light, but Yui could tell he was barely holding back his fury.

"It means that the Associations have gotten a better deal. If we stay or if we go, they're covered."

"Any movement on their side?" Domonos asked.

"Nothing official yet or in the city. We're not planning to do anything either way. Most of the issues have come from the traders and the bandits that have cropped up."

"What's the intel saying?"

"That someone—not the Willful Institute—is targeting us. Our sources indicate that they're linked to the surrounding cities. Dad's looking through it. How are things on your side? How have my people been?"

"You their mother now?" Domonos cracked a half-smile and rubbed his worn face.

"Willful Institute is playing the waiting game. Most of the sects don't understand this shit takes time. We can't just run in and take it. The conflict has pulled the Institute together, but not everyone else. They're vultures looking for the biggest prize." Yui shook his head. "They've increased in number and hired more mercenaries to help out. If not for Dad's spies, we would have been led into a few bloodbaths. Your people have done well. They're well-trained, switched on. Haven't had any issues, yet. Even with the battalions being different, they are working together as if they're one unit. I trust them as much as I trust my own people."

"What about the halls being hit?"

"Are you asking what I think, or what the reaction has been?"

"Any of it."

"The military members understand. It is a hard decision. Erik and Rugrat trained with us every chance they got. We know they're not cold, unreachable sect heads. The guild members, we mostly trained them. They don't know Erik and Rugrat. They're pissed that they weren't told. They're looking at their people being hit. Don't see how they tried to limit the damage. How Erik and Rugrat's primary focus is to defend the people of Alva. Don't acknowledge how their own families have been hidden and protected. So they're pissed at Erik and Rugrat, but it will pass with time. In the meantime, it's increased their rage toward the Institute."

Domonos coughed. "The people that haven't been trained here and don't know about Alva, they're more driven than ever. All of them that can have been signing up to join the battlefields."

"How is the guild on the battlefield now? There were issues in the past."

"When we started, they were fighting like mercenaries. While they're not soldiers, they're coming together. Having the Tiger and Dragon Battalions fighting alongside and supporting them, they've matured quickly. One has to learn fast in war." Domonos stared at the opposite wall, tapping his finger softly against the table. "What about Mistress Mercy?"

Yui frowned. "She's looking for information."

"You're not happy?"

"She's poking around in the Second Realm. Went to see Elder Hui that recruited you and teleported into what was Chonglu. Zahir, it's called now. Talked to the lord there, then disappeared."

"Do we know what she found out?"

"No, but she's got a direct line of contact with Cai Bo. There's no knowing what they've learned."

The door opened. Rugrat and Glosil walked in. Yui and Domonos snapped to attention.

"Be seated." Rugrat returned the salute, his voice somber. He moved to Domonos and held out his hand.

Domonos shook it.

"Good to see you back here, boy."

"Sir." Domonos nodded.

Rugrat patted his shoulder and moved to his chair. "All right, Glosil, how are things going out there?"

"We lost nearly one hundred guild halls in the attacks, and nearly one thousand dead. Since then, half the guildhalls have been closed with the fighters consolidated. The Willful Institute lost sixteen cities at last count, over a third of their total holdings. Twenty-five locations are under attack or monitored by at least one sect army. The guild has been hired to watch seven different cities. Their tactics have changed, which Domonos can expand upon."

The room looked at Domonos.

"The enemy are not idiots. They call the special teams wraiths, assassins that appear out of nowhere to cause chaos. The effects of Operation Doomsday persist. The different factions work together, but they don't trust one another. It's dropped their combat effectiveness. They're used to duels and battles between small groups, not siege warfare. Still, they're learning." Domonos sighed and leaned back, battle-weary. "Lives are cheap to them and it shows. Certainly cheaper than pills and concoctions. If someone isn't strong enough, doesn't have the connections, or doesn't offer enough contributions to the sect and they get wounded, there is no coming back. While infections might kill them through a graze, our casualty rate is high, but the number of them that die is incredibly low."

"How is that on our people?" Rugrat asked.

"Reassuring. They know that if they're hurt that someone will look after them, so they work more like our military than a group of fighters. The Guild members have matured a lot. Sieging is supply intensive. It takes us a lot more people and supplies to take a city than it takes for them to defend it."

"Don't worry. You will have all the supplies you need. We finished the latest factory and are building another two. One in Vuzgal and another in Alva," Rugrat said.

"Yes, sir."

"How are things on the ground?" Glosil asked.

"People are focused. We haven't had many issues. A lot of them are pissed off with the sects. The one we're fighting primarily, but we're always butting up against the sects we're allied with. Right now, the leadership has had to play games with the sects to get them to dedicate more resources."

"Such as?" Rugrat asked.

"We make a feint, not for the enemy but the other sects. We make it appear that we're going for a treasury. Looks like we're getting more rewards. Then they'll take more risks and push their people harder. They only care about the rewards."

"It makes me think of medieval feudal systems. Going to war for profit gain." Rugrat shook his head.

"Anything major?"

"The leadership might be annoyed by what happened, but the general guild members are angry at the Institute. All of our people understand it. We've started to pull out our people from leadership positions, turning them over to the guild members. We've been able to reform squads to use as quick reaction forces. Fighting is slow. That is it." Domonos coughed, pulled out a canteen, and drank.

Glosil picked up from where he'd finished. "The Institute has been searching for information around Vuzgal in any way they can find it. After the guild attack, Elan wiped out most of the Institute spies. We know who the remaining ones are and where to find them. We have to watch out for not only the Institute but other powers moving against us. We've set up a lot of hidden fallback positions across the realms, but we're still low. Something that should be fixed shortly." Glosil glanced at Yui and Rugrat. "The Institute is pulling together but they're on a shaky foundation. There are plenty of others interested in gaining a new city or settling old debts. Here is the information book."

Glosil took out the tome and slid it to Domonos.

"Light reading." Domonos opened the book, getting caught up on the operations of the rest of the Alva army.

Elder Lu Ru re-read the orders he had just received.

"Understood," he said to the messenger, putting the scroll on his desk.

The messenger bowed and left Elder Lu Ru's office.

Elder Lu Ru stood and moved to the windows that looked over the Fourth Realm Blue Lotus Headquarters. Through it, he commanded all the Blue Lotus locations across the Fourth Realm.

Lei Huo marched into the office wearing her armor. Cui Chin came with her, wearing his scholarly robes.

Elder Lu Ru turned from the impressive view.

"An agreement has been reached between the Blue Lotus and the Willful Institute in regard to Vuzgal. Cui Chin, Lei Huo, make the necessary arrangements to remove families from the city and prepare for a warring state."

"Sir…" Lei Huo's frown deepened. "There are honorary elders among the Vuzgalians."

"The Blue Lotus comes above personal relationships. The other Associations have all agreed. We have made it clear that they are to try their best to not kill the honorary elders. You will have to tell them to evacuate. If they do not, they will not be under our protection." Elder Lu Ru couldn't hide the harshness in his voice or the way he gripped his hands behind his back.

18
Shifting Landscape

Erik's focus centered on the alchemist cauldron in front of him, and the flames dancing around it. Beasts moved around in the flames, refining the ingredients.

A large slumbering wolf lay in the center of the cauldron. Inside its half-translucent blue body was a small, slowly revolving mass of pink and neon yellow liquid.

Flame beasts charged the wolf. Their flames mingled with one another as the prepared ingredients within the flame beasts were combined. The pink and yellow liquid changed to greens and reds, blacks and golds, combining ingredients.

Sweat beaded on Erik's forehead as he controlled the flame beasts and maintained the perfect conditions throughout the cauldron.

The cauldron rumbled slightly as the beasts continued to consume one another, combining their ingredients at an ever-increasing rate. The flames of the sacrificial flame beasts turned into the greatest supplement for the central fire wolf.

With minimal movements of his fingers, threads of red, green, and black energy entered the cauldron. They merged with the flame beasts, altering the flames. The pure fire, earth, and metal affinities were a tonic to the ingredients.

The ingredients changed. Grasses that had been dried and turned into a fine brown powder took on a deep azure appearance with metallic hints throughout. A rough metal-looking ingot of silver and black drew in the earth element. It bloomed. The covering cracked, spreading to the sides as it opened like a flower. A healthy, pale, fruit-like flesh opened. Inside, a pale fuzzy pear rested upon the petals, inviting one to take a bite.

Erik used his connection to the earth and metal elements. They had become part of his refining process. "Reinforce. Compress!"

The cauldron stilled while the ingredients shuddered.

The last combinations were completed, leaving just three flame beasts around the wolf.

They turned and charged the large wolf. It stood and howled, causing a tremor in the reinforced cauldron.

The beasts struck the fire wolf like rain hitting the surface of a lake.

Their ingredients, like a hidden payload, continued on. Flames embraced the ingredients and the partial concoction.

"Increase compression, decrease the temperature, and increase revolutions," Erik said. The elements leapt to his command as the ingredients were pushed together. Impurities and smoke came off the bean-shaped item forming in the middle of his cauldron.

"More earth and metal mana." Threads spread from Erik's moving fingertips, passing through the flame holes of the cauldron and into the forming concoction.

The beasts wrapped together, combining with one another, forming a nebulous cloud of pure blue flame. The concoction rested in the middle of the cauldron and its flames.

The cauldron strength and temp were good, the ambient air temperature, too, and the pill's internal temperature was low. If he increased the metal content of the pill slightly, it would heat up faster.

As he thought it, the black mana threads danced in response. The cauldron was a realm of its own, and Erik was the god controlling it.

Erik's eyelids were closed, but his eyes shifted underneath. His newly altered senses allowed him to see the cauldron, the flames, and into the concoction. His senses had all locked onto his task.

He took a slight breath as the concoction spun. It was a myriad of ugly colors spreading into one another. Smoke continued to rise.

Slowly, painfully so compared to the action of moments ago, the concoction became smaller and rounder.

A large chunk cracked and released a powerful black gas, smoothing out a large part of the concoction.

Crap. Erik's fingers flew, altering the flames. *Come on! Stabilize, will you?*

Erik's clothes were covered in sweat. The mana in the room danced to his rhythm and command.

The concoction stabilized, its molasses-like surface hardening.

Newborn pill. Erik relaxed slightly. He rolled his tight shoulders and neck, refraining from trying to clear the sweat on his face.

"Compress, lower temperature."

Erik used his flames and earth spells. The rough, pitted, and bumpy surface of the pill released more tiny gas vapors, smoothing slowly.

He had to keep the compression and heat high enough to purify, but not too high that it would burn the ingredients. Some of the ingredients needed a high temperature over a short period to burn off, while some needed a low temperature over a long time.

He increased the mana flow, but again it was too much, too little, and different amounts. *Okay, lower temperature, increase mana flow.* That would balance out the Elder Weed so it didn't evaporate.

Sweat beaded his forehead as he carefully introduced the Elder Weed.

"Condensed." He sighed in relief, continuing to adjust the temperature, slow and steady with bouts of furious speed.

The bumps on the surface smoothed out, but there was still pitting.

Erik slowly drew away his flames and canceled his spells.

He used mana manipulation to open the cauldron and pull out the pill, storing it in a waiting pill bottle.

"One Expert grade Revival pill."

Revival Pill (Condensed) *Grade: Mid-Expert*
Increases natural regeneration by 450% for 5 minutes. Increases Stamina regeneration by 800%. Heals blood vessels. Heals respiratory system. Heals bones

Skill: Alchemy *Level: 88 (Expert)*
Able to identify 1 effect of the ingredient. Ingredients are 5% more potent. When creating concoctions, mana regeneration increases by 20%

He needed to make a lot more of those pills to get to the high Expert ranks, which was more involved than just making a high-level pill. They only increased a level a certain amount. When he had helped Old Hei, it had taken him months to reach the skill he needed to produce pills that would increase his skill level more. Now that he had a higher skill level, he had to prove it again and again to the Ten Realms.

Erik grunted as he shifted, his muscles tight and weary.

"Ah shit." He let himself drop on his shoulder, stretching out his legs and reaching his arms out, the stretch opening tight places in his body with pops and cracks.

"Quick Heal."

Erik groaned as the aches fell away.

He canceled the spell and stood up. He stored his gear and used a clean spell on himself. He had lost track of time, but guessed he must've been in there for a few days.

He yawned, pulling out a stamina potion. At least he had found some better flavoring for these. "Faster than eating a meal." Erik drank from the potion and walked to the door. He opened it with his mana manipulation and stepped out into the hall.

His special team had switched again. Special Team Four waited for him.

"Hey, boss." Han Wu, the second-in-command of Special Team Four, looked up from the card game he and another team member were playing. Two others were watching the hallway of alchemy rooms. Alchemists entered and left the different rooms without a second glance.

"Rugrat told me to tell you that once you're done, you need to go dungeon raiding." There was still a great need for dungeon cores to create secure locations for Alvans to hide in and to spread Alva's influence under the developing Beast Mountain Range and Vuzgal.

"What's he up to?" Erik asked.

"Been at the range, training in the dungeons, teaching." Han Wu stored the game away.

"All right. I need a shower first." Erik started walking, the group moving into place around him.

"Anything change?" Erik sipped from his potion again, letting the others guide him out of the crafter hall.

"You've been in there for five days. No change. Domonos came back. Director Silaz has been gathering information on the traders and bandits at Vuzgal." Han Wu passed Erik an information book.

"Yay." Erik opened the book.

Information Book: Summary for Lord West
Do you wish to activate this information book? Doing so will destroy this information book. *YES/NO*

"Sure."

"Well, you look like shit," Rugrat said as Erik wandered into the house, followed by special team four.

Erik flipped him the bird and put it away quickly as he heard a cough. Erik bobbed his head in apology and spared Rugrat's grin a glare.

"Come on, we've got lunch ready. Bring your friends," Momma said as she turned back for the dining room.

"Momma." Rugrat moved out of the living room and followed the procession into the kitchen.

"What? I had free time on my hands. What else am I supposed to do? Sleep all day?" She waved people around the table. She'd put out a full spread. The special team members looked at one another.

"Sit your asses down." Erik rolled his eyes.

They grinned and did so as Rugrat sighed.

"Here is some thick chicken soup and fresh-baked rolls. Eat up!" Momma patted two covered items. "Then we have enchiladas and sides." She went down the table.

Erik opened his mouth and then closed it.

"You best all eat up. Can't work properly on an empty stomach." Momma Rodriguez raised an eyebrow at the special team, pulling out a spread from her storage ring, setting it out.

Rugrat opened his mouth, looking at Erik. They grinned wryly and shrugged. *Momma is a force of nature when she sets her sights on something.*

"Dig in!" Momma said, sitting at the head of the table. It seemed only natural.

"Who wants soup?" Rugrat said as he picked up bowls and a spoon.

"Bread?" Erik asked.

Everyone passed food and plates around the table.

"Could you pass the guac?"

"Is that sour cream?"

They served one another, settling into chit chat.

These hardened warriors would have fit in perfectly with any family at Thanksgiving, eating and drinking together, relaxing, praising the food.

Rugrat patted his stomach. "I couldn't eat another thing," he said as Momma Rodrigeuz watched over them all with a smile; it faltered as the special team members stood up. Rugrat stood as well. "Got a job to do, Momma." His voice was quiet, but strong.

She put a hand on his arm. "Be safe out there."

Rugrat covered her hand with his.

"All of you hear me?" She looked at the rest of the group.

"Yes, Momma Rodriguez."

"Good!"

Almost as quickly as the feast and tables had come together, it disappeared, cleaned, and then stored. Rugrat waved as they headed out, taking the road toward the totem.

"Where is this dungeon?" Erik asked.

"Third Realm."

"Great. Swamps."

"Haunted swamp."

"Even better. Sounds like you'll be right at home."

"Call me crazy, but I feel stronger after Momma R's cooking," Erik said through the sound transmission device inside his helmet. The team had spread out as they moved through the swamp trees. The ground seemed solid, but it was just dirt that had piled up on roots over the water below for centuries.

"Her skill level is high enough, everything she makes has an effect on it," Rugrat said.

It was dark, and the air was wet and heavy under the thick canopy of the swamp's trees. Erik wasn't affected by the heat, though others were covered in sweat from pushing through the mangrove swamp.

"I think I have something," Jackie said to everyone on the team's sound transmission channel. "Trees look different, stronger, and bigger. They make a circle. Think that there might be an entrance at the center."

"We're moving to your position," Gong Jin replied.

They converged on Jackie's position.

"Yup, definitely a dungeon entrance. I can feel the change in mana," Rugrat agreed. He used dungeon sense, confirming it.

"Dismount. Han Wu, secure the entrance."

"Got it." Han Wu took four people. They walked between the circle of mangrove trees. They were twice as thick as a man. Veins of mana traced up the side of the gargantuan trees, bringing light to the surrounding area.

A low-lying mist covered the ground.

"Got an entrance. Moving in," Han Wu reported.

Erik checked his repeater and waited.

A wave illuminated all living beings around the entrance to the dungeon and beyond.

"Doesn't look like there's anyone in the area." Gong Jin glanced at Erik and Rugrat.

"Dungeon core is close. It's to the northwest. A hundred, maybe two hundred meters." Rugrat pointed in the direction he sensed the dungeon core.

"Let's go conquer a dungeon." Erik walked toward the circle of giant mangrove trees.

"Contact!" Han Wu yelled.

The ground shook as Erik picked up his pace. The second half of the team pushed ahead.

"Water elemental! Two of them! Focus your Metal and Earth attribute spells!"

Inside the ring of trees, an entrance formed of roots lay in the middle. The special team ran through the entrance with their weapons at the ready, following the tunnel down.

You have entered the dungeon: Black Spring of Souls

Erik heard the sound of rushing water as the tunnel stopped

descending and they reached their first room. The entire dungeon from roof to wall and floor was a series of roots crisscrossing one another. It was like a mangrove had grown into the form of the dungeon. Water descended from the ceiling, creating a large pond to the back left of the room. It spilled over into smaller, root-rimmed pools.

Among the pools were dozens of water elementals. Their amorphic shifting bodies formed weapons as they rose and charged Han Wu's special team.

They were cut down like wheat by the repeaters.

"Fucking big boys!" Rugrat raised his repeater, firing on the two water elementals whose heads almost touched the ceiling of the room twenty meters above. They had more humanoid bodies.

One turned his arm into an ice shard and threw it. The special team members ran away. The spear tore up the tree roots and broke through the floor, revealing the level below.

"Spread out, create a firing line!" Gong Jin ordered.

Erik and Rugrat joined the line.

Erik pulled out one of the metal needles that he had used to temper his body. He activated the formation all the way. "Iron enhance!" The needle shook in his hands, the formation burning with power, distorting from the mana flowing through it.

Erik drew back and threw the metal needle. He hit the spear-thrower in the chest.

It shook as black tendrils spread through its chest, causing it to stumble.

"Focus on the closest one!" Gong Jin yelled.

Arrows struck the elemental. Earth and metal, the water elemental's weaknesses, spread through its body. It collapsed, leaving a tombstone.

"Shift fire!" Gong Jin ordered.

"I have enemies coming in from the three other entrances!" Han Wu yelled. "Jin, take out the elemental. Simms, Jackie, cover the western doors!"

The second water elemental stomped his foot, shaking the room.

"Duck! Barriers!" Rugrat yelled.

Water from the pools turned into spears that shot out in every direction. They smashed through the roots, leaving splintered wounds.

Erik dismissed his mana barrier.

"Go to rifles!" Gong Jin yelled.

"Thank you." Rugrat pulled out his rifle, dropping his repeater. Erik formed mana in his ears.

Rugrat sat back and hooked his arm around, resting the rifle in the crook of his elbow.

Erik stored his repeater as Rugrat fired. The water elemental's body distorted as a massive ripple cut through it. Water sprayed on the wall behind him. It began to shrink as the second round struck.

It penetrated the water elemental before it exploded. The metal shards killed it from the inside, creating another massive tombstone.

Rugrat held his rifle in one hand and took in his repeater with a storage ring on the other.

"We're moving! Head for the northwestern door. Jackie, Simms, hold your position and cover us!" Gong Jin yelled.

There were creatures and beasts boiling out of the three doors to the western side of the room. Beasts from the floors below were tearing at the holes left behind in the fighting.

"Move it!" Gong Jin yelled.

Erik ran, jumping over the roots and obstacles. He reached Simms and Jackie.

A flesh golem made of beast bodies crowded the middle doorway. Han Wu and his people were pushing for the closest doorway in the direction of where they'd sensed the dungeon core.

Erik fired on the golem with his railgun. "Covering!"

Bits of flesh and bone came off the golem.

Erik switched his point of aim to the water elementals that had survived their entrance; it took a single round to turn them into tombstones.

"Change weapons," Erik yelled at Simms and Jackie.

They stored their repeaters and pulled out railguns. Erik switched to the furthest door where fire elementals dimmed upon entering the room.

Erik sensed *a lot* of concentrated fire mana moving toward them through that corridor.

Shooting came from the closest door. "Covering! Simms, Jackie, Erik, get moving!" Gong Jin had established a firebase, firing on the other two doors with Rugrat and Tyrone. The rest of the team was clearing the corridor and pushing ahead.

Erik turned and started running.

The beast golem stood up again, repairing itself. Around it, furred beasts with yellow eyes, duckbills, and powerful claws covered the ground. Their bodies were drawn to the golem as it grew in size and power.

What the fuck!

He thought he had killed that thing! No way should it be standing up. Erik slowed and fired his rifle. The beast golem took the impacts and collapsed, but there was no tombstone.

Erik rushed past the fire-based elementals and pushed into the corridor. It was warm. Burn marks covered the ground, as did tombstones. Erik missed the roots that would have twisted his ankles. The corridor turned to the right. Erik came around the corner with his rifle raised.

Han Wu and his people were in the room beyond.

"We've got fire elementals and something big is hitting the damn wall to the west!" Han Wu yelled.

Erik used his Dungeon Sense.

"The core is in here!"

"Find it!" Gong Jin yelled.

Erik ran into the fog-filled room behind the extended line of Han Wu's five-man team. They were focused on slowing the tide of fire elementals that were contained in the western doorway.

He saw a door in the southern wall parallel with the corridor. In the middle of the room, roots had formed pools, as they had done in the first room. The steaming water covered the room in fog.

Erik used his Earth mana, and the roots shifted to create platforms. He jumped up, using the steps to climb up the pools. The eastern wall exploded, revealing four fire elementals. They pushed through the dirt and roots. Something had started pounding on the second door.

Elementals were spreading out and running across the root floor.

Erik gritted his teeth and reached the top of the pools. The water bubbled and frothed in the center.

"Grow!" The roots grew under his spells, creating a platform above the middle of the pool.

He took a knee and aimed at the large fire elementals. Two had fallen. The third was pushing forward. Under the larger elemental's feet, smaller fire elementals swarmed. The fog shifted as Rugrat fired. Erik hadn't noticed him.

"The wall is going to collapse!" Han Wu yelled.

Erik fired on the smaller elementals coming from the western wall. He cut down dozens, but more poured in from the broken wall. Two more large elementals appeared as Rugrat killed another.

"Reloading!"

"Covering!"

"Grenade!"

"Han Wu, how are things back there?" Gong Jin asked.

"We're taking them down."

The southern door and wall exploded. Small fire elementals fell over one another. Two more large fire elementals came with them. Rugrat killed another large elemental at the western wall.

"Reloading!" Erik yelled as he tore out the magazine and replaced it. He glanced at the water. It was bubbling frantically. He could see a light in the depths.

"More coming in from the south! Erik!" Han Wu stood and fired his grenade launcher into the new opening. It stemmed the tide.

Even in this chaos, they were controlling the situation.

"Just need some more time!" Rugrat finished off the last large elemental on the western side. The ground erupted with Earth spikes, stabbing through the smaller elementals. Rugrat's round spread a southern elemental's fire across the wall. Fires started here and there among the roots.

Erik reached down into the steaming pool. The metal-melting heat didn't affect him as he grabbed the dungeon core.

You have come into contact with a dungeon core. With your title, Dungeon Lord, new options are revealed.
Do you wish to: Take command of the Dungeon Remodel Dungeon Destroy the Dungeon

"Take command!"

You have taken over the Black Spring of Souls
Construction ability unlocked

Erik released the dungeon core still in the water, rolling awkwardly to his side. "Stop!" Erik's voice spread through the entire dungeon. Like puppets on strings, the elementals were pulled up short.

Erik pushed up from his side to see rail gun rounds cut through dozens of the paused elementals.

"Cease fire! Cease fire!" Han Wu yelled.

The weapons' fire died down.

"Fire elementals, stop the fires, and return to your rooms," Erik ordered.

They drew the flames into their bodies, leaving charcoaled roots as they moved back to where they had come from.

"Consolidate in the dungeon core room," Gong Jin ordered.

"I've got control over the dungeon now. Just give me a minute. I have to check out things," Erik said.

"Understood. Han Wu, set up an all-around defense on the dungeon core."

"Yes, boss."

Erik pushed his slung rifle to the side so he wasn't lying on it and reached into the boiling water again.

"Rise up."

Erik guided the dungeon core out of the water. He checked through the notifications that had come with taking control of the dungeon.

Resources
Monster Cores: 23194x Low Mortal Grade 8712x Mid Mortal Grade 52x High Mortal Grade 61x Low Earth grade 14x Mid Earth Grade
Minor Fire Elementals blueprint Minor Water Elementals blueprint Minor Air Elemental blueprint Minor Earth Elementals blueprint Large Air Elementals blueprint Large Fire Elementals blueprint Large Water Elementals blueprint Large Earth Elemental blueprint Dara-bird blueprint Beast Core Golem blueprint Diseased animated objects blueprint
Diseased rabbit fur bracers Small bag of exotic spices Tapestry Continual Flame Spell Scroll

Continual Water Spell Scroll
Powerful Earth Manipulation scroll
Strong Invisibility Spell
Ghost Shield medallion
5x Broken Ballista
152x Broken armor
118x Broken spear
4x Shrine
5x sealing scrolls
6897x Wobbergol Fish
19238x Wobbergol Spawn
14x Teleportation formations
1x Armageddon Formation
3x Mana Chaos formation

Upkeep costs:
150 Mortal Mana Stones per day

You have gained control of:

Dungeon Core (Grand Earth Grade Dungeon Core)

Beasts:
2139x Minor Fire Elementals
5123x Minor Water Elementals
874x Minor Air Elemental
15748x Minor Earth Elementals
17x Large Air Elementals
38x Large Fire Elementals
53x Large Water Elementals
73x Earth Elemental
1923x Dara-bird
13x Beast Core Golem

Rune of Fear
4x Energy drain
14x diseased animated objects

"Fucking jackpot." Erik knelt next to the dungeon core, getting it to display a map of the dungeon.

The dungeon was a mass of semi-interconnected rooms. "This place is chaos, small rooms here and there. Everything has been formed with roots. The dungeon core acted as a keystone for all the beasts populating the area."

"How are we looking, Erik?" Gong Jin asked.

"Place is five kilometers by eight, roughly. We're lucky we found the entrance that we did. This place is a damn maze. There are thousands of elementals in here. Three floors in total. Top two floors are built out of the roots. The bottom floor is underground. The dungeon area was created more by the mangrove trees than by the dungeon core. The dungeon core was only responsible for creating the dungeon beasts, I think. Got teleportation formations as well."

"Gonna install a mana gathering formation."

Erik pulled out a blueprint and held it up to the dungeon core.

Blueprint accepted

Black Spring of Souls Dungeon can now create: Mana gathering formation (Large)

On the map of the dungeon Erik manipulated the formation. It didn't work on the upper floors, only the bottom floor. The Dungeon core couldn't manipulate the living trees around it.

The ambient mana decreased as the dungeon set to work.

"Okay, we're going to need formation masters in here to finish inlaying the mana gathering formations. Let's get that teleportation formation set up. We need the crafters' help and Matt's. This place is much bigger than we realized. If we copy Alva dungeon's setup, we'd lose a lot of room. There are fish living in the dungeon. The roots will act as a natural carbon sink and it's frankly massive."

"Another backup position. Good and ready to go?" Rugrat asked.

"Shit, who knew there were so many damn elementals, and what's with the fire boyos?" Han Wu said.

"We're sitting on top of a series of hot springs. There's an active magma flow beneath us. There's also Air Elementals in here," Erik answered.

"Well, we can turn this work over to another squad and Matt," Gong Jin said.

"Got what, another two dungeons on the roster?" Rugrat raised his rifle.

"You heard Lord Rodriguez, check your gear. We're going Dungeon hunting!" Gong Jin couldn't quite hide his eagerness.

"What are your plans to deal with the increased attacks?" Punita Pakesh asked. The middle-aged woman had been trading in the Fourth Realm for decades, building up a trading empire. Her caravans crossed the Chaotic Lands to the east, the Northern White Wastelands, and across the seas in the south.

Chonglu was sitting in the main seat in Vuzgal's public hall. Behind him were two empty seats.

In front of him were the leaders of the traders and merchants within Vuzgal.

"We are looking into the situation. This is the Fourth Realm. I am sure you know that bandits are not uncommon. With the fighting that has just cleared up in Aberdeen to our west, and between the sects to our north and south, there are sure to be fighters turning to banditry."

"What do you expect from a city that allowed another sect to attack someone under their protection, Pakesh?" said Olivar Murillo, a trader specializing in the trade of smithing goods.

He is part of the group controlling the warehouses.

"Do you think I need you to fight my battles, Murillo?" Pakesh drew out her voice, lifting her lip in disdain.

Murillo's lazy eyes sharpened.

Chonglu pushed on. "What happens outside of Vuzgal is not our concern. We—"

"That is clear! Can you even defend Vuzgal?" Arleta Melnik said.

Murillo snorted and looked toward Chonglu.

All the traders were looking down at Chonglu.

"The Associations have started to move their people out. Others will be allowed to attack if they meet the Association's desires!" Arleta continued.

"What the Associations do is not our concern," Chonglu said.

"Bah! You think that you will remain much longer with this?" Arleto threw up her hands.

Chonglu sighed and stood. "Vuzgal is open for trade. You are all supposed to be adults. Hire more guards. You will be protected inside Vuzgal. If you cause trouble, not even an old monster from the Sixth Realm will be able to protect you."

"There was no way that was Sho Tolentino!" Murillo said.

"Are you so sure?" Chonglu asked Murillo.

"There is no way that he would have fallen in such a cowardly attack!" Murillo argued. His supporters among the other traders agreed.

Chonglu showed an ugly smile and snapped his fingers. A door opened to his right, to the side of the three chairs. The pressure in the room skyrocketed.

A skeleton walked out wearing repaired robes. Embroidered on the robe was the Tolentino crest. A Willful Institute medallion hung the man's neck. Each step seemed to increase the pressure. Only the sound of the skeleton's footsteps and medallion hitting his breastbone filled the hall. He stopped, the fire in his eye sockets looking over the traders.

"I have to thank the Willful Institute for supplying us with such a powerful fighter. In Vuzgal, we don't let *anything* go to waste."

"That could be any skeleton!" Murilla yelled.

"It could be." Chonglu's smile had a bite to it.

"The Willful Institute will destroy you if you've turned one of their people into a skeleton!"

"One person? They sent us such good talents. We couldn't let them go to waste either!" Chonglu chuckled. Some of the traders shuddered while the veterans among them showed impassive faces. "Might makes right in the Ten Realms. Starting today, Vuzgal will supply discounted heavy repeaters and ammunition contracts to any sect attacking the Willful Institute. We also offer contribution medallions. Those that wear our medallions and attack the Willful Institute will be rewarded. For every member they kill, they will gain contribution points that they can use in Vuzgal. We will place contribution points above mana stones in purchases. One can get memberships to the Battle Arena, concoctions, gear, even bid in auctions! We have made the same offer to the guilds hunting down bandits in the area."

The traders leaned forward in interest.

"How many repeaters are we talking about a week?" Pakesh asked.

Chonglu looked up. "We have twenty thousand for sale right now, with up to three thousand per week. We'll offer discounts on stamina and healing potions, as well as spell scrolls." Stunned silence fell over the room.

They could sell all the old stock they didn't use anymore. The factories were already producing higher level potions and spell scrolls compared to what they were selling. They could buy ingredients with the money and feed the factories and the true Alva military. These people weren't used to having items produced on such a scale. *Just wait until they see all the looted gear we have for sale.*

Several aides moved up, pulling out papers.

"Please, take a look. These will also be posted on notice boards across the city. Prices have been listed on the pages. Thank you for your time. I know you must have other things that require your attention."

Chonglu turned and walked away. The traders grabbed papers from the aides, talking to one another as they looked at the gear lists in surprise.

The undead Sho Tolentino turned and followed Chonglu out of the room.

That should stir things up a little.

19
An Unfortunate Partnership

"Elder Elsi, I was happy to receive your invitation to meet," Low Elder Kostic said. The hum of a sound canceling formation filled the air around them as they sat in Elder Elsi's office in the Fourth Realm.

Elder Elsi chuckled. "It is my honor to host such a venerated elder."

"I was most interested in the content of your letter."

"I have heard *whisperings* that Vuzgal city's leadership is due for a change. It's a shame, but the Elsi clan is most excited in the rumors about the valiant Willful Institute leading the charge."

Kostic's eyes narrowed. "Oh?"

This was the Elsi Clan, not the Stone Fist Sect. What did a middling clan of the Fourth Realm think they could accomplish? They had barely gained a foothold in the Fifth Realm!

Elder Elsi laughed off Elder Kostic's change in tone. "To be honest, I'm not much of a fighter anymore. I have a new passion now: trading. I find warehouses bring the greatest source of income. They can turn a city on its head if they are not managed well."

Elder Kostic had heard that the warehouse district was under the control of the new gangs in Vuzgal. *That was his doing?* "Certainly, they are one of the main arteries of a city."

"Much like the roads. I've certainly noticed they've become more dangerous around Vuzgal." Elsi pressed his lips together, shaking his head. "It's most sad, the state of affairs. Luckily, my own traders have been able to make it through unscathed."

"Bandits are a help and a hindrance." Low Elder Kostic caught on.

"They are, aren't they? Such a trouble to manage! There are always plenty of ex-fighters in the Fourth Realm looking to make some extra coin." Elder Elsi sipped his tea, never taking his eyes off Elder Kostic.

Elder Kostic smiled. "The Willful Institute is *always* appreciative of allies with proper foresight. Especially those with the ability to say, disrupt our enemy and guarantee our members safe passage."

"I couldn't agree more."

"I think that we would be able to cooperate." Kostic's voice turned serious. "What would you want?"

Elsi's playfulness disappeared. "Chonglu's head, one hundred training slots at the Battle Arena per month, and thirty slots per month at the training dungeons."

"That depends on what you can offer." Kostic sipped his tea.

"Totems and guides to Vuzgal."

Kostic's smile gained some warmth. "I'll have to talk to my sect, but I think the Sect Head will be pleased."

Julilah sat on a bench, watching the water weave through the small stream in the park. Couples walked hand in hand. Others laughed with their friends around a picnic under the shade of large trees. She let out a grumbling sigh and looked at the pond the streams drained into without seeing it. The formation had failed, even with the new modifications. What was she doing wrong?

She rested her elbows on her knees as she picked at her fingers, rolling blueprints and plans through her mind.

The bench shifted with additional weight, and she looked over in alarm. Her mouth twitched, unsure what expression to show.

"Don't worry. I'm not as loud as my boys." Momma Rodriguez gave her a genuine smile.

Julilah let out a dry laugh and pulled her wild hair back behind her ears, her actions rough and jerky as she blushed.

She waited for Momma Rodriguez to say more, but she just sat there, taking in the park.

Julilah pulled herself from her thoughts and looked at the happenings instead of simply existing within it. Students raced through it to class, passing others on a walk on their work break. Some played games, kicking balls across the open ground, or read books, or were on a date.

The world continued to move, even with so many fighting against the Willful Institute.

The newest miniaturized formation might not have worked, but it's just a matter of time. She was so tired of it all. She wanted to do more and wasn't as if it was her body holding her back or if she was making excuses.

Julilah rubbed her temples to fend off the impending headache.

"Something bothering you?" Momma Rodriguez asked, dragging Julilah out of her thoughts.

"Sorry, just tired is all." Julilah smiled.

"I've raised three of my own children and countless others. There's more to this than just being tired."

Julilah opened her mouth and rapidly closed it, staring at the pond under Momma Rodriguez's pursed lips. She slumped forward, showing the weight upon her like a physical force. "I'm not sure if I'm tired or making excuses. There's so much going on, so much that needs to be done."

"And you're overwhelmed with it all, suffering in silence? Praline?"

"Huh?" Julilah looked up to see a box of caramel-covered nuts.

"Pralines." Momma Rodriguez shook the box.

"Thank you." Julilah took one, biting into it. The sweet and slight saltiness, and the texture of the nuts, made Julilah perk up.

"Feel free to have another," Momma Rodriguez said, putting the box down between them and taking one herself. "In hard times, one wants to do so much. Though doing too many things is a sure way to get nothing done. Focus on one thing and only that thing. What will have the greatest impact? Get excited about it. If you treat it like a chore, you'll make excuses to get away from it and do other things, and you won't get anything done."

Julilah took a second praline, nibbling on it. "That makes sense. Just getting my brain to obey is hard."

"Ah, you're young, and there's so much to do in the world. There is a reason why we work with others. Because we can't do everything ourselves."

Julilah's stomach rumbled. She grimaced and reached for a stamina potion.

"Another thing I know is that you can't live off stamina potions alone. You need some food, a shower, and some sleep."

Julilah turned to make an excuse, but bit into her praline when she saw Momma Rodriguez's expression.

Momma's eyebrow lowered, and she ate her own praline.

"You're right." A weight lifted off Julilah's shoulders. She had been hard-charging it all by herself. She avoided asking Qin, thinking she would look down on her for doing less, but they were good friends, and she might have an idea that could help. She could ask others for help, too.

"Thank you."

"So, you haven't had anyone to talk to and you let it bottle up."

Julilah nodded.

Momma Rodriguez pinched her cheek. "You have so much on your shoulders. Come on, let's get you something to eat. Fresh food is the best, no matter what my son says about these storage rings. I just got a new kitchen. It would be a waste not to put it to use."

Julilah rubbed her hands together nervously. "I don't want to interrupt your break."

"Girl, I don't have anything I would rather do than make you something to eat." Momma Rodriguez put her hands around Julilah's and looked into her eyes.

"Okay." Julilah smiled.

"Good, I'll need your help in the kitchen!" Momma Rodriguez patted her hands and stood up.

Erik woke with a start and glanced around the Expert alchemy room. He wiped the drool running from the corner of his mouth. "Crap."

A knock at the door came again.

"I'm coming!" Erik stretched out his legs, getting creaks and pops, his body shaking. He'd fallen asleep cultivating mana, reading a book, cross-legged on the floor.

Hip needs to pop.

Erik collected his belongings into his storage ring and opened the door.

"What?" he yelled at Rugrat.

"Gonna go check on Gilly and George. Plus, we've got a training slot in the dungeon."

Erik rubbed his face. "Sure," he mumbled, yawning and stretching out.

Rugrat pulled out a breakfast burrito and stuffed it into Erik's mouth.

Erik glowered at the grinning redneck, grabbed the burrito, and took a bite.

"Let's go!" Rugrat led the way out of the workshop.

Damn, this is a good burrito. Rugrat was a genius sometimes, and an idiot the rest of the time. "How have things been?"

"Since you laid the smackdown on the Tolentinos and Willful Institute? Quiet. At least on that front." Rugrat's voice darkened. "The Adventurer's Guild has sent more people for training and healing. It's becoming common practice for them to burn their cultivation in moments of need."

"We can only help so much. We don't know enough yet. With time, we can improve techniques to help them. It will be a long and slow journey to understanding, I fear."

"What would you do in their situation? Would you choose to burn your cultivation to help your fellow guild members or roll over?"

Erik held up his burrito to speak, but paused, shaking his head and sighing. "I'd do the same thing."

"Right. Anyway, I've been switching from Vuzgal to Alva while you've been hiding in that alchemy room. Done some work in the factories. They can make the gear faster than I can. Besides, making custom weapons can take days."

"And one of us should be at least aware instead of locked away crafting. Sorry, brother," Erik said.

"No worries. The revival pills and concoctions will save lives. I'll take sentry duty this time."

"Thanks, man."

Rugrat waved him off.

Arriving at the teleportation pad, light enveloped them.

"You been training much?" Erik asked as they reached the Wood Floor.

"Every day, if I can." Rugrat struck a pharaoh pose.

"You're going to blind the kids." Erik munched on his burrito, tilting his head to Storbon and Special Team Four, who were protecting them.

Rugrat flexed his back, completely ineffectual through his body armor.

"Got the team on my back! The beach is over there. Take a *right.*" Erik rolled his eyes, smirking at Rugrat's elaborate poses.

They were walking toward the beast training stables when Erik and Rugrat sensed something above.

"Geo—" Rugrat disappeared as a missile of blue flames and pink tongue dragged him backward, his feet leaving grooves in the ground. "—rge!"

"Gilly!" Erik yelled with wide eyes, stuffing the last of the burrito in his mouth as a shadow covered him.

She let out a happy squeak. Closing her *wings,* she dropped the last several meters to the ground. People ran for their homes as the buildings shook.

It's Godzilla!

Erik dropped to his back as the Special Team *literally* jumped through walls.

Quest Completed: Beast Cultivation 1
One's power is great, but the power of two united in a single cause is greater than the sum of its parts.
Requirements: Increase your Beast Companion's cultivation
Rewards: Your Beast Companion has reached Body Like Stone.

Quest Completed: Beast Cultivation 2
One's power is great, but the power of two united in a single cause is greater than the sum of its parts.
Requirements: Increase your Beast Companion's cultivation
Rewards: Your Beast Companion has reached Body Like Iron.

Quest: Beast Cultivation 3
One's power is great, but the power of two united in a single cause is greater than the sum of its parts.
Requirements: Increase your Beast Companion's cultivation
Rewards: Your Beast Companion has reached Body Like Sky Iron.

Gilly took the impact easily, not giving Erik time to read the notification fully. Her powerful legs were as large as a man. Adjusting her wings to lie along her back, she flicked her tail.

She stretched out her neck, licking Erik's face.

Hi! Hihihihi Hi master!

"Gilly?" Erik held her head with both hands, pushing her away as he looked into her big eyes.

Hi!

Her thoughts were not only filled with emotions. She could communicate. Somewhat.

Erik laughed, rubbing between her eyes. "Hey, you!"

Ohh scratches, yuss.

Gilly's leg bicycled in the air, shaking the ground. She half-closed her eyes, her tongue falling out.

"Stop slobbering all over me." Erik got back up. Gilly's body was as large as an SUV. Her neck as long as he was tall. Her tail was twice as long, and her head was the size of a chair.

She had a base color of deep blue with yellow stripes running from her neck to her back and down her tail. Her markings were brighter. Her wings had developed enough to fly. She was a true dragon now, proud and powerful.

"Who's a good boy?" Rugrat wandered over with George, who was as large as an armored personnel carrier. The markings around his face had turned white and blue, extending into his coat. Except for the tongue hanging out of his mouth, he looked regal and proud. He pushed against Rugrat, making him watch his steps to keep from falling over.

"Hey. Sorry. They got a little excited," Rex said as he jogged over. He glanced at the people recovering in the small Wood Floor village. "Shall we get out of here?"

"Whoops! *Gilly get small.*"

She jumped up, turning smaller, and landed on his shoulders.

Erik waved his hand, smoothing the ground. Rugrat fixed the walls that had been broken. The Special Team watched the area, patting off the dust that came from jumping through buildings. Erik's reprimanding finger turned into a hand as he scratched Gilly. He couldn't punish such an innocent-looking face.

Erik and Rugrat winced at the annoyed stares they got from the people of the Wood Floor village and escaped to the training areas beyond.

Gilly and George returned to their full sizes as Erik and Rugrat petted them.

"So, a few things have changed since we started training," Rex said. "First thing was that I got them food that aligned with their natural element.

Then we ran tests, saw what increased their strength even more. Attribute dense mana beats pure mana every time. Their bodies absorb it rapidly. They also learned a lot by training and working with beasts on the lower floors. It accelerated when they went into the dungeons to fight against beasts of the same attribute. Their attacks are stronger, and they now have more of them. Through what I've learned, their advances are closer to the body cultivation side of things than magic and spells. The attributes have purified their bloodline, altering their bodies. A bit different from how we cultivate, but faster."

"Wait, bloodline?" Erik asked.

"Yes, all beast cultivation is based on bloodline. Their heritage and environment, at a young age, creates their bloodline. The element that the beast draws in, usually environmentally dependent, is the first element they'll master, unlocking their bloodline and gaining sentience."

"George already communicates a few words with me," Rugrat informed Rex.

"Same."

"They might know small phrases through communicating with you all the time. Think of them as babies on the human scale. Once they get their human forms, they're like young children. They supposedly get knowledge through their bloodline, so they mature rapidly."

"So, we've got kids?" Rugrat asked.

"No, no. They're still tamed beasts. It's just the way of things in the Ten Realms. Beasts retain everything from before and can change back into beasts. that is when they are strongest, though they can now learn."

"My body cultivation says that I need to purify my bloodline." Erik pulled up the quest. "Well, it... I guess it is its own cultivation path?"

Quest: Bloodline Cultivation 1
The power of the body comes from the purity of the bloodline.
Requirements: Form an Earth Grade Elemental Core with 2 elements
Rewards: Earth Grade Bloodline +100,000,000 EXP

"Purify your bloodline?"

"He also formed a monster core." Rugrat tapped his chest.

"What?" Rex looked at Erik's chest.

"Yeah, I tempered my body to Diamond and that unlocked my bloodline. Now it wants me to purify my bloodline."

"Well, a monster core is similar to a mana core, though instead of storing mana, it stores the elements. Have you checked what elements are stored within it?"

Erik turned his sight inward, focusing on the small clear marble within his chest. "Nope, nothing. Wait, I'm sensing it with mana sight, I'll search for the el—Woah."

The clear marble turned into a nebula of drifting smoke that intertwined with one another.

"What are you seeing?" Rex asked.

"It's filled with elements. When I was watching my tempering, I was looking for the mana the element was attached to, not just the elements. It's easier because all of my skills, spells, and sights tend toward mana. It's like the vapor stage of the mana core. There's red, yellow, and black vapor drifting around in there."

"Fire, earth, and metal elements."

With just a thought, the elements slowed their movements, separating into their own clouds.

"I can control them, but what do I do with it?"

"Beasts eat a ton of elemental ingredients and cores to overload their bodies, storing it in their core. Can you try to cultivate the elements?" Rex shrugged.

"I'll give it a shot." Erik sat down. Gilly and George watched him with interest. Erik took a deep breath. His body drew in the ambient elemental mana. Elemental energy spread throughout his body. He drew it into his veins, then through his arteries, before drawing it into his elemental core. The clouds of elements increased in size and density as Erik felt a warm feeling in his chest.

He let out an easy breath. It was like stretching after waking. The very fiber of his being was crying out in joy.

His elemental core grew larger for some time before Erik started to feel a tension in his veins.

He pushed onward, but the pain increased while the elements dried up. Erik released his hold and relaxed. He looked through his body. Faint green shoots had pierced through his skin. Each of them felt like a bone burr driving into his soul.

The wild elements that filled his body had decreased, contained within his elemental core, which had grown several times. Now it was the same size as the tip of his thumb to his first knuckle.

"I'm on the Wood Floor. Those green shoots must be the wood element," Erik muttered as he watched them fade away, released from his body.

"What was that?"

"I'll need to go to the Earth, Fire, and Metal Floors to make my elemental core bigger. I can't cultivate water or wood elements within my elemental core yet. I can absorb and temper my body with the water element, but skipping ahead and tempering it with the wood element isn't a pleasant experience."

"You want to try consuming a monster core?" Rex asked, holding one out.

"Not the worst thing you've eaten. Remember that snake whiskey in Asia?" Rugrat teased.

Erik shuddered right to the base of his spine "That was an affront to whiskey and snakes." Erik took the monster core, inspecting it.

Monster Core
Do you wish to absorb this Lesser Mortal Grade monster core? *YES/NO* You will gain 5,000 EXP

"Yes."

The monster core melted, entering Erik's hand. A thin sliver of experience entered his body. Erik used his mana sight to watch the changes within his body.

"Yeah, that doesn't happen to normal people," Rugrat said.

Erik ignored him.

Earth, fire, and metal elements were refined out of the absorbed monster core. It was barely a drop in the ocean compared to the elements that had filled his body moments before, but they were there.

He drew the energy into his elemental core, increasing the density of the swirling clouds by a small amount.

"Okay, that works, but I don't see how this helps me unlock my bloodline?"

"When beasts get their monster core to the Greater Sky Grade, then I think that's when they develop human characteristics. If you get to that stage, maybe something happens? Do you feel different?"

Erik stood up, shaking it out.

"I feel deflated, but in a good way. It was like my body was under stress all the time, but now it's relaxed. Like I was squeezing every muscle in my body, but now they've unlocked." He threw out a few punches. "No decrease in power. It seems to flow easier now. What the hell is it with this quest? It's going to take me forever to increase my elemental core to a high level, I'm guessing. But won't I need all the damn elements to complete it?"

"I have no answers." Rex shrugged. "This is all new to me."

"Maybe it's like the mana gate quest? A lot of people have that quest but never complete it because of how hard it is. Plus, they don't have the right information. We did it and got a bonus. Sounds like something you can only complete after you've tempered your body all the way, if you need all the elements, right?" Rugrat said.

"While beasts get access to more of the human mana cultivation system as they increase their power, we get more access to the beast cultivation system?" Erik looked at Gilly and George, who looked at one another, then back at Erik.

"Possibly." Rugrat shrugged.

"I just deal with beasts. I'm not sure what's right or wrong. But that is a hell of a thing if you can use not only the experience but also the monster core. Have you absorbed a lesser mortal monster core before?"

"Nope."

"Try absorbing another." Rex held out another lesser mortal monster core the size of a twenty-sided die. "If a human uses one, they usually get experience, and that's it. If they use the same class of monster core later, they get a much smaller amount of experience, so it's considered a waste. Beasts are *always* consuming the flesh and body of their enemies because of the elements they contain."

Erik absorbed the monster core. There was no experience, but the core melted into his hand, entering his body instead of turning to dust.

He drew the elements into his elemental core.

"It works. Different break down of elements but it has power in it all the same. I wonder if I took tempering pills if I could absorb the elements directly into my body."

Rex eagerly pulled out an earth tempering pill.

"It's a little strong. I use them to train Gilly. Should work with your body tempering."

"Good thing you work with animals. They're more robust. You go around trying these out with people all the time, and someone is going to say something," Erik muttered but grabbed the pill.

He smelled it, using Reverse Alchemist to understand the pill and its ingredients.

"Should work."

Erik took the pill and swallowed it. It started to fall apart before it hit his stomach. His own body was stripping out the earth element from the pill.

"They still taste like dirt." He wiped his tongue.

"Like you weren't going around tasting all the ingredients in every market we could find when we first got here." Rugrat yawned and stretched.

"This is,a ton of earth element. They've upgraded the formula since I used them for my earth tempering. It is smoother, though. Still, it would be a lot for an untempered body to contain."

The earth element spread through his body. Erik directed it through his veins. Like rivers toward the ocean, the earth element flooded through his veins and into his elemental core.

"Okay, more energy than the lesser mortal monster core, all earth. This time not as much as what I dragged in from cultivating the elements. You're going to have to tell Melissa Bouchard about all of this," Erik told Rex.

"Why?"

"Because she'll have us in there for hours if I tell her, and I want to go dungeon training. We got sidetracked. How are Gilly and George doing?"

"They've been growing crazy fast. They train in the dungeons and eat tons of concoctions. Their bodies are heartier than humans, so pills and concoctions that are too strong for humans, they can take just fine. They spend a lot of their time on the floors associated with their element. They are both level sixty-eight. Seems they're a little competitive. Gilly's power increased faster. She has two elements, and they were unbalanced. Once they balanced out, she increased steadily. They're peak Seventh Realm beasts, I would say."

"So, they could train with us?" Rugrat asked.

Rex looped his thumbs into his belt. "Sure, exercise is the best, and fighting brings about the fastest increases in power."

Gilly and George clearly understood part of it as they perked up, bristling.

Erik looked from them to Rugat. *So who wants to show off the gains we've made more?* Erik coughed at the errant thought.

"Something wrong?" Rugrat asked.

"Nope, nothing. Something caught in my throat."

"Okay, well, see you later, Rex. Thanks for looking after these two."

"No worries. It opened up a whole new area of beast raising. I've been talking to the other trainers. It will be much faster to raise beasts and make them stronger."

Erik and Rugrat jumped onto Gilly's and George's backs, respectively.

"This is going to make protecting you a whole new challenge," Storbon complained.

His mount complained in a low whine.

"And it's going to cost a lot." He sighed.

"Training is the most valuable exercise a person can do." Erik waved his finger, being teacherly.

Then everything became light as Gilly jumped, launching herself into the air. Erik clamped down with his legs and his throat to stop the building scream.

Gilly snapped her wings and tail out. With a few powerful flaps, she was just meters away from the ceiling. She banked, the wind gliding over her and Erik.

A fiery comet appeared to their side. Rugrat had a massive smile on his face.

Erik laughed. "Woo-hoo!"

"Yeee-hawww!" Rugrat yelled.

Gilly and George joined in with their roars.

They circled the floor. It was covered in orchards that produced food for the Alvans. Alchemy gardens. The signs of Davin's great fire were fading with time.

Erik nudged Gilly, who flew toward the teleportation area within the village. She batted her wings as she came in, coming to land lightly on her feet.

Storbon and his team were there waiting for them.

"Egbert!" Rugrat yelled.

"Jackass!"

Light enveloped them as they appeared in the dungeon training area.

"He still pissed at you?" Erik asked as Gilly padded off the teleportation area and toward the dungeon entrances.

"Yeah. Guess that while he was asleep, he was still recording everything."

"You dropped me in the bathwater! Twice!" Egbert's disembodied voice rang out.

"Just won't let it go for some reason."

"You tried to drink beer out of my skull!"

Rugrat sighed. "Petty of him."

People stared at them as they passed. Some saluted, others bowed. Erik and Rugrat nodded and saluted back, reaching the dungeon they'd requested.

"You sure we can't come with you?" Storbon asked.

"You'd steal all the damn experience." Rugrat laughed as he dismounted and checked his gear.

Erik jumped a few times to get his carriers moving in the right way, opening and closing his gauntlets and moving his shoulders.

Rugrat took out his modified rail gun and adjusted the two-point sling, raising and lowering his rifle to make sure it wouldn't catch on anything. "So, we've got different capture points inside. We need to hold those for a certain period of time to control the area. As we advance and control more of the points, more creatures will come out and attack us."

"Lovely dungeon," Erik muttered.

"Dude, it's a level sixty to sixty-five dungeon in the First Realm. Shit, I talked to the formation masters that worked on it. Place is practically its own world. Also, with it so deep, the elements are concentrated as hell. So concentrated you need to have Body Like Iron to deal with it!" Rugrat smacked his chest.

"Well, shit." Erik pulled out his helmet and put it on. The formations activated inside.

Rugrat pulled on his helmet as well, their faces hidden behind formations and enhanced metal.

"You hear me?" Rugrat asked.

"Loud and clear. You good to go?"

"One sec, prepping grenades." Rugrat looped a drop-down panel to his carrier and tied it around his left leg. It had ten pouches filled with twist-top grenades.

Erik checked his larger medical kit and the back of Rugrats' gear to make sure everything was secure. "Good to go."

They walked through the open dungeon doors.

Light flashed, and they were teleported into a large cavern.

Rugrat grunted.

Erik took the increased pressure well. The gravity change wasn't severe, but with the high elements, it would be harder.

"That's new," Erik muttered as earth and fire elements were drawn in through his mana gates. They entered his body as he refined out the other elements, purifying and compressing his mana through his body.

They were all on alert. George and Gilly were practically glowing with power as they looked around.

Water dripped somewhere in the cavern. A kind of moss grew in random places, creating bright spots and abyss-dark shadows. The ground was uneven, filled with divots, half-steps, and drops. Stalagmites jutted out of the floor. The ceiling was lumpy rock, carved out in some places, hanging low in others.

Several entrances led into the cavern they were standing in.

"Love what they've done with the place."

Capture Dungeon
Capture different areas within the dungeon. The more areas you capture, the more dungeon creatures will attack. Kills and holding more area will get you dungeon points, redeemable through the dungeon kiosk.
Capture Area 1

In the middle of the cavern, a pillar lit up with the number 1 above it. There was a table with four medallions.

Erik grabbed them, putting one onto his carrier, then onto Rugrat's, and lastly onto Gilly and George.

A notification floated in his vision as a circle on the totem turned green and started to light up.

Capture Area 1
1/100

The circle kept growing as they all faced outward, looking and listening.

"The hell is that?" Rugrat asked.

Erik heard a noise in the distance like heels on a hardwood floor. "Your new ex?"

The creature rounded the corner. It looked like a dust-mite, but blown up to the size of a large dog or small pony, and was three times as wide.

Erik turned with his rifle, but Gilly was faster. Eight Earth spikes compressed until they burst out of the ground with a release of pressurized water vapor.

Five spikes failed to penetrate, but three succeeded.

The creature clicked and chittered in pain, a white ichor coloring its carapace.

Pillars of stone slammed the dust mite against the ceiling, cracking the mite's exo-skeleton and killing it.

A tombstone appeared below it.

Erik checked the slowly growing capture percentage as light traveled up the pillar.

Capture Area 1
27/100

More of the mites' pointed feet hit the ground. Rugrat fired. The helmets deadened the sound as it rang through the cavern.

The unlucky mite showed a hole in its head as its back blew out, splattering the tunnel behind it.

Erik fired at another mite. The first round broke its exoskeleton. The second went through, killing the beast.

George released a blast of flame that melted a mite's armor and the surrounding ground. The mites' rate of attacks picked up.

Erik switched between three tunnels. Mites were pushing past their fading brethren. He'd killed about twelve of the mites. Scanning the area, he lowered his weapon.

"Clear on my side!" Rugrat yelled.

"Same here!" Erik yelled.

No hard beasts. Gilly relayed into Erik's mind as she let out a yip.

George did the same.

Capture Area 1
100/100

The pillar they were standing next to showed a complete green circle. Erik and Rugrat scanned with Gilly and George.

"I don't hear anything," Erik said.

"Me either. Not sensing any changes in mana around here. I think that's it."

A notification popped up.

Capture Area 2
0/100

"Guess we have to go find the next one," Rugrat said.

"Hold up. Let me check out these big bastards before we move on."

"Got you covered."

Erik moved to the nearest one. "Okay, what the hell are you?" He used Scan, encompassing medical scan, then inorganic scan, filtered through his elemental and mana sight. "From what I can tell, this thing is earth and metal attributed. Strong exo, not so strong internally. These antennae are element sensitive. If there is a spike in the element, they'll lock onto it and go after it. I don't think they really eat anything."

Erik opened the tombstone.

3x Carapace sections
1x meat
1x Earth Grade Earth Variant Monster Core

Erik looted the beast. It released a burst of Earth element that Erik absorbed. The rest drained into the dungeon.

"What do you mean?" Rugrat asked.

"I think they just draw in the earth and metal element. That's what keeps them alive."

"Don't creatures need food?"

"Not necessarily. Elemental energy can restore your body. If I have enough elements, I won't get hungry for years, possibly forever. Though I'd need a lot of elements and to not do so much."

"So, wait, will it eat us?" Rugrat asked.

"Probably, beasts eat one another for their elements to increase their monster core. In the past, we always thought they were trying to get one another's mana and experience."

"So, still dangerous, and weird."

"Yes. And they have bodies that are nearly as strong as Iron. Before we step into the area around the next capture point, let Gilly and I put up some barriers," Erik said.

"Works for me."

Gilly and George reduced to the size of large dogs. Erik checked his experience bar. A smile spread across his face. *It's sweet fighting stronger beasts.*

You have reached Level 63
When you sleep next, you will be able to increase your attributes by: 5 points.

18,484,039/217,100,000 EXP till you reach Level 64

"Okay, so where the hell do we go?" Erik said.

"I think it's higher in mana down that tunnel." Rugrat gestured to a tunnel with the barrel of his rifle. "You take the front. Gilly, George, in the middle. I can be at the rear."

"Let's go." Erik nestled his rifle tighter into his shoulder. He scanned the tunnel as he walked down it. The others followed behind closely.

"Turn to the left, piecing the pie."

Erik aimed around the corner, taking steps to the side and coming into line with the corner. In a burst, he stepped out.

"Clear!" He pushed down the new tunnel. It dipped down, but there was more light. He scanned ahead, seeing nothing moving. "Gilly you look right. I'll look left."

Master.

He stepped out with Gilly, churning up the gravel and mud, looking out along the wall. Still, there was nothing.

The room was smaller with a mound in the middle with another pillar. The ground was a gravel-mud soup. The walls and three other tunnels were made of worn rock with compressed clay in between. Some of the rocks glowed red as if they were still partially magma. Others were covered in the glowing green moss.

"Bit tighter than the other one," Rugrat said.

"We'll get some spikes set up around the mound and in the tunnels. Keep a watch."

"On it."

Erik connected to the ground at the entrance of the tunnels through his elements, fueling his commands with mana and raising sharpened stakes of stone and metal from the ground. Erik conjured flames around the spikes, hardening and tempering them.

Gilly was drawing up other spikes, while George used his flames to temper hers.

Erik took out poison and poured it out into the air. With mana manipulation, he coated the spikes.

He raised blocks from the bedrock around the pillar, creating two defensive walls with more spikes.

"Are you building defenses or trying to recreate the hedgehog?"

"Shut up and watch the tunnels. I'm going to test something out."

"What?"

"The pillar. When it activates, it must be releasing elemental power. I'm going to use a metal tempering needle, see if it distracts the mites."

"Okay."

Erik activated a needle and threw it down a tunnel. If they were interested in the needle, they wouldn't advance toward them as long as it was stronger than the pillar's power.

"Good to go."

"Let's get this show on the road."

They stepped up the mound and into their defenses.

Capture Area 2
1/100

Gilly raised the last defenses, sealing them in as Erik felt the spike in elements.

"Shit, this thing is like an elemental well."

Spiked feet splashed in the mud.

Several red crystals formed around George and flew down a tunnel striking a mite. The water in the tunnel vaporized in a moment. A wave of heat surged around the pillar.

Erik waited, watching. The mites rushed down the tunnel, lunging for the metal needle.

They crashed into one another as their bodies expanded. Their exoskeletons opened as they drew in the surrounding elements.

"Explosive shot." Erik fired into the open exoskeletons. The explosive rounds tore the unprotected beasts apart, turning them into ichor as they started to dissolve.

"Reloading!" Rugrat yelled.

Gilly turned her neck, letting out a yell. Brown waves shot into the tunnel. The ceiling collapsed around the mites. Time seemed to reverse as the tunnel reformed, using the mites as building materials.

"Back in!" Rugrat fired at the mites.

Erik moved to Gilly's side, firing into her tunnel. The mites ran into her spikes. One had already died from the poison.

Gilly, focus on your area first! Help others only if you can!

Gilly hung her head lower but kept using Earth attacks.

Erik checked his tunnel; mites had gathered around the metal needle again. He let his rifle hang from his sling and pulled out a grenade launcher. "Fire in the hole!"

The explosion tore through the mites.

Erik dropped the grenade launcher into his storage ring. *No movement.*

He smacked the side of his magazine. It was half full. He scanned Gilly's area. She'd crushed or slammed the mites into the walls and spikes in the tunnel. George was looking at his tunnel with more of the fire crystals. Molten stone dripped from the ceiling of his tunnel as mites collapsed.

Rugrat's rifle was silent while he scanned as well.

"Stand ready," Erik said.

They watched the tunnels, but nothing else rushed toward them.

Capture Area 2
100/100

Capture Area 3
0/100

"I guess we must have scared them off. How many was that? Thirty or forty? I'm reloading." Rugrat pulled out his magazine and put in a fresh one.

"I think it was closer to fifty. The needle worked, by the way. When they got close to it, they opened their exoskeletons. Easy targets. Have to make sure they don't get too close, or they'll strip the elements right out of us."

"What happens if they do that?"

"Think of it like a slowing spell. We get slower, weaker, and our resistances weaken. In this place, if we don't have a high resistance, we'll die."

"Back in. So, they're working with their environment against us."

"Yeah. Reloading."

Erik changed out his mag for a fresh one in his storage ring. "Back in."

"This experience gain is sweet," Rugrat said.

"They're a higher level, plus nearly Body Like Sky Iron. Yeah, they're going to be an experience jackpot."

83,395,078/217,100,000 EXP until you reach Level 64

"Let's go find pillar three."

"More mana in that direction." Rugrat pointed down a tunnel.

"Let me grab my needle and we'll head out." Covered by Rugrat, Erik used an earth-moving spell to grab the needle and throw it in the air. He grabbed it with mana manipulation and returned it to his hand.

"Damn, nearly drained it." Erik looked at the pillar. "If I can draw in the element as well, would that reduce it overall? Maybe the creatures wouldn't charge as much."

Erik put the needle away. "Let's get moving." He led the way again, lowering the spikes in the tunnel.

"We can use this as a fallback position," Rugrat said.

"Good call."

It was a long path to the third area.

"Ah, shit." Erik entered the cavern. There were five paths leading to the middle of the room with a bottomless dark pit between them.

"That doesn't look like it would be a fun drop."

The paths were big enough for Gilly to grow to her full height and walk across comfortably.

The central area was a ruin. Collapsed stone lie around arches and pillars, jutting from the ground like ribs. Metal and earth attribute plants had grown between the stones. In the middle of the ruin stood the pillar they were looking for.

Motes of light drifted through the area. Moss lay among the ruins and on the ceiling, making it brighter than the other rooms.

The tunnels and paths leading in showed veins of rare metal and stone. Some gave off light; others reflected it.

"I never really got interior design, but dungeon design is stranger still. Want to spike the paths leading in? I was thinking of laying mines, but don't want to break these bridges."

"You think they reach all the way down or are they just arches?" Erik asked.

"You want me to answer that?"

Erik glanced at the darkness at the edge of the path. "Nah, I'm good."

Erik, Gilly, and George got to work while Rugrat patrolled the ruin. He moved the stone blocks outside the capture area, creating defensive positions.

"Spikes are set." Erik finished poisoning them all and laid down a few metal attribute needles.

"Okay, I'll take those two paths. Split the kids up to take the others," Rugrat said.

"Got it. Shall we?"

They all entered the capture area.

Capture Area 3
1/100

Rugrat took a position in some broken rubble. He pushed rocks and chunks away to get comfortable.

Erik used a broken wall to support his forward arm. Gilly and George hid among the piles of debris, looking at the paths leading to the ruins.

Rugrat fired first, dust shifting around him.

Erik double-tapped the first mite that appeared. George went with his fire crystals, hurling them into the entrance of the tunnel. Against earth and metal attribute creatures, he had one hell of an advantage.

Gilly created brown gems that dropped from the sky, struck the ground, and turned into stone spikes.

Erik's penetrating shots cut through the mites. He drew in the earth and metal elements of the surrounding area. He was like a vacuum. The rate of mites showing up slowed.

"The hell is that noise?" Rugrat asked.

Erik listened; it was coming from the pits. "I dunno, sounds like bones hitting one another?"

A centipede-like creature shot out from the pit. It shook its body, letting out a shuddering roar as its exoskeleton clacked together. The top half of its body leaned forward, crashing to the ground. It was over ten meters long.

Three rapid-fire rounds went through its teeth-filled mouth and into its body, detonating at different points, spraying ichor and exo-skeleton everywhere.

Another one came out of the pit with its battle cry.

Erik fired on the creature. His rounds cut through its body but didn't hit anything vital. "Blunt shot!"

His attacks did more damage as the creature dropped. A spike grew out of the ground to meet it.

It must have not seen the spike as it landed on it. The spike drove through its body and exploded.

Rugrat fired on the mites that were getting closer, excited by the earth and metal elements released by the dead centipedes.

Erik fired on his own paths and on Gilly's as she took care of the centipedes.

"Need some support here!" Rugrat said. Erik drew in fire mana.

"Firestorm coming in on your paths, Rugrat!"

A spell formation appeared; the air twisted faster and faster, bursting into flames. The fire storms rapidly moved down the paths, burning and throwing mites into the pits, stopping before the tunnels.

Rugrat got to his knee, turning and shooting the head of a 'pede that had crawled up from the pit. He swiveled like he had eyes in the back of his head. A penetrating shot took two mites out as George created fire rain that tore through three other centipedes.

Erik fired on Gilly's path and then switched to his own.

Gilly roared. Earth spears stabbed through two centipedes and exploded.

Erik scanned the area, but there was nothing. He forced out a breath, his eyes flickering across the area.

Capture Area 3

100/100

"Ah shit," Erik let out a breath.

"I fucking hate worms. Reloading," Rugrat muttered, sliding down behind his cover.

"Got you. You mean centipedes?"

"Anything long, round, and with lots of teeth!"

"Makes me think of the sandworms."

"Fuck those worms. I nearly died."

"I got the damn One Foot in the Grave title a second time doing that." Erik tapped his magazine.

"Back in. Wasn't it the mana spirit knight things that nearly killed you?"

"Reloading." Erik checked his notifications.

You have reached Level 64

When you sleep next, you will be able to increase your attributes by: 10 points.

132,701,878/273,500,000 EXP till you reach Level 65

"Good to go. Maybe. I dunno. It was years ago now. You want to try for area four? Or call it?" Erik asked.

"I don't have anything else I need to do right now."

"So forward then?"

"Sure." Rugrat shrugged, scanning the area. "When you drew in earth and metal elements, the mites slowed right down."

"Yeah, I never really paid that much attention to elements. I thought they were only useful when combined with mana and became attributes."

"You ever think that elements and attributes are confusing?"

"I guess. Element is the pure form, without the mana. Attribute is where the element and mana have combined. The purer mana is, the fewer attributes it has, or the lower the elements-to- mana ratio."

"Yup, guess it's that whole thing. Where the more you know, the less you think you know," Rugrat said.

"So, where we heading to?"

"That way." Rugrat pointed to a path.

Erik stood up, shaking out the kinks.

"Let's do this. Cover me so I can examine the centipede and some more of those mites. I want to figure out what their weaknesses are. Just need more test subjects."

"Bro, you know you sound all mad scientist an' shit when you say that, right?"

"You've watched too much TV."

Erik examined the bodies before they dissipated.

"The mites have a weakness."

With a wet noise, Erik flipped the mite over. Its limbs were splayed out, and it was starting to drift away. "See where the limbs connect right there? That'll kill them. Otherwise, go for where their head connects to their neck."

"The centipedes?"

Erik moved to a headless centipede. "Sixth section down where it bulges out." Erik pointed at the section with his rifle.

"Yeah."

"Vital organs are right in there. Sixth, seventh and eighth sections have extra armor, but the fifth and ninth don't."

"So hit the fifth with a penetration round and it'll tumble right through its vitals."

"Yeah. They're strong against direct hits. Between the sections and the leg joints, they're weaker. Hit them from an angle or as they rear up. Much better chance to get through."

"And that, kids, is our lesson on creepy crawlies and their weaknesses. Got it." Rugrat nodded.

"Let's head for the next area then."

Erik led the way down George's path. He dispersed the heat as he walked toward the tunnel.

"Contact!" Erik fired on the mite that came down the tunnel. His rounds smashed through the thinner skeleton around its neck; it collapsed instantly.

Erik scanned the area for any more moving around.

"We didn't kill all of them?" Rugrat asked, looking around.

"Maybe more of them spawned?"

"Moving."

Erik continued forward. He cleared his way through the tunnels. It took them longer to get to the fourth area. They ran into more of the mites. The further from the ruin capture area, the more of them there were.

Erik entered the room that housed the fourth capture room.

"Well, this looks like a fucking pain in the ass. At least the holes in the ceiling aren't *right* over the capture point, cause as sure as shit something is going to fall out of those. Hope you can catch them, Gilly!"

"Blind corners, pillars in the way."

The center of the room had a much larger capture pillar atop several half-steps. There were several tunnel entrances along with holes in the ceiling and ground. Five large pillars as big as George surrounded the capture area, blocking their line of sight.

"Well, it should funnel them a bit. I'm using the mines."

"Extreme dungeon makeover?"

"C-four style."

George and Gilly covered for Erik and Rugrat as they laid down mines between the pillars. Spikes were stuck in the tunnels that led into the room.

"Contact!" Rugrat fired twice and went silent.

"Talk to me," Erik said. He couldn't see Rugrat with his rifle up and ready in his hands, watching the other side.

"Think it was just the one. Think it was just roaming the area."

They kept working on the minefield and traps.

"Okay, that should work," Rugrat said as they met up around the central pillar. They'd made a wall around the capture area for defenses.

"Minefields are primed, spikes all over the place."

"Let's start."

Capture Area 4
1/100

Chittering and the sound of armored feet against stone filled the room.

Erik flicked to automatic. He didn't try to draw in the earth and metal elements, testing out his new theory.

He fired as soon as he saw mites. The tunnels curved close to their entrance, giving only a few meters before the spikes.

They smashed into the spikes. Even if the leading mites had wanted to stop, those behind them pushed them into the spikes.

Erik's rounds cut down through the tunnels, killing dozens.

Rugrats' rifle sounded like it was on automatic with how fast he was firing.

"Reloading!" Rugrat tossed off a magazine and grabbed a new one.

"Above!" Erik looked up as a centipede launched itself from the ceiling. Earth spears shot out of the ground like missiles, striking centipedes in the air. There was a stream from Erik's rifle arcing across the open area between the pillars.

A centipede rose from the floor, stepped on a mine at the entrance, and its front half disappeared.

Erik's rifle clicked empty.

"Reloading!" Erik yelled as he tossed the magazine, grabbed a new one, smashed it into the magwell, and hit the bolt catch.

Rounds went downrange.

"Mites on the pillars! Back in!" Erik yelled.

He hosed the mites and centipedes, aiming at their weaknesses. His arms blurred as he switched targets, rounds drilling holes through armor plates into the mites and centipedes' vitals.

His reactions, honed by a lifetime of both medical training and fighting, came together with the enhancement of the Ten Realms. In his vision, he was overlaying the internal structure of the creatures.

It was a slaughter, but it was just a dent compared to the surging numbers.

They had broken through the spikes in some places, using the bodies of those that had gone before them as a bridge over top.

George let out a fire breath like a laser. The red light left scorch marks on the pillars and needed just a few seconds to cut through the mites. The centipedes cried out, but they were only more pissed off.

Erik gathered the mana and elements within his body. He tossed his rifle to his side, securing it with a tie.

He threw a punch, scooping up the ground. A fist the size of Gilly swung out, smashing through four centipedes and several mites.

Erik drew on the stone around him, creating fists he sent into the oncoming centipedes, crushing them against the walls and floor.

Gilly swiped her claw, earth condensing along her Frigate's path, cleaving through mites.

Erik channeled the power of the fire element and mana through his leg, injecting it into the ground. The ground shifted and broke, spreading out and exploding, tossing mites and magma everywhere.

"Switching!" Erik pulled out a grenade launcher, firing it into the clumped groups near the tunnel entrances or around the pillars. He swung out the empty magazine, dropping it into his storage ring. "Fuck!"

A centipede screeched, dropping out of the ceiling and aiming for George below.

Erik dropped the launcher, grabbed his railgun, and pulled the tie off.

He fired one-handed. His tempered body took the recoil easily as he wrapped his hand around the handguards. The rounds punched holes in the centipede as it smashed into the ground and faded out of existence.

Erik turned to fire on the mites that had made it to the minefields when two explosions rang out, killing most of them. He tossed his rifle to the side on his sling and knelt to grab the dropped grenade launcher. He pulled out a full chamber, slotted it into place, and snapped it shut.

He fired wherever he saw groups of creatures, using magma explosion spells underneath those he couldn't hit.

"Reloading!"

Another centipede came up after the minefield, just meters from Erik.

"Motherfucker!" Erik formed a hammer in his hand, infusing it with earth, fire, and metal. He threw it with all his power. The hammer smashed through the centipede's mouth, going through it lengthwise before it exploded.

"Fuck centipedes!"

Erik finished reloading, looking for groups. He had time between shots as the groups had slimmed down, the ground filled with the dead and the dying.

"Reloading!" Rugrat yelled.

Erik threw out a hammer, catching a mite that came around a pillar, and jumped. It was tossed backward as Erik's hammer exploded behind it, striking the ceiling.

"Back in!"

"Switching!" Erik changed to his rifle, firing on the mites.

Capture Area 4
100/100

"Isn't this shit done?" Rugrat yelled.

"They're attracted by it."

"Shit!"

The mites slowed their progress as Erik fired on them, targeting their necks. They dropped faster than before.

"Reloading!" Erik tossed out his magazine and threw in a fresh one. "Back in!"

The mites' forward line was getting pushed back. The centipedes had been slaughtered. Some of the mites were moving to their dead brethren and opening their exoskeletons to draw in the ambient mana.

Erik fired explosive shots into the open mites, leaving smudges on the stone. Scanning, he didn't see anything.

"Good on my side, I think!" Erik yelled, looking at Gilly's and George's areas filled with tombstones.

"Good here. Shit, I think we got them all. Should we get out of here?"

"Yeah, let's go."

They broke their medallions and reappeared at the dungeon entrance. The doors opened, revealing the training dungeon lobby.

"Shit! That was a tough last wave." Rugrat pulled off his helmet.

Erik followed suit. "Got a little messy there with the centipedes coming from the ceiling." They walked out with Gilly and George, who had shrunk down padding along with them.

"The earth spears were a good idea. You learn a new fighting technique with the fists?"

"Yeah, from the library. Someone watched too much anime. They wanted to make a magi-tech mecha. You can clad yourself with earth, fire, wind, and whatever. But it takes a lot of damn mana to do it. And you should temper your body with that element. Else, you need to wear armor to protect against it."

Rugrat rolled his eyes as he stored his helmet, cradling his rifle in the crook of his elbow.

"Anyway, it didn't work the best. Though, if you use parts of it, like that magma fist, you can create stronger versions of your own punch, and it doesn't even hurt your fist."

"Great to know you're putting my gauntlets to use."

"I thought that I would use them more often, too. Might be a better idea to get a formation that increases my spell damage."

"There are new beast hide gauntlets. The armored ones are okay. They're nice, but the plates rub on your finger. Starts to hurt after a while. The beast hide lasts longer and doesn't restrict you as much, but the formation is sewn in."

"Might be a good idea." Erik looked at Storbon and his team. "Let's head back up top."

"You got it, Boss."

Gilly and George grew, allowing Erik and Rugrat to sit on their backs.

"Guess we were in there for what, four or five hours?" Erik asked.

Rugrat sniffed his pits. "Smells like it."

Erik grinned and checked his notifications as the group headed toward the teleportation pad.

Skill: Throwables *Level: 58 (Journeyman)*
Your throws gain 5% power Stamina used for throwing is decreased by 15%

You have reached Level 65
When you sleep next, you will be able to increase your attributes by 15 points.

146,596,128/344,700,000 EXP till you reach Level 66

"Shit, it's hard to increase any skill now."

"You could take on another set of skills to increase levels quickly. Cooking, for one, or something like that."

"Maybe once this is done." Their party moved forward toward the teleports.

Erik saw Rugrat off once they were on the living floor. He headed to his private quarters in the Dungeon Mansion and took a sleeping potion.

You have 15 attribute points to use.

Erik looked at his stat sheet. His strength was a little high, but the agility was enough to control that. Stamina was regenerating at forty-one points per second. *No wonder I needed two doses of the sleeping concoction.* His mana pool was at 1160 while his stamina showed as 1845, with a mana regeneration of fifty-one per second. "Mana pool it is."

Erik dumped in all fifteen points. His body started to change as he sunk deeper into sleep.

He opened his eyes sometime later.

"Better than waking on the damn floor," Erik snorted. He was still wearing his armor and boots.

He opened his stat sheet.

Name: Erik West	
Level: 65	Race: Human-?
Titles: *From the Grave II* *Blessed By Mana* *Dungeon Master V* *Reverse Alchemist* *Poison Body* *Fire Body* *City Lord III* *Earth Soul* *Mana Reborn* *Wandering Hero* *Metal Mind, Metal Body* *Mortal Grade Bloodline*	
Strength: (Base 90) +51	1410

Agility: (Base 83) +77	880
Stamina: (Base 93) +35	1920
Mana: (Base 37) +94	1310
Mana Regeneration (Base 40) +61	61.60/s
Stamina Regeneration: (Base 142) +59	41.20/s

"Time to go train some people," Erik grunted and got up. "A shower might be useful."

20
Counterattack

Cai Bo walked into the planning room.

Marco Tolentino turned around from the detailed map model he was studying.

Her eyes drifted over it, taking in key and familiar features.

"Elder Cai Bo." Marco bowed his head slightly.

"Vuzgal city, some call it the Gem of the North." She indicated to the map, putting it to their side as Marco pursed his lips, eyes flickering over it.

"It is on the higher end of cities in the Fourth Realm. Though they made a key mistake thinking that their reputation would make up for their defenses. What do you make of these?" Marco pointed to a desk which showed a scaled model of Vuzgal, the Battle Arena, workshops, various towers, the inner walls, and the bunkers along the outside of the city.

"We couldn't get any information on the boxy buildings. We know there are people inside, but that is it. They don't allow people to get close, and strong formations protect them from any sensing spells."

Marco leaned on the table, looking at the bunkers. "They are a blind spot. Do you think that your numbers on the Vuzgal Defence Force are accurate?"

"They all wear the same gear. There is no way to know their numbers."

"Thirty thousand." Marco didn't look up. "That is the estimated number of Blood Demon Sect bodies that could have been recovered. If what they did to Elder Sho is true, then they have at least fifty thousand undead soldiers. They're slower and weaker than humans. They consume a massive amount of power, though they're extra support. How many people join the military every training cycle?"

"There are around three thousand joining every month. We do not know where the Tiger Battalion's main strength is located. Many think that the tigers and the Dragons are the same regiment to make them appear bigger than they are."

"What do you think?" Marco asked, looking at her sideways.

"I think that it would be an incredible smokescreen to hold up for so many years."

Marco smiled slightly. "Yes, their city lords are fighters, though they don't care about how they achieve victory. In the fighting with the Blood Demon Sect, they employed unknown whistling weapons, magical traps that couldn't be traced, along with ambushes. There were reports that they used weapons similar to the Sha. But they have only shown the repeater weapons. They didn't directly attack the enemy until they had no choice but to do so. They were tens of levels lower than their adversary, but they leveled up rapidly in the fighting. These square buildings, they have a purpose." Marco pulled out a piece of paper. It was a drawing of a repeater.

"They are low to the ground," he continued, "with thin slits that would be hard to attack through. Bows are great from up high; see the enemy, aim, then attack. Their repeaters are powerful. Plus, they shoot fast. They must have a massive stockpile by now. These squat buildings, they're built with the repeaters in mind. They can attack more people rapidly. The ground here…" Marco pointed to the area in front of the buildings. "It is sloped, giving them a height advantage. It is slight and discrete. Most people would miss it. We won't know where their people are in these buildings. We can't see anything. Even if we attack them, there are no external entrances. We'd need to breach them and clear them out individually, and there's no knowing what's underneath."

Marco stood up, holding his chin, looking over the model.

Cai Bo was interested. She felt she could work with someone like him. *Seems his father may not have been boasting as much as I thought.* "Just what do you think of Vuzgal?" she asked.

"It is best to fight an enemy you understand. Vuzgal has many mysteries." His faraway look focused on Cai Bo. "I'm sorry, Elder. I was lost in my thoughts. What did you want to discuss?"

"We made contact with a local resource. He can get the city lords to the north and west of Vuzgal to let us use their totems. Guides toward Vuzgal, hidden in the woods. He can also create chaos with the traders under his control."

Marco nodded. "Good. That should make it easier to launch our opening attack. They'll know we're coming because we have to warn the crafters and others to leave the city. We can crush the city, but if we piss off the powers behind the crafters, we'll be worse off than when we started."

"We still believe that the Adventurer's Guild and Vuzgal are working together." Cai Bo held her breath.

"It would be good to assume that they are the same force."

Cai Bo was a little stunned, thinking that he would rebuff her idea.

"We have hidden forces. Why can't other groups? It isn't that strange. We underestimated the Guild, and now they are leading the war against our cities. They have even claimed several, breaching the walls and cutting paths into the city centers. They even tried tunneling and all manner of other ways."

"What is your plan?"

"Siege. Under the pressure, their secrets will have to come out, one by one. Then, with the sects' armies added to our own armies, we will take Vuzgal."

"That could take weeks."

"I have plans to shorten that. We must seize the initiative or else the Willful Institute will collapse."

There was a knock at the door.

"Come in!" Marco looked over. The door opened to reveal five armed and armored men and women. Each of them was a powerful instructor of the Institute. In these times, they were the leaders of the different armies.

They came in, bowing ninety degrees to Cai Bo, then gave Marco a shorter bow.

"We have come as commanded," said a woman with long green hair that clashed with her purple eyes. She wore gold and silver armor that showed off her figure. Her hand rested delicately on the sword at her hip.

Sword instructor Feng Dan.

Behind her was a tall man with a fine mustache wearing armored caster's robes. Another shorter, well-muscled man, with a mohawk and a beard that started at the tops of his ears, stood next to the caster. At the rear was an unremarkable man wearing beast hide armor, with a bow on his back and daggers on his hips. His dull grey eyes took in the entire room. The last was another woman. She had whips on either hip. Her red hair was pulled back into a single braid that ran down her back; a blade had been tied to the end of it.

"Mobilize your units. In nine days, we will be attacking Vuzgal."

"'Bout time we got to do something," Onam, the mohawked, muscled man said.

Sergeant Bai Ping of the Dragon Regiment grunted as he sat on the broken wall. Adventurer's Guild parties dotted the courtyard. Squads were up in the buildings or on the roofs, watching for attackers.

Bai Ping surveyed his party. They'd cleaned their weapons. Some were napping while others were eating or drinking water.

He pulled off his helmet and set it to the side. He wished he could use his body armor. *This Ten Realms armor is restricting as hell.*

"What's our next move?" Bradley, a man that had aged years in just weeks, asked Bai Ping.

"The Institute turned this place into a death trap. Spell traps all over the place. Got some tunnels we found as well. City is so damn big it's going to take time to clear it all."

"House by house." Bradley nodded in understanding.

"Fuck, that could take weeks!" Rana threw a rock she had been playing with at the wall.

"Slow and steady." Bai Ping pulled out a canteen, drinking from it.

A man walked over to the group.

Bai Ping lowered his canteen with a smile. "Well, well, well! Look who the war dragged in. You testing out some new armor?" Bai Ping laughed, standing up.

"Heard you needed a hand." Sergeant Bolton smiled as the two clasped arms and hugged.

"You been here long?"

"Two weeks or so," Bolton said as Bai Ping indicated for them to move over to the side.

"How're things back home?"

"Good. The old man is focusing on the defensive. There could be more action at Vuzgal. Other sects and groups see that the Associations aren't with us and all that."

"Do you think it'll come to anything?"

"This is the Ten Realms, buddy. If someone thinks they can steal it from your cold corpse, they'll have a blade in your back the next second."

Bai shook his head.

"You got people there?" Bolton asked.

"Yeah, most of my family."

"They staying?."

"Vuzgal gave us everything. They aren't going to leave unless someone's battering the damn door down."

"Shit." Bolton's words came off as praise.

"Yeah, we're a stubborn bunch. What about you?"

"I ain't got nothing waiting for me. Just feel sorry for leaving you sorry bastards behind. How's it been up here for you?"

Bai Ping rubbed the back of his neck. "Shitty, and it's gotten worse. Traps and ambushes all over the place. Institute members fighting to the very end. We might rag on them, but they're good fighters. Now there is nowhere to go but to die. They're vicious bastards. Had several detonate their cultivation just to take out more of my people. It's slowed us down."

"What do you think is going to happen to Vuzgal? If it gets hit?" Bolton asked.

"I know one thing, if we have to pull back everything, the Institute is going to come out of their holes, add in more traps, and make it ten times harder to take these places. I wish we had just bombed the shit out of the place and fucked off."

"That ain't gonna happen, not while there are innocent people in the cities."

"Yeah."

"Do you think they would call us all back?"

"Nah, I don't think they'll call the Adventurer's back."

"Why?"

"They're a formidable fighting force. They aren't the Alvan military, but I'd trust them to watch my back. As time has gone on, there're fewer Alvans in the command structure and more of the Adventurers. They're pulling it together."

"So, you think we'll go back to defend, and the Guild would keep fighting?"

"I think that's the way it has to be. If it isn't, we'll lose all the progress we've made." Bai pulled out his canteen again.

"You think that we'll be cleared for all weapons?"

"I ain't a Colonel. I don't know that." Bai chuckled.

"Just wondering. Those railguns are a little terrifying."

"You get issued one?"

"Yeah." Bolton's mouth spread in a smile. "Fresh out the factory, man. Sweet as fuck."

"All right, get ready to move, we've got houses to clear and Institute fucks to kill!" a group leader said as he walked through the units, getting someone lower down the totem to pass the message on.

Soldiers complained and muttered, storing their gear and pulling on their armored helmets.

"Looks like we're heading out." Bai held out his hand. Bolton shook it.

"Catch you later, brother." He headed off toward his own party in the courtyard.

Mistress Mercy looked outside the carriage as she arrived in Henghou city. The headquarters of the Willful Institute were filled with schools, academies, training squares. Crafters, fighters, and people from all over the realms wished to enter this city. She passed through the streets.

As she got closer to the Willful Institute, there was less traffic and more guards. She passed through several checkpoints before she reached her destination. Unwilling to wait, she opened her carriage door and jumped down. She walked as quickly as possible to the main entrance.

"Identity, purpose of visit."

"Mercy Luo to see High Elder Cai Bo. Information gathering." She pulled out a medallion. They checked it, then took a sample of her blood before letting her pass.

She stepped onto a rising platform. The formation powered up, accelerating it upward.

It wasn't long before the platform slowed and the door opened. She walked through, passing another checkpoint, finally reaching Elder Cai Bo's office. A guard announced her through his voice transmission device.

He listened for a few moments before opening the door.

Mercy's pace faltered as she looked around the room. It had always been immaculate before, with only a few items inside. Now, there were three planning tables. A model of Vuzgal with flags of different colors spread across the city. There were also maps on the walls showing arrows and directions from surrounding cities toward Vuzgal.

Another wall showed the leadership of Vuzgal. There were rough images of two men wearing masks at the peak. Chonglu was underneath. Domonos was in parallel with rough information and people across the wall.

Cai Bo talked to a mustachioed man wearing casting robes.

Mercy closed her mouth as Cai Bo glanced over, continuing her conversation with the man. "These locations will need to be altered for passage. Once you have them, they will give the elevation to the siege weaponry to hit Vuzgal well outside their range."

"They won't have a chance to counterattack. We'll have almost twice the range of our Journeyman siege weaponry. I have other things I need to attend to, High Elder." He bowed to Cai Bo and turned to leave the room.

Mistress Mercy bowed to the man deeply.

He paid her no attention as he walked out of the room.

Mistress Mercy held out her cupped fists to Cai Bo.

"Stand up. What did you find out?"

"Chonglu used to be a city lord in the First Realm. The Silaz family has mostly disappeared. Only one family member remains. He is a big trader within a nearby rising kingdom." It all spilled from Mercy's lips.

"Clearly, something is happening down there." Cai Bo frowned. "There are plenty of Institute members from the lower realms that can be put to use. The lower realms don't get information from the higher realms. Get the kingdoms in the First Realm to join you. Use them as cover for our people. Attack this kingdom and bring me this remaining Silaz."

"Yes, High Elder Cai Bo." Mercy paused.

"What is it?"

"I feel there is something hiding in the Beast Mountain Range. I was only able to scratch the surface."

"Are you scared?" Cai Bo's eyes narrowed.

"No, High Elder!" Mercy bowed again with her clasped hands. "The more information I have found the more questions I have."

"It is good to have questions, but it is also good to know when to follow orders. Go and destroy this kingdom. It will be a great opportunity for you to gain standing within the Institute."

"Yes, High Elder!"

21
A Change of State

"How are you feeling today?" Erik asked Kim Cheol who was sitting in a chair next to his bed, hooked up to an IV drip, looking out of the window at Alva.

"Stronger since last time, but just achy."

Erik checked his charts. "You been sleeping well?"

"Off and on. The pain can wake me up in the middle of the night."

"I'm hesitant to use sleep aids and painkillers. The body can become too reliant on them." Erik flipped the papers back down and hooked the clipboard back up.

"Ah, I knew what I was doing when I did it. I made it through, which was more than I was expecting."

"And you'll be using that shield soon enough if I have anything to do with it." Erik grabbed Kim Cheol's wrist.

Scan.

Erik had hoped to heal Kim with the same pill that his teacher had created for Rugrat, but Kim's mana system had been crippled. More than that, his bones were fractured. His entire body was a wreck. Instead of healing him, the pill would kill him. Painkillers and stamina drips sustained him. Too long without either, and he would quickly regress.

Anywhere else, they would have discarded him as a waste of resources and squandered talent. He was nearly impossible to heal and would take an astronomical amount of resources to do so. But this was Alva, and Erik took his oaths and promises seriously.

"How do I look, Doc?"

"You're one of the few people that I would say your interior is scarier than your exterior. You could still crack a mirror with your smile." Erik smiled, hiding his frustration and guilt. "Thankfully, we've been developing our techniques and understanding of a human's body in the Ten Realms. Your body is a mess, but with time and concoctions, you will recover and be stronger than ever."

"Good thing I was never much of a mage," Kim grinned.

"Well, there's no knowing if you won't be able to use mana. Today, I'm going to remove your scar tissue and the blood clots that keep forming. With that out of the way, your body should heal faster. The concoctions will help you heal, followed by earth tempering to get your natural regeneration to peak. Your body will be stronger than ever. You will then naturally start to rebuild your mana channels."

"Sounds like a lot of work," Kim said.

Erik raised an eyebrow. "I didn't think you'd be the kind of person that would give up after a little work."

"Ah, shit. Well, better get started, right?"

Erik went to the door and opened it. A team of medics came in with a hospital bed. They helped Kim stand and get onto the bed.

Leaving the room, they headed to the operating theatre.

"Thank you," Kim Cheol said.

"Don't thank me. My decision put you and everyone else in danger. It's the least I can do."

"Don't think I haven't heard of the blue-eyed medic that's been running around Vuzgal and the hospital, helping out my wounded guildmates. You were doing what you hoped was the best for everyone. Now you're putting us back together."

"Wish that I didn't have to."

"Well, I'm going to get a Body Like Sky Iron. Damn, never thought I'd be able to get such a high cultivation." Kim Cheol grinned, making Erik smile a little.

They went through the operating theatre's doors, passing through a cleaning formation that pulled all the dirt and muck from their bodies and clothes.

Erik went to the side. A nurse helped him get into his medical robe, adding goggles and a mask, then helped him put on his Healer's Hands gloves.

He turned back to Kim Cheol. An assisting alchemist had just finished using a bag-valve mask to deliver a powerful sedative, putting Kim into a deep slumber.

A nurse stepped forward and connected an IV tube to a cannula inserted into his left hand. Another nurse attached a breather over his mouth and nose. The air being pumped in had an aerosolized stamina potion added to it. The newly hooked-up potion entered his bloodstream as well.

Erik ran a Medical Scan as the nurses and medics moved around Kim, running checks, moving gear into position. The formations under the table were powered, but inactive. A formation master stood at a command console that controlled the different medical formations. It was the culmination of the concepts learned from Julilah's stack formations, Rugrat's formation sockets, Qin's interlinking formations, and the work of dozens of other experts that enabled their operators to have control over the formations necessary for medical use.

Erik could see Kim's body was trying to heal itself. Where there was necrotic or heavy scar tissue, the healing ramped up, overworking his body, draining his stamina.

The new potion was working through his body, obliterating blood clots as it passed through his veins.

Erik used his Medical Scan to locate the worst clumps of necrotic or scar tissue.

"Okay, ready on the retractors?" Erik looked at the nurse opposite him.

"Ready."

"Scalpel."

He was handed a thin blade.

"As we talked about, the first place we're going to target is his right thigh."

Erik saw right through Kim Cheol's body as he used the scalpel.

The nurse moved in with the retractors, opening the incision.

"Forceps." Erik held out his hand, feeling them land in his palm. He grabbed the necrotic tissue in Kim Cheol's thigh with the forceps. Using the scalpel, he cut away sections of the blackened tissue. A nurse offered a bowl for him. He deposited it, moving on to the next section of dead tissue. He worked quickly, efficiently removing the damaged tissue.

"Status."

"Stable!"

He worked through the thigh.

"Let's seal him up. Heal Muscle." The muscles started to regrow and reform faster. Erik stopped when thin bands of muscles connected to one another. He went muscle-by-muscle. The nurse released the retractors.

"Heal Skin."

The line down Kim Cheol's leg closed, becoming a pale, thin scar. He had only laid the framework, but his body could build upon that.

"How are we looking on stamina?"

"Eighty percent and increasing," an alchemist reported.

"Okay, we'll move to the other thigh, then to the left arm. I don't like having so many problems near the heart."

Erik repeated the same process with the other thigh. He made multiple incisions so he wouldn't have to cut through healthy tissue, prolonging the healing process.

Time faded into the background as he worked.

He closed up the arm.

"Dipping to forty percent. Recovering slowly," the alchemist warned.

"Okay, I want a minimum fifty percent of stamina. Crank up the healing formations till he surpasses that and maintain balance."

"Understood."

"Okay everyone, good work! There is still more tissue to remove, but this is a good start."

Erik left the operating room, moving to the clean room. He stripped out of his gear and washed his hands.

"Erik, Glosil is requesting your presence in the command center." Egbert's voice came through the ceiling.

"He say why?" Erik conjured flames in his hands, drying them.

"The Willful Institute is mobilizing. They appear to be targeting Vuzgal."

"Understood." Erik passed through a clean formation. "I'll be there as soon as I can."

Rugrat watched the range as the shooters took their time to aim before firing. The sounds of shooting were thrown off cadence, each shooter entirely focused and in their own world.

He had five squads' worth of people out on the range, working on their skills and with their weapons.

The shooting died down and the shooters cleared their weapons, holding them out for inspection. Rugrat canceled the spell on his eyes while the range officers checked the weapons. They finished quickly, holding a thumb out to Rugrat.

"Range clear! Everyone stand!"

Everyone got to their feet.

"Okay, let's go check out those targets."

They walked toward their targets. It wasn't mandatory shooting, just a fun shoot. Rugrat and Erik had introduced it. Rugrat was as good as he was at shooting thanks to practicing in his backyard. He could barely hit a target marginally better than a regular person before then, though he wouldn't be any kind of a good shop past a few hundred meters.

"How's it going, Lieutenant Acosta?" Rugrat asked as he neared one of the shooters.

"Not bad. I think that I got them all on paper at least." She smiled as they kept walking.

"I don't doubt that." Rugrat grinned as they walked over the grassy ground. The range was attached to the first barracks. With formations, they could stop the noise from spreading to the rest of the floor and make sure none of the rounds went flying off and hit someone.

"You up for rotation soon?"

"Got my marching orders. There's going to be an attack on a Fourth Realm location in a week. Whole combat company is going. We'll be dressed down, though."

"How are your people?"

"Eager, excited, scared. You know how it is." Acosta shrugged. "I'm just glad we're getting the opportunity. Some time or another, they're going to face a fight. Best to get it into their bones now."

"You just don't want the CPD's taking all the jobs." Rugrat laughed.

"Shit, I'd damn well jump into the next spot on the CPD training rota just to get out there."

They reached Acosta's target. "So how did I do?"

Rugrat looked at the target. "You're looking good. Haven't forgotten what you learned in your sharpshooting course. You'd be an ace shot back on Earth with a grouping like that at three hundred meters."

"Just we'll be using bows and spells instead. I hope we don't have to use rifles in the future."

"Why?" Rugrat asked.

"Well, if we're using rifles, something will have gone horribly wrong."

Rugrat saw motion as Colonel Yui walked over to the firing line.

"And if a colonel is looking for your ass, it's never a good sign," Rugrat said out the corner of his mouth.

"Better you than me." Acosta snorted.

"Aren't you due for a promotion?"

"When we're back, they're making me a captain. Gonna have my very own combat company. Yay." She turned to look at Yui Silaz.

"Well, congratulations on the impending promotion. Piece of advice? *Never* become a lord of anything." Rugrat looked at her. "You've got control of the range. Make sure people don't start spontaneously forgetting how rifles work."

He waved at Yui and walked over to him. A hundred thoughts ran through his head as he mentally reviewed the different units in the field, none of them good. There were fourteen CPD squads deployed, and an additional five thousand Alva military personnel. Three hundred and twenty thousand Adventurer's Guild members. Seven battlefields in total.

Nearly fifteen thousand Alva military members were housed between Alva and Vuzgal, not including the undead legions and the four thousand that were training.

"The Willful Institute is mobilizing. The people of Vuzgal just got word from the Associations to evacuate. Glosil is in the command center. He's stepped-up defenses in Vuzgal."

Rugrat jogged away from the range, Yui right beside him.

"Erik?"

"A messenger has been dispatched."

Niemm and his First Special Team fell in around Rugrat and Yui.

"We knew it was coming."

Erik was last to arrive in the command center.

"As of four hours ago, the Willful Institute mobilized five main armies. Messages posted across Vuzgal confirm there will be an attack," Glosil said.

Officers in the command center moved with purpose, but there was no panic. They updated plots on the different realms, sending and receiving information.

"Do we know if they have support?" Erik asked.

"Director Silaz is still gathering information on just who is aiding them, but we believe the Elsi clan is working to support them along with city lords around Vuzgal."

"You've been planning for this for months. What are your thoughts?" Erik asked.

"Recall Colonel Domonos and his Dragon Regiment to man the defenses. They've been on the ground and know Vuzgal's terrain and defenses better than anyone."

"The offensive led by the Adventurer's Guild?" Erik asked.

"We've already turned most of the control over to them. We can leave with minimal ripples."

"Do you want to pull out Tiger Regiment's people as well?" Rugrat asked.

"Yes, and call on the reserves. They can return to Alva, get organized into units, and armed."

"Gives them time to get acclimatized to one another instead of fighting together with strangers." Erik glanced at Yui, who was nodding in agreement. Yui was eager and young, wanting to prove himself, cut his teeth in a real battle, but he had the strength of character and confidence to wait. To do his duty. It might not be the most valiant looking role, but it was nonetheless vital.

"It will take time to pull back Domonos. In the meantime?"

"In the meantime, Yui will head to Vuzgal to prepare the defenses before turning them over. After which he will return to Alva with Tiger Regiment. Do you want to talk about your actions, Colonel Yui?"

"Thank you, Commander," Yui nodded. "We are currently locking down the city. All leave passes have been canceled. We will run a full preparedness check on every weapon system. The bunker network will run through ready drills. All nonessential personnel will be pulled back to Alva or to the fallback dungeons. Kanoa is already stationed in Vuzgal. His people will fly recon over the passes, in addition to our sensing net and information from Director Silaz. We'll get a clear picture of everything we're facing."

"Once we confirm the enemy is coming, our next moves will depend on the situation. Specifically, which weapon systems we are escalating to," Glosil said. "We have come up with four levels of weaponry to use. Level one starts with repeaters and gear that is commonly used in the Ten Realms. Level two progresses to the use of mortars, explosives, the air force's bombs, stack and interlocking formations. Level three allows the use of firearms such as the regular machine guns, semi-autos, and bolt actions. At this point, our troops would be free to use all their abilities. Level three also allows the use of enhanced non-direct weaponry, such as artillery cannons and the conqueror's armor to double our people's stats. Level four permits the complete use of all abilities, all of our railgun weaponry, as well as our conqueror's armor dialed up two hundred percent."

"Your recommendation?" Rugrat asked.

"We'll begin with Level two and escalate as needed. If they learn all our trump cards, they're going to wonder where the hell we got it from. It won't make people run away. They'll attack us for our secrets. If we keep pulling out powerful weapons, they wonder just what other secrets we have. It allows us to lull them into a sense of security, then wipe that away when we reveal a new weapon. It will be a morale killer."

Erik looked at Rugrat.

"Are you going or me?" Rugrat asked Erik.

"What do you mean?" Glosil asked, his brows pinching together.

"You need heavy hitters, and we're the biggest damn hammers you have. Erik will command the First and Second Special Teams. I will command the Third and Fourth. One of us will be in Vuzgal, the other in Alva. We won't hide in the rear for this. Our people need to know that we're in this fight, that they have our support, and we won't leave them behind." Rugrat's words were firm.

Glosil swallowed. "As a commander, I'm not pleased. But knowing you two, I'd expect nothing else. As an Alvan, I'm proud."

"You're gonna make me blush." Rugrat smiled and fanned his face like a southern belle.

"If I go up there," Erik said, "I can help the medics and on the front line, but you can do all that and work on people's gear to maintain it and create more ammunition and weaponry."

"I can do that from here too," Rugrat said.

"But you have long range abilities. Your rifle, your spells. I'm up close and personal. I'm no help unless they enter the city. You go. You can help in more ways."

"You sure?"

"I'll work on getting people fighting fit. I can create the concoctions needed for the front lines as well. You're more useful on the front lines." Erik reassured him.

"All right." Rugrat looked at Glosil. "Though I would suggest that Erik commands the First and Fourth Special Teams and I get the Second and Third. Roska and her people are up there right now. They know the situation. The First is still deployed with the Adventurer's Guild."

"You are the commanders of the special teams, but I agree." Glosil nodded "Colonel Yui, prepare to move your forces to assist Vuzgal in five hours."

Yui snapped to attention. "Yes, sir."

Rugrat slapped the front of his vest, making sure it was secure. He breathed, feeling his body press up against the plates. It felt comfortable and familiar.

"You talked to her yet?" Erik grabbed Rugrat's chest plate, returning Rugrat's checks.

"Yeah, she ain't pleased, but she understands."

Erik turned to Rugrat, checking his gear. He pulled out the medic pouch, making sure everything was accounted for.

"She never is when we go off." Erik closed the rip-away pouch and attached it back onto Rugrat's lower back. "All set, brother."

Rugrat turned around to face him. "Ah, shit, feels like the old days." Rugrat rubbed his clean-shaved face.

"Got the haircut, too." Erik smiled. "Look like a proper marine now."

"Feel like a teenager."

"'Bout as smart as one, too."

"Asshole." Rugrat held out a hand.

Erik grabbed it, and the two men embraced. "Stay safe, brother."

"Ah, you know me. Fucking hard to kill, man."

The door opened as Momma Rodriguez walked in. The two released one another. She looked at Rugrat, who was tucking a few straps away.

"You look after yourself and the others now." She held it together, focusing on his gear instead of him.

"I will Momma," Rugrat said in a soft voice and leaned down, hugging her.

Her breath caught in her throat as she wrapped her small arms around his neck.

Rugrat held her tighter as he heard her sniffle.

She let out a breath and kissed him, pushing him back.

"All right, you go now and finish up quickly. When you come back, we'll have your favorites." She put on a smile, even as her eyes brimmed with tears.

"Yes, Momma." Rugrat pressed his teeth together. He couldn't bring himself to say he would be back. *What happens is what happens.* Rugrat looked at Erik. *Look after her for me, brother.*

Erik nodded.

Rugrat kissed Momma Rodriguez on the cheek and walked out of his and Erik's shared office.

He exited the front door to find Gong Jin and Special Team Three waiting for him.

"Off to Vuzgal we go."

22
Man-beast, Man-elemental

Erik walked into one of the clinically clean body cultivation testing rooms again. "Nice display."

He looked at the table where there were eleven monster cores lined up. There were assistants preparing testing equipment while scribes readied their various pencils.

"Lesser Mortal monster core all the way to a Lesser Sky grade monster core," Melissa Bouchard said.

Erik let out a low whistle. "In the name of science."

"Yes, *expensive* science." Melissa gestured to the reclined chair next to the table.

Erik laid back and a nervous-looking assistant came up with a formation-covered band. He smiled. "I don't bite." He lifted his arm to make it easier.

"You *are* the city and dungeon lord, Erik. I was scared to meet you the first time." Melissa checked her always present clipboard.

"And turned me into a guinea pig." Erik looked at the assistant as she finished putting the band around his arm. "Don't trust the researchers."

The assistant tried to hide her smile, moving away with a blush.

"So, what you got me doing today?" Erik asked Bouchard.

"You want to increase the power of your bloodline, to purify it. So, we're going to test to see what these do." She waved at the different monster cores.

"Never seen them all lined up like that. As they get bigger, they get less murky."

"Yes, in the higher-level cores the elements separate out. Past the mortal grade of monster cores, variants are much more likely."

"Because the beasts only take in one kind of element?"

"That is the running hypothesis."

Erik was strapped, hooked up to, standing on, under, and around dozens of different sensing systems, with at least another dozen spells being targeted at him by the testing staff.

The things I do in the name of science.

"We're ready." Melissa looked at Erik, her eyes a thermal peering purple.

"Thank God. About ready to fall over with all this testing crap." He indicated to the stuff stuck to him, took the Lesser Mortal monster core, and consumed it, eager to get through this.

Nothing happened for a second. Then the built-up elements entered his body, flowing through and straight into the core at the center of his chest.

Medics and formation masters described what they were seeing while scribes diligently recorded everything. Melissa moved around the room, checking the influx of information.

It quieted down after a few moments.

"Next."

Erik picked up the next monster core.

Monster Core
Do you wish to absorb this Common Mortal Grade monster core? *YES/NO* You will gain 10,000 EXP

Erik consumed it.

"What are you feeling?"

"My elemental core draws in the elements naturally, through my mana channels, and my pores and veins. But only the elements I've tempered my body with. It's like mana gathering, except with elements, and I'm using monster cores instead of mana stones. I can draw some elemental energy through my mana gates."

"Hmm. So, do you think that tempering, while it increases the body's abilities, is training you to refine your bloodline?"

"Sure, that's a possibility."

The different scribes and medics in the room started to quiet as they finished recording their information.

"Next core then."

So it went as Erik consumed monster core after monster core.

Melissa pulled out another monster core. "This is a water variant Mortal monster core. Could you try to consume it?"

Erik took the core and used it. The water element entered through his skin and he tried to draw it into his elemental core like he had with earth, fire, and metal. It didn't move.

"I don't get the sense that it will harm me. It sank into my bones and started to temper them. With enough of these variant cores, I could temper my body, I think. As the mantra goes: The foundation Tempered, the soul grounded, the mind forged, bones reformed, muscles that flow, and blood with the power of the realms.

"My foundation was tempered with flames. My body had an explosive rise in regeneration under the pressure of the earth. My mind was altered with the metal tempering, while my overall defensive ability grew, the bones reformed. I guess that has to do with water, but I think that it might have been part of the metal tempering, Muscles that flow sounds water-based."

"What do you think of the last line?"

"And blood with the power of the realms." Erik pursed his lips. "Well, the only remaining element is wood, but the mention of blood makes me think of the bloodline. It has to be connected."

Melissa nodded and made a note, flipping over a page on her notepad, and looked up again. "We found information that talks about monster cores being used in body cultivation. It talks about concoctions, which are stronger but also gentler on the body. There are fewer complications and it is harder for someone to die or be crippled."

"If we can use the cores in combination with the tempering instruments, it could assist. The more we know." Erik shrugged.

"Exactly. Okay, shall we move on?"

Erik continued to consume the monster cores, moving through the Earth grades and into the Sky grades.

His experience increased at a massive rate as his own core increased in scale.

"Well, congratulations! You have reached the Variant Earth grade monster core. Some of the energy is lost, so consuming a grand monster core. Doesn't mean that yours will be the same grade. You have a three-attribute core. Once your elemental core reached the Earth grade, you started to draw in more of the water element passively and increased the amount of fire, metal, and earth you drew in as well."

"I thought it was easier to pull them in. I thought the water mana was just from the cores." Erik stretched in the chair. "Feel tired, even with my high stamina stat."

Erik pulled up his experience.

226,356,128/344,700,000 EXP till you reach Level 66

"Are you ready for the last one?" Melissa handed the core over.

Monster Core
Do you wish to absorb this Earth Lesser Sky Grade monster core? *YES/NO* You will gain 450,000,000 EXP

"Level sixty-six here I come."

Erik consumed the monster core.

His pores opened to the electrifying chill of metal, the deep calming energy of the earth, and the heat of the fire element. His bones itched as he gritted his teeth against the water element that scoured through his body.

His elemental core was a starved scavenger that had found scraps to eat.

The elements had nowhere to flee as the air shifted in the room. Erik's body glowed with elemental power.

His muscles bulged and his veins popped. The mana within a meter around him stilled; the mana beyond created a storm. The formations within the room flickered as the elemental power of their formations was drawn into Erik's body.

Paper and equipment were torn free and sent flying around the room.

The wind disappeared and the formations brightened as Erik opened his eyes. He scratched his head, looking around the room. "Uhh, crap."

Quest completed: Bloodline Cultivation 1

The power of the body comes from the purity of the bloodline.
Requirements: Form an Earth Grade Elemental Core with 2 elements
Rewards: Earth Grade Bloodline +100,000,000 EXP

Title: Earth Grade bloodline
You have brought 2 elements to the Earth grade in your Elemental core. Strength, Agility, Stamina and Stamina Regeneration increase by 5% Mana and Mana Regeneration increase by 2%

You have reached Level 66
When you sleep next, you will be able to increase your attributes by: 5 points.

431,656,128/434,200,000 EXP till you reach Level 67

"Well, that seems to have had an effect. Next, we'll look at consuming meat. We've prepared some samples for you."

Erik went through similar tests throughout the day, using every idea any Alvan had thought up.

"Okay. So in summary, you can only increase an element in your core if your body has been tempered by it. And you should only draw in elements that you have tempered your body with or should use next. Water works for you, but wood is dangerous right now. Monster cores are effective. So is drawing in mana heavy with the element, as long as you have the capacity for it. Eating monster meat is less effective, and concoctions heavy in the elements can be the best way to increase your elemental capacity. For now, I don't think it is useful for anything but your ability to control the elements."

Erik pulled up the last notification.

Quest: Bloodline Cultivation 2
The power of the body comes from the purity of the bloodline.
Requirements: Form a Sky Grade Elemental Core with 3 elements

Rewards:
Sky Grade Bloodline
+10,000,000,000 EXP

"Okay, so what should we do?"

"I think that you should increase your body cultivation. Right now, your monster—sorry, bad habit—*elemental* core is lopsided. There is more room within it. Once you temper your body with water, I would be surprised if it doesn't start to get absorbed into your elemental core. Maybe something will happen then, too?"

"Bleeding edge of research. We'll find out eventually." Erik stood and stretched.

"With that, I have some work to do."

Erik said his goodbyes and left the training facility.

He climbed onto Gilly and they headed toward the crafting sector, through the streets.

"Did you know that the basic standard of every person that becomes a soldier of the Alva military is to have opened all of their mana gates and reached the Vapor Mana Drop stage? And they have to have reached Body Like Stone," Erik said to Storbon as he rode alongside with half of Special Team Four.

"I think I heard that somewhere."

"You reached Sky Iron the other day?"

"Yes, I did," Storbon said.

"Congratulations," Erik said as he pulled out a box and passed it to Storbon.

"Sir?"

"Something to help you out. I had to get reports from Niemm on what stage everyone in the special teams is at."

"These… they're body-altering concoctions?"

"Yeah," Erik said, rolling his shoulders. Everything had transformed now that the traders were moving supplies to the front line.

"Sir?"

"Take them. We can mass produce the concoctions needed to form liquid drops and reach Body Like Iron. Beyond that, we have to rely on ourselves." Erik looked in the distance. "Just trying to do everything I can to prepare for this war."

Storbon put the box away. "Thank you."

"No worries, time to get back to work."

They had reached the crafting district. People flowed into the workshops along with materials, while carts filled with provisions left. Crafters staggered out of different shops and into their beds to rest, only to do it all over again hours later.

Erik dismounted and joined the stream heading into the workshops district with four special team members.

He went into the alchemist workshop, taking a key for a vacant Experts level crafting room. He looked at a board filled with concoction requests.

"Earth level tempering pills." They were always in need. It allowed those that tempered their bodies with the earth element to recover faster and be stronger. Revival concoctions only reacted to the people who are wounded.

He took the request to the quartermaster and put it on the table.

The quartermaster glanced up, eyes wide, and snapped out of his work. Erik pushed the request forward. The quartermaster accepted it with both hands and headed to the shelves behind him. He brought out a box with prepared ingredients.

Erik checked the box. "Who prepared these?"

"I-I'm sorry. I can get new ones," the man squeaked.

"I was just wondering."

"Uhh, it was Apprentice level alchemists. They're organizing the ingredients and portioning them out according to the formulas."

"They did a good job! This will save me a lot of time." Erik stored the box away. "Thanks."

He checked his key and went up to his crafting room.

"Gonna need a nap first to sort out these points."

Erik took out a sleeping concoction, drinking it.

You have 5 attribute points to use.

"Strength. Fastest way to increase my fighting power," he muttered. "Though it's getting hard to control it all. Fine, three in agility, two in strength. Or should I do mana pool? No, all my spells are cheaper, and I can recover naturally or with potions. Strength and agility it is."

Name: Erik West	
Level: 66	Race: Human-?

Titles: *From the Grave II* *Blessed By Mana* *Dungeon Master V* *Reverse Alchemist* *Poison Body* *Fire Body* *City Lord III* *Earth Soul* *Mana Reborn* *Wandering Hero* *Metal Mind, Metal Body* *Earth Grade Bloodline*	
Strength: (Base 90) +53	1501
Agility: (Base 83) +80	937
Stamina: (Base 93) +35	2016
Mana: (Base 37) +94	1336
Mana Regeneration (Base 40) +61	63.62/s
Stamina Regeneration: (Base 142) +59	43.26/s

Darkness fell and faded all too quickly. Erik opened his eyes, filled with energy. He stretched as he woke, and rolled to his feet, perched on the edge of the cot.

He pulled out his cauldron and placed it down. Flames appeared around and within it, starting to heat it up. Erik opened the box of ingredients and organized them on the side.

"Time to get to work."

The flames grew in temperature and started to dance, turning into beasts that roved across the metal surface.

Several hours later, Erik was sitting looking at the cauldron. The flames receded as he collected the pills in the middle of the cauldron.

He stood and stretched, feeling the satisfying pops through his body. He pulled out a stamina bar with a groan and started eating. With his higher cultivation, he needed stronger potions to have an effect, but he wasn't really eating much more than he had before.

He flexed his right forearm, feeling it tense and the rush of blood.

I wonder how my blood has changed.

He finished off the bar and stowed the wrapper, frowning. What if he was to do a blood transfusion? Would others with a lower cultivation be affected? They didn't really do blood transfusions as the stamina potions increased the speed that the body created blood. But would it be worth having a blood bank or doing blood transfusions instead of using the stamina potions?

Erik started pacing, holding his chin as his brows furrowed. It might be a good idea to look at what happened with blood transfusions and see if they were better than stamina potions in some situations. If someone's blood with a higher cultivation blood worked on people with a lower cultivation...

What would the effects be? Would it increase their cultivation? Would it help them to heal faster?

Erik smacked his hands together. "If I took a stamina potion, would it show up in my blood?"

Erik turned, snapping his fingers. "Wait. Hell, what if we were to use the blood as if it were a potion in itself?" It would help them recover from the blood loss *and* take a straight hit of potions.

He stopped, his skin tingling. He turned back to the cauldron, on the cusp of an idea. "Furnace, cauldron, blood, body." He held his hands to either side of his face, framing his vision, blocking out everything but the cauldron. "What if… what if the body was the cauldron? The blood the product?" The rampant energy in his body stilled as if a train had arrived suddenly at its destination, his energy directed to his brain.

"If I were to ingest different ingredients, my body would break them down, consume and use them, add it into my blood. If I were kept supplied with stamina potions, my high body cultivation would replenish the blood fast." Erik pulled out the revival potion he had made in his crafting session.

"What if I make a potion like this, but from blood? Wait, backtrack. If I knew what ingredients made my blood like this potion, wouldn't I have a revival potion in my veins? If I could eat the right things, then I could increase the stamina and healing effects of my blood, right?"

He conjured a mana pin in his hand and pricked his forefinger. He pulled out the mana pin, and the wound healed fast.

Erik muttered, but saw the red stain on the mana pin.

He held it above his mouth and removed the conjured mana pin from existence. The bare drop of blood fell into his mouth and he used his reverse alchemist and his alchemy knowledge to understand the breakdown of his blood.

Erik stood there, unmoving, for several minutes.

When he opened his eyes, his lips lifted into hearty laughter. He moved to the preparation table and pulled out ingredients. First, he needed to experiment, test it all out. He pulled out a sound transmission device and called Jen.

"Erik?"

"Jen, do we do blood transfusions?"

"No, stamina potions work well enough, and we would need to get another IV or IO line into the patient to get blood into them. Why?"

"Do you have kits to draw blood?"

"Uhh, I don't think so."

Erik checked his gear. "I'm going to need some empty IV bags."

"What are you doing?"

"I'm looking into combining blood and the potions using my body to create the revival potion instead of using a cauldron. I should be able to produce it faster and in greater quantities. I'm going to need you to get some medics together to test it out and see how it works!"

"Okay, boss. I'll head over."

"Thanks."

Erik put the device to the side and worked on different ingredients. He took out a pad of paper and a pen, writing out his ideas.

"Hmm, first I'll take my blood and combine it in the cauldron with different ingredients. Then I'll see how it works within my body. It might be that we have to combine the potions and the blood afterward instead of inside the body."

Rugrat walked into the training room and pulled off his shirt. An assistant took it away as he stripped off his boots and pants and stood there in his short shorts.

He looked at the formation-carved pod in front of him.

Rugrat turned around as medics inserted IVs into his veins. He grabbed the hydration mouthpiece they offered him between his teeth, drinking from it deeply. His body seemed to wake up. His cells felt revitalized as his mana gates opened, passively drawing in mana.

"The mana pod will increase the density of mana to twice the predicted density in the Eighth Realm," Qin said as she stood off to the side.

"Sounds like a lot of juice." Rugrat breathed in and out, feeling the warmth of mana building within his body. He moved toward the pod.

"We will be monitoring you from the exterior. If there is any danger, we'll shut everything down," Tanya informed him.

"Combining formations, pure magic, and mana gathering; I like it."

"There are a lot of experts in mana gathering. I just volunteered to be up here in Vuzgal," Tanya replied.

"Don't sound so excited! Let's do this shit. For science or something." Rugrat got into the pod. Medics attached the IV lines that ran through openings in the pod.

Rugrat looked down at the formation between his toes and felt it on the carved metal under his back.

The pod closed, and he was tilted backward until he lay flat.

Locking bolts engaged as Rugrat breathed in, focusing and calming his mind. He turned his gaze to his Solid Mana Core.

He shifted, getting comfortable in the pod.

"We're going to activate the formations now," Qin said.

"Give'er."

The formation plate under the pod glowed with energy. It was as if liquid mana were spreading through the formation, passing through the carved-out rune before reaching the base of the pod's support.

"We're starting at the same density as the Sixth Realm."

The mana traced the formations and spread across the pod like branches reaching for the heavens.

Rugrat pulled in a sudden breath as the mana surged through his body.

Using his domain, he drew in the mana, compressing it externally and circulating it to increase its density, creating a cloud of mana vapor. It increased in density as it passed through his mana gates, creating snakes of mist. Circulations compressed it further, forming into liquid as it reached his solid core, nourishing it and causing it to grow slowly.

"We'll increase the density now," Qin said.

Rugrat drew in more and more mana. The mental strain piled up. He was trying to focus on everything and maintain control. Even with his domain, the mana was at two times the Seventh Realm's density. He grunted, trying to refine the mana through his domain to make it easier to consume.

His control kept slipping. It was like holding back the ocean with wooden box panels, and the box had fallen apart completely.

Rugrat released his external control and focused on compressing the mana within his body.

"Huh." Rugrat increased the size of his Solid Mana Core. There was a ton of mana entering his core. *Wait. Is this like negative pressure?* "I have the capacity for more. If the density in my body isn't as high as the outside, will it be easier for me to draw in enough mana?"

"What are you saying?" Qin asked.

"The mana here is so dense that it's got more pressure than most of the mana in my body. I could increase my cultivation by just sleeping here. Compressing it internally just speeds it up like I'm creating a vacuum in my body!"

Rugrat laughed and focused on the compression. The amount of mana he drew in was *increasing!*

His frustrations fell away as mana mist formed within the pod. He didn't need to compress it as much to create drops.

The pod slowly filled with mana mist and then mana vapor, twisting and creating vortices which Rugrat's open mana gates drank in greedily.

His Solid Mana Core shook as it reached a bottleneck. He drew in all the surrounding mana in one go, clearing the pod.

Drops shot toward his mana core, assaulting it again and again, the pressure of compression and expansion fighting one another.

A cracking noise sounded. Then a howling wind as the mana entering the pod shot into Rugrat's body. He groaned.

"Increase the pressure!" Tanya yelled.

Qin worked her console as the lines leading to the pod increased in brightness.

The IV bags' levels started to drop as if someone were drinking from them.

"Increase the IV flow!" Medics moved to add on new IV bags.

Rugrat's mana channels appeared as he consumed mana like a ravenous beast.

"More!"

Qin looked at Tanya.

"Do it."

Qin increased the density. Mana mist formed within the pod again, creeping around Rugrat, covering him. One could see the mana channels, the gates through his body, all leading to the mana core under his belly button.

Rugrat's solid core had broken through into the higher stage. The amount of mana it drew in was immense, nearly four times that of his mid-grade Solid Mana Core.

Newly formed, it seemed to be starving and consumed more mana.

The mist once again formed into vapor around Rugrat.

Time lost meaning for him as he drew in more and more mana.

23 War Footing

Bai Ping looked around the secluded courtyard between houses.

The Alvan Soldiers were covered in dirt and signs of battle, their eyes cold as they accepted their new orders.

Everyone there was a true member of the Alva military. They talked in low voices, excited at the prospect of seeing their friends again. They all knew that Vuzgal had been targeted and could be attacked soon.

Colonel Domonos walked into the square.

Everyone snapped to attention.

"At ease."

Formations overlaid the place so that no one would be able to spy on them.

"We have reports that the Willful Institute will attempt to attack Vuzgal. You are the first group that will be shifted back home. There you will resupply and reorganize. Tiger Regiment will support Alva and the mobilization of the reserve units, while Dragon Regiment will return to their posts in Vuzgal." Domonos let his words sink in.

"You have been the backbone of the Adventurer's Guild offensive. You helped to transform them into the fighting force they are today. While you come from the Dragon or Tiger Regiments, we have trained and worked together constantly. We are two units, but the same military. Grab your gear.

We'll be rotating out in four hours."

Colonel Yui stood in a mana barrier tower on the inner wall that broke up Vuzgal. He had been to the city nearly every week, working with the forces there. Now he commanded them all.

He straightened up in his armor, his eyes tracking the traders and caravans streaming out of Vuzgal.

His eyes drifted to the totem with lines of people extending out of it.

Major Kanoa walked up. "Guess we'll need a second totem for them streaming back in."

"Thankfully, that's for someone else to worry about," Yui said. "Anything?"

"Nothing. I've got my people patrolling in the air, though your dad's the one who'll find out when the United Sect Army arrives first."

"I always thought he was a seer when we were growing up. He'd always predict what was going to happen before it did. When I got older, I thought he was paranoid as hell. Now I think it was just prudent planning."

"Good to know that you had such faith in me." Elan reached the top of the stairs, his lips pressed together in a bemused smile. "There is still no word from the cities, though they are all preparing."

"How long until they attack?" Yui asked.

"At least a few days."

"Well, we have a few options depending on how much information we want to give away." Yui looked at his father and Kanoa. "One: we repeat what Erik and Rugrat did in the first battle of Vuzgal. We bleed them as they try to reach Vuzgal. Hit them with traps. Hit them with artillery and bombs from the air force. If we use traps, we can kill many more, as it will be under their mana barriers, though they will know that we are tracking them somehow. Two: if we don't use artillery and bombs, we will cause less damage, but they'll think that we can't see them all the time, which opens them up to make more mistakes. I personally think we should go with the first option. What do you think?"

"I agree," Kanoa nodded.

"I think the first as well. Information is power. But once they enter the valley, they won't be able to hide from us, anyway."

"Okay. Well, let's start with this inspection." Yui led them into the center of the tower. Mana barrier formations took up the ceiling and the floor, a thin thread of mana rising from the bottom formation into the formation above.

They moved off to the side, stepping onto a teleportation formation. Yui nodded to the officer working the console.

The room changed; strips of light formations lit up the transportation room. One could hear movement through the corridors that led out of the room.

Yui led them out of the room and through the corridors.

"If they do attack, I don't think they'll expect our defenses to be so dense. Hundreds of bunkers, miles of tunnels connecting them. Teleportation rooms to keep people and supplies moving," Kanoa said.

"It's an impressive network." Yui stepped onto a rising platform. The formations activated, and they shot up.

They stepped off, seeing more people moving around. They nodded to the trio, but didn't stop walking.

"We're in the belly of the bunker fortifications now," Elan said as they walked upstairs to the next floor.

"They built an entire system to move ammunition as fast as possible. Matt and his blueprint office went wild. With the dungeon core and its size, they could move all the earth they wanted."

They got to the top of the stairs. Straight ahead was a full bathroom and shower. On the left side, there were a few bunk beds stacked so closely one couldn't turn over.

"Stamina and mana recovery formations." Yui pointed at the runes carved into the beds.

"Coupled with their cultivation, they'd need what? An hour or two of downtime to reach one hundred percent?" Kanoa calculated.

"Scary." Yui opened a heavy metal door to the right. "Imagine fighting an enemy that has people with the energy to fight for days on end, then rest for an hour and be ready to fight again."

They passed through a switchback corridor, entering the true bunker with natural light streaming in. There were two people set back from the thin slits that showed the outside world. They were looking through formation-enhanced binoculars at the open ground in front of Vuzgal.

The others rushed to their feet, disturbing their card game.

"Sir," one man said, going pale.

"You're not going to be alert all the time just watching the fields. We're on twenty-five percent. Only need one spotter per section," Yui reminded them.

"Ah, yes, sir." The man nodded.

"Those weapons ready?" Yui pointed at the repeaters and FAL style rifles that were loaded and ready behind the firing slits.

"Yes, sir. They're ranged and readied. When given the word, we just need to put them in their mounts and we'll be ready to fire."

"Good work! Make sure you get some sleep and food. Can't be alert all the time. Take this time to get ready." Yui turned and left the forward section of the bunker. He passed the supply elevator and moved down the stairs.

"Air exchanging formations are working well, and the heat-dissipating formations look good in there," Kanoa said. "One hell of a piece of engineering."

"Over-engineered to hell. Maybe I'm not the paranoid one. Erik and Rugrat worked on the first series of designs, updating them all the time," Elan said.

"Oh, I don't doubt it."

They went through more corridors before reaching another bunker. The rear section of the bunker was largely similar.

Yui waved the troops hanging out to sit back down. He looked at the ladders that ran up the rear of the room to yet more rooms.

"There are two armored gunner positions, dual repeaters or machine guns if needed. The lift goes up there so they can get ammunition if they need it. The trap door to the front of the bunker is bigger for the shells," Kanoa said.

"I haven't seen the new artillery cannons yet."

They went through another metal door, through a switchback.

"Shit," Yui said, smiling.

"One forty-centimeter, reinforced Earth Iron shield."

The artillery cannon was just that. An artillery cannon.

"It's in a hidden position, so the metal exterior doors have been closed over. Moving to the ready position, the exterior doors open to allow the barrel clearance. Then they will rotate from side to side with the artillery cannon to act as a second shield. The interior shield moves with the barrel, protecting the crew from incoming fire that makes it past the exterior doors. The cannon can elevate from zero to forty-five degrees. Its design is based on the railgun, but with that base charge cartridge." Kanoa said.

"Right, because of its weight of a hundred and fifty kilograms, the cartridge allows it to gain an initial velocity right into the teeth of the formations along the barrel that increase its velocity. It saves having to use the heat-dissipating blocks that are seen on the regular railguns." Yui grinned.

"With the same discarding sabot system as the railgun covered in formations. Damn thing is scary as hell." The three men admired it.

"It certainly sounds like it," Elan said, bringing them back to reality as the artillery team stood around, not knowing how to react.

"Ah." Yui coughed. "Good work. We should head over to inspect the other bunkers. There are still the mortar bunkers, command bunkers, and supply caches."

"The whole roof comes off the mortar bunkers. With the mana barrier, they're protected from the air. The Willful Institute will have one hell of a time trying to get close."

"If they can make it past your air force."

"Can't let you ground-pounders take all the glory. About time you saw what we can do. Our shells start at one hundred kilos and go up to one thousand."

"Well, looks like the valley might be a little remodeled in the near future."

Mistress Mercy's office was filled with people. While her uncle was away, she still had plenty of people within the Kostic Clan to help plan out the campaign she was put in command of.

"Cousin Niklaus." Mercy walked up to the scholarly man looking at the maps of the Beast Mountain Range.

He turned and bowed to Mercy. "Cousin Mercy."

"Have you had progress?" She walked to the table past him.

"The different units have been pulled together. Messengers should reach the lower realms shortly to apply pressure and incite attacks against the Beast Mountain Range. Once we arrive, we will clear up the rest."

"Very good. The quicker we can complete our mission, the better. High Elder Cai Bo is watching. If we can complete this task, our entire clan's standing will increase."

"Yes, Cousin."

"Tell the commanders to pull it together or else they will have to tell the High Elder why it takes them so long to prepare." Mercy's voice dropped into a growl.

"I understand."

"The clan recommended you for this position. I hope they were right to do so."

Niklaus cupped his hands and bowed. "I shall endeavor to do my best for the clan and the Institute."

"Good." Mercy turned and walked away. She didn't have time to waste on wars and planning. She had to keep training. While it was odd that there was something happening in the First Realm, it was only the First Realm—nothing useful ever came from there.

"Stand to! Stand to!" The voice rang through the bunker complex as Lieutenant Acosta jumped out of her bed with the rest of her command staff. They pulled on their clothes as they ran into the adjacent communications room.

"Report!" Acosta yelled, pulling on her shirt.

The night staff was fully awake, talking through communication devices. On the main wall, a projection formation showed the exterior of Vuzgal more than thirty meters above their heads.

To the left side of the command center, a formation enhanced artillery cannon rested, hidden beneath layers of armor to defy the enemy's sensing spells. Its hardened painted metal waited on shiny greased gears, ready to extend forward into firing position.

Hopefully, you'll remain our dirty little secret. Acosta averted her eyes.

"Batteries are readying!" the sergeant on watch said as the first linked formation switched from red to green.

"Artillery cannon five ready!"

Another green.

"Mortar bunker three ready!"

Green lights appeared as the artillery company came alive, standing by, ready and waiting to open their metal shields and rain hell down upon their enemies.

Acosta pulled on her body armor as she looked at the other bunkers. The machine-gun nests were at the ready, locked and loaded with guns mounted. The medical bay was ready and waiting to receive. Reserve and quick reaction forces were holding ready.

The air force had pilots mounted and ready to fly. The whole of

Dragon Regiment was alive and buzzing ready in their bunkers.

In just minutes, all of Vuzgal's forces were ready for battle.

"Stand down, stand down. This is a drill! Assess all units and conduct an AAR. Command staff, send reports in two hours," Colonel Yui's voice sounded through the defensive bunker system.

Acosta sighed, looking at her people. Only a few of them, like herself, were resting. With such high body cultivation, they didn't need much sleep.

"AAR in ten minutes. Let me get some damn coffee. Call in the company to the briefing room. Then we'll break them down into squads," Acosta said.

The soldiers started talking with one another, smiling and grinning as the adrenaline bled off.

24
Ripple Effect

Marco clicked his tongue. His majestic horned mount moved forward from the teleportation pad and into Aberdeen city proper. Its armor matched his own: whites, golds, and blue with polished enhanced iron. There were fewer golds and whites in his guards' armor, but it was no less effective as they pushed back others using the totem, their hands resting on their swords as they dared others to make a move with their eyes.

He stopped studying the surrounding defenses, his eyes falling on Lower Elder Kostic and the group with him.

"Master Marco of the Tolentino Clan." Lower Elder Kostic bowed.

"Lower Elder Kostic?" Marco looked at the people with him that weren't of the Willful Institute.

"Please let me introduce you. These are the great allies that have come to support us in removing the blight that is the Vuzgal leadership." Lower Elder Kostic introduced them all as Marco nodded to them as their names were called out, not paying particular attention after the first few.

"They have brought supplies and fighters to join our cause," Lower Elder Kostic informed him.

"I thank you all for your support. There are many riches to be had working together." Marco smiled. They were all weaklings within their sects, people that could be cut away as rogues if their attack went badly. There were enough of them standing to make it look like they were, at the very least, supporting the Wilful Institute, but they just wanted Vuzgal.

More Willful Institute fighters passed through the totem behind Marco and headed into the city, a constant river heading out of Aberdeen, driving toward Vuzgal.

"I hope to see you all on the front lines, but I must take care of my soldiers first. Lower Elder Kostic, may I steal some of your time, esteemed elder?"

"Of course, young master!"

Marco extradited them both, his guards closing around Lower Elder Kostic, who pulled out his beast and mounted up.

Marco made sure no one could hear them. "What is the situation?"

"They have brought one hundred and fifty thousand people in total."

"So, ten thousand each. While we have one hundred thousand. Enough to overwhelm our numbers and spread their losses out."

Elder Kostic remained silent.

"What about our paths and guides?"

"They are ready and waiting to take us to Vuzgal."

"Very well. Once we have fifty thousand gathered, we will head through the passes toward Vuzgal. Have all of our allies' forces arrived?"

"Yes, young master."

"Good. If they see us preparing to move, they'll want to get ahead of us. A disagreement between our commanders will slow our deployment. Let them get ahead of us. What of the situation inside Vuzgal?"

"People are fleeing. Most of them have left already. The defenses have remained quiet. We cannot see inside, and we do not know what they are doing. The Associations have reduced their staff. Vuzgal is nothing but a ghost city."

"Good. Make sure that all information is reported to me right away. Remain here with a force to keep us supplied. I'll make sure that they're strong enough to deter others."

"Yes, master Marco."

Marco picked up his pace, he and his soldiers leaving Elder Kostic behind.

He rode down the road, passing the marching units. A sea of fighters spread across the open land beyond the walls. Two hundred and fifty thousand to take a single city. He would make sure the other sects went first. He expected Vuzgal to put up a terrifying defense. Or he had guessed entirely wrong.

"They've arrived," Elan said to Yui, Kanoa, Roska, and Chonglu. They were all standing in one of Vuzgal's command centers.

Yui took in a breath and let it out slowly, nodding his head.

"How many?"

"Two hundred thousand to two hundred and fifty thousand at a rough estimate."

"Two hundred thousand?" Kanoa shook his head. "They're determined, all right."

"You might be making a wrong assumption," Elan warned. "One hundred and fifty thousand servants, fifty thousand fighters."

"What about the Blood Demon Sect? They didn't have that?"

"Well, the Blood Demon Sect Army left their camp followers behind. They were expecting a lightning raid and then to run away. This army is expecting to siege Vuzgal. The Willful Institute has the least amount of camp followers, showing their confidence in taking Vuzgal quickly."

"How strong are they?"

"We expect thirty thousand Fourth Realm fighters, twelve thousand Fifth Realm fighters, eight thousand Sixth Realm fighters."

"So, two to one to our forces?" Kanoa asked.

"Yes."

Kanoa frowned. "Everything I know says you should have a *lot* more than the guy you're attacking."

"I don't doubt that they will get more. They have been talking to a lot of allies," Elan said.

"Well, then it's time to begin." Yui looked at Roska and Kanoa. "I want your scouts at high altitude watching their every move. Roska, with the support of our close protection details and artillery companies, make them remember just what it means to attack Vuzgal."

"Sir!" They both snapped to attention and saluted.

Yui saluted them back. "To your commands."

They released salutes and headed off.

"Director Elan, Lord Chonglu, it is time we dealt with those traders in our city and start to expediate the evacuation of our people quietly."

They both nodded.

"What about Rugrat?" Chonglu asked.

A smile spread across Yui's face. "Ah, I'm sure he'll wake up in time. If we evacuated him, there would be hell to pay. I'd rather face the Wilful Institute, alone."

A guard barged into Evernight's office. She had finally taken a room for herself to deal with all the operations in the First Realm. Several agents were working around her. In the middle, there was a globe showing the First Realm. A glass with formations rested on an arm circling around the globe. The scene under the glass was reflected on the large main table. Pins were added to it, reflecting on the table.

The guard rushed to Evernight's desk and put down a report.

She picked it up, breaking the seal. She rose to her feet before she had finished reading. "The Willful Institute has started to move in the First Realm. They have been contacting the different nations and forces that surround the Beast Mountain Range. Their targets are the outposts and King's Hill. From now on, we must assume that they know some secrets about the Beast Mountain Range."

The intelligence agents all looked up.

She scribbled a note on a new piece of paper and handed the report and paper to an aide.

"Send this to Alva. In the meantime, I want to know which nations were contacted. What is their military strength? Bring me Aditya and Pan Kun." Her last words were for the guard, who bowed, heading out of the office. "Well, let's get to work, shall we?"

The door to the office opened to reveal Aditya, Old Quan, and Pan Kun. Evernight bowed with the rest of the room.

"No need for that. We have a fight to plan out," Erik said, looking at Glosil and stepping to the side.

The door closed as Glosil spoke. "We planned for this kind of attack in the past. The Tiger Regiment is prepared to support the BMRA as needed. Colonel Yui has had extensive training. You would do well to listen to his advice."

"Yes, sir," Pan Kun saluted Commander Glosil, who returned it.

"We will go with your poison outpost trap plan," Glosil said. "Could you explain it?"

Pan Kun nodded and turned to the table.

"The outpost trap is simple. We pull back all our non-essential forces to King's Hill and leave fighting forces with plenty of consumables and the fastest mounts in the outposts. They will act as a rear guard and use spell scrolls and consumables to wreak as much havoc as possible on the enemy. Then they will flee the outpost. We will leave traps in the outposts to allow our people to flee." Pan Kun drew a line down the roads to King's Hill.

"The road traps will all be activated to make sure that the enemy does not get a clear shot at us. Forces will use the teleportation formations to attack the enemy as they enter the Beast Mountain Range.

"There are teleportation formations hidden under each of the outposts. The enemy will probably use some as their forward bases. Teams will sneak into the outposts and into the camps carrying a powerful poison. The poison is slow acting and highly infectious. It will quickly spread through the enemy camps and through their lines." Pan Kun looked to Erik.

"The poison is something that people in the Fourth Realm would find hard to cure or treat," Erik said. "Everyone deploying the poison will have tempered their bodies with poison and we will have an antidote in the water and food served to the general population so our people will not be affected."

Those around the table had grim looks. It wasn't a fair battle, nor was it honorable, but it could save their lives and the lives of those underneath them.

"It will last for three days in the open air and die out with our enemy's forces. Any longer than that and it could spread to the rest of the First Realm and wipe out entire populations."

Pan Kun nodded. "When they are weakened, we'll attack their supply lines. Storage rings are a rarity in the First Realm. They'll have a hard time supplying their armies. The BMRA will hold the Beast Mountain Range while the Alva Military head into the different kingdoms and nations that have attacked us and steal from their granaries and treasuries. It will destabilize the rulers. While through the information networks, we will increase the unease within the population, arming and supporting rebellions across the First Realm." Pan Kun said.

"What if the Institute provides fighters that are strong enough to overpower us?" Evernight asked.

"Use tools and items to deal with them. Otherwise, the Alva Military will deal with them," Glosil said.

"Seems that we have plenty to keep us busy," Erik said. "I talked to Elise. She's handling the traders through the First Realm and is meeting with as many of them as she can. The traders in the First Realm will stop trading with any of the nations that turn against us."

Evernight took in a sharp breath. "There are some kingdoms and nations in the first realm that are wholly reliant on our trade. The impact will not be small. They'll know something is wrong."

"Problems?"

"No, the more war supplies we can buy now, the more expensive it will be for them to wage war."

The rest of the meeting was spent organizing and settling the smaller details. Leaving it to them, Erik took the opportunity to get five minutes in a secure room to complete his level up.

You have 5 attribute points to use.

He looked through his character sheet.

"Put five into Agility. Help me with aiming and working with alchemy and healing."

He reviewed the new changes to his stat sheet. There was still much to be done. He felt the changes spread through his body as the darkness took him.

Name: Erik West Level: 66   Race: Human-?
Titles: *From the Grave II* *Blessed By Mana* *Dungeon Master V* *Reverse Alchemist* *Poison Body* *Fire Body* *City Lord III* *Earth Soul* *Mana Reborn*

Wandering Hero *Metal Mind, Metal Body* *Earth Grade Bloodline*	
Strength: (Base 90) +53	1501
Agility: (Base 83) +85	966
Stamina: (Base 93) +35	2016
Mana: (Base 37) +94	1336
Mana Regeneration (Base 40) +61	63.62/s
Stamina Regeneration: (Base 142) +59	43.26/s

"Form in your squads! Two lines facing me! Move it!" Bai Ping yelled at the rabble loitering at the side of the parade ground.

They stepped onto the parade square. Their marching made Bai Ping wince nearly as much as their mismatched outfits.

"Right hand out, size off of the person beside you and in front!"

They bounced like a caterpillar, stretching out and getting into some semblance of an organized unit.

"Thank the gods we're not relying on you to do drill! Drop your arms, eyes forward!" The group looked at Bai Ping.

"I am Gunnery Sergeant Bai Ping. These are Staff Sergeants Yi and Baines. You have all tested high in your ability to fight as mages."

Bai Ping waved the quartermasters on. The ex-traders went down the lines, checking everyone's sizes and dropping off gear at their feet.

"You are now being issued a belt, three complete uniforms—with a week's worth of underwear—shirts and socks. You're also getting one carrier with a set of plates, boots, helmet, sound transmission device, repeater crossbow, notepad, pencils, as well as formation plates. You will be issued meals and potions upon deployment. They will all be geared toward increasing your mana regeneration. Ammunition for your repeater will be issued at the same time. You will be going into battle in the coming weeks. Everything that we do here could save your life. I do not care who you were before or what you did before. You're all soldiers in Alva's military and we have a reputation that will not fail." Bai Ping raked them all with his eyes. "You will fight for the person beside you, those that you can't even see. Yours is not a glamorous job, but it is a necessary job and essential to winning."

The quartermasters finished laying out the gear in front of the reservists.

"All right, grab your shit and get changed. I want you back here, formed up, in fifteen minutes." A few started running.

"Did I tell you to move yet! Get!" Bai Ping barked.

The shame-faced members returned to the formation under his dark eyes. He checked his watch.

"Listen to orders. Follow them and you might survive. Act on your own and you will kill those beside you. Damn, I feel like you're smarter already! Hell, I think you might not need that extra five minutes." Bai Ping gave them a smile unique to training sergeants. "You have ten minutes. Go!"

The formation broke apart as they grabbed their gear into their storage rings and rushed toward the tents that they had been thrown up, tearing them up in an orderly way that only near-panicked soldiers could.

"Going to be a long three days," Yi said.

"Good thing we don't need to sleep. We'll train them as much as possible." Bai Ping sighed.

"The more they sweat, the less they bleed." Baines sighed, showing no outward signs.

"We'll have to make sure they're properly hydrated. Don't want them to become dehydrated, sweating it all out. I thought I saw a few water buffalos around. They should have somebody tempering right?" Bai Ping shared a smile with the other two. "Let's get started."

They dispersed into the crowd, vipers filled with curses, their own brand of venom.

People started to stream out of the tent around the seven-minute mark, forming back up where they had been before.

"Get your asses moving! Have you never been dressed in your lives?"

"Get the hell out there!" The gunnery sergeants and staff sergeants hurled their own abuse getting them out. They harried the last of them out of the tents, toward the lines. Bai Ping waved the sergeants over and looked at Baines.

He nodded and met the sergeants.

"Seems some of you have forgotten how to get dressed!" Bai Ping yelled as Baines was speaking with the other sergeants.

"You have all been issued with mana-suppressing medallions. Put them on!" They pulled out the medallions, putting them around their necks.

"Check the person to your right and left to make sure it is on. Set it to fifty percent!" They adjusted the medallions.

The formations activated as they let out grunts.

It sucks having half of your mana pool and regeneration cut off, like losing a limb.

"Good, now tuck it in your shirt. I want you to do something simple. Hold out your right hand and create a flame that is ten centimeters tall."

They conjured the flames in their hands.

"If your flame goes out, then your entire squad will have to do moving and covering in the high earth element training rooms until Staff Sergeant Yi is happy. Sergeant Yi *loves* long walks in the high earth mana rooms!"

A few flames quivered but didn't fall apart.

"Right turn!" The group moved somewhat sloppily, still with flames in hand.

"All right! We're heading to camp two. Perseverance, keep pace!" Baines released the sergeants who moved around their squads.

"By the left! Left, march!"

The group started marching out of the training area.

"Left wheel!" Bai Ping said.

"Holy shit! Sergeant, did you forget what a left wheel is?" Staff Sergeant Yi jumped on a leading squad member that had fucked up.

The squad member gritted his teeth and half shut his eyes.

"You better not fucking let that flame go out! I feel a need for a nice stroll! Open your damn eyes! You good at walking blind? I didn't know you developed your domain already! Less mana more air, dumbass."

Yi growled as the offender adjusted, his features relaxing in surprise.

"Right wheel!" Bai Ping barked.

"Who's a little flame?" Yi growled, the training sergeants circling as they smelled blood, yelling and seeding in corrections to form and to casting at the same time.

Holding out their flames they marched out of the parade square.

"All right! By squads, form up!" Four other squads were pulled out from the sidelines and into formation to repeat the process.

"Don't you let that flame go out, Hendricks!"

Bai Ping marched them through the streets. The staff sergeants ran ahead, blocking the cross streets so the squads could move forward unmolested. Other squads, platoons, and companies were on the move too. The totem flashed every few minutes. Alvans from across the realms returned home.

"Open the gates!" Bai Ping called out.

The gates of the base opened, revealing different stations around the first training square.

"Left wheel!" Bai Ping called out as they snaked along the inside wall.

"Right wheel!" Bai Ping yelled as they turned right. Ahead were several chairs and barbers wielding hair clippers.

"Halt!" The group came to a stop.

"Now time to get you cleaned up! While waiting you will maintain your flame. Since neither I nor the barbers trust you with a flame near anything remotely flammable, you will extinguish your flame when getting your hair cut and reignite it before returning to formation!" Bai Ping made sure his words made it into their skulls. "Good, first eight get in those chairs! Go!"

The first eight rushed the chairs. The barbers used enchanted metal wands that removed all beards, mustaches and fuzz.

Sergeant Yi walked around to the other side.

Buzzers worked rapidly, dropping hair on the ground, leaving the seated recipients with the same haircut. The men all had short hair with fades while the women had their hair cut to their mid-back.

"Use cleaning spells. I want flames in your hands before you're formed up!" Yi yelled.

"When there's a seat free, move to take it! Others are waiting!" Baines yelled.

Quickly, people flowed through the barbers. On the other side they all had the same clothes and appearance.

Bai Ping saw Staff Sergeant Akachi leading in four reserve artillery squads.

"Halt! Once Gunnery Sergeant Bai Ping's people have cleared the barbers, you will be next!" he yelled. Bai Ping moved to the side and Akachi met him to talk away from their charges.

"How you doing, Akachi?"

"Not bad. So, what's the game plan?"

"Get them cleaned up, looking like they belong in the same army. Get their carriers together, run through specific training, then throw your group and mine together to make sure they can work together?"

"Sounds like a plan to me."

Bai Ping checked his watch. "Say we start cross-training in eight hours?"

"Can we call it ten?" Akachi asked.

"Ten works for me. Let me know if you need more."

"Will do." Akachi and Bai Ping turned to face their two groups.

"What do you think of them?" Bai Ping asked.

"Haven't seen them in action yet. Gonna have to shock them back into it. They haven't trained in a long time. Most of them got their position because they did well with math. All of them have completed their basic training, but fewer completed their sharpshooter course."

"Same with mine. Gonna have to squeeze in as much refresher as possible."

"What about if they get hit head-on?" Akachi looked over.

"The mages should have some spells to protect themselves. Want to do a range day to get them checked on their repeaters?"

"Yeah, all of them took defense courses. But it was years ago for some of them. Few have used the repeaters before."

"I'll put in the request for range time, but we only have seventy-two hours with them. We'll have to make every minute count."

"I heard that they want to get all the reserves prepped."

Bai Ping let out a breath through his teeth. "All of Dragon Regiment is back in Vuzgal. We should have all of Tiger back in a few days max. There is what, nearly a division worth of reservists? I hear the plan is to get them all qualified and checked out. Then if we have more time, we teach them and the recruits that are getting processed out of their training. We fill in the training that they don't have."

"With them all on defensive operations, it's a lot easier than training them to fight offensively in the forest." Akachi shrugged.

"Agreed." Bai Ping couldn't help looking at their fresh uniforms. The colors were vibrant. Plus, their shoes were brand new.

"At least we have healing spells for their feet as they break in their boots."

"Would suck if they didn't. We have thirty-five thousand reservists to dress, shave, clothe, and check to make sure they haven't forgotten anything."

"Take us to what, close to fifty thousand under arms? Good thing we didn't throw away the old armor and repeaters." Akachi grinned.

"Yeah, all the old gear is coming out of storage. The City Council is pushing to double the number of factories we have."

Akachi blinked, shaking his head.

"'Til then we're handing out all the old armor we've got and formation medallions so that the reservists can link into the conqueror's armor network. Most will just get the regular helmets with formations to see out of. Our people don't really need them. The rifle companies are getting them though."

"Needs must. How long till they guess the sects will reach Vuzgal?"

"Week and a half if they rush with nothing in their way."

"So, what, three batches of reservists before then?"

"Yeah, two regiments are going to Vuzgal. Two will remain here. Way I hear it, they're going to split us up, one reg force to every three reservists. Going to mix us all together. They fill the bodies; we bring the knowledge."

"Shit! I thought I was done training other people." Akachi rubbed the back of his head.

Bai Ping just grinned.

Blaze stood in his command tent, facing another battlefield with another siege against a different Willful Institute City. The cities changed, the allies changed, but the mission remained the same, as did the self-serving Sects that employed him and his people.

"What do you mean?" Blaze demanded from the Sect messenger.

"Sect Branch head Hoazin, your *employer,* has expressed that he wishes to conserve our strength in light of the current situation."

Sect-speak for slow the attacks so they might get a better position. "We have the advantage. We need to hit them harder. If they have time to recover, build up their defenses, it will take twice the effort to get this far again."

"I am sure that your forces need rest too, Guild Leader. If you are so adamant, then we will have to ask to change your contract," said the messenger, one of the sect branch head's lackeys.

What I'd give to punch your idiot face in. They were just hoping that more of the Willful Institute would be called away to fight Vuzgal so they could save more of their fighters.

Blaze clicked his tongue. Such words would only cause more issues.

"Ah!" Blaze kicked a random box in his tent. "Dammit! The loot, though! What about the loot? You think they're going to keep it all there? As soon as they can, they'll send it away! The longer we wait, the less there will be for us. I bet they'd consume their training resources just to spite us!" Blaze kicked the box again, apparently not paying any attention to the messenger, whose eyes shone with a hidden light. "Fine! I'll do it." Blaze leveled a finger at the messenger. "But I keep the agreed share, even if it has to come from your branch head! It's not my fault he wants to wait and lose this opportunity!"

"I will pass your sentiments on." The messenger bowed and left quickly.

The fire went out of Blaze's body as he sighed. *Fuck, I'm tired of all this positioning bullshit.* He moved to his desk as a new shadow darkened his doorway.

"Heard you might be in here," Elise said.

Blaze stood as his expression melted. She nearly toppled him as she wrapped her hands around his neck and kissed him.

He put his arms around her and kissed her back. A few minutes passed before they came up for air.

"I missed you," she said.

"I can sense that." Blaze grinned. "How long you here for?"

"Not long enough." She kissed him again and released him, pulling on her tunic.

"Business?"

"You know me, babe, business before pleasure." She gave him a sly smirk.

Blaze quirked his lips and nodded.

Elise's smile faded as she pulled out a worn ledger. "I have supplies from Alva. Production has increased to nearly two hundred percent. We're producing faster than we can use it. Running us ragged to purchase supplies."

"How is it in Vuzgal?" Blaze grimaced.

"The United Sect Army is pushing through the woods, day and night. Don't know much more than that."

"And the First Realm?"

"The armies are assembling. Don't know when they'll attack. The outposts are quietly redeploying. All reservists are being issued gear. Everyone was recalled."

"Yeah, I lost some people to the recall."

"How is the guild?"

"Stronger and bigger than ever." Blaze ran his hand through his hair."And constantly fighting. There are a lot that take a few days or weeks off, but most of them come back to the fight. They can't leave their people to fight alone, though, I've been getting reports from Jasper and the rest of the branch heads. Either the sects are attacking more aggressively, or they're pausing, not sure of what to make of the attack on Vuzgal. Scared that the Willful Institute could get support and wash them out."

"Glosil wants to draw their strength to Vuzgal. Clear out the problems in the First Realm in one move, then support the Adventurer's Guild to crack cities. If we can do that, then the Willful Institute's support will dwindle."

"Sounds like a nice plan. Let's see if it works out."

Elise shrugged and pulled out a scroll, handing it to him.

"Yay, more paperwork," Blaze said dryly, opening the scroll.

"Well, if you finish up quickly, maybe you can have a little treat," Elise said with a wink.

Blaze's brain short-circuited, rebuilt itself, speed reading through the scroll without letting anything slip.

He stamped it, rolled it up, and passed it back in record time.

Elise laughed as she took the scroll.

Blaze grabbed her hand and pulled her to him. "Now, where were we five minutes ago?"

25
Silencing Eyes and Ears

Roska looked at the soldiers and police officers gripping their weapons, standing ready inside the empty tavern. She looked through a crack in the wooden shutters. They closed with a gust of wind, then opened wider, giving her a clear view of the warehouse district.

For the past few hours, she and her people had been preparing. Across Vuzgal, police officers backed up by Alvan soldiers were waiting patiently for their targets.

"In position."

Roska heard the last squad leader report in as she took a breath. "Go!"

The doors of the tavern were thrown wide open as the waiting squads rushed out with their weapons at the ready.

"Vuzgal Police! Put your hands up! You're under arrest!"

Stunned traders looked around with wide eyes as police officers and soldiers appeared. They stormed out of abandoned buildings that seemed lifeless a second ago, pouring through the alleyways and roads, surging toward the warehouses. There was not a single gap for the traders or their guards to slip through.

One man tried to draw his sword; several arrows pierced his body, leaving a tombstone as he collapsed.

"Don't try to stop me!" another yelled, pulling an axe from his storage ring. He coughed as arrows slammed home. His eyes went wide as he collapsed.

The police officers reached the first traders and their guards, pushing them to the ground and securing them.

Roska's sound transmission device beeped as the special team members reported in.

"Target Delta secured."

"Target Foxtrot secured."

Across the city they locked down the traders and guards linked to the Elsi family, as well as the spies that were connected to anyone but Vuzgal.

Roska used her sound transmission device to connect to Director Elan. "We have the rats."

"Carry on. Send the spies not affiliated with the groups attacking us through the totem. The rest of them, bring them in for questioning."

Roska looked over the sad group of traders that were hauled before the court.

The court had been sealed off, but there was a lawyer for each talking in the pews leading up to the front bench.

"Good hunt?" Storbon said, sitting down beside her.

"Not too much of a problem. You?"

"Smoothly enough, just supporting the Close Protection Details."

The judge used a gavel to bring quiet to the room.

"Jonas Elsi, you have been charged with smuggling, illicit gathering and selling of information, and conspiracy to harm Vuzgal. Please go through the information." The judge waved forward a police officer who spoke about meetings, timings, and the contents of them, listing the items that were smuggled in and out of Vuzgal.

Jonas Elsi paled. "I'm an Elsi. There's no way!"

The judge leveled her gavel with him and the silence spell returned peace. "If you cannot be civil in my court, I will keep you quiet to save us all a headache and wasted time." She removed the spell and looked at the information in front of her.

"In this case, I think that the verdict is rather clear. You will serve a sentence of fifteen years under contract. Take him away."

"Do you know who my grandfather is? He will have all your heads!"

The judge hit him with another silence spell. "Yes, we do, even if you changed your name, Mister Elsi." The judge raised an eyebrow as Jonas's wriggling stopped and the police officers pulled him away.

And so it went, through the ranks of traders and others that created information networks throughout Vuzgal.

"What happened with the other groups?" Roska said.

"Got a quiet chat from the Close Protection Details or a message to do their actual jobs and to keep their lips sealed, or to take a long vacation and not come back," Storbon said.

"Smart. I think we have enough enemies as it is. I don't know how Elan keeps it all straight."

"Well, unless you want to watch this all day, beer?"

"Oh, that sounds like a good plan. Beer it is."

The duo left the courtroom as the judge listened to the next case's prosecution and defense present their arguments.

Klaus stood at the top of his Fighter's Association's building, watching Vuzgal.

He sighed and looked around the Association's Circle. The other buildings stood proud and unyielding. Their gates closed as guards patrolled their grounds, mana barriers protecting them from the outside world.

A messenger ran up on the roof.

"What did Lord Chonglu say?" Klaus turned.

"He read the letter and burned it. He said that he did not have time for the Associations until the Willful Institute was crushed."

Klaus sighed and shook his head. "He's still too young." Chonglu could escape with his family and Mira. The blame would fall upon the associations rather than him. What made these Vuzgalians so damn loyal to Erik and Rugrat?

He thought of the weeks he had spent training the duo. His lips were sealed from telling anyone about their abilities and strength.

They were powerful enough to bring many to their side. *But they are just two people.* They must have consumed all the resources that Vuzgal had to spare to get as strong as they were. The Willful Institute had fighters that were as strong as they were. Even if they defeated someone of the Seventh Realm, could they fight ten of them together? A hundred?

Klaus looked up at the skies. Odd aerial beasts flew out in every direction, covered in wooden armor.

"How is the evacuation going?" Klaus asked the messenger, his eyes looking over the city.

"All family members and non-essential members have pulled back to other locations."

"What's the situation at the totem?"

"People are fleeing as fast as they can. The Vuzgal leadership is not stopping them, though, they do warn that all land that is left unattended for more than one month will be repossessed by the city, and they are not liable for damages."

"They make it sound as if they can hold back an army of hundreds of thousands with only a few thousand people." A sad and tired smile spread across Klaus' face. "They would have made fine members."

"Sir, the military and police conducted lightning raids across the city last night. They targeted traders and their guards. Most of them around the warehouse district."

"The trader community has a long memory. If they attack traders now, that could work against them. Turn the traders against Vuzgal." Klaus frowned. "What is happening, and why am I only hearing about this now?"

"They struck without warning in the middle of the night. We didn't discover anything was wrong until it was announced by the Vuzgal Police." The aide took a breath. "They took out all the spies and informants within the city, too. They questioned them last night and have been dumping them at the totem. Spies of the attacking sects were sentenced. Several were executed, others banished."

"Just what is happening? They have been so quiet, meek even, not leaving their city walls. Is this really the Vuzgal we know?"

"The news is causing more people to leave *en masse*. Vuzgal announced that they will stop people from leaving tomorrow morning. Everyone is fleeing while they can."

"They must have a reason for attacking the traders, or else they've just killed themselves no matter what. What are they thinking?" Klaus frowned, looking at the central tower that stuck up in the middle of Vuzgal. *Why do I feel like I have been blind for too long?*

Early morning light fell on Alva as the members of Dragon Regiment organized into squads, talking to one another in low tones, checking their gear and trying to fill the remaining time.

They held their heavy repeaters with comfortable ease. Weapons of war had become as familiar as a farmer's shovel. Their carriers and gear showed signs of wear and tear. Frayed scars marked some carriers, faded camouflage from having to scour the dirt out.

"Move into formation!" Lieutenant Colonel Zukal called out.

The groups pulled their helmets on, closing them off from the outside world, moving into position with the lazy competence of veterans.

Domonos walked out into the training square. They had cleared out all the spies two days ago and locked down the totem and communications the day before. Only Alvans could communicate or travel freely. Now, just like in the beginning, Vuzgal had only Alvans and the associations within its walls. *How things have come full circle.*

He looked at the men and women under his command. When they had defended Vuzgal, there were only one hundred of them. Now, there are nearly ten thousand in Vuzgal alone.

He picked out familiar faces among the ranks. "I heard that some bastards want to take what's ours," Domonos said. "I think that it's time we educated them on what happens when they attack our lands, our homes, and our people." He felt his anger in each word, and saw it reflected in his soldiers as they stood taller, set their shoulders, and gripped their weapons tighter.

"Let's rejoin the rest of the regiment. To Vuzgal! Turn to the right!"

They moved as one, drill turned instinct.

"March!"

Those at the front led, not needing any guidance as they headed out of the Alva training center.

The gates opened for them and Domonos saw Commander Glosil outside, waiting for them to pass.

"Dragon Regiment, eyes right!" Domonos and the other officers saluted Commander Glosil, who held the salute as they passed through the gates.

"First Battalion, Alpha Company, eyes forward!" The group through the gates snapped their eyes forward. Their feet fell at the same time, born of ingrained training and a deep desire to not trip up the person ahead or behind.

"First Battalion, Bravo Company, eyes forward!" The second group passed through.

Domonos caught Glosil's eyes and nodded. *I'll do my duty. I'll bring back as many as I can. Alive or dead, I will leave none of them on the field.*

He passed the gate and looked forward. Two thousand members of the Dragon Regiment snaked through to the totem.

Domonos felt a deep sense of pride, of anticipation mixed with fear and determination. It was *his* regiment and *his* city. He had been entrusted with both. Any bastard who thought they could take Vuzgal would have to walk over the entire Dragon Regiment to do so. *Bring it on, motherfuckers.*

26 Handover

Domonos blinked as the light of the totem dissipated. He marched forward with the rest of his people. The gates opened, allowing the Dragon Regiment to return home. Family members and other Alvans cheered. The totem flashed again as another part of the regiment arrived.

Domonos saw a familiar face in the crowd. His brother's armor stood out among everyone else.

Father and sister as well. Domonos held his smile and nodded in their direction.

The regiment separated into battalions, each heading to their own training grounds. The whole city was quieter, subdued. Carriages were infrequent and only heading in one direction: out of the city. People had gathered their belongings and fled to safer areas. His face hardened. Soon, this would become another battleground, and they would fight for every damn inch of it.

This was their city; they had spent blood to gain and hold it. They had poured out resources and time, turning it into a city that filled him with pride.

They marched through the gates into one of the military compounds. Several units stood off to the side, waiting for them.

"Halt!" Domonos called out, and everyone snapped their feet down.

"Left turn!"

They all turned to face him as he faced them.

"Dragon Regiment, Second Battalion, Fourth Company, you are released until fifteen hundred this afternoon. Dis-missed!" Domonos signaled their release.

They all turned to the right, walking three paces before they dispersed, meeting up with their friends and heading out to see families they hadn't seen in weeks or months.

How the hell…?

Elan and Domonos' siblings walked out of the depths of the training center. Domonos smiled. Qin grinned and hugged him, moving aside. His father patted him on the back. Yui stretched out a hand and Domonos took it. The two brothers pulled one another into a big hug.

"Good to have you back! Don't worry. I think I only annoyed them a little with all the drills," Yui said as they released one another.

"Well, we can either go to the command center to do our debrief, or I hear that the Sky Reaching Restaurant has a new Peking Duck recipe," Elan said.

"Uhh." Domonos turned, as if to ask if it was really a question.

"Sky Reaching Restaurant, of course. You go there so much, you're going to need to watch your waistline, Dad." Qin poked him.

"Hey," he muttered, drawing himself up straight, smiling and rubbing where she'd poked him.

"Not the normal family greeting," Yui said.

"We're not exactly a normal family," Qin shot back.

"What she said," Domonos agreed. "Though seriously, Yui, how have things been?"

"I've had the recruits completing full readiness checks, including all of the pre-set locations in the forests. They were using teleportation formations, so there shouldn't be any way for the Institute or the Elsi Clan to get any information."

"How did they do?"

"Four set-ups and take-downs at two locations a day for each platoon. They got quick, taking five minutes on set-up and three on tear-down. Room for improvement, for sure. With the readiness tests in the bunkers, full readiness in two minutes."

"Now that we don't have anyone around, we'll get them to set new firing positions. Do we know what routes the enemy intends to use? Father?"

"Nothing yet, our spies have got several clues but no specifics, we do know they are using local guides."

"Have their numbers increased?"

"Yes, another fifty thousand have joined them, bringing their numbers up to around three hundred thousand. Their leader is Marco Tolentino, cousin to Nico. He is a powerful cultivator and fighter in his own right. Marco excels not just at training but in tactical fighting. He has captured five cities. Three as a fighter, two as a commander. He learned how to fight as a child and went to war when he became a teenager."

"He's not the only one, Father," Yui said.

Domonos nodded in thanks. "It's good to know your enemy. He's dedicated and has experience. He also has backing and a lot of people. In assaulting a city, you have a few things you can use to tilt things in your favor. Have more people, have more long-range weapons, have more food and water. If you can, get better people, better weapons, and better food."

"Why's that?" Qin asked.

"With more people, you can charge into the enemy, absorbing the deaths to reach them. With more weapons, you can cover the enemy's barriers, stopping them from seeing or breaking their mana barrier. If you crack the enemy's mana barriers, they're naked before your weapons. If you have more food and water, you hole up and wait, starving the enemy out. Let them get desperate. If you have better items, you can speed things up."

"Can't you use tactics?" Qin asked.

"Yes, you can use combinations of all three to tilt the situation to your advantage, though tactics are about positioning, timing and information."

"Come on, let's get something to eat and we can talk about something not so grim," Yui said. He led them into the city and to the largest Sky Reaching Restaurant in Vuzgal.

"A lot of people have gone into hiding, but there's enough staff to keep the restaurants open. For today, all meals are free for military members." Yui grinned.

"I taught you well." Elan laughed.

Domonos and Qin smiled as they were guided to a table.

"When do you head back to Alva?" Domonos asked Qin.

"Why would I do that? You need crafters, metal workers, and formation masters here."

"Qin," Domonos started, looking to his brother and father for support.

"Brother." She stopped him with a fierce light in her eyes. "I might be your younger sister, but I am no less an Alvan than you. I know what will happen. You'll need formation masters to create bombs and mortar shells, to repair damaged formations if needed. Vuzgal has nearly as many formations as Alva. I helped design many of them, or my students did. You need me here, and that is it. If there are any signs of trouble, I will take a teleportation formation out of the city to one of our backup locations. This I swear."

Qin went back to eating the snacks that had been brought out.

Domonos choked out a laugh, sharing a look with his father and brother.

"Once Qin Silaz has a goal in mind, there's nothing we can do to stop her." Domonos' voice softened.

"It really has been a long time since then," Yui recalled.

"Maybe to you all," Elan reprimanded, mock serious. "It has been the best years of my life, for sure. You have all grown up so quickly in your different areas. Some of them closer than others."

He looked at Domonos and Yui with an amused smile and drank from his cup, letting out a refreshing breath.

"You have truly soared." Domonos rubbed the bridge of his nose, feeling awkward.

"Dad," Qin said, and hugged him from the side.

Elan laughed and stroked her head.

"My daughter healed! My son returned to me! My family given great opportunities in a land that doesn't wish to enslave, but supports us. Wren has expanded the trading company across three realms. Erik and Rugrat would have gained my loyalty for any of these things, though they have done all of this and more without asking for any kind of compensation other than to defend the land we created together."

Elan's eyes grew wet as he looked out at Vuzgal. "If only your mother could see you now."

He stared at Yui and Domonos with tears brimming in his eyes; the fierce intelligence director of Alva's lips trembled with bittersweet loss and pride.

He pulled himself under control and patted Qin's head once again. "She would be so proud of you all."

His shaky whisper created heat deep within Domonos' chest as his nose flared and he swallowed to hold in the tears.

Yui looked over his people from the Tiger Regiment. Now that the Dragon Regiment had returned, he and most of his Tiger Regiment would move to Alva to support the work-up training for the reservists and others that would be supporting them in the coming fighting.

He spotted Domonos walking toward him.

"Came to say goodbye?" Yui asked with a smile.

"To apologize. Commander Glosil sent me to fight alongside the Adventurer's Guild and now I'm taking command away from you again."

"Domonos, I'm not angry, nor do I think that you're trying to steal being on the front lines from me. It doesn't matter who leads the fight. What matters is that they are the best person for the job. You know Vuzgal like the back of your hand. If you hadn't fought the Willful Institute with the Adventurer's Guild, it would have been a big hit to your confidence. Alva needs confident commanders. You needed to fight them to prove to yourself that you could. You gained firsthand knowledge of the enemy, their tactics; it bloodied our troops. Now going into battle is no longer a worry. You are focused on the job, not on just the enemy."

"Shit, when did you get so mature?"

"You're my brother. I know how you think. After you got nearly killed by them and healed up, you've been holding a grudge. Fighting them got your confidence back and you're a better leader for it. You are the best person for this fight. If you need support from me and the Tiger Regiment, we'll be there."

"And my Dragon Regiment will be there for you."

They hugged and patted one another's backs.

"You've got some good people! I think you poached them all from my regiment!" Yui grinned and walked out in front of his regiment. "All right, you lazy bastards! I hope you enjoy training because it's up to us to get the reserves into fighting condition! Atten-tion!"

Soldiers snapped to attention, rank upon rank.

"Forward, March!"

Tiger Regiment headed out from different bases and training centers, heading through the totem back to Alva, unseen by scrying spells, tamed beasts and even the association's eyes hidden under the city itself.

Good luck, brother, Yui thought as the light of the totem swallowed him.

27
Starting Positions

"What the hell are we doing out here?" one of the artillery corporals complained.

"What we're doing, Corporal—" Acosta's tone dropped. "—is checking and sighting our guns along the southern artillery positions. You see, the Silaz family are a paranoid bunch no matter what branch they're in. There are pre-set artillery positions through the forests and we're going to check they haven't been messed with, and that they're free of debris and ready for us to use."

There was a whistle up ahead.

"Not everything we do is just for fun, Corporal," she finished off and headed up to the front on her mount.

"What you got, Jakovac?"

"Found it. Just up ahead."

"Lead on."

They rode ahead of the main group. The ground kept rising, reaching a grassy knoll covered in weeds, bushes, and trees. In the middle, nearly hidden in the thick bushes, a boulder peeked out.

Acosta checked her map again and reached out her hand. "Let's clear it up, shall we? Plant Command."

Bushes and vines pulled back, revealing pre-made mortar pits and bunkers underneath.

"Bring it in!" Acosta said as the new artillery personnel and mages looked around the forest.

"These locations have been covered in different ways to hide them from passersby." Acosta got off her mount and dropped into a mortar pit. Her people fanned out, clearing out the brush and debris that had fallen in the hardened dirt pits.

Acosta squinted, spotting rocks out away from the knoll to site the mortars off of. With that done, they just needed to consult the pre-made range cards. They would be ready to fire just as soon as they had set everything up.

She climbed out of the pit and walked to the central boulder that reached her hip. "Clean."

Her spell removed the mud and dirt off the stone, revealing markings.

"Your squad leaders all have range cards. We're going to go through setting up and tearing down. Back up to the entrance. You've all trained in this. It is a core skill. You must move in, ready your mortar, and be ready to fire within minutes or less. These tactics held back the Blood Demon Sect and we will use it constantly to fight the Willful Institute and the sect bastards they brought with them!"

Acosta checked they were at the entrance of the opening.

She glanced at her watch. "Go!"

The first squad went around counterclockwise to the position at nine o'clock, with the other squads filling into the positions behind, from the nine o'clock to twelve o'clock, three, six, and linking up to nine o'clock.

Mortars were pointed forward and checked with sights against the different markers as Acosta moved her mount around, watching them all and taking mental notes.

"Everyone's here," Lieutenant Colonel Zukal said into Domonos' ear as Major Kanoa walked into the Vuzgal command center.

Colonel Domonos looked up from the map showing the terrain around Vuzgal. He nodded to Kanoa and cleared his throat. "All right, gather around."

The officers quietened, ringing around him and the map.

"The enemy is coming for us from every direction. We have them moving up the roads in the east and west." He used a map pointer to circle the markers that were updating, crawling forward at the edge of the map on either side. "Everything in Vuzgal Valley is covered by sensing formations, and we're getting real-time information on their movements. In the north,— "Domonos circled the mountain range "—the south, east, and west."

He circled either side of Vuzgal and looked at the officers around the table. "That's where we're expecting the enemy to appear, and it's a blind spot. Once the enemy enters the valley, they have a four-day march to Vuzgal. Lieutenant Lei, what do the mana barriers need to have the greatest effect?" he asked, testing the newly minted officer.

"Heat dissipation, access to mana stones, centrally located, even, clear terrain."

Domonos nodded. "Very good, Lieutenant. Key part for us is even, clear terrain." He circled the lines of advance. "None of those mountain passes offers even and clear terrain. They'll be pressed together in close quarters. Hell, once they get into the valley, they'll have to cross through the damn forest. Even if they have mana barriers, there are going to be openings. What do mortars need to know when hitting the enemy? First Lieutenant Cardoso?"

"Where the enemy is."

"Bingo! Without the formations to reveal their position, we're going to have to go old school. Maps and the Mark One eyeball. The recon flights will spot the enemy, find out which passes they're using. Sharpshooter squads, dropped off by Kestrel flights, will observe the enemy and call-in mortar fire. We'll create a network of eyes watching every pass coming into the valley, extending the ground we control and observe. Now, there are going to be locations where we can't get our mortars into position to hit a target. Those targets will be yours, Major Kanoa."

"Sir." Kanoa tilted his head to the side. "The sparrows and kestrels are fitted for close air support and bombing runs. We might not be able to hit the enemy with mortars, but they can't escape the skies. I want them to come in dumb and happy. We get our people into position and hit the enemy all in one go. We use the element of surprise and hit them with mortars and bombs before they raise their mana barriers."

"Sir." First Lieutenant Cardoso raised a hand. Domonos nodded to him. "We're going to be spread thin."

"Yes, we're putting our strength in the essential places. All medics, engineers and CPD units have mortar and mage training, and we can borrow mortars from Alva. Scout squads will be broken down into teams of two. Rifle squads will act as support for the artillery platoons unless we need more scouts. Then they'll get a crash course on spotting and be pushed out as well."

The Alvan's dedication to cross training meant they could quickly switch from one role to another with minimal issues.

Kanoa held up a fist.

"Major?" Domonos asked.

"To cover that much ground and have downtime for the birds, I'll have to move my sparrow fighters in pairs. Then group them together again into their complete eight person wings before they can strike. I only have twelve Sparrow wings and twelve Kestrel Wings under my command here."

"I intend to use your sparrows to drop fast and quick, come in low to rake the enemy in open ground where they have a greater chance to counterattack. In tight quarters where our mortars can't reach, I hope to employ your kestrels. Your air force will play a vital role in the coming fight. Also, the spotters will not be just looking for the enemy. We will be using the new spell trap dispersal mortars." Domonos looked at Zukal. "Do you want to talk about them? You know more about them than me."

"Sure."

Zukal stepped forward. "The spell trap dispersal shells are just what they sound like. Fired from a mortar, these shells explode in mid air, releasing spell trap formations over a one-hundred-meter area. We can use them ahead of the enemy and cover a lot of ground. While their mana barriers can cover the sky, the trap formations will be under their feet. They get within range, the formation activates just like any other spell trap formation.

"We know where they're coming from. Our people are surveying the land and laying in some surprises. They'll wait for the main body to arrive and act as spotters, call in fire, guiding it onto the sects."

The lieutenants looked at the map, and to Colonel Domonos.

"Organize your people and coordinate with the air force. Use teleportation pads and personal mounts where possible, kestrels where it's not possible. Make sure they have exfil plans. We're going to need them back here. Once the enemy is in the valley, our artillery platoons can hit them without needing spotters. Kestrels will be used to leapfrog the artillery units to pre-set firing positions. Sparrows will do strafing and bombing runs continuously. They're going to have to move through the treeline. We'll hammer them the entire way, just as we did against the Blood Demon Sect! Defense in depth with overlapping devastating mortar fire and spell traps!"

Major Hall raised his hand. "They're going to find our spell traps, though. It was only the explosives they couldn't find. They thought that they were spells when it was actually chemicals."

"Once they catch on, we won't have to use as many. If we throw down one or two random shells of spell traps, won't they need to move slower to make sure they find all the spell traps?" Domonos asked.

Hall pressed his lips together.

Even if there were no spell traps, how would they know? It would weaken them initially and slow them from then on. *Devious.* Kanoa looked at the officers around the table. A shiver ran through his body and the hairs on the back of his neck raised. At one time, he had looked down on these men, believing them to be immature and playing at being soldiers. *They learned the hard way.*

Kanoa mentally chastised himself. They were all Alvans now. *No matter where we started.*

Domonos kept talking. "If the enemy runs forward without caring about them, then we sow them as dense as the fields on the Earth Floor."

Major Choi raised his hand. "The road?"

Domonos smiled and stood upright. "Well, Major Choi, you were here when the Blood Demon Sect came knocking. We're just gonna go big with it." Domonos turned to the others. "For those of you that don't know, we have pre-sighted artillery positions covering every inch of the Eastern and Western roads." Domonos pointed out the positions. "Spell traps and explosives lay ready under the ground. What's worse than being at the edge of a minefield? Being right in the middle of one."

He tapped farther down the west road, ahead of the red mass heading for Vuzgal, and swept forward. "We'll let them advance into the minefield. When we hit the other locations, we'll switch it on and hammer the piss out of them with artillery. If they want to go backward, they're welcome to activate every damn trap we've laid." Domonos turned to the men as he gave his orders. "Major Choi, you get the roads. Major Mitchell, you're in charge of the south. Hall, you have the north. Major Moretti, you will be running support here in Vuzgal."

The majors nodded.

"Kanoa, you will be in support under my direct command. Your people may be seconded to other units as needed."

"Sir."

Domonos looked at Roska. "Special Team Two will support artillery in the north and south. Special Team Three will remain here to protect Rugrat. I'm told that he will wake up soon. I know he won't want to miss this fight."

Roska smiled.

"All right, I want the first group of spotters heading out before it gets dark. There are fifty thousand coming down each road, so there must be another two hundred thousand moving through the mountain passes. I want to know where every last one of them is."

Corporal Nicholas Landrith stifled a yawn as he and the rest of his team waited, their Kestrel coming to land on the pad in front of them.

"I heard that other special teams were taking teleportation formations," Private Zhan Kun said.

"That's just for the locations that you can access with teleportation formations," Landrith said.

"Great, up a fucking mountain. I was wondering why they told us to check our cold-weather gear."

"You bitching again, Zhan?" Sergeant Cao asked, returning from his talk with the other scout squad sergeants.

"Why couldn't we take the teleportation formations?"

"I see that's a yes, and because we're the best spotters they have. We've done cross-training with the artillery platoons so recently that you haven't even forgotten it all!" Cao's presence brought the rest of the squad over. "We're heading out soon. Everyone has two weeks of food and water, right?"

They held up their arms in agreement.

"Good! We'll recon different spots and drop off pairs at the best locations we can find that you can exfil on your own. You all remember your mission brief?"

"Watch for the enemy. Confirm enemy routes. Emplace traps. Call in mortar fire on the enemy once given the command!" They repeated together, a mix of boredom and drudgery filling each word.

"Good, I'm so happy to know you're excited and focused," Cao crowed in mock-joy.

"Ready to load!" The kestrel's rear ramp gunner called out to them, standing to the side of the ramp.

The first squad moved, heading for the ramp.

"Come on!" Cao was serious as he pulled on his helmet and followed the first group. Two other squads followed as they ran into the kestrel's cabin, grabbing onto the handholds above.

The ramp gunner was the last in. He tapped a formation. The ramp grew back into place as the tree arm supporting his repeater swung back. "Good to go, Chief!"

"Got it. Hold on to your lunches; they're firing up the launch formation."

"He knows it's not even morning yet, right?" Zhan said.

"Zhan, buddy, shut up," Basheer said as she got comfortable and closed her eyes.

Zhan grimaced, but shut up.

Landrith looped his fingers under his vest and leaned against the cabin's side, looking at the rear gunner, who was making sure his repeater could move side to side, up and down.

The two side door gunners were hooked into their harnesses. One passed a packet of herbs to the other.

Some things were the same the world over. At least this chew was just to increase stamina and wake people up. Hell, they were using birds to imitate fighter jets and Chinooks.

Landrith wasn't from the Ten Realms, but an Earther who had been about to finish his final accounting exams when he contracted the Two-Week Curse and appeared in the First Realm. Now he was heading off into some mountains to call in artillery on the sorry bastards who wanted to kill their people and take their land. *Feels like some medieval magi-tech screwed-up world. Shit, I sound like Zhan now.*

The kestrel extended her wings. The formations underneath powered up, pushing them slowly into the air. The kestrel added her own strength as they rapidly ascended. The kestrel flew out of the formation's area of effect, picking up speed and altitude.

Landrith looked out over the rear of the cabin. Other squads were still loading up on their kestrels. Formations were lighting up, pushing the first loaded Kestrels up into the air.

One of the door gunners talked into Cao's ear against the wind.

Cao stood up and grabbed the handholds, using them to walk toward the cockpit to where the other squad's sergeant was sitting.

Hope you find the bastards and make it easier for me.

Landrith closed his eyes and tucked his chin into his vest.

He must've fallen asleep as he felt the bird jolt.

"First two prepare for drop off!" Cao's voice came through all their sound transmission devices.

The ramp gunner hit the formation, causing the ramp to regrow and swinging his gun to the side.

"We won't be touching down. Cliff is too steep! One minute!"

Landrith was next to the door gunner. He looked out into the cold wind; mountain ranges stretched ahead of him. It was an impressive sight of nature, stone and land that had turned into waves, crashing into one another, and ascending into the heavens.

He pulled his cold-weather gear tighter against the wet wind. They were closing in on the side of a mountain. The first two scouts stood up and were ready at the ramp. The gunners watched for threats.

The kestrel turned and beat her wings, slowing their speed and bringing them to a hover in mid-air with the ramp just feet from the ground.

Landrith let out a snort. "Shit, that is some piloting and flying." He patted the cabin.

"Move it!" Cao yelled.

The two scouts ran off the ramp and jumped onto the cliff that would be their temporary home.

One held his repeater up in his hands.

"We're clear," Cao said. The kestrel left the cliff and climbed again, looking for another perch to drop more scouts on.

28 Artillery Moves

Rugrat felt the mana thrumming throughout his chest and his body. His mana core had graduated upward into his left chest cavity, transforming into a second heart, a mana heart.

The mana within his veins had condensed into liquid. His mana veins became perfected, interweaving and interlinking with his circulatory system. One would not be wrong in saying he was a man with two hearts, two sets of lungs, and two circulatory systems. His mana gates drew in mana from the surroundings, much like lungs drew in air.

He moved his hands. Controlling mana was like moving a muscle he hadn't used in a long time or didn't know it existed. Before it was like waving his hands in the air and expecting to make ripples in the water.

The surrounding formations dimmed as the mana gathering formations pulled it down into Vuzgal.

Rugrat unlocked the pod, and the formations powered down as he rotated forward. The front of the pod opened as two medics helped him out.

"Situation?" he rasped, his throat painfully dry.

A medic fed him water as Tanya passed him an information book. Rugrat opened it and drew in the information contained inside. He staggered with the overload and forced himself upright. A medic readied a needle.

"Hold off. You can use that on others." Rugrat staggered to the tray where his gear was kept. He used a clean spell and grabbed his storage ring, pulling out a tube. He tore it open and poured the wet oatmeal textured food into his mouth, swallowing it as he quickly started to recover.

"Qin?"

"Qin is helping to manufacture more bombs," Tanya said.

"You have more important things to do than watch me put my pants on," Rugrat said as he grabbed his clothes.

"Yes, sir." Tanya looked at the rest of the people in the room. They quickly left, heading up to Vuzgal.

Rugrat got dressed, finishing four more of the high calorie stamina recovery tubes.

"Kind of like applesauce, or baby food. So much better than Chicken-ala-king," Rugrat said to Han Wu and his half special team that was waiting there.

"What's the plan, boss?"

Rugrat checked his time piece. "Scouts are already deployed; artillery is preparing to move. Roska is supporting them already. See if she wants to take the north. We'll take the south and support Arty."

"Can ask," Han Wu said.

Han Wu used his sound transmission device as Rugrat checked his map. Scout squads had created a ring around Vuzgal Valley, covering the north and south. The artillery platoons and support-platoons- turned-artillery platoons were set to leave in the afternoon.

There were still a few hours to go. Rugrat checked the map. *Good plan.* The sensing formations didn't reach that far, but their mortars would—guided in by the sharpshooter's coordinates.

Han Wu finished on the sound transmission device. "They say we're good."

"Sweet. When do we step off?"

"Four hours. Colonel Domonos wants to meet you at the second airfield."

Rugrat's mana radiated through his entire body, power beating in his very cells. His veins glowed with power as he looked at Han Wu. "Sounds good to me. Hell, I wonder just how powerfully I could enhance a mortar shell."

The eyes of the others darkened as they circulated their own mana, feeling the power that had laid dormant, ready, waiting, and wishing to be freed.

Rugrat was looking out of the window at the waiting kestrels as the door opened. Domonos walked in and saluted.

"Am I supposed to salute you, or vice versa?" Rugrat asked, returning the salute and reaching out his hand.

"Hell if I know." Domonos shrugged as he shook Rugrat's hand.

"You're in charge of Vuzgal. I'm just your backup. Good to see you back home."

"Thanks." Domonos smiled and sighed. "You really want to go out there?"

"Sure. You have Roska's team support to the north. Special Team Three and I will go to the south."

"All right, then I have one more request."

"What is it?" Rugrat looped his fingers into his belt, waiting for the other shoe to drop.

"Speech."

"Huh?"

"Talk to the troops. They're going into a fight that's going to be nasty as hell. Hearing from you might boost their morale."

Rugrat sighed. "All right, for fear of saving them from some damn general that talks for three fucking hours. I'll do it."

"Good, let's go," Domonos said.

"Great."

Rugrat followed him. They reached a balcony overlooking artillery platoons that were ready to board kestrels. Others checked gear and ammunition, preparing to leave after them.

They must be the support platoons.

"Form up!" Officers called their platoons into position facing Rugrat.

Other officers were waiting for him and Domonos at the balcony. They had set up a sound transmission formation.

"Once this is activated, it will broadcast to all Alva military sound transmission devices. Even the scouts in the field and recon flights will hear you," a lieutenant said. Behind him, the groups were moving through drills.

"What about the Associations?" Rugrat asked.

"We sweep the bases constantly and there are formations that stop any noise from leaving. They're all active."

Rugrat nodded. The platoons settled in the at ease position with their repeaters. Their legs spread out at shoulder width as they pushed their repeater out with one arm and held the other down at their side, their eyes locked on the balcony.

Domonos stepped up to the sound transmission device. "Attention all members of the Alva Military! Lord Rugrat, who will be joining you in the field, has a few words he wants to say."

Domonos turned to Rugrat.

Thanks for the lead up!

Rugrat exhaled through his nose, looking at the ranks of soldiers. "Today I stand here among fellow Alvans. All of us have come from somewhere else and *chose* to become Alvans. The Alvan Nation was nothing more than a village when we started. Now, we control a kingdom, a city state, and too many fucking dungeons to count. Seriously, I think Erik went a little nuts with that."

The soldiers grinned and laughed as Rugrat became serious once again.

"Alvans took Vuzgal with their very blood. We defended it when it was nothing but broken walls. Since then, your families, your friends, and your fellow Alvans have put their determination, sweat and lives into Vuzgal, building it into the proud city you see before you. Vuzgal is ours by blood, and if those sects think that they can take it from us, they don't know a fucking thing! You have gathered your mana, endured and tempered your bodies as your leaders have trained your minds and ingrained into you the skills you need."

Rugrat paused, hearing repeater butts hit the ground. Pride burned in his chest as he gritted his teeth, stabbing his finger out at them. "*You* are Vuzgal's wall. You are Alva's sword. You are the mother fucking Alva Military!"

Roars and yells came from across the defenses, across the bases.

"We do not fight for riches; we fight for our people! We do not train for our own gain; we train to lift up one another! Trust in yourselves, trust in Alva, trust in one another! And kill the bastards that want to kill your brothers and sisters on either side!"

Repeaters slammed into the ground again. The military yelled out, building into a chant.

"Al-va, Al-va, Alva, Alva!"

Rugrat joined in and smacked his chest, the noise ringing out across Vuzgal.

"Shoulder arms!" His Marine drill instructor voice *rocked* Vuzgal as his body glowed with mana. Each and every soldier's cultivation was pumping out, distorting the mana in the air.

Repeaters snapped up into the ready position.

"To your *duties!* Dis-missed!"

Those ready turned to their right, slamming their feet into the reinforced stone ground so hard it cracked in places.

They marched off as a single being. Soldiers headed into the depths to take teleportation formations to the forward artillery positions or headed to the air force strips to board kestrels.

"Move it!" The Artillery Platoon's Second Lieutenant Couto yelled as everyone streamed out the rear of the kestrel.

Rugrat and Special Team Three ran down the kestrel's ramp into the forest as the platoon broke into individual squads and spread out to get ready for the second part of their journey.

"I remember the first time we did this all," Rugrat recalled.

"Yeah, I do too. Han Wu was practically humping your leg to find out more about explosives," Gong Jin said as he got on his mount.

"It was strange," Rugrat agreed.

"Then he blew up half the damn road to Vuzgal. He learned fast." Gong Jin laughed.

"The bigger the explosion, the better."

Gong Jin scoffed. "Rednecks."

"Heh." Rugrat half-shrugged and grinned as he whistled.

George shot out of the sky, expanding into his full size as Rugrat jumped on his back.

"First Mages Squad, move out!" Second Lieutenant Couto ordered.

The platoon shook out as the mages led the way, using tree moving spells to clear a path.

"Seems almost peaceful," Simms said, riding with the ease of someone that had done it most of his life. His eyes scanned the right side.

"What, other than the people rushing toward us to kill us?" Tyrone asked, looking over the left side.

"Well, that's just part of the job," Gong Jin said.

"Everything is nice and peaceful until it isn't. Peace and chaos." Rugrat snapped his fingers. "Just that close to one another."

"Like hurrying up and waiting?" Gong Jin asked.

"Smart ass. Aren't you supposed to be a team leader?" Rugrat laughed.

"Some days."

"Halt!" an officer called out as the convoy came to a stop. Mages dismounted and used their spells. They stood on top of a large hill that commanded views over the mountain ranges in front. The remote hill was only reachable through flight.

Spells pulled back the vegetation covering the hill, naturally and purposefully placed. The remote and wild hill turned into a series of mortar pits and interlocking trenches.

"Shit, these are a bit big," Rugrat said.

"These are newer, built to not only house mortars, but the new artillery cannons," Tyrone said excitedly.

"Too much time around explosives." Gong Jin sighed. The squads set to work clearing out the pits and preparing ammunition.

"Let's work on the most important stuff—rooms," Gong Jin said.

They moved away from the guns.

Rugrat jumped into a trench and reached his hands out to the side. As he walked forward, the plants moved, revealing trenches.

He stopped at the plots where the first squad would be staying. "I've got this one. Just want to test out my limits."

"All right, Tyrone, Simms, watch him. Rest of you come with me." Gong Jin walked off.

Rugrat increased the trench width. Compressing the dirt made it nearly as hard as stone, but porous enough to take water. He turned to face the cleared ground, creating three ten-by-twenty-meter outlines.

He reached out with his domain into the ground, and felt through the dirt, deep into the ground. *Those streams will be useful.*

He looked deeper into the ground, passing through dirt into the stone of the hill.

He fused the stone together, checking the clear patches of ground above ground.

"Up you come."

Twelve stone pillars as thick as a tree shot up through the rubble and the dirt.

Rugrat stopped ten meters below the surface; stone spread out between the pillars, creating a fifteen-centimeter hyper-compressed slab of stone as strong as iron.

He pushed it up on the pillars, causing the dirt above to mound over.

In the space underneath, Rugrat created walls with compressed stone A-frames. Compressed soil created a door and stairs leading down.

The stone walls of the bunkers appeared. Rugrat compressed the dirt in bands to disperse the kinetic forces and cover.

He stopped raising the three rooms and formed the floor. "Let's check it out, shall we?"

Rugrat went to the first of the bunkers. He conjured mana blades to cut through the stone. They turned into hands pushing the slab in, grabbing it before it fell.

Rugrat took out light formations and stuck them to the ceiling. He saw the simple grey-flecked room he'd created.

"Need to make a bathroom; pull that wall out a bit. Have the showers in the right, shitters in the left."

The wall on the right grew out, creating a dividing wall as the entrance section flew opposite, fusing with the floor and wall before growing into another dividing wall.

"Stalls, and more drains. Connect them to the wastewater chute and stream."

The walls and pipes grew unseen.

Rugrat checked the field showers. They had holes in the wall and drains.

The bathrooms were a series of holes in the ground leading into the unknown.

"Simple, but effective. Always get a better dump squatting. Feels more natural," Rugrat said to Simms who was admiring the bunker.

"If you say so."

"Got bathrooms, sleeping area." Rugrat altered the area around the steps, creating a trough leading to the drain. "If it rains, the water will drain away nicely. Just need to repeat it on the other bunker and make sure the other bunkers don't use my wastewater stream for their showers. That would suck!"

Rugrat walked to the entrance. Simms followed. Rugrat created a switch back entrance so they wouldn't need a door to protect them from the elements, growing it from the floor, ceiling and walls.

"Not even a dent in my mana pool. Shit, I wish I could have done this in some of the other places I had to fight. Damn hooch hotel around here. Get all that Gucchi shit."

Rugrat saw the plan of the first bunker with his domain; sky, ground, stone, air. The bunker's walls grew and reshaped according to the first bunker's layout.

"Come back here plants."

The trees and bushes moved. Their roots entombed the bunkers, creating a living camo net from vines and bushes, hiding them from above.

"Okay. Now that I've done it once, it should be easy to repeat it!"

Rugrat finished creating the bunkers, impressing the artillery platoon who'd sighted in and readied their mortars and formation plates. Cold wind kept most of them in their new bunkers, waiting. Sentries watched the hilltop, scanning with their binoculars. Rugrat had a sheet tossed out, his custom railgun broken down into parts.

Rugrat used his mana-smithing abilities to alter the parts. He enhanced them slightly, decreasing their size, reinforcing the threading a bit more.

"That's plain weird," Gong Jin said as he walked up.

"With my domain increasing, I can sense things clearly. Seeing that everything isn't perfect would annoy me to no end. I'm sure that, later on, I'll want to change it all again. For now, she's the best I can make her."

Rugrat picked up his cup of coffee and drank from it, looking out over the mountains.

"Are you sure about this, sir?" Gong Jin asked.

"Sure about what?"

"Being out here. You're the lord of, well, Alva. Everything."

"I ain't sitting in the rear with the gear. I know I shouldn't be on the front lines. Simple matter of fact is that I ain't built for command. I'm built to be where the metal meets the meat. Commander Glosil, the Silaz, they're better at that officer shit than I ever will be. Damn. I don't think I could be them, holding back, coordinating, watching and planning. That's one hell of a burden to carry and hold."

29
Support from on Far

"You sure you don't have anything better to do?" Kim Cheol asked as Erik studied his medical report at the base of the bed.

"You're my little guinea pig. How you been feeling? Your vitals are stabilizing, and it looks like your body is starting to make its own headway on some of the scar tissue. Going to need a few more treatments still."

"You cut any more out of me and there won't be much left," Kim complained with a smile. "But nah, I can feel it getting better. Just want to be back out there and doing something."

"You been eating everything?" Erik pressed his hand to Cheol's leg. He sensed increased stamina and mana regeneration, but it would still take a lot of time for his body to remove the scar tissue on its own. They had cut out the really bad internal shit over the last two surgeries.

"Yeah." Kim nodded.

"Okay. So, we've gotten rid of most of the scar tissue affecting your vitals: heart, lungs and such. You had a few burst blood vessels in your brain when I first saw you, but those have healed nicely and shouldn't trouble you anymore."

"Don't use it all that much." Kim grinned.

"*Anyway,* we're going to move onto stretches and non-invasive therapies. We need to bulk you up again, replenish your energy and stamina, and get your body working to heal itself."

Erik pulled out some tools, placing them on the bedside table.

"Why do those all look like torture instruments?" Kim said warily.

"There are two ways we can do this. One, we go light and careful; two, we don't. The second way will mean that you will heal faster, but it will hurt more."

"Ah, so they are torture instruments. I don't like it when I'm right," Kim grumbled before sighing reluctantly. "Option two."

"All right, let me know if it's too much."

"Okay. What do they *actually* do?"

"These allow me to dig deep into the muscles, break up the scar tissue and promote blood flow to the area. You up for it?"

"Sure."

Erik smiled at Kim's uncertain tone.

"Ah shit, when you're smiling like that, I know it's not good."

Erik rolled his eyes and grabbed a simple wooden dowel from the table among his other soft tissue mobilization tools. "We're going to start on your legs first. Specifically your shins." Erik positioned himself alongside Kim's leg, placing the dowel against the top of his left shin under his knee.

He pushed down and along Kim's leg.

"Oh-fuck-that-fucking-SUCKS!" Kim's eyes bulged as he grabbed the sheets, clenching his jaw shut and stared up at the ceiling.

Erik continued working. "Back in the army, they used to do this if you got shin splints. Crude way to break up the tissues. Keeps you going because training didn't stop. It does suck though." Erik commiserated as he worked the length of wood, scraping it up and down Kim's left shin. He sent bolts of electricity through the area, tiny amounts that were just enough to stimulate the tissues.

He moved to the other shin, then started to take out applicators. He activated the crude ultrasound formations and went to work on Kim's feet.

"Sucks in places, but feels kind of nice, not so tight." Kim hissed and tilted his head to the side with a wince. "Good spot," he said breathlessly.

"Yeah, your feet were pretty bad. You were driving all your power through them, gripping onto the ground. It's built up real bad. We need to break it down and ease things out. These tools are basically a last resort. I'm going to give you stretches to get you moving again. Pain is bad; resistance is good. Stretching will allow you to open the muscles and get them moving more regularly. These applicators speed up the process, and with stretching, you'll heal faster."

"I'm up for some movement. Getting stuck in bed is enough to drive anyone mad."

"Good. We'll do these sessions. You do your stretching. Then we'll add in fighting drills and sparring with others. Then we'll move to body tempering. Your mana system is a wreck, though you can still draw some mana into your body. The stronger your system is, the more mana you can hold. I found out that tempering is just the method to hold elements within your body."

Kim's eyes were sober, even through the pain. "Will I really be able to fight again?"

Erik kept working on the calf. "I swear on my life."

Kim held his eyes for a solid minute before he slumped back. "Tell me what I need to do, and I'll do it."

Even after I let them suffer to protect Alva and Vuzgal, to keep our secrets.

"Okay." Erik focused on Kim's leg. A swirl of emotions ran through his mind and turned his stomach.

Nearly an hour and a half later, Erik was done. Food arrived and Kim dug in with gusto.

"Okay, so do you have all of your stretches?"

"Add in movement. Make it easy. Do it for thirty seconds. Pain is bad, resistance good," Kim said, holding up the page of stretches.

"The more stretches you do, the better. Means you'll be out of here sooner. Now, I've got other patients to see."

"I wanted to ask… Is something happening?" Kim asked.

"What do you mean?"

"Most people moving around out there are soldiers."

"Willful Institute is targeting Vuzgal and we have an issue in the First Realm. The Institute stirred up people to attack the Beast Mountain Range."

"They know about Alva?"

"No, but they have suspicions. Sects are messy things. They might be using this to bind the different kingdoms together, bringing them under their control. Shit's complicated."

"Better you than me." Kim snorted and went back to his food.

Erik smiled and left the room, checking his clipboard.

"Thank you." Kim's words were soft, but Erik still heard them.

"You can thank me by getting better!" he called back.

Erik smiled as he walked down the corridor and into another room. It was a larger ward, with a few people that were talking among themselves.

"Lord West!" Fatima said. The three with her looked up and made to stand.

"Will you sit your asses down?" Erik growled.

They gave meek smiles and ducked their heads as they sat back down.

"You'll be cursing me in a few minutes, so no need to act like your mother is gonna come around and smack you for not minding your manners."

"I'll smack you for not minding yours!" Momma Rodrigeuz's drive-by comment passed the hall and Erik saw her amused smile as she winked at the people in the room, waving and continuing on.

Erik ran his tongue over his teeth and turned back to the group who had sucked on their lips so hard they'd inverted, letting out half-hidden snorts.

"All right, yah morons, let's have a look at you." Erik moved to his first patient.

They made to clear away the game of euchre; it had spread through the army after Erik and Rugrat had taught it to the Special Teams and through Alva shortly afterward.

Another group was playing board games. It gave them something to do, and the board games make them think tactically, which they could apply in fighting.

"No need to stop on my part." Erik looked at the table and Rafael's hand.

"Got a good hand, too."

Rafael's partner glowered at him, trying to decipher his cards as Fatima and her partner watched them.

Erik laughed to himself quietly and studied Rafael. They had burned their cultivations for one another. It could have crippled them and would take months to recover. *I'll make sure they're stronger than ever.*

"How was Kim Cheol?" Fatima asked.

"Probably cursing me in his dreams, but he's a tough bastard." Most of the damage was just scar tissue. His mana system was torn up, but sowing treated Lidel leaves into his mana channels created a latticework for his mana system to grow along. Using tough Lidel leaves to replace mana channels had worked surprisingly well.

The group laughed as Erik held Rafael's arm.

"Let me have it." Rafael released the tension. Erik cast Medical Scan and reduced the strength he was using.

"Euchre!" Fatima said as the round came to an end.

"I'll need Rafael for a minute," Erik said.

"Okay," Rafael said, dropping his cards.

He moved him to a bed and got to work with the applicators on his shoulders and arms. Rafael was worn out as Erik put a sheet of stretches on his bedside table.

"Fatima, you're next."

Erik moved through the room, examining them, giving them stretches and working their worst spots over with the applicators.

They were lethargic and slow afterward.

"See you all tomorrow," Erik said to a cacophony of groans that made Erik smile.

"It's good to see patients with a healthy appetite!" Momma Rodriguez said as she walked into the room. Erik moved out of the way. The Adventurer's Guild members perked up and smiled. *They don't do that when I walk into a room.* Erik grumbled, but his smile only widened.

"Fatima, all vegetarian with extra onions." Momma Rodriguez pulled warm meals from her storage ring and handed them out. "And will you stop getting out of bed, or I'll make Erik put you back in it!"

She looked over and winked at Erik as if to say: *Good work! I have this now.*

Erik thanked her with his eyes. He left the ward and walked down the hall to a reception desk.

"Lord West?" The lady smiled. He was around enough that she knew not to bow.

"Jen around?"

"She's in her office."

"Thanks. I just took a look at the guild members." Erik passed the receptionist his notes. "Make sure they do their stretches and correct their posture. Maybe put a mirror in there so they can see what they're doing?"

"I'll see what I can do," the receptionist said brightly.

"Thanks!" Erik rapped off a tune on the counter and headed for Jen's office. Yao Meng and his people, who had been waiting in the hall, followed him.

"Time for the needle?"

"Yes, Yao Meng. Time for the needle." Erik rolled his eyes.

"You're already as pale as a sheet. You trying for see through?"

Erik looked at his glowing forearm. *Shit. I'm white. Need a tan.* He still flipped off Yao Meng for his accurate description.

"Heh."

They wandered through the halls. Things were peaceful, most of the rooms were empty and the staff sparse. They passed a group of soldiers circling their first aid instructor, jotting down notes, taking in everything.

Erik knocked on a simple door.

"Come in," a distracted voice called through the door.

He opened the door to find Jen, the head of Alva Healing House, slowly raising her head, drinking in the last words she was reading. New lines had worked into her face and she had a gravitas that hadn't been there before. She had been so young and eager when she started. Now that eagerness had been tempered with time and experience.

"Lord West." She blushed.

"Don't worry. You ready?"

"I should be the one asking that. You're the one we're draining."

"Ah, with my stamina, it's nothing much. I'll work on tempering my mana at the same time."

"Do you ever take a rest?"

"I sleep for a few hours a week."

Jen sighed as she stood up wearing her lab coat. Erik made way for her in the doorway.

They went down the corridor. She opened a door to a room with chairs reclined over formation plates and one rolling chair.

"Are you sure about this?" Jen asked, taking a seat on the rolling chair.

"I'm sure. Feel like a bit of a fucking vampire, but I don't care if it saves people's lives. I have Reverse Alchemist for a reason."

Erik moved to one of the reclining chairs.

"Okay, let me get my gear." Jen pulled out needles, catheters, saline, tubing, and bags. With additional gauze, she connected what needed to be connected. Yao Meng stepped outside with Jamie, while Rajkovic, Tian Cui, and Lucinda moved to the couches, pulling out books and a set of cards.

Erik retrieved several ingredients and started eating them while taking off his shirt. They were meant to increase his blood production, and if he was right, increase the stamina regenerative properties of his blood.

Jen set up her gear. "Good?"

"Yup." Erik opened and closed his fist, his veins bulging against his skin.

Jen used a tourniquet, finding the vein with her fingers. She pulled on the skin and inserted a large-gauge needle. Blood rushed into the flash chamber. She pressed down ahead of the needle with one hand before pushing the catheter forward. Then withdrew the needle and released the tourniquet. She attached tubing before taking her prepared tape and securing the catheter to Erik's skin.

She secured the tubing to a thick plastic bag, putting it on a formation plate before she passed a ball to Erik. "Squeeze this." She tapped the formation under the chair.

Erik felt the wash of mana run through him, and a cooling sensation through his arm as he squeezed the ball. He drew in the mana, concentrating.

Compress it in the outer reaches of my mana channels, draw it through my elemental core.

The mana was filled with earth, fire, metal, and a small amount of water elements. His core sucked in everything but the mana and water element as he drew it around his body. He was still regaining his strength from the metal tempering and getting used to it. Jumping right into water tempering would only increase the learning curve later.

Erik circulated his mana until all the water element had been absorbed into his body before he drew it down deeper through his mana system. There, he compressed it further, then poured it into his mana core.

Jen checked everything and sat back in her chair. She smirked at Erik as she crossed her arms.

"Something interesting? I got salsa on my cheek?" Erik rubbed his face but didn't find any of his lunch.

Once he started cultivating, it was easy to maintain it.

"Just you, turning your *entire* body into a Revival potion factory."

"Well, I didn't think it would actually work at first. Was more asleep than awake when I thought about it."

"How did such a thought occur to you?"

"I was making the potions and needed to get some rest. So, I was eating the nutrient dense bars that we have and thought about how my blood must be nutrient rich. I eat so much damn food. The idea stuck with me. I cut my finger a bit and tasted it, used Reverse Alchemist on it. With a Body Like Sky Iron, I extract a lot more out of my food and environment, my blood is a pretty decent stamina potion. So, I put it in my cauldron and started working on it, adding ingredients. Figured out that if I ate some things to increase my blood flow, and then some other ingredients to increase the effects of my blood… Well, here I am."

Erik watched the blood filling the bag quickly.

"I'm going to need bigger bags." Jen pulled out another, ready to switch it out.

Erik half-closed his eyes when Jen started talking again.

"Thank you for saving Alva. For still trying to save us all," Jen said.

"Wouldn't change a thing. Maybe get more beer." Erik smiled.

"Please don't. The people taking your blood would be as drunk as a damn skunk. Food isn't the only thing you need a lot of to do something to your body."

The door to the room opened. The special team didn't move, expecting it.

"Reports." Yao Meng walked in holding out a box, filled with information books.

"Dammit," Erik sighed as he grabbed the first book.

"Blood donor, mana cultivator, and city lord," Jen laughed.

"Keeps me out of trouble and keeps my hands occupied," Erik winked.

"Yes, like if you actually said you wanted company, you wouldn't have three wives and four girlfriends by the end of the day." Jen's comment made Yao Meng snort as the rest of the special team laughed.

"Gah, the curse of wives!" Erik looked shocked as he held out a hand to Yao Meng who dropped the box into his hand.

"You'd have to do something other than train, work, train, work. You know he wanted to try to do this while he was sleeping?" Yao Meng said to Jen.

The door opened again.

"Will you stop doing so many things, Dame Fuerza!" Momma Rodriguez waved her hand at Erik and looked to the heavens, quickly doing the sign of the cross.

Jen's mouth was half open. A smile threatened to split her face apart as her eyes crinkled at the corner.

She switched him to a new blood bag, and rolled backward, crossing her arms to watch the show with the rest of the special team. He'd filled the first two in under two minutes.

"What are you doing? Are you trying to give me a heart attack, Erik?" Momma Rodriguez grabbed the box of papers and put them on a spare chair. She pulled over a table on wheels and pulled out plates, filling the table.

"Momma," Erik protested.

"I know, you have a lot to do." She waved her hand at him as she continued to draw out food. "You still need to eat—and sleep."

Erik wanted to fight, but it would be useless while his own stomach was rebelling after smelling the food.

She pulled out containers and walked over to Yao Meng. "Take that to Rajkovic as well."

"Thank you, Momma Rodriguez."

"Ah, you're a growing boy. You'll be strong like my Erik and Jimmy soon enough. Make them go and find some wives!" She sent a pointed look at Erik who wiped his face and groaned, maintaining his mana cultivation.

She tsked and pulled out more containers. "I made too much. Come on, come on, otherwise it will go to waste!"

The special team members bowed their heads, thanking her for the food and accepting it.

Like it can do that in a storage ring. He wasn't going to be the one to argue with her, though.

She moved back to Erik and pushed the table over. "Come on. Here, these tacos you can eat with one hand. Do you want me to feed you?"

"No! Uhhh, um, I got that. All good, yeah." Erik coughed, going bright red.

"Okay, okay." She raised her hands and put the reports on a table, taking the next seat over.

"Thank you, Momma," Erik said.

"Now will you get a wife? Then I won't have to slave in the kitchen every day!"

"You wouldn't leave the kitchen even if I had *five* wives!"

"Well..." she considered it for a minute and nodded at his faultless logic. "They would have to be as good as I am."

So, none of them will.

Erik picked up the taco and bit into it, letting out a groan.

"See! Can't see you getting all skinny again. Girls like a big, strong man. Why not get a new wife?"

"I'm not going to go out on the street and wear a signboard with looking for a new wife written on it."

"It's the Ten Realms. Things are different here. There were all those dating apps you used. What about that girl before you went to Africa?"

"How did you—" Erik bit back his words.

I'm going to murder Rugrat.

"She wasn't a girlfriend." Erik staved off other words by eating.

Momma Rodriguez tutted and sighed. "You fighter types." She waved her hand next to her head as if the Lord himself was giving her strength. "Bah! You need a wife. Someone to look after you, someone to come home to."

"You just want *un nieto*!"

"So what if I do? Do you not want children?"

"I didn't mean that."

"You need a wife before you can have children."

Erik gave up on the long-lost argument.

Momma Rodriguez sat there smug in her victory.

Erik got his bag changed again. He licked his fingers as Momma Rodriguez talked.

"Anything from Jimmy?" Her voice was softer.

Erik used a clean spell and reached out a hand.

She looked at the offending limb, then at the table of food before she sighed and grabbed the reports, passing them to Erik.

Erik braced himself, then opened and activated them.

He finished all three of the thick information books. Their dusty remnants covered his lap as he closed his eyes, concentrating on the information that flooded his mind while his brain organized it. He focused on his cultivation as something to hold on to.

The headache faded and he looked up, sighing. His eyes moved to pull it all into perspective.

"Rugrat is safe. He finished tempering his mana core. He has a mana heart now. He's with the mortar crews." He looked at Momma Rodriguez. "He's more of a threat to them than they are to him. He's been building bunkers with his mana abilities."

Momma Rodriguez nodded and looked away. "It is good to know he is safe."

Erik watched her, feeling that there was more.

"When you and Jimmy were out *wherever,* I never knew what was happening. I know, but you're my boys. I won't stop worrying." Her shoulders sagged.

Erik saw flashes of being in the field. Weapons were like a cellphone to them. They carried them everywhere, treating them fondly at times or hammering on them when they screwed up. Dust-covered faces, wire-thin bodies in sweltering heat or howling cold. The distant sound of firing, the hair-raising whiz of rounds, the crack as it hit the wall behind, the rush of heat and adrenaline. Death was everywhere, but doing nothing was worse.

Red filled his vision. Faces filled with pain, a forgotten memory as he tore away plastic and paper-wrapping bandages, tightening tourniquets. The blood on the threads of his shirt button, he couldn't get off.

"When I watched the tv, I was looking out for you, your units, but also fearing it. Hearing you were in some battles, about the wounded. Then my heart would clench so tight. I knew that I would know before the news. But maybe they forgot me. Maybe the chaplain was on his way over right now and the news went out early."

Momma Rodriguez let out a shuddering breath. Erik stretched over and held her hand.

"You'll mess up your needle!" she said but only gave a light push away, letting him hold her hand.

She gathered herself, but tears still filled her eyes. "It was worse with the private jobs. There was no information. You would just leave one day and come back another." She picked up his hand, kissed it, and put it against her cheek. "War took one of my children, but the army gave me another."

Erik felt something catch in his throat, his own eyes wet.

"You have such capacity for good. That is why you do what you do." She wiped away her tears, patting his hands. "My Erik and Jimmy. I knew you would do great things together. It is harder in some ways to be so close, but so far from you both in this."

He gripped her hand in his, unsure what to say, so he just sat there as she held tight to his hand. Erik saw the lines on her face, the weariness and exhaustion that had snuck into her bones. She had such energy, but there was a greater toll than just the physical one.

30 Sighted

Domonos looked over the most recent map information. The grey markers indicated the locations of the sects pushing toward Vuzgal. They took into account when they had left the different cities, how fast they were moving, and the direction they were going in, but there was no recent information on just where in the mountain ranges they were.

His eyes fell on the iron ring around Vuzgal, showing the patrol routes for the air force and the scouts' observation posts.

Zukal walked into the command center. "How are the reserves looking?"

"Good, they're listening to their training staff and working hard. Haven't slept in three days, since they were recalled."

"You get them sorted out?"

"They have their weapons. Tomorrow we'll take them out on the range and get them used to their equipment."

"Good. Then we'll push them into the defenses," Domonos said, looking over the underground city that peeked up out of the ground in front of Vuzgal.

"You sure you don't want them to support the front lines?"

"Too much can go wrong. Their cultivations are all over the place. So, what a normal soldier does, they might not be able to. They need time to adjust. Run them through using the defensive weaponry. Easier than figuring out new gear, new tactics, and having to use them all in a few days. We have plenty of forces in the field." Domonos pointed at the artillery units. "With all of our units turned into artillery platoons, we've created a double-ringed defense." The artillery positions were spaced out like a W that repeated over and over again in a crude circle.

"We have two lines of artillery so the guns will never go silent as we pull back. Our people have been working alongside one another for years now. They work seamlessly. Adding in new units will only add complications, and we won't have a place for them. Instead of increasing their combat effectiveness, it will reduce it, turning our lean fighting machine into a bloated whale."

"Understood." Zukal looked at the map. "So, what do we do now?"

"Now?" Domonos exhaled and stood up. "Now we wait and watch for the enemy."

Captain Wazny moved with his sparrow mount against the air. His eyes never left the diverging black lines. Like a river of poison, the different sects flowed between mountain paths toward Vuzgal.

"Hey Joe, you seeing this too?" he asked Joe Santos, his wingman for the recon flyover.

"If you mean the thousands of people flooding through the mountains, yeah, I see it."

"Well, shit."

"Take them another three or four days to reach Vuzgal and they're in our range now," Santos said.

"You're one positive bastard, aren't you? Just give me a second. I'm gonna call it in."

Wazny used his sound transmission device to connect to the Vuzgal command center. "Vuzgal Command, this is Recon Flight Alpha Three. Message. Over." Wazny checked the map on the inside of his arm.

"Recon Flight Alpha Three, this is Vuzgal Command. Say message. Over."

"Vuzgal Command, be advised I am seeing the enemy moving through the northern mountain range, grid square whiskey-November-two-six-one-zero. Heading south. Over."

"Recon Flight Alpha Three, understood. Would you be able to give exact locations for the different passes they're using?"

"Vuzgal Command, understood. Wait, one. Over." Wazny checked his map against the ground terrain and went through the process of passing back information to Vuzgal Command.

Rugrat leaned against George, looking over the artillery positions from his section of trench.

"Why did you take the worst sentry shift?" Simms asked.

"Not like either of us need too sleep much anyway," Rugrat said as he shifted his sling, raising his rifle that was between his legs and scanning the forest beyond.

"Yeah. But boring as hell in the middle of the night."

"Don't worry. You'll be back in your warm cot in no time." Rugrat grinned as he kept scanning.

"All forward artillery platoons, this is Vuzgal Command. Stand to. I say again, stand to!"

Rugrat stood as Simms raised his rifle a little higher.

The artillery position came alive as lighting formations lit up. Artillery squads rushed out to their prepared guns.

Rugrat pulled out his map and checked it. Symbols appeared across the map in the north and the south. "Looks like the recon flights found them."

The red river of enemy seeped into the mountain ranges. Secondary markings showed possible routes they might take into Vuzgal.

"Load for spell trap dispersal. Our observers should have some coordinates for us shortly." The Second Lieutenant briefed his squad leaders through the linked sound transmission channel.

The mortars' coverings were removed, revealing their runes. Enhancing formation plates were activated as mages prepared spells to increase the mortar's range.

Rugrat and Simms seemed to be outside of the craziness happening all around them.

"Lay down the spell traps, then wait till they get into range. How do we know they're not going to reach the spell traps before we hit them with mortars?" Simms asked.

"We don't. The scouts have to radio in coordinates to the command center. They'll check them and agree. It's up to them to make sure that the spell traps are far enough back that the enemy shouldn't run into them first. Starts a timer, really. We have to hit them with mortars before they reach the spell traps, or we lose the element of surprise." Rugrat grinned. "Don't worry; it won't be long now." Rugrat patted George, who let out a low growl.

"Target is pre-set Charlie!" Second Lieutenant Couto yelled out.

"Target is pre-set Charlie!" The mortar squad leaders called back. "Deflection change!"

The squad leaders called out changes to the mortar teams who adjusted according to their pre-sets.

The guns turned in line, their sights adjusted and checked onto their markers before setting the guns again and adjusting the elevation.

"Mortar One-One ready!"

"Mortar Two-Three ready!"

Mortar teams finished positioning their mortars. They operated in teams of four. The gunner on the gun checked the sight. Ammunition bearer one stood on the other side, ready. The second ammunition bearer was checking on the mortar rounds in his storage ring to make sure they had the right amount of additional charges.

Two mages stood at the rear with the squad leader, a Staff Sergeant or Sergeant. The formations they were positioned on glowed with power, linked to the mortar.

"Mortar Team One-One, Illumination round. Fire when ready!" Couto yelled.

"Illumination round!" the Staff Sergeant called out. The first ammunition bearer took out a tracer round.

"Hang it!"

They held the top of the round.

"Fire!"

They released and ducked.

The formations flashed, and the mortar fired, illuminating the dark hill.

Everyone waited in silence as Couto waited on his sound transmission device.

"Shift one-five-zero, drop one hundred!"

"Shift one-five-zero, drop one hundred!" The squad repeated as the squad leader turned that into changes, the gunner inputting them as the first ammunition bearer readied his next round.

"Looks like a real military now. Shit," Rugrat said.

The other mortars adjusted their point of aim off the changes happening with Mortar One-One.

"Ready!" the squad leader yelled.

"Fire when ready!"

"Hang!" the Staff Sergeant ordered.

The ammunition bearer loaded.

"Fire!"

The mortar fired once again.

They waited, looking at one another.

"Good shot! All guns load T-D rounds! Twenty rounds each. Increase deflection two turns after each round. Fire when ready!"

Ammunition bearers dropped their rounds and ducked out of range of the blast of hot gas. Gunners changed the deflection before the next round was placed in the mortar's mouth.

The six mortars fired off of one another. The waves of constant air hit those standing on the hill as they worked methodically.

"Rounds complete, rounds complete! Change to new target!" Couto yelled as they finished coating their target area with three hundred and twenty artillery shells.

In the silence as guns were cleaned and repositioned, Rugrat heard the rumblings of the other artillery platoons nearby.

He checked his rifle and looked out into the darkness.

"If everything goes well, I won't have to use you." He tapped his forefinger against his rifle's body. *I have a feeling that I'll have to, though.*

"Been a day since we spotted them, but they're all finally in range," Zukal said.

New yellow zones appeared on the map, marking out where trap formations and shells covered the ground.

Domonos' eyes focused on the crooked red lines that weaved through the mountain paths into Vuzgal Valley. "What time is it?"

"Around seventeen hundred hours."

"They should be settling down in a few hours to camp. Do we hit them as they're going to ground or as they wake up and start moving? If it's when they set up camp, they'll be spread out. In the morning, they'll be packed together again." Domonos looked at the trap fields.

"They will be deeper in our range and they shouldn't hit the trap formations seeded over the area."

"I vote for morning," Zukal said. "Our people can set their ambushes, pre-set their impact zones, and they'll be more alert. They will also see the enemy situation clearly. At night they have spells, but it isn't the same."

"Director, what time do they break camp in the morning?"

"Oh-seven-hundred hours. The Willful Institute dictates when they move." Elan was standing off to the side.

"Do we have any information on where their leadership is?"

"No. We know where their units are, but Marco Tolentino doesn't want to be found, apparently."

Domonos grimaced.

"We would do the same thing. Hell, we did with the Adventurer's Guild's assaults," Zukal said.

Domonos looked at the lines in the rear, the supply lines and camp followers. "That's where I would be if I were him. They're well back from the artillery, though. Kanoa, you think your people could hit their supply lines?"

"The sparrow flights have the maneuverability to hit them multiple times. The kestrels are too slow."

"Our artillery will prioritize forces moving along the mountain passes. The air force can target the supply lines. The camp followers aren't under the same restrictions as the fighters. If they collapse to the rear, the forward forces will lose their support and luxuries," Domonos said.

"Most of the fighters are pampered," Elan explained for Kanoa's benefit. "Their every need is sorted out by someone else so they're in the best condition when they fight. Without having those luxuries taken care of, it'll impact their morale,"

"Sorry, it's still hard to get my head around. Won't we be hitting, you know, civilians?"

"Would you consider our quartermasters and supply lines to be civilians?" Domonos asked.

Kanoa frowned. "Well…"

"The traders? They've been conscripted into the military. The camp followers are actively supporting the fighting forces. They came out here knowing the risks. They want to gain from our corpses. I don't like it, but, they're vultures while the army is the tiger. The difference, in the Ten Realms, between fighter and civilian is a thin one. Most have experienced death, and the majority have killed to survive. Whether they killed beasts or humans, it's a degree of difference."

"I understand, sir. I have my orders."

"Good. Hit the supply lines and camp follower trains in time with the artillery barrages."

"Yes, sir."

"Make sure that everyone rests as much as possible tonight. Tomorrow it begins."

Bai Ping was with the rest of the training staff watching their charges' training exercise. Bai Ping's face screwed up into a frown, looking through the different formation screens showing the training area.

"Tommins focused too much on getting the formation pad down," Staff Sergeant Baines said.

"Xi is sitting in the rear, focusing on healing. Hasn't moved since the start," Staff Sergeant Yi Do-Hyun pointed.

The two Staff Sergeants grumbled as they stood in the observation tower. Gunnery Sergeant Bai Ping had his arms crossed, watching the battlefield below.

The village looked like it had been shelled out. The walls were in disrepair, and the stone walls had been collapsed in several positions. Buildings were half-intact from battle damage.

Spells flashed between buildings.

Skeletons were on one side, and Bai Ping's reservists were on the other. They were wearing sparring barriers, so once they took enough damage, the amulets that the barriers were carved into would sap the user of stamina.

The skeletons had special instructions. Once they took a certain amount of damage, they would allow themselves to collapse as if dead.

"They've stopped watching their flanks," Bai Ping said.

Yi Do-Hyun let out something between a growl and a sigh.

"And here they come." Baines pointed at the group of skeletons that had peeled off from the fighting and flanking through the buildings.

The reservists didn't move, holding in position as they fought. *They should have put out flank security, trap spells, or warning spells at the least. There are si—five of them left.* A skeleton's arrow reduced the number of mages.

Two fell before they realized that they were being attacked from a different direction.

"All right, call it. We'll do an AAR," Bai said as the last of his mages slumped.

Baines pulled out a medallion and talked into it. "Return to your ready positions."

The skeletons reformed and went back to their side of the village.

Yi Do-Hyun canceled the stamina draining factor of the amulets. The mages let out a collective groan as they picked themselves up.

"Form up outside the village for an AAR." Baines projected his voice over the training village as the squad congealed together, relaxing and forming a semi-circle to wait for the instructors.

The two staff sergeants looked at Bai.

"Well, at least we've got another week to get them into fighting shape."

"Sure, Gunny. Their casting speed has increased dramatically, and it's stronger. The cultivation work is having an effect," Baines said.

"They're using more than just one spell in a panic. They're breaking into groups based on spell use. They should spread out those different spell-wielders instead of bunching up. In our full-time squads, everyone is supposed to do everything, but we have nearly a year of training, and who knows how long we've spent in the field. Not expecting this behavior at that level." Yi Do-Hyun derided.

"But tactics are a problem," Bai explained.

"Yeah, they're a bit of a mess. They're tunnelling. They get some kills and focus on getting more," Yi agreed.

"Kill hunger. They treat it like a game. Once they have a few kills, they try to get more to show off and get a higher score."

Bai chewed on the inside of his cheek. "Change the settings on the amulet and give them a shock. That should wake them up." Bai saw flashes off to the side. He looked over to another training village where reservists were being put through their paces, putting what they had learned to the test.

Bai felt the weight on his shoulders. He would be fighting side by side with these reservists in the future. More importantly, his brothers and sisters from the other units would be fighting next to them. He didn't want them to fuck up and get asked who taught them.

"We have three days in training village eight. Let's use it to our advantage. Get them to siege the village, put down a camp. The whole nine yards. Then get them to defend. Switch it up so they can't get into a rhythm. I want them to see what both sides are thinking. If they know how to attack, then if they use their heads, they can counter what their own actions would be on the defense and vice versa," Bai directed.

"Nice bit of sleep deprivation training. Shouldn't be so bad with their cultivation," Baines chuckled.

Bai led them toward the stairs of the observation tower, one of a dozen that surveyed their own training villages on the metal floor.

"How many are there now?" Commander Glosil lowered his hand, returning Colonel Yui's salute.

They stood upon the walls of Alva's main camp.

"Reservists, thirty thousand altogether. Enough to form two divisions. Reg force, they should have another four thousand by the time they are fit to move. Another one hundred and fifty thousand have signed up so far."

Glosil shifted his head from side to side. "Thankfully, we had the reserve program in place. It will only take a two-week refresher for the reservists we already had, and a slimmed-down month and a half for those that we didn't."

"Having the self-defence classes for everyone really helps. We don't need to teach the basics of fighting; just get right into the tactics and the stuff that's linked to their task. Not as mobile as the regular army, but on the defensive? Much easier to train and deal with than leading a complicated attack."

"If Domonos can get us two weeks, we can get him the first reserve division. Another month and we can deliver him two more." Glosil tapped on the camp's stone wall and turned, walking over to the other side, looking into the camp and its nine different training squares.

"It's a race for time now," Yui surmised as Glosil looked at ragtag groups under the yells of their sergeants. Other squads that were better put together were going over key equipment such as mortars, repeaters, and grenades along another wall, making sure that their hands and minds remembered their old drills.

Teachers conducted lectures on how to improve spell casting, and what to look for in wear and tear of weapons and gear. Movement was constant. People headed to the cultivation centers to open their mana gates, and temper their bodies.

"The cultivation centers are like a factory now. I never thought I would see anything like it. In less than a week, one can go from no cultivation at all to all their mana gates opening and form the foundation for their body cultivation. Fifty thousand." Glosil shook his head.

"I'd think it was madness just a few years ago."

"It still is madness." Glosil looked at Yui. "I'm afraid we aren't giving them enough training and are putting too much on our people. I'm thinking of sending the first reserve division to Vuzgal with the newly trained soldiers."

"Sir?"

Glosil smiled at the question he heard in the word. "Your Tiger Regiment is stretched thin. We went from four instructors to three on the reg force riflemen that are coming out. Then we threw them and everyone at corporal and higher into training the reservists. We're just hammering them into shape here. Vuzgal can temper them quickly, turn them into veterans, and give us a few thousand more fighting hands."

"What about the personnel drawn from the Dragon Regiment?"

"It will weigh on the Dragon Regiment some, but they need people. They've got the basics down, at least."

"Which leaves thousands of soldiers in the rear with nothing to do," Yui said.

"Right, who can take in the reservists and new soldiers, pull them into shape, and get them ready for the defense, shoring up holes in their training quick-like?"

"Shit, what do you think the Willful Institute would think if they knew that in just a few weeks our forces would shoot from seven thousand to forty thousand?"

"I don't think they'd care, but they've never engaged the Vuzgal army on the field of battle. We'll have to teach them."

They stood in silence for some time.

"What do you think about the actions of the kingdoms and the Institute in the First Realm?" Yui asked.

Glosil frowned. "That, I can't predict. It's clear that they're shaking the tree. I think they're also using it as a means of recruitment. They lost a lot of people; quantity over quality has always been the motto of most sects. Let the lower-level people grind it out 'til something appears."

"The kingdoms have said that the Institute will support them personally. Then we heard that there are mortal level armies preparing to move. They're too weak to affect the battles that rage across their lower positions. I think they want to use this as an opportunity to sharpen their people."

"Mhmm." Glosil indicated for him to continue.

"We both know that sects don't care about the number of casualties.

Right now, they have a big problem. They have plenty of fights ahead of them, but no one is joining their sect. They need bodies to fill their ranks. Whoever survives this fight will have fewer people, but all of them will be stronger for it. Have a taste of fighting. Perfect for the Institute to use as cannon fodder in the higher realms. They'll get some low-level training aids and gear in return for an army that can fight in the lower realms for them."

"I agree. It's easier to hire in the First Realm and have the kingdoms fight it out. They confirm their rumors, or at the very least, they get people with higher levels who have been through a fight already."

"But it's preferable for us. If we can take out the kingdoms, make them look weak and fight it out without showing our true strength, the sect might get annoyed with the people in the lower realm and refuse to take the Beast Mountain Range because it would be too much of a problem."

"That is not to say they won't send down powerful reinforcements."

"No, there isn't, and there is a limit to what the Beast Mountain Range can do on its own. If it is anyone from the Third Realm or higher, we will have to have some people step up."

"What if they escalate?"

"We will have to deal with it. Alva can't and won't abandon the Beast Mountain Range."

Yui went silent as he processed what Glosil had said.

Glosil looked back over the training square. His gaze expanded to the other squares. The other bases were at full capacity, training and preparing. Smoke rose from the factories and workshops.

The factories hadn't ceased production once, only increasing their capacity. To see all of it mobilized... *Do you realize what lurks in the dark, Willful Institute? Today you attack a snake, but tomorrow you might just find out that snake is the tail of a dragon.*

"If we're found..." Yui said.

"Colonel Yui." Glosil held his hands behind his back. "We need not worry, if we are found out. It is our job and task to carry out the orders given to us. We stand to defend Alva. Focus on that and that alone. Other decisions do not matter. That is for the council and for the dungeon lords to decide."

"Yes, sir."

"Plan for the worst and hope for the best. We'll need to work fast to get our reserves trained and ready to deploy. Come on, we'll head to the command center."

"Yes, sir."

They walked along the wall, looking at the line of men and women that reached the recruitment offices and the constant flow of squads to and from the different camps.

Alva moved with Vuzgal.

31
The Skies Whistle and the Ground Shakes Once More

"Move it! Get those formations powered up already! The Willful Institute isn't going to wait for your sorry asses!" Kanoa's voice bellowed across the landing strip as casting enhancing formation plates were slotted into position in the Kestrel cabins.

He surveyed the airfield, badly wishing that he were heading off with his people.

The warmth of the sun kissed their skin even as the cold of night licked it away. Pilots and crews rushed out to their takeoff points. Their mounts were prepared for them as they boarded.

Support companies were split into their squads and sent to waiting birds.

"Launch!"

Formations shot out warm air underneath waiting sparrows. Their wings spread wide, catching the wind, and ascending into the air. A path of formations lit up, carrying them higher and increasing their speed before they left the airfield.

Other acceleration formations lit up, sending kestrel wings of three and sparrow wings of eight into the skies.

The military might of Vuzgal was roused. Formations across the city flashed with power. The slumbering beast was waking up.

"Prepare to rearm and resupply as needed! Get the reserve birds ready!" Kanoa yelled. "Those fuckers want to take your city. Are you going to let them?"

The wind cut across the mountains north of Vuzgal, right through the spotter hidden in the snow and rocks of the mountain. Corporal Nicholas Landrith couldn't see Vuzgal city tens of kilometers away.

He turned back to his target in the opposite direction. Sect fighters were packed into the dry riverbed that snaked between the mountains into Vuzgal Valley.

Morning had arrived, reflecting off the picturesque, snow-topped mountains.

He lowered the enhanced binoculars, letting them hang from the strap around his neck, and consulted the map strapped to his forearm. The wind chilled his exposed skin and ruffled his winter gear. He pulled out his compass; setting it, he used his binoculars again, checking features against map lines and the compass bearings.

"How are we looking?" Sergeant Cao.

"Coordinates look good," Landrith said as he pulled his jacket tighter to his body to block the wind, holding out the checked numbers to Sergeant Cao.

"All right, punch them up, Earthy!"

"You just don't want to freeze your fingers off holding this damn board," Landrith muttered. The Earther jokes didn't phase him anymore.

"I'm living it up with my rank privileges." Cao grinned under his cold-weather hood.

"On this fine, wind-swept, cold-as-shit-asscrack-of-the-world mountain."

Landrith chuckled as the other members of the sharpshooter team grinned into their scarves. He keyed his sound transmission device. "Firebases Group Three, this is Spotting Squad Four-One. Targets at coordinate uniform-whiskey-three-four-seven-niner by eight-one-five-zero. Requesting shot. Over."

"Understood, shot."

Landrith raised his binoculars, as did the rest of the sharpshooter team, watching the dark river of people. A flash hit to the west and north of the winding stream of enemy fighters.

"Correction. Twelve hundred mils. Add three hundred. Over." Landrith didn't lower his binoculars.

"Correction. Twelve hundred mils. Add three hundred. Out."

A few seconds rolled past as Landrith watched on.

"Shot out!"

Landrith watched with his heart in his teeth. There was a flash on the east side, bracketing the riverbed. "Drop one hundred. Fire for effect. Over."

"Drop one hundred. Fire for effect!"

It wasn't a perfect call for fire, but if it worked, it worked.

The route was filled with members of different sects. The winding path was wide enough to let three men abreast push forward. The mountains and stone gave them nowhere to go as they wove through the dry stream.

The walls and terrain made it nearly impossible to use mana barriers. The sects didn't have theirs active, thinking themselves safe and secure.

The first shells had been unenhanced marker shells. The ones that followed were enhanced by formations and mages. Instead of just one gun, there were two artillery companies, part of Firebase Group Three firing.

Destruction flashed upon the riverbed as tens of mortars landed. It took several seconds for the rumbling noise to reach the sharpshooters.

Stone that had lasted untold years turned into flying shrapnel, cutting through the unprotected fighters, and creating craters in the riverbed.

"Shift fire! Six-zero-zero-zero mils. Add two hundred. Repeat!"

The wave of fire followed the river's route. The rumblings rolled back at them as they forever altered the landscape ahead of them.

Landrith called in correction after correction until he had nothing else.

He turned to Sergeant Cao. "You see anything?"

"Nope, I don't see shit down there, man. You got 'em." Sergeant Cao patted him on the back.

"Firebases, this is Spotting Squad Four One. Fire mission complete. Over."

"Understood. Coordinates for trap placement. Firebase Group Three out."

Landrith called in corrections. New mortars exploded above the ground, tossing out trap formation plates, sowing them down the river on the dead fighters.

"Anyone trying to come through there is going to have a shitty day," Sergeant Cao said as the wind rushed over them, dusting their white and grey coverings that blended into the mountain perfectly.

Landrith let out a breath. The hit of adrenaline dropped off as thunder rumbled in the distance.

"Looks like rain is coming." Landrith gestured to the ominous clouds to the west.

"That's not thunder. The flashes are on the ground, not in the sky," Cao said. "Those are the other mortar positions. Get some food in you. I've got first watch. Make sure that anyone coming through our sector gets a welcome surprise."

"Okay." Landrith pulled out snacks, numbly putting them into his mouth. *How many did I kill with those mortars? How many more will die from the traps?*

He rubbed his face, covering his eyes as he took a breath in and out.

"Looks like we have some new customers," Cao said. "Firebases Group Three, this is Spotting Squad Four-one. Targets at pre-set position. Charlie moving to position Delta. Fire for effect."

Marco frowned at the noises echoing from the south, shifting in his saddle.

"We made good time over the last day. Tomorrow afternoon we will reach Vuzgal," said Leonia. She was one of the Tolentino's younger generation, waiting on his every need, acting as his second, learning from and supporting him.

Marco responded with the same indifference he had always treated these hangers-on. Leonia was of the rare breed that didn't care if she was ignored. More of a glorified messenger and squire, looking to get introduced to powerful people in the sect and among others.

"I don't get why we had to use the smaller tents. The greeting hall only fits ten or so people." She sighed.

And your bedroom, bathroom, kitchen, dining room and reading room. Marco stretched. It felt like someone was watching him but was probably just excitement for the upcoming battle.

He settled down. Just part of another long line of soldiers and supplies.

Their force was broken into dozens of smaller groups following their guides, moving through the northern and southern mountain ranges, before taking smaller paths that were a person to two carts wide in places.

What are those sects doing?

As he'd expected, once the Willful Institute prepared to charge ahead, the other sects had rushed out. His commanders had played their part well in slowing them down.

The other sects were well in the lead. Some were about to enter the valley. Now Marco Tolentino was passing sects that had rested through the night and were waking up slowly, rekindling their fires from the night before, servants brewing tea and preparing the morning's meals.

Another noise rose from the south.

Marco frowned. "What is that?"

"I will check with the sect ahead," a nearby aide said, pulling out a communication device.

Marco released his reins and pulled out his map. Once they got into Vuzgal Valley, he would use the planning cart.

He turned the map so Vuzgal sat in the center. The southern mountains were impossible to cross with anything but aerial beasts, which were rare and expensive. *They also have defensive ringed walls around the Alchemist's valley.*

He traced the sweeping lines in the south and north that splintered into smaller lines, like roots digging through the mountains themselves. The Valley was filled with wild forests other than the area around Vuzgal and the roads that cut to the east and west.

His eyes fell on the two force markers moving down the main roads toward Vuzgal.

"Still nothing." Marco put the map away.

"You keep frowning like that, cousin, and you'll scare all the girls away!"

Leonia faced his glare. Her smile disappeared, and she lowered her head.

"We have reports of whistling devices being used!" an aide said.

Marco had been going through every piece of information on Vuzgal and in the first defense of the city, the whistling, exploding weapons had been used to devastating effect.

"Raise mana barriers!" Marco ordered.

The aide hesitated.

"Do it," Marco snarled.

Marco's personal guards turned to their formation cart and activated their mana barrier. It materialized in the air and covered the ground.

"Skittish, must be their first fight to put up a barrier when we haven't even seen the enemy yet," a nearby sect elder muttered, loud enough to be heard.

"Waste of mana stones," another fighter agreed.

Others repeated similar statements, but Marco paid no attention, pulling out his map again. There were more dull noises in the distance, falling like a constant rain. *If we are here, then those sounds are coming from the west. Here.*

Marco looked around, his finger pointing at the mountain paths.

"Paths are being hit with that whistling rain spell," another aide reported as they updated their linked maps.

"They knew where we were coming from and how we would attack," Marco said calmly, as if it was all within his expectations. *Just a simple trading city in the Fourth Realm.*

"I want all of our mana barriers up, *now*!"

Toufpht, Toufpht, Toufpht.

Marco looked up to see sparrows descending from the heavens like the Devil's own messengers. Repeaters along their sides fired twin angry red lines projected out of their chest.

The explosions came before the screaming.

The birds flew in formation, three in the lead with four trailing behind, dropping glowing boulders.

Formation covered metal shells?

They struck the ground like the gods own hammers. A fifty-meter area was *vaporized* instantly. Winds tossed around people, carts, trees and beasts like playthings. The aerial formation swept down the convoy.

Marco watched the red lines rake his mana barrier. The formation covered metal shells ignited on the barrier's surface. The explosive force rebounded, clearing trees, and killing those outside the barrier, but it held.

As fast as they arrived, the aerial formation climbed into the heavens. In its wake, a path of devastation.

A few of the fighters had pulled up mana barriers in time, but the several thousand strong convoy had been reduced to less than two thousand.

Even Marco's elite guards were shaken by the sheer destruction.

"Order our armies to charge toward Vuzgal as fast as possible!"

It seemed that the Vuzgalians were well-prepared for this kind of a fight. If the convoy continued to move slowly, they would destroy them as they had the Blood Demon Sect. Marco turned to the aides who were hunched over their maps, trying to get as close to the ground as possible.

"Give my orders now!"

The aides pulled out their sound transmission devices.

"Come on! Hyah!" He snapped his reins and increased his pace, forcing the rest of them into movement. They had to throw the Vuzgalians off-balance, close in on them as soon as possible.

He didn't look down as his mount's sharpened claws drew cries and screams from those that didn't move fast enough or weren't able to move.

"Faster, faster!"

His riders moved with him as they charged forward, feeling the pounding of their beasts' charges.

Gong Jin sported a limp as he walked through the gates of Aberdeen. He was covered in bloodied bandages, leaning on Asaka. The diminutive woman looked like a weathered camp follower, complete with wrinkles and tired eyes. His other hand gripped onto a rough wooden limb fashioned into a cane.

They passed into darkness under the portcullis. Carts rattled forward on the stone. Traders still came, selling their wares to whoever would purchase them. Wars were good business. Several had picked up paying wounded to cart through.

The wounded capable of movement shuffled forward.

The smell came first, a mix of offal and death, with well-churned mud and medicinal herbs. Exiting the wall's tunnel, the groans and cries of the wounded filled their ears.

Gong Jin stumbled, Asaka holding him aloft, a work of acting to make herself look feeble.

"The Blue Light's Healing house has limited room," a healer called out. "Ten Earth mana stones to secure a bed in the finest healing house of Aberdeen!"

"Have a case of the slow death? Drink this golden fire potion! Removes your fever! Match it with this mild healing powder to heal your wounds!"

Alchemists and healers cried out their prices. Wounded cursed as they suffered without the funds to pay for even the simplest of services.

Gong Jin saw several questionable low-quality healing potions exchanging hands.

A group of horsemen rode in through the tunnel, the noise warning Gong Jin and Asaka as they pushed to the side.

"Move you damn beasts!" a man yelled as four horsemen, bloodied from battle protected a wagon with several wounded and an emblazoned sect crest.

"Over here, my lords!" A man lowered his herb-filled rag and waved the group forward. "The Golden Light healing troupe has been hired out to your sect!"

The group wheeled around, and the man ran forward, guiding them down the street.

"The bigger the sect the better the treatment," Asaka muttered as they headed deeper into the city.

"Look at their crests. There are others from the same sect among the wounded. Just they don't have such a grand position. Bodies to fill the charge, little more."

The city was in motion. Crafters worked continuously, repairing and supplying the front lines of the United Sect's Army. Traders came and went via gates. The totems were controlled by the sects, bringing in a sea of supplies and reinforcements, sending out wounded and empty wagons.

The sects controlled the city; everything was put toward the war effort.

The farther they moved into the city, the less wounded there were. Either they had found aid or hadn't made it this far.

Asaka and Gong Jin headed into an alleyway. Asaka pulled off the colored wax from her face, her wrinkles disappearing as she tore away the bloodied clothing, revealing plain work clothes of a laborer.

She cracked her back audibly as Gong Jin wiped the last of the blood from his head wound. The skin healed without the poison covered wrapping on it.

He shed his other bandages and the stick he had used. He pulled on a shirt, another nameless citizen, tired from the long hours and new residents.

He glanced at the sky, the fresh breeze of morning tainted with iron, oil and medicines.

"Ready to go, boss?" Asaka asked.

"Yeah, I'm good."

They had been here a few months back on a reconnaissance operation. Each of the special teams and Close Protection Details took turns keeping an eye on their neighbors. It kept the city fresh in their minds.

They moved through the alleyways, passing others using them as a shortcut home, and walked out into the crafter district. Carts rattled down the street at a constant pace. Some entered crafting warehouses, others left.

The heat of the smithies and the alchemy workshops had burned away any of the surrounding moisture. Soot-covered smiths and assistants moved behind doors, feeding the smithies' flames.

They walked the length of the crafting quarter, weaving between places, gathering dirt and dust as they traced the carts back to large compounds, staging areas filled with supplies.

Gong Jin's sound transmission device buzzed twice before going silent. "Let's head somewhere we can think," he said to Asaka.

They weaved through the traffic to a quiet area where they could lean against a wall, using a covert sound transmission device.

"Han Wu?"

"Boss, we're inside the city, I've got everyone with me."

"Good. Meet us at the first rally point. We'll be there in fifteen."

"Got it."

He stepped away from the wall and indicated to Asaka with his eyes, walking to the street and checking for a gap between carriages before they ran across the road.

"Good news, I hope?" Asaka asked.

"Yeah, the others are ready to work."

"Nice."

Gong Jin knocked on the door of a house that looked no different from the others around it: small, stone and soot-stained in this part of the crafter's quarter.

A woman opened the door. "I was expecting you later. Come in, come in!" The woman waved them in with a smile as she cleaned one hand under her apron, then closed the door. Her cheer faded as the formations on the door activated and she moved her hand out from under her apron, holding a mana pistol.

"The rest are downstairs. All the way down that corridor, and the door behind you to the right."

"Thank you." Gong Jin and Asaka walked through the house. The front had a plain table in one room, and a bed in another. They entered the kitchen and found the door leading down.

Asaka closed it behind her. Formations glowed, illuminating the stairwell. They passed a picture on the wall and entered the basement. The large open room had been broken into an area with bunk beds, a bathroom, and a table with chairs. Several doors led to tunnels and a map of the city with different markings hung from a wall.

Han Wu came out from behind the picture wall with a grin, making Gong Jin flinch and curse.

"Hey, boss." He jerked a chin at the only person in the basement that wasn't part of their team. "That's Ming, our contact."

"Good to meet you, sir," the man said, standing up and shaking his hand.

"Tell me what we're looking at here." Gong Jin indicated to the map on the wall.

Ming moved to it and pointed at several red dots. "These are all supply depots for the United Sect Army. They're stored, sorted and sent out from here to the front lines. There are seven in total. These—" Ming pointed to the orange markings in the crafting quarter. "—are sect-controlled crafting workshops."

"We're here to blow the supply dumps. Why are you telling us about the crafting workshops?" Han Wu asked.

"The sects check everything and anything that comes into their supply depots from an outside source. They don't check the carts coming from their sect workshops."

"Useful how?" Gong Jin asked.

"Useful as in they won't check the carts too closely when they return to a supply depot from a crafting workshop, and those on the front lines don't check their supplies as they're busy fighting a war."

Gong Jin took in a cold breath. "Nasty. Real nasty."

"Complacency will kill a soldier faster than a round," Asaka agreed.

Han Wu yawned in the early morning sunlight. He paused as people flowed around him on the sidewalk, trying to avoid being late. They grumbled as they passed him and created a cover as he stood in front of the gates to a workshop.

He reached into the ground under his feet, using his control over the earth element to part the rocks and dirt to create holes. He moved his leg to the side, releasing the explosive charge in his cut pocket. It slid down his leg into the left hole.

He moved to the side, sealing the left hole as he released the charge down his right leg and into the second hole. The stone and dirt washed over the charge, hiding it from view. He moved to an alley, his work unseen in the busy street. He changed clothes from worker to trader and doubled back, entering a restaurant, ordering noodles and tea. He pulled out a notebook filled with markings and took his time sipping his tea. He didn't have to wait long as the first supply cart appeared, it forced the walkers to either side and pushed past the gates.

More carts showed up through the morning.

Han Wu finished his noodles and ordered some more tea, spotting different team members planting more explosives.

The first cart made to exit. The driver yelled at the people in front of the exit as he pushed through with his beasts.

Han Wu opened the ground underneath the cart. A pillar of dirt tipped with the explosive-wrapped charge pressed against the bottom of the cart. "Wood Manipulation."

He muttered the spell, altering the underside of the cart to grow over the charge as he released the dirt and covered it in stone.

There was no sign anything had happened as the cart rattled onto the street.

Han Wu drank some more tea, feeling the sweat on his brow.

More carts departed, but Han Wu had to wait until there was a slower one. He spent the morning pushing charges to the undercarriage of several supply carts.

When the explosives ran out, he paid his bill and headed out.

He went to the side of the crafting workshop. His flowing robes covered the ground underneath him as he tied his shoe.

Last little present.

He dropped in a much larger charge, covering it, and pushing it under the ground and wall as deep into the workshop as he could in the time it took him to tie both shoes and stand up.

He took out his sound transmission device.

"Hey boss, planted at the target. Moving out."

"Understood."

Han Wu ducked into an alleyway. Tyrone was already there, wearing sect armor and gear. He nodded to Han Wu as he continued to stand on lookout.

Han Wu took off his robes and pulled on pants, a shirt, and boots. He strapped a sword to his hip and pulled out a bandana emblazoned with a sect's symbol. "How do I look?"

"Passable," Tyrone said.

They moved through the city and toward the gates. By then it had turned to mid-afternoon. The guards barely spared them a second glance as they walked through the gates.

Carriages lay waiting to transport reinforcements. They found some of Special Team Four and Eight waiting for them and got on a carriage that had been checked for explosives.

"Be good to get to the main army," Han Wu said. The sect members in the carriage looked over but kept to themselves.

"Yeah, we've got a lot of work to do," Gong Jin agreed.

The driver called out to his beast, and the carriage lurched forward, onward to the United Sect Army's front.

They rode for a few hours. Asaka checked her watch. Gong Jin pulled out a clacker, hidden in his hands under his arm and squeezed it three times, black smoke shot up into the sky, the sound of the explosion reaching them minutes later.

Secondary explosions went off in several locations and Han Wu saw the signs of fires starting around the city.

Han Wu's sound transmission device buzzed. He picked it up and listened. "Each of the supply depots were hit with varying levels of destruction. The teams at the supporting cities are reporting success. Some carts exploded along the road, killing reinforcements headed to the army as well. The targeted workshops don't exist anymore." Ming reported.

"All right. Stay safe, Ming. See you back at base."

"You got it, boss man."

Han Wu closed the transmission device.

"Some spell formations went off in the city. Looks like an enemy attack!" he said to the people in the carriage, acting for the sect members in the carriage.

Murmurs went through the carriage.

One sect member snorted. "I can't hear anything."

"I'm telling you, I have a friend in the city. He said everything was attacked in one hit."

"How could they do that? Teleport into the city and attack us? My master says that they know nothing about how to fight properly. They keep retreating and use formations and spells because they can't cast powerful spells and their combat skills are weak," another sect member said.

"I'm telling the truth," Han Wu said.

They snorted and stopped talking to him.

Han Wu looked at those around him before falling into sullen silence. *Part one complete, now for Part Two.*

Night fell as they rolled off the road, coming to a wayside camp. Tents had been thrown up to create sleeping and eating areas. Carriages were lined up ready to continue their journey for the next day.

The team left the carriages, stretching and moving to the food tents. The wounded were fed weak soup outside while the fresh fighters got cooked meats and stamina potions.

The teams moved around the camp, planting attack formations in the ground. They snuck past the guards who made sure people didn't desert, and grouped together, pulling out their panther mounts, and headed into the forest.

Moving in silence, they removed their sect clothing and reached a cave.

Gong Jin halted them. "Great night for some fireworks."

Two Close Protection teams appeared out of the forest. "You're the last," one of them said and waved them forward. The team dismounted and entered the cave, the details collapsing from their watch positions.

"How about the rest stops?" Gong Jin asked the CPD leader who had led them into the cave.

"We got nearly every damn one of them."

"Good," Gong Jin said as one of the mages used a spell. The dirt at the side of the cave moved and a stone slid away, revealing a teleportation formation.

"Back home we go."

"They did what? Charged?" Domonos stared at the map, deciphering the ever-changing symbols and placements. Trees that appeared one moment disappeared into craters as aerial forces bombed the fighters hiding underneath.

Glowing markers showed where artillery platoons had set up and the path of the aerial forces.

Aides created a buzz of conversation, transforming and changing the map as new information came in.

The swords had turned into arrows and were charging forward.

"Yeah, they must have thought we were leading an attack into their teeth. Don't think they're used to an enemy hitting them from far away and not getting in close to steal their shit. Command and control is a mess. There are lost units walking in circles. Reinforcements and supplies are stuck in the passes as we keep hammering them. Some units are using mana barriers, but the terrain is fucking them up." Zukal smiled. "They're a fucking mess."

"I love good news, but they reacted faster than I thought. While they're fucked up, spreading out and pushing forward as fast as possible is the best move for them," Domonos said.

"They rushed through the mortar fire. Looks like panic or orders. Groups ran right into the trap fields, although some made it through," an aide reported.

"Must not have known if they were mortars or traps," Zukal added.

Domonos used his sound transmission device, his eyes flicking over the map. "Kanoa, launch all your people. Hit them with everything you have. Break their forward momentum or they'll cross our lines, and we'll have their units among ours. I'm ordering the mobile artillery to pull back. They'll cover and move, shooting over one another to hit the enemy. Once they're inside our sensing range, they'll be free to pick out their own targets. The reserve support units will assist your kestrel units."

"Yes, sir! Target priority?"

"Hit the runners. Make them turn back with the sparrows. Use explosives and firebombs. Create lines in the forests to funnel them. Use kestrels to hit the larger groups."

"Yes, sir."

"You heard what I said." Domonos looked at the aides. "Make it happen. The reserve support units will board the kestrels and act as attack mages. Enact plan Scorpion. Activate all spell traps across the valley. Make sure our scouts pull back before they're encircled. If they need aerial extraction, they'll have to hold in place."

Domonos' eyes never left the map. *Was there an order to disperse and charge or did that happen in a panic?* With the enemy spread out, one mortar wouldn't be able to kill as many. Their command and control would be hampered, but they had numbers on their side, and they knew where they were going. Domonos gritted his teeth, trying to see through the enemy's plan, to scry the future.

"If I were him, I'd charge forward as fast as possible to disrupt our lines, create chaos. The farther they get, the better. If they can cross and confuse our lines, that would be the best. Okay, so we need to make them group up and slow down." His eyes locked onto the mountains. "The traps will slow them, but they're streaming out of the mountains now."

"Most of their forces still need to cross them," Zukal said.

Domonos grabbed a pointer and studied the mountain ranges. "We need to cut off these paths here. This is where most of the units are splitting. Cutting off these routes will force them into the central paths." Domonos pointed at non-circled lines. "It will slow how fast they can move people into the valley and give us time to deal with the leakers. Track them down with sparrows and kestrels, forcing them together for safety in numbers."

Zukal nodded.

"If they're charging forward and get deep into our territory, their supply lines will have to go farther than before."

"Blow the rest stop locations?"

"I think so. We'll only get one chance to do it. From then on, we'll have to do harassing attacks on their supply lines. They're already feeling the pinch after losing supplies in the last operation."

"Anyone's bound to feel it when that much armor, ammunition, and mana stones are destroyed," Zukal said.

"Send the order. Blow the rest stops. Pass orders to Kanoa to have the aerial forces harass the supply lines. They won't have the coverage or the protection of the front lines.

"Yes, sir."

Rugrat grabbed the shell from the second ammunition bearer. The formation plate lit up as mana flexed in the air, dashing into the mortar shell as the spell completed in less than a second. He passed the shell to the first ammunition bearer who grabbed it and released it down the tube, then ducked as Rugrat got another shell, casting Explosive Shot on it.

The mortar pounded into the dirt with a tinny metal noise and a blast of hot air.

Rugrat passed the new shell to the first ammunition bearer as the gunner worked the traversing gear and the elevating gear with quick, professional movements before bracing the front bipod legs.

The ammunition bearer hung the massive mortar shell, longer than his arm and as thick as his leg, before releasing.

There was no time to think as they operated as one machine, feeding the metal beast.

"Rounds complete! Rounds complete! Shift one-one-five-one!" the mortar team leader yelled.

"Shift one-one-five-one!" the gunner repeated as he adjusted and checked the sight.

"Five rounds. H.E. Double charge!" the team leader said.

"Five rounds. H.E. Double charge!" the second ammunition bearer yelled back, pulling out rounds from his storage ring and tearing off secondary charges.

"Bunker bust spell!"

"Bunker bust spell!" Rugrat yelled back, casting the piercing shot spell. "Ready."

"Ready!" the gunner yelled.

The assistant gunner passed the first shell to Rugrat.

The mana fluctuated as his spell overlaid the formations carved into the shell before he handed it to the first ammunition bearer. "Fire when ready!"

The first ammunition bearer released and dropped. Rugrat cast the spell on the second shell and passed it to him.

They repeated the process again and again.

"Target destroyed. Shift fire!"

Rugrat felt the waves of mortar fire from the dozen or so mortar pits on the mountain side.

"Artillery line Alpha is pulling back to the rear. Be ready to move if necessary!" Second Lieutenant Couto's voice rang out.

"New targets!" the Staff Sergeant yelled, focusing the mortar team. "Target pre-set Foxtrot. T-D rounds and T shells!"

32
Adapt and Overcome

Captain Wazny checked on the rest of his sparrow wing. Early morning had turned into midday. "Follow me in!"

His sparrow tilted downward. The formations in his goggles activated to keep them clear of mist as he broke through the clouds. Below lay the forest. In their rush, the sects had made it into the forests of Vuzgal Valley. Confusion had made them spread out. Their convoys—a black snake filled with war beasts, fighters, and supply wagons—were trying to claw their way through the wilds.

The life detect formation in Wazny's goggles lit up with the thousands of fighters just beneath the canopy. With that many trees and chaotic terrain, there was no way they could use their mana barriers.

He lined up his sights on the convoy and pulled on the trigger. His wooden cockpit shook as the two modified heavy repeaters under his sparrow's wings and along her body unleashed destruction.

Leaves and branches turned into splinters as the explosive bolts carved a path into the trees below.

His wing, seven strong, was spread out in an arrowhead formation. Their fire raked the canopy, destroying trees and tearing apart the fighters hidden underneath.

"Leveling off!" Wazny looked through a looking glass, which had carved lines to range bomb drops.

"Bomb drop!"

He opened his storage ring. Streams of bombs dropped from the sparrows.

Arrows and spells tried to respond, appearing randomly in the air.

"Break!" Wazny guided his beast and stopped dropping bombs.

The wing of seven split into two groups, four banking left and three banking right as their sparrows regained altitude.

The bombs struck the ground. Explosions shook the sparrows even from their height of several hundred meters and well past the drop zones. Fifty-meter-wide areas were cleared of fighters, carts, beasts, and underbrush.

Fireballs spread across the ground as the incendiaries went off.

Wazny grunted against the force of his sparrow as they banked in the direction they had come from.

He was in the lead. Two other sparrows were with him, moving into arrowhead formation once again. The four that had banked to the left flew away from them and along the enemy lines of advance.

His voice cut into their communication devices. "Bombing only!"

He looked through the bombing sight, seeing the fighters through the thick tree cover. "Release!"

He once again activated the storage ring. Bombs tumbled out, one after another. Their fins grabbed the air, positioning them as their formations glowed with destructive power, called down to exact vengeance upon the ground below.

Wazny saw the impacts before he heard them through the tearing wind that whistled through his cockpit.

The bombs spread out, not impacting one after another.

"Cut speed!" They slowed, their blast radius nearly overlapping one another.

Wazny glanced at the path of destruction they had left. The forest turned into a broken trail, with fires rapidly spreading throughout.

"Sparrow Wing One-Three, group up on wing leader. We're heading northeast."

Marco Tolentino didn't look over at the sound of another trap formation going off. The rivers, woods, mountains, and the roads were filled with trap formations and spell traps. Not even Leonia was cracking jokes anymore.

While weaker than they might be in the higher realms, the traps wore on the fighters' minds and could be hidden anywhere. They were smaller than a palm but had the power to kill dozens of fighters in their range.

It was one of the things Marco was thankful of, fighting in a mana sparse realm.

The mana barriers covering the advancing Willful Institute army shuddered as kestrels cut overhead. Marco bowed his head as meteor rain screamed out of the air, crashing into the barriers, and lighting them up with ripples as the world filled with noise.

Metal weapons fell from the kestrels, exploding below.

A few weakened mana barriers either didn't have the power to support the barrier anymore, or their formations had burned out from the force upon them.

Spells shifted targets, slaughtering the unprotected fighters.

Ranged fighters turned to the sky, casting attack spells that caused the kestrels to split and weave, trying to escape.

"Push forward!" Marco had to use his sound transmission device to be heard by the commanders.

The melee fighters cut forward, clearing through the forest ahead as they advanced under their mana barriers.

Marco and the rest of the Willful Institute leadership had kept ironclad control of their fighters, pulling them together, unlike the sect groups that had spread across Vuzgal Valley.

The sects had pushed out of the paths, entering the forest valley itself. Aerial beasts continued attacking the paths into the valley, cutting down supply lines and reinforcements. They had been attacking them all morning and into the afternoon, and hadn't yet seen anything other than their aerial beasts.

A scream rang out with a flash of spell activation. Another melee fighter on his mount had found a trap formation.

They were just days away from reaching Vuzgal and needed to get there as fast as possible.

"Sir," the aide was interrupted by a whistling sound.

"Push forward!" Marco yelled. The pace increased as the whistling ended and exploded.

The Willful Institute surged once again. People were claimed by the trap formations as another whistle filled the air, exploding in a different direction from the first one.

Those near the mana barrier formations were charging them with mana stones as fast as they could.

The pace increased as they cut a wide path through the forest, spread out to minimize the number of fighters that could be taken out in one attack.

The sky filled with chilling whistles.

Was it the deaths or the mental pressure of constant attacks that broke the Blood Demon Sect in the end?

33 On Both Sides

The telltale flash of distant spell traps didn't raise alarm anymore.

"Waste of resources. Do they have an endless supply of formations?" Onam muttered, rolling with his mount's gait as he passed over broken trees.

"It is surprising," Feng Dan agreed, riding on her lizard mount.

"I sense that you have more thoughts on the matter," Onam asked.

"We have no reports of crafters working on these weapons. They got a lot of people into their academy, but all crafters look to increase their skill level. They won't waste their time making hundreds of these spell traps. As soon as they can, they'll work on something to advance their level."

"So, they purchased them from somewhere else?"

"Something is not what it seems with Vuzgal. The screaming weapons are like trebuchets, but they must have formations. They're weapons that burn through money faster than mana cannons. Though they keep using them without caring. They have their own forces to train their soldiers and to create these weapons."

Onam opened his mouth as shadows passed overhead.

"Hold in place! Secure the edges of the mana barriers!" Feng Dan ordered. Explosions rocked the forest, punctuating her words.

Men, women, and beasts were torn apart. The trees shattered, collapsing as firebombs went off, tearing air from men's lungs, a wave of heat greeting them.

Onam used his reins and legs to control his mount uneasily, shying away from the destruction. All the beasts had been trained for war, but this was beyond their training.

A tree that stuck out of the barrier was struck. It splintered within the barrier, killing or wounding the surrounding fighters.

People jumped from their mounts, hiding in the ground and dirt.

Like a curtain of rain, the bombs arrived and passed.

Onam watched the birds that had appeared just above the trees, unseen and unheard, circle.

"They're coming back around!" he yelled.

Groups broke, rushing forward into the trees as if the cover would save them. Others ran to the mana barriers in the cleared sections of forest.

The shadows arrived, bringing death behind them once again.

"Mages, hit them!" Feng Dan yelled.

Mages cast spells, but they were drowned out by the second rain of destruction. The birds took to the skies again. A trail of spells followed them as they split apart, weaving and altering their flight path randomly.

Suddenly, the explosions and bombs stopped.

Cracking and spitting fire fought against the screams and cries of the wounded and dying.

Onam gritted his teeth. "Fucking cowards. They don't even face us, just run away as fast as possible!"

"Seems that Marco wasn't exaggerating how effective they are. The whistling weapons are silent now. At least we *knew* they were coming before."

Knowing when you were being attacked and suddenly being in the midst of destruction would make even the most courageous fighter nervous.

Spell traps went off as people at the front found them, returning or running away from the main group.

"Aggh!" Onam spat on the ground to hide the tremble in his hand.

"We face a determined enemy," Domonos said to his Battalion Majors. "They lost a day in forward momentum. But at the cost of thousands, they have gained entry into the valley. They pressed forward as fast as possible through every path. Now, they have gathered their dispersed forces once again. We successfully withdrew our artillery platoons and scouts to Vuzgal. With the enemy out of the mountain passes, they're in our sensing formations' net, but they can employ their mana barriers with greater effect. The air force will be taking on a larger role from here on. Major Kanoa..."

"Yes, sir." Kanoa stepped forward and cleared his throat. "Our kestrel forces are harassing the mountain passes with heavy fire power. Sparrows continue to conduct lightning raids on the enemy's positions. With eyes on target, they can inflict greater casualties." Kanoa nodded to Domonos and took a half step backward.

"There it is. Mortars and the air force will be our weapons in this coming advance. Our enemy has shown cunning and ability. We must be ready for changes as they occur. Problems? Issues? Queries?"

Major Hall raised his hand. "Have our targets changed?"

"No, artillery's first target is the camp followers. Second, attacking enemy formations as they come together, third laying of traps. Kestrels target the mountain passes. Sparrows take targets of opportunity and have priority, then kestrels, then artillery."

Hall nodded.

"In the meantime, we have two regiments worth of reservists that are on their way or will be shortly. It will be their task to prepare our defenses while our remaining frontline units will coordinate as needed. I want them ready for what's coming. I think it is time we started using the silence spells on the mortars," Domonos informed the command staff.

"We must increase our speed. These traps and airborne attacks only slow us. The slower we move, the more time our enemy has to hit us. We need to reach Vuzgal as fast as possible." Marco tapped the map on his lap as his mount carried him forward.

Master Teacher Eva Marino rode beside him. "Thankfully, their focus is on the camp followers instead of the fighters."

"As long as our fighters aren't affected, they can have as many camp followers as they want. Create groups of ranged fighters and mages to attack these aerial beasts. A few random mages and archers won't have much effect, but a group of them can fill a small area of the sky with spells and arrows."

"The whistling attacks?"

Marco pressed his lips together. "We need to find out where they come from and counterattack. Have our people spread out more. Keep a spear's spacing between fighters and have them lie down when they hear the whistling. That should kill fewer of them."

Marco paused. The mountain passes were their greatest weakness. Should they use the teleportation formations now and bring more people directly into the valley? Either they used the teleportation formations to bring them forward, or have them back out of the passes, use their mana barriers to protect against the larger birds and their mages. The smaller birds brought destruction with them, but the larger birds were like ships of the air. Their mages must have been enhanced for them to call down such powerful attacks.

Marco looked toward Vuzgal as if he could see through the hills and forests between him and his goal.

What will their next move be?

"For every action, there is a reaction."

"Hmm?" Master Marino turned her head to look at Marco.

"Have those in the passes regroup behind the mountains. We will clear areas for teleportation formations in the valley."

"Then they will know we have the teleportation formations."

"We need more people in the valley. We'll abandon the roads and the passes." Marco stored his map away. The afternoon was swiftly changing to night. "Our first day in the Vuzgal valley."

"They failed to keep us out," Marino sneered.

"At the cost of a sixth of our force."

"Only three thousand were actual fighters."

"Our enemy knew when we were leaving the cities we rallied at. They knew we were coming through the mountain paths and killed our eyes and ears. Now they attack the camp followers?"

"What does it matter? Usually, we are the ones dying."

Marco looked around at the people with him. His guards, the soldiers beyond.

"What do you think would happen if we didn't have the camp followers?" Marino asked.

Marco sunk into thought. He watched a man run up to his lord, a powerful fighter. He pulled out food and drink, holding it for the fighter as he rode, talking to his fellow fighters.

Fighters were treated like gods and goddesses on the field of battle. If they needed anything, it was supplied. If their gear was worn, it would be repaired and honed. Injuries were handled by healers and alchemists, and as for frustrations, there were ways to relieve them.

"Oh, you are smart, very smart and devious. You have clutched onto our weakness," Marco muttered and shook his head. "Sorry, Master Teacher, you were right."

"Why is that?"

"If they were all dead, who would erect our tents? Who would we trust to mend our armor, hone our blades? Treat our wounds—"

A devious grin spread across Marco's face. "Make them fighters."

"What? That takes years of training!"

"I don't mean true soldiers. We'll give them armor and weapons to wear, have them move along like the other units. How will the enemy be able to pick them out then?"

34

Dawn of the Second Day

Captain Wazny scanned the ground. His sparrow flapped her wings, carrying him forward. His wing of seven stretched behind him.

"Shit, looks worse in the daytime," Lieutenant Lovren said through their communication channel.

"Last flight bombed the hell out of them all night. Twenty-four hours of random attacks," Lieutenant Bell chimed in.

"Good thing it's not late summer or fall, else the whole forest would be on fire." Wazny looked at the smoldering pockets among the cratered landscape.

"They wanted a fight." Lieutenant Nilsen sighed.

"Clear the channel. In ten minutes, we're going in low and fast. Spread out more. Their mages and archers are getting bold." Wazny pulled on his harness, feeling the metal hooks stick into the material. "If you have to, break off. Got it?"

"Yes, sir!" all seven yelled back.

"Let's get this done, then. Follow me in."

Wazny's mount led their arrowhead formation as he dove, searching for the target. They picked up speed, coming up just meters from the tops of the trees. Adrenaline filled his body and mind. Everything was clear.

Where are you bastards? Ah, there!

Several trees fell down.

"Prepare to drop! Climb!" Wazny surged into the sky as his speed turned into elevation. He didn't want to be next to the treetops when the bombs went out.

He held the storage device, checking his drop sight with a glance.

The spread-out army, huddled together in their mana barrier groups, appeared ahead.

Wazny's stomach tightened, the wind tearing at him as he checked the drop sight again. "Release!"

He activated the storage device, sending bombs tumbling to the ground below. He checked and altered his heading. The rest of the wing moved with him.

That ground is rough enough to disrupt a mana barrier, I'm sure.

Lights flashed around him and the wing. Spells came in, hot and heavy.

Shit!

This wasn't like before.

"Break, break, break!"

The sparrow wing divided away as the mass of spells and arrows checked and altered their aim.

Nilsen banked to the left, dropping bombs as she went. Spells filled the surrounding air, tearing her mount and wooden cockpit apart.

Wazny's sparrow cut, dove, and randomly banked as spells and attacks shot past. He gritted his teeth as air blades struck his cockpit, tearing it open to the spinning trees below.

"Suzy! Suzy!" he called to his mount.

His mount's wings were limp, their connection severed.

Wazny grabbed the pull tab on the side of his cockpit and was hurled free of his mount. A special formation activated, destroying his cockpit and mount as he hurtled away. He grabbed a second pull tab in his armpit. The second spell scroll activated; wings of air appeared on his back, shooting him forward.

Wazny was clear and away from the enemy. He banked toward Vuzgal, activating his sound transmission device. "Report in!"

"Two KIA. One wounded heading to Vuzgal." Lovren held back a curse.

"Shit. I'm on air wings. I'm moving to the closest teleportation formation. Send a report to Kanoa. They have anti-air units now." Wazny sped forward. He pulled his map out of his storage ring.

He saw Nilsen and her mount in his mind's eye.

Now's not the time. Deal with it later. He could feel a pit, waiting, ready for him to give in and let it consume, but duty held him.

I'll make those fuckers pay. Nilsen was right; They came for a fight, and we'll fucking give it to them.

Domonos read over the reports. "What is Major Kanoa suggesting?" Domonos looked to Zukal.

"Increase the altitude. It will decrease the accuracy of our fire, but it will be harder for them to hit the sparrows. Have the kestrels work as a mobile fire support base instead of being over the enemy. Decreased accuracy as well."

"Very well. Do it. The enemy is smart and cunning. I'm sure he has other plans too. Are we sure that the forces in the mountain paths are being recalled?"

"Yes, they're pulling out of the mountains as fast as possible. The order came from Marco Tolentino," Elan confirmed.

"What the hell is he doing? He needs people in the valley to push his advantage. He's stopped movement on the north and eastern roads. Has them holding position." Domonos' hooded eyes looked from the roads to the mountain paths as he scratched his cheek, trying to solidify the feeling he had into words.

"What about the pressures from the rear?"

"They have mounted. The sects have lost more than they expected already."

Marco had thirty-five thousand in the valley. Ten thousand were fighters, and a third of them were his own people. Was he using this to increase his position? If he could get to Vuzgal first, the Willful Institute would lay claim to more resources. The people with him were from his faction as well. *Greed, even now. All they care about is rewards.*

"At the core, we are fighting the Tolentino faction of the Willful Institute. They do not have large numbers in the field, but that is a strength. With fewer people, they can act and react faster. They adhere to orders better. If we can defeat the force within the Valley, the other forces will retreat." He tapped the valley, feeling sure of his knowledge as he pointed at the mountain ranges. "Otherwise, they have to push the mountain paths again. They lost over fifty thousand in those paths. Focus everything we have on the forces inside the valley."

"Then there is the matter of the disappearing camp followers," Elan said.

"The enemy has given them uniforms to wear, and some got mana barriers. It's smart. and a huge pain in our ass now that we've recalled the scouts. Sparrows and kestrels will be flying higher, so it'll be harder to pick the followers out. The formations just give us the position of everything."

"Camp followers are still followers. They won't be in the lead." Zukal said.

"No, but they sowed fighter units among their ranks. We have no idea who we're hitting."

"A dead enemy is a good enemy. We can't focus on plans that are ruined. Just the ones we can make to win," Elan said. "With this move, the camp followers' security will be fixed and they will feel cared for, giving the best they can to the enemy. That is the end of it."

Domonos nodded. "For now, our focus is on anything inside our Valley."

Acosta checked the information on her linked map, showing the target as it got hammered with mortar rounds.

Her twelve mortars were firing rounds as fast as possible. The cooling formations running down the tubes were working overtime to expel the heat. Heat exchange blocks raised on their rails, waves of heat shimmering off of them as the teams worked as a machine.

They had gotten into a rhythm over the last few days. She was just the guidance as they operated. Everything else was lost. Worries, fears, their past and futures… All that remained were their actions.

Acosta saw the markings of the mana barrier disappear.

"Impact H.E. Rounds Explosive shot spell! Impact H.E. Rounds Explosive shot spell," she yelled.

The squad leaders repeated it as the ammunition bearers grabbed Impact H.E. rounds, tossing away auxiliary charges, passing it to the mage who added the explosive shot spell, and then to the first ammunition bearer who hung and released the round.

There was only a half-second lull as rounds that had already been released continued to hit the barrierless sect. Mana barrier busting piercing shots smashed through people, dirt, and stone.

A new rain rose.

"Drop five hundred. Drop a turn each round!" Acosta's words echoed through the mortar pits as gunners whirled, elevating gears.

Her eyes tracked the enemy running into the forests. Others laid down on the ground.

The impact rounds fell as the newly adjusted guns were loaded and fired.

A wave of destruction covered where the barrier had stood and swept forward.

Spread out to all hell and most of them lying down. Shit.

Acosta watched her brand of retribution. The air force had taken a heavy blow this morning. Twenty-eight dead, another forty-two wounded. Of that, five were behind enemy lines and still working toward a teleportation formation. If they were captured, death would claim them through torture or suicide.

Master Sergeant Sirel, her second-in-command, smacked her on the shoulder. "Command said there's a group of aerial beasts headed for our location. Four minutes."

"Shit!" In the same breath, she used the platoon-wide channel. "Enemy aerial forces incoming! Defensive positions!"

The last rounds went off, and the gun units covered their weapons. Mages gathered their power, remaining on their enhancing formations. Close Protection forces ran to their ready position at the four cardinal points of the ring of mortar pits. Artillery gunners moved to the front of their pits, pulling out their repeaters and aiming at the heavens.

"Use flak spells!" Squad leaders reminded them of their anti-air drills.

As they rushed to their positions, Acosta grabbed her own repeater, her head snapping to Sirel. "Direction?"

"Northeast."

"Be ready on the northeast!" Acosta repeated on the platoon channel.

The silence of the artillery position only added to the tension.

The aerial mounts came in all different forms, grouped together by sect as they cleared the trees.

"Fire!" Acosta's platoon fired their repeaters. Their arrows shot into the sky. Their spells activated, generating air blades that blasted out along the path they were heading, shredding what lay before them. Personal mana barriers stopped many.

Spells ignited in the sky. Spears and blades of air became red lines as they cut through unprotected beasts and fighters.

They were a half second faster than the sects who attacked. Spears of flame, water, and air crashed into the mana barrier covering the artillery position. Meteors roared, creating ripples.

A group of fighters worked together, their hands shining with runes to create a spell formation between them. The land seemed to darken, drawing the sunlight into the formation before it was released.

Acosta ducked as the formation created a second sun, a pillar of light as bright as the sun and lightning struck the mana barrier, drawing a line across its surface and passing over.

Stone melted and burned while trees were turned to charcoal without time to catch aflame.

Acosta blinked the light out of her eyes. Seeing movement in the sky, she aimed and fired.

They paid the reaper's bill for their attacks.

Dozens fell from the skies. Repeaters left lines of spell-enhanced bolts. Their unnerving aim that came from Rugrat's teaching and had been honed through years of training, plucked riders from the sky.

They broke and fled.

Acosta turned, leading her target as she fired. Their barrier appeared; several other repeaters added their attacks. The barrier cracked as a red spray and tombstone filled the air.

The beast and rider dropped from sight as Acosta looked for more targets.

"Sirel?" She turned and yelled.

"Don't see anything coming in." He looked over to her from the covered command center.

Acosta changed to the platoon channel. "Pack it up! Moving out in ten! CPD, watch the skies."

She reloaded her repeater as she walked into the command center again. "We're moving position. Advise higher. I want our CPD's on aerial protection. Fuck, that sunlight spell was a bitch." She stored her repeater. "Sirel, you head to the next location with the first squad that's ready. Start prepping the position for us."

"Yes, ma'am. I'll hurry them along." Sirel ran out of the command post.

"Well, this looks promising," Colonel Domonos said as he walked into Matt's blueprint office. He waved off several officers and foremen from Alva's construction companies, moving to the light display showing Vuzgal's growing defensive plans.

"You wanted impossible to cross." Matt walked up beside him.

"Care to explain?"

"Okay, so, we have plenty of barbed wire traps and shovels. Earth moving spells, same thing." Matt waved off Domonos' smirk.

"This all looks rather intensive."

"Not all that complicated. Get a few earth movers making the trenches, some laborers pulling out the barbed wire. Triple Concertina wire. Basically, just posts nailed into bedrock with these coils of wire with razor-sharp barbs. Put two on the bottom and one on top, link them all together."

Domonos nodded with the air of one who was intimately familiar. "What about removing the earth and leaving stone?"

Matt paused. "Manipulating stone takes more mana and going deep enough, in the range of the dungeon core."

"We can put the reservists to work," Domonos said.

"That should help."

They devolved into planning, the officers and foreman mobilizing every dastardly part of their brain. They came up with trap enchantments on the ground, the barbed wire, the posts affixing it to the very ground, random hidden holes and slit trenches a few centimeters to meters deep to capture beast and human ankles. They went through several iterations of obstacles, changing Matt's plans, and creating three different areas.

Matt felt the cold stroke at his spine. "That'd be nasty."

"So would sticking our strongest mana gathering formations right under their feet," Domonos said.

"And we use it all to charge our barriers." Matt let out a low whistle. "The more people they throw at us, the more spells they use, the faster we gather power."

Domonos snapped his fingers and pointed at Matt. "Turn the dirt into mud. The should have the stamina for it, but should make some of them trip and it's a pain in the ass to wade through every damn day. All churned up they'll get stuck deeper and deeper."

"We could pull in a weather spell to saturate the place with rain. But it's just mud."

"Even better. Morale, Hall. If they believe that they won't take Vuzgal, they won't, and we make it a damn hell for them to try. Rain and sloshing through mud rarely makes one's day."

"Could we tunnel under the battlefield and have some undead mages casting spells to turn the ground into mud? They could wander around randomly, making sure that it's a soupy mess. Then if the enemy mages cast hardening spells, they'll get broken up." Matt asked.

"Have them casting spell traps as well. Sow them all over the place."

Matt made some notations on the blueprint, and the light display changed. He tapped his pencil on his lips before pressing on. "So, for the second line of defense, they hit the trenches and terrain obstacles. If it's connected to the dungeon, then there is little chance in hell they're going to be able to fix that. Create chasms under the ground so they have to create bridges to cross them and thin sheets between so they have to be a damn cat to not fall down. Add spikes in the bottom and razor-sharp protrusions on the wall. Have the dungeon maintain them as well. Make them progressively deeper as they get close. Put barbed wire on the spaces between the pits."

"Traps inside the chasms?" Matt looked up.

"Link them to the razor walls or the floor." Domonos paused and nodded. "Why the hell not?"

"It will take time to do that up to the wall," An officer said.

"Anything we link to the dungeon will have a power cost," Matt added.

"We have access to all of Vuzgal's resources, including the mana stones we've saved up."

"Okay, then what about alchemy poisons? We could toss those on the barbed wire and any pits. Turn any scrape into a potentially lethal wound."

"We'd have to have the reg force do it. They've tempered their bodies with poison. Not all the reservists did," Domonos said.

"Fair," Matt nodded.

"What about fuses on the different traps? That way they could go off immediately or a few seconds later. Say they stuff it into their storage ring. They pull it out later and it could go off, or they break through, think they're safe, charge ahead, and it goes off behind them," a devious officer said.

"Done," Domonos said.

"So, the first line is the mud, roving mages, and traps. Second are the random potholes, chasms, and trenches," Matt said.

"Three," Domonos said, taking over, "a field of barbed wire. Reaches to the mountain walls on either side of us, semi-circle around our defenses, out three and a half kilometers. Fields of it. Posts, trap enabled. Chasms hidden underneath, traps, roving mages underground. Everything. The whole thing should follow the incline up to Vuzgal. Dug right into the bedrock."

"To add in randomization, we could sow reserve squads all over the place, have them take care of different areas. They just update and repeat, butt up against other squads doing whatever they have thought up," Matt said.

"That'll make it a damn mess. I like it! Give them time to improve, update, talk to one another, and come up with more traps." He shared a look with the officers in the room who had all added their own nasty touches to the plan.

"I'm starting to feel a little sorry for the bastards," Matt said.

"Why? We're just warming up. They haven't seen *shit* yet," Domonos said.

35 Trading Blows

Marco and the other master teachers half-ducked in the command tent as explosions boomed in the distance.

"Come down here and fight, you damn cowards!" Onam yelled, covering for his embarrassment.

"Since we started attacking their aerial forces, they have increased their height to the point where it is hard to see them. When their attacks land, they are already gone. The roads are covered in spell traps and hidden traps. The forces moving down the east and west roads have had more issues than us," Hae Woo-Sung, the mustachioed Willful Institute teacher-turned-commander, said.

"Have a force remain where they are. The rest of them are to teleport over and catch up with us," Marco said.

"What about the forces in the south?"

"They have been moving slower. There are fewer of our people among their ranks. With word sent back of how far ahead we are, I'm sure they'll speed up," Feng Dan said. Her armor had remained untouched through the fighting.

Bombs went off one after another, making it difficult to see through the tent as the mana barriers fought to hold on.

The group waited for the noise and light to die down.

Only the agonized cries and sounds of freshly burning wood were left behind.

"We will push ahead to Vuzgal until we reach the city. Then we will lay down teleportation formations to move our forces as fast as possible. Teacher Medina, do you think that you and your students will be able to move faster if I set you free?"

Everyone turned to look at the covered man standing at the rear of the room. Their hands moved closer to their weapons in unease.

"We can reach Vuzgal by tomorrow afternoon and place the teleportation formations."

"Take anything you need." Marco bowed his head to teacher Medina, maybe a little lower than the others.

Out of them all, Medina was the strongest. He didn't rely on just his strength to kill the enemy. He used anything he could to win.

"I believe the enemy already knows where we are. I do not think that all of my students will evade detection."

"I understand, teacher, but this is the best option. We will use the teleportation formations to shift our forces forward. That should focus their attention," Marco said.

"I do not mind their deaths. I just have to remind you of the cost it takes to train someone to their level. I hope you don't waste it."

Teacher Medina turned without creating a ripple in the air and left the tent.

"Knows where we are. They would have to be casting searching spells all the time," Onam, the muscled, shorter man said.

"Crafting," Marco said. "Teacher Hae Woo-Sung, I hope you can split up your mages among the other groups. They are our only effective way of engaging the aerial beasts and their riders."

"If we were to have casting wagons, we would be more effective."

"Though it would make you a greater target. I agree with Teacher Medina. The enemy must know our every move."

"Wait a minute, lad. What do you mean by crafting?"

"Vuzgal is a city of crafters. It has the crafting dungeon, the Vuzgal academy, and one of the largest and most advanced crafting districts in the Fourth Realm. Most cities in the *Fifth* Realm can't meet their abilities. The whistling spells, the formation carved metal barrels… They are all crafting items. With tens of Expert crafters backing them, their crafting is unrivaled in the Earth Realms. Spells would certainly exhaust them. We know that the people of Vuzgal, while capable, are not high in level. They use crafting to make up for their weaknesses. They're using sensing formations and they have shown a high capability in other formations in the past and tonight."

Explosions rumbled in the distance as another group was attacked.

"You think they seeded the valley with sensing formations?" Eva Marino asked, her hands resting on her waist, just above her whips.

"I think they've covered the entire valley with them. We must assume that they can see our every move."

"That would take a massive amount of resources and time." Teacher Feng Dan's brows pinched together.

"They have been here for several years, and while construction might have stalled within their walls, their defensive box structures only multiplied. Their watch towers were constantly upgraded, as were their military bases. If the Battle Arena is as strong as reported, how much stronger must their military training facilities be? They never once slowed on defense, or on advancing their own people's training."

"You make it seem like you admire them," Onam said.

Marco shook his head and let out a frustrated breath.

"Boy," Onam warned.

"How much do we truly know about them? Some surface information at best? It's not like we will learn anything else. Our spies and informants stopped reporting to us days ago. Vuzgal purged their city and plucked out the eyes and ears within it. Do you know how hard it is to find out *all* of a sect's sources? They did it to *every* informant within their walls. That fact alone should make you respect them, should make you brace for what is to come, and understand why I am marshaling these powerful assets."

"Gather all the earth alteration spell scrolls among your ranks. Once the sun rises, we will use them to create a path forward. We won't be able to avoid the buried traps, but it should remove the threat of the traps that are being dropped from the sky."

Marco nodded to the teachers and left the tent. The forest had been torn apart by fighting techniques and stomped into submission by the hundreds of feet that passing through.

Marco jumped onto his waiting mount and headed off toward his clan's army.

The moonless night didn't give them any indication of where the aerial beasts were; their silent bombs arrived suddenly.

If it is bad out here in the forests, just how many traps have they prepared in front of the city?

Captain Wazny woke with a start, taking in a deep breath, sitting up on his bed. He looked around the ward, feeling one hundred percent rested. *Damn, I need a piss.*

He got off the bed, the formations underneath and carved into the frame dimmed. *Stamina regeneration, healing, increased mana density. No wonder I feel like a million mana stones.*

He headed out of the hyper-recovery ward, checking the time. Only an hour had passed.

He exited, heading for the closest teleportation hub.

The under-city was lit up. The factories and crafting workshops were a hub of activity. Crafters passed him, rushing back to work. Others, like zombies, shuffled to the hyper recovery ward, their eyes dull and arms limp from overuse. Just how hard had they been working? They were Journeyman crafters with body and mana cultivation.

Wazny grit his teeth and jogged toward the teleportation hub. He stepped on a teleportation formation with several supply carts and other air force personnel. All the time he and the others in his team had been resting, the crafters had kept working non-stop to create the supplies and gear they needed.

Wazny balled his fists as light covered the teleportation formation. The crafters were doing so much for them. He *had* to do more.

He and the rest of the air force personnel left the teleportation hub at a run. He rushed toward his squadron's hangars. Sparrows were resting on their perches. Formations all around them were lit up, increasing their recovery rate.

"Wazny!" Major Sullivan waved him over to a group of pilots.

Wazny nodded to them, seeing a few familiar faces.

"They're fresh in from the First Realm. I need someone to take them out, show them the ropes."

"Anything change?"

"Altitude increase. They got smart about using ranged spells. Started using wind and thermal spells. Out of range for the repeaters, but not the bombs. They're using some of their own aerial beasts in the air now. Make sure you're scanning for them. Wing Eleven got hit."

"Bad?" Wazny's chest tightened, familiar faces flashing by.

"Four wounded, one dead. Aida."

Wazny and the other pilots winced. Their unit was a small one. They had just been training together in the last few months.

Sullivan nodded. There was nothing else he could offer.

"Get them prepped for flight, and head up with them. Once they're good to go, report back. Either your people will be in the air or you'll pick them up here."

"You got it, Boss."

Sullivan walked away, leaving them to it.

"What have you heard?" Wazny asked.

"Two eyes on the ground and four on the sky," Captain Vesik, leader of the sparrow wing said. "They're using spells and aerial forces against us. Stay as high as you can, then dive to bombing level. Drop your load and back up into the heavens.

"They keep their casters under mana barriers and they're getting better at hitting us out of the sky. If you do another pass, coming in from a different angle, vary it. Hit them lengthways, then cut off the end of their lines and get going. The longer you attack one target, the greater the chance of getting hit. Also, they've taken a fancy to spell scrolls which can really fuck up the skies. Watch out for that shit. You feel mana building, put on the speed and fuck off."

The pilots nodded.

"Okay, let's get going. I'll lead the first, then we'll AAR. Vesik, take the second; we'll do the same. Then I'm just along for the ride and to bomb some fucks." Wazny clapped his hands together.

"Your AO, your call." Vesik held out his pinky and thumb, shaking his hand.

"Appreciate it," Wazny said.

He led them to the aerial beast masters. The sparrows were energetic and ready to fly; their stores of ammunition had been reloaded and prepped.

Wazny climbed into his cockpit. Support staff checked to make sure that he was secure and that the emergency spell scrolls were ready.

In the event of emergency, pull on the red silk to activate spell scroll. Wazny repeated the lines from his training, checking his controls.

He scratched the sparrow he was on, getting a chipper sound from the war beast. He smiled a little before focusing.

The sparrows flitted forward, half-stepping, half-flapping their wings out of the hangars.

Wazny pulled on the cocking handle, readying his twin repeaters.

The sparrow wing, all eight of them, moved to the acceleration platforms. The sparrows gripped onto recesses in the ground.

Vesik went through the takeoff procedure before the formation activated.

The sparrows hopped and spread their wings, flapping them as the formation's power increased.

Wazny's stomach was forced into the back of his spine as they caught the air and pushed into the path of the other acceleration formations, climbing up and into the pitch-black night sky. As the speed decreased, he found he could breathe again.

The acceleration slowed as the sparrows glided, their heads twitching from side to side, taking in the change of location.

Wazny's goggles picked up on the special bands that had been added to the sparrow's legs, allowing him and the others to find one another without alerting the enemy of their position.

Vesik talked to flight control.

"Looks like we have our target." Vesik pinged his map, linked to the rest of them.

Wazny looked at the map, checking the elevations of the surrounding mountains.

"I'm thinking that we come in from the southeast. Ride low and dirty, come over the mountains as fast as we can, and start dropping as soon as we clear them and bank off to the west. I don't like how closed in the area is there. Target rich, but they could have more mages in there."

"We'll follow your lead."

"Okay." Wazny checked his position against the target and altered his direction. The wing rose higher, accompanied by only the creaking of their wooden cockpits and the flapping of their sparrows' wings.

Wazny checked his gear and the map. He couldn't see the other wings, though he thought he saw a few of the identifying bands on kestrel or sparrow legs.

"Nice and high up here," Vesik said through the sound transmission device.

"Altitude is our friend. Kind of peaceful," Wazny said.

"I just get antsy. Want to get in there, get the job done, and get the hell out."

Wazny snorted. "Don't worry. We'll be there sooner than you think, and it'll be over faster than the first time you met your wife."

"Shit, it was a solid second!"

"Hah! What was it, self-serve?"

"I was satisfied."

"Fuck." Wazny shook his head, grinning.

Time went by slowly until they were nearly there.

"All right, wake up you lot," Vesik said.

Wazny checked his map. "Get ready to dive."

The wind was with them, their mounts only needing to flap a few times to keep them aloft.

Wazny contracted his muscles, getting the blood flowing, ready for what came next.

"Once we're over the mountains, three seconds drop, ten seconds climb, and bank to the left. Got it?"

"Over the mountains, three seconds drop, ten seconds climb, bank to the left," they repeated.

"Good, let's do this. Follow me and maintain spacing."

Wazny's mount tilted forward. The speed picked up as his sparrow kept them level. Wazny scanned the ground for life and watched their position on the map. He felt the air fighting him as his mount caught it and leveled off. They were silent as death, riding on invisible waves of air. He saw the ridgeline ahead. There was light on the other side from its occupants.

He looked across the sky for aerial beasts. "Here we go!"

Wazny and the rest of the wing passed over the mountains silently. Their speed caused the trees at the top of the ridgeline, just tens of meters below, to shift and shake. The ridge disappeared to reveal fighters pushing through the crater-like valley to the forest beyond. Even at night, they were pushing ahead. They had light formations and fires to guide them.

"One dungeon lord, two dungeon lord, three dungeon lord. Release!" Wazny and the rest of the wing released their bombs, sending them tumbling out.

"One dungeon lord, two dungeon lord… Ten dungeon lord."

Wazny stopped the flow of bombs and banked; the rest of the wing followed.

Their sparrows flapped wildly, gaining altitude and regaining speed as the first bombs reached the ground. Force was converted and amplified into fire spells that tore apart the shell, sending shrapnel and dirt in every direction. Like a rock skipping across the ground, the bombs fell one after another, tearing the forest and valley apart.

Firebombs drew in air greedily as they spread through the valley.

"Welcome to Vuzgal Valley, mother fuckers! I hope you enjoy the stay!"

Wazny and the group disappeared into the night. "Watch for aerial beasts. They could launch them after we hit them."

They didn't see anything as the adrenaline faded in their veins.

"Captain Vesik, next one is all yours."

"I have the feeling it's going to be a long night."

Rugrat and the special team were the first into the opening, clear of trees. In the distance, flashes of spells and explosives marked the enemy's advance. Rugrat blinked, his eyes filled with mana as he looked to the skies.

"Clear!" He lowered his repeater, casting a spell. The covered ground cleared, revealing new pre-set mortar pits.

"Fan out, defensive positions. Second Lieutenant Couto, we're clear up here."

"On the move."

Rugrat and the rest of the special teams got comfortable and adjusted their positions to cover the others.

Couto and his people arrived a few minutes later. They broke into squads with mechanical precision. They drew out mortars which hadn't been given the chance to cool in their storage rings. Mages set to cooling the guns as the gunner and first ammunition bearer sighted the weapon. The second ammunition bearer readied everything else in the pit while the squad leaders held a conference through the platoon channel, checking their position and range cards.

"We have two groups in range. They're both spread out in the forests. We will target the group to our northwest. Grid square one-three-three-two. Confirm target." Couto paused as squad leaders checked their maps.

"Confirm target at grid square one-three-three-two," the squad leaders relayed back.

"Chain lightning rounds, fuse to air burst formations. Spell: Lightning Enhance," Couto ordered.

"Lightning rounds, air burst fuse, lightning enhance!" a squad leader near Rugrat called out.

The second ammunition bearer pulled out the rounds. Their dark grey body was covered in formations that crackled with power. They unscrewed the round's nose and replaced it with formation carved fuses.

The gunner and first ammunition bearer had set the gun. The heat dissipating blocks slid back down along the barrel, covered in a cold wind from the mage's hands.

The squad leader moved beside the gunner and ammunition bearer with his map in hand.

"This is our target. Heavy forest cover. Our target area is one-three-zero, three-two-four to one-three-five, three-two-six. We'll move from the southwest corner serpentine up to the northeast. Got it?"

"Got it." The two nodded.

"Good." The squad leader pulled out the range card and checked his map, studying it with his team.

Rugrat flexed his shoulders and studied the area.

The mortar crews changed their elevation and traverse, some re-sighting their guns so they could cover their two-hundred by five-hundred-meter squares, breaking down their one-kilometer-wide target grid square.

The cooling blocks rang out with metal hitting metal. The mage waved his hands; the cooling spell dissipated.

"Mortar Squad One Three ready!"

The squad leaders radioed into Couto.

"Have your second ammunition bearer ready. Arm and then dump them to your mages. Let's hammer the bastards. Fire when ready!"

The second ammunition bearer dumped their ready rounds into the mage's storage rings and continued to ready more mortars.

"Been some time since I did this," the mage said. The formation under his feet glowed while his spell covered the round. He passed the now-live round to the first ammunition bearer.

"What, a whole two months? Hang!"

"Fire!"

Conversation was ripped away as ten mortars fired, lighting up the night and sending their payloads skyward.

Mages pulled out the rounds, checked them, and cast their spells, passing them to the first ammunition bearer. They dropped and ducked as the mortars fired one after another, recoiling and filling the air with tiny rings.

Rugrat checked his linked map. The mortar crew had fired three rounds before the first landed. Red markers disappear, while others remained in a semi-circle.

Barrier must have stopped the chain lightning.

He checked the area around his position. *No fast movers coming for us yet. Should be dawn in a few hours. Day four.*

36 Redeploy

Marco watched as Leonia rode up to him with her own group of guards, fading back as his own guards made a hole for her.

"What is the situation?" Marco demanded.

"The enemy has been using different attacks. These don't make a noise before they strike. They explode at head height and release chain lightning that jumps from metal to metal, killing anyone wearing armor or carrying weapons. The northwestern force is getting hit hard, but no less than us. Spell traps cover the ground."

"We lost nearly half of the force to death and injuries. It is more than I expected. They will not be able to bear it again."

Mana barriers powered up as the mana in the area fluctuated. Soldiers ran in every direction. It looked like panic, but they quickly started casting spells, raising the ground to create defenses. Others drew out formation plates and placed them down, powering them up.

Dirt, stone, and trees weaved together into rising walls, creating several defensive structures.

The first teleportation formation flashed as dozens of fighters appeared. The mages waved them off as they looked around in surprise.

Drums beat as the forces gathered in a coordinated move. The camp followers separated from the fighters, clearing away into two clear groups.

Marco used his sound transmission device. "Gather your fighters and we will charge forward. Use spells to clear a path!"

The teleportation formations flashed with increasing regularity. Dozens quickly turned into hundreds as fighters poured out of the rising defenses.

A horn bellowed and the Willful Institute's people moved forward. Leonia turned her mount with Marco.

Spells blasted into the ground, tearing it apart and destroying any traps that might have laid there. The ground was then leveled and smoothed, creating a road as powerful mages wove their spells from their mounts.

Beasts gathered speed as the stalled formations surged once more. Sects organized into their own fighting forces and charged. Reinforcements streamed out of the teleportation formations, joining the charge.

Aerial beasts unlimbered their wings as they soared into the open skies.

The roar of lost frustrations tore from thousands of throats as they cleaved a path toward their enemy.

Good luck, Teacher Medina. I hope we don't beat you to Vuzgal.

Marco watched the aerial beasts wheel away, heading toward the whistling attack sites. He allowed himself a smile, feeling the power of his mount, seeing the forward charge.

Momentum was on their side once again!

"Cease fire! Aerial forces coming in. Prepare to retreat!" Couto yelled.

The mortar squads released their last rounds and threw their gear into their storage rings. The CPD teams grabbed their repeaters, scanning the skies.

Rugrat checked his map. "Shit! There have to be fifty or so aerial fighters."

"Fucking awesome." Han Wu checked his repeater. "How'd they get so many people?"

Rugrat opened the map some more. "Oh fuck, they're making a couple of new castles. They must have snuck teleportation formations up!"

Spell formations appeared in the sky as the first of the mortar teams jumped on the back of their mounts at the mouth to the covering.

Meteors shot out of the sky, striking their mana barrier, and making everyone duck as the barrier took the impact. The shock wave left a clean line on the ground around the barrier, tossing trees away, clearing the hillside, and opening the sky.

Spell formations appeared in the hands of the aerial mages as they unleashed beams that raked the artillery platoon's mana barrier.

Rugrat cast flak shot on his arrows as he aimed and fired his repeater.

Magical attacks mixed with repeater bolts in mid-air.

"Fire!"

A squad of Alvan mages unleashed their own firepower. The air shifted around them as birds made of still air shot out of their spell formations. Their razor lines detonated spells and slammed into the mana barrier covering the aerial riders, outlining the barrier.

The two close protection details and the special team fired into the sky. The barrier became a darker sheet of rolled glass.

"Fire!" The second squad released fiery spears from their revolving spell formations like war ballista.

The riders were diving and turning away.

They didn't expect such a counterattack.

The fire spears shattered the mana barrier.

Rugrat's bolts passed the limit of what had been the barrier. With a twist of magic, he activated his spells. Air blades cut through his targeted mount and rider.

He fired bursts of bolts that swept across the sky like whips, reaching out to meet the aerial forces.

"Fire!" The first mage squad's formation spells appeared around the aerial beasts. Lightning covered the aerial mages. They and their beasts screamed out; tombstones bloomed.

Rugrat lowered his repeater and checked the side window on his magazine. George grew to his full size. Rugrat got on his back.

"We're moving!" Couto yelled. Everyone mounted up, charging away from the artillery position. Mages cast spells, throwing the flattened trees out of the way, clearing a path.

George and the special team members' mounts jumped out of their firing pits and toward the exit. They rushed out of the position as Rugrat turned back and closed his hands. The trenches exploded and collapsed. The central sitting rock cracked and fell apart.

"We have a kestrel en route," Gong Jin said as the special team members hemmed Rugrat in.

Rugrat grunted. He hooked his repeater to the mount on George's harness as he checked his map. "Slippery shits. They must've placed the formations last night. They've got six different camps rapidly expanding and charging toward Vuzgal."

"No one said we were the only people with a sense of tactics," Gong Jin said.

Rugrat looked at the six lines reaching toward Vuzgal. "I'd prefer fighting arrogant bastards to smart ones."

The panther mounts were at home in the thick Vuzgal forests. They wove between trees like a black flood, leaping over fallen logs and nimbly crossing roots that threatened to twist a man's ankle. Their riders rolled with their steeds, leaning into the turns, their lower body moving with their mounts as they scanned the area.

George jumped over a fallen log. He half-opened a wing, turning himself as his paws found purchase on a tree, hurling them forward as his wings flicked out slightly again. Rugrat dipped with the impact, letting it ride through his body.

His mana-covered eyes searched the canopy above.

The only noise came from the panthers' breathing, the cracking of twigs underfoot, and the random *clinking* of equipment.

Rugrat *felt* like a blade had passed over his skin as spells entered his domain.

"Spread the fuck out!" Rugrat yelled through the sound transmission device.

The units spread out to either side as Rugrat felt pinpricks against his skin and the chill in the air as the skies above were gathered into a spell.

Like giants surfacing from the depths, mana transformed through spell and elements, stilled, given new purpose. The sky screamed as ice and formed air were released, cutting a path through the ancient forest.

Rugrat covered his face as ice hit trees with such force they turned into fountains of wood.

George barrelled forward, under the falling tree, and through the rain of splinters the size of Rugrat's forearm.

They hammered the riders and their beasts as they charged onward. Rugrat willed George to move faster out of this hell.

The air shimmered as air spears rained down on an artillery member.

His back armor took the impacts while his panther let out a horrible *mewl* as spears lanced through his hindquarters, tearing off its rear half even as it continued forward.

The rider yelled as he was thrown free, hitting the ground and rolling. Another rider diverted. A meteor slammed into where he had been just moments ago, causing the panther to half-stutter as he regained his footing.

The rider grabbed his thrown comrade and pulled him up. His leg and arm were at an unnatural angle as he was pulled in front of his savior.

Rugrat gathered his mana, using his senses instead of his eyes, searching the skies.

George rushed forward, taking care of the path ahead.

Rugrat heard and felt the trees being torn apart all around. He ducked from ice arrows that buzzed past his head and struck the mana barrier of a special team member.

Meteors tore through trees and crashed into the ground, jolting Rugrat and George, sending others flying and clearing trees. Rugrat's insides twisted into jelly, ingraining the fear of the random and sudden death.

Where are you, you bastards?

Rugrat gathered his power, drinking in the mana around him as George jumped over a stream that had cut deep into the earth.

Rugrat lunged, taking the impact of landing on the other side. The platoon bounded over without a pause.

"To the east! Follow me!" Second Lieutenant Coutu's words were punctuated with shifting shadows as meteors barrelled down.

The forest shook and rumbled once more.

"Found you!" Rugrat locked onto where the spells were being created. Aerial beasts held their positions in the sky as mages formed spells between their hands, unleashing them below. Formations appeared all around them.

Two unlucky souls were hit by the meteors. Another's mount was killed, everything below his stomach torn away as he screamed.

Rugrat's open hand gathered the elements needed into a swirling mass. He infused his will into the spell and powered it with his mana, then finished with his cast.

He threw out the spell. Like a bullet, it took off into the sky and erupted among the aerial mounts, outlining them through the thick canopy.

The aerial beasts lurched from the light and their spells failed the last stages of casting, creating feedback as they spat blood.

"Target marked!" Rugrat channeled power.

The spell clicked together as he directed the resonant power and pressed it into the ground. Stone and metal shot out like rain recalled to the heavens. It lengthened and sharpened, turning into a net of projectiles as reins of red appeared along their lengths.

They crossed the downward spells, which rippled across the sky with explosions that shook trees that had stood for millennia.

The ground behind the retreating artillery platoon was sucked into the sky.

The aerial casters hurriedly used counter-spells. They formed sheets of solid air using their mana barriers, while Rugrat's stone and metal rain struck like a tropical thunderstorm across a calm lake. The mana barriers lit up. Their golden hue darkened to brown, but held as the aerial casters rained down air spears and meteors.

The special team and mages joined in.

In a rush of air, the sky twisted, compressing and solidifying into spears and blades.

Trees bent and shifted, weaving the canopy together like intertwining hands, creating a lattice overhead.

The skies were pulled together into a faint mist. Clouds darkened and swirled as lightning crackled in its depths; water, like blue gems, shone brighter, turning white with a chilling edge.

Spells hit the latticed trees, tearing apart their cover. It tried to reform even as more holes punched through it like a drunk fighter that just wouldn't stay down.

The formed air, released from their bonds, shot into the skies above, shifting the sun's light into a rainbow of color.

Ice, rain, and lightning intertwined in blinding light, hitting the aerial casters' mana barrier.

The aerial casters weren't expecting such a counterattack as they poured their power into their defenses and tried to lash back at the enemy below.

Rugrat ducked as a meteor hit a latticed tree above and kept coming. *Shit.* He flexed his domain and yelled, creating a crude spell that drew in surrounding mana into a beam of blue, almost white light. It crashed into the meteor, shattering it, and piercing through.

Rubble fell as Rugrat's metal and stone spell faltered for half a second.

There were screams of pain among his people, but if they could scream, they could be healed.

Rugrat exerted his command on the mana. It lit up the canopy as it flowed from the ground to his fingers, into the stone and steel, adding blue veins to the red.

How do you like me now?

The spells struck the mana barriers in a twist of red and blue streaks.

The casters drew back as their barrier exploded. Without the barriers, the casters were forced to draw from their mana reserves, creating thinner personal mana barriers. They broke, looking to escape.

The attacks threaded through the aerial formation, hitting some, missing others.

The attacks on the ground disappeared as the special team members tore through the mages.

Rugrat reshaped the purpose given to the spells within his domain. They bloomed into chains of fire and mana, raking the aerial casters as they passed, capturing some and then detonating their energy in a directed blast.

Barriers gave way as lightning arced and razor ice slashed. The wind howled, cutting and tearing at those unlucky enough to be in its path. Then the casters dispersed and flew out of range from Rugrat and his fellow mages.

The spells canceled as the artillery and special teams kept their forward momentum. Instead of being used for destruction, the mages used their spells to heal the screaming wounded, carrying out immediate first aid as they continued to weave through the forest. Those too wounded to ride were stored in beast storage crates.

Rugrat looked at the scars and fallen trees that lay in their wake.

"Birds are eight minutes out! Keep it moving. Make sure you're getting stamina into the wounded! Second Mages Squad, watch the skies!" Master Sergeant Warren, Couto's second-in-command yelled.

If he's talking, Couto must be out of action.

There weren't many left standing. Soldiers used revival needles, bandages, and salves on their mounts and friends, storing them away into beast storage crates where medics could work into them.

Rugrat tore his eyes away and looked to the sky.

"What the fuck happened?" Jackie asked on the Special Team's channel.

"They have teleportation formations." Gong Jin's words were like iron in Rugrat's gut.

"So, when they were pulling back to the rear…" Jackie's words trailed off.

"They were gathering their forces, reorganizing them for a push. The sects are charging Vuzgal in every direction right now. Came with a bunch of aerial forces it seems," Gong Jin said.

They continued to ride.

"They have momentum on their side now," Rugrat said. "We're not just facing a few thousand anymore. They can bring all their strength to bear and who knows if they have more teleportation formations out there. They'll get their reinforcements and more allies now."

They rode in silence, darkness holding over them.

"Special Team Three, left side. Mage squad two, right side perimeter defenses!" Warren called out.

They exited the forest, reaching a hill that looked out over the valley and their pickup point.

Gong Jin led the special team. They looped around to the left, creating a semi-circle as the mages did the same on the other side.

"Dismount and get low!" Gong Jin yelled.

Rugrat unlimbered his repeater and slid off. He hit the ground and dropped into the prone position. George shrunk to the size of a dog, lying in the grass beside him. The wounded were pulled from the mounts into a casualty point in the middle of the defenses.

"Rugrat, Simms, go help the casualties," Gong Jin said.

"On it!" They both replied. Rugrat got up, leaving George watching his position as two artillery members took it. Rugrat stored his repeater, looking at the bloody stained mess in the middle of the grass.

Camouflage was darkened with fresh or drying blood as healers-turned-medics worked on their patients.

The patients' carriers had open flaps. The formations underneath had all been activated. The conqueror armor linked them to everyone, increasing their recovery speed.

Simms and Rugrat jogged over together, spotting a gunnery sergeant covered in blood.

The sergeant pointed to different groups. "Pri Alphas, Bravos, Charlies, work your way down." Blood covered his hands as he worked on the patient in front of him; his assistant squeezed an IV bag under his knee while he secured a clotting bandage.

"Got it." Rugrat and Simms ran to the twisted forms in the grass.

Rugrat moved to a soldier covered in burns along his right side, down his face, his neck and arm, splattering against his ribs and leg. The man was whimpering and gargling blood. Rugrat grabbed the tag stapled to his shoulder. *Artery right side, bleeding into main body cavity, draining out of a hole in right side. Rib cage.*

Rugrat's domain told him all he needed to know. The man was bleeding into his thoracic cavity, the pressure was weighing on his lungs. The hole in his side was draining the blood out, thankfully, but it was hard to breathe, and he was still bleeding.

He healed the man's trachea and held his hand above the man's mouth. Threads of mana went down the man's throat. They encircled the blood inside his trachea and built in his lungs.

Rugrat pulled out the ball of blood and flicked it on the grass as he moved to the next person.

They were a collection of broken limbs and shards of wood.

"I'm sorry. I'm sorry," the man sputtered through bloody lips.

"You shut the fuck up now, Delan!" The mage working on him yelled.

Rugrat pulled out additional tourniquets. "Get his arms. I have his legs."

The mage grabbed them and tore them open, looping a second tourniquet around his still bleeding legs.

Rugrat secured the tourniquets around the man's bicep's, tightening them with a groan from the patient. *That should concentrate the healing and stamina potions into his torso. Fucking mess. Stamina is waning.*

Rugrat pulled out a revival needle and stabbed the man in the heart. He let out a small gasp as Rugrat injected the potion payload before he drew the needle out. "Keep him awake and focus on healing his head. Swelling around there," Rugrat told the mage.

The mage saw his medical patch and nodded. "Okay."

Rugrat patted him on the shoulder, leaving a bloody handprint, and was onto the next.

"Birds incoming!" someone yelled.

Rugrat was too focused on the wounded to look up.

The woman he was treating had been badly burnt. A near hit with a meteor spell had sent burning hot stone through her body, cauterizing the wounds as they went.

Rugrat was securing her tourniquets when he felt her heart still. "Clear!"

The other mage leaned back as Rugrat rubbed his thumb across his two left fingers as if he was snapping them. A spark formed on his fingers as he pressed them to the woman's side.

She jolted from the electricity. Her heart fluttered.

"No, you don't!" Rugrat jolted her again, increasing the lightning.

Her heart fluttered again.

The mage put a breather to her mouth and squeezed the attached pump, forcing air into her lungs.

Rugrat hit her again. Her heart picked up pace.

Wind, getting stronger every second, washed over the field.

"Landing!"

"Wounded are first to load!"

Rugrat leaned over his patient to cover her. Dust, grass, bits of discarded medical packaging, and empty IV bags hit Rugrat and flew on over the shimmering grass that bowed under the powerful wing beats of the first kestrel as it landed.

The mage, with Rugrat shielding the woman with his body as well, pumped air into her lungs as her heartbeat grew stronger.

The wind died down.

"Move it!" Warren yelled.

Rugrat pulled out a revival needle. He'd needed too many already.

He stabbed it into the woman's heart and injected it. She took a fresh breath, sputtering as the mage moved the breather to the side. Rugrat extracted the needle.

"Recovery position."

They rolled her onto her side as she coughed and convulsed. Rugrat used his mana manipulation to draw everything out of her lungs in one shot.

"We have to move her!" a mage yelled.

Rugrat nodded to the mage holding the end of the tarp she was lying on. "Go for it."

He stood and got out of the way with his helper. The two mages at either end grabbed the tarp and hauled her for the waiting kestrel, its wings out and ready to take off at a moment's notice.

There were too few helpers for so many wounded, and Rugrat turned to the mage that had been working the breather. "We'll grab another one."

He gave Rugrat a thumbs up. They moved to a man in a tarp and grabbed either end. Rugrat barely felt the weight as they ran with the line of mages carrying wounded into the kestrel. The wooden cabin had been transformed, creating three rows of cots four high. Formations were on each cot, promoting stamina and low-grade healing spells.

A stack formation was strapped between where the gunners would link to the conqueror's armor.

Mages ran out of the kestrel as soon as they had released their payload.

Rugrat and his helper brought their wounded in. The gunner slapped a cot, indicating to Rugrat and his helper where to put the soldier.

The gunner glanced at the tag as they ran out, slapping another cot for the next wounded.

Rugrat and his helper moved to the walking wounded, helping them into the kestrel. The cots at the rear turned into seats.

The gunners were working up and down the cots, checking on their new payload.

The gunnery sergeant Rugrat had seen before waved him over. His clothes were covered in more blood than before, creating dark stains. "We need healers on the bird. You up for it?"

"I'm with you." Rugrat looked at him and the three other staff sergeants. All of them had to have trained as medics to get their current rank.

Rugrat and the sergeants moved between the cots, tending to the wounded. Able-bodied men and women filed into the last remaining seats as quickly as possible. Rugrat sensed the second kestrel waiting in the air to take the remainder of the platoon.

Follow Gong Jing, George. Rugrat thought to his mount.

He got the feeling of an acknowledging woof as he checked IV lines and bags hanging from carabiners on the kestrel's cabin ceiling.

The cabin darkened as the rear ramp closed.

"Hold on." The chief's voice was tight in a way that *promised* his best skill and speed for the souls that relied on him.

Enhancing spells covered the kestrel as the crew, gunners included, added their own buffing spells.

They shot into the air, rising quickly as they piled on the speed.

Rugrat leaned into it as he moved up and down the cots. He added more bandages to those that had come free as they burned with power. The kestrel showed her full might as she surged forth, cutting between the mountains in favor of speed.

"Hold on."

They went into a dive. The cabin shook as the formations glowed with power and the left door gun opened up.

"Left side!"

The gunner's repeater sent vibrations through the kestrel as the rear door gunner added in his own attacks.

"Pump and dump!" The chief yelled as shells ejected from the top of the cabin. They ignited their alchemical payload and formations, creating illusions to confuse the enemy's spells and cover the kestrel in smoke.

Their speed shot them past whatever enemy they had seen. Rugrat continued to work.

"Landing in one minute!" the chief yelled.

They kept coming in fast.

"Ten seconds!"

Rugrat braced as the kestrel shifted her body, her wings battling the wind as she brought them down.

"Prepare to open casualty bays!" the chief said as the gunners both opened a box on the ceiling and grabbed a handle.

The kestrel landed with a loss of momentum, taking the weight on her back easily.

"Open, open, open!"

The gunners pulled their handles, activating a formation as the limbs of the cabin walls unlinked and creaked open, revealing platforms on either side of the kestrel with medics ready and waiting, tables at the ready. They ran forward, following branches and vines that wove underneath their feet, hooking into the lower section of the Kestrel Cabin as it opened to greet them. The branches and vines created a floor as they shifted the wounded from the cabin cots to gurneys before they were rushed away. A medic attached to each of them as they read their tags, did their scans, and started to save their lives instead of just hold onto them.

In just seconds, the outer cots were emptied; the gunners pressed another formation and the cots' roots folded up, allowing access to the central cots. The able-bodied and walking wounded were unloaded from the rear. Rugrat and the rest of the attending sergeants-turned-medics moved out of the way to let others do their job.

Then it was quiet, the whimpers, screams, whispers, and cries were carried into the two buildings on either side of their landing platform.

Rugrat rubbed his face, finding his helmet there. He unclipped it as he stepped through what had been the cabin wall and onto the sides. New fresh gurneys, assistants, and medics moved into position with grim expressions.

He pulled his helmet off, feeling the cool wind against his face. He took a breath as another kestrel came in to land one bay over. Its sides peeled open, revealing more cots and samples of mangled meat and broken bone.

"All right! Let's get out of the way," Rugrat said.

The able-bodied soldiers followed him and the sergeants down a ramp to the ground. Their kestrel was released, its cabin sealing back together as the chief moved them out of the way before taking to the skies once again. The cabin was still threading itself back together as he banked and headed out beyond Vuzgal's walls.

Rugrat reached the bottom of the ramp. Another kestrel streamed in filled with wounded.

We weren't the only ones hit.

He raised his hand to rub his face, letting the fatigue born of emotion rather than stamina wash over him for a second.

"We're going to head to our barracks," the gunnery sergeant said, looking decades older as his adrenaline crashed.

"Good work, all of you." Rugrat nodded at the sergeants and then the corporals behind them.

"We got them here, even if there is only a thread of life left in them. We've got the best damn healers in the Fourth Realm working on them. You did Alva proud today." Rugrat patted the man on the shoulder and pressed his lips together, nodding. He let out a breath and released the man. "Stay safe."

With that, he turned and headed toward the nearest teleportation formation that could get him to the under-city's command center.

Lord Chonglu was studying the maps on a wall of the command center when Rugrat walked in. Rugrat secured his helmet to his vest and scanned the room with a hard eye before he rested his hands on the edge of the map. His hands were clean, but his face was covered in soot and dirt. There was a faint line of an already healed cut on his cheek. Unmistakable stains on his clothes were covered in dirt that had clumped to the blood.

He took a look at the evolving details, then moved to the main map where Domonos stood. He focused on several wide paths that spread from three locations in the north and two in the south.

"Teleportation formations," Domonos spat out. "Suggest: We were so focused on hammering them with attacks we stopped watching the mountains."

"What's done is done, Domonos." The finality in Rugrat's voice closed

Domonos' mouth. "This is war. We can't control everything." Rugrat's words were quieter, spoken to the table, and spread to everyone's ears. He looked at Domonos directly. "What's our next move, Colonel?"

Domonos tilted his head slightly. The muscles of his jaw outlined, tensing, bringing himself back under control.

"If they have teleportation formations, their supply and support are secure. They've gained the momentum and are charging. Kestrels are bringing back the wounded and artillery platoons in proximity to the enemy's forces. We're in the process of withdrawing all artillery and pressed artillery units from the field."

"What of the sparrows?" Rugrat asked.

"They are observing the enemy."

Chonglu saw it happen as Rugrat looked at the advancing spears of sects.

Domonos' eyes tightened and then opened.

"They're in the valley, using spells to tear apart our traps and clear the ground, but the terrain isn't flat." Domonos' words started slow, turning into a waterfall. "The sparrows don't need to come in low to hit them. They can do that from up high. The enemy will have two choices: to keep sending their aerial units after our artillery, or to return to fight our sparrows."

"Aerial units are rare in the sects, right?" Rugrat asked.

"Yes, to have a force of them is a massive expense. They are useful, but there are so many ways they can be killed," Domonos said.

Acting instead of reacting.

He grimaced and opened his mouth only to close it again, chewing on his own thoughts.

"I hate feeling like we're letting them cross the valley unmolested. If we hit them with mortars, we might kill a few dozen, but it won't do much more than waste ammunition and leave our people tired. We'll have to have kestrels on station to move the artillery out. If we have them putting traps all over the place, the spells they're using to clear a path will destroy or throw them away."

"Feels wrong, but got to do what's right," Rugrat said.

"Extract everyone in the field. Get them ready in their defensive positions. The sparrows and kestrels will be our way of attack. Once the enemy gets in close, we'll recall them as well. The enemy aerial forces will all be gathered, making it easier to overwhelm and counterattack our own aerial forces."

Domonos tapped on the surface of the map.

"We'll do that then. Zukal, contact Kanoa with new orders."

Rugrat caught Chonglu's eye and gestured to a corner of the command center.

"Sir?" Chonglu asked. He could smell the earthy dirt and wood mixed with smoke and tang of blood.

"How many dead and wounded?" Rugrat pitched his voice low enough that none but Chonglu could hear.

"Twenty-nine dead, three hundred and fifty-three wounded at last count."

Rugrat exhaled through his nose, bobbing his head. Pain cut across his features before he steeled himself again. It was better than he had hoped, which hurt harder, thinking that having some die was *somehow* better.

"Our soldiers' cultivation, gear and training kept our wounded high, but the deaths low," Chonglu pressed. He must have seen Rugrat's pain.

Rugrat gave him a forced smile and a nod of thanks. His eyes unfocused as he thought. "Evacuate anyone non-essential to the city's defense. Any word from the traders?"

"They're pissed off. The different sects are offering up elders to sign truth contracts that say they're not a part of this. The Stone Fist Sect is posturing. I think the entire sect will use this as an opportunity to enter the conflict. Elan is listening in."

"And the sects with this?" Rugrat gestured at the map.

"More will support them. There are others that are interested in an alliance with us. Their offers are dwindling with time."

"They want a piece of our city without paying too high a price in blood." Rugrat showed the decades of fighting on his face. "The second defense of Vuzgal. At least we've had time to prepare. The first time, we had less than a hundred people."

37 The Butcher's Bill

Erik watched as mages from Tiger Regiment solemnly carved out each letter on the polished black stone.

They cleaned the smooth lines.

The carver placed his hand on the fresh raw names that had not worn away with time, adding to those that had been there since the founding of Alva.

People stood in their own groups. Some cried, others were solemn while children looked around, confused by the significance of those names and the people they represented.

Mothers, fathers, sons and daughters, sisters, and brothers. Alvans. That gave their lives to defend Vuzgal.

Erik tightened his hand on Momma Rodriguez's shoulder as she shuddered; tears covered her cheeks. He looked at the mana gathering formation in the sky. It gathered strength as a lieutenant marched out and stood in front of the wall.

"Ro-ll, Call!" His voice rang clear and true across the fields.

Tears burned the edges of Erik's vision as he gritted his jaw and faced the wall head-on. Momma Rodriguez squeezed his hand on her shoulder, giving him strength.

"Sergeant Alvarez!"

A choked sob came from within the park. No one turned to look, their eyes fixed on the stone.

"Sergeant Marcio Alvarez!"

Silence greeted the lieutenant waiting for an answer.

"Corporal Guiying. Corporal Guo Guiying."

The name sounded off the wall and across those that filled the park.

"Lieutenant Couto! Lieutenant Elvin Couto."

A young woman holding a baby in her arms and her daughter's hand bent as she choked on her tears.

"Corporal Celeste Lopez. Corporal Celeste Lopez."

Thirty-two more names were called out, but silence greeted the lieutenant.

"To the fallen!"

Erik and the other military members straightened.

"Salute!"

Hands snapped across chests throughout the park before slowly lowering.

The lieutenant's arms returned to his sides. He turned to face his audience, looking above them. "You may now approach the wall. Please move from the left to the right!" His voice caught slightly as he turned to the side and marched away from the wall.

The families walked up to the black stone wall carved with gold names, the names of their loved ones.

Erik and Momma Rodriguez slowly walked away, just two more among the masses that had come to pay their respects. The special team kept their distance so as to not draw attention.

Doesn't matter if you have a body like divine iron, or a Solid Mana Core of Mist. None of it is enough to armor against loss.

Erik looked back at the stone wall, looking at those names.

Storbon looked at Erik with a grim expression.

"You sure this is necessary?" Yuli asked him.

"Create as many revival potions in an hour as he would produce in a day and increase his cultivation. You think you can stop him?" Storbon smirked.

Yuli said nothing more as they watched their dungeon lord. He stood in front of a mana cultivation pod. There were several in the room; most of them were already under use. Medics walked among them, checking on the occupants, members of the Alva Military.

Erik had more machines around his pod. Two lines ran from his arms, pumping blood into the large blood bags on either side.

He had another tube taped to his mouth like a rebreather.

He swallowed the sludge in the line and vat behind him.

"Good feed. Doesn't taste the best, though," Erik joked, getting a weak smile.

It wasn't just food; it contained ingredients half concocted together for him to suck in and consume, increasing the power of his blood and allowing him to produce more.

Erik stepped back into the pod. Medics made sure that the tubes wouldn't get snagged before he was lowered backward.

The pod turned into a table, locking into place as the formations activated.

"Ready?" Julilah asked, standing at the formation panel.

"Ready," Jen said.

"Good to go!" Erik got around his tube.

He caught Storbon's eye and nodded to him before closing his eyelids.

"Increasing the mana density," Julilah said.

She and Jen worked together, increasing the mana density, and quietly returned to the room. Storbon and his team moved to the chairs provided.

Time sped up as Jen and Julilah saw to other work, Jen visiting occasionally to check on him. Medics changed the blood bags as they filled up. Soldiers entered and left while Erik lay there drawing in the impure mana. He only talked to say when to change to a different element.

Occasionally, he would slurp from his concoction, keeping his body supplied with all he needed.

Storbon could feel Erik changing, rapidly regaining strength, his metal tempering stats no longer just numbers. What was the toll on his body and mind to take so long to heal?

Erik's domain grew, increasing the mana that he drew in. Mana mist hid him from view. Only the slurping and fresh blood bags that started filling the instant they were connected revealed that there was someone beneath it.

Hours turned into a day and then two. Storbon and his team slept in the mana cultivation pods, increasing their own cultivation as they too donated blood enhanced with concoctions.

On the second day, a soldier not on the special teams wanted to get his blood drawn.

"Look, I have Body Like Iron. It isn't Body Like Sky Iron, but if it could help, I don't need it," the soldier said to the medic.

"Okay," the medic agreed. While it would be weaker, it was still as strong as some of their stamina and healing potions.

Alchemists started to bring in vats of the sludge for people to eat while they started their cultivations and were bled.

It was limited to those with Body Like Iron and higher, but everyone wanted to help. Erik remained oblivious, drinking in mana, growing his elemental core and mana core.

38 Construction

"Well, the devil makes use of idle hands, but when devilish minds are mixed with industrious hands…" Rugrat shivered, peering into the deep pits below. The light caught sharpened metal and stone in the ground below.

He rode on George. Han Wu and his people seemed to have been permanently attached as his security detail. They flew around him, along with several undead aerial mages.

Matt moved from behind Rugrat, using his sound transmission device instead of fighting the rushing air. "The reserves have been working for close to three days, pretty much since they showed up. We put the undead put to work as well. We have three areas."

Matt pointed at the intersection where east and west roads turned south toward Vuzgal. "We have area one from the road circling to where the forest meets the mountain range on either side. A two-kilometer, sometimes wider, band of mud fields and traps. We call it the soup dash, or The Soup for short. Area two extends five and a half kilometers from the forward bunkers and extends out of the valley."

Rugrat didn't have to follow his finger to notice the dark, almost polished stone that cut lines in the ground, going from thin and annoying to large and nearly a hundred meters apart. They lined up row upon row like a kid had been drawing with a pencil and then picked up a fat marker.

"Trenches, potholes of all kinds, every protrusion sharpened and covered in poison. We call it Deadman's Fields."

"Got it." George banked, bringing the last area into greater view.

"Finally, Scarecrow's Hill." Matt waved in the direction of the last area. Squads dotted the ground, instructing the undead and weaving their concertina wire across their imaginative traps. They were moving back toward Vuzgal, turning the ground into a deadly landscape.

"Barbed wire, traps, trenches, wandering undead attack mages underneath, poison, and anything else our people thought to add."

"The trenches, the mud, the barbed wire; no way a mana barrier is going to cover people through all that."

Matt remained silent.

"When will people get in range of our guns?"

"Area three, Scarecrow. We can hit them with mortars and spells out in the soup."

"And we aren't freeing up any other weapons right now. What about the other weapon systems?"

"Bolt rifles are good sub-one kilometer. The semi-autos and full autos, if they're mounted, good out to four and a half kilometers."

"So, into Deadman's. What about the guns in the valley pillboxes?" Rugrat pointed to the squat buildings that lined the sloping valley, bowing out toward the defensive fields around the main gate and outer wall.

"Deadman's and Soup's border is at five and a half kilometers from the main gate. They're up higher yes, but they're farther back." Matt sounded unsure.

"Maybe not as accurate as we want. Have a few guns working together. Reach the border, possibly," Rugrat surmised. "Mounted grenade launchers will get right into Scarecrow, close and dirty. Railguns give accurate fire while shoulder-mounted for one and a half klicks." He sucked on his lip. "Mana cannons have a ten-kilometer range, so they'll cover all zones, same as the mortars. The Artillery Cannons can out and smack anything fifty klicks out."

Rugrat looked at the polished stone that made up a good chunk of Deadman's and covered Scarecrow.

"Solid, dungeon-hardened stone." He could imagine the explosive rounds striking it, sending shrapnel in every direction. "Gonna be honest, Matt. I'm fucking puckered up tighter than the new fish on the block who dropped his soap in the prison shower, looking at this."

"That's a fucking image."

"Got a creative imagination." George turned lazily from the defenses, making it easy for the security detail to follow them. "Well, we have a day, maybe two, until the sects show up. A good army knows how to fight. A terrifying enemy knows how to prepare," Rugrat said into the wind as George straightened out, flying them back toward Vuzgal nestled between its two valleys.

39 Head-On

Master Teacher Medina felt the chill of the night air as he checked the teleportation formation. It had been two days since the united sect's armies had redeployed and chased the Vuzgalians and their whistling weapons away.

He looked into the darkness, catching his disciples' eyes. Without a word, he drew out an earth mana stone. Threads extended from it lit up his hands and face, turning into smoky tendrils that touched the teleportation formation. The metal glowed as tendrils of greater density flowed into the formation. Parts of the stone dissolved into sand, carried away by the wind as the mana poured along the teleportation formation's runes.

Around him, several disciples hidden in the night's darkness were illuminated by their mana stones and the formations they powered.

Spells ignited as trees collapsed, clearing the area as several meticulously placed mana barrier formations activated.

Mana flowed through the runes of Medina's teleportation formation like water filling words written in sand.

The entire formation lit up; the runes glowed with power as light flashed.

Twenty mages appeared, rushing out in every direction, pulling out more teleportation formations and setting to smoothing the land and raising defenses.

Medina's disciples were replaced with mages. They flickered like shadows, following Medina, who left the teleportation formation to others.

Twenty turned to forty, then one hundred, then two hundred, then four hundred.

They streamed out, drawing walls from the ground, preparing secondary mana barriers, readying spells for a counterattack.

Medina and his students stood behind the growing wall. Medina examined the forest, the three kilometers of cleared land before the road that branched east, west, and south. Shacks that had sold food at the intersection lay abandoned. The shutter that would have shaded the shack's merchant from the summer sun lifted and closed with the wind, a skeletal memory of times past.

Medina observed Vuzgal, the crisp clear lights that rose with the city. Towers stabbed into the sky like polished sabers. The rounded defensive towers stood like scepters at the inner wall and the main castle that surveyed all.

Most of the city was dark, empty, and dead. He looked at the proudest lights in Vuzgal. *The Associations remain.*

Melee fighters ran out, moving to the growing walls that were being continuously reinforced as aerial mounts took to the skies with their riders, looking for Vuzgal's infernal birds.

Medina jumped without a sound, landing on the rising wall that attempted to block his view.

"Master, their city is so open without a wall. How can they defend themselves?" Turren's voice was calm, analytical.

"They have their repeaters and odd weapons. I am sure we will learn more soon." Medina pointed at the fields between the shacks and the city. "What do you think those are?"

A few of his students used spells to enhance their vision or pulled out tools.

"They look like fields, but they give off a metallic light," one said, perplexed.

"Did Vuzgal ever have fields?"

His disciples focused harder.

"They look like bushes of metal, and range for kilometers. A measure to slow our forces?" Turren said.

Good, they took some of my lessons to heart. "They can slow and trap us in the land in front of their city, disrupt our mana barriers with those metal fields." Medina's tone was one of musing interest as his student's gazes sharpened.

"What are my first three rules?"

"Everything can be used as a weapon. Use whatever you need. There is no honor in dying; only honor in surviving by whatever means." Even as they repeated the ingrained words, their voices didn't rise or carry farther than the wall.

"Today, I am interested in what lessons Vuzgal will give us."

He felt their eyes turn to him. *Too much confidence by far.*

Medina looked away from the unblemished Vuzgal and walked off the edge of the wall that stood nearly fifteen meters tall. He treated it as if he had just stepped down the stairs as he walked toward the stone tower growing from the ground under the power of fifty mages.

Its sides smoothed out and openings appeared as the dirt fell from its sides.

Marco rode out of the teleportation formation on his mount, slowing his pace as he took in the developing camp.

No whistling weapons, no spells, no attacks? Marco raised an eyebrow and chuckled at his own joke. *We must be outside of their range.* Instead of attacking them and wasting their supplies, the Vuzgalians were waiting and conserving their strength. Or maybe they had lost most of their forces in the forest?

He thought of the trained birds that had dropped attack formations one after another on the United Sect's Army. He suspected that not as many had died in the forests as they first thought. Still, the Vuzgalians only had a few thousand fighters, while the united sect armies would have four hundred thousand by tomorrow's nightfall.

"Young Master, the command center is ready," a guard said, indicating to a simple castle-like structure that jutted out of the ground.

Around the camp, other sects were creating their headquarters and mages were reinforcing the mainly dirt walls with thick stone.

"What about the secondary camps?"

"They are being raised as well. Five secondary camps along the northern side, two on the eastern, and two on the western. The first of each flank has been created. They are waiting to gather more forces to create the last camps."

"And there Vuzgal sits, calmly and patiently," Marco mused. He clicked his mount forward toward the headquarters.

Medina was waiting for Marco, looking at the maps that covered the main table. He didn't take the time to look up at Marco.

"Master, you and your disciples have done excellent work. We are but a few kilometers from the enemy's city now."

"We both serve the Institute. We have other matters we must attend to once this matter has concluded."

Not one to waste words.

"We caught them by surprise and cut days off our travel time. Now we can directly draw our reinforcements into battle and pressure them instead of fighting in the forest."

"They are silent, but they are not blind." Medina put his finger on the area in front of the city and circled it. "Here, they have created fields of metal. I believe to entrap and slow us."

"With no wall, they had to have something."

"It extends from halfway down their road to their odd buildings."

"They might not have expected our teleportation formations the first time, but they predicted their use. Instead of engaging us with ground forces, they chose to attack through the skies. If they had been on the ground, we could have moved our forces around with teleportation pads, encircling and defeating them." Marco let out a breath with a snort. "Some have said that we killed half their number in the forests. Do you think that we did?"

Medina's and Marco's eyes met.

"No." Medina's face split into a rare smile. "You always were a cautious and observant disciple."

Marco cupped his fist and bowed to Medina. "Thank you, Master. You made sure I realized that cultivation is just our own strength to borrow and use others through whatever means." Marco rose. There was a crazed, excited smile on his face. "And to not underestimate the enemy. Do you feel as excited as I am to fight a worthy enemy, Master?"

Medina let out a low, choking laugh. "Who knows if they will be worthy? They are smart and resourceful, but we have yet to see what other secrets they hold."

Marco felt something shift at the edge of his sensing range. His expression flattened as he released his fists. Medina's eyes lowered to the map of Vuzgal once more.

Marco's house guards moved to the side, and Leonia was allowed in.

"Your forces are organized?"

"Yes, sir."

"Good, make sure that you do not engage in any lasting fighting and pull back once you have shut down their totem."

Leonia bowed and left the room.

Her attitude and bearing had become much more manageable. Maybe the sleepless nights and threat of death had changed her for the better.

"We will begin testing them with the light of tomorrow's dawn."

Rugrat squinted across the outer defenses, spotting the force of five thousand advancing on Vuzgal. Roska and Gong Jin stood at his side.

"Domonos deactivated the outer traps," Roska said. "He doesn't want to waste them on a small force. It would give away our range."

"Five thousand is a small force?" Rugrat grunted as he watched the lines jog forward. "Ten kilometers isn't a short distance. On Earth, they'd be at most three, maybe five kilometers away, in medieval times. Take them a day to organize, march out, attack, retreat. Ten kilometers would take an average human two hours to cover and have plenty of energy left to fight it out. Though ten kilometers isn't much for our artillery."

"Why didn't we open up on them as they moved into position?" Gong Jin asked.

"More surprises to hit them with later. Right now, there isn't much we can do if they're in the valley. Consolidated, right in front of our walls, we can implement our defenses. We're secure and safe here." Rugrat shrugged.

"Feels shitty letting them get so close," Roska said.

"Just imagine what their expression will be when they find out our mortars can reach fifteen kilometers and our cannons can go nearly twice that."

Gong Jin shivered from more than just the cold.

Rugrat lifted his eyes from the oncoming army to the nine bases, forming an opposing semi-circle, closing off Vuzgal completely. "They're quick builders for a bunch of dickwads."

Roska and Gong Jin snorted and the corner of Rugrat's mouth lifted ever so slightly, just covering the simmering rage underneath as he rubbed his storage ring.

George raised his head from where his small form rested on Rugrat's shoulders, his eyes mirroring his master's murderous intent.

Leonia heard the change from the road back to the swish and thud of feet, hooves, and paws over grass, the heavy breathing of warriors, and dull *shoosh-shoosh-shoosh* of shifting armor with every step.

Her hands were cold as she rode, looking ahead to Vuzgal.

They had passed the seven-kilometer marker at the road. The towers of Vuzgal reached into the sky and the short wall reached from one side of the valley to the other. The road they rode on could fit ten carts beside one another.

It's much larger than I thought.

She and her army of five thousand rushed across the land, their noise like thunder in her ears.

Silence greeted them, reflecting their noise back at them.

She didn't miss the shifting eyes, the confused looks. These were veterans from multiple battlefields. The enemy's silent retort set them all on edge.

Leonia cleared her dry throat, pushing aside the uneasy feeling twisting her guts, the one that begged for something, anything to happen. She also wished that today, right now, would be an abnormality, that nothing would happen.

They reached six and a half kilometers. With her heightened vision, she could see the outline of the city. The flat plane was an illusion. It had a slow and steady incline to the fields of broken ground and metal fields. Behind it lay unseen defenses and squat buildings that rose with the smaller valley Vuzgal had been built into. The edge of the city expanded where it met the edges of the valley and then rose along the valley sides to a height of several hundred meters.

We have to be inside their range now, right?

"Prepare to halt!" Leonia said. They slowed their pace, looking at the sleeping city ahead. Leonia felt eyes looking at her from the darkness with their deadly intent. She gritted her teeth.

You think I'm scared of you cowards hiding in your city! She shook herself, turning her frustration into anger.

She checked her map. They were exactly where they needed to be. "Halt!" The formations rolled to a slow and then to a standstill. "Run the cannons!"

The formations moved apart as cannoneers pulled out mana cannons and powered them up, the reduce mana slowing the charging process. If they wanted to charge them faster, they'd have to burn mana stones.

The realm was already thin in mana, but this close to Vuzgal she could feel the mana being pulled from her body, reducing her mana regeneration.

"They are ready commander," one of her aides, a battle-scarred man nearly four times her age, said.

"Fire!"

Formations lit up along the mana cannons. A series of rotating spells lined up with the cannon as it drank in mana.

The mana cannons made a noise halfway between lightning and a bee passing one's ear. Leonia held her shudder, watching as dozens of attacks lit up the darkness of night, illuminating the ground more completely.

The attack spells tumbled toward the ground. She held her breath and was rewarded with pinpricks of light that caught in mid-air like dying embers meeting water.

Not even a ripple was thrown out. Leonia blinked as the rolling thunder of impact came back across the battlefield.

Did they not hit the city's mana barrier?

Event
The city of Vuzgal is under attack! Pick a side!
Defend Vuzgal Attack Vuzgal

If there was a notification, then they must have struck it, but why did nothing happen?

A new light bloomed from Vuzgal. It shot across the ground, aiming right for Leonia's army.

"Stand steady!" The scarred man's voice steeled their bones. "Mana cannon won't break our barrier."

A swirling collection of chaos arrived with all the subtlety of a bull in a chicken coop.

Leonia lowered her eyes and braced herself to not react.

She heard the sound of rushing air before the world turned into pure noise and light. She ducked her head and raised her hand to protect against the light as her mount shifted and shied away from the attack.

What the hell was that?

The noise faded into ringing as she blinked her eyes open. The formations had shifted. Their barrier held, but its entirety was lit up like a golden hill.

"Bah, I was looking for a little light, anyway!" The scarred man snorted, his voice reaching the formation as they laughed nervously. He turned to face Leonia. "Commander?"

"Let's head back. Our job is done. Vuzgal won't be able to use their totem now." She pulled herself up higher, trying to look the part of a commander as she brought her mount around. The beast fought her slightly, but gave in under her iron grip.

"Yes, Commander." The scarred man cleared his throat. "Turn around. We're heading back to camp! My legs are feeling tired so let's take it at a march!" he said as if forgetting he rode upon a mount.

They headed back at a more sedate pace.

"Show our confidence," Leonia whispered Marco's words in a sour voice. She glanced back at Vuzgal, sitting and waiting for them. She bit her lip before glancing at the scarred man and clearing her throat, then moved closer.

He bowed his head. "What can I do for you, Commander?"

"What happened with our mana cannon attack spells? Why did they fade away in the sky?"

His face bore a solemn expression. "Their mana barrier was strong enough to take the attacks without needing additional support. The power of the barrier was enough. It didn't need to direct more to the point of impact or spread the attack's effect outwards."

Well, it was a city, so it made sense, and they had only used a few cannons.

"Have you seen this happen before?"

"No."

His answer broke Leonia's thoughts. "Huh?"

"That has to be one of the strongest or *the* strongest mana barrier I have ever seen. To have the power to defeat nearly two-dozen mana cannons at once without so much as a flicker of power… Those Vuzgalians have mana stones to burn and formations as strong as my own shield."

"What about their counterattack?" she asked, leaning in her saddle.

He looked to either side. "Strong as some I've seen in the Sixth Realm."

She saw something in his eyes that she hadn't expected. *Fear.* She recognized it well and sat back in her saddle. Maybe his outward appearance didn't reflect who he really was. He could be a coward. No, Marco might not like her, but he would never send her out on my own without an experienced leader for support. He had needed this to go well and given her some of the better units from the different sects to command to make sure nothing went wrong.

She looked at the other leaders with her. They were all silent with their thoughts. The soldiers and sect fighters were unworried, although they complained about being out during the night, talking about sleeping, eating, or rutting. There was a casual laziness to them as they covered the anxiety and fear from before, using the opportunity to talk about lighter topics as if unafraid of Vuzgal.

Slowly, she looked back at Vuzgal, the slumbering dragon that had made its nest within these remote mountains.

Marco opened his eyes, instantly awake.

He sat up in his bed, looking out the window. Beyond it, he could see the compound that had grown around his personal quarters, staffed with members of the Tolentino clan and their attendants.

Past the walls, he saw a growing city. Four hundred thousand people took up a lot of room, and he wondered how many more people would join the fight.

Marco walked out of his room to find his guards waiting there and an attendant, a straight-faced, simple-looking woman.

"Your bath is ready for you, Young Master." She bowed with the composure of someone that had done this for a lifetime, indicating to another room.

"Good, get me Vivaldo."

Marco moved into the other room. A bath had been poured and readied for him. His maids took off his clothes before he got into the warm water.

He glanced at his cleaned, repaired, and oiled armor that stood in a corner of the room as he stepped down into the bath of two meters by three meters.

Marco felt his pores opening, drawing in the concentrated mana within the water. His body relaxed as he expelled dirt and impurities from within his body. He sunk into the water, gathering mana, clearing his mind.

"Leave me."

The maids fluttered out of the room, allowing him to luxuriate in the feeling. He breathed in, the vapor coming from the bath drawn into his body as the mana spread throughout.

Footsteps approached the private room. Opening his eyes, he formed mana into a hand on the door handle and opened it just before Vivaldo, his guard captain, reached it. He walked in without pause and bowed to Marco as he shut the door behind him.

"I am sorry to interrupt you, Young Master." Vivaldo remained bowed.

"You would have waited outside if it wasn't important. Go on." Marco pursed his lips as he drew in the mana, faster and with greater purpose now.

"All nine camps have been formed and are now being reinforced."

Marco pictured them in his mind. The camps were set out in a W that faced Vuzgal with long sides and a short base. Two small bases made up each side, with his main camp taking the middle peak with two smaller camps taking positions at the base of the overall formation.

Thirty to forty thousand fighters remained in the main camp, with ten to fifteen thousand in each of the other camps. With camp followers, the main camp swelled to one hundred thousand, and the secondary camps to forty.

"We have been unable to find the mana draining formations at work against us. I have teams working around the clock, but we have not found any of them. They are either massively powerful and cover a large area and are few, or they are too deep for our spells to detect them."

Marco pursed his lips and waved for Vivaldo to continue.

"Our mana regeneration has decreased by ten percent at this range, mana pools decreased by five percent. Based on the mana cannon performance last night, the formations must only get stronger."

"How much stronger?"

"Thirty percent we guess at the walls."

"I sense more?" Marco's face tightened.

"Inside the walls, it could be more. That's what I would do."

Marco sighed, his nose flaring. "It seems to be about right. I am sorry about that. This campaign has been tiring." He waved to dismiss his outburst, continuing. "They have a mana barrier that seems to eat our cannon shots and cannons that have power that is only common in the Seventh Realm. Begin construction on the tunnels. I have a feeling Vuzgal will have more surprises, but a siege is a series of attacks and feints. Just we do not know which feint will turn into an attack and which attack we will divert into a feint."

"Yes, Young Master."

"Anything else?" Marco's light tone returned.

Vivaldo's words caught in his mouth as he opened it twice, closing it as he organized his thoughts.

"Raise your head." Marco's voice deepened.

"The iron fields that Master Teacher Medina talked about. They were hard to make out in the night. With the morning sun, we were able to see them. Vuzgal is not what it was a week ago.

"I sent up aerial riders to better understand. Lines that have been cut into the ground. They cover an area of one kilometer and ring the entire metal forest beyond. The forest covers a semi-circle of three and a half kilometers in front of the city. Under the metal forest, all the dirt has been removed, covered in stone. The low squat buildings are fused with it, creating a protrusion out toward us before running up the sides of the hills on either side of the city."

"Four and a half kilometers of defenses. Troublesome."

"It's a monumental undertaking to complete it in under a week without outside assistance. I would guess it to take a month for them to build such defenses."

He needed to see this for himself. "Maids!" he yelled as he stood up. His skin dried as it touched the air, a spell wicking the water away.

The maids rushed in, cupping their hands and bowing.

"Help me with my armor."

They rushed to obey as he stood there, quickly clothing him in his layers and armor.

Marco pulled out his sheathed sword and belt from his storage ring, pulling it around his waist as he walked out of the room, causing eddies in the foggy bathroom.

"Take my helmet."

The maid bowed to Vivaldo, who accepted it and followed his young master out.

"Lower Elder Kostic is due to arrive today with the other sect elders," Vivaldo said as guards opened the doors to his quarters.

Waiting guards moved to encircle him.

"Are they not worried we could be attacked at any time?"

"Comes from the Head."

Marco sucked in a breath as the door leading into the compound opened and noise flooded in.

"If it is the Head's wish. I guess he is looking for more to join the fight." Marco took Vivaldo's silence as agreement as he walked into the early morning sun. He was greeted with a courtyard that had stables on either side. They'd been spelled into existence from trees and stone and filled with mounts.

The stable attendants quickly readied his and his guards' mounts.

A wall and gates circled the courtyard now, made from compressed stone and wood to create a fence of upright spears. He could see the movement beyond.

The compound was busy with Tolentino soldiers moving between groups from one task to another. The sound of hammering came from the shimmering smithies, maintaining and fixing armor and weapons that had grown dull or uncared for in the march.

Houses of compressed dirt and trees lie around Marco's larger manor. Tents were corralled into lines and groups while a ten-meter-tall wooden wall had risen in the night to circle the entire Tolentino compound.

They got on their readied mounts. The gates of his manor were opened by waiting guards.

As he left the courtyard, Marco looked around, taking it all in. His mount kicked up dust from the hardened dirt path, heading for the gate into the rest of the camp.

"Use stone to create new roads. Send people out to get boulders or have supplies brought in. How are our walls?"

"The outer walls are twenty meters tall and ten thick. It has been hard to build much of anything. The mana here is so thin that our mages need much longer to recover between castings. More building supplies are coming in."

"Good, the wall is the priority."

"Yes, Young Master."

The other sects and powerful families had set up their own smaller compounds within the walls that ringed them all.

Two kilometers wide with room to expand and nearly no stone left at all. Forests were being cleared of lumber and stone to speed up the process instead of just relying on their building mages.

The sea of tents was hemmed in by main roads marked by the sects or pathways that had organically grown out of necessity.

The command center in the middle of the camp stood at seventy meters tall. It was the only building and was made purely from stone to support its height.

Marco dismounted, leaving his mount to be attended to by another stable hand. His guards followed him into the command center. A formation pad took them up to the highest room in the tower to the noise of voices.

"About ten meters to the southeast it stops. Then there is a ledge of about a half meter."

"Ten meters to the southwest is the corner of another box, same dimen—"

Talking slowed or stopped as the cartographers noticed Marco's presence.

Marco looked through the windows, seeing the forest to the north, and the opening left by the Eastern road before facing south at his target.

Rows of cartographers created new maps while others relayed what they saw through viewing glasses.

The cartographer watching through mounted viewing glasses was pulled to the side by his partner, the two of them bowing deeply.

Marco stepped up to the viewing glasses and looked through them. The land was barren now, leaving bare polished stone that must have been hardened. Their whistling attacks and the formations they dropped would have a greater effect now. The lines in the ground and the iron bushes would make it impossible for mana barriers to give soldiers complete coverage.

The room remained silent as he studied Vuzgal.

Time passed slowly; the only noise came from the joints on his viewing glasses which squeaked as he moved them.

Finally satisfied, he stood back up.

"Well, let's test it out then."

Kim Cheol breathed in as he rolled up through the stretch, and exhaled as he bent down again, slowly. He completed the series of moving stretches that limbered up his body, causing him to sweat and feel some heat in his muscles.

He moved to tension and backed off before it got too painful.

His movement was coming back, and he was stronger than before. His mana channels were still a mess, but healing took time. Kim stood up straight and let out a breath, opening his eyes to the view of Alva beyond his window.

He didn't even glance at the chair which he had relied on to recover from his exertions when he had first started exercising. He hadn't believed that he would actually recover. He thought Erik was making that up to make him feel better.

Kim flexed his arm. He was still weak and had a long way to go. "It won't be done in a day. Every day just a little bit more." He recited the words Erik had repeated and again. "He was right." Once he recovered, he would be stronger than before. Then he could start to rebuild his mana channels."

There was a knock at the door.

"I like to see a patient adhering to his recovery plan! Love a bit of stretching, all the right angles." Nurse Tollins gave him a flirty wink.

Kim couldn't help but laugh at her outrageous behavior. The indomitable nurse had been watching over him. Her flirts were only surface level, but it built up his confidence. And her quips kept him on his toes.

"Let's take a good look at you."

Kim gave her his wrist, feeling the spell that appeared around her hand and deep in her eyes. It spread from his wrist through his body like a wave. "Okay! We're looking pretty good! Let's get you up on the bed. I'll torture you a little bit and then you can have your afternoon mana cultivation session."

Kim got up onto his bed. "I'm holding more of the fire element in my body now." He held out his hand. It turned red as heat emanated from it. "I can only infuse it into what I'm holding. Without mana, I can't use it at a distance."

"Color me impressed! You'll be able to enhance your weapons and armor with that still."

Kim smiled, proud of the praise.

"After tomorrow, we should be able to discharge you. The other guild members you came in with have mostly left."

"Yeah, they came by before they headed out. Will Erik be done training before I leave?"

Something flashed in Tollin's eyes.

Did something happen to Erik?

"I don't think he will, he's..." Tollins paused.

"Is something wrong?" Kim asked calmly, too calmly. *If someone...*

She sighed in exasperation. "He's being the dungeon lord."

Kim released the tightness in his muscles.

"He's cultivating his mana and bleeding himself dry. Say someone from the First Realm could only give five hundred milliliters of blood at most, in a three-month period. Erik has pumped out a liter every ten minutes for the last two days, nearly three hundred liters of blood."

"How is he still alive?"

"He is Lord West. Some might know more in the medical field than him, but none of them can draw on as much power as he can. Add to that his Body Like Diamond and the fact he's basically using his body as an alchemy cauldron, turning his blood into a highly potent revival potion that one can use on the worst wounded."

"Is he in pain?" Kim asked as Nurse Tollins applied her applicators to his feet, making him wince.

"Nope, just lying there, cultivating and being a human blood machine. Now all the soldiers are donating their blood. We haven't used blood in the past. With the blood, it deals with blood loss right from the start, and it has stamina properties, and healing effects if it comes from someone with a higher body cultivation."

She found a problem area on his foot he didn't know about until the flare of pain forced him to not clench his jaw.

"I've been wanting to work on that one. Breaking up nicely."

"Yeah, feels good," Kim said, stretching it out.

Tollins laughed at his pained expression.

She worked him over good, leaving him sinking into his sheets.

"Eat this. Got some time before your mana cultivation." She put down lunch in front of him and cleared up her gear.

The meats, vegetables, and gravy made Kim take a deep breath in.

"I'll be around later to grab the dishes and take you down."

"Okay, thanks!"

"No problem It's my job."

Kim dug into the heaping plate of food with gusto. He woke up several hours later to Nurse Collins again.

"Training time."

"Yup, yup." Kim smacked his lips together and pulled himself out of his half comatose state, blinking his eyes around the blurry room as he got his feet over the side, resting on the edge of the bed.

He took a deep breath and stretched out, feeling things pop, crack and move into place before he slid his feet into his shoes and slowly stood up.

"Okay," he said.

She led him through the hospital. There were more staff than patients. Most of them were showing and teaching members of the Alva military basic first aid courses, how to use their medical supplies, and—for the more advanced medics---battlefield medicine.

They passed them and went through a corridor into the adjacent mana gathering center.

"The body cultivation center is located down the hall. They're hooked up to the hospital for recovery. If anyone has any injuries from cultivating, we can help them right away."

Kim nodded with approving noises.

"We redesigned the room from the standard mana training rooms to the mana cultivation pods. Easier to monitor, takes up less space, and less wasteful in creating a highly mana dense area."

She led him past a lobby and into what looked like an open warehouse. Sheets of formations covered the floor. Long and wide boxes sat on one another, covered in runes, with stairs bolted to their sides to reach up to the second and third stacked container. Windows provided a view into the rooms, which were filled with cultivation pods; some were filled with mist, while others pivoted backward, laying those inside on their back.

There were several in a row in each container.

"They were made specifically for the military to help them train faster. Lord Rodriguez was the first tester. That's why they look like stacked bricks, with as many pods stuffed into them as possible and with windows. I certainly wouldn't want people staring at me while I'm cultivating!"

She pointed at a room where a few men were standing outside. "There's Lord West."

Through the window, Kim could see men and women inside the pods. Tubes disappeared into the mist-filled pods. Others gave them food or were taking blood.

Medics unhooked the bags and added new ones as they filled up.

A courier put the full bags in his storage ring. Two guards accompanied him as he left the room and headed past Kim toward the hospital.

"Now alchemists will check the blood and add active ingredients. Then it will be stored in blood packs, waiting to be put into people. The strongest will go into revival needles." Tollin's face turned grim as she led Kim toward a specific cultivation room. "Army types joke that they'll bring you back from the brink. They're extremely powerful Expert concoctions with the single purpose to keep one alive, no matter the damage. This is you." She waved to the room.

Kim opened the door.

Medics were watching panels and wandering between the pods three rows deep and ten across. They helped people out of the pod, checking them. Several pods were empty, but the majority were occupied.

So many.

"Medic Tollins." A man with a smile came over and smiled at Kim. "Branch head Kim Cheol. I hear you will be in my care this afternoon. My name is Researcher Xun Jun."

Xun Jun was as strong as Kim but he wasn't talking down to him. *This place is weird compared to the rest of realms.* He expected him to be weaker based on how the man was speaking to him.

"Yes, he's all yours," Tollins answered for him.

"Sorry, my mind wandered. It is good to meet you researcher Xun Jun." Kim smiled.

"No worries! So, I've seen your medical records and we've been thinking about your recovery. I'll be watching the entire time. We increase the mana density in the pod to see what will happen. Then we will increase the fire element, just to test it. We won't go too fast. Today is about discovering what your limits are."

"He has been able to maintain and draw more fire mana into his body," Tollins offered.

"Good, good!" Xun Jun wrote down some quick notes. "Any increased ability to hold mana?"

"No."

"Is there a stationary amount you can hold when relaxed?"

"A small amount."

"Half of your original total, less?"

"Uhh, about..." Kim thought of the numbers he had learned with his training in Alva. "Ten percent?"

"Okay, okay, we can work with that. I'm excited to get started!"

"What do you do?"

"I am primarily a researcher into body cultivation techniques. I study how people temper their bodies. I do tests and studies to see if there are ways that I can improve the process. I second in mana cultivation. Tollins came to me once she saw Lord West's notes on your recovery."

Such a person would be a guarded secret in a sect!

"All right. I think I should be good. Thank you, Miss Tollins."

"No problem." Tollins left as Xun Jun waved him to follow.

"Okay, so this is like normal cultivating, but we're controlling the environment a little bit more. No need to take off clothes. We only do that for extended periods of cultivation. We clean the pods after every use so don't worry about putting your head where someone's boots were. Now you're thinking about it, right?"

Kim nodded and smiled at the bubbly and energetic Xun Jun.

"Don't worry! You'll be fine. I've done this hundreds of times. I have more than thirty patients training right now!" He grinned and indicated to the rest of the room then leaned in to Kim and hissed behind his hand. "Very captive audience." Xun Jun winked and smiled as he hit a button on the panel beside him. The pod rotated backward.

The pod locked into place.

"Everything good? Any questions?"

"Will this help with my mana channels?"

Xun Jun's voice slowed as he held his clipboard against his stomach. "I make no guarantees. Today is the day that we find out what we're working with. We can figure out treatment from there. If I don't know how to help, I will find someone that does. The only goal I have is to make sure that you leave my doors in peak condition, physically and mentally."

He gave him a soft gaze. One of the quiet and smaller departments that had risen from Erik and Rugrat were the therapists. Healers of the mind. They were a quiet group, but if one was having issues, they were always there for a talk.

"Okay."

"Good, then hop on in and let's get started!"

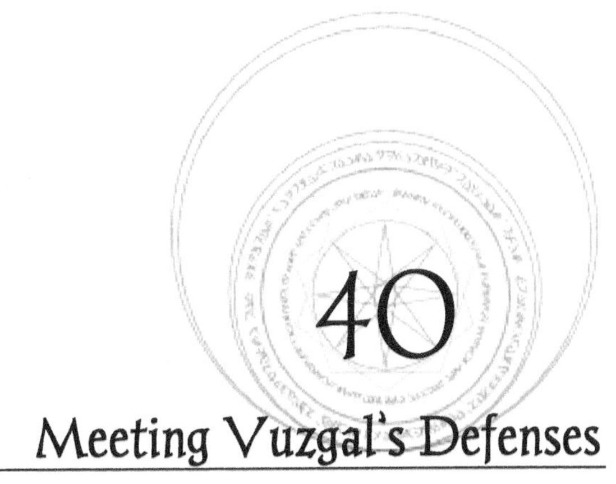

40
Meeting Vuzgal's Defenses

Acosta looked through the periscope. Adjusting the formation on the side didn't make it any clearer before taking out a cloth to wipe it. "Dammit, Brines, are you sweating out of your eyeballs? Looks like I walked into a damn sauna."

"Stand-to! Stand to!" Colonel Domonos' voice carried through the defenses as Acosta turned her periscope, watching the enemy camp's gates open.

Fighters marched out twenty abreast. Banners fluttered in the wind, declaring their sect and familial connections.

The United Sect Alliance formations raised a dust cloud as they marched toward Vuzgal.

It stalled her heart and stole her breath.

Shit. Well, that's a lot of them, huh? She quickly joked with herself before the fear could take hold.

"Damn, wish they'd let us go weapons-free, like fish in a fuckin' barrel!" Master Sergeant Sirel sighed as he stepped away to let someone else use his periscope.

"Hell, yeah," Acosta drawled, moving the periscope from side to side.

There had to be thousands of them. Not their full force. A probe to test their defenses. *And my patience.* Knowing they would be fighting thousands and actually *seeing* them...

Clans packed into tight squares, grouping together with their sects. They spread out in the open flat ground between camps that jutted out of the forest.

Or what used to be the forest. They had cut down a ton of it and pulled it into their camps. They only had dirt and grass to work with otherwise. She smirked. *Ha! You're on Vuzgal rock now.*

She pulled back and glanced at the top of the periscope where a degree circle had been placed and bracketed any enemy formation. The handy and simple invention meant that merely by pointing their periscope on target they could give the mortar crews pinpoint accurate targeting.

A line had been carved into the side of the periscope's glass, creating a runway of numbers. As one zoomed in on a point, the bracket would get bigger, showing the range.

Acosta mentally recorded the degrees and range.

"Staff Sergeant Neumann and Staff Sergeant Pok, please sight me some targets, degrees, and bearings. Since we have the opportunity to do some practice, let's try it out! Gives the crews something to do other than sit in their bunkers and take turns playing with the periscope. Go blind doing that all day."

The platoon command staff laughed as Pok and Neumann stepped up to the periscopes.

"All right, Fourth Artillery platoon, we're going to do some practice. No live rounds, but you will be getting real coordinates. Stand by on your guns!" Acosta said.

She waited as green lights appeared on her command boards.

Her mortar crews stood by, ready and waiting in the bunkers around her own.

"Ready and waiting, Staff Sergeants."

They started rattling off degrees and ranges, passing them to their respective squads. They waited, counting out the time it would take to target before picking out new targets and engaging them.

Sirel walked over to Acosta. She lowered her voice so only he could hear her. "Keep their minds from turning in circles and show them that they can do something. Better than just playing with their thumbs."

"More periscope training? Haven't tested them out thoroughly enough for my liking," Sirel said.

"Add it in. We don't know if this will be a long or short engagement."

"The mana cannons are getting the first shot at them," Sirel said in dark tones.

"And you wish it was us?"

"Damn right. Mana cannons? Shit, just a big damn rifle with a scope."

"Wouldn't want to be looking down that scope when the cannon went off." Acosta smiled.

"Hell, fucking no." Sirel shared a grin.

"When are they going to hit them?"

"Six kay range. They're holding the soup and thunderstorm."

"Nice clear day for the mana cannons."

"Should be an interesting show. Wonder if they upgraded their mana barriers." Sirel crossed his arms contemplatively.

They went back to watching the staff sergeants, Acosta with her thumbs in her belt and Sirel's face dimming, although there was still a glint in his eyes. "You think they'll break at Deadman's?"

"I think they've got a way across, though once they reach Scarecrow, they're fucked. Mana barriers won't know what's open sky, spikes, post, or concertina wire. They cut the wire or the metal, the formations will lose containment. Thirty seconds later it'll go up."

"Nasty. They could cut it, move forward and then it blows up."

"Or it blows up in their faces," Acosta agreed.

"How does it work?"

"Uses the same stuff as our light flares: phosphorous. Lights into flame when in contact with air and keeps going when it is underwater. It has explosive powders added in, so if the phosphorous or the mana goes off, the whole thing will go off."

Rugrat looked at Han Wu and the rest of the special team. They had sighted-in their mounted mana cannons along Vuzgal's bunker lines waiting for the United Sect Army to come into range.

"Prepare to fire," ordered Domonos.

Everyone's hands rested on the formation pad next to the cannon.

"Fire."

The latter half of the word was drowned out as the cannons recoiled at nearly the same moment. Wind and mana recoiled, pulling at their clothes as the area suddenly increased in mana.

The flash of spells and mana was gone, faster than the eye could track.

The guns were at the rear of their firing tracks. Turning formations pulled on cables, dragging the cannons back into position. The formations glowed, recharging the cannon. The whole action took three seconds before the cannon was charged and ready to fire again.

"Hold ten seconds!" Rugrat yelled.

The cannons returned to their ready positions, gunners looking out of their thin slits over Vuzgal.

Rugrat watched the sand drain through the hourglass, marking time before their next shot.

He grabbed his periscope, watching their mana cannons' spells arcing up and then returning to the ground. They hit within ten meters of one another, peppering their targeted barrier.

Rugrat turned his periscope to scan the area. Mana cannon fire rained down on the barriers. They flashed into existence with multiple impacts greeting the United Sect Army's advanced units.

Damn. They hadn't popped any of the barriers, but he didn't think they could take another hit; he was sure he'd seen some brown patches.

He checked his aim and looked at the degrees; the hourglass was getting low.

"Get ready! Minus eight degrees."

They turned their traversing gears. The rotating platforms the cannons were placed on turned, orientating onto their new target.

The last of the sand ran out on the hourglass.

"Fire!"

The cannons expelled their payloads again. Rugrat watched for the splash. The cannons reached their ready position as the spells hit the mana barrier.

The grouping was even tighter now, like a sledgehammer striking water.

"Good shit! Rang it like a bell."

The barrier shimmered and shook; definite brown patches appeared. They didn't have time to smooth as another cannon crew with the same target had fired right behind the first.

The barrier took three hits and two went inside. The barrier broke like melting plastic, folding toward the ground and disappearing.

"Change to AOE spells!" Rugrat reached down and turned the triggering formation plate. He felt the resistance as he turned it, the click as it fell into a new fire setting. The formations within the panel altered and changed to the new attack spell.

He heard the other panels switch.

"Minus four degrees, drop two hundred!"

Gears turned the cannons on their new targets, their rotating barrels locking onto their new targets.

Rugrat checked his degrees and range one more time and glanced at the hourglass, waiting for the cannon to charge and cool before his next shot.

"You all dialed out?" Rugrat asked.

"Yup!"

"Dialed up and out!"

"Ain't my first roh-deh-o."

Rugrat pulled a bizarre expression, reeling from their ready call returns. "Mutha-fuckas, a 'yes' would suffice and when did you see a rod-eh-o?" He stared at Tyrone, who shrugged.

"Hourglass," Han Wu said.

"Fire!"

The cannons recoiled, and Rugrat looked through his periscope again.

"Dialed in and out, the fuck does that even mean?" Han Wu asked.

"If you're dialed in, then you're right on target," Rugrat said absently.

He watched the spells strike the ground. Light and smoke dotted the rock where United Sect Army units had been moments before.

"Good hit." His voice was dull.

"Minus fifteen degrees. Add one hundred."

The cannons shifted as Rugrat scanned. The second cannon crew shooting on the barrier went with area of effect spells as well. The AOE spells erupted into lightning above the ground. It arced through anything metal: armor, swords, spears, harnesses. Where the lightning hit the ground, it sent up dust and light, leaving burn marks.

Rugrat looked at the eight other mana barriers.

A second wavered as new rounds took out its last remaining strength.

Rugrat checked his targets. "Minus another degree." As Rugrat looked at the hourglass, it emptied. "Fire!"

The AOE-spells dotted the forward edge of the oncoming formation to the rear. Blue appeared under the explosions.

"Barrier! BP rounds!"

Rugrat turned his fire selector back. "Drop fifty, minus one degree."

He turned the gears. *Come on hourglass!*

Sand finished running. "Fire!" His voice was choked out with the cannons.

Rugrat grabbed his periscope. The rounds arched, taking their sweet time as he counted down silently.

"Splash." His whispered word brought destruction with it, raking across the impact zone.

The first round was too far right. The second and third hit right after one another, the blue sky turning black. Round four broke the barrier; the remaining rounds swarmed the impact zone, obscuring his view.

Rugrat held his hand above the panel.

The smoke started to dissipate; a hole had been torn out of the fighters' ranks.

"AOE, minus one degree,"

He switched the formation, turned his traversing gear a degree, and looked at the hourglass. "Fire!"

The cannons bellowed again. Rugrat looked through the periscope, watching the impacts.

"Good splash!" He swung his periscope, looking for new targets. Another barrier had fallen, bringing the number to three.

The United Sect Army was in Deadman's Fields now. Mounted forces had been forced onto the ground for fear of laming their beasts. A few had run afoul of the obstacles. Rugrat grimaced. *Poor beasts.*

Those at the trenches pulled out bridges of different kinds and threw them out. Those without barriers rushed forward under the press of people. They pulled out more bridges as they reached ground of some kind to keep going.

The people running on a bridge ran to the end and throw another bridge down, but the stone they'd rested their first bridge on turned into a fulcrum and, as it tilted, they dropped into the trench.

The trenches weren't all on the same level. The Sects charged across, their weight tilting the bridges like see-saws over the stone blades that stuck out of the ground. The fighters went screaming down into the poison-covered spikes inside the trenches.

It happened multiple times to the groups without barriers. They just wanted to get out of where they were as accurate fire rained down.

Another group under a barrier was taking their time. Part of the group was resting their weight on the bridge so others could run forward without it tilting.

They deployed multiple bridges.

"Load BP. Add seven degrees, drop three hundred."

Rugrat did the changes and waited, the others watching through the bunker opening, ready.

"Fire!"

Rugrat looked through the periscope as the spells arrived. The smaller sect barrier shook and shuddered but stood firm.

Rugrat threw the canon's lock back into place as the hourglass tilted. He glanced through the periscope again. The United Sect Army was rushing now, but they were packed in against Deadman's Fields.

Rugrat looked at the hourglass. *Come on, come on, dammit!*

"Fire!"

The cannons recoiled, the wind rushing over Rugrat as he looked through his periscope. The rounds landed. He couldn't tell which one broke the barrier as the rounds impacted lower, hitting those below.

AOE to clear the area? Wait, never mind. They're running.

He searched for a new target as the dust plume from the impacts reached up into the heavens, dragged away by the wind.

"Come on! We can't let Roska's people beat us!" Han Wu yelled.

"New target!" Rugrat checked the top of the periscope, "Minus forty degrees, add four hundred."

Domonos watched the live feed from Vuzgal's main gate, mana cannons pounding on the barriers relentlessly.

"Well, they are the special teams," Domonos muttered to Hall. "I don't know what's scarier: how damn tight their groupings are at five and a half kilometers out, or the fact they aren't using an ounce of their actual power."

Hall grunted in agreement. "Before I joined the Alva army, I had no idea about grid squares, about enfilade or defilade fire. Didn't know about cover and movement, first aid. It doesn't feel like much, but they just crammed information in our heads."

"And then we started to act on it, think and exploit it. Takes a certain kind of power to not only build something, but pass it on to others and let them take the reins."

The map updated.

"Damn. Sects going to need better barriers than that. It's been what, three minutes? And they've lost four?" Hall checked his watch. "Look, they're starting to crack."

The Sect's fighters broke and started running back toward their camps, turning from a few into a tide.

"He'll come up with something else," Domonos said.

"Still, not bad for what, sixty cannons?"

"Yeah. They have to be a Fourth Realm force. Don't think they're Fifth, and there is no way they'd waste a Sixth Realm group."

"Where's Zukal? In the front or the secondary command center?"

"Secondary." *In case I die in some bizarre accident. He'll be able to take command immediately.*

"You know, while it is one hell of a show of firepower, our enhanced and mounted cannons might be scarier. One person can control dozens through the dungeon core, or all of them."

"Looks like they have more for us." Hall pointed at the seer stones as the gates opened once again. A second force marched out, toward those who were retreating.

"We have a reading on how strong they are?" Domonos asked.

A few moments later, an aide turned to face them. "They appear to be all above level forty. They have formed their mana core with some among them reaching Body Like Stone."

"Fifth Realm force. You think they'll send a Sixth Realm group at us?" Hall asked.

"No, this is just a test. That second force was holding behind their gates. If the first force made any progress, they would have charged out to assist, but they ran into a wall so now they need stronger people to take on the defenses to learn anything."

"Have to say I'm not jealous of them. The mana focusing formations decreasing their mana regeneration has to cost them, while increasing ours, of course." Hall clicked his tongue.

"The first force is turning and retreating," another assistant reported.

"Good. Have the gun crews switch off. Clear any of the bridges and scaling gear in area two with the cannons. Make sure I get a report on the mana usage from the cannons after this is complete. I want a report on mana gains through mana gathering formations. Siege warfare is all about resources in the end."

"Yes, sir." Domonos' head assistant nodded, jotting down notes as he remained a step away.

"You think they brought stronger barriers?" Domonos asked Hall, his eyes flicking from the different information inputs.

"Unless they're brain dead."

The first attack had been a failure.

Marco had expected as much. There hadn't been any aerial attacks, which was a relief. Just mana cannons. A powerful weapon, but one he was familiar with.

He turned his viewing glasses, watching the battlefield directly. He grimaced at the Fourth Realm forces that were coming back. Only three barriers had survived. Another had slowly started to recover, a single barrage away from collapse.

Marco felt a warm thrill in his stomach. He held back the smile that threatened to appear on his face.

Eva Marino was the first to speak up. "Such coordinated fire. Their batteries must be hitting within ten meters of one another at six kilometers."

"And take in the fact they are over a kilometer apart. They've been well trained," Marco agreed.

"Well," Onam grunted. The Willful Institute's Master Teachers lifted their eyes from their glasses. Marco turned as well, interested to hear their thoughts.

"It is as we thought. Those odd box buildings hold their weapons. Their tactics are based on using strength other than their own." Hae Woo Sung drew the corners of his mustache through his fingers.

"It matters little if they use their strength or not. Their aim, their coordinated skill across their entire front." Feng Dan's eyes thinned as she watched the Fifth Realm forces form up two assault groups per camp under their own mana barrier, preparing to march out. "From what we know, they have not called for support. They are using sixty cannons, which require three to five people to operate. Three hundred people."

Feng Dan's words hung there. She turned under that quiet. "A *twentieth* of their people manned those cannons. They have nearly seven thousand professional fighters and they coordinate like a family clan."

"They have not used their repeaters, mages, ranged fighters, or their whistling weapons. The information that we got on them previously should be thrown away. Their defenses, *this,* they have a fighter's mindset, not just a crafter's."

"It will be a slow process to take on their defenses. We will continue to use barriers as cover, attacking them in concert to open a path. I am interested in those metal bushes that cover the second part of their defenses." Marino rested her hands on her whips.

"They should be getting into range now." Marco grabbed the mounted viewing glasses and focused on the Fifth Realm assault groups.

They were broken into sects and individual clans, creating similar squares moving together, holding their own banners. Each group held one thousand fighters, making it eighteen thousand on the battlefield.

Flashes appeared in the darkened slits of the squat buildings.

The spells arced slightly, rising and then falling, igniting the mana barriers as they lit up, outlining their reach as they fought back against the attacks.

The guns paused, recharging and altering their aim as the Fifth Realm fighters increased their pace.

The next barrage came. Only half the guns fired, but with tighter groupings. The barriers that had faded flared up once more. Marco saw the streams of light underneath. The mana barriers were being carried by the strongest of the fighters. Around them, mages pulled out mana stones, feeding them into the barrier. Streams of light flowed like water between the mana stones and the barrier, drinking the power in greedily.

Mist fell from the streams, falling to the ground and being dragged away. A mist covered the barrier formation as well, power draining away slowly.

The second half of the cannons fired, their hits striking where the first half of their battery had.

The assault groups forged on.

"They are picking only six of the barriers to attack. They must not be confident to destroy them all," Onam said.

"Or they want to find out how much our barriers can take before they fail," Marino said.

"The activation speed of their cannons is precise. They are firing with the same lulls between each attack," Hae Woo-Sung said.

"They fire precisely on time," Feng Dan said.

"Is that coordination or necessity?" Marco asked.

The impacts on the barriers were gradually darkening it, like blood on white cloth.

"The barriers aren't getting time to recover between strikes. I would say a mix between coordination and necessity. They could have fired rapidly and slowed. They are monotonous in their attacks," Marino said.

One barrier collapsed, spells converging across the Sect fighters. It tore through their ranks and then stopped, having visited death and destruction upon the Sect fighters.

"They've switched targets. Look at the assault group from the second camp," Feng Dan said as a new barrier started to color.

The previous thrill in Marco's chest chilled.

"This isn't a fight. It's a slaughter, cold and calculated. Maximum destruction with the least work," Marino spat.

Magar marched with the rest of his Takar clan, gripping his spear tight. Sweat covered his back and ran down his forehead.

He wiped it away as light appeared above. He braced like it would help as the mana cannon fire drowned out all noise. The barrier penetrating spells made the barrier darken, going from clear to blue and then darkening through yellows, greens, and reds—dependent on the barrier—until it would crack like glass and evaporate like a popped bubble.

"Just a city of crafters," Ghazar spat.

"Prepare bridges!" The sect commander's words fell on the clan's ears before cannon fire washed away the sound once again.

They stored their weapons and pulled out their siege gear. Magar was at the front, looking down at the shadows in the grass.

"Ah!" The rolling booms, monotonous and chilling, were louder than any yell or scream. A man in front of Magar stumbled into a knee-high hole. The weight of his body, armor, and bridge broke his leg. The fighters holding the bridge tried to not step on him as they ran.

Magar turned his eyes to the ground again, doing his best to avoid potholes and obstacles.

They were well hidden and small. Sometimes a divot, enough to make one trip. Other times it was a hole with spikes to cut up one's leg.

Magar didn't have the time to glance up at the barrier now.

Vuzgal was still so far in the distance. *Run!* He held back his instinct with the experience of battles across the Fourth Realm.

"Make su—" The rest of the sect commander's words were stolen as the cannon fire speed almost doubled.

Flashes of the mana cannon's spells struck the barrier so close together the barrier had little time to recover. The bombardment paused, but the ringing in his ears remained.

They passed the dirt and stepped onto hard stone. Magar ran forward. To stop was to be trampled by those behind him. His animal instincts forced him forward like a rabbit away from a fox. If he broke down now, the clan would kill him for cowardice.

He slowed as he readied his bridge, a ten-meter plank of wood. Others carried planks in rings while some carried plants.

Magar tossed down the plank of wood. Those with plants summoned their magic. The vine plants grew rapidly at first, entwining their limbs around the planks, but the mages' spells and bodies weakened under Vuzgal's formations. Mages that should have been able to grow a house from a tree in minutes struggled. Their brows dripped in sweat, and exertion marred their faces.

Come on, hurry up!

The different bridges spread out and fell to the side when they grew too heavy, falling on other planks and wrapping around them, creating a sturdy bridge of vines and planks.

Magar pulled out another plank and moved forward. He put it down on the bed of vines. Others did the same, rushing up as the vines grew up their new latticework.

Magar focused on his task, pushing up, placing more planks, letting the vines connect them, repeat.

Their speed was slower, but they advanced constantly.

Magar looked between the vines before quickly looking away with a shiver. The trench was filled with spikes and sharp edges. *What sadistic bastard made this place?*

The sound changed, and his ears popped. Magar rubbed his ears at the sensation.

He felt a punch in his side and glowered at the clan member responsible. The man had no mercy in his eyes. He glared at Magar and his plank.

Magar quickly judged if he could toss the clan member off the bridge into the spikes below, covering his own frustrations.

Too many eyes.

Magar threw down his plank in anger.

Vines sped along it as the terrain changed. They grew thicker and thinner in places. The bridges were up and over at odd angles, but they created a path forward.

Magar ducked as the sounds of the mana spells changed. The cannon strike fizzled against the barrier just meters above, causing it to darken like the coming night.

He grabbed another plank and forced his way forward, putting everything into his task. He still had his personal barrier, the best he could buy, and his armor was all charged. He had a defensive scroll, too.

He touched the piece of cloth that ran along his wrist and attached to a spell scroll as he watched the vines grow and curl forward. The vines neared completion, and he threw down a new plank. It hit the vines and tilted forward. Instead of coming to rest on the other side, it tumbled into the chasm below. Magar looked ahead. It had to be at least twenty meters across.

He turned to the side. He was ahead of the main body of fighters, who were quickly catching up.

Another plank fell to his side and vines wove upwards. Mages moved up with fresh plants, putting them down near the edge of the bridge. They had archers with them.

The mages grew thin vines that the archers attached to their arrows. They checked the amount of vine they had, then drew back and fired their arrows across the chasm. They hit the other side, burying themselves into the stone.

The mages focused on the mana. The vines attached to the arrows grew over the wall and split, then burrowed into it or grew along it, covering the side in vines. The vines turned back on themselves as they weaved a bridge back toward Magar.

Magar looked down at the movement, shuddering with more impacts. They were stretched out more than the attacks on the main barrier, and it was a matter of time now. Not if, but *when* the barrier collapsed.

Spells struck the other side of the chasm, exploding and peppering the barrier with stone shrapnel.

"Extend the barrier!" he yelled, turning toward the sect commander, but his words were drowned out by cannon fire.

One of the lightning spells struck the vines on the other side of the trench and they exploded as lightning ran down them, falling in flaming ruins as it came toward Magar.

Magar drew his spear. Stepping to the edge of the chasm, he severed the vines that were growing out to meet the exploding vines.

The bridge fell into the chasm, the lightning running its course. The vines burst into flames as they dropped to the bottom.

Other vines exploded to his right as the lightning jumped from the vines to those standing on them. Sections of vines collapsed, sending them tumbling into the waiting spikes below.

The mage closest to him pulled out another plant, and the archer readied a new arrow. Retreat was not an option, and they repeated the process. Magar held his spear at the ready. He worked his jaw as his ears popped. The cannon fire and sounds of battle became clearer.

The barrier!

He fumbled with his necklace, activating his personal barrier.

Lightning spells crashed into the press of fighters. It *smashed* through them, tossing them like chaff in the wind. Tendrils of lightning continued to stretch out, too bright to look at directly, but searing an image of the bridges' and vines' destruction into Magar's eyes.

Waves of mana and air buffeted him before it was suddenly his whole world. He was thrown aside, an inconsequential fighter among many. He grabbed his wrist and tore the spell scroll, his spear forgotten as he fought to survive.

His barrier collapsed under the energies as the spell scroll activated around him, throwing him up and back.

Magar struck stone and rolled. He felt his bones break and shift, causing him to hiss in pain, but he had to move—now—or risk being hit by the mana cannon spells.

He pushed up from the ground, facing away from Vuzgal.

Other groups had pushed ahead, unmolested and untouched.

Magar dove into a crater, away from the fire, flinching at the noises all around him. He curled up, trying to become part of the ground as a silence-spelled mortar rained down on him.

"Shift down fifteen degrees, drop one-five-zero! Fire for effect!" Acosta barked. She looked from the degree marker and through the periscope into the chaos beyond. *Shit, the Colonel's done messing around.*

Three hundred cannons and one hundred and sixty mortars had left lines of dissipating mana trails, crashing into barriers, ground, and enemy fighters. Main barriers were darkening at a visible speed now, hit from several directions under constant fire.

Acosta tracked her target, a group that was attempting to bridge Deadman's Fields.

"Should've called it Deadman's Drop."

The first of her mortars illuminated their barrier like the sudden onset of rain-turned-deluge. Other shells struck, revealing the boundaries of the barrier, and covering it in a haze of expelled mana and stone dust.

Shells continued to drop around them as her crews ran through their five-shot payload.

The barrier collapsed under withering fire.

"Switch to H. E! Switch to H. E!" she barked, with Staff Sergeant Neumann relaying her orders.

Their rounds hit the bridges. The barrier penetrators cutting through all that was in their way and diving into the depths below.

The high explosive struck, throwing out clouds of smoke. Stone shrapnel, metal and anything in the blast zone tore through fighters, turning bridges of different kinds into flying debris.

"Rounds complete!" Neumann relayed.

Acosta shifted her periscope. "Change in target. We'll go right to fire for effect, five rounds B. P, ready on the H. E," Acosta said, scanning her designated sector.

"Be ready five rounds B. P, ready five rounds H.E."

"Make it three rounds H.E. No need to waste ammunition."

"That's one way to tell them to fuck off back home," Rugrat said.

Han Wu grunted.

They were in a repeater pillbox looking out at the break in hardened stone and metal with the gun's crew.

"Last of their main barriers," Simms said in a dull voice.

"What was that, less than a minute?" Tyrone shook his head.

"The mortars are tearing apart whoever makes it into Deadman's. The shrapnel is turning that place into a mess," Rugrat said.

"Looks like they've realized what's going on." Simms pointed out to the west. Rugrat pulled out his viewing glasses. He saw glimpses through the smoke of different clans and sects falling into disorder and disarray. A complete turnaround from the segregated mass that had made it to Deadman's Fields. Some tripped and fell but kept going as they left muddy footprints, straying from the hardened dirt paths they'd advanced on, trying to escape like the devil himself was chasing them.

Rugrat felt the slumbering formations activate through his connection to the dungeon core. The wind picked up, chilly and wet. Formations inside the pillbox fought to warm the pillbox against the wind.

"They activated area three," Rugrat said as trap spells erupted from the ground among those fleeing back toward their camps.

The sky darkened as nearby clouds gathered over the battlefield, stretching out in a perfect circle six kilometers across. Lightning flashed through its depths as the thick white clouds turned gray, and finally black. Even with the mortar and cannon fire, all eyes shifted toward the massive clouds that had been gathered by spells.

Lightning ripped through the heavens and a gray sheet fell from the sky.

"Damn! That's so much rain I can't see more than a kilometer into it without spells," one of the gunners said.

While the dark skies hung over the battlefield and all but the most westerly and easterly camps, it stopped just five hundred meters from Vuzgal which was still bathed in sunlight.

Light flashed among the clouds, pausing for a moment.

"I can't hear the lightning over our own guns."

Han Wu looked at him and then slowly back toward the battlefield. "I don't suppose they can either."

Klaus entered the Vuzgal Fighters Association main hall. There, three guards wearing the armor and helmets of Vuzgal stood, totally at ease with five unconscious forms at their feet. They stood there unaffected and seemingly uncaring at the mana the silent association members were gathering.

Klaus could tell a fight was a spark away. He hid his frown. The unconscious members looked like the spies he had sent out.

Not dead, thankfully. Klaus waved his arms at his unconscious fighters. "What do we have here?"

"These are your people. They were found in areas they shouldn't be in. For your own safety, we ask that you only visit the Battle Arena and the other Association locations. Any that are found lost or wandering will be exiled from Vuzgal. Have a good day." The trio turned to leave.

"A moment of your time," Klaus said, feeling his fellow association member's anger building, hands silently creeping toward weapons.

The trio turned, greeting him with faceplates of blank armored metal.

"Even if we wish to leave Vuzgal, how could we? We have no totem anymore."

The leader of the trio pointed to the north. "Through the front gate," she said and turned once again. The other two waited for her to get close before they left as well.

"They think that they're gods! No damn respect!" someone yelled, spitting into his tankard and hurling it.

Klaus punched out without looking, a wave of force shot from his hands, shattering the ceramic tankard in mid-air, covering the thrower in his own drink.

He turned without a word and looked at the unconscious five. "Bring them to the healers and don't piss off the Vuzgalians. We already stepped on their honor." Klaus's footsteps rang through the hall as he walked into the rear of the association.

Klaus stood on the roof of the Fighter's Association, looking at the dark clouds in the distance. The door to the roof opened as Nane walked out, one of the five that had been left in his hall.

"Feeling better now?" Klaus turned, asking her.

"Yes, Branch Head." She bowed, embarrassed.

"We suspected the Vuzgalians had a way to track people. There were few disturbances during the fighting competitions. The Vuzgal police appeared at opportune times and the perpetrators were always found."

"Wish I didn't have to confirm it with my face," Nane said as she rose.

Klaus laughed softly and indicated for her to join him. "So?"

"We didn't get far, a few hundred meters to the outer walls."

"There aren't any people; the city is empty. Carts do not move to the front, or return."

"They have to have a hidden system. We know as much from their defenses, but it must be larger than I suspected. The crafting workshops work day and night. They must have tunnels to the front. A smart way to prepare away from prying eyes. I wonder if they made the defenses beyond the gates before this and just raised them, or if they really did make them in less than a week."

"If you knew this, why did you send us?" Nane asked.

"I wanted to test their reaction, but I also wanted you to confirm it if you could. We'll show that Vuzgal has the ability to maintain this siege indefinitely. Then the Associations could be tempted to mediate the situation."

"Mediate?"

"Vuzgal creates a lot of profit, items that the Associations want, and training. The Associations may try to cut a deal. They'll get more from Vuzgal to lift the siege. Then they pay off the Sects, get an agreement in place, and things will return to how they were before."

"Will the Sects go with it?"

"Yes, they will get concessions from the associations. Something to make up for their losses and more. They won't be looking over their shoulders for counterattack, either."

"Though Vuzgal would still lose something," Nane said.

"Of course. Vuzgal is the lonely island with little in the way of support to call upon. They might be able to get the Blue Lotus and the Alchemist Association to lessen their terms, but they'll want something. It is best for them as well because the Sects will not be able to attack them in the future." Klaus sighed.

"What do you think will happen, Branch Head?" Nane asked.

"That remains to be seen." Klaus crossed his arms. "The Willful Institute needs a win here to turn the tides in the lower realms. Vuzgal needs to show their strength to secure their position."

"I think they might have done that with the last attack."

"Ten thousand dead, seven thousand wounded, only one thousand made it out, somehow, without losing a limb." Klaus felt the sun on his back, but inside he was as cold as the rain clouds that hung in front of Vuzgal. The association had learned much about their hosts and the sects that fought them.

41 Moving Pieces

"To think that all this was built in a single night. It is impressive what our sects are able to do together!" the bejeweled Sect Elder whose name Elder Kostic had not spent the time to learn, said.

"It is a grand achievement. Now the enemy cowers behind their walls and in their boxes."

"Walls! Hah, they have but those odd metal things. Their walls are barely five meters tall!"

The larger sect elder got the laughter of the others as they perused the food that had been laid out for them. They looked at the updated maps which dotted the room and peered through viewing glasses at the waiting city.

Groups of sect elders floated around the room, introducing different leaders and fighters they had brought with them, tightening sect ties. *And showing others why they shouldn't think about attacking them,* Kostic thought wryly.

Marco found Kostic as he bowed to the group of sect elders that had engaged him.

"I am sorry, but we must talk on sect-related matters," Low Elder Kostic said as he indicated to Marco to lead.

He bowed his head to the elders in the room, who returned the gesture, before leading Kostic down the corridor to a guarded room.

The door closed as Kostic's smile dampened. "The Head is eager to hear how things have progressed here. Several groups wish to ally with us."

"Vuzgal will be tough. I cannot guarantee anything right now. I will need greater support if we want to get to their walls."

Marco told Kostic about the defenses.

"I think it would be best to rope people into alliances now, before they realize it could take months to take the city or even years if we do not get support from the powers in the higher realms."

"Years?"

"Vuzgal had a population of nearly eight hundred thousand. There are seven thousand soldiers, maybe fifty thousand people inside Vuzgal right now. They have massive stores of supplies, the ability to grow food, and have crafters to make weapons. The crafter dungeon alone will keep them well stocked."

"You think that seven thousand can hold us back?" He sounded amused.

"Yes. I think that if we were to go face-to-face with them, there would be no contest. But the fight here will not be on the ground, it will be in the air. Whoever gains air superiority wins. A rush on the ground will leave dead and dying in such numbers that the other sects won't stomach the losses."

"Press them for mounted aerial forces and spell scrolls."

"That would be for the best. If the aerial forces can harass the city, that will open a gap in their defenses. If the Vuzgalians are beaten back on their front lines so they can't attack, we can advance our fighters into the enemy lands."

Kostic needed to gather more forces from the other sects to support Marco. Else, this campaign would fall apart. All Oskar Elsi had achieved was to get his people within the city imprisoned. *And guide us down paths for the Vuzgalians to attack us.*

"Elder Kostic," Oskar Elsi greeted as he entered the office. A compound had been turned over to the Willful Institute, to act as their headquarters closer to Vuzgal.

"Elder Elsi." Kostic indicated to the couches, giving the man behind Oskar a questioning glance.

"This is Commander Lovak of the mortal realm's armies."

"Elder Kostic." The commander bowed deeply, coming up slowly.

"Oh." Elder Kostic drew out the word as he sat; Oskar followed a moment later. Commander Lovak stood behind them, a silent statue.

"So, what is it that you wish to talk about?" Kostic pulled his eyes from Lovak.

"I am sorry that I was not a greater help at the beginning of the campaign. The Vuzgalians have kept much a secret from all of us."

Kostic waved his hands. "You provided passage through the totem and the mountains. It was no small deed."

"Thank you, Elder Kostic; you honor me. You see, I have always admired the Willful Institute. Your ability with mana gathering cultivation is impressive in the extreme. We body cultivators are many in the lower realms, but it is hard for us to progress further. I share these problems with the rest of the Stone Fist Sect."

Kostic glanced at Lovak, again deciphering Oskar's words. It was true that mana gathering cultivation was a faster way to gain strength in the Earth Realms. In the Mortal Realms, there were few resources, so hurting oneself to temper their body was easier. But Oskar was speaking of the Stone Fist Sect, not just his clan, and he had brought someone from outside who must be closely aligned with the sect or else he would quickly lose his power.

"The lower realms are indeed a headache these days," Kostic ventured.

"Surely, as friends, we could help one another?"

Support in the lower realms? Kostic's mind turned it over, and he extended his senses toward Lovak.

Body Like Iron in the mortal realms. There was a strong earth presence about him as well. He hadn't reached Body Like Sky Iron yet. He was the commander, but Body Like Stone must be common and there would be plenty of leaders with Body Like Iron.

Kostic turned to Oskar. "You have an offer?"

"Friends helping one another. The Stone Fist Sect will support your cities in the lower realms. We have a great number of friends that would be honored to assist the Willful Institute in clearing out these pretenders in the lower realms and take a chunk of their flesh as well. We just hope that the fine Willful Institute will take some of our talented youth and teach them mana gathering." Oskar sat back comfortably in his chair. "I hear that cultivation in body and in mana is highly sought after. Our heritage and knowledge has extended to the Body Like Diamond level."

"While we hold the enemy at our gates, would it not hurt them more to hit their cities?" Kostic put forward.

"Indeed, Elder Kostic has a brilliant mind!"

Maybe Oskar wasn't as useless as he thought. They could gain access to their body cultivation heritages, and the support of their armies in the lower realms as well.

Kostic pulled out a tea set. "Elder Elsi, please have some of my personal Fuchen mind-calming tea. It comes directly from the Sixth Realm and is a great elixir for assisting in their cultivation and rejuvenating the mind and body!"

"Elder Kostic, you are too gracious!"

Ringing and lights filled Erik's pod. He opened his eyes, letting his mana settle. The density around him dwindled, breaking his concentration.

Something must have happened.

He studied his elemental core. It had become denser since he got in the pod. His mana core had achieved the vapor stage.

He checked the litany of notifications.

Quest Completed: Mana Cultivation 2
The path to cultivating one's mana is not easy. To stand at the top, one must forge their own path forward.
Requirements: Reach Vapor Mana Core
Rewards: +20 to Mana +20 to Mana Regeneration +50,000,000 EXP

Quest: Mana Cultivation 3
The path to cultivating one's mana is not easy. To stand at the top, one must forge their own path forward.
Requirements: Reach Liquid Mana Core
Rewards: +40 to Mana +40 to Mana Regeneration +500,000,000 EXP

Skill: Alchemy *Level: 95 (Expert)*
Able to identify 1 effect of the ingredient. Ingredients are 5% more potent. When creating concoctions, mana regeneration increases by 20%

You have reached Level 67. When you sleep next, you will be able to increase your attributes by: 5 points.

254,487,951/ 547,100,000 EXP till you reach Level 68

Name: Erik West Level: 67 Race: Human-?	
Titles: *From the Grave II* *Blessed By Mana* *Dungeon Master V* *Reverse Alchemist* *Poison Body* *Fire Body* *City Lord III* *Earth Soul* *Mana Reborn* *Wandering Hero* *Metal Mind, Metal Body* *Earth Grade Bloodline*	
Strength: (Base 90) +53	1501
Agility: (Base 83) +85	966
Stamina: (Base 93) +35	2016
Mana: (Base 37) +94	1336
Mana Regeneration (Base 60) +61	76.02
Stamina Regeneration: (Base 162) +59	47.46

Erik opened his eyes. The medics and Storbon stood outside the pod. He grabbed the handholds, and the pod rotated upward and opened.

"Report." Erik looked at Storbon over the medics who moved to check him.

"The enemy sects used teleportation formations to set up nine camps in front of Vuzgal. They have attacked five times. Each attack has ended in failure. They appear to be feints. Elan has information that they are seeking out support from the different sects in the way of aerial forces and spell scrolls."

"Attack from the sky."

"Yes."

"How long have they been under siege?"

"One week."

"Reserves?"

"I sent all of the First Division and the newly graduated soldiers out. Another two divisions are being trained currently.

"Otherwise?"

"The kingdoms have started to move in the First Realm. The Willful Institute has not appeared, but civilians are fleeing the Beast Mountain Range."

"Anything else?"

"Nothing major."

"What are we doing?"

"Glosil has ordered the special teams to King's Hill. Niemm will remain with the Adventurer's Guild. You have battlefield command. If needed, you can turn over to Colonel Yui, who will be ready to deploy his regiment within eight hours."

The needles came out of Erik's arm. The holes left by them pushed out drops of blood as they healed completely.

Clean.

A wave of mana ran over Erik's body, refreshing him.

"How long have I been out?"

"Ten days."

"Okay, the blood?"

"All good. You supplied so much that the alchemists were working on everything but the revival potions."

"Good. There are other things we need like the buffing potions as well. Do we have numbers on the kingdoms?"

"Each army is about fifteen to twenty thousand strong with core troops, with around five thousand mercenaries. At least two people to support each fighter."

"Armies of twenty-five thousand with fifty thousand camp followers and a massive supply route back to their lands. I love supply routes instead of people just bringing all their shit in a storage ring," Erik said as he started to get dressed. "Anything else?"

"Hearing noise with the Stone Fist Sect. A bunch have joined the Willful Institute to fight Vuzgal. There are rumors that even if they don't take the city, they will get a share of the city's holdings. The Blue Lotus and Alchemist Association have sent you a message."

Storbon held out a scroll.

"Read it." Erik buttoned up his shirt.

"They offer to lead the negotiations against the sects. They do not want to take anything, just continue the relationship. They will do all they can to get rid of the sects."

"Rugrat's response?"

"He hasn't made any. He wanted to leave it to you. Said you knew them better."

Erik paused. If they took the deal, they would lose some of their power. *And they will figure out our secrets soon enough, so it won't matter. Everyone will come for us.*

"Who is it from?"

"Elder Lu Ru."

A good man in a bad situation. Erik already knew that Old Hei was behind the Alchemist Association's message. He sent them a silent thanks. Even before they were using their status as honorable elders to save as many of them as possible, they were part of something much larger. Their hands were tied. The Willful Institute had greater reach, more locations. Vuzgal was just one place. Of course, they would side with them. *But we have the opportunity to prove we can hold what we have, which allows the Associations the power to step in and leverage between the two groups.*

"We cannot agree to anything other than them leaving. Those are our conditions. We will not attack the other sects if they retreat. But we will make no such agreement with the Willful Institute. That is it," Erik decided.

Yao Meng jotted down notes.

"Check with Commander Glosil to see if he would like Rugrat to write the message in such a way as to piss the sects off."

Yao Meng paused.

"Based on the defensive plans I saw and the fact they're trying to pull aerial forces together, they'll come out worse on the other side. We piss them off, draw them into a fight and hammer the shit out of them."

Yao Meng kept writing.

"So, King's Hill?" Storbon asked.

"Yes, I think it's about time I met with these outpost leaders and took things in hand. If Colonel Yui is free, get him to join us."

Flames appeared as wisps around Erik, twisting into beasts curling around his hands and arms, happy to be close to their master. They moved around his clothes without burning them. Mana blades flew around his other arm without cutting a hair.

"Good." He dismissed the spells and tied his boots. "Let's get going. No time like the present. How long till the kingdoms reach the outposts?"

"A week."

"Plenty of time. Make sure Aditya knows to expect us."

Erik pulled out his vest and threw it on. then pulled up its front flap, securing the undone side and slapping it back down.

Tian Cui opened the door for him as he looked out at the cultivation pod rooms.

The other special team members, seeing Erik armor up, were pulling out their vests, tightening their gloves, and clipping on their helmets.

Erik kept walking, testing out the new limits to his body. He had finally consolidated Diamond Body. There was None of that weird disconnect where he felt like there was more power just out of reach. It was slowly coming back. He wondered if he could make use of the parts in his title yet, beast transformation and such.

Erik pushed the thought away. He didn't have time to fuck with new things; It was best to use tried, tested and true.

Erik's sound transmission device shook. He quickly read it.

"Change of plans. Off to the Dungeon Headquarters. The Council has called a meeting."

Delilah took her seat at the head of the council table. Blaze was still off fighting the Willful Institute in the other realms; same with the Silaz brothers and Rugrat. Elise had just come back from across the realms. Jia Feng looked tired. Her student population had just switched into soldiers. The teaching staff had poured as much information into their heads as possible in a short period.

She studied Erik, who sat at her side, looking for any signs of harm.

Teacher, you are too much! Turning yourself into an alchemy cauldron to make more revival potions out of your blood! You could have hurt yourself.

Some of her thoughts must've leaked through her eyes as Erik winced and ducked his head.

She turned to glare at Rugrat, who grinned, making her blush and look away.

She cleared her throat, bringing the smaller conversations to silence.

"All right, this is probably one of the rare times that we can meet like this in the coming months. Let's make sure that we're all on the same page. We'll go from Jia Feng, to Elise, Commander Glosil, Lord West, and Egbert."

"Thank you, Council Leader." Jia Feng bobbed her head. "The Vuzgal academy staff is working within the city, taking on jobs to create the supplies needed for the Army. The Kanesh Academy has been working with the military to give the soldiers the best information possible. We've streamlined our courses to get them done in a few days instead of weeks. Those that are not teaching have been drafted under Taran. He has taken over the operation of the factories. Or they are under Melissa Bouchard and Hou Jun to increase the soldier's cultivation." Jia Feng looked at Elise.

"The traders from across the realms are returning to Alva," Elise said. "Most of them have outside help operating their companies. There are three major fronts we are working on. First is moving materials to Vuzgal and Alva in support of the crafters, then getting the finished products into the hands of the people that need them. Second is moving supplies to the Adventurer's Guild and Beast Mountain Range. Finally, supporting the Intelligence Department. A lot of our traders are also intelligence agents, so they have remained in place." Elise turned to Glosil.

"The sects in the Fourth Realm are testing our defenses," Glosil said. "They have not made any major attacks. They are gathering support for the next assault. The Dragon Regiment has been reinforced with a division of reservists and two battalions of fully trained regular service riflemen. We have thousands of people undergoing reserve training to get them up to speed as fast as possible in Alva. All of Tiger Regiment has been turned over to training these people.

"The Adventurer's Guild has made small advances in their different battlefields. The Willful Institute is consolidating their forces, and that has made them harder targets. First Realm kingdoms have gathered their forces and are marching on the Beast Mountain Range. We expect them to arrive at the external outposts in one week. They are supported by the Willful Institute. We are not sure what their aims are at this time."

Glosil sat back.

Erik shrugged. "No change for me. I have to wrangle a beast and head to King's Hill after this. I think now is the time to reveal that there is a power behind Aditya to the other outpost leaders."

A ripple ran through the room as people sat up and looked at Erik.

"How much information and why?" Delilah asked.

"Get them into a contract to support Aditya or get out of his way. Consolidate the leadership there. Just showing up, throwing out some power, and saying that we support Aditya. Don't tell them anything about Alva or otherwise."

"Commander?" Delilah raised an eyebrow at Glosil.

"The range has been Alva's cover since we got the binding contract with Aditya years ago. Colonel Yui has been giving me reports on the situation that Aditya has been sending to you. The outpost leaders are in a panic. They're collapsing. This move will tie them to us."

Erik nodded and looked at Delilah. She took in a breath, organizing her thoughts.

"The situation in the Beast Mountain Range is mostly with the outliers. Aditya has done well to integrate people into roles that they fulfil and excel at." She sent a silent apology to Aditya. "Do what you did to Elise and I."

"Install him in power and step back?"

"Yes, throw him into the deep end." Elise gave him a wry smile. "He has the support, and he knows everything that is going on. This just allows him to exert greater control. Have him form a council to spread the load: trading, army, banking, the consortium, the farmers, the healers, and the mercenaries. He will need to make more offices instead of fewer to fit in the different outpost leaders. Then, over time, he can trim them. For now, it doesn't matter; he just needs the control."

Erik nodded. "I have a question."

Delilah indicated for him to go on.

"Where are the family members of the Adventurer's Guild?"

Delilah looked at Elise.

"Before the Guild went to war, they were moved to secure cities," Elise said. "They are living and working in those locations across the realms."

"What about the back-up dungeons?"

Glosil cleared his throat. "They are all up and operational. They have plans to extend themselves as they gather enough power. We were able to capture a few more than expected."

"Do we have the capacity for all Alvans?"

"Yes, sir."

"What about the Guild member's families?"

"You're thinking of bringing them into Alva?" Delilah asked.

"They have been fighting for us. The least we can do, *if* it comes to it, is give them and their families refuge. If nothing comes of this, I still want more of the Guild to get access to Alva. We have been hiding for so damn long and they have proved their ability."

"I agree." Delilah nodded after a few moment's consideration. She looked around, seeing the general agreement. "Then I guess it is my turn. Egbert?"

He rose from a chair in the corner of the room. Back to his complete form, the formations tattoos had spread down through his bones and he'd gotten a new robe, black on the outside, blue inner layer with *lots* of sown in formations in the material.

"You learn anything else from your memories?" Erik asked.

"Some things are coming back to me. I know more about the dungeon, what it can do, and the things that were built in."

"Anything immediately useful?"

"A range increasing formation. It stretches out for kilometers. It was broken, but I can pour power into it and it will repair and increase the range that the dungeon cores can link."

"Link?"

"You know how we have to be within the dungeon's area of influence to control it? Well, I was annoyed with being restricted to the dungeon, so I created an extending formation. It allowed me to travel kilometers outside of the dungeon on the surface and not collapse."

"How far are we talking?"

"About twenty kilometers in any direction, but more importantly, it works above ground level. Look at Vuzgal. The dungeon core has a range of ten kilometers, but the undead can't go higher than two kilometers and they can't go out more than seven and a half kilometers on the surface. This formation increases the sphere of influence above ground. It does not increase the range of the dungeon's influence below the ground."

"Okay, so you can then move around and provide support above ground?"

"Yes, also, you can draw on the dungeon's power above ground."

"Draw on the dungeon's power. I remember seeing that, but won't that burn through me?"

"Yes," Egbert contemplated. "You'd be like a bug in a lightning formation if you tried to do it when you first arrived. Now, you've tempered your body and your mana; you can cast spells reinforced with external mana. This is like that, but on a larger scale. You complete your spell and use your body like a conduit. Mana pours through your body and into the spell, going from using your personal power to a portion of the dungeon's power. Thankfully, you have me because I can limit it so you don't explode like popcorn."

"Lovely."

"Bite me."

"You'd like that."

"Wah, uhh I'm bones! Are you a dog?"

"Anything for you, Baby."

"I—jus—y-you!" Egbert wagged his finger, full of impotent, confused fury.

If a skeleton could have turned red or melted into a puddle, Egbert would have. Erik broke out into a big grin.

Delilah worked her lips to hold her smile at bay. Clearing her throat. "Egbert, you were saying?"

"Otherwise, I've been working with the formation masters to create a battery buffer system. And I found Alva's defenses."

"Defenses?"

Egbert shivered at Erik's tone but continued. "Most of them were destroyed, but I have all their plans and can modify them with what I have learned."

"So, we can add tactical attack spell formations to our command center?" Glosil asked.

"Yes, the key part is the targeting. That has been our problem with adding them ourselves. I was a rather good formation master, and my friends were good at it as well, so we fixed that issue. Also, the cooling problem and creating super massive formations. There is a reason the water floor is the size it is and freezing, and why we carved power formations into every damn floor. Alva dungeon is a massive battery."

"What?" Jia Feng asked as everyone looked at Egbert.

"Yeah, you know how I changed the whole Beast Mountain Range, and diverted a river? That's why there are ships in trees around here. Well, I was double casting. I can use a lot of the Dungeon's power, but not all of it. Like, I tore apart the ground, crushed an army. This was all plains. There is a reason that the mountains are a hellish landscape. I was using forests and mountains as *weapons.*" Silence fell over the room.

He said that he had altered the area, but not to this degree.

"Pre-tty sweet," Egbert said in the silence. "Never been curious as to how I lost so much damn power, and why there is a random mountain range in the middle of nowhere, and the kingdoms aren't around here much? Those that attacked us seemed to have forgotten what happened here. Short memories. I think I've been down here a lot longer than I realized."

"Just how strong is the dungeon?" Erik asked.

"Well, if we were to turn off everything and only power the attack formations..." Egbert looked up, his skull turning in a slow circle. "Yup, a lot of power."

"How much is a lot?"

"Dude, we have a freaking laser that is cutting through the damn planet!"

"What?" Erik reeled.

"Sorry, I've been around more of you Earthers, learning things. But the drilling laser is a precise combination of elements and mana combined into what is effectively a spell. Looking at you, Tanya... Sorry, off-topic. Ahem. That laser is cutting through stone and iron buried tens of kilometers in the ground. On Earth, the deepest you went was twelve kilometers, from what I've been told. The plan for the drill is to punch a one-meter-wide hole down a hundred kilometers."

"How deep is this thing?" Elise asked.

"We're at like fifty kilometers deep. With the power we have, we could make it through a kilometer a day and still support the dungeon."

"Anything else?" Erik asked.

"Nope, I think that's about it. All the other memories seem to be personal stuff."

Delilah felt a stab of pain. *All of those memories coming back decades, centuries later and knowing that no one survived. That must be hard.*

"Well, you've made some new memories. You are an Alvan. If you need something, reach out, you hear?" The rest of the room nodded, reinforcing

Erik's words.

Egbert lowered his eyes. "Thank you," he said in a small voice.

"Don't worry about it, Brother," Erik said. "These attack formations, how long to bring them online?"

"A few weeks, I'd think. We can create smaller versions to speed it up. It depends on what you want to do. If you want to increase the range, then we can focus on that. But it will take up resources that other projects would need."

"So, either we do the range extender, or we do attack formations. If we want the attack formations, then we have to put the ranged formations on hold. Or else, if we do them both at the same time, they'll take longer?"

"Yes."

"I would vote for the extender. You and Egbert are already powerful enough by yourselves. We'll look at the drill and the attack formations next," Glosil said.

"You want to start the drill up again?" Delilah asked.

"If we need it. I want to make sure it is ready. It is a fallback for Alva."

"I was doing it out of desperation, but if we were to use the dungeon to carve in formations, it would be more effective, and we could channel the power more easily. But yeah, more engineering formation talk," Egbert said.

"Do we have permission?" Glosil asked.

Erik looked at Delilah who turned it back to him.

"Do it. Any way we can gain power, and increase our security, as long as it doesn't go against our core values and laws," Erik shrugged.

"Yes, sir." Glosil made a note and Erik looked at Delilah.

"I guess I am last. All of Alva has returned in the majority. We have expanded housing on all the floors. Most of our population is training in the army or working in industries related to our mobilization. While this is going on, I have been working with the Alva administrators to prepare for what might happen after these fights, and working with the council on the predictions.

"Otherwise, mostly all I've been doing is putting loans on hold. We've started a ration point system so we don't cut into our mana stone supply. Everyone gets rations for food. We have plenty.

"Wandering Inns and Sky Reaching Restaurants continue to operate. Most of their staff is external now. They continue to grow with our other businesses, allowing people's savings to grow continuously. We have spread out the bank's reserves across the first four Realms. Even if we lose one, it won't cripple us. All essential services have been backed up. While all the Alvans are working on the war effort, there's a lot of money to be made and traders have networks across the lower realms that don't know about Alva. The dungeon cores are expanding faster in Alva with so many powerful people around," Delilah checked her notes. "That is all."

"You make it sound so simple." Erik smiled and looked around the table. "Thank you all for what you have done. I can't put into words the thanks for your tireless efforts."

"There is always more to be done. Is there anything else?" Delilah asked, clearing up her papers.

No one said anything.

"Okay, then I call the meeting to an end. I'll see you all, but good luck and keep doing what you're doing. You do Alva proud. And you, Dungeon Lord, need to go scare some outpost lords."

"Just have a quick stop on the water floor first."

Erik headed to the armory and quickly added his new attribute points putting all five into his strength.

Name: Erik West Level: 67 Race: Human-?	
Titles: *From the Grave II* *Blessed By Mana* *Dungeon Master V* *Reverse Alchemist* *Poison Body* *Fire Body* *City Lord III* *Earth Soul* *Mana Reborn* *Wandering Hero* *Metal Mind, Metal Body* *Earth Grade Bloodline*	
Strength: (Base 90) +58	1554
Agility: (Base 83) +85	966
Stamina: (Base 93) +35	2016
Mana: (Base 37) +94	1336

Mana Regeneration (Base 60) +61	76.02
Stamina Regeneration: (Base 162) +59	47.46

After his nap, he and Storbon's Special team headed to the Water floor.

"Place is huge, still."

"We're going to need the room," Storbon said.

Erik grunted.

Around the teleportation pad, a small town had grown out of the snow and ice.

"Clothing used to be a rarity and a pleasure, but people can buy it so easily now. My sisters keep going on about their different outfits nowadays," Yuli said.

"Isn't that a new casting robe?" Foster asked.

Erik's lips twitched. He didn't have to turn around to feel the glare Foster was getting. "Rather nice still." Erik walked forward. The village dwellings were made of stone. Carved formations kept out the weather and decorated the walls in blue hues. It made the village feel lively. Snow clung to the roofs of the houses, falling occasionally, dissolving before reaching the ground.

They passed a park where people had turned off the formations, creating ice sculptures that dotted the area as children ran and threw snowballs at one another. A group of parents nearby drank warm drinks leaving dragon breaths of steam in the air as they talked.

Water wagons and wagons with Alva's alchemy symbol rolled through the streets, heading to the other floors.

They reached the edge of the village, walking out onto the paths.

"The formation masters really didn't want anyone to slip and fall," Storbon muttered.

"All the roads across all the floors are formation-enhanced to make sure that they can withstand the test of time." Erik looked out over the snowy expanse. Snow fell in the distance, covering a forest of trees made of sparkling ice.

Hills wove together, creating ranges that stabbed into the sky. The light of the sun shone off the dark cold waters that covered most of the floor.

"It's the same harbor the Tiger Regiment launched from to take back the floor." Storbon followed Erik's gaze. Proper docks had been added, with roads and loading equipment.

The sheer cliffs the Tiger Regiment had used to launch from when originally taking the water floor had been carved down.

Set with stairs, overhanging lifts, and a sprawling warehouse district, a proper fishing village had grown around the icy harbor.

A fishing ship that had returned from its early morning departure moored across from the warehouses. The crew moved to secure the ship. Formation-enhanced rollers and cooling boxes were brought out as the warehouse crews and fish buyers talked with the fishermen, joking and laughing with one another as they brought in the day's haul.

Traders that had come from the other floors, mainly the Kanesh Academy, and the restaurants and taverns on the living floor eyed the fish coming off the boat.

"Rich fishing in these waters. Been left alone for a few hundred years so their population has swelled," Storbon informed them as their path diverted away from the harbor.

"Still, we need to make sure it remains that way. Back on Earth, we fished the waters so much that there was little of anything left. Here, fishing is as dangerous as going in the forests. You're liable to be eaten by your prey."

"Open the gates!" An NCO's call carried the distance as the gates of the floor's military camp opened.

The camp had its own harbor cut through the land and into the water. Roads connected them to the harbor and the small town in one straight line.

"The army has a barracks in the town too, right?"

"Yes, sir. Eight reserve rifle squads and one reg force rifle squad on this floor. We keep two of the squads in the town at all times, one squad ready to go out on their corvette to help fishermen and the others as backup. With everyone joining up, their normal four squads shot up. They're training the reserve squads as much as possible." Foster pointed at the mounted squad that passed through the camp's gates, heading off toward the mountain ranges in the distance.

"Must be doing patrols, teaching them. Most of our winter training is done down here. Recruits get to spend a week down here to understand it."

"You know a lot," Erik questioned.

"My brother is a fisherman and joined the reserves. I looked into it." Foster scratched his head.

"Seems that everyone is in Alva's military now." Erik studied the camp and kept walking.

"There are what, a million Alvans now?" Storbon asked.

"Something like that."

"So, about a hundred thousand are traders or work doing something related to the outside of Alva or Vuzgal. Twenty thousand people to run the administration. Ten thousand to run the farms across the different floors. Fifteen thousand in the military factories. Three hundred thousand crafters of the mid journeyman level or higher?"

"That sounds about right. Probably two or three times that in apprentices and low journeyman," Erik nodded.

"Then twenty thousand-ish in the reg force? People working as intelligence agents, in the Alva Healing Houses, the Alva bank, as teachers, as staff in Wandering Inns and Sky Reaching Restaurants... How many people were out in the realms taking courses or adventuring?" Yuli asked.

"The rest? Don't forget all the stable hands, the people doing odd jobs in the realms or in Alva," Jurumba added.

"A million people. A lot of people owe their future to Alva." Storbon pressed on as Erik opened his mouth and closed it, looking at the walled stables that shared an offshoot of the army's harbor, their intended target.

"Terrifying, powerful, exciting. Did I mention terrifying?" Storbon chuckled.

"Yeah, all the above. Shit, in three months we'll have another eighty thousand soldiers, ballooning our numbers to one hundred thousand. I'm a little scared that we're not giving them enough training and just throwing them into the deep end."

"I guess, but with their body tempering, they don't need that much sleep,; just a few hours a day, if that. The damn training centers are working at all times." Erik chuckled. Add in information books, then it's death by information book instead of death by PowerPoint. In one day, they went from a farmer to a farmer filled with a mind full of military tactics and understanding their role from a technical perspective. The rest was taking that information and hammering it into action.

"The fact that you're worrying about these things…" Storbon shrugged. "I'm sorry, boss, but I'm happy that this is what you're worrying about. The level of ability for our people is what we rely on. We have quality; now we've gained quantity. If we can spread that quality to them…" Storbon opened his hand.

"Gonna fucking suck for the Willful Institute," Yuli said.

Erik let out a huff of laughter, smiling at the two elite warriors.

A keening wail came from within the stables just a few hundred meters away. A familiar head appeared as Gilly flapped her wings, quickly rising in the sky and sending out eddies of snow as she shot forward, covering the ground in seconds.

"Show off!" Erik said examining Gilly.

Blues and browns mixed in her scales. Her powerful leathery wings flicked at the ends as she banked, the tip of her wing nearly touching the ground as she circled the group. Snow was thrown everywhere in her passing as she adjusted her tail and wings, cutting into the skies.

Gilly dropped toward the ground, reducing her size. She flapped her wings, making everyone cover their eyes as their cloaks were thrown back and the air ruffled.

She landed before Erik, shrinking to the size of a horse as she licked his face.

"Hey!" Erik said as she nuzzled the side of his head and used her lips to pull at his hand.

Master! Treats!

Her thoughts had become clearer with the increases in her cultivation. Erik sighed and threw out a slab of meat the size of her head. Gilly expanded, snatching it out of the air and hacked it apart with razor-sharp teeth, looking at Erik expectantly.

"Come on, you." Erik patted the scales between her eyes, turning it into a scratch. She lowered her head, her back foot kicking up as the others chuckled.

"Well, I've got the beast. Let's go to King's Hill."

They turned and headed back the way they came.

Gilly padded beside Erik, her tail wagging with her tongue hanging out.

Are you a dragon or a poodle?

Poodle?

Erik patted her, feeling better with her by his side.

"If Gilly showed up, I think she would make the Kingdoms think twice about joining the Willful Institute's path," Sang So-Hyon, the last member of their squad said.

Gilly flared her nostrils, her eyes sharpening.

Erik clicked his tongue in light admonishment.

She let out a complaining growl.

"Yes, but it would gather more attention. A level seventy dragon of dual elements with heavy body cultivation. I don't doubt Gilly could take down the First Realm by herself. We're busy fighting across the higher realms. We can't get locked into a prolonged war down there. We need the reserve forces to support Vuzgal once we have enough troops."

The air distorted around Erik. "Then we'll crush our enemies at Vuzgal. We can move to support the Adventurer's Guild. Win or lose, it hangs in the balance. We need time; every day is another day we can increase our strength."

The teleportation formation hidden deep under King's Hill flashed, revealing six people. Their matching gear was worn and used. Their helmets hid their faces completely.

Lord Aditya cupped his hands and bowed deeply with clear eyes and respect buried deep into his bones.

Consortium Leader Quan stilled his cultivation in reverence. The wild ex-mercenary's bow was sloppier, but held the same sentiments.

Pan Kun, Commander of the Beast Mountain Range Army, saluted as Jen, head of the Alva Healing House, and Evernight, spymaster of the First Realm, all struck ninety degrees.

Erik had a miniature dragon curled around his shoulders. Her eyelids blinked sideways, her brown and blue eyes studying the people in the room.

"Stand up, will you? Can't get all this bowing stuff still. Is Yui in the command center?"

The corner of Aditya's mouth lifted slightly as they all stood upright. "Yes, he's watching the developments."

"Good, let's go bug him. Please, lead the way. This place is as confusing as Vuzgal. How are things going with the other outpost lords and the people?" Erik asked.

Aditya indicated for them to follow him. "The outpost lords are ready and waiting for you. We are pulling back people from the outposts to King's Hill with mixed results."

"Go on, you clearly have more you want to say."

"Lord." Aditya ducked his head as he led the group through the tunnels. "Telling the outpost leaders about your presence? Are you sure?"

"It is something that I have been thinking about. You have been managing them up to this point, but they're all over the place. If they know there is a power behind you, they'll fall into line. We need command and control," Erik said.

Aditya nodded and glanced at the special team members.

They reached the command center in short order.

"Every time I see you, Colonel Yui, you're hidden underground in some command center." Erik saluted the other man.

"Someone has to keep an eye on things," Yui replied, returning the salute with an easy smile.

"So, how are we looking?"

"Beast Mountain Range Army is forty thousand strong. Outposts have an additional four thousand they can add to that number. Add in eighty thousand mercenaries. It is the Beast Mountain Range, after all. Plenty of people come here seeking fortune and fame, hunting powerful beasts and resources."

Yui got a nod from Erik to continue.

"The army is speeding up the retreat to King's Hill. The city needs expansion, and quickly. If we just throw up unplanned buildings to fit the masses, it could lead to dysentery, fights, riots and other issues in our backyard."

Aditya stepped forward. "We have plans for the expansion of the city drafted by the blueprint office. We just don't have enough mages and construction workers to make it happen as fast as we'd hoped."

"Colonel Yui, what about your engineers?" Erik asked.

"I'm sorry, but they're tapped for training. What about the civilian builders?"

"That could work; could you coordinate?"

"Yes, sir."

"Anything else?"

"No, not really."

"All right, let's go and scare some outpost lords," Erik said as the group left.

Aditya and Quan looked at one another. The corners of their mouths lifted. *He might be an odd one,* thought Aditya, *but he's our lord.*

Emmanuel Fayad closed his eyes, trying to calm the headache that raged in his skull. His clan had started to make noises, with different kingdoms sending their armies toward Vermire. All the noble students had been called back to their nations. *No doubt carrying information on our layout and military.*

Groups of outpost leaders talked in hushed tones around the chamber. A few sent furtive glances to Fayad who had taken his seat as head of trade. He pinched his brows and opened his eyes.

So, it has come to this. He didn't regret turning his outpost over to Aditya and taking up the role as the head of the alliance's trade, despite it being a difficult job. He was more of a mediator between the remaining outpost lords than anything else.

He looked at the seat in the middle of the long desk he sat at. Aditya's seat. Behind it were three seats, largely forgotten, and to the sides of them were the seats for the lords and assistants to take notes. He wondered if Aditya had put them there to show that, one day, he would be king of all this. King Aditya? It would be interesting to see. Maybe the kingdoms would lose too much and run away. But there are the rumors of a sect from higher realms supporting them.

The headache returned as the door to the room opened. Aditya walked in with Pan Kun, Consortium head Quan, and Jen, the leader of the Alva Healing House.

What is she doing here?

"Please take your seats," Aditya said as he moved to the table.

People broke up their groups and sat, waiting.

Aditya sat down. His secretary sat down on his right with Quan beyond her, causing Emmanuel to frown. Quan *always* sat on his right, Pan Kun to his left, and Jen between him and Emmanuel.

Everyone was watching with questioning glances.

"Okay, I call this meeting to order." Aditya stood up, gesturing for the others do so as well.

What the hell is going on?

The doors to the meeting room opened. Emmanuel had tempered his body to Body Like Stone, a rare talent in the First Realm. But he staggered, feeling like the sky was collapsing on him, as masked guards walked into the room, flanking a man, wearing simple yet expertly made clothes.

The pressure came just from his guards. *Who is this man?*

"Lord West!" Lord Aditya bowed with the rest of the people who had come in with him. The power of these people made Fayed and others in the room hurry into bows, not wanting to get struck down for pissing him off.

Most of the leaders stared at the man in shock.

Two of the guards remained at the entrance, closing the doors. The other four guarded Lord West as he moved behind Aditya, everyone turning with his path. He stepped past the standalone chair and sat in one of the two chairs behind and to the side.

A man stood beside him, ramrod straight. Emmanuel saw familiarities between his body language and Pan Kun's.

"Rise." Lord West's voice was filled with power, making Emmanuel's blood and mana shake.

"Your orders, My Lord?" Aditya asked, his voice flat.

"Continue." Erik sat back in his chair, leaning his elbows on his armrests, clasping his fingers together. His gaze was heavy as he looked over the men and women in the room.

"Yes, My Lord." Aditya bowed his head and turned back to the room. "Please be seated."

An assistant came around with a contract.

"This contract seals your lips," Aditya said. "This meeting and what we're about to talk about is not to be leaked to anyone, including the existence of our benefactor, Lord West."

His words were not up for debate.

The lords had awkward looks on their faces as they dripped blood onto the contracts before they were all collected.

"First, some information. When I was the leader of Vermire, I came under Lord West's charge. My forces played a part in the fall of the Zetan confederation under the guidance of Lord West and his subordinates. The consolidation of the outposts was done under his authorization. The crafters, the teachers we have been able to attract, all serve Lord West, as does the Alva Healing House. The army was trained by his subordinates. I am but a caretaker of the Beast Mountain Range. Lord West is my lord."

There were no disturbances in Pan Kun or Lord Quan's expressions, confirming Aditya's words. They looked a little relieved, their eyes shining as they stood straighter.

Lord West's expression remained neutral as he weighed the room and its occupants. "We face war with the First Realm kingdoms and with the Willful Institute that supports them. If we are to win, then changes are needed." An aide passed out another piece of paper. Emmanuel looked at it; it was an organizational chart.

"These are your new positions."

The mutters spread, gaining volume.

"Quiet." Aditya's power came out like a wave, shutting people up before they could start yelling.

When did he get so strong?

Emmanuel felt the cultivation power of Quan, Pan Kun, and Jen flooding out. In fact, Jen was stronger than the other three. *How did she get so strong?*

Jen gave him a small smile. The secretary Evernight, Fayad thought her name was, had a flat expression that revealed nothing. He still didn't know why she was up there. She normally never came to these things. While she was Aditya's personal secretary, that didn't make her more powerful than the outpost lords.

More than Aditya's words, his display of power confirmed the truth.

"You have all been given positions in accordance with your skill sets. We need your talents. I'm not tossing you aside. You will continue to gather your percentage of the Beast Mountain Range's earnings. You will have to obey Lord West's rules and be bound to his service. We will consolidate all the outposts. A united front."

Aditya scoured the room.

"Beast Mountain Range will not be a kingdom with a single ruler. Lord West has more important things to do. It will be run by a council, a slim one with a few heads to get things done. This will allow us to coordinate our efforts more effectively." Aditya's eyes roved through the chambers. "I want to assure you, this is not a time of loss, but a time of gain; cultivation resources, information, all of it is accessible. The consortium, its teachers and information come from Lord West's subordinates. From the higher realms."

People muttered, now with approval. There were some thinned eyes. Every single one was a fox to have held their position in the mountain range for so long. The nods and covert glances at Lord West weren't missed.

Emmanuel looked at Lord West and the others through the corner of his eyes.

But will they be strong enough to defeat the Willful Institute as well?

Lord Salyn finished swirling the water in his mouth and spat it out. His clothes were covered in dust.

All I can taste now is dirt.

He assessed the lines of fighters. They all wore different gear, but those that were part of noble's personal guards wore similar coverings and colors, representing their houses. They created a sea of different colors, grouped together behind kingdom and regional banners. Fighters were hard to raise and maintain, and they would quickly leave to join the higher realms if possible.

He looked down on the mercenary companies. They wore the signs of battle on their armor and bodies. They walked in a greater semblance of order compared to the personal guards, though their equipment was varied and rough.

Dozens of wagons trailed after them all, carrying their necessary supplies.

The sound of marching armored soldiers, beasts snorting and pulling their creaking wagons filled the air. A low hubbub of conversation lay over it all. Salyn held up a perfumed handkerchief, covering the smell of the unwashed and sweaty beasts and fighters mixed with the animals' waste.

The road was filled with people behind the supply wagons, pulling their own carts and materials.

There he is, finally. Lord Knight Ikeda and his Red Falcon Knights rode forward.

Salyn had always thought that they were just powerful fools. While many of them were idiots, Ikeda definitely wasn't. Salyn couldn't help but think of the mission he had been sent on with Ikeda, and now they were heading back to the Beast Mountain Range. He wanted to destroy them but had never imagined it would be like this. Either way, he could silence the people from the Alva Village while also getting rewards.

Ikeda and his Knights rode up in their red armor. The ground, dry from the summer heat and loose from the press of feet, released a cloud of dust that Salyn shielded his eyes from.

He held his tongue through a powerful force of will as the dust dissipated.

"Lord Knight Ikeda," Salyn greeted, when he felt he wouldn't be spitting out dirt the next second.

"Crossing the army into Rodenheim's lands. I didn't think that day would come," Ikeda said, looking around his saddle.

On a hill in the distance, a group of mounted knights watched the Shikoshi Army marching down the road.

Ikeda waved to them. "That's sure to piss them off." He laughed, turning on his mount with the sound of shifting armor and stretching leather he moved in his saddle.

"Anyway, Salyn, you will be part of my command staff. You have been to King's Hill twice and have been in the Beast Mountain Range for weeks. I need your knowledge. The Captain of your guard as well."

Being among the leaders could give him an opportunity to make new contacts and grow his network. He wouldn't be able to sneak off and kill the Alvans, though. With Drev with him, his personal guard would have to handle the rest of his guards. Maybe he wouldn't need to kill the Alvans. Maybe someone else would save him the trouble.

"I am honored, Lord Knight Ikeda. I will do all in my power to assist you."

"Good. We're meeting the Rodenheim, Turkell, and Di armies tonight. Make sure you attend."

42 Slow Drag

Rugrat and Roska sat in one of the defensive towers playing rock helmet. A miniature defensive fort, one out of tens that dotted Vuzgal, created interlinking spheres of coverage and support.

Rugrat threw his rock, getting it into the helmet with a satisfying clink.

Roska's rock followed his and landed inside.

The rest of Roska's Special Team Two sprawled out in a corner of the map room, some sleeping, some talking, others playing cards or reading.

"Oh!" Davos wind-milled his arms on the balcony as he tipped over and fell backward.

The CPD members he was talking with rushed to the bannister.

Rugrat reached out with his domain, ready to grab him, but spotted the grin on Davos' face as he fell. "It's only forty meters, right?"

"Yeah." Roska threw another rock and raised her voice. "Stop falling off the buildings and scaring people, Davos!"

Others on Special Team Two snorted and laughed at the close protection detail's reactions. They were used to this kind of messing around.

Davos used spells to level off and land.

The group of CPD members looked back at the muffled noise below.

Rugrat spotted a cup and threw his rock. He heard the plop as it hit liquid. He stopped, hand mid-air to throw another rock, and looked at Roska who stared at him with wide eyes.

Who the fuck's cup is that?

Fuck if I know.

Rugrat changed his point of aim and threw his rock into the helmet as if that was what he intended the entire time.

Roska cocked her head to the side. "Sounds like the reservists are back."

Rugrat heard the footfalls with a sergeant calling out the cadence. "Two weeks refresher and right into this. They're not doing bad."

"Doing better than I expected. The training staff gave them the basics. Now they're putting it to practical usage."

"What practical usage they can." Rugrat tossed another rock.

"One attack every three days. Marco is biding his time until he gets the support he wants. Do the Associations really want to mediate a deal between the sects and Vuzgal?"

"Yeah, they do. They love being the middleman and picking up something to get things going again. Sneaky, but it keeps the balance and assures that they have the greatest control over the situation. Though we're not going to take the deal."

Roska grunted in understanding, tossing her rock to bounce off the wall and into the helmet.

Rugrat picked up the rocks in the helmet with his mana manipulation and brought them back between them, creating a pile as they started throwing them again. "Erik told me to write the letter, try to piss them off and draw them into an attack instead of this parade of creating hardened earth paths over the soup."

"Guess that's what we get for having defenses that are so good?"

"There is always a way to defeat them."

Sergeant Major Stenbock, second-in-command of Third Battalion, walked into the room. Roska and Rugrat looked over, lowering their stones.

"How was the view?" Rugrat asked.

"Same shit, different day." Stenbock shrugged, taking off his helmet. "They expanded their camps, created stone roads. They're trying out new spells on the ground."

"I thought they might pack it in after the last thrashing we gave them." Roska sighed.

"They might not have been pleased seeing that many Fifth Realm fighters torn up, but I guess we're more valuable," Rugrat said.

Stenbock grunted in agreement, and they turned back to what they were doing. Rugrat weighed the stone in his hand, seeing the broken enemy formations that had fled every time they engaged the Vuzgal defenses.

It made him think about World War One. Just enemies separated by a strip of land. *They have a camp over there; we have ours here.* If they had used their mounted aerial forces, the pressure would have stretched the Alvans a little more.

"What the fuck! Why is there—was that a rock? In my coffee! I fucking swallowed it!"

The other special team members laughed as Rugrat stored the rocks in his storage ring and used his domain to sneak the helmet full of them across the room and to his side.

His secret was safe with Roska, but then he caught the gazes from the other members of the team. *Shut the fuck up. Stop looking at me!*

Lord Salyn rode over the hill with Lord Knight Ikeda's group. Behind them was the Shikoshi army, weary from travels that had worn on for weeks.

"There it is, the United Army's Host," Ikeda said.

Rough camps had been thrown up in five distinct groupings. They were like a dead flower that had forgotten to release its petals. Wagons wore a path through the camps, heading off along different roads, old or freshly created, carrying the supplies needed for such a vast collection of people. With the support needed for the host, the number ballooned from one hundred and forty thousand to over four hundred thousand, including the Shikoshi Kingdom's own warriors and the mercenaries.

"Come on, we're expected." Ikeda snapped his reins, and they made their way down toward the massive tent in the middle of the different army camps. People grumbled but cleared out of the way as they rode through the tent city to the main tent at the center.

The breeze carried dust into Salyn's face, and he felt the grit on his teeth. He hid his groan as he dismounted, moving his legs side to side, feeling the wear of riding for days on end. A bath and a bed were much needed, maybe some nightly company from some of the ladies among the camp followers.

He walked with generals, knight troop leaders, noblemen, and mercenary leaders who trailed after Ikeda; there were about ten in total.

They passed into a different world as braziers at the entrance of the tent burned incense, fighting against the smell of the camp beyond. Inside, flooring had been laid down, food and drink laid out, people sat on couches or meandered around the room. A few were looking at the maps that depicted the Beast Mountain Ranges.

Salyn looked at their clean armor and freshly shaved faces with jealousy.

"Ah, Lord Ikeda!" a rotund man wearing fine beast fur clothes said in greeting.

"Lord Aras, it is good to see you," Lord Ikeda greeted the other man.

No wonder he was so large. The Aras family had been a power in this area for generations. The city of Shida was a key access point between the Beast Mountain Range and several other nations. Salyn had only had food rations over the last few days and couldn't afford to get too skinny or they would think him poor.

"Come, have a look at the main map. New information has come in," Aras said.

Ikeda glanced at Salyn.

They moved to the map. It was crude, made of pieces of hide that had been sewn together into one large map. It was impressive, though there were a few flaws.

"With your force now joining us, we have our military commander! The other two hosts, smaller in comparison," Aras assured Ikeda, "are still amassing in the north and to the east."

The force in the east was to strike Vermire before heading inwards. It would get them accolades, but Vermire was Lord Aditya's outpost and wouldn't fall easily. On the map, it looked like a large kidney bean.

The outposts and King's Hill created a sort of disjointed wagon wheel shape. The outposts were dotted around the uneven Beast Mountain Range. Roads connected them to the outside kingdoms and to one another. Razor-straight lines cut through forests, mountains, and over hills to connect to King's Hill in the center.

"People have been fleeing the Beast Mountain Range for several weeks now. The children that attended the Consortium have given us detailed information on the internal layout of the outpost." Aras waved to a large map showing the entirety of the range. Various nobles examined it as if they knew what it all meant, muttering to one another like war generals plotting their next move.

"Has the Willful Institute showed up?" Ikeda asked.

"They have not appeared yet." Aras sighed.

"Okay." Ikeda looked at the plan. "We will wait for them to arrive. They may have orders for us." Ikeda pointed to the smaller markers that lay opposite the outposts.

"With our main armies camped back from the outposts, they will not know where we will attack first," Aras said.

"It will be hard to maintain the secret for too long."

Aras nodded in agreement.

"If the Willful Institute does not have orders for us, those guarding forces will remain in position while the armies attack their designated outposts and drive toward King's Hill in a lightning strike. If we hit them hard and fast, they won't have time to move people to support the outposts we plan to attack. Then we can cut up the roads into King's Hill."

"Brilliant, brilliant plan, Lord Ikeda!" Aras raised his ring-covered hand, clasping a glass in salute.

"The simplest plans are the best plans when we have strength on our side." Ikeda chuckled.

"Indeed! With enough people, no one can stop us."

"New orders from High Elder Cai Bo," the messenger announced, passing the scroll to Mistress Mercy.

She opened it as he bowed and left her office. Once finished, she passed it to Niklaus, who stood beside her.

"We are to prepare our forces for immediate redeployment to the lower realms to support the Flaming Sword Operation. Forces from several sects, mainly the Stone Fist Sect and the Willful Institute, will attack the cities of the forces opposing the Willful Institute. Secondarily, they will conduct attacks to recover stolen cities and strike out against forces deployed against the Willful Institute," Niklaus read out the scroll aloud for the benefit of the other commanders in the room.

It had taken months to pull together all these different factions and groups and prepare them for war. Fighting in the Fourth Realm was consuming all their resources. Instead of leading an attack on the First Realm and finding out what secrets there were, they were expected to divert their efforts. Mercy shook her head, lost in her thoughts and paying no attention to Niklaus.

"This is the counterattack we have been waiting for," Niklaus declared as the commanders talked excitedly amongst one another.

Their force would be one of the most coordinated. They had the greatest number of resources, and if they did well on the battlefield, they would gain greater supplies to take the Beast Mountain Range and make it their own. It was a small power, but it would become *her* small power, completely under her control, feeding much-needed people into the Institute.

She smiled and stood from her chair. The commanders paused, looking at her.

"Prepare the army to move. It is not our original mission, but the rewards are much higher! Niklaus, I leave the planning to you, but I do not doubt that we can capture a city in the Second, or the Third Realm!"

Cheers rose, and the commanders eyes shone. Loot and plunder motivated any sect fighter.

"Your contributions will be noted and passed on to the sect. This is a grand opportunity that comes only a few times in one's lifetime. Let us seize it!"

Greed ignited in their eyes as cheers filled with savagery.

Mercy looked at Niklaus. "Send some of our people to the First Realm to oversee things there. Have the First Realm kingdoms attack to prove that they are worth coming under the Willful Institute banner."

"Yes, Mistress Mercy." Niklaus bowed his head.

Blaze watched the attack on the city of Lasco.

"We've broken through their outer defenses. They only had two inner walls. Soon, we will take the city," the sect elder, from the force leading the attack, said. He wore intricately carved armor that was more a work of art than functional, much like his impressive mustache.

So many of these fools. What's his name? Ronald? Gerald? Timold? No, it's R-something... Rosinal? Yup, yeah, I think that's it. Bit of a fool or plays the part well. They may have taken the outer wall, but the inner walls wouldn't be so easy.

Blaze raised viewing glasses to his eyes.

The inner wall was a sea of spells and siege weaponry firing into the outer city as sects charged through the holed wall. Blaze saw his guild's units organizing their forces, getting them focused and out of the bloody vanguard.

There was the sound of feet on the stairs that led to the top of the observation tower.

Blaze checked on the positions of his people, consolidating within the wall. It had happened more than once that the sects rushed in, eager to get inside the walls only to lose so many people that they lost their foothold. *We'll just say that a lot of our people died, that we were disorganized. They'll make some snide remarks. I can take the hit to my pride if it saves my people's lives. And what the hell is this messenger doing here?*

Blaze looked back as the messenger passed a letter to Jasper, who quickly read it. He frowned as Jasper looked up and indicated with his eyes for Blaze to join him.

"Excuse me for a moment," Blaze said as he moved to Jasper and took the offered letter. He opened it and read the scrawled message.

Willful Institute and Stone Fist Sect are preparing to counter-attack sects currently attacking Willful Institute cities. Targeting cities that armies came from. Advise withdrawal from battlefield ASAP.

The cities were poorly defended and filled with supplies to support the fighting. If they could pin the sects against their walls and attack the supporting cities, they would gain a quick victory, supplies, and a base to attack the sect's rear.

Blaze looked at Jasper, who nodded.

"I'm sorry, esteemed elders. An issue has come up that I must see to personally."

"Go, go, everything is well in hand," the elder, whom Blaze thought was Rosinal, dismissed him.

Blaze's mind buzzed as he headed down the stairs with Jasper and his guards. He used his sound transmission device so no one else could hear them. "This is across all battlefields?"

"Don't know at this time; we only know the overall plan, not their targets. It could happen in the next three days. Our spies are getting flushed out of the Willful Institute as the sect is forced to work together."

Blaze clenched his jaw. "If we pull back our people and the attack doesn't come for several days, we'll look like cowards. Fuck, what do I care what we look like? We've hit the enemy hard. Send word to all the branch heads. Retreat from the battlefield. Where are we going to go though?"

Jasper passed him an information book.

Blaze took it, using his blood to unlock the seal.

Adventurer's Guild Retreat plan
Do you wish to activate this information book? Doing so will destroy this information book. *YES/NO*

"Yes."

The book dissolved as information flooded Blaze's mind.

"Do you have the box?" Blaze asked.

"Yeah." Jasper pulled out a chest.

"Commander Glosil is a busy man."

"What do you mean?"

"He made an entire fallback plan for our forces. In that chest are three sets of orders that we can issue to our people to tell them how to retreat based on the situation. We don't have to plan it out, just follow them."

"Where are we going, though?"

"The backup dungeons."

"What? I thought those were a secret?"

"They are. Everyone will have to take a contract to seal their lips. But the dungeons, if you don't know about the dungeon core, look like underground bases. They're massive, large enough to hold all our people. The guild members' families can also be evacuated there. They have training facilities, and we have been given permission to invite the people we trust to become Alvans. There is no maximum anymore."

"Well, this will change things a little."

"A little." Blaze coughed and cleared his throat, feeling his eyes itch with a small smile on his face. The Alva Army had supported them with training and fellow fighters. Alva's crafters had supplied their food, their armor, their weapons. Alva's medics had saved countless Guild members. Alva hoarded its secrets, but they did not have secrets between one another.

To be an Alvan. His heart beat faster and he blinked against his increasingly itchy eyes, pride filling his heart as purpose marshalled his thoughts.

Blaze sniffed and looked at Jasper. He patted him on the shoulder. "Pass our Alvan recommendations on to the recruiters. I will disseminate the information to the branch heads and the guild members."

"What will this mean for the guild?"

Blaze cocked his head to the side. "If we go to the dungeons, there will be a lot of our members joining Alva with their families. The guild will change; we will not be a free entity. It changes the dynamic. We will have a clear backer to our guild members."

Blaze sighed. "Always thinking ten steps ahead." He looked up at the tent's roof. "First, we get them to safety, then we figure out what to say."

"This is a big risk. It could reveal Alva," Jasper said.

"It comes down to a single question. Do you trust the council, Erik, and Rugrat?"

"Yes," Jasper said without pause. "But—"

Blaze waited, but Jasper twisted his mouth, his following words failing as he frowned. He opened it twice, but his arguments were countered before they left his lips.

Blaze smiled and patted his shoulder. "So simple, but that's the heart of it. I can see steam coming out of your ears. Don't need to think that hard." He grinned.

Jasper's furrowed brows released and smoothed as he smiled, laying down a weight upon his mind.

"Come, we have a lot of work to do and not much time to do it."

"Yes, Guildmaster."

"Will you stop that? Have we not known one another for long enough?" Blaze growled.

Jasper laughed and patted Blaze on his shoulder. "Very well, my friend, as you said, we have much to do."

43 Movement

Three days went by in the camp. Lord Salyn spent his time in the meeting tent planning with the other lords and ladies. Most were making deals and trade alliances or talking about other lords and ladies and the latest gossip.

Few talks were about the enemy or the Beast Mountain Range. In their minds, it was already owned by the Willful Institute. There was no way the enemy would be able to hold.

The only thing that had really changed was the fact that all the outposts were emptying. People were either fleeing the range or heading deeper, going toward King's Hill.

Salyn swirled his wine, looking at the table as a commotion broke out at the front of the tent.

Several aerial beasts had landed. They wore dressage with the Willful Institute's emblem sewn on.

A group of eleven people walked into the tent. Three of them pulled off their helmets. A clean-shaven, expressionless young man led the group. A younger woman with a bob cut stood to one side, and an older, scarred man on the other. The rest kept their helmets on and stood at the entrance. *Their guards?* Four men followed behind them, carrying chests.

Lord Ikeda stepped forward to greet them.

"My name is Juri Kostic. I have been sent as a representative to oversee things here. You are Ikeda?"

"Yes, My Lord."

"Good." Juri waved the chests forward. "Weapons, armor, and items to assist your endeavors. You will attack in no more than two days. I expect good results."

Ikeda took the hint. "Yes, My Lord; you are most gracious. Do you want to see the map, or I can show you to your quarters that have been prepared?"

"I have seen your plans already. I will retire to my quarters. Lead on."

Ikeda guided them out of the meeting tent. Salyn and the other Shikoshi representatives looked at one another, moving closer to the chests. They milled around them with placid smiles and steely eyes, like wolves guarding their kill.

Aras clapped his hands once and rubbed them. "Good! Now it really starts. We have but two days to set our plans into motion and show our glory to the Willful Institute!" He walked to the table, drawing everyone with him. Even those that were there simply to add numbers suddenly seemed to have become military savants, discussing their plans intently.

"The Stone Fist Sect and their allies in the lower realms are ready. Our combined forces have started to move and are teleporting into position." Elder Cai Bo read the message to Head Asadi.

The latter studied the scene outside his window, looking at the Henghou city beyond. "Good. the Stone Fist Sect has good eyes. Depending on how they do, we can see how our partnership will go. What about that force you created for the First Realm?"

"They have been fully mobilized and are heading to attack the enemy cities as we speak. We have coordinated forces in the First Realm to lead the attack and soften up the enemy. Once our forces secure their objectives in the Second and Third Realms, we can funnel the resources and loot into our treasury to pay for further expansion and draw others into our sect and alliance."

"Good. Very good. Increase their abilities in the First Realm fighting, use them as support and bodies to fill our needs, and add relief in the Second and Third Realms. There are always so many people in those lower realms. It surprises me; they're like human rabbits." Asadi snorted and shook his head.

"How are things in the Fourth Realm?"

"The Associations have reached out to the two parties to mediate the situation."

"*Bah*, they just want more resources without offending anyone. Are their defenses that strong?" Asadi peered at Cai Bo.

"Marco believes that only a combined attack in the air and on the ground will allow him to break into the city anytime soon."

Asadi looked out of the windows at something only he could see.

"Now it is a race to see if we can get the aerial forces that we want, or if the associations strong-arm us into mediation."

"You think Vuzgal will go for it?"

"Do they have any other option? They are alone with no support. The Associations are in their corner—for now. With the new contract, they'll lose some wealth and control, but they have proven that not even major sects of the fifth Realm can breach their walls." Head Asadi went silent. "Use external recruiting. Offer rewards to people to join the fight. Specify aerial forces. And offer recruitment into the Institute."

"That will burn through our resources."

"Yes, but we are about to take several cities in the lower realms and reclaim some that are ours. But… we *must* take Vuzgal."

We were running low on resources before this fight started. With most of their trading routes and partners cut off, they hadn't been able to replenish anything. They were burning through resources to support the cities in the lower realms, to gather and support armies. The cost of the force in the Fourth Realm was astronomical. Each day they burned as much as a medium-sized city in the Third Realm used in a year. Retaking those cities in the Second and Third Realms, then rebuilding them… Even the cities they took from others would not have enough to increase their supplies.

"Sect Head, we only have a few months of resources remaining at our current rate."

"I am very well informed on the state of our resources, which is why we need everything we can get from our attacks."

Win or lose, it comes down to this. Cai Bo's heart felt like it had been grabbed in her chest. *We could collapse and fail. What would happen then?*

"Is there anything else that you require, Head Asadi?"

"No, continue to keep me apprised."

She bowed to his back and retreated before turning and leaving the room.

44

Words Meet Action

Salyn assisted in checking the gear contained within the chests after Lord Juri left the command tent and Lord Knight Ikeda returned. The chests were treasures in themselves, spatial chests that could carry as much as forty wagons.

They were filled with high Novice-grade weapons and armor, various powders that could be mixed with water to increase stamina or mana regeneration, and some gear of the mid-Apprentice level. The most valuable were the spell scrolls, mana stones, and mana cannons.

They distributed the goods to the other kingdoms and empires, forging stronger alliances and drawing everyone under Ikeda's command completely.

Salyn rode on his mount, looking at the amassed armies. They had all eaten well last night in preparation for this battle.

Powerful mounts towed mana cannons behind them, and the commanders and noblemen were all wearing Apprentice-level gear.

"So, Lord Salyn, how long do you think it will take to breach the Hunter Frontier outpost?" Ikeda smiled.

"If it lasts until the end of the day, I will be surprised!" Salyn laughed.

"A single day? I doubt it will last more than a few hours!" another lord joked to the laughter of the group.

Salyn smiled with them. He felt good after a clean bed, good food, and good company in the shape of some of the courtesans that visited him in the night. He also wore a new set of low-apprentice armor.

"What do you think, Lord Knight?" the same lord asked.

Ikeda smiled, but didn't say anything.

"Look, I can see it now," one of the ladies said, breaking the somewhat awkward silence as she raised a gauntleted hand to her brow.

Soft rolling hills covered the area, most of it farmland that met up with the outpost. It was made to defend against the Beast Mountain Range, not the kingdoms beyond it.

Hunter Frontier Outpost sat at the top of a valley between two hills, creating a U shape toward the Beast Mountain Range.

Towers, used to fire down on beast tides and pick off wandering beasts, dotted the hills.

"Just open for the taking," a general said.

"Well, about time they showed up," Lukas said. The large man opened and closed his hand.

"You still feel it?" Pan Kun asked him.

Lukas looked at his hand. "Ah, this? Yeah, sometimes it feels tight. I know it's all in my head. You know, I didn't have a hand for a couple of years. Just got used to it and now I have a new hand."

"Yeah. For the first few months after I got my eye back, I kept my eyelid closed and I would get dizzy with both eyes open." Pan Kun sighed.

"Aditya's broken guards." Lukas laughed.

Pan Kun grinned. "Shit, makes me feel old. Been working in King's Hill so long."

"Well, a lot of shit has happened. Feels like just the other day and a lifetime ago you dumped us in the Beast Mountain Range with secret trainers to teach us how to fight. Took the outposts, secured the range, made King's Hill, and now these dickheads want to take it from us." Lukas tilted his chin toward the army that was slowly covering the hills toward the Hunter Frontier.

"Too bad for them our training expanded to the Beast Mountain Range Army, and we knew exactly which outposts they were going to attack." Pan Kun looked behind the defensive wall. Houses had been leveled for the catapults and trebuchets.

Tents were being packed up and secured in groups, the organized rows dissolving as people checked their gear, unpanicked, as if they had done this a million times before.

"Cold as ice," Lukas said.

"A real military, built with people with experiences from all over who spend their time fighting bandits and beasts."

"Or in dungeons," Lukas added.

"Or in dungeons," Pan Kun agreed. "The poison pots, they all ready?"

"Ready and waiting. We positioned them across the outpost for maximum dispersion. Though if the wind changes, it could get carried in different directions. It is a dust, after all."

"Ten thousand of our people against a hundred and fifty thousand of theirs. I like our odds."

"I'd like to be having a beer with a nice-looking lady on my lap, too."

"Pervert," Nasreen said as she walked up.

"How are the ranged?" Pan Kun asked.

"Set and ready. We'll crank them back once they get within a kilometer."

"Wait for my command. Once they get into range, we'll open fire, stun the shit out of them. They shouldn't have mana barriers, but the Willful Institute showed up and gave them a lot of gifts, so be ready for it. We need to blunt them here, hit their morale, and make them fight for the outpost. Mounts?"

"Secure and ready. We have them under cover so if the enemy flies beast scouts or uses viewing spells, they won't be able to tell." Lukas pointed at the buildings close to the gate leading into the Beast Mountain Range.

"Healers?"

"They're set up and ready." Nasreen glanced at several buildings that had been thrown up; they dotted behind the wall with large openings on each side.

"Got casualty points. Then we'll feed them into the field hospital." She pointed to a squat, sturdy compound. "Mana barriers and the works over it, just in case. Teleportation formations to take them off to the Alva Healing House in King's Hill. Got charges on everything so if we can't pull it out, we can blow it to nothing."

Soldiers moved up onto the wall, taking up places among the guards that had been standing there.

Behind the defenses, oiled leather was removed from the siege weapons and team leaders began checking the machines with their people. Ammunition of stones and pots were moved into position from cellars. Archers and mages marched into position; the mages circulated their mana, and the archers strung their bows. Runners carried baskets filled with arrows.

Others circulated with warm soup and bread. People ate and chatted with one another.

Everyone was served before Lukas and Nasreen, then Pan Kun.

Lukas made appreciative noises as they ate their soup.

Pan Kun soaked his bread in the rich broth before taking a bite.

Stamina Regeneration increases by 5% for 6 hours. Agility increases by 3% for 2 hours. Strength increases by 3% for 2 hours.

"That's some damn good soup! Have to get seconds after we've dealt with these assholes," Pan Kun said in a loud, clear voice, heard easily in the quiet outpost, making some grin and laugh.

"Wish they'd hurry up then! I need thirds," Nasreen replied, getting chuckles and cheers among the troops.

Tea was handed out as the soup bowls were taken away.

Calm mind 10% for 3 hours Increased mana regeneration 5% for 6 hours

Pan Kun finished his tea, and the cup was taken away.

"Well, that was a good breakfast! Now, let's get to work, shall we?"

Spears and yells agreed as Pan Kun laughed freely. His gaze sharpened on the approaching army. "Looks like they've already formed up a little, and they brought their new mana cannons."

"They'll want to hold them back. The cost in mana stones would pain them," Nasreen said.

"Shooting all of them would cost the same amount as most of the lord's cities make in a year."

Wooden siege weapons pulled by beasts captured Pan Kun's attention. "So, trebuchets and catapults, range of three hundred, maybe four hundred meters."

The others nodded. *Well within our plans.* They hadn't had anything to do but look at the information Evernight had gathered and battle out what we to do against one another.

The trio watched the oncoming army.

"Six armies all accounted for," Lukas said.

"Still spread out from marching from their main camp. They'll need to form up again before they can attack. Put half of our people to rest in place," Pan Kun said.

The minutes ticked by as the ranged archers and siege weapon teams started to shift around. Those on the wall could see the enemy clearly now.

"What's that, six hundred meters?" Lukas asked.

"Stand to!" Pan Kun frowned. "Something is weird. I'd expect them to stop at eight hundred meters at the most."

"You think they'll charge?" Lukas asked, bewildered as he looked at Pan Kun and then through his viewing glasses.

People moved back to their positions, feeling the growing tension in the air.

"Looks like they're forming up," Nasreen's voice rose. "And not slowing down."

"Load!" Pan Kun barked.

Wood creaked and team leader voices rang out as gears were engaged, drawing back the catapults and trebuchets. The archers pulled arrows from baskets and laid them along bows. Mages sped up their circulation of mana.

"Wait," Lukas warned "they're speeding up. They… They're charging!"

Yells rose from the field as hundreds and then thousands of voices rose in bloodlust.

"Prepare to fire!" Pan Kun didn't remove his field glasses.

Shaped rock was loaded into the Beast Mountain trebuchets.

Flags were raised in front of the siege weaponry by each Trebuchet commander. They worked the same way as the Alvan artillery units.

"Ready." Nasreen tapped his shoulder twice.

Pan Kun looked for the marker stones. He felt the rumble of the charging enemy through the ground.

Their formations barely had time to rebuild before they charged.

Pan Kun watched the range markers out in the fields beyond. He knew he was trying to ease his mind. "Be ready on the wall!" he yelled.

"They have ladders and ropes with them," Lukas said.

The leading edge rushed past the five-hundred-meter mark and kept coming.

Come on. Pan Kun gritted his teeth, looking from the marker to the approaching human tide. The ground rumbled and the yell of men grew louder.

They crossed the marker in a wash.

"Fire for effect!" Pan Kun yelled. Nasreen repeated the order as they were drowned out in the creak and *whump* of siege weaponry; the order rippled down through the lines.

Pan Kun raised his viewing glasses; the teams behind him worked to crank their weapons back into position and reload them.

He scanned the enemy lines and checked markers.

Nearly three hundred meters.

The siege weapons' payload of stone balls crashed into the enemy, leaving bloody trails as they threw up dirt from their initial impact and bounced, crushing more men and armor.

Holes appeared through the enemy tide as lines were broken, fighters scattering.

He heard wood on wood as the siege weapons fired for the second time.

"Hold steady!" Lukas yelled to the forces on the wall, commanding his melee forces.

"Mages at the ready! Two hundred meters!" Pan Kun yelled.

"Mages, range two hundred!"

Pan Kun could feel Nasreen waiting beside him, a ball of tension.

The enemy surged across the two-hundred-meter range, speeding up as they came down the slight incline toward Hunter Frontier outpost.

One hundred and fifty meters.

"Fire!"

"Fire!" Nasreen repeated.

The light of the spells flickered at the corner of Pan Kun's eyes as he scanned the enemy.

"Ready archers!" Nasreen called out.

Spells carved a shorter path over the battlements, striking the ground and spreading out rapidly, leaving broken and twisted remains, their enemies' screams consumed by the yells of the United Army charge.

What I'd do for a hundred more siege weapons and ten times the mages.

The defenders on the wall yelled as the enemy closed in on the one-hundred-meter range.

"Fire! Ready on the walls!" Lukas and Nasreen yelled out. Pan Kun scanned the enemy. They were bunching up as they got close to the wall.

It was a tide of killers, their weapons held high as they charged. Spells and siege weapons reaped a heavy toll.

Bows twanged as arrows flew skyward. He swore he could feel a breeze as the arrows hissed overhead and plunged into the enemy ranks beyond, cutting down sections of fighters. Those behind them were running too fast for them to slow and raise their shields. Some tripped over others hit with arrows, tumbling and left to the mercy of the feet of those behind them.

The front line reached fifty meters and disappeared.

Some stopped, only to be pushed forward, screaming and windmilling as the ground collapsed beneath them, revealing deep pits filled with spikes.

"Crossbows!" Lukas yelled before Pan Kun could give the orders.

"Fire when they're ready," Pan Kun said in a quiet voice. His stomach turned in knots as he tried to clear his wet throat. He lowered his viewing glasses. Crossbows raised from behind the wall and aimed at the enemy who were being rolled into the massive spike pits, the sheer number of bodies filling the holes.

"Fire crossbows!"

It was like a scythe cutting through wheat as people stiffened in pain and shock. Dropping to the ground, they grasped at their wounds in confusion.

Pan Kun forced himself to breathe.

Don't go into the black; watch the whole picture.

"Change to fire pots on evens! Ready fire spells!" Pan Kun said into Nasreen's ear.

She yelled and used flags on the rear wall to the team leads. Flag bearers relayed the message.

"We have breakthrough." Lukas grabbed Pan Kun's arm, pointing with his viewing glasses.

Paths between the pits became the enemy's lanes, like water through rocks. Some lost their footing and tumbled into the pits. Ladders were tossed down, creating chaotic crossings. One misstep, putting a foot through an opening, could break a leg, while those behind used your back as support to rush forward.

Nothing but stable ground to cross and dirt to fill in the pits.

A flare of light drew Pan Kun's attention.

Pots smashed on the ground, spewing brown liquid. Soldiers cried out as they tried to spit out the liquid. Steel and flint within the pots drew against one another as flames ballooned through the oncoming ranks.

Some of the pots merely broke and flung out their contents. Fire balls from the mages landed among the flammable contents.

"Those spotters are doing well," Pan Kun muttered as the enemy reached the base of the wall.

Pan Kun grabbed Lukas, bringing his mouth to his ear. "Rocks!"

Lukas gave him a thumbs up and pulled out flags. Noise washed away words.

Pan Kun grabbed Nasreen. "Decrease the siege machine range. They're clumping at one-fifty! Bring the fire pots to the walls!"

She gave him a thumbs up and worked her flags.

Pan Kun raised his viewing glasses. An arrow flew at his wall. His gut clenched before the arrow smashed apart, seemingly in mid-air.

Mana barrier. Pan Kun gritted his teeth, chastising himself and purposefully ignoring the arrows.

Siege weapons continued firing just over the wall. Their payloads sent out waves of dirt, their bloody path longer than it had been.

Pan Kun turned and raised a green flag, waving it. He looked to the left and the right. Small groups of Alvan army mages threw pots the size of a man's fist up into the air. Mana flashed around their hands, striking out and destroying the pots, dusting the battlefield below with the poison hidden within.

The wind is at least going away from us, for now.

Pan Kun grabbed Nasreen. "Have the mages shoot from the wall!"

A ladder reached the top of the wall. A soldier threw a rock down beside it and grabbed his spear to throw it off.

Lukas raised a new flag and pulled out a whistle. Its piercing shriek rose three times. The last of the rocks were tossed down. Soldiers fired the last crossbow bolts, leaning them against the rear wall.

The drilling had paid off as Pan Kun watched them transition to spears without the slightest hitch.

Fire pots were brought to the top of the battlements and rolled down the walls.

Commanders stood next to braziers, holding a simple stone covered in wax rope.

"Ready on pots!" Nasreen yelled.

"Go!"

Two soldiers lifted the fire pots and threw them off the wall.

The commanders threw their wax roped covered stones after them.

They ignited with a *whoumpf* of heat and screams.

Pan Kun raised his hand at the wave of heat, feeling it trying to draw the water from his eyes.

Beast Mountain Soldiers used pears and staves on the ladders to toss them back.

Light flashed below the wall, different from the flame pots igniting.

Mages' ranged spells appeared along the base of the wall, right against the press of bodies. The spells activated, tearing through iron, cloth, muscle, bone, and wood. Ladders collapsed and fell. Fighters screamed, and the stench of bad meat and the tang of iron mixed with the thick smell of flammable liquid rose as flames wafted over the wall.

Pan Kun spat to the side and looked at the battlefield. The charge had slowed to a crawl. Those at the rear began bunching up, waiting for the front to make room. The thick carpet of fighters were perfect targets. The archers and siege weapons continued to fire into them.

The enemy archers and mages responded in kind, striking the mana barrier that lay atop the walls.

A spell formation appeared on Pan Kun's right flank.

A flaming spear shattered like glass against the mana barrier. He blinked the flash away. The barrier sent out ripples where the enemy's attacks landed.

He choked on the smoke and his eyes watered. Mages used air spells to clear the air and throw the smoke into the enemy's front as a ladder hit the wall in front of Pan Kun.

He grabbed a spear to push it off. A spell activated below, shredding the ladder, and it fell away.

Pan Kun grabbed Lukas. "Rocks, fire pots, and crossbows!"

"Sir!" Lukas' ragged voice was nearly drowned out. He used his whistle and waved his flags, checking that people up and down the line saw it.

Runners brought baskets on their back with fire pots and stones. Soldiers hauled them off their shoulders and sent them running back as they tossed their payloads into the enemy.

Pan Kun looked back behind the lines. His people carried out their tasks without pause in opposition to the enemy's floundering, chaotic efforts. Runners replenished baskets of arrows. Siege weapons bucked as they released their payloads. Their teams moved before the weapon had settled back down.

Good, good. Pan Kun raised his viewing glasses. *They're getting torn the fuck apart.*

The rear of the army had spread out. He scanned beyond, looking at the mounted forces and the leadership in the rear. He didn't have to look through his viewing glasses at the closest parts of the army. People jumped into the pits, walking across the dead that covered the spikes and climbed up the other side.

Pan Kun could feel the battle shifting. Every second his people reaped untold lives. *They've lost their momentum.*

He looked at the Alvan mages. They threw pots out, smashing them with a flash of spell, covering the enemy.

Good, good, coat the bastards in it.

Pan Kun felt his stomach twitch.

The rear of the army turned and rushed back the way it had come. Drums and instruments called out to them.

What is it?

Pan Kun grabbed Lukas. "Crossbows!"

He pulled in Nasreen. "Attack what you want!"

BMA soldiers grabbed crossbows from the rear wall. Shooters put their foot in the stirrup using the cocking lever, drawing the wire back, loading it and aiming into the enemy; they couldn't miss.

Archers fired as fast as they could, going for speed over coordination.

Like a string being pulled, the enemy's rear was collapsing.

Pan Kun looked at the siege weapons. On Nasreen's orders they hurled pots skyward, smashing into the ground and sending a wave of flame through the enemy ranks. The retreating army bunched up between the cones of flame the pots left.

The people behind the pits and those in them started to run away.

Those with crossbows shot them in the back. Once again, the enemy had to cross the pits and the thin, foot-wide dirt track between them.

Crossbow bolts nailed those climbing out of the pits.

The remains of the United Army's first wave cleared the pits, wounded trailing behind trying to limp or drag themselves to the rear.

Spells rained down on the runners as fire pots cracked in the distance.

Pan Kun grabbed Lukas. "Cease—" He lowered his voice at the new silence. "—Fire."

Lukas waved his flags, giving two long blows on his whistle. Those on the wall lowered their weapons and looked around as if seeing the world for the first time. Wounded were pulled from the line, carried off to the healing huts.

Pan Kun watched the markers. "Have the archers cease fire."

"Sir." Nasreen waved out as the hiss of arrows slowed and stopped.

"Siege machines," Pan Kun said.

The creak and *whumps* finally stilled. The noise fell away like a dull pain.

Someone lost their soup over the wall.

Pan Kun's throat was raw from the smoke and yelling. He took a drink from his canteen and passed it to the others. "Get sand on those fires and issue face coverings for the smell."

"What about the wounded?" Lukas asked.

Pan Kun had tried to ignore the crying and sobs on the other side of the wall. He gave them both a grim look. "Have the mages put them out of their misery. We don't have the arrows to waste."

"I'll see to it," Nasreen said.

He nodded and patted her shoulder. She nodded in thanks and turned, heading down to her ranged forces.

Pan Kun stopped Lukas. "Get me a count on wounded and dead. Make sure that everyone took the damn recovery potions. Anyone has even a cut, get them to see the medics. I don't want anyone getting sick. That powder is powerful."

"And make sure they drink water?" Lukas asked.

Pan Kun gave a glimmer of a smile. "And make sure they drink water."

Lukas headed off as Pan Kun realized he was still holding a spear. He put it back into the rack, letting out a breath, feeling tired and lightheaded.

The army slowed as they reached the mounted forces and leaders at the rear. A few tried to keep going and were hunted down and killed for cowardice. Salyn thought that most of them had stopped because they were too tired to keep running.

He looked at their faces. Some were bent over, coughing or throwing up. Others collapsed to the ground, bone-weary, or stumbled, looking around with blank eyes and weapons in their hands as if they were startled and panicked beasts.

Wounded, some with burns across their bodies, others with broken bones and missing limbs, stumbled back and were sent to the healers and alchemists to purchase their services if they could.

The smell of sweat, smoke, and offal lay in the air as Lord Salyn raised his hand, breathing in the perfumed handkerchief tied to his wrist, clearing his mind and calming the growing nausea.

"Well, now we know their abilities," Lord Knight Ikeda said.

Salyn looked over. The Lord Knight leaned forward on his mount, peering out at the outpost. He lowered his viewing glasses, a treasure from the Willful Institute, and passed it to Lord Aras.

"Yes, tricky fellows." Aras accepted the viewing glasses and studied the walls.

"Regarding the charge?"

He had paid off some of their knights and low-level commanders to start the charge, and the rest followed afterward.

"It seems that they came from uneducated forces, unfortunate." Ikeda clicked his tongue.

"It is a shame, hot-headed but well-intentioned younger commanders," Aras agreed, still studying the wall, and talking as if he was appraising a horse's value. "Stronger than I guessed, didn't think they would hold."

"Nor did I." Ikeda frowned. "Those pits take more than a day to prepare, and our scouts didn't see any digging."

"They must've put them down, what, weeks ago?" Aras lowered the glasses and handed them back.

"Maybe, or they worked in the night."

"We should assume they have an information network to know our plans."

"Agreed," Ikeda tapped his reins. "Salyn, order one of the cannons to be brought up and fired on the outpost."

"Is that wise?" Aras asked.

"We cannot have the army stewing on their losses. The cannon will keep us out of *their* range, show the fighters something exciting and powerful. Promise them increased rations and an extra portion of beer for the night."

"That will bite into our supplies," Aras warned.

"We have supplies for one hundred and fifty thousand; the rations of those we lost will make up for it. Who knows? Some of them might have a breakthrough in their body cultivation. Battles are known to push people past their limits."

"Lord Ikeda, you are as brilliant as always."

Ikeda smiled and nodded before looking at Salyn. "Go, now, get me that cannon."

Lord Salyn rode toward the cannons. The personal guards of each kingdom stood guard, protecting the cannons and the mana stones that would power them.

Pan Kun stood on the wall with his two seconds in command.

"What do you think they're doing?" Lukas asked him and Nasreen.

"Well, it's a cannon," Nasreen said.

"Gives them something to build up their morale." Pan Kun shrugged. "Keep our people working. The barrier will stop it."

Melee and ranged fighters threw sand on the fires that blackened the wall's stones, checking gear and stowing it, ready for the next battle. Siege weapons were checked and repaired as needed, the fire pots secured once again.

"I'll leave it to you." Pan Kun walked toward where the Alvan mages stood on the wall, using their magics to stifle the fires.

"How do you think it went?" he asked the lieutenant leading them.

"Sir, they're covered in it."

"You think it'll..."

A blast of light made Pan Kun turn. He steeled himself as the mana cannon's projected spell hit the mana barrier, making his soldiers duck and stare as a ripple splashed across their barrier.

The cannon started to charge again.

Pan Kun noticed that the lieutenant didn't duck either. "You've had experience with these before?"

"Yes, sir. I was at the siege of Meokar and several others."

"What do you think of their cannons?"

"They're cute. Pain in the ass to figure out how much they hit for. Best to fire them in groups, pile up the damage before the formation has time to recover." The man smiled. "But now, with that single shot, they just told us how powerful their cannons are."

"That's useful?"

"Sure thing, sir. We can figure out how much power we need to defend against each shot, the kind of attributes they're using, and switch out parts of the interlinked formation. Make it stronger against that combination of elements and feed it the power it needs to take the hits."

The cannon fired a second time.

"John-o! You got a time between rounds?"

A mage, John-o, turned back. "Forty-three seconds."

"Rei?"

"Agreed!" another mage said, staring intently at the cannon. Pan Kun saw her lips moving as she counted.

The spell struck, making people recoil, but not as bad as before.

"Also means that our people can get used to it. Fight through it," the Lieutenant said.

That should scare them if we're standing there not caring about the cannon and just firing back.

"Keep me apprised and see that the adjustments are done to the mana barrier."

"Sir," the Lieutenant nodded.

Pan Kun turned to leave and paused. "The powder, how long before it takes effect?"

"About twelve hours, sir. It'll start hitting them tonight. They'll have the colds and the shakes all night. Do you mind if I have everyone drink another round of the antidote? Should make sure that everyone's bodies get tempered with the poison, then they could drink it if they wanted to."

"Good idea, do it. Make sure the team leaders watch them."

"Yes, sir."

Pan Kun walked along the wall. Soldiers carried out their tasks before being led back to their quarters to erect their tents again. New fires were lit, and food was prepared for lunch.

They needed to do something about the bodies, too. They stank, and if the wind turned, the smell would come back this way. They would deter the enemy though, having to cross over their dead.

The cannon flashed as Pan Kun's hands twitched.

Don't let them see you panic.

The mana cannon hit the mana barrier, flaring.

"Mother fucker," a soldier spat before dousing a brazier.

Pan Kun looked over the battlefield. The cannon crew moved out of their positions and the beasts needed to tow it were pulled over, skittish with the new weapon.

Hopefully, that's the last for today.

Colonel Yui entered the King's Hill command center and joined Erik by the map table. "Lord West."

"Colonel, you're up early."

"And I doubt you've gone to sleep."

Erik just smiled. "What do you think of yesterday's attacks?"

"They were crushed at Vermire. The outpost is one of the largest, with ten thousand army members, a lot of spell scrolls, mana barrier, and the city cornerstone. Brigadier General Donner knew how to eke out every last bit of her combat potential. Estimated twenty-five thousand dead, unknown on wounded. No dead on our side, light injuries. They lost a quarter of their force and they're shaky."

"You think they'll try again?"

Yui shrugged. "I wouldn't."

"If you were them?"

"Create a camp, leave twenty-five thousand of my people. Send the rest to reinforce the group at Hunter Frontier. Defenses aren't as strong, the army is a few days march, and they have the strongest weaponry." Yui pointed at the map, tracing the ring road that connected the outposts.

"I agree. Latest reports say Lord Ikeda is leading, and he's told them to attack again."

"It'll be a bloodbath. They were overconfident yesterday. Thought they'd walk over us; might be the new equipment they got, or just idiocy. It was the first big engagement for the BMRA. Now they know what to expect, and how strong the enemy is. Lieutenant Lee is running two mage squads there in support. They figured out the element distribution of the spell and adjusted the barrier and mana stone consumption rate. He warns that under sustained fire, in forty minutes the barriers will fail."

"Including being hit with the siege weaponry?"

"He didn't add that in, though he calculated for firing every thirty seconds with the four guns broken into two sets."

"How fast are they firing?"

"They shot one cannon, and it varied from fifty seconds to forty-two seconds."

Erik grew silent. "So, it depends if they're willing to spend the mana stones and if they have the fire control."

Yui nodded.

"Expectations?" Erik asked.

"Their plan is to siege Hunter Frontier and then attack. It could succeed. If not today, then tomorrow I think we will lose Hunter outpost. Then Major General Pan Kun is going to have to sprint into the forest. If the enemy leaks around Frontier, he'll have to run through enemy attacks to retreat." Yui took in a sharp breath. "He says his confidence is high. But he has ten thousand people to get out once they break into the outpost. It'll be messy, but that is why he's there with Brigadiers Nasreen and Lukas."

"Messy," Erik muttered.

"Yeah. Thankfully, they have some teleportation formations to pull the wounded and support staff back with."

"What about Dryfall?" Erik pushed on.

"The enemy made it to the walls. The twisting path through the cliffs prevented the enemy from using siege weaponry, but the defenders can only see the enemy for two hundred meters up to their walls. We have fifteen thousand there because of this. Brigadier General Veli was smart though. She created a false wall." Yui was impressed. "She had the mages raise another wall in front of the original outer wall, with the same gate placement and battlements, but with a two-meter gap and a hole that goes five meters deep.

"How high is the wall?"

"Ten meters."

"So, a fifteen-meter drop." Erik shook his head. "They climb up one wall, get to the top and are still two meters from Veli's people. Guess they're using spears?

"Yeah, and long staves to throw the ladders off. Still, some of them got across; not many but a few. Dryfall will be hard to take."

"So Vermire and Dryfall are good. The other outposts all have guards in them watching the enemy and Hunter Frontier will break under enough pressure."

"Yes, sir. We have the rest of the army working night and day to cover the roads and forest behind the outposts in traps. Five thousand from the BMRA, three thousand Alvans and forty thousand mercenaries."

"Construction crews are making false roads that look like the originals but on a slightly different heading, taking them miles away from King's Hill. The original roads have been submerged and covered in forest."

"Tricky, tricky," Erik said and stretched. "Now to wait and see what happens today."

45
To the Bone

Some warm food, drink, and useless speeches; that's all it takes for them to forget yesterday.

Lord Salyn sneered as he brought his mount to a halt behind Lord Knight Ikeda. Dawn had broken earlier, the sun's rays already warming the day. The pace was slower, in keeping with the armies that had come to a halt.

Siege weapons had been assembled, adding armor to give their crews a bit more protection.

A rider arrived from the siege weapons. "We are ready to advance my lords."

"Very well. Send the siege weapons forward," Ikeda said.

The rider saluted and headed back out of the tent and to his mount. A dirt trail followed him through the army's formations and to the armored siege weapons.

"How many of the attacks will you use from the cannons?" Aras asked.

"I told the commander to make sure that he has the right aim first," Ikeda hinted.

"Quite. It is a timely process to make sure one's aim is correct."

"What time will you send the soldiers in?"

"I think in the early afternoon, out of the heat. Otherwise, they will collapse." Ikeda snorted derisively.

"They are stupid creatures indeed."

Lord Salyn and the two powerful mens' retinues dismounted. Servants took their mounts away as they entered the cool tent to watch the day's fighting.

The men pushed forward the siege weapons, rolling through the gaps in the fighters' formations.

"They look like turtles with a tail with so much armor," Aras mused.

Salyn stayed close to them both as they stood before the tent and watched from the shade.

The siege weapons trundled forward in staggered rows, boring and monotonous. There had to be a hundred of them, at least.

Salyn got a drink from inside the tent, picking out some prepared food that was circulating before returning to the watchers.

Dots appeared in the distance, growing bigger.

"Looks like they've fired. Our siege weapons will be well within their range." Ikeda passed his glasses to Aras.

"We assumed as much."

Salyn watched with interest as the enemy's stone balls arched over the outpost's walls and then dropped, coming to rest among the advancing siege weapons.

"Must be the limit of their range."

"They're rather good at bouncing their stones. They've left great big gaps in our formations." Aras cringed slightly. "Ough, that one looks nasty."

It had struck a siege weapon's armor. The force nailed its front right corner into the ground, slamming it to a halt.

It was the only casualty in the first attack.

The other siege weapons pushed on.

"The stones, I think they're painted." Aras handed the viewing glasses to Ikeda.

"Why would they be painted?"

"Odd to decorate stone. Stick out a bit, don't they?"

Ikeda snapped his fingers. "They're using the stones to see where they land and adjust."

"Smart, very smart indeed." Aras rubbed his chin in appreciation.

"Here comes the next volley."

The arm of one trebuchet exploded into splinters. Another armored covering was hit, planting itself into the ground with a dent in its forward side. Another was rocked back, the front end coming up as the stone struck the top, tearing apart the wooden structures underneath as it slammed back to the ground and stopped moving.

The rest of the siege weapons continued to advance, spreading out, moving around the old hills over the bloody streaks, avoiding where stones rested from the day before.

"What will you do with the forces at Vermire, Lord Ikeda?" Aras asked.

"I'm not sure. I hope they were able to break the outpost. Otherwise, I have overestimated their abilities and confidence. We shall have to leave a force there and consolidate here. I bet they will be eager to show their fighting spirit."

"Quite." Aras and Ikeda shared a smile.

Soak up more of the damage for us. Salyn sipped his drink as more stones struck the siege weapons.

Another five were destroyed or put out of action. Crews from the first armored siege weapons ran to the rear, wounded came with them, many victims of shattered wood or crushed bone.

"I told the commander to get them in closer. I want to hammer their mana barrier and then we can bounce the stones into their walls," Ikeda said.

"There is plenty of rock to be found. And I would guess their commander believes he is in range."

The armored siege weapons slowed to a halt, weathering another volley from the outpost. Only three were on target, many hitting ahead of their targets.

Trebuchet arms cranked down into the armored walls and loaded.

"They shot before we could load. I will have to talk to the commander about speeding things up. Can't let them fire faster than us," Ikeda muttered.

"Quite."

Salyn stood there, a statue as he watched the trebuchet arms fling forward.

"There they go!" Aras said excitedly.

All the nobles and powerful figures looked over as the stones rose and then slowly descended before smashing into the invisible mana barrier, lighting it up with ripples.

"Bravo!" Aras laughed, clapping. Salyn and the other lords joined in, smiling and nodding to one another.

Under this barrage, they are sure to collapse.

Ikeda was the only one not clapping or smiling.

What's the old fox looking at now? Salyn looked at the wall to try to figure it out.

"Bold." Ikeda lowered his viewing glasses. "It appears that they too have viewing glasses."

Another volley struck the armored siege weapons.

"You, come here." Ikeda pointed at an aide.

"Look at where the gate is. To the left of that, two protrusions in the wall over. I want them to hit right where the wall is."

The woman squinted.

"Use these." Ikeda pushed the glasses to her.

"Uhh, yes, sir." She raised them like her family's greatest heirloom.

"You see it?"

"Yes, sir!" She nearly jumped out of her skin.

"Good, hit it." Ikeda's words promised nothing good otherwise.

"Yes, sir!"

She passed the viewing glasses back, looking relieved, and ran off for her mount.

Siege weapons traded fire between the outpost and armored trebuchets.

"Send out ammunition runners."

Beast drawn carts rushed into the stone rain, carrying ammunition for the trebuchets.

The cannons fired off-time with one another, striking the mana barrier.

Ikeda made an appraising noise. "Must be their commander, Hiraga!"

"Lord Commander." She stood only a short distance away.

It's hard to keep track of her.

"Tall man, bald, commands forces of the outpost. Who is he?" Ikeda offered her the glasses. She looked through them for a few seconds before passing them back.

"Pan Kun, old captain of the Vermire Guard, and Lord Aditya's personal guard. Now the leader of the outpost alliance forces."

"Very good. Salyn, have someone tell the cannons to shoot at where the outpost's siege weaponry is firing through."

"Lord Ikeda." Salyn bowed and moved to the messengers.

Pan Kun is here? They must have been prepared for this fight if they brought their leader here. *And they must've known this is the main force.*

Pan Kun looked across the battlefield. Spotters called out to their crews, watching their stones crash into the ground. *Damn stones are all different weights.* They could shoot the exact same way, but their aim could be off.

He looked at the hill where a large tent had been erected in the early hours of the morning. *Just out for some entertainment?*

Pan Kun spotted one in red armor looking through viewing glasses. He stopped, looking at him.

"Asshole's looking at me, I think."

"Sir?" Lukas asked.

"I need a volunteer!" Pan Kun said.

"What for?" Lukas asked as soldiers looked over.

"Too smart for your own good. Who wants to moon the enemy commander?"

"What do I do, sir?" one yelled out.

"Put your lily-white ass between two battlements."

Pan Kun heard a collection of belts being undone and dropped.

He smiled at the sour expression on the red-armored man's face as he lowered his viewing glasses.

"Yup! Good show!" Pan Kun grinned as he lowered his own glasses. Twenty soldiers were mooning the battlements.

"Put your pants back on." The soldiers grinned as they got dressed again.

They laughed as Pan Kun looked back at the tent. Someone was running down the hill. He traced a line from them forward.

"Looks like we'll get some cannon fire soon. Might've pissed him off."

"They're moving ammunition up," Nasreen said. Spells enhanced her vision just like the spotters.

"Forget them, just hit the armored ones."

"Should we hit them with fire pots?"

"Not until we see where those cannons are firing."

Pan Kun held out the viewing glasses to Lukas.

The cannons fired.

"Brace yourselves, troops. I think they're aiming right at us." Pan Kun rocked on his feet with a smile on his face, clasping his hands behind his back.

"First one to duck owes us all a beer!"

The spells hit the mana barrier. A few of the soldiers clenched their hands, but they didn't move. Instead, they stared at one another to see who owed beer.

"Well, shit. I was hoping to get a beer out of this," Pan Kun complained to Nasreen.

"You're always trying to get a beer out of your bets!"

Pan Kun laughed as the soldiers chuckled. *Good, puts them at ease. Worst thing in a siege is to get tense and nervous.* "Wonder what's for lunch. This siege crap is boring."

"Soup?" Lukas asked, lowering the glasses and holding them to Pan Kun, who waved for him to hold on to them.

"I could go for some soup. I think there might be fresh bread, too."

"Fire pots?" Nasreen asked.

"See where the cannons are aiming at in the next volley."

Pan Kun patrolled the wall, talking to the various soldiers and looking over the edge.

"How was the clean-up?" he asked Nasreen.

"Messy. We looted the bodies and used spells to bury them in the pit. Took us thirty carts to collect everything."

"The heat's starting to get to them. Taking their loot through their tombstone, the bodies will fall apart faster. It'll affect our troops otherwise. What about those that went out last night?"

"Had them up for stand-to and then the morning off."

"Good, ready for the afternoon." Pan Kun looked up at the stone that hit the mana barrier.

"Looking a lot bluer," Nasreen said in a low voice.

"They've been hitting it for four hours. They'll need to hit it all day, or pick up their mana cannons' rate of fire, and hit the same spot if they want to crack that barrier. Right now, they're doing nothing more than making a light display and I'm more than happy if they keep at it."

Nasreen snorted.

"Must be trying to save up their mana stones."

"First Realm thinking. Sieges are over a long time, grinding the enemy down, demoralizing them and breaking their shit. Leave them in fear. They should have fired those cannons as fast as possible."

Cannon fire hit up the line, meeting a stone as it was crossing the barrier. The stone exploded, raining debris. The spell hit the underside of the mana barrier on the other side of the outpost.

A mage punched a spell out into the air, smashing into the falling debris and turning it into pebbles.

"Fricking prick!" someone yelled back at the cannon as they were hit with stones.

The catapult crews released fire pots, arcing into the distance. Pan Kun watched as they smashed around a group of enemy trebuchets. One fire pot shattered on top of one directly, bursting into flames. Other pots failed to ignite on their own, but caught fire from the others.

People ran out on fire and screaming.

Effective, but a horrible way to go. Pan Kun gave them his silent thoughts and continued walking. Most of them were just farmers forced to fight, though they were still the enemy.

The midday sun dipped into the afternoon. Pan Kun drank from his canteen. Boxes and other makeshift chairs were given over to those on the wall. They rested in the shade with some watching over the wall.

"They're moving," Nasreen said to Pan Kun. He took another gulp from his canteen and secured it, casting far-sight.

Soldiers stood up from where they'd made their ad hoc camps, getting back into order.

Pan Kun used a hand to shield his eyes. "Barriers should hold. Depends what they bring us."

They waited and watched.

"Wake up those that are sleeping. Make sure they're all watered, and their buffs are active," Pan Kun said.

"They're not looking so hot out there, coughing, pale, tired," Nasreen said.

"Yeah, not the best way to be fighting, that's for sure. That powder was supposed to have started working last night. They've had it in them for nearly a day now."

"Shit." Lukas shook his head. "Think they know?"

"It should just look like dysentery at first."

Salyn stood off to the side, listening to Aras and Ikeda hissing at one another.

"That should have depleted their morale. They must be ready to break by now!" Aras said.

"Where did they get a mana barrier that strong, and the power to support it?"

Salyn stepped up. "The Beast Mountain Range and the King's Hill Outpost generate approximately ten Mortal grade mana stones per day, I'd estimate. Traders from the Second Realm have come down in the past and there are known traders from the Third Realm, or at least those that had connections with it."

Ikeda and Aras turned from Salyn to one another.

"I have been out of touch. I did not know they could create that much per day." Greed flashed even in Aras' eyes.

"With that wealth, I wonder what other things they've purchased. If one has a mana barrier, then they must surely have spell scrolls."

"They could have used them under the cover of their mages' spells," Ikeda mused. "It seems like they have a lot more mages than I would expect."

A horn blew, calling for the advance of the formed-up army.

Twenty thousand fighters, broken into five squares of four thousand, moved forward. The formations gained spacing with two up front, one in the middle, and two at the rear.

Cannons and trebuchets fell silent as they passed, building up speed into a run. Fire pots crashed into the ground, occasionally landing among the formations or on the armored siege weaponry, their flames licking at the sky. Stones came in low, hitting the ground and bouncing, crashing through those unfortunate enough to be in their path.

They slowed as they reached the thick carpet of bodies and flies before the outpost. Spells, arrows and then crossbow bolts reaped lives.

"Not as many dying in these smaller formations. The first will collapse," Aras observed.

"Agreed." Ikeda watched all through his glasses.

Salyn squinted, imagining what was happening rather than watching.

"Simple, but effective," Pan Kun said, looking at the planks the enemy threw out, covering the pits and creating a bridge across.

"Get the mages to hit the pits. The wood looks fresh, be hard to burn."

"Sir," Nasreen used her flags.

"Their other formations are coming in," Lukas said.

The first formation close to crumbling surged in number as its two supporting formations ran through the path they had created. They'd added their own planks at different pits to create passage across.

"They're moving a second unit into place," Pan Kun said, watching a group of five formations pushing forward.

"They've got more equipment for the walls in the last groups," Lukas' voice rose.

Pan Kun studied them intently, seeing what looked like massive pikes and mounting devices. "Damn, that's going to be annoying. Target them first."

"Spells to the walls and pits, Brigadier General Nasreen!"

"Sir!"

The spells ran along the walls and over the pits, tossing over the new planks, slowing, but not stopping the tide.

Yells reverberated off the outpost walls as ladders were thrown up.

Hundreds were dying, but the fourth and fifth formation of soldiers appeared, pouring more bodies into the fight.

A ladder reached the top of the battlements with a man wielding a sword on top of it. Lukas jabbed out with a spear, punching through the man's leather armor. The man's yell died in his mouth as he looked at his wound drunkenly.

Lukas flipped the spear, using the butt against the top of the ladder, and heaved, throwing the ladder off.

"Draw spears!" Lukas yelled. Soldiers put their crossbows to the rear and readied their spears as ladders arrived with fighters already on them. Their ladders were spread out so they couldn't hit so many with spells.

Pan Kun pulled on his helmet with a blue fringe at the top. Nasreen and Lukas wore helmets with white fringes.

Pan Kun's guards jumped into the fight, keeping the area around the trio safe to command the battle.

"The second unit is here," Lukas said.

Pan Kun saw a battlement collapse. The pike-looking siege weapon was akin to a battering ram and drove its hardened point into the wall. The hooks around it grabbed on, pulling the wall apart.

The BMRA engaged the enemy on the walls. More ladders appeared as fresh forces moved in. The second unit's forward two units crossed the pit bridge.

"Third unit preparing," Nasreen yelled.

"Mages, focus along the wall," Pan Kun said and raised his green flag. Lieutenant Lee's people hurled out poison pots, covering the sick and lethargic-looking enemy. *They sent the ones showing the worst symptoms at us first. Trying to pass it on to us, perhaps?*

Pan Kun grabbed his war hammer, taking several steps forward, and drove its spiked top forward, throwing a fighter off the top of a nearby ladder.

"Push!" he yelled at a soldier who had blood running down his armor.

The soldier gritted his teeth, turned his spear, and threw the ladder off as another fighter's head appeared. They reached through the rungs, grabbing thin air as they swung backward and away from the walls.

"Sir," one of Pan Kun's guards said, as the group moved closer.

"Get that seen to," Pan Kun said to the wounded soldier.

"Sir."

Pan Kun looked up and down the wall. People engaged in fights all along it. Reserve forces ran up, supporting those on the wall as runners carried away the wounded.

He moved to the edge of the battlements and looked over. The pits were bridged. Arrows cut down from overhead, causing fighters to drop to the ground as spells lit up along the wall, taking out ladders and those waiting below.

More ladders were raised. Fighters ran up as they started to tilt forward to get to the top of the wall.

Shit. The new ladders in the fresh units had wheels and a supporting base. They wouldn't be able to push those off, just hack at the wood.

Pan Kun turned back to his position on the wall. He couldn't use the lightning scroll, either. They were wearing more armor than the enemy and were too close.

Air Scythe scroll it is.

"Hold things here. I'm going to the right flank to use a scroll." He grabbed Nasreen, who was closest.

"Yes, sir!"

Pan Kun waved to his guards and hefted his war hammer, taking off at a jog that broke into a run.

Four ladders hit the wall ahead of him. Fighters jumped off and bowled over the two soldiers on the wall. The attackers' blades found openings in their armor, coming out red. Other fighters poured up and over into the battlements as the soldiers on either side turned to fight and cover their own section of wall.

The team leader yelled orders to the reserve below and charged in.

Pan Kun picked up his speed, just five meters away.

Three attackers went down, but new ladders appeared.

Mages attacked the bases of the first four ladders, dropping them from the wall, but more ladders replaced them.

Pan Kun let out a yell as he swung his hammer. "Air Blade!"

His hammer crushed a man's breastplate, tossing him over the wall as the air blade created with his hammer sliced through two others behind him. A man stabbed out at Pan Kun's side, but his guard's spear punched through their side before they could make contact. Pan Kun brought his hammer around and, using momentum, he crushed the skull of one of the attackers atop his downed soldier.

Another swing took the other in the chest as he raised his sword. The fighter crashed into the wall, looking at his caved-in chest.

Pan Kun stood over the two downed soldiers facing the wall.

"Air Blade!" The spell wrapped around his warhammer as he swung it. The blade of air cut out across the wall, striking ladders and attackers.

Reserve forces pushed to the wall, stabbing at the fighters, and regaining control over the wall.

Pan Kun looked at the two beneath his feet. Their tombstones floated above them.

Medics moved to the downed soldiers, tearing off their armor and stabbing needles into their hearts before sticking rebreathers over their mouths. Some lost their tombstones. They were alive, barely. Others gained more attention as the medics turned back fate on the ten realms.

"Let's go!" Pan Kun waved his bloody war hammer forward. "Move out the way!" Pan Kun barked, clearing a path as they rushed past supply runners and moving soldiers.

He reached the limit of where the United Army was attacking. He grabbed onto a ladder with one hand, holding his hammer in the other, and climbed up one of the wall's towers. An archer turned with an arrow ready.

"Sorry, sir!"

"As you were."

Pan Kun looked from the tower over the battlefield.

He dropped his warhammer next to him and pulled a spell scroll from his storage ring, staining it with the blood on his hands.

Pan Kun aimed the scroll's attack into the enemy below and ripped it. The paper burned, releasing the spell within.

A spell formation appeared beside the main wall, running parallel with it as it gathered power. The wind surged, pulling at Pan Kun's gear and the blue fringe on his helmet.

The spell formation stilled and flared with power, then raced along the wall.

Air blades nearly a meter wide shot out from the spell formation. They sliced through the packed-in enemy lines, sometimes two or three blades striking a single person before they fell.

It cut a bloody path ten meters wide right through the enemy formations.

The archers paused for half a second at the stunning loss of life before they started picking out their targets and firing as fast as they could.

Pan Kun pulled out another spell scroll as the first formation was dying. He could feel the enemy on the edge.

He aimed and tore it.

The air blades cut through the wooden bridges over the pits, setting the flies off and covering the battlefield with the stench of death and decay.

Pan Kun activated a medallion around his neck. "Kill them all! For the Beast Mountain Range!" he yelled, his voice ringing over the battlefield.

Yells and roars responded from along the wall, driving back the small footholds the United Army had gained.

The front lines of the United Army fractured, turning and fleeing across to where the air blades had just torn their people apart.

The new First realm forces were just beyond the pits. Having seen the horror of the air blades first-hand, they were slowing their pace even as officers and horns ordered them forward.

The fleeing front-liners were attacked by the leadership of the second wave, only to find themselves hacked up for getting in their way.

The archers slowed their attacks until finally stopping. Siege weapons hurled fire pots out at the United Armies.

Pan Kun looked at the tombstones that littered the ground. Ladders and broken siege equipment lay between them.

The wounded cried out; some were trying to make their way back to their lines.

Others walked around the battlefield with blank expressions before crossbow bolts dropped them to the ground.

Soldiers tossed bodies from the defenses and threw off the ladders. Wounded were carted away as reserves took their positions. Sections of battlements were broken where the siege weapons had struck. Craters lined the wall, showing where the damage had been done.

Pan Kun stood on the edge of the tower, grabbing onto a roof pillar and holding out his bloody hammer. "Beast Mountain Range!"

Cheers dotted among the lines returned.

"I said, Beast Mountain Range!" The cheers doubled.

"I don't think they can hear you all the way back in their camps! BEAST MOUNTAIN RANGE!"

The cheers rose across the wall and in the outpost, chasing the enemy back to their position.

"See to your duties and be ready!"

The mana cannons fired.

"Looks like they want to play with their expensive toys!"

Pan Kun turned off the medallion as his people laughed. "Good work," he told the archers and headed down the ladder.

Pan Kun, Lukas, and Nasreen patrolled the walls. They'd been cleared, reorganized and prepared for the next wave. Stone from inside the outpost had been scavenged from buildings to reinforce and repair the walls.

Many in the army had leveled up or increased their skills, though it was secondary to surviving.

"One hundred and fourteen dead, four hundred and twenty-nine wounded. Most will recover by the end of the day. Some are being shipped back due to missing limbs or healing that will take longer," Nasreen reported.

"The survey of the walls?" Pan Kun asked.

"They punched some nasty holes in it with those super-sized hooked pikes. I've got teams gathering wood to mount on the walls. Slow them down so they can't get so deep."

"How are the walls?"

"We repaired them, but they were the worst hit."

"The loot?" Pan Kun asked.

"We collected it all and sent it to the rear with carts, no issues. There were fewer casualties on the enemy side than last time, probably because they spread out more."

Pan Kun looked over the wall. "If you were the enemy commander, what would you do next?"

"Under pressure from all sides, including Dryfall decimating their forces and Vermire remaining a thorn in his side?" Nasreen gave Pan Kun and Lukas a knowing look. "Hit us with everything he has. Damn the cost and drive us into the range. Colonel Yui advises that sixty thousand of the Kingdom's army are coming from Vermire. They should arrive by tomorrow afternoon. They brought their siege weapons."

"He'll wait them out, send them first so he doesn't lose people," Lukas said.

"Lukas, it's your turn for night work duty."

"Sir." He managed to *just* keep the sigh out of his voice.

"Pour that napalm, as Rugrat calls it, over the pits. Take the siege weapon and hand pots, remove the flint starters and bury them under ground, ahead of and behind the pits. Pierce holes in the pots and connect them with napalm so if one goes up, they all go up. Go no further than one hundred meters past the pits. Take two more groups and have them lay more pots out to our right and left flanks. I want to make a wall of fire so that when we pull back the enemy can't chase us, or at the very least, it slows them."

Pan Kun looked at the body-covered, smoking ruins in front of the outpost. A smoking siege weapon collapsed in the distance.

"That's a lot of digging. I'll use the bodies as cover."

"Good, start once the sun is down."

The atmosphere in the planning tent was stale and dark as many drank themselves into their cups. Quite a few of the leaders had retired as early as possible. Salyn didn't have that luxury.

"Tomorrow, Lord Fletcher will arrive with his forces from Vermire. With their siege weapons in support, we will attack the outpost until we defeat their mana barrier and open their walls. We have the numbers, but they have that wall *and* powerful spell scrolls," Ikeda said.

"At least our fighters proved themselves. We lost fewer people than yesterday, and they kept pressure on the enemy," Aras said.

"Can you think of anything *useful*, Salyn?" Ikeda said.

"Once we defeat their barriers, they will only be able to hide under the attacks. What if we are to send mounted forces in?"

"Mounted forces?" Ikeda chuckled. "I do not have the coin that the queen would tear from me if we lost those mounted forces. They are our most expensive forces. Fighting in cities is not their strength."

"We could move some forces up behind the siege weapons with the ammunition carts," Aras said.

"Give them less time to react?" Ikeda thought it over. "They'll be a small force, and we'll have to stop attacking with our siege weapons for them to advance. Better to go with a larger force to crush them."

"What if we sent people out under the siege weapons fire?" Aras counter-proposed.

"Under it? The possibility of hitting our own people would be high," Ikeda said.

"It so happens that there are a group of deserters in the stockades. Why don't we give them a chance to redeem themselves? There are also some criminals turned slaves. What if they were to earn their freedom?"

"Clear their names and accept them into the army again?" Ikeda nodded. "That should motivate them. We'll send Fletcher in after them as the second wave."

A messenger came in with a small scrap of paper from a bird carrier. Ikeda took it and read it before passing it to Aras.

"Lady Talan has had more trouble at the Dryfall Outpost. They created a false wall. Combat is hand to hand most of the time, but the enemy has proved themselves capable, and any attempt at breakthroughs have been thoroughly halted."

Aras finished reading the slip and looked at Ikeda.

We have to break Hunter Frontier. The cost at the other outposts will be too high.

"I want to know how they found out which damn outposts we were going to attack." Aras muttered, casting a glance at the nobles in the back of the tent.

Salyn saw Drev enter the tent and walk toward him. Salyn tilted his head to the side.

"Our forces are sick," Drev whispered. "Forty thousand were claimed by their wounds, another four thousand by sickness."

"See that it does not spread. Make sure the sickness doesn't come near my personal guards or our mounted fighters."

"Yes, sir."

"If need be, cut out the infection."

"Sir." Drev lowered his head with a knowing look.

"Problem?" Ikeda asked.

"Just some sickness. I will give orders to make sure it is dealt with quickly."

"Yes." Ikeda frowned. "It seems camp sickness has spread much faster than I thought it would. Must be those bodies in the field. Make sure to add those who are sick into the vanguard. Might as well get some last use out of them. If the enemy catches it, all the better."

The early morning was crisp and Salyn wished he could remain in bed. Instead, Ikeda pulled him out to the forward tent.

Most of the other lords were still in their beds while he and Ikeda sat outside with the army watching the morning attacks.

"Brilliant move, pushing out the siege teams in the middle of the night so the enemy wouldn't spot them." Salyn moved his mouth against his thoughts.

"Unfortunately, there are few of our siege weapons remaining. They spent all of yesterday creating new ones and taking shields from the army to create their cover. Not as strong as their first weapons. Thankfully, Fletcher has plenty of siege weapons and two mana cannons."

Salyn coughed, but it seemed to bring more with it. Ikeda watched him closely as he cleared his throat after the fit and sniffed.

"Don't tell me you've got the camp sickness."

"Just a cough." Salyn cleared his throat again.

"Best to not stay around the peasants and mercenaries. The surrounding air is ripe with it. We lost many in the night due to it."

The women he had chosen were of good stock, not regular peasants. They didn't have anything.

Salyn shook his head and looked out at the blue barrier-covered outpost as trebuchets flung their rocks at it, striking the barrier right in front of the wall. Some fell short between the pits and the wall.

A returning stone smashed through their siege weapons, turning into an explosion of splinters and metal.

Salyn grunted. Most of the stones struck the ground around the siege weapons.

"Their fire pots must not reach that far," Salyn said.

"No, and many of their stones fell short. We're at the limit of our range to hit their wall, but their weapons are back from the wall. Their weapons are better made, and their range is further as a result."

Ikeda looked at the outpost, wrapped in his own thoughts.

Salyn fell silent as the morning wore on and more of the lords appeared.

Some coughed or sneezed while others made excuses to remain in their tents.

46
Build and Destroy

Blaze toweled off his face as he walked to the side of the training square. It had been broken up into several different areas. Nearest to him, parties ordered into squads were training in hand-to-hand combat. He grabbed a ladle and poured water into a cup, drinking it.

The weak stamina concoction in the water helped to revitalize him as Emilia walked over, decked in Alvan gear.

"Well, you look the part." Blaze grinned, drinking from his cup.

Emilia examined her armor with a wry smile. "I swear it's been worn by at least three or four people."

Blaze gasped as he finished his cup and stored it away. Laughter coiled in the back of his throat.

"I come with orders and updates."

The laughter faded. Blaze waved for her to join him as he walked down to the training area.

"Are we moving out?"

"Not yet. Once the United Sect Army is committed, they'll have us attack. Preparations and routes of advance into the fourth realm have been readied and organized." She pulled out a folder and passed it to Blaze.

He checked the rough maps and plans, storing it away.

His eyes passed over his guild members. Some of them were wearing rag-tag gear; supply was still trying to catch up with all the new people. Even if they didn't have the newest gear from the Alva army, Alva's armories had been opened. Journeyman armor was the norm, with pieces of Expert gear.

"You think they are ready for it?" Emilia asked.

"Ready?" Blaze shook his head. "Are any of us ready when the spells start landing and iron meets meat? We're stronger than we've ever been with the cultivation pods, direct training, and gear, but we're not as strong as the main army. Although, we have experience on our side.

"If we can crush the United Sect Army at the gates, then we can change the balance of power, bring the enemy down. The beginning of the end starts at Vuzgal."

"What about afterward?" Emilia asked.

Blaze's eyes focused, pulling them away from the training to Emilia.

"Afterward." He exhaled. "The guild will continue. I have had assurances from the council and the lords. Those that prove themselves in the guild can train in Alva and their families will be allowed to live there. They will all need to be checked before they gain residency. We will continue to operate through the ten realms as we have in the past. A subsidiary of Alva. If more fighting comes in the future because of being part of Alva, the guild members will get the same option. They can fight for Alva, or they can leave the guild and take care of themselves."

"How are the talks with our old allies?"

"I've talked to some of them. They're non committal, for the most part. The Silver Dragons are sending over reports, as are some others." Blaze shrugged.

"They're protecting their own asses if we lose."

"Yeah, and this isn't the time to ask for their support. When we win or have something to show for it, it will make our cause stronger."

"Makes us sound like sects, power plays."

"We might not want to be a sect, but we have the power of one. We have to play the game, at least. If we don't, then we'll die without knowing where the final blow came from."

"I just want to get back to running security on convoys, drinking beers, and making fun of Derrick and his pointy swords."

Blaze chuckled, turning somber, seeing something within his mind. "We all do, but peace, is a plant watered with blood."

Emilia stood straighter. "Command wants to start moving us into the fourth realm as soon as possible to reinforce our people there."

Blaze smiled and looked at her. *I wonder if she realized she didn't call them Vuzgalians or Alvans.* He stood straighter, it was time they returned the support they'd gained in the shadows over the years.

Evernight opened Aditya's office door to find Erik looking over King's Hill.

"Sir," she greeted.

"Construction is going quickly," Erik remarked, turning his head from the window.

"We have the inner keep now, the main city, and the outer quarters," Evernight said, moving to stand next to him.

"Tripled your size in just ten days."

"The mages did most of it." Evernight looked at the ringed walls standing twenty meters tall, interspersed with stone towers and walkways wide enough for two carts to travel side by side. Siege weapons were being prepared at the tops of the towers, massive things, twice the size of mobile versions.

More towers dotted the quarters, some in different stages of completion.

Tents were set out in grids running up the hill to the inner walls. Crews were going along, growing trees into houses. Others, without mages, were using wood from the lumberjacks toiling away in the forest, clearing the area of trees.

Carts rolled in day and night, carrying refugees with nowhere else to go, as well as dirt, stone, and lumber to aid the massive building project.

"Wish we could do better than tents," Erik said.

"The bunkers are coming along. We'll have enough room to hold all the refugees," Evernight assured him.

"I hope so." Erik sighed.

Evernight felt the air contract and release with his movements. Then any sense of mana manipulation was gone, as if he was just another person from the first realm without any cultivation.

Seeing him there, it feels like everything will be all right. Evernight mentally shook her head, clearing her thoughts.

"Did you have something you wanted to talk about?" Erik turned in the silence. His hair had been cut to regulation, and he was clean-shaven.

"Sir, I wanted to talk about what happens after we push back the kingdoms."

"I think it might be a little premature to talk about that," Erik said.

"People are going to have questions. Where all this support came from, mages that can pull walls out of the ground. We should be ready for that."

Erik grimaced. "Feels like bad mojo to plan for it."

"If we don't plan now, we'll end up reacting rather than acting."

"Okay, so what are you thinking?"

"First, we get the people on contracts to make sure that our secrets hold, at least most of them. Two, we expand the Consortium to bring in people from among the refugees. Make them loyal to us. A negotiation with the other kingdoms. Control land around the Beast Mountain Range. Set down farms, put up defensive towers and add a buffer zone for warning in case of attack. Keep bandits from entering the Beast Mountain Range." Erik reeled off his thoughts.

"Why the farmland?"

"A nation needs food."

"A nation?"

"Sir, if we win, we will control the Beast Mountain Range under a unified and complete council. It will have a standing army and a population equal to most kingdoms. The outposts could swell into cities and King's Hill would be our capital. The Consortium will be one of our powerful levers and a major draw to the surrounding kingdoms. We will have shown we can defend ourselves. Those that didn't attack us will seek alliances."

"So, we'd really create a nation?"

"Yes, one hundred thousand of ours against nearly four hundred thousand of theirs, with a dungeon, resources, room to grow and train. That sounds pretty damn good in the First Realm."

Erik nodded. "All right, what else?"

Evernight took a deep breath and braced herself. "Do we want to control the First Realm or just the Beast Mountain Range?"

Erik shrugged. "Never owned a planet before. What're the pros and cons?"

"Pros: we would get a large draw of people. Cons: massive administration issues, turn into a quagmire."

"And for just the Beast Mountain Range?"

"We control it completely. We raise it to be a symbol in the First Realm. It makes us a target, but it allows us to control the realm in different areas and gather the best people. A change here could ripple through the rest of the First Realm."

"Let's just deal with the Beast Mountain Range then."

"Okay, so then I have some other questions."

"You ask Delilah about this?"

"Yes, and she answered all the ones she could and told me to ask you the rest."

"Awesome," Erik grumbled. "Keep going."

Evernight smiled. "The military will need to expand to support all the Beast Mountain Range. How do we want to organize them as a supplement to the Alva Military, or as an isolated unit with Alvan training as they are now?"

"Gonna be a long night," Erik said before his eyes wandered, thinking.

Marco accepted the letter from the Blue Lotus messenger. He quickly opened and read it, raising an eyebrow.

Impressive. He didn't think that someone could write as if they were yelling. It was obviously written to piss off the Willful Institute. It slighted the other sects, but gave them an option out. Blood for blood, it seemed.

Marco read the letter twice and then passed it to Master Teacher Feng Dan. He was calm reading through it. It was antagonistic and played right into his hands. He needed a reason to keep on fighting to win. It was the first domino that could send the others falling across the realms.

This letter had been written to piss him off and drive him into action. *They want me to attack them?*

His eyes sharpened. It felt as if a hidden set of eyes was looking at him. He unconsciously looked in the direction of Vuzgal.

"They want a fight. We'll tear down their city," Feng Dan snarled, practically tossing the letter to Hae Woo-Sung.

"We will not accept the mediation. Clearly, the Vuzgal city lords wish to use this opportunity to insult our armies and our sect," Marco snarled, looking at the messenger.

"Do you have a letter you wish to pass on?"

Marco knew that he had to play his part; a life at the peak of the sect had taught him well. "Tell them this. We will tear apart their city, kill their families, and search out any of their ancestral lines and erase them!" he snapped.

The messenger was unfazed. "I will pass it on." The woman bowed her head slightly and left the command center.

We'll have your fight, but you must be hiding more. Vuzgal, you have not failed to impress me.

"How are our forces?" Marco asked Leonia, making sure his voice would only pass to her ears.

"We have eight hundred thousand in the camps."

"How many in fighters and aerial forces?"

"One hundred and seventy-five thousand in fighters, thirty thousand in aerial fighters."

He needed to decide whether to continue sending out testing attacks to learn more about the enemy or go all-in on a larger attack to overwhelm and smash Vuzgal open. They needed a quick victory. They had been here too long already, with no direct action. *We'll do a test, make it look like a test and then attack.*

"Okay, let's plan our next offensive. I wish to reply to the people of Vuzgal with more than just words!" Marco's words were at odds with the calm surety of his mind.

Other sect commanders and personnel growled in agreement.

Angry, remorseful, yelling or being quiet, they're all just tools.

"How long will it take to mobilize all of our forces for an attack?"

"It would depend. For an assault without support, we would need a week; with our siege weaponry, add in another week."

"Move up our ranged siege weaponry. I want to see just how strong their mana barrier is." Marco grabbed a tile on the map that represented the siege weaponry and pushed it up toward Vuzgal. "Prepare our ground and aerial fighters. We'll test their defenses throughout the day and night. We'll exhaust them. At the same time, have stealth fighters find the gaps in their defensive structures. In three weeks, we attack!"

He'd need to play things close to the chest to make sure that Vuzgal's spies wouldn't have time to react to the real attack. In the next week, he'd attack with everything he had. He was betting it all on this one attack. *If we lose our aerial forces, then we won't have another chance.*

"Those must be the forces from Vermire. Haven't seen those banners here before," Pan Kun said, passing the viewing glasses to Nasreen.

She checked quickly before passing them to Lukas.

"Sooner than I thought." Pan Kun glanced at the mid-morning sun that had burned away the morning chill, warming the wall and those behind it.

The first realm kingdoms' siege weapons were firing from extreme range. Behind them, fighters had been organized into squares.

"Those mounts have to be guards," Pan Kun phrased it as a question.

"You think they'd waste mounted on us? Not sure who those sorry bastards are, but they're not here because they want to be," Nasreen said.

"I agree. They're in groups with spears, watching the infantry. Vanguard suicide force, I'd guess."

"Probably the runners from yesterday." Pan Kun shifted his armor around. "I don't like how close they're hitting to the bottom of our wall, or the fact some rounds are skipping over the damn ground. They're smashing the pots up. Barrier is cracking the rocks for now, but if they get through the wood cladding and hit the walls, that's gonna start throwing up some sparks."

"Good thing we only have the small ones and we packed them in groups of nine." Lukas said.

"Not like they're going to call off the attack," Nasreen said.

"Nope, not for those poor fuckers." Pan Kun rubbed his face and took in a deep breath.

The Army that was supposed to have taken Vermire now took up position behind the guarded members stuck behind the siege weapons.

"Here it is," Lukas said.

Mana cannons bellowed, releasing their spells as they hit the mana barrier.

"Six of them now. That should be all the cannons that the Willful Institute gave them."

The cannons charged up again and fired.

"Looks like they don't care about the mana stones anymore," Lukas muttered.

"Get everyone that we can fit underground into the bunkers. Have the forces on the wall ready to rush down as well," Pan Kun said. "I don't think they'll come until they crack our wall this time."

47 Rebuttal

"Barrier can't take much more of this," Pan Kun told Lieutenant Lee. "We can use the stronger mana barrier, but that'll give away that not everything is normal around here."

"Yeah, an impenetrable barrier. I hate making these kinds of decisions." Pan Kun looked at Nasreen.

"Evacuate the wounded to the rear, pull out our supplies. Prepare everything for the retreat. I only want those fighting left inside the city. If people are wounded, soldiers will take them to the medical carts at the rear and provide security. Once the carts are filled, they're to head to the rear. Shut down and remove the teleportation formations. Lee, you and your people check the poison pots. Set them off before we get out of here. Your people will form up at the western gate into the range. You'll be my quick reaction force."

"Sir," Lee nodded.

Nasreen took notes.

"Lukas and his people will break off once they're driven past the first row of houses. It will fall to you, Nasreen, to cover their retreat and create distance between the enemy and us. Use your archers and the outpost buildings to funnel them and slow them. You have your spell scrolls?"

"Yes, sir."

"Good. Use them as you need them, and your commanders as well. Leave the siege weaponry where it is, light it on fire if you can. It should slow the enemy. I don't want anyone or anything left behind. Once you get clear of the buildings on this side—"

"Get on our mounts and pull the hell out, at which time you will activate one last spell scroll to flip them the bird. Regroup at rally point Alpha unless otherwise ordered," Nasreen finished for him.

Pan Kun nodded.

"Putting our back to the enemy and retreating like this, I don't like it. Too many things could get fucked up."

"Simple enough. When the attacks stop, we get up on what's left of the walls and bleed them." Nasreen shrugged.

"One part I don't like is you waiting to go last," Lee said to Pan Kun.

"I want to make sure all my people are out before I bring down hell on this place."

The lights on the mana barrier formation in the middle of the room started to change.

"Let's get our people into cover! Lee, you sure about keeping watch?"

"Little bit of stone rain didn't hurt us. I'll have one of my people down there with you. Tenzin, she's a beast tamer and has comms, so she can keep you updated."

"Good." Pan Kun and Nasreen jogged for the exit.

The barrier lit up with stones and mana cannons blasting through the early afternoon sun.

The walls were thinned out, the reserves no longer holding behind them. Siege weapon crews continued to fire as their spotters called out corrections.

Pan Kun waved a flag at Lukas, who was on the wall. He pulled out another flag and waved it. The soldiers on the wall formed and ran down the stairs. Pan Kun looked at the sides and rear of the city. Soldiers were still on those walls.

If they advance the siege weapons, then we'll have to pull them into the cellars and bunkers too.

"Good luck, sir! See you in the Range," Nasreen said as she ran off toward her bunker.

"Stay safe!"

Pan Kun saw the wall clear of soldiers. The barrier started to break; attacks crashed through the walls and the buildings beyond with titanic force.

The siege weapon teams turned and ran to the underground areas. Pan Kun's two guards grabbed him and pushed him toward their bunker. He hurried down a set of stairs into a large cellar. Boxes had been thrown up to stop people from just running right inside. Pan Kun slowed down and turned through the maze.

It opened up again. The cellar had been heavily reinforced and connected to the cellars of nearby buildings, giving them multiple entrances and exits. Benches lined the room, as well as stools and other boxes. Soldiers kept to their squads, finding somewhere comfortable. Their team leads counted them all as they filed in and tried to relax.

A woman walked over to Pan Kun. "Sir, I'm Tenzin."

"Good, you're going to be my eyes and ears," Pan Kun said. A waiting guard indicated a corner where some chairs had been scrounged. The other guards were standing around.

"Let's take a seat."

She nodded and followed.

The sounds changed above.

"Lieutenant Lee reports that the enemy are moving up their siege weapons, the cannons are—"

Dust blew in through the switchback entrance closest to the wall.

"Targeting the walls."

"Great."

They waited in the cellars. Pan Kun heard the mana cannon's spells tearing chunks out of the defensive wall, obliterating the wooden cladding.

"Siege weapons firing," Tenzin said, her eyes covered in spells.

The sound of stone on stone rang out.

"They're targeting the wall."

"Are they skipping them across the ground?"

"Some of them, yes."

"Shit." *They're going to ignite the damn fire pots. If it slows them down, it doesn't matter.*

Pan Kun sat there, listening to the wall falling apart. There was a deep thud as something hit overhead, dislodging dust that fell on the soldiers in the cellar.

"They took out some of the supports. The wall has collapsed in sections so they're hitting the buildings," Tenzin reported. "A group of pots sparked. There're fires on the ground, but the rubble is covering most of it."

More thumps came from overhead as stones hit the buildings above the cellars-turned-bunkers.

"They've stopped using the cannons and are advancing the siege weapons again."

Stone rained down outside the doorways, throwing up dust into the cellar's defensive boxes, causing those closest to cough.

What if these things aren't as strong as we hoped? Just one hit at the wrong place and the whole thing could crash down on us. Pan Kun looked at people playing with threads of their clothes or fiddling with their weapons. They looked pale and clammy as they closed their eyes at every near miss.

"Be good to get out of this outpost and into the forest. If they think that this is all they have to face before they reach King's Hill, they are going to be in for a rude awakening," Pan Kun said to Hajjar, the leader of his guards.

"And I have no doubt that you will be dangerously close to where we set the traps."

Pan Kun just smiled.

"That's strange," Tenzin said.

"What is?"

"The force that was right behind the siege units are running forward, but the siege units haven't stopped yet."

That's why they had to have the mounted guards.

"On your feet! Prepare to fight!"

Someone pulled out a metal drum and started hitting it. Other drums were being beaten around the outpost.

Team leaders got everyone on their feet and ready, facing the passages to the surface that were clear. Some were closed off by buildings falling on them.

"What about the second force?"

"They are ready and moving forward as well, slowly. The siege weapons have stopped firing."

Pan Kun stood. The outpost was just that, an outpost. It didn't have a cornerstone, so it wasn't recognized as a village or town, meaning no alerts when under attack, and no debuffs against the enemy.

"It hasn't landed yet," she warned.

"Weapons at the ready!" an officer called out. The soldiers drew their swords and mages layered on buffs, the glow of mana sinking into their bodies.

The thudding stopped.

"Go!"

The boxes were torn out of the way and soldiers rushed out. Pan Kun waited for two squads to pass, jumping into the line with his guards and Tenzin.

Pan Kun's feet faltered as he reached the top of the stairs. The towering wall was sprayed across the outpost. A rough higher mound showed the foundations. Some sections were still up or half-destroyed. Houses had been crushed by the siege weapons, the stones going right through the wooden houses and scattering the few made of stone.

"Move into formation!" Pan Kun yelled, seeing the movement of others emerging from their cellars. "They're coming!" His voice carried across the outpost with the medallion.

Melee fighters rushed out to create shield walls between buildings and behind the broken wood of their siege weapons. Archers lined up behind them, aiming between the melee fighters as they hunkered down, shields ready and swords out. The mages were kept in groups at the back, away from the front line.

"Front line, steady!" Lukas barked.

"Archers, pick your targets! Get them coming over the rubble. Mages, be ready with fire spells!" Nasreen yelled.

Fighters appeared over the wall; their yells died in their throats as arrows knocked them backward. More started to come over the wall, two or three, then dozens. They slipped on the broken stone, archers claiming their lives.

Team leaders had back up melee fighters ready and fired their crossbows.

"What does it look like?" Pan Kun asked.

"They're all spread out. They're throwing down planks and crossing over, a big group now."

"Mages be ready!" Pan Kun yelled. "Tell Lieutenant Lee that, once the second group is in the middle of the flame pots, to hit all but the ones on our flanks."

"Yes, sir."

The wave that had gathered behind the pits trying to cross them came over the wall, yelling as spells appeared above the shield line, cutting through their ranks with the combined arrows and bolts.

Pan Kun grabbed his war hammer as they made it down from the rubble wall and ran at the shields, madness in their eyes.

The melee fighters shoved their shields out, smashing into the chargers and throwing them back as they lashed out with swords shining in the afternoon sun as blood stained the ground and soldiers' gear.

"Hold the line! Do not advance!" Lukas yelled.

They were no match for them one on one. It was a slaughter; the wave thinned out.

Streaks of light appeared in the sky. Pan Kun looked over to see meteors raining down on the enemy. They disappeared beyond the wall and he felt the impacts through the ground; they got closer and closer until they were landing on the other side of the wall.

"Hold!" Pan Kun barked as the shield lines started to bow in slightly.

The meteors stopped as flames and screams were heard on the other side of the wall.

"We caught three of the enemy units in the flames," Tenzin said. "They're looking to go around. There are two more large units behind them."

Advance onto the wall or hold?

Pan Kun took it all in. They were about twenty meters from the base of what was the wall, among the houses, most places without clear sight. The wall was still their greatest defense, acting as an obstacle and bad footing. They needed space to react, but if they went on top of that, they were going to be the ones falling over and breaking ankles.

"Withdraw thirty meters! All support personnel, retreat!" Pan Kun yelled.

The team leads took over, pulling everything back in order.

"Set fire to the siege weapons and push debris into the road!" Nasreen yelled.

They threw fire pots among the siege weapons, which butted up against the houses. The enemy would have to come down the roads unless they wanted to jump through flames on the broken houses.

"They're coming through the flanks," Tenzin said.

"Watch the flanks!" Pan Kun yelled.

"They have shields in the front."

The new enemy units appeared at the side of the breaches, shields pulled together to protect those underneath trying to set their footing.

They're not charging. Scared?

Arrows and bolts struck high and low, aiming for openings.

People dropped as arrows found openings. The shield wall collapsed on the left flank as mages cast spells into the openings created, killing dozens.

Arrows came over the wall.

"Shields!" Lukas yelled. The shields raised to cover. People cried out as they were hit.

Archers fired back blindly over the rubble.

More fighters crossed over the wall, building momentum.

"Withdraw ten meters, wounded to the rear!" Pan Kun yelled.

They picked up their wounded and ran out of the outpost to the waiting carts.

"Team leads, take command!" Pan Kun yelled. *It's all up to you now.*

"Sir?" Hajjar said, indicating to the rear.

Pan Kun looked at the archers appearing on the wall, trading fire with his own. His people's spells cut through the enemy as arrows punched through armor.

He turned and made for the rear.

"Tell Lee to break the pots."

"Yes sir," Tenzin said.

Nasreen watched her people falling back slowly. A mage grabbed out with her hand and dragged a half-collapsed building down on the road.

The siege weapons' fire was spreading to the rest of the buildings.

"They're breaking down more of the wall!"

A section of wall on the left flank crumbled and collapsed.

Damn oversized pikes.

Archers fired as the enemy fighters tried to clamber over obstacles.

Nasreen smelled something in the air. *The pots?*

She looked to the stands where the poison pots had rested. There were just ceramics and a dispersed cloud.

Nasreen glanced at the wall above the gate into the range. Signal flags snapped in the wind against the smoke and destruction. "Keep pulling back. Archers, move to the alleys. Shield melee fighter group one, pull back to the range!"

The archers and the melee fighters from group two moved into cover along the road. Fighters were moving in force. Arrows caught them as they focused on their footing, trying to cross the broken house.

"Moving!" Archers and melee fighters up front crouched and ran back, taking up positions behind their fellow archers.

Enemy fighters ran out from the alleyways past the downed house. They turned and charged, yelling and wielding their weapons. Nasreen raised her bow and fired, her arrow going through several before it stopped.

"Hold your ground and shoot!" she yelled. Archers fired into them, thinning their ranks. An archer next to Nasreen went down with an arrow to the neck, clawing at the air and at his neck.

"Medic!" she yelled, covering the retreating front line.

A soldier grabbed the archer and ran to the rear.

Mana blasts lit the street as the United Army pushed into the streets. BMRA Mages waved their hands, creating air blades that cut down the street at neck height. Bodies kept going as their heads or part of them remained still.

"Pull back!" Nasreen yelled as the momentum returned in her people's favor.

They peeled back. One soldier struck in the back was grabbed by another and carried behind the archers and toward the gates.

Mages threw spells into the cover that the enemy fighters and archers were trying to use.

Nasreen ran back with the next group, reading the flags. "Second group melee fighters! Head off! Keep peeling back!"

Now there were only the archers and the mages. They kept moving back, giving ground and taking casualties. But they made the enemy pay dearly for it.

They were just twenty meters from the end of the road when the buildings caught fire. The wind shifted, bringing smoke over the group, making Nasreen's eyes water.

She grabbed another arrow. The first punched through a wooden wall and hit the archer on the other side, then shot at a group of fighters running forward, killing two.

"Covering!" the second archer line yelled.

"Moving!" She turned and ran with the archers, straining against the smoke to look at the flags. "Pull back once more and then get the hell out of here. Mages, move to the gates!"

Mages gritted their teeth and rushed to the rear; now it was only the archers.

Nasreen got to cover and pulled out a spell scroll.

"Covering!"

She and the archers with her yelled out, their voices hoarse from smoke and running.

"Moving!" The archers that had covered them turned and ran to the rear.

"Keep going all the way out!" Nasreen yelled.

Come on! Run faster!

They cleared the front of Nasreen's line. Archers fired on the fighters that were getting bold, seeing their enemy run.

Enemy archers and mages fired at them; a wall exploded, throwing back the archer using it for cover.

"Cover me!" Another archer ran as the rest fired arrows down the streets.

Nasreen ripped her spell scroll.

Mana surged above as spell formations opened in the sky.

"Get under cover!" Nasreen yelled.

Meteors rained from above. The first struck ahead of the lead fighters running down the road and detonated. The blast collapsed houses, sent shrapnel through the rear guard.

The noise was deafening.

"Move it!" Nasreen's amulet glowed, her enhanced voice nearly drowned out by Armageddon raging down the street.

The group turned and ran. Nasreen made sure that her wounded archer and the one that had grabbed him were past her, giving a five-count before following.

She grabbed her bow in her left hand, looking at the meteor rain before turning and running.

They broke out of the buildings and into the large clear area around the rear gate. Their beasts had been prepared and laid out in groups. Team leaders got people organized and onto their mounts, then rushed out of the gate as fast as possible.

Pan Kun sat atop his mount with his guards, waiting for them.

The man working the flags ran down the stairs and jumped from the wall to his mount.

Nasreen leaped up, landing on her mount with ease. She grabbed her reins with her right hand, her bow in her left hand still. "Get going!" she yelled at the archery team.

"You heard her!" The team leader led the group forward, bringing empty mounts with them for people that had been wounded or were being carried out.

Nasreen saw people running, some carrying wounded, down and out of the outpost as a large explosion caught her eye. There were tongues of fire on the northern side of the outpost.

Her mount moved nervously under her as she surveyed the burning destruction that was the outpost over to the south where spells struck buried flame pots, making a second fire barrier.

"Nasreen!" Pan Kun called out, bringing her back.

She turned and rode over to him. "How is it going?"

"All melee are out. Just waiting on your archers now," Pan Kun yelled over the heat and flames. "Just one more team from the south needs to come in."

She looked over, seeing the teams race out of the outpost and through the gate, making sure to not bunch up. *We trained them well.*

Just four groups of mounts remained. Spells lanced through a section of the outpost.

Spell scroll.

Two teams with wounded got to their mounts. The wounded were tossed on their own and lashed down quickly, the reins taken as their team members got on their own mounts before the groups rode out.

A third group ran out just as the last of the groups left.

"Where is the last group?" Pan Kun asked.

"They have to climb over buildings. Their road was blocked," Tenzin said.

Nasreen grabbed an arrow from her quiver, using her legs to move her mount.

Pan Kun's guards moved into a skirmish line, eyeing the entrances into the square.

Nasreen saw movement. She drew her bow and aimed. Not seeing the army's uniform, she released, the force of the arrow threw the fighter backward as it punched a hole in them.

"You two, cover that area. You two, that area. You two, this." Pan Kun smacked people on the shoulder, giving them arcs.

The first enemy runners appeared. Nasreen killed one, but another ran ahead of them.

They're gaining ground!

Mana gathered behind her. She didn't have time to look. Targets appeared faster than she could shoot.

The mounts started to complain as they got closer.

"Lightning's Descent!" Tenzin cast a spell.

A bolt tore from the heavens, striking the ground. Nasreen covered her head against the dirt and stone.

A crater lay where fighters had once been.

"Radiant Pulse!" A blast of force struck another group of enemy fighters, throwing dozens of them and their fellows back into buildings.

Nasreen fired into the fighters still coming down paths.

"Ligh..." Pan Kun grunted. He breathed heavily. "Lightni..." He gasped in frustration before the area fluctuated madly. "Lightning Sphere!" Pan Kun screamed.

A sphere no bigger than a marble shot out toward the intersection of three streets. Nasreen's world turned white and loud. She ducked her head, squeezing her eyes shut, but she swore she could see through them.

The noise died down as she blinked. Tears rolled down her face.

The ground had been turned to glass. A smoking crater ate part of the ground and the surrounding buildings. Black markings like burnt vines stretched across the surrounding buildings as the smell of ozone mixed with the stench of cooked meat.

Pan Kun looked exhausted, his body heaving up and down as Hajjar forced him to take a mana potion.

"Holy shit, sir," Nasreen said. He cracked a partial grin.

"Where are my damn archers?"

Nasreen looked out over the destruction. In either fear or because they were building their numbers back up, the enemy wasn't pushing the square just yet.

She saw movement among the buildings. She pointed at it, squinting. "Those are our uniforms!"

The archers rushed over the buildings, haggard as they had to find their footing. They were carrying the wounded on their shoulders.

Thank the gods for our partially tempered bodies.

The archers jumped off the buildings and ran to their mounts as the first enemy fighters bold enough to walk through the destruction appeared. Two of Pan Kun's guards fired, killing them.

The archers rode their mounts out of the outpost as fast as they could.

"Time we got going, Tenzin." Pan Kun passed the woman a spell scroll. There were runes within the pages, altering the surrounding air with the dense mana contained within.

It seemed he was using the last of his strength as he barely held himself upright.

"Pull back!" Hajjar yelled for his Major General.

Nasreen fired her last arrow, hitting a fighter in the neck as they turned and wheeled out of the outpost.

The guards formed to the rear as they raced down the hill, gaining speed quickly. The forest spread out ahead of them. The last archer team was riding for all they were worth.

Tenzin's eyes were unfocused, watching something else.

Nasreen felt a shiver run through her spine. How many others like her were in the Alvan Army? Would she have even noticed them subtly changing the battle if she hadn't known know they were there?

Her eyes dropped to the scroll in Tenzin's hand and then to her bow. There was little you couldn't do if you have the right gear and the proper knowledge.

Arrows struck the road behind them as the fighters shot from the open gate.

"Tenzin!" Nasreen yelled, to pull her out from whatever she was seeing.

"Wait." Tenzin's voice was calm, as if removed from this world.

Archers appeared on what was left of the walls.

"Get low!"

They hugged their mounts, trying to get them to go faster.

Arrows landed closer. One guard hissed as they were struck.

"Now." Tenzin tore the spell scroll. Like the air itself had been drawn out of her lungs, so was the mana around them ripped from the area, pouring into the burning page of the spell scroll. Nasreen looked back, seeing the spell formation appear above the Hunter Frontier Outpost.

"Holy shit," she said as the wind picked up. The outpost was largely *gone.*

The air twisted as the flames within the city rose higher. The wind gathered, creating tornadoes that reached the ground, drawing up debris as they travelled through the outpost erratically. Flames ignited in some of the tornadoes, turning them red as lightning exacted vengeance upon the ground.

A section of wall was hit, blowing out and scattering across the ground before a tornado slammed into it, tearing up the wall and flinging stone in every direction and drawing it up into the winds. Stone, wood, and people were sucked up and thrown, no longer able to control their fate.

Are the gods that powerful?

The spell formation moved toward the enemy, carrying its destruction with it.

Nasreen looked ahead as they continued their mad dash into the welcoming cover of the Beast Mountain Range's trees.

48

Occupy Hunter Frontier

Lord Salyn watched his footing on the mound of stone and charred wood as he made his way toward Lord Knight Ikeda, Lords Aras and Fletcher. He arrived behind them, looked over what remained of the Hunter Frontier Outpost.

Stone and wood shifted as fires broke some of the half-ruined buildings. Soldiers cursed as they picked their way through the rubble.

Siege weapons and stores had been put to the flame, leaving the outpost wreathed in smoke.

"So?" Ikeda asked, turning to Salyn with that imperious glare only aided by Salyn's lower position on the rubble pile.

"No one left behind, not even a body."

"Not even a body?" Fletcher was a tall man with greying hair and thick black eyebrows against his pale, almost sickly looking, skin.

Salyn coughed. *Damn all this smoke and dust.*

"No, Lord Fletcher, not a single body has been recovered from the outpost. We did find out how they counterattacked so well. They hid in reinforced cellars that connected under the houses."

Fletcher ground his teeth. He wanted someone to blame, someone to pin this to. He had just arrived and lost ten thousand in the attack, with thirty thousand wounded. With the sickness going around, not many of them would survive.

"They probably took their dead and dying so we wouldn't know how many we killed," Ikeda said.

Salyn looked over the outpost. *If it can be called an outpost. It's just mounds of stone and wood. There's nothing here.*

Some sections of the wall remained, but nothing above one story remained standing.

Salyn shivered, thinking about the spell scroll storm that had washed through the outpost and into the teeth of the unit.

"Bring the camp forward. Have the soldiers and laborers clear the ground and stack the stones against the walls facing the Beast Mountain Range."

Explosions went off inside the outpost.

They all ducked and looked over.

"These fucking outpost lords! When I get them..." Fletcher's threat ran off as veins appeared up his neck and on his hand gripping his sword.

"Tomorrow the mounted forces will lead. We'll push them from the rear all the way to King's Hill," Ikeda said.

Salyn felt like he had just fallen asleep when he was awoken by one of his servants.

"What is it?" he demanded.

"There's been a problem in the outpost, sir. Ikeda is demanding your presence."

It had taken all afternoon to get the ground cleared and get some tents thrown up. Then the damn peasants had complained about having to sleep near the pits where their fellows died.

"Is it about the towers where we sent the peasants so they'd stop complaining about being near the dead?"

"No, sir, there's an officer here."

"Show him in," Ikeda said.

The servant nodded and lit several lamps before leaving.

Salyn rubbed the sleep from his eyes as the servant returned with an officer.

He bowed, shaking as he cupped his hands.

"What is it?" Salyn demanded.

"A fight has broken out in the army camp, My Lord," the officer reported nervously.

"Why is that of any interest to me?"

"It escalated and now there are a number of nobles involved."

"What would draw them into it?" Salyn demanded.

"A weapon, My Lord." The man was sweating as he stared at the ground, still bowing.

"Instead of spitting out parts, why not tell me everything?" Salyn demanded.

"I am sorry, My Lord. There was a spear. Someone took it from the Hunter Frontier outpost and used it. The weapon was powerful, and he bragged about it to others. They doubted him and he showed off its abilities. Others learned about it and a fight broke out. Then a passing noble took the weapon and was about to leave with it when the noble of the man who had found the spear arrived. They got into a fight with one another."

"Over a simple spear?"

"It is supposed that the spear is of the high apprentice grade."

Salyn snorted and stood up.

"Send word to Ikeda," Salyn said. He was on thin ice with him, and this could be a test. "Bring me my armor."

The servant hurried out and several others appeared quickly, dressing Salyn in his armor.

They headed off to meet Ikeda, who had been going over reports instead of requiring anything so mundane as *sleep.* Salyn could only curse him as Four Red Falcon Knights came over with mounts while the officer waited off to the side.

Ikeda mounted up; the others followed suit. The officer moved ahead.

"Move faster than that. I have other things to deal with."

"Uh, ah yes, sir!" The officer stumbled and regained his footing, taking off at a jog.

They followed him through the camp that took up the interior of the Hunter Frontier outpost.

Salyn could hear the fighting, the clash of metal on metal before they saw the flames. One tent had caught fire, others that had been smashed over lay flat on the ground as fighters yelled. Allies this morning were at one another's throats barely hours later.

"Halt! In the name of Lord Knight Ikeda!" one of the knights yelled from his mount.

Salyn wished dearly he was back in his bed instead of dealing with this *mess.*

They must not have heard, as Ikeda indicated to one of his falcons.

With a hellion scream, Hiraga charged forward.

That caused heads to turn. Her blade slashed through several men, her horse crashing through others that were too slow to move.

She came out the other side, expressionless as she flicked her blade clean and wheeled to the side, slowing her mount, ready for the next charge.

The fighting stalled as the groups looked at Ikeda's knights and Salyn's ragtag group of guards.

"Whoever has this spear, bring it to me." Ikeda's dark eyes looked over the groups.

A woman shivered as she walked forward, holding the spear out with both hands.

Ikeda motioned to a knight. They took the spear from her and presented it to Ikeda. It wasn't much to look at, just a strong piece of wood with a metal spearhead. Ikeda's eyes widened as he held the spear. "Salyn!"

Salyn obeyed and took the weapon.

It was well-balanced, and the wood had been treated against the elements. The wood was supple, allowing for some flexibility without snapping. The spear head was finely made. The smith working on it had sharpened it to a razor point.

He moved the spear around in his hands and studied it again. *No markings, no decoration, just a simple looking spear.* But how was a lord expecting to get this back if he lost it?

He looked at the hardened butt of the spear, fixed with an iron cap. A name had been scrawled near the bottom, barely legible from their writing. It had been burned into the spear.

What lord would scar such a weapon with an ugly brand? It looked like writing from a child.

"I will not have fighting in my camps," Ikeda said, looking at the groups of ten to fifteen men. "Leave the nobles."

The fighters yelled, trying to put up a fight. The Red Falcons cut them down easily.

Salyn waited as Ikeda held court.

"Each of you will pay ten gold coins in compensation." Ikeda looked at the nobles, taking the spear with him as he turned, his knights following.

Salyn hissed as a splinter from the spear caught his hand. He plucked out the dark wood and shook his hand.

"Salyn?"

"It is a fine weapon. I'm not sure who owned it. Looks simple in make, but no denying its quality."

Ikeda reached out and Salyn passed it back. Salyn thought he saw something in his eyes. *Recognition?*

"Hiraga, the other spears. Where are they?"

"With the loot train."

"Take us."

She led them to the most guarded part of the camp, several open areas with treated leather covered crates filled with loot. Guards from different armies and noble houses patrolled, keeping one another honest.

Hiraga led them to a stack of boxes. She undid the ties on the leather tarp with one of the knights and pulled out a long crate. They cracked open the top with their swords, showing several spears.

Ikeda dropped down from his horse and compared the spears. He waved Salyn forward.

The brands were all badly made but in the same spot. They were adjusted a bit higher or shorter with more or less metal bands around the spear head or cap to maintain balance.

Salyn hefted two spears and checked them against one another, then laid them side by side.

These spear heads.

He pulled out another spear and laid it down next to them.

"What do you think?"

"The spear heads, they're almost identical; same shape, same sizes. These were crafted by the same person." He looked at the sheer number of spears. "Or his apprentices."

"Aoki, I want a bounty put up. I will buy any weapons found for five silvers."

"Yes, my lord." Aoki bowed his head from his mount.

"Go pass the word now."

Aoki turned and brought his mount up to speed, racing back to Ikeda's tent.

The spears were higher than mid apprentice, much higher.

"Do you think these weapons were used by the nobles?" Ikeda asked.

"No, the markings are crude, and these weapons show signs of wear. They are well cared for, but they have been used repeatedly."

"Do you think…? No, that would bankrupt them." Ikeda shook his head and waved the thought away.

"Low-apprentice level gear would be a low noble's family heirloom. Even powerful nobles might only give out a few pieces to their personal guards."

"There are few able to create such items. All come from higher realms that rarely come down here," Salyn agreed, but he felt uneasy.

"There are many that come from the higher realms to trade with the Beast Mountain Range." Ikeda looked toward the Beast Mountain Range. "With their treasures and the Willful Institute's backing, we could enter a new age."

Salyn's heart beat faster as he saw the outline of that future.

"I want to ride at first light. We can catch up to their foot soldiers and cut them down. Gather all the weapons you can and pass them out first to the rest of the Falcons then to the army commanders and mounted forces of the Kingdom," Ikeda said.

"Salyn, make sure you get some sleep. We have a long road ahead of us."

"Yes, sir." Salyn half bowed as Ikeda mounted up and Salyn quickly left with his guards, his mind far from thoughts of sleep.

49
Home Ground

"We have withdrawn from Hunter Frontier, completing phase one of our plan."

"Dryfall and Vermire?" Erik asked.

"We're bleeding the enemy, but Veli and Donner have reduced the number of troops in their outposts. They don't need them all. The Willful Institute people have been getting reports on what is happening, but they remain in the main camps and send people to report to the higher realms every day."

"Anything on what's happening there?" Erik looked at Evernight.

"They are talking to the leader of Mistress Mercy's army, Niklaus. He is leading a campaign in the other realms to recover their lost cities and take the cities of other sects. Right now, he is wrapped up there. There are more rewards to be earned."

"Hmm, I don't like having that particular sword hanging over our heads. Sorry, Colonel."

Yui gestured that he wasn't bothered.

"The army sent to attack Vermire has about one hundred and twenty thousand effectives. Another forty-ish thousand are wounded or so sick that they cannot move. Those are the estimates from yesterday. Today the numbers will definitely increase."

"They've been fighting through it so far," Lord Quan said.

"The poison doesn't take effect for twelve hours. It's a powder, so it gets into people's faces and clothes. They're spreading it right now—or contracting it. The poison on the weapons and spears you left behind will cause in-fighting and poison the strongest people who touch them." Erik muttered as he looked at the map. "Okay, so while we've lost ground. Situationally we're doing damn well."

"Yes, sir. We just need to make sure that we don't get too cocky. We've got them charging toward us. They don't know how bad their situation is. We need to maintain discipline; no stupid shit, just a slow, grinding withdrawal."

"Agreed, Colonel. Any changes in the higher realms?" Erik said.

"Testing fights. The Associations are stepping up the pressure to have talks. They're gathering a lot of aerial forces and resources to lead an all-out attack. Numbers at Vuzgal have swelled on both sides." Yui pulled out a piece of paper and passed it over. Erik took it and scanned quickly.

Training is going well with the new people confident in their roles. Soldiers have been freed up to work on their cultivation. The enemy is wary of our weapons. New barriers are stronger but burn through damn mana stones.

"We need to sort this out to support the Fourth Realm and hit the Willful Institute where it hurts." Erik looked up.

"What about the Adventurer's Guild?" Yui asked.

"They're secured in the dungeons, recovering and seeing their families."

"Yes, but they're hot-blooded. You think they want to stay down there?" Flames appeared in Yui's hands, setting the letter on fire.

If they went out fighting, Erik didn't want to keep them in the dark anymore, at least not the key ones. *Damn secrets are a pain in the ass.*

Erik held his hands behind his back as he walked away from the table, looking at the ground.

"Adventurer's Guild. The mercenary guild?" Aditya asked.

"Yes," Evernight said.

"I know they have some reach in the higher realms. I'm guessing it's not small?"

"No, definitely not," Yui said, sharing a smile with Evernight.

"Alvans." Aditya sighed.

Nasreen woke with a start, grabbing her sword as she noticed Lukas standing in the darkness a few feet away from the tree she was sleeping against.

"What's up?" she asked as her heart slowed back down.

"Few hours till morning. Came to wake you."

Nasreen let out a heavy breath and grabbed clothes from the pack she'd readied before going to sleep.

Lukas looked away as she changed her underclothes under the blanket.

"Any change?"

"Nothing yet. They're holed up in the outpost. Pan Kun is sleeping off his mana fatigue. Heard what he did from some of his guards."

She saw him shake his head in the moonlight as she grabbed pants and a shirt, pushing off the blanket to the cool night air. Goosebumps ran along her skin. "Fuck, it's cold."

Lukas chuckled. "Better than doing this in winter."

"I'll take the heat over walking in those damn snowshoes any day of the week," Nasreen agreed, pulling on her remaining clothes.

"The mages shifted all the trees into place. I sent the wounded with a security detail down the new road to make it look like we went that way. They'll circle back through the woods, with the mages erasing any signs of their passing, and take a teleportation formation to King's Hill."

Nasreen looked around in the darkness. She couldn't make out the sleeping soldiers that lay in an all-round defense, back from their firing positions. Sentries talked to one another in the darkness, keeping one another awake.

"You think the road thing will work?" Nasreen asked.

"I hope so. Their maps are shit. Only new arrivals get updating maps. All they've got is some rough drawings unless the Willful Institute gave them real maps. They haven't had the time to wander to King's Hill to plot one out."

Nasreen pulled on her armor and tightened up the side ties before looping her sword belt. "Are they doing anything up at the outpost?"

"A fight broke out, but it got put down. They're getting sick and losing a lot of people. Nearly half of their reinforcements were wounded. The poison is spreading across them all. The nobles and commanders slept in the outpost. Just a matter of time now."

"We have to buy that time."

Nasreen grabbed her quiver. She'd unstrung her bow and secured it.

"How did the prep on the ambush location go?"

"We've got a hill switchback about six kilometers down the road from the outpost. Let them build up some speed, bunch up as they climb." Lukas turned around as Nasreen stuffed her sleeping gear into her pack. "Some people from the Special Teams came down to assist and teach us how to do it right."

"Shit, no way. I thought they hid in the shadows till the last moment." She turned, heaving the pack onto her shoulder.

"Nah, they were out there teaching. Most didn't know who they were. They were there at Vuzgal against the Blood Demon Sect. Just smart, how they planned it out, picked firing positions, where to place the traps and charges, what kind even. They picked out the hill because they'll see over the trees and should be able to see King's Hill in the distance with the road looking like it's straight on. Then throw in some curves around different terrain and lead them off target."

"You think the mounted are going to come after us, or they'll come in formations?" Nasreen hiked her pack up on one shoulder as they walked toward where their mounts were secured.

"Mounts. They want in on the action. They moved them up into the outpost. You won't believe this, but they have their infantry on this side of the outpost. They camped them on the dead. Instead of pushing them back, they pushed them forward."

"That's stupid. Sure, they have the high ground, but we come in, mounted in the middle of the night, or use some spell scrolls from the edge of the tree line..."

"Yeah, shitty way to wake up. Though they have mounted ready to charge out. So, we attack, we better be doing it at range and then running the hell out of there or else they'll be on our asses."

"Plant fire pots and blow them when you pass?"

Lukas paused. "Pretty good idea actually."

"Not part of the army just for my good looks."

"Who would think that Nasreen Fayad, daughter of the famous Emmanuel Fayad would be sleeping on the ground in the forest while fighting the kingdom's armies?" Lukas laughed.

"Who thought that the leader of a mercenary company who lost his hand and most of his leg as tiger treats would become an outpost guard and rise to a Brigadier General?"

"Even got the hand and leg back," Lukas said as Nasreen secured her pack to her mount's back.

The sky was starting to brighten as team leaders were woken by the sentries. They gathered at the large metal urn that held the highly coveted coffee.

Nasreen took in a deep breath, drinking the entire contents of a cup in a few big warm mouthfuls. "All right, teams for the ambush point, grab your squads. We'll be moving in ten," she said. "Rest of you, get your people up and moving."

The team leaders finished off their drinks.

"Grab food for your people too." Lukas picked up a small crate and passed it to the team leaders as they passed.

"What is it?"

"Something called breakfast burritos," Lukas said.

The team leader shrugged and headed off.

Lukas tossed Nasreen the wrapped package. She opened it and bit in.

"Mmm!" Her eyes lit up as she took another bite.

Lukas opened his and chomped down on it.

"Frig, the Consortium's new cooks know a few things about cooking. Damn I could go for four more." Lukas picked the last remaining pieces out of the wrapper.

Stamina increased by 2% for 1 hour Stamina regeneration increased by 7% for 3 hours

"Stats are fucking decent too."

"Now just ambush the hell out of these United Army pricks, and it'll be a perfect day. Looks nice and warm, good breeze and shade in the trees," Lukas said as they headed away.

Teams cleared their gear. Those moving on packed their mounts and prepared to leave, aiming to eat on the move.

Other teams packed their mounts and ate near the coffee urn, huddling in groups as their team leaders briefed them.

The teams, mainly archers and mages with a group of melee fighters thrown in, got into marching order. The most senior team lead walked up to the two officers.

"Ready to go?" Nasreen looked at the forty or so people, all armored and geared up.

"Yes, sirs."

"Let's get going then," Lukas said.

They moved through the forest. After about five minutes, they reached the hill.

It looked just like they had left it the other day.

"Move into your positions. Let's make sure we're ready to give the United Army a nice good morning," Nasreen said.

The teams spread out, taking the high ground of the hill. The melee team split to either side, covering the flanks with the mages and archers between them.

They pulled out formation plates and laid them down for the mages.

"How are the spell traps looking?" Lukas asked the mages' team leader.

"Still strong, we'll make sure they're charged up.

"Good positioning. You put traps in the ground and along the hills?" Erik asked, lowering the scope of his rifle and glancing at Storbon beside him.

"We took what we learned from Vuzgal's defense. Using just the road is one way to slow them, but taking out the sides of the road is more effective. Who checks a hillside?"

"Too right." Erik shifted the camouflage sheet around him. "Jerky?"

"Sure."

Erik pulled out some and passed it to Storbon.

They were on another hill looking through the trees at the switchback position the Beast Mountain Range Army was set up on.

"They're moving like a good unit. Still using melee and ranged groups," Erik said.

"They don't have the gear or weapons for different group types. Functions well for them, greater command and control."

"Guess all we can do now is just wait."

Erik shifted in his position and got comfortable.

The BMRA got into their positions and settled down, lying in wait, not realizing who was monitoring them from above.

The sky brightened as the sun started to rise.

"Movement on the road," Storbon said.

Erik used his scope to look. "They're mounted, which makes me think that they're impatient, but they're here well after the sun is up so they slept in?"

"Kingdoms, sir. The people that have mounts have wealth and

position, so they have people to take care of them."

"Stupid way to run a fighting force," Erik muttered.

The beasts' footfalls thundered through the morning.

"Anything behind the first group?" Erik asked.

Storbon checked his map and relayed the question.

"Three more forces on the road. They're racing to meet up with them. Each are about twenty minutes apart."

"This is a prime little spot. Make sure that the army knows."

"Sir."

Storbon sent out sound transmissions before falling into silence once again.

"Here we go." Erik tightened his grip on his rifle as Storbon raised his own.

The riders slowed at the switch back, bunching up as they fought to get up the hill. The rear forces pushed up as well.

They reached the top as the spell traps went off; riders and beasts were torn apart in the attack. Archers and mages stood from their cover, firing down on the enemy, focusing on those in the rear of the group. Many fell without even knowing what had hit them. Some riders tried to turn around in the tight quarters to flee. Their panicked beasts caused a stampede, fear overriding their rider's commands as they charged forward.

It was over in a few short minutes. Erik scanned the ridgeline and the switchback road.

Mages finished off the dying and wounded and lay down more spell traps before taking their positions again.

Erik watched the second force ride up the hill. They paused at the base, looking at the bodies of men and beasts. A rider turned and rushed back to the rear. The leader slowly took his people up. Two people, side by side, picked their way through the dead, looting as they went. They pushed up to the other side, making it past where the attacks had been carried out. They seemed relieved, watching the hill for attacks. The force sped up.

Traps went off as mages hurled spells from cover.

Archers fired on the leading units outside of the trap's range. Others focused on the riders in the rear that were fighting to control their mounts.

Some of the riders fired arrows up at the forest.

Erik reached out with his hand, feeling his connection with the earth element. He seemed to reach through it, to the ground under the riders in the rear.

He twisted the power of earth and infused his will, his mana, into it.

Spikes shot out of the ground, piercing beasts and riders, rolling forward like a wave through the mounted force in seconds.

Erik released the spell, and it collapsed into dust.

The archers and mages quickly cleaned up the remaining forces. Some threw out powder, using spells to spread it over the dead.

Tombstones dotted the ground. Not one of the army went down to loot, focusing on their mission.

"Looks like they listened to your advice." Erik lowered his rifle.

"Nice spell at the end there."

"I could do something, so I did. Not like they'll be telling anyone." Storbon shrugged.

"Let's head to the next rally point. We'll get in on the AAR and check out their positions up and down the road."

"Don't want to go back to the command center?" Storbon asked as they cleared away their gear and crawled back from the edge of the ridge.

"Bite me, Storbon."

50 Unified

Erik blinked away the light from the teleportation pad. His vision cleared, showing Niemm's special team fanned out around him and Jasper standing with branch heads Derrick and Lin Lei.

"Hey, Erik."

"What's up, Jasper?" Erik looked around.

"Blaze has *administrative duties* to take care of."

"Got it." Erik pressed his lips into a smile. "He never was a great lover of meetings."

"No, not really," Jasper snorted. "We have a meeting room set aside."

"I've been in enough damn meeting rooms to last a lifetime. Let's see what you've made of this place."

Niemm made a noise in the back of his throat, but Erik chose to ignore him.

"Yes, sir. I guess Blaze isn't the only one?" Jasper smiled.

Derrick and Lin Lei openly stared at Erik as they left the teleportation's defenses and entered the town growing beyond it.

"If I could get away I would," Erik muttered, clearing his throat and raising his voice as they left the defenses, looking out over the dungeon. "Looks pretty similar to Alva's living floor."

A dungeon core headquarters lay in the center, surrounded by administration buildings. Houses and apartment buildings had been crafted from different materials, creating roads. A section of the city was turned over to crafters. Another section was dedicated to training, another looking after and teaching the younger generation. Fields and animal pens were sown throughout.

Water dropped from above in a small waterfall, the stream weaving through the floor.

"The backup dungeons were all based on it. Instead of parks we have fields, and we have rows of apartment buildings to fit many people into the smallest area. Training grounds for mana cultivation and fighting, taverns, smithies, water treatment... All the things one could ask for in a city," Jasper said.

They walked down the road. People nodded to Derrick, Lin Lei, and Jasper while staring at Erik and his special team.

Women washing laundry and hanging it out on their balconies chatted with one another as they stared at the group, making guesses.

"How are your guild members?"

"They're happy for the rest. Most of them were fighting in the higher realms. We've passed on the information on the attacks," Jasper said.

"We're eager to fight. Either we or the Willful Institute must be destroyed," Derrick said.

"I don't think anyone is doing any destroying anytime soon," Erik said.

Jasper gave Derrick a sharp look, making him close his mouth.

"So, the Lord of Alva doesn't pay visits for no reason, especially when I hear he has been on the front lines in the First Realm. How are things going there?"

"Their army made some advances, took an outpost, but now they're all sick in their camps and can barely move. Major General Pan Kun and Colonel Yui are picking the time to strike. I don't have much time here. I will be heading back to the First Realm after this." Erik stopped and looked at Jasper. "I've come to ask the support of the Adventurer's Guild."

"What do you need?" Jasper asked.

"Fighters. For Vuzgal."

"Do you have a plan?"

"Two groups, one to fight in Vuzgal. The second will be our strike force to make good on our counterattack."

Derrick and Lin Lei shared a look, their hands curling into fists.

"It'll be nice to have us all under one banner. I wonder what people will think when they see the Adventurer's Guild and Alva Army fighting side by side." Erik smiled.

Lord Salyn coughed, pain wracking his entire body. His lungs felt like they were made of iron; he had to force them to open and close. It was almost as if his chest was collapsing under that weight.

He had his feet in an aromatic bucket, the steam washing over him to cleanse him and heal him.

The dividing sheet between him and the other nobles was drawn to the side. Beyond, people were lying everywhere, fighting to breathe. Healing houses moved between their clients, using their healing spells on the nobles and those with enough coin for their services.

"What news?" Salyn wheezed as Drev approached, a scarf over his nose and mouth.

In the three days since taking Hunter Frontier, their forces had been driven to a stop by the sickness passing through them.

"Supply carts are dumping their goods away from the camps now. Many of them are fleeing with our supplies. Lord Ikeda has fallen sick, as have his Red Falcon Knights. Everyone thinks this is something the Beast Mountain Range people thought up."

Drev paused to catch his breath. "We made it five kilometers up the road yesterday. Camps have been established, but we haven't had messengers since yesterday."

"We didn't—" Salyn wheezed, trying not to cough. "—send people."

A horn sounded nearby. Salyn looked around blearily and tried to stand.

Should greet them. Good word.

He got his feet under him and looked at Drev.

Drev jogged away to find out what was going on. Salyn tried to stand, groggily determined as his vision and head were swimming.

When Drev returned, he gripped the wooden pole that supported the dividing sheet, struggling to catch his breath. "They're... coming."

Salyn felt the power drain from his body. He grabbed the same pole and started to pull himself upright.

"H-orse." Salyn tried to cough out.

"Soldiers," a voice cried out across the outpost. "Your masters and lords do not care about you. Your kings and queens hide in their cities away from the battlefield. They send you forward to attack our outposts and people out of greed!

"They sent you here, not knowing of the sicknesses that came with the area. It is their fault that you have fallen ill! Surrender and we will take care of you! We have dealt with this sickness before, and we know how to treat it!"

They have an antidote? This is part of their plan! Drev helped Salyn up and supported him out of the room. Salyn leaned heavily on his guard captain. His wet feet chilled as he walked barefooted on the cold floor.

"The healers and alchemists only want your coin," the voice continued. "They do not care for your lives! You have heard of the wealth of the Beast Mountain Range. It is a hard place, but it is fair. You will be treated fairly! We are in need of farmers, of laborers! We will heal you without asking for payment!"

Salyn coughed as Drev paused to gather his breath. Salyn wanted to punch him for slowing.

"We do not want more death. We were protecting our homes as you were forced to fight us! Surrender and we will heal you!"

"Move," Salyn rasped as Drev continued huffing.

Drev looked at him in a way he had never in the past. "My... cousin—" Drev cleared his voice as he recovered his breath. "—was in Alva."

Salyn looked at him, confused and leery.

Drev turned, hugged Salyn, and slipped a blade into his guts. He stabbed him again and again before dragging him out into the night.

Salyn covered his stomach and gulped for air like a fish out of water.

Drev dropped him between the bodies of the dead that were piled up outside the tent. He cleaned his blade on Salyn's shirt, looting his rings and patting him down, then pulling out anything in his pockets.

He leaned down so Salyn could hear him. "Alva still stands even when you betrayed our trust." The weakness left Drev's expression as he stood, a different man.

Salyn's head rolled back, looking up at the sky. Coldness came as darkness overtook his vision.

"What do you mean they surrendered?" Juri stood up from the mana gathering formation he was cultivating on.

"Sickness spread through their ranks. Apparently, it is a sickness of the area. All the soldiers in all the armies were affected. Last night the Beast Mountain Range offered them a concoction to heal their afflictions if they surrendered."

Juri had been given this mission by Niklaus for the clan. It was supposed to be easy, but the kingdom's armies were useless. "Send a message to Niklaus immediately. Ask what he wants us to do."

"Yes, sir." The man tapped his Willful Institute emblem and left the tent.

Juri walked out of his quarters and across the rear camp for a view of the distant Hunter Frontier. In the massive camp of hundreds of thousands, few were moving.

He heard a commotion and saw mounted forces riding toward the Kingdoms camp.

"Please do not be alarmed! We are from the Beast Mountain Range Army! We do not wish you harm! Please surrender so that we might treat you! Your loved ones on the front line have already given up this illegitimate war! We will treat everyone, not just the lords and nobles!"

"To me!" Juri gathered his power as his guards and advisors ran over, less than ten in total, brimming with power.

Juri's steps faltered with the rest of his people. His bones creaked under a newfound pressure.

"Well, what do we have here?" a woman asked as she walked out from between the tents. Her head was covered, like the two men beside her. She made a tutting noise. "Juri Kostic of the Kostic branch family, from the Second Realm. Made it up to the Third though, didn't you? Not the brightest, but good at following orders. Niklaus has a soft spot for those loyal to him."

Who is this that she could be this strong and want to come down to the First Realm? He couldn't sense how strong the two men were beside her, like throwing a pebble into a lake.

"Who are you?"

"I am an interested party who wants to be left *alone*." The woman's voice dipped as the pressure increased. "Something your Willful Institute and the surrounding kingdoms are making *harder*."

Juri's body dipped under the new pressure before it lightened.

"Thankfully, you will make sure this little problem is dealt with."

"Did Domonos put you up to this? The Silaz's?"

"Who the hell is he talking about?" the woman asked one of the men beside her.

"There is a Silaz Trading house in the range." The man tilted his head.

"Do you think I would take orders from a fucking merchant?" The woman yelled and marched forward. The pressure redoubled, dropping several of the weaker members to the ground and nearly doubling over Juri.

"No, My Lady, no!"

Fuck you, Niklaus. What fucking viper's nest did you walk me into?

She let out a disgusted noise. "At least your dead will be useful. More to work with. The kingdom's losses will create some interesting chaos. Other than my research, things have been boring."

She had to be a dark mage. Why else would someone so powerful be in the First Realm? It would be easy to hide and people wouldn't question her practices.

"Give them the contracts." The lady waved her hand and walked away, one of the men leaving with her.

Four others, cloaked, walked out from among the tents, surrounding the group as the man she left behind pulled out a set of contracts.

The pressure decreased as two of Juri's people ran out with a yell.

A cloaked fighter smacked one in the hand, breaking it, then kicked out, buckling his knee and dropping him with a stunned expression. The pain hadn't set in yet. The cloaked fighter smacked him in the face casually.

The other Willful Institute fighter went down even faster.

"They're fragile. Try to not kill them," the man with the contracts said as if nothing had happened.

"These contracts will serve to save your lives. You will communicate with your superiors that this was a grave loss due to the stupidity of the First Realm kingdoms. You will do your best to persuade your superiors to not interfere with our lady's experiments here in the Beast Mountain Range. If you reveal this information, your strength will self-detonate. Now, sign."

The contract was put before Juri's face with a knife. Gritting his teeth, he cut his finger on the knife and pressed it to the contract, binding him.

Pan Kun rode through the Hunter Frontier, seeing the destruction, ad hoc tents, and the dead laying everywhere.

He looked at the two camps that formed up on either side of the road leading to the Beast Mountain Range.

The dead were tossed into mass graves while those that surrendered had signed binding contracts before being fed the antidote from large pots and put to rest in large open tents.

It looked like one massive field hospital.

Nasreen rode up with her advisors. "Sir!"

"Nasreen, how are things?"

"They have all surrendered. Some have already recovered and are eating to build their strength. Lukas went out with ten thousand of his people to the camp."

A bird screeched in the sky and headed for the arm of Nasreen's advisor. He fed the bird and passed the message to Nasreen.

"Good. Mages and construction crews will arrive soon to build defensive towers. In the meantime, organize the people, mix the groups up from different kingdoms. Have any families reunite and work out who has family and who does not. I want to know who everyone is and what their skills are."

"Sir?"

"The Beast Mountain Range is expanding. Veli and Donner led their forces to capture their attacking armies and camp followers as well. For the first time, we'll own land beyond the Beast Mountain Range to farm and harvest with towns and cities to support them."

"Sounds like a lot of land to cover," Nasreen warned.

"We won't be covering it all right away. And it's a good thing that we're looking to hire more members into the Beast Mountain Range Army."

"Still have to train up the guards from the different outposts, and our animal problem is getting worse."

"Land of opportunity, Miss Fayad. We're just here to keep the peace, protect the people, and keep the roads clear."

"I'm feeling tired already." Nasreen grinned.

"You did good; the army did good. Forty thousand against four hundred thousand fighters. Ten to one and we kicked their damn asses."

"Most of them were farmers and peasants thrown into service."

"Yes, but who else will be able to pull a force like that together?"

51 Ascend

Niemm opened the door to Erik and Rugrat's shared office. The duo had one in Vuzgal, another in Alva's dungeon headquarters, and this, the third, inside the command center that commanded Alva's military forces across the ten realms.

Like all of them, this one had papers stacked to one side of the desk.

Erik opened one eye mid-way through rubbing his face.

"You ready to go?" Niemm asked.

"How are the preparations looking?" Erik finished rubbing his face and stood, stretching.

"Towers are going up along the new border staffed by the army with a few of the Willful Institute's mana cannons defending King's Hill. The former outpost lords are getting used to their new positions. People are returning to their outposts. Those that surrendered and clear their trials are being sent to the outposts to work on farms and other tasks they're suited for."

"Five days sure do change things." Erik sighed. "First Realm secured. Now we need to direct all our energies toward Vuzgal."

"Are you sure about this?"

"I remained down here one, to help out, and two, to be here in case shit went sideways. Now I'm not needed, and things are well in hand. I'm doing paperwork that other people can do."

Erik walked out of the door with Niemm. The rest of his team was waiting. They fell into position, heading up and out of the Alva command center. Glosil and Yui were waiting at the gate out of the camp.

"Good work, both of you, supporting the people of Beast Mountain Range and training up the army. They might never know what you and your people did for them, but I will."

"Thank you, sir," Commander Glosil said. "Your performance with Evernight. Do you think it will stop the Institute from coming to the First Realm?"

"I'm not sure if it will. But it might confuse things at the very least. I guess we'll just have to make sure that we give the Willful Institute something bigger to focus on. Egbert is building formations to cover the entire territory of the Beast Mountain Range. With them, we'll be able to hide our presence completely, enough so that we can activate the drill again. It is an advantage we can't let go of."

The two men nodded.

"Colonel Yui, I will be waiting for your Tiger Regiment and Second Division of the reserves in Vuzgal."

"Yes, sir. We'll be there," Yui said.

Erik shook both of their hands and left the camp behind. Outside the totem's defenses, Storbon and his team were geared up and waiting. Erik took the lead with Niemm and Storbon behind him. Walking to the totem pad, the rest of the special teams checked their gear one last time. A screech came from the skies as Gilly flew over the defenses; she shrank and banked, landing on Erik's shoulders.

He pulled on his armored vest and opened and closed his gloves, feeling the power surging through his body. "Egbert, Fourth Realm please!"

"See you later, Lord West!"

In a flash of light, they appeared in a new city. They paid their tolls and headed for the warehouse district, where they joined a convoy of traders.

"Off we go!" The leader of the convoy said as the carts rolled away from the warehouse district and toward the gates.

There were more guards than usual with the convoy, but it was the Fourth Realm, and bandits were part of a trader's life.

Erik breathed easier as they left the city.

They rode for a few hours before coming to a bridge across a stream.

Mages used spells, causing the forest a few yards back from the road to open and reveal a new path. The carriages continued, the trees closing behind them as if waves were forming and collapsing around the convoy.

Erik watched the ground open, creating a ramp into darkness.

The lead cart ran over a teleportation formation plate, disappearing in a flash as the next followed.

They don't even blink about it anymore.

Darkness consumed them as the ramp down to the teleportation formation rose, once again becoming a part of the forest above.

With the flash of teleportation, the light of Vuzgal's busy under-city greeted Erik.

Vuzgal City is under attack!
Stats buffed: 15% Enemy stats decreased by 10%

Erik guessed that, being the city lord, there was no way for him to turn down the defense of the city.

He dismissed the screen, rolling with the cart toward the bunker complex when he heard a familiar voice.

"Erik! How was the vacation?" Rugrat yelled as the cart kept on moving.

"Thanks for the ride," Erik said to the driver.

"Any time, My Lord." The man grinned.

Erik snorted and jumped off the carriage.

Rugrat walked over with Roska's team. The two hugged.

"You look like shit," Erik commented.

"You look like you're twelve without a beard."

"Look who's talking!" The two fist bumped as the Special Teams greeted one another.

"I heard that you pissed off the enemy commander." Erik turned aside with Rugrat.

Rugrat opened his arms and shrugged. "Well, not my fault he's more on the sensitive side."

Erik laughed. "Fuck, feels good to be here, man."

"How're things down south?"

"All good, just what I sent in the reports," Erik said.

"Don't worry, you'll get plenty of chances to shoot at something up here. Glad you took that, man, I'd be up the fucking wall, bored. Come on.

Domonos is waiting, probably trying to figure out his retirement plans now that we're both here."

Erik laughed as Rugrat turned to the others.

"Fall in for the briefing. You've got your old quarters."

"Don't worry. We only took the best spots," Roska assured.

"Four teams in one city. Shit." Storbon laughed.

"Four teams? Hell, two fucking dungeon lords. I'm scared," Niemm added.

"Fucking kids these days." Rugrat gestured as he led the way.

"I know. they grow up so fast and steal all of our tricks."

"Welcome to Vuzgal, the Willful Institute's greatest and latest pain in the ass."

"Gonna need some hemorrhoid cream soon," Rugrat quipped.

Domonos smiled and pointed at the map. "Their forces have swelled, with near two hundred thousand in fighters, and forty- five thousand in aerial fighters spread out across their camps." He circled the W of camps facing Vuzgal. "From the left to the right we've got secondary camps one to four, main camp in the middle. Then secondary camps six to nine. Forces are split up among them, but most of the aerial forces are held in the secondary camps one and nine.

"Some people call them Parrot City, one on the left, and Bird House on the right, formerly known as secondary camp one and nine. Forecast is rain and thunderstorms in this area all day every day." Domonos circled the area in front of Vuzgal. "Otherwise, we have cold days and colder nights. Winter's coming, but that doesn't matter much to you body-tempered freaks."

The special team members chuckled as he continued.

"We've got three layers of defenses. The largest and farthest out is area one, or as we call it, the soup. Whole area is a bog with the constant rain feature. The soup is our special mess. Undead mages go around swirling it up and casting trap spells. Even if the enemy creates hardened ground, it'll eventually get wiped out. Even if they can get through the soup's traps, they have to come back through them if they retreat." Domonos cleared his throat and tapped the second area.

"Area two is Deadman's Fields. Major Hill here had a troubled childhood, loves digging holes and sharpening rocks."

Major Hill smiled, getting nods of appreciation from his fellow warriors.

"Holes and trenches of all shapes and sizes, trending from the small to the large all throughout the area. The enemy has taken to creating different bridges across our fields. We don't much like that, so we like to play a game of fuck your bridge. Most effective bridges are growing bridges, using plant life to span the area and cross after it. We made the ground wavy with ups and downs between the trenches. They seesaw side to side, up and down. Otherwise, they came up with a new bridge. Major Hill?"

"Sir, we call it the ballista bridge. Two ballistae are fired into Deadman's. They have cables attached to them, between the cables are wooden slats. They wheel in the fired ballistae, hooking them into the edge of a trench. Then they run up these bridges with barriers. Can get a few hundred meters in. Once they secure ahead, they use these ballista bridges to cover our fields." Hall stepped back and looked at Domonos.

"I don't much like them covering our beautiful fields. Grass needs blood to grow and these fuckers are *smart.* Been testing us for weeks now. Last area is Scarecrow's Hill. There was a going out of business sale with concertina wire phosphorus metal and some dangerously unstable explosives from the alchemy department, so we thought we'd make an art installation. Even if they destroy the spells, they won't stop the alchemy.

"Wire runs through the entire area, added in pitfalls and trenches, layered with traps, explosives. We let the squads go wild with their imaginations and they did not disappoint. That is the situation beyond the wall. Inside..." Domonos tapped ahead of the castle complex.

"Association's Circle hasn't gone anywhere; they're sitting up on their roofs and watching the show. We have limited their movements in the city and closed off the dungeons as we're using them ourselves for power generation and management. Workshops, Battle Arena, fields in the valley, they have access. Everything else is us."

"Bunkers?" Erik asked.

"We've added some new ones, but no real change in their placement. Machine gun nests are focused on the leading edge and dotted around the place. Mortars and cannons make up the second line and are the first line on the valley flanks. Heavy artillery cannons are in the rear. We've not been using spells, just weapon systems at this time, with the exception of the regular cannons. We are set to tier two weapons, use of mortars and explosives. The air force's bombs, stack and interlocking formations are allowed. No rifles or machine guns.

"We have also been limiting the weapons we use," Rugrat said.

"Yes, one hundred cannons and twenty mortars. We use the same ones so they don't know what the other bunkers house. We haven't been using the repeaters either. That used to be over half of our cannons and mortars. With the reserves, we have seven hundred manned cannons and two hundred mortars."

"So, what do you need from us?" Erik asked.

"You and Rugrat are our nukes. The teams are our quick reaction force. Now we'll have two teams always close to the frontline. We'll put you in these towers, nineteen one-one and twenty-two eleven, just back from the front. CPD is an immediate quick reaction. Anything happens they can't handle, it's over to you. Also, you'll have aerial mounts and undead support. Erik and Rugrat, one of you will be on the line and the other at the rear doing whatever you want with the two other special teams. Just be close to the castle compound if needed."

"Got it." Erik nodded, looking at Niemm and Storbon, who nodded as well.

"Our mission is to hold. Once the Second Division of reservists are trained, they will move to support us under the Tiger Regiment. The teleportation formations have lain dormant, and we intend to use them to our advantage. We will hit them from the rear, smash their camps and force them into the open. Then we'll hammer them with all we've got and drive them off. We don't need to defeat the Willful Institute here. We just need to break their alliance. Without it, they won't have supply routes and they won't have the extra bodies."

Domonos looked at the men and women of the special teams. "You will all be part of that assault. This is no First Realm skirmish. These people are strong, and they have plenty of their own tricks. Do not underestimate them or they will give you a bloody nose. Expect them to be as strong as you, if not stronger. We've had a lot of cultivation training and gained a lot of levels. It does not make you gods. We're only in the Fourth Realm. There are six more realms above us. Understood?"

"Sir." Everyone responded.

"Good. All right, that is all I have for you. Lieutenant Colonel Zukal should have given you a rotation schedule?"

He looked around as Roska held up her hand with a list.

"Good, and welcome to Vuzgal, ladies and gentlemen." He nodded to them and headed out of the room to the command center.

"Okay, listen up," Roska said. "We'll be operating in duos. Team one and team three will be working together, as well as two and four. Change up our dance partners. We will switch each rotation between the towers so we know the layout of everything. Don't want to have to figure shit out in the middle of a fight. We've all been here before. Team leads on me. Rest of you, get your gear stowed. Teams One and Three, we will be heading out to the front towers tonight, so three hours to relieve Team Two, which is on watch right now."

The teams dispersed as Erik and Rugrat waited with the other team leaders.

"I heard that both of the lords are here now!" Acosta heard one of her corporals saying to his friends as she passed him on the way to the leadership tables.

She nodded to a few leaders and sat down opposite Meehan, who was reading a book as he ate.

His eyes flicked up with a grunt as he kept eating. "You hear about the First Realm?"

"There anything else anyone is talking about?" Acosta said.

"Nope."

"Yeah, I heard. Three hundred and seventy-five thousand massive fricking army steam-rolled. Lost twenty percent to the fighting or wounds, another fifteen percent lamed unless they get treated. Rest of them hit with poison to stop them."

"Better they use the poisons than fight them on the roads."

"A mercy to some." Lieutenant Meehan shrugged, throwing more food back.

"You think it's wrong?" Acosta asked.

"Do you?"

"Doesn't sit well with me. I understand it, but..."

"But we're stronger than them. We could've subdued them. Act like the adults and they're the children?" Meehan snorted. "They came to kill our people and steal our shit. We used poison and a lot of them died. But shit, if we fought them straight up, we'd have killed a lot more. Saved more than we killed, and they're the fucking enemy. They tried to go toe to toe. The Beast Mountain Army put them in their place."

"You hear that people think Erik is going to cook up some new poison here?"

"I doubt it. Down there, it might work. There are few people that know about poisons. Up here, people are poisoning one another all the time and alchemists make a lot of money from poisons. They know the lord is an alchemist; we have an academy full of them."

"Yeah." Acosta took a bite of her meal.

"Bets are going around about seeing the lords fight." Meehan grinned.

"One another?"

"No, course not. Why'd they do that?"

"They need to spar sometimes. Not many others they can fight with safely."

"Didn't think of that. But no, the bet is if they'll get a chance to fight against the pricks outside our walls." Meehan tossed his head in its direction, grabbing more food.

Acosta finished what she was chewing on. "I don't think they can get the lords to go full power. We're not even using all of our weapons right now and we're still at level two."

A siren went off. People stood up and started running for the doors.

"Fuck, I just sat down!" Acosta shovelled a few more mouthfuls down. Meehan did the same, marking his page in his book and tucking it into a cargo pocket as they ran with their mouths full.

"Probably just another tester attack."

People pulled on their combat gear as they used the teleportation formations to shoot off across Vuzgal to their stand-to positions.

"Maybe, never know which one will be real!"

Erik and Special Team Three were on watch when the attack started.

"They used to come in from all different directions. Now they group up and drive through the soup in one direction. Takes them longer, but they can clear an entire path. They think they're out of the range of our guns," Gong Jin informed them.

"What will they do once they reach Deadman's fields?"

"Spread out along the trenches and start making their bridges. The more spread out they are, the harder it is for us to crack their individual barriers and get the people underneath."

"Looks like they're getting smarter," Gong Jin muttered.

"How so?"

"See those people at the end wandering along the hardened earth?"

"Yeah?"

"They must be looking for new spell traps and maintaining their passage."

"Give them a route to retreat or push supplies up through." Erik held his chin watching the slow work of the two sects.

"If it turns into anything, let me know." Gong Jin turned back and headed for the rest of the special teams who were sitting around finding something to do with their time.

52
Ripples

"Those idiots." Mercy tossed the scroll to Niklaus.

Niklaus raised an eyebrow in question and read the scroll.

He shook his head, and read from the scroll.

"Idiots! Spineless idiots!" Mercy put one leg over the other in frustration. "The kingdoms were useless. They couldn't even take an outpost! At least we found out how useless they were before any of them joined our ranks! Can you imagine what would have happened?"

"What do you want me to do?" Niklaus asked.

"Focus on the campaigns here. It looks like the Silaz family was close to Chonglu. They lived in his city. They could be the ones that protected his life, seeing as they were able to ascend and gain power. The secrets are hidden in Vuzgal. Once Marco can crack the city, we'll find out just what they're hiding. We need to take as many cities as possible before we are told to go to the First Realm again. When we do, I want to make sure that no damn sickness takes out our army."

"Yes, Mercy."

"Niklaus, capture this city quickly. The faster we move, the better."

"Yes, My Lady." Niklaus bowed. His eyes flickered to the two men behind Mercy that she had tamed.

He walked out of the tent.

Through the flap, Mercy saw siege weapons attacking the grand city's walls, its barrier looking shaken and weak. Spells and cannon fire flew overhead into the defenses while they, in turn, fired back at the encroaching armies.

This is only our third city. There are still many more to capture.

Esther found her uncle sitting in his workshop, looking at the flintlock. This one didn't have the formations and carvings. It was worn, tired, and old. The treated wood had been rubbed smooth over time.

Was that the one her uncle had entered the Ten Realms with?

"Come to sneak into my workshop again, Little One?" Edmond Dujardin didn't miss a beat as he used oil to lubricate the weapon, working the action.

"I didn't want to interrupt you, Uncle."

Edmond turned around with a light smile on his lips. "What new information do you have for me?"

"You are invited to an auction of rare goods by the Blue Lotus. The Alchemist Association wants to talk about the ingredient order you put in, and one of the younger generations of the Raj family was dishonored in a match."

"Which Raj?"

"Talem."

"That boy needs to learn some manners. Are they doing anything about it?"

"They are preparing to offer a challenge to the family that beat him."

"The opponent's family?"

"The young man's family is from the lower realms and do not have much. Their son has great ability."

Edmond's gaze tightened. "Tell the Raj family this will be a good lesson for their son, and I will not let them kill people just because they're embarrassed."

"Yes, Uncle." Esther paused. "Vuzgal has held their position. We do not know what they are doing within the city, but powerful fighters from the Sixth Realm have attacked them repeatedly to test their defenses. They have been rebutted with heavy casualties every time."

"Interesting. What do you think? You went to the city."

"It was an interesting place. I did not think they would last long against a force so powerful."

Edmond played with his thin, but well-maintained, moustache. "If we send aid, then we show our hand. We would need assurances from Vuzgal." He paused. "Have the Associations started to mediate?"

"They have, but it fell apart almost immediately. The lord of Vuzgal sent a message to the attacking commander that upset him."

"Idiots and their pride." Edmond sighed.

53 Feint

"Here they come," Gong Jin announced.

A flash of a half-formed spell appeared in front of the enemy formation.

He and Erik were in their defensive tower, back from the front lines. Erik used binos to study the enemy. Flags depicted different factions in each sect as Fighters from different camps formed up beyond the gates, on their march toward Vuzgal.

Rain and lightning covered their path. The enemy mana barriers flared when lightning struck. The rain couldn't be stopped. Fighters hunkered down against the constant deluge, soaked to the bone in minutes. Mages hardened the ground and searched for spell traps.

The flash had been them destroying a spell trap.

"They look pleased." Erik chuckled.

"Their barriers will probably hold up, but it'll take some time for them to get across." Gong Jin slumped into a chair and yawned.

Erik watched, studying them wandering around. It took nearly three hours before the enemy showed any signs of speeding up.

They reached Deadman's fields and spread out as fast as possible.

Cannons fired.

Fuck, that's a lot of firepower.

They lit up the main mana barrier and new ones popped up as groups activated their own.

Bridges extended over the trenches as mortars landed. They struck the leading edge of the barriers like rain on an umbrella.

The approaching sects worked quickly, extending their bridges and testing them before they pushed up. Remaining under their barriers, their bridges quickly progressed.

"I think they'll make it to Scarecrow," Erik said.

"They must be using those strong barriers again. Shit burns through mana stones like water in the desert. Thank you for your mana stones!"

Erik snorted and shook his head, watching the fighting.

"Why don't they use magic on Deadman's? Long range?"

"The mana gathering formations would literally eat the spell apart." Gong Jin shrugged.

Erik let out a low whistle, watching the enemy's advance over the bridges. A barrier went out, the attacks landing among the bridges, sending dozens down into the sharpened stone lining the walls and bottom of the pit.

They crossed their bridges, using a patchwork of different methods.

The barrier reached the edge of Deadman's as a group of fighters reached the barbed wire extravaganza.

Mortars struck among the barbed wire. The leading fighters were cut down in a hail of shrapnel. The barrier pulled back, no longer touching Scarecrow Hill's boundary.

"What the hell?

"Barbed wire fucks with the barrier, leaves gaps in it. Can't get full coverage. You need somewhat flat ground and no obstacles for a barrier to work correctly. Great for defense, but shitty for offense."

"And the barbed wire is still there. Shit, I can't even imagine how much hell that must've been in World War One."

"The one with trenches, right?" Gong Jin asked.

"Yeah, sorry. Earth references."

"No worries, man. I've already pulled some info out of you Earthers. World War One was where people were fighting one another from trenches. They had artillery, rifles, the first machine guns. Barbed wire was used all over the place."

"Yeah, and tens of thousands died in a day because, to take the other guy's trench, you had to run across the open ground, then jump into the opposite trench and kill them."

"Not too different here, but we've got barriers," Gong Jin said.

"Yeah, and they keep on throwing the people at us."

"And we keep sending bodies back."

People at the edge of Deadman's used spells against the barbed wire. Explosions tore through the area. Sometimes, entire sections of barbed wire went up. Sections were inert so the whole area wouldn't go up in one shot.

Sometimes they'd advance only to have the remnants of the obstacles explode. It was impossible to destroy it completely.

"They're not using their spells on the stone and metal anymore," Erik said.

Erik held out his binos as Gong Jin turned around. "Thank you." He looked at the fields.

"Well, they're not as stupid as they look. Shit. They can stay protected under their barrier, pushing forward slowly, and have mages and spell scrolls cut into our defenses. Be slow work and costs a lot," Gong Jin spat and passed Erik the binos again.

Erik watched the mages working together to figure out the best system to overcome the defenses. Runners grabbed sliced concertina wire using their storage rings.

A trap went off inside the barrier under a group of mages, taking out the bridge they were on. The others behind them yelled as they dropped to the spikes below.

"What was that about spell traps on the bits of ground that remain in Deadman's?" Erik asked.

"The Colonel has a plan for that. He wants to put traps up that will only activate if a person goes over them. That way, if someone runs over on a bridge, suddenly the bridge and the people on it aren't our problem anymore. He's holding it as a trump card."

"I'm hoping we can use them sometime, but shit is seriously fucked up if we have to," Erik said.

"Like if they let you fight?" Gong Jin smiled.

Erik shrugged. "Not like you aren't eager to get in on the action. Now we're all a quick reaction force. Not even in the rotation on the cannons."

"I'm working on my euchre game."

The two of them snorted.

"You any good?"

"Nah, absolute shit."

Erik laughed.

"Fuck, well good thing you've got some time to practice."

Rugrat spotted Qin, Tanya, and Tan Xue sharing a table in the cafeteria, and altered his path to sit next to Qin.

"Hey," she said, stifling a yawn as she went back to her food.

"How you all doing?" he asked. They looked exhausted.

"Tired. We've been running around repairing what the Sects are breaking," Tan Xue said.

"You sleeping at all?"

"Here and there. Just a lot of work to be done," Tan Xue admitted. "All the students that call Vuzgal home and nearly all the teachers stayed behind. We've been throwing ourselves into work."

"Where's Julilah at?"

"She headed down to the First Realm again. Don't want to have the two of us together. Redundancy," Qin said.

Rugrat grimaced but nodded, scooping up his potatoes and vegetables.

"It's led to a massive number of upgrades and a lot of new ideas. Now the crafters are seeing not just their abilities used in the real world, but the effect of what they've created," Tan Xue told him.

"All of this wouldn't be possible without everyone working together." Rugrat waved with his spoon at the bunker complex they were entombed in.

"What about the Adventurer's Guild, the Wayside Inns, and Sky Reaching Restaurants?" Tanya asked.

"The Adventurer's Guild is in our backup dungeons training. Blaze and Jasper will be telling them some of the truth. That they're not just another guild with no backing and have connections to Vuzgal. Not the full truth, but close enough," Rugrat said.

"The Wayside Inns and the Sky Reaching Restaurants have a lot of people working in them who aren't Alvan. A few of our people are still operating them. They are a core part of the intelligence department and they generate a massive amount of income. They've been able to keep everything operating during this time," Tan Xue said. "Is the fighting in the First Realm going well?"

"You don't get out much, do you?" Rugrat asked.

Qin gave him a side-look as she ate her food.

Rugrat smiled and cleared his throat. "We won. Took over the forces that attacked us and bound them up with contracts. The Willful Institute ran off. They're too busy attacking sects in the Second and Third Realms. They've reclaimed ten cities and captured six more. Gathered more support. They look to be coming out of this stronger than before."

"Isn't the Adventurer's Guild fighting them?" Tan Xue asked.

"We pulled them back so they wouldn't get stuck in the middle. Right now, the lower realms are getting stirred up; peace is crumbling."

"Won't we have to deal with that as well?"

"Everything with time. Have to deal with our current problems first," Rugrat reminded them.

"Won't the Alchemist Association tell them to stop fighting in the third realm?"

"As long as the associations are left out of it, the rest of us can fight as much as we want." Rugrat tried to keep his disgust out of his face. From their expressions, he'd failed.

"They keep things stable for the most part," Qin said softly.

"I know, reminds me this place isn't like Earth."

"No, on Earth, people don't wage wars because everyone has weapons that could wipe out all life," Tanya said.

"Created the longest period of peace."

"They just found how to fight one another without weapons. Money, position, and other nations without those weapons," Tanya said. "The associations are the Ten Realms' Nukes and the treaties that kept Earth tied together."

Rugrat didn't really see it that way, hoping it was just because people were decent instead of scared that they would get wiped out.

"While I'm angry with them, I can't deny that they do look out for their own people. That shows there's some good in them."

Marco finished outlining his plan of attack and stood up straight, looking at the army commanders that ringed the map.

"I'm sorry I didn't tell you about this plan earlier. Vuzgal has a powerful ability to find out what we are doing. I didn't even tell my own people. The testing attacks I've had your people carry out over the last several weeks have been to test our mana barriers, tactics, and scout the ground for the best routes through the obstacles ahead of us. Now we have accumulated the knowledge, weapons, and the forces that we need to act."

"The plan is simple but thorough, using our regular testing attacks as a lead-up to the true attack. What I don't understand is why we didn't siege them beforehand?" a severe-looking commander asked.

"We've tested their mana barrier with our cannons and different ranged siege weapons. Vuzgal's barrier formation is one of the strongest I have ever seen, and they have the mana stones required to power it."

"Our crafters studied it. They believe the formation has reached the level where it uses the external mana of the area to reinforce itself. It's completely balanced in the environment it lays in," another commander added.

"Attacking the barrier would be a waste of our resources. We must get past their barriers to inflict casualties," Hae Woo-Sung said, backing up Marco.

"We haven't tested their aerial capabilities yet. We know that they have them from the advance, but we haven't engaged them head-on," another commander said.

"We will have one test attack in the air. Your people better learn fast," Marco informed them.

The different commanders looked at the map and markings, trying to picture it all.

"We have much to do to make sure that everything works. Let's get to work. Vuzgal awaits us, ladies and gentlemen." Marco turned and left the room with the Willful Institute's master teachers at his back.

The room shifted as commanders talked to one another or headed off to pass on orders.

"What do you think our odds are?" Feng Dan asked once the door to the private suite was secured.

"Eighty percent if we catch them off guard. I know there is more in those defensive buildings, but they only have a few thousand fighters. They can't cover the entire city. Even if we can take over the skies, we can't take out their defensive structures. But we can fly our fighters in to create chaos in their rear. We *must* control the skies, or this plan will fall apart. The ground forces are there to lock up their people into defending."

"Well, we have four hours to prepare. We shouldn't waste it." Onam scratched the right side of his scalp before running his hand through his mohawk.

Acosta checked her watch.

"Come on! The enemy is eight hundred meters and closing. They're from the Fourth Realm. They can reach you in a few minutes!" Sirel yelled as the reserve mortar team worked to bring the gun to the ready.

"Hang!" the team leader yelled as the ammunition bearer held a dud round above the barrel of the mortar.

Acosta checked the time, watching the other two teams finish at nearly the same time.

Sirel walked over.

"A minute and a minute and a half," she said into his ear.

"You want to, or want me to?"

"I'll take a crack at it."

"Yes, ma'am."

Sirel turned back, all the heat directed at the gun teams who were looking at him and Acosta nervously.

"Stand by your guns!" Acosta yelled, holding her hands behind her as she walked in front of the guns.

They assembled, twitching nervously.

"It is the role of the artillery platoon to support the actions of units in the field. We are not on the front line, but that does not make our job any less vital. If you are on the frontline, the support we provide can mean the difference between life and death! This practice will hone what you were taught in basic training. Make sure that you pay attention."

Her expression twisted as she stopped walking and turned to face them all; her eyes scanned them.

"You all did well in your training. You earned the right to be here. But that does not give you the right to strut around and be assholes now. Yes, there is inter-unit rivalry, which can be healthy and lead to lasting bonds between one another. Being an asshole just means you're an asshole." She didn't single out anyone but saw eyes turning toward a few among their ranks.

"As a reservist, you have learned one job, one task: how to be a member of an artillery platoon. It takes a lot of resources and time for people to get to this position in the regular force." Her tone was conversational, disappointed even. "To reach this same stage in the reg force, if they had come in early, they might have just taken the same course as you. But they trained in other roles before they were allowed to progress. For organizational reasons, you have been given the rank of Specialist Corporals and Specialist Sergeants.

"Your training is specialized, more advanced than what riflemen and scouts would learn, yes. *But—*" The word came out like falling bricks "—You *do not* have the training or experience of people in the reg force who have earned the true rank. A sergeant has done the training of rifleman, scout, mortar team and mage! You can give him a compass and he can cross a continent. Give him a rifle and he'll take your nose hair off at five hundred meters. Give him a mortar and he can run the entire damn thing by himself, if you give him coordinates. He can call down the power of the Ten Realms and sow destruction. He can also lead a squad of riflemen and scouts, be a second-in-command of a mortar squad and team leader of a three-man mortar team."

Silence fell in the bunker.

"Respect the men and women around you. That is what the rank is for, to show that you have earned the respect of others. That others put you forward for a promotion based upon your skills. Do not use it against others! If someone is out of line, deal with them. If you are having a fucking pissing contest..." Acosta's expression made some shoulders rise. "I will personally take you through every damn qualification course to adjust your damn mindset so you will know what it is to not just earn your qualification but your rank."

The silence was deafening.

"You are good at mortars, but you are not yet the best, so we will make you the best. We are Alvans and we produce the best. Am I understood?"

"Yes, sir!" The bunker rang.

"Good."

The siren went off.

"Stand to!" Sirel yelled. "Looks like we'll be putting your skills to the test for real today!"

"I'm heading to command," Acosta yelled to Sirel.

"Yes, sir!"

Acosta ran out of the rear of the bunker, opening and closing the thick metal bunker door.

She ran down the stairs and into the tunnels. Other people were rushing back and forth, running up the stairs to their assigned bunkers.

The tunnels were numbered, marking their grid location, but they were thrown together like someone had tossed wooden beams on the ground in no semblance of order.

She ran up the right side of the stairs to the command center, two at a time.

"Make a hole!" she yelled, hearing people coming down.

She passed members of her platoon who rushed down the stairs behind her. She opened the bunker's sealed door to see the remains of a card game and a book turned over in the ready room.

She closed the door and entered the command center.

"Report!" she yelled, feeling her heartbeat starting to calm down.

"They're gathering forces for another test." Staff Sergeant Neumann stepped away from the periscope.

She put her eyes to it, seeing the forces pouring out of the main camp as well as secondary camps four and six on either side.

"We've got movement in all the camps coming out to watch."

"Twisted pricks, aren't they?" Acosta muttered. She looked at the other camps. Fighters moved to the walls to watch.

"Learn what worked and what didn't," Neumann said.

Acosta grunted.

"Have all guns readied and checked. Make sure that they're set. I want to be the first with effective rounds on target."

"Yes, sir."

Acosta let the periscope go and went into the right observation room. The enclosed room looked out over the defenses through a slit in the wall. Mounted viewing glasses and a mount for a repeater were the only things in the room.

The mounted viewing glasses gave her a greater field of view. She studied the different camps before peering out through the slit at the other bunkers. She couldn't see into the darkness. Special formations made it hard to see in but were fine to look out.

She sighed, gathering herself and clearing her mind. "Okay, let's do this."

She took another glance at the enemy formations before walking back inside.

"Okay, looks to me like the secondary camps are going to rally up on the main camp units before they attempt the soup."

"Agreed," Neumann said.

"In ten minutes, if there is no change or they are just advancing, we'll step down to seventy-five percent. We have a threat assessment from higher?"

"No change."

"Stand-to," Niemm said.

Rugrat stood and stretched.

"How goes the world?" He approached Niemm, who was watching the oncoming enemy through binos.

"They just made it through the soup." Niemm held out the binos.

"Yup, right down what was the road. Gonna be a bitch to fix that," Rugrat grumbled.

"The path behind them, the mages, aren't they a bit spread out?"

Rugrat watched the trailing mages who had the job of keeping the ground clear of traps and solid for the withdrawal.

"Hmm, yeah." Rugrat focused the binos more. "Their mana barriers are some of the stronger ones. Pain in the ass to crack and we only get one person. Whoever is leading this is... What are *you* doing?"

Rugrat looked at a mage as a trap spell, away from the path they had taken into the soup went off.

He studied more, watching the mages. His frown turned grim. "Niemm, you good to relay a message to higher?"

"Ready."

"Mages are thicker along the road. They are pushing out to either side, expanding it to much larger than what they had before."

"Message sent. What are you thinking, boss?"

Rugrat lowered the binos. "I'm wondering why they need so much space."

"You think this is it?"

"A real attack? We'll have to watch and wait."

Rugrat passed the binos back and pulled out his own as he whistled.

George was lying on the roof in his small form and glanced around blearily before Rugrat whistled again. He bounded off the roof. His wings snapped out as he wheeled around and landed on the railing Rugrat and Niemm were leaning on.

Rugrat watched and waited.

"Pushing pretty aggressively into Scarecrow, aren't they?" Rugrat asked.

"Seems they brought a lot of mages and people with fighting techniques to cut that deep in."

Attacks were raining down on the enemy barriers, making them flare with mortar and cannon fire. At the same time, the mages and fighters inside the barrier were attacking the defenses, cutting up the wire and posts that would explode randomly. Once they cleared around the barrier, they advanced.

A barrier faltered and failed. Some turned and ran, activating secondary barriers.

"I hate how quick they're getting at doing that shit," Rugrat muttered.

Mortar and cannon fire killed some and savaged the bridges.

Another barrier started to fail, and they threw up a second mana barrier before the first could collapse completely.

"Victor Zero Actual to all command units, be advised movement has been spotted at Parrot City and Bird's Nest. Prepare fire plan Bravo. I say again…" Domonos repeated his message.

Rugrat glanced at Parrot City. Towers had risen out of the camps with the arrival of more aerial forces. They filled with activity as a group took off from the different towers.

"I've got a bad feeling about this," Rugrat admitted.

"You and me both, boss. Get your gear ready!" Niemm yelled to the team.

Rugrat looked over to the air force's bases. The sparrows were ready and waiting in their hangars. Locked and loaded.

Close protection detail members moved to mount positions around the tower, ready to pull out their repeaters and mount them if needed.

"They're banking!" Niemm said.

The enemy aerial mounts turned in their groups toward Vuzgal. They flew along the mountains so the bunkers couldn't see them.

Sparrows rushed out of their hangars and over the formations, shooting up into the air in their formations. They circled as the first wing of eight turned into three wings, then five and nine.

Kestrels launched, patrolling Vuzgal.

"This is Victor Zero Actual. Fire Plan Bravo activated!" Domonos barked.

Rugrat pulled out a repeater as Niemm pulled off the weather cap on the mount.

Rugrat lowered it. Niemm made sure it lined up with the mount, and secured them with locking pins.

"Good! You're secure!"

Rugrat grabbed the charging lever and pulled back on it, looking through the aiming reticule as he swiveled from side to side.

"Good!"

All around the tower, repeaters were mounted and aimed into the skies.

The team moved to the covered stone balcony or went up to the roof, where more gun nests had been set up with clear views over the city.

Rugrat tracked the group coming in from Parrot City.

Too far for me to be sure.

"Niemm, keep a watch on those pricks down in Scarecrow." He cast air shot through the transfer plate to the bolts.

"On it!"

The aerial forces crossed through Vuzgal's mana barrier, unleashing attack after attack on the bunkers. Their own mana barriers easily dealt with the attacks.

Tower gunners fired, tracers weaving lines that exploded into black puffs of shrapnel.

Their fire halted as the sparrow wings dove, scattering the aerial forces as they tried to evade. The Sparrow wings side-mounted repeaters left black streaks across the sky, exploding flak rounds—modified air shot spells spraying out hundreds of air blades—raked the sect's aerial mounts, cutting them from the sky.

Spells were hurled back and forth between riders and mounts.

"Get some, mother fuckers!" Rugrat yelled. *Formations for the win, baby!*

Soldiers in the towers resumed firing.

"Coming into range!" Rugrat barked. The enemy was banking away, having lost a third of their force already. Their barriers had been smashed apart in the crossfire.

All the repeater gunners were watching. Rugrat's repeater mount squeaked as he adjusted his aim, sighted on the aerial force.

"Follow my trace!"

Rugrat's dual repeater bucked, sending out twin streams of air shot-enhanced bolts.

The tower's gunners joined him. He was firing well ahead of the aerial forces. The air shots were like a swarm of flies through a fan, but the fan was the thing getting torn up.

Aerial beasts plummeted as their riders used every trick they had to get away from their impending doom.

The enemy cut out of the barrier, diving and running back toward their bases.

"Reload! Must've been a test."

"I'm not so sure. They're opening their gates.

"Fuckers. Tell higher! Go linked!"

Rugrat reached to the ground, grabbing a bolt feeder. He pulled the magazine off, hooked the bolt feeder on, secured it with latches, and moved to the other side.

"Aerial forces are mobilizing!" Niemm yelled.

"This is not our fucking day," Rugrat grumbled as the camps came to life. Formations of fighters marched out. Mounted forces rushed out of secondary camps four, six, and the main camp.

"Well, now we know why those mages were fucking about on the damn road!"

Rugrat turned his repeater from side to side, making sure that the belt feeders wouldn't get fucked up.

He cast spells on his eyes and his sight zoomed in as if he had flown through the air. He saw streaks in his vision as the cannons opened up. Seven hundred mana cannons fired straight into the mana barriers of those pushing into Scarecrow's fields.

The rolling thunder reached Rugrat as the enemy barriers fell in the dozens.

"Looks like they've been working on their aim," Rugrat yelled to Niemm.

"Target destroyed. Leave it to the repeater crew!" Sergeant Cao Jing yelled as the cannons started recharging.

Nicholas was looking through his own periscope, watching their cannon fire rake those under the barrier. Repeater bolts, glowing red with explosive shot, tore up the ground traversing side-to-side while also cutting deeper, the impacts throwing up mud and stone.

"New target! Drop fifty, minus forty degrees!"

Nicholas and his fellow scouts moved the gears next to the firing panel. The cannons shifted along the firing slit.

He could *feel* the other cannons firing across the defensive bunkers.

Sergeant Cao was watching the timer.

"Fire!"

The cannons bellowed again. Their grouping was tight. As it smashed into the barrier, it was struck by two other batteries before Nicholas'.

"Same target! Repeat!"

The timer ran out and they fired again. The cannon rocked the floor as it came back with a hot rush of air before pulleys and gears moved it back into place.

"Repeat!"

The barrier was taking a pounding.

More cannons focused onto it. Nicholas watched the barrier break under the attacks. The cannon's spells landed on the forces pushing into Scarecrow and in Deadman.

"Add one hundred, minus thirty! Landrith!"

"Sorry, Sarge!" Landrith pulled his eyes from the periscope, altering his point of aim.

The barrier around the bunker lit up with impacts.

Sergeant Cao looked through his periscope.

"Just the air force beating the piss out of their parrots! On task!" Sergeant Cao glanced at the timer.

"Fire!"

"Here comes their second wave. Rake them, break away, and maintain height. Whoever has the height and the speed wins! The kestrels will pick off anything that gets past us! There isn't anyone in the city to get hurt," Captain Wazny ordered as he banked hard, pushed into his harness. He leveled out, checking the rest of his wing right behind him. Not a feather was out of place.

"As long as we don't have to pay for damages!" Second Lieutenant Santos quipped.

"The lords have you covered. Come on. We've been sitting in the back for several weeks now. Let's show them that they shouldn't just fear us on the ground."

"For Nilsen," Lieutenant Lovren said.

"For Nilsen," Wazny agreed. "Follow me in and break on my command."

Wazny looked out to the other sparrows. Seeing the wings flying behind one another, he felt like the dominator of the skies.

"All sparrow wings, dive!"

The sparrows dropped, passing through the low-lying clouds that were being pulled into the massive lightning storm over the battlefield, picking up speed. They came from behind Vuzgal, crossing the aerial mounts that were flying from Bird City up over the mountains that butted up against Vuzgals' eastern flank. The bunkers, which were unleashing hell, provided cover while mounted forces rushed up the cleared path of what had been the main road.

The infantry was pushing into the soup, forging their own paths to Vuzgal's front.

This is it; it has to be. Get your fucking head in the game, Wazny.

He shook himself and studied his targets. Formations of different aerial beasts were doing everything they could to get over Vuzgal.

He blinked against the flash of a spell scroll being used in Vuzgal. It struck a tower's barrier that returned fire through lances of golden light.

Kestrel's door gunners banked their repeaters unleashing hell down on the aerial forces.

Hits appeared on the barrier around the heavy birds like moving fortresses. They were getting smashed but succeeding in drawing their attention away from the main fight and doing the most damage.

Wazny checked his aim as the wings separated.

"Shoot when you've got a target."

They spread out to keep from hitting one another on their gun run.

Shit.

The riders of the aerial mounts cast powerful spells. *They must be strong to cast spells that powerful with all of our mana gathering formations pumping that shit away.*

The wings opened and fired on the unsuspecting aerial mounts below.

Wazny's sparrow shook with the repeater's fire, the air shot creating clouds of expanding flack ahead of the sparrows.

"Break!" Wazny yelled.

They pulled up and broke apart. Mages from Bird House on their right fired at them, but they were too far away for the spells to do any damage.

Wazny's group reformed on him as they banked back and above the enemy formation that raked the defenses.

"Follow me down!"

Sparrow wings dove after the aerial mounts. The mages hurled spells into the sky. One attack made three sparrows' barriers flare alarmingly ahead of Wazny.

They tried to break off. Spells tracked them through the sky, breaking one barrier then another. The beasts and pilots were torn apart in a spray of wood and red mist.

"Wingman, wingman, wingman!"

They broke apart into their pairs. Santos stuck to Wazny like glue.

"Going heavy!" Wazny pulled on a spell scroll tab. A spell formation appeared under and in front of his sparrow's chest.

Mana was drawn in and fired out in mana blasts.

Wazny guided the mana blast over the mage that had killed the sparrows ahead of him. His shots struck the ground, tearing up buildings as the mage dodged and flung spells back. They were wild and wide. Wazny unleashed a stream of mana bolts breaking the mage's mana barrier sending him careening into the side of the building in a spray of debris.

Wazny shifted his aim and targeted the other riders with his mana blasts. Santos rained down air shot onto them, covering him as they tore up the rear of their group.

"Break! Break! Break!"

Wazny and Santos turned away, heading deeper into Vuzgal. Kestrels flew overhead, laying down heavy fire into the aerial mounts. Wazny fought to push higher and gain altitude.

"Captain, I think they're dropping off things at the edges of the city," Santos said.

"What things?"

"Yeah, I think they might be formations."

"You take lead, show me where. I want to confirm if they're dropping teleportation formations. This just got a lot more fucked."

He followed Santos. They were lower than he liked. If someone dived at them, they were fucked. *But we need to know.*

They were quiet against the fight that raged on their left flank as the front of Vuzgal unleashed her rage.

He saw a street. One of the building's roofs had caved in and rocks littered the street, half covering a big metal plate that lay upside down in the street.

"Ah, fuck."

"Sparrow Wing Alpha Three reports that the aerial forces could be dropping teleportation formation plates in the city."

"Activate the undead legion. Prepare to deal with attackers inside the city. Activate conqueror's armor. Company leaders have freedom to increase buff as needed." Domonos checked the map.

"The mounted forces have reached Deadman's field and are pushing on foot to Scarecrow," Hall reported.

"Traps activated in Deadman's?"

"Yes, sir. They're having a hell of a time, but they have people across into Scarecrow."

Domonos looked at a communications aide. "Have the undead focus on putting spell traps in Deadman's and Scarecrow. Give up on the soup."

"Sir!"

"What's happening with our cannons and mortars?"

"They're tearing up mana barriers, but they've been playing this game with us for weeks now. They're well spread out to reduce casualties. The mortars and cannons are focused on breaking the barriers. The repeaters are online and hitting the enemy that are not in cover."

"How are we doing in the air?" Domonos asked.

"We're tearing them a new one, but they have strong mages and a seemingly unending supply of spell scrolls. We just don't have the weight in numbers. My people are getting cut up by their massed fire. Not even the stack mana barriers can take that much punishment," Kanoa said.

"Release the undead aerial mages to assist."

"Yes sir."

"I want the towers reporting any formations that drop in Vuzgal. Have the Undead Legion go investigate and destroy any formations they find. If we start losing contact, send in the QRF primary."

"Yes, sir."

54

Feed the Beast of War

"Looks like they were hiding more than a few cannons," Eva Marino said from beside Marco.

"They have to have more than seven thousand inside the city. There are more than that in those repeaters alone. If we have teleportation formations, why shouldn't they? They've been getting support and reinforcements, but from who?"

"Something to figure out at the end of this all?" Marino asked.

"Yes, yes." Marco peered through the viewing glasses again.

Eva Marino received a report from a nearby aide. "The metal obstacles explode or burn randomly. A group dumped out the metal of a storage ring to understand it and it exploded, killing the crafters just minutes ago."

"More tricks," Marco growled, flashes illuminating his vision along his force's path. "They have forces jumping from the mana barrier towers. Must be the Undead. They used them in the fight against the Blood Demon Sect." Marco watched as they exchanged spells with his aerial forces. A few collapsed here and there, but they drove headfirst through the formation, flinging spells that made Marco feel a chill. "What?"

"Looks like they got some high-level undead," Marino muttered.

"Their aerial riders are well-trained and using all the same mounts."

"We have three teleportation formations live at the front."

"Push people through them as fast as possible. Have the aerial mounts focus their attacks on the crafter workshops!" Marco turned back to the battle. He had to win this. If they didn't, they wouldn't have the mana stones to teleport people forward. *Damn their mana gathering formations.* They must have been buried too deeply for their sensing scrolls to pick up.

"Our ground forces are making progress. If we win in the air, around the teleportation formations, or reach their gates with the armies, we'll change this battle." Marino said.

Spells and spellbound weapons flashed across the skies and ground. Barriers weathered the storm and pushed forward, sometimes failing as smaller barriers snapped up into existence, continuing forward.

Mounted riders teleported from the other camps to the main camp, charged out of the main gate, and down the cleared road, giving a clear path forward.

They pushed into the metal forest and spread out so that a single whistling attack or mana cannon blast didn't take them all out.

Spell traps flashed, taking out bridges, dropping people into the large trenches or killing those trying to clear the metal forest.

"Have the dismounted go through the teleportation pad. Have the mounted charge out of the bases to attack directly. We have them now; we just need to keep up the pressure." Marco smacked the table.

"Yes, lord!"

Now it is just a matter of bodies. Do we spend too many lives or bleed theirs?

"Report in from Vuzgal!" The command center went silent as Glosil looked up from the desk he was working at. "They are under attack by the enemy. They have employed aerial beasts to attack the city. Ground forces are pushing up into area three. Reports indicate that they're using teleportation formations dropped inside the city and new ones have been placed in area three."

Glosil stood and walked toward the map table, which showed Vuzgal. "Get me Colonel Yui and Guild Leader Blaze. I want all our people, including the Second Reserve Division, ready to move. I need situation reports and maps for what is happening along the entire valley. Inform Colonel Domonos that we intend to support."

The room turned to action.

It wasn't ten minutes later when Colonel Yui ran into the command center. "Sir!"

Glosil returned the salute. "Seems that they finally committed. Now it is our job to make sure that they regret it. How is the Second Division in your mind?"

"They're so new that they squeak, but they know how to use their weapons. I would count on them for simple maneuvers, nothing crazy."

"Then we'll have to rely on Tiger Regiment and the Adventurer's Guild. Get me Blaze now!"

"What are you thinking, sir?"

"I'm thinking that the enemy isn't the only ones with teleportation formations in the Vuzgal Valley. We need to move people through every damn route we have into the Fourth Realm yesterday."

Blaze read the summons and passed it to the rest of his branch heads. The message was short as they quickly passed it on to one another. Kim Cheol was the only other one sitting.

They walked right into our trap, and it's up to us to close it around them.

"Sir?" the messenger asked as he looked at the people in the room.

Blaze cleared his throat. "As Alva has trained us, supported us, and protected our families, the Adventurer's guild will heed the call. We will head to Vuzgal to support the Alva military in defeating the combined Sects. The Willful Institute committed, we'll close the trap."

"Yes, sir." The messenger took out his sound transmission device and started talking into it.

"Then we go to war," Kim said.

Blaze grimaced and opened his mouth. Kim raised his hand with a smile. "I might not make it for this battle. If I can help from the rear?" Kim's eyes shifted to Jasper.

"I could certainly use the help and you know more of our military capabilities than me." Jasper said.

Blaze nodded.

"Kim, you will be our liaison with the Alva military. The rest of you, begin mustering your people for the fight ahead. There is much to do."

"Undead have run into problems here. There are three suspected teleportation formations." Roska circled a section of the city on her map, showing her Special Team Two, Special Team Four and Erik.

They were on one of the side movers, a moving platform that rushed through the under city sideways instead of up and down.

"This will be our first target, but not the last. The aerial forces are dropping plates all over the place. We will move in, engage the enemy, figure out their displacement, and take momentum of the fight with suppressing fire. The team with the best cover and vantage will become the fire base. The other team will flank and drive through their flanks. Special Team Two will take the ground. Team Four, you're high and mighty. Erik?"

"I'll be with Team Four in support. Need to work on my tan and parkour."

"Yes, sir." Roska had a note of question in her voice.

Erik smiled. "And yes, I am allowed to use my complete power. We just have to make sure none of them can report about it."

The special teams glanced at one another and then Erik.

"Looking forward to it. Conqueror's armor is not buffing right now. If this shit goes sideways, I'll take us to one hundred percent. We're inserting east of the target. We'll be on foot to give us more mobility. Clear as mud?"

"Good to go," Storbon said as the others nodded and checked their gear.

They pulled their face-covering helmets down and secured them.

Erik buddy-checked Storbon. "Good to go. Comms check."

"You're loud and clear. Me?" Storbon said, turning Erik and checking his gear.

"Loud and clear."

Storbon ran his gloved hands over Erik's carrier, hitting his pouches and pulling on them before turning him around and repeating the process.

"Good!" He patted Erik's shoulder.

Erik pulled out his repeater, loading it.

Roska walked over to them. "We'll take control of the undead in the area. Make sure you have some people picked out for that. Erik, you want lead on this?"

"Sure, I'll take it." Erik nodded. "I've got the domain, which'll help with seeing everything that's happening."

"Can't wait to increase my cultivation." Roska checked her repeater.

"Yeah, it feels awesome being walking charcoal with silver coming out of your veins."

"You bleed silver now?"

"Bleeds like the fucking rainbow. Looks like blood, but there's all these flecks of color in it. Like someone injected glitter into him," Storbon answered.

"Thank you for making my blood seem like a four-year-old's clown party."

"I had nothing to do while you went full blood donor."

Roska snorted at them both.

Memories, unbidden, came back as Erik slung his repeater. His voice softened. "You remember when we were defending Alva? Like the village?" Erik's voice softened.

"Yeah, I thought I was over all that," Roska said.

"I was nearly shitting my pants the entire time." Sadness colored Storbon's voice.

Erik let his repeater hang as he flexed his jaw. Neither Roska nor Storbon had any family to speak of. He had relied on them and they had not failed him, rising to the challenge.

He felt a deep pride in them. It had always been there, but now it hit him with full force. His eyes watered as he lifted his helmet and put his hands on their shoulders, looking at their mirrored lenses.

"I'm proud of you, both of you." *Shit. Pull it together, man. Maybe this is what it feels like to be a dad?*

He shook his thoughts free and tried to think of how to express how proud he was.

"That means a lot, bBoss," Roska whispered as she patted his hand.

Storbon nodded, but Erik could feel the weight of their sentiments.

He patted them once more and sniffed, pulling his helmet back into place. "Now, time to earn our pay."

"Don't you technically pay us?" Storbon asked.

"Terrible fucking investment."

The three laughed, storing away the moment, and focused.

The lift they were on slowed rapidly before it rocked to a stop. They moved sideways with the momentum and recoiled backward, a few stumbling.

"Off the pad!" Erik yelled.

They jogged into a series of tunnels, passing through a secret door built into a shelving unit. They took the stairs up two at a time and exited a cooling room that was powered off with the contents removed.

The first two out of the freezer had their repeaters up, clearing the room.

"Clear right!"

"Clear left!"

The rest of the teams poured out.

Erik could hear the distant sounds of fighting.

"Team Four high!" Storbon yelled. They went for the stairs and headed up.

"See you on the flip side!" Roska said.

"You got it." Erik ran up with Special Team Four as Roska pushed Special Team Two out through the ground floor to the street.

Erik ran with Team Four up the stairs, slamming through the roof access door. Four scanned the other rooftops in the area. Lucinda released her tamed birds to give them overwatch.

Chaos ruled the skies and land.

A sword of ice missed a kestrel and hit the city. Ice, like cracking glass, spread over a path a hundred meters long across buildings before it shattered in a frigid shower, crushing the buildings.

Repeater bolts enhanced with air shot filled the skies. The towers were bastions of fire as kestrels' door gunners earned their pay.

The sparrows dove and weaved, hitting the aerial mounts and flying off. Erik couldn't see the front lines outside Vuzgal, but he could hear fierce fighting.

Erik closed his eyes for a second. Instead of holding all his power in, he released it. His senses expanded in every direction, through the floor beneath his feet and the door behind him.

It wasn't like he could see in every direction, more like he resonated with it. He felt the elements that made up the materials around him: the metals of armor and weapons, the compacted dirt used as tiles, the heat of the sun, the mixture of air. He could so easily call out to those elements, bringing them under his command. He felt the flow of mana through it all. It permeated the world, but it was thicker in the buildings than it was in the air. The members of the special team were beacons of mana density to Erik.

Erik thought the sensations of a domain were similar to when someone touched another's arm.

"Yao Meng, you take this side of the street. I'll take the north," Storbon said through the team channel.

"Got it."

Storbon and his four ran and jumped, clearing the thirty-meter-wide street with ease.

"Good?" Erik asked.

"Good and ready to rock."

Erik flicked to the command channel. "Roska, ready to move?"

"Yes, boss. Split up into two teams to take either side of the street.

"Okay, good. We're heading west, then dog legging north. Move out, Storbon. Yao, make sure you're always in visual contact with one another and see Team Two."

"Sir!"

"On it."

"Let's move. Head on a swivel."

They took off. Erik scanned as they ran and jumped between buildings.

Their light jog ate up ground as they utilized their Body Like Iron cultivations.

"We're getting close. Storbon, push right. Yao, let's jump onto the other side of the street we'll orientate north and—"

"Contact!" Storbon yelled as spells struck the building he and his people had been on. The structure collapsed under the attacks.

"Returning fire!" Storbon yelled.

Erik watched the explosive bolt trace as it connected with a rooftop.

"Calling in spell scroll!" Erik took out a scroll and tore it.

A spell formation appeared above the building.

Chaotic power swirled together and turned into a lance that blasted through the building.

Erik checked the map on the inside of his wrist. "Use the next main street to orientate north. Storbon, I want your people on the west side. You take the point. Yao, we'll hang back and go farther west."

They leapt across the street, over Roska's people, who were pushing hard up the street for the next large intersection.

They organized on the run, two half teams on the road, with two half teams on the roof like the left side of an arrowhead.

Several buildings collapsed beyond where the spell scroll had struck.

"Buildings went down in the distance. They must be clearing out an area around the teleportation formation," Erik relayed.

"Roska, move your people forward to this building." Erik put down a pin on his linked map.

"Got it."

"Storbon, take this roof. Yao, this one."

"Got it."

"Okay."

"We'll establish a fire base there and react. Be ready to shift as needed. They have the ability to crack buildings, so they'll probably try to bring it down on our heads."

They crossed the buildings in no time. Yao Meng was on the left flank, Storbon on the right, with Roska in the middle.

Arrows and spells lanced the building they landed on.

Erik threw his hand up. A building was torn apart, thrown into the air. Red magma threads appeared in the stone as Erik landed on the other roof and threw his hand forward.

The building sections hammered the cleared ground as the special teams added in their own spells. The ground was pounded with attacks, giving them the cover they needed to get to the edge of the building.

Erik raised his repeater using the explosive shot spell. The repeater arm bucked and recoiled as a line of tracers broke up across buildings. They raked the mana barrier, following after the spells.

In what had been a park, there were now hundreds of soldiers fighting the undead soldiers that raged in their formations. The undead were powerful, but they were few, getting isolated and cut down. A barrier covered the formation in the middle and the soldiers around it. Buildings had been torn apart by mages that were readying new spells.

"Barrier buster?" Storbon yelled as they fired into the barrier.

"Roska, prepare your mounts at the rear of the building for a charge," Erik yelled. Gilly grew on his shoulders in anticipation.

"We'll charge. We don't know if the buster will break them. Two will lead. Four will follow on flanks. We run through them and into the formation."

"Mages, smoke!"

Spells appeared in front of the mana barrier, pouring out prismatic smoke and making it impossible to see through.

Erik saw movement below. Roska made her entrance. Her war mount, a purple-streaked panther with lightning crackling through her fur, blew through a wall with a flash of lightning, coming out of the building he'd ordered her to move up to.

Her team punched holes out of the building, spreading out behind her in an arrowhead, dodging between the remains of buildings as they drew their weapons, and charging for the smoke.

"Here we go!" Yao yelled and jumped with the rest of the half team. Erik leapt from the five-story building. They hit like rocks, leaving craters on the ground as the team members waved their beast storage devices.

Gilly expanded to her full size and Erik sprang onto her back, grabbing her harness with his left hand, hoisting his repeater in his right hand.

"Move!" Yao barked. Their mounts' claws dug into the stone and rock, throwing it up as they raced toward the smoke.

Erik felt the thrill of wind against his body as he checked left and right. Gilly moved underneath him as she tore up the ground, her body shimmering with power. He checked on the masked riders to his sides, who held their repeaters as they rushed to the enemy.

He gathered his power as Roska dove through the smoke, the rest of her team right on her heels.

They disappeared as Team Four hit the smoke in a skirmish line.

Erik was anything but blind. He saw the enemy through the mana-filled smoke and solid mana that represented the barrier in his domain.

An oldie, but a goodie.

They passed through the smoke and right into the infantry that had been softened up by Roska's team, driving headfirst toward the teleportation formations.

Erik lowered his repeater and fired as Gilly breathed out her power. A beam of water cleared a path ahead as her head traversed from left to right and back again.

He fired his explosive shot into the infantry; spells appeared inside the barrier. He raised his left hand, using his legs to hold on as his body glowed. He punched forward, sending a mana blast tearing through the air, leaving a trail of mana vapor before it struck the ground, exploding.

He changed his aim with his repeater, his domain acting as his eyes while he sprayed explosive shot spells into the groups of enemy fighters trying to pull together.

The mana barrier over the formation plate popped, bringing back the noise of Vuzgal.

Roska and her team cut down those controlling the mana barrier and reached the teleportation formation just as a new force arrived.

Team Two's spells covered the formation plate. It broke, sending out a wave of power that threw fighters to the ground.

Erik grabbed onto Gilly's saddle and ducked low as the wave rushed over them.

He stored his empty repeater and gathered his power. Spell formations appeared around him as he closed his eyes, looking at the world through his domain, locking onto the fighters around him. The spells completed. Tens of mana bullets fired out of them, striking fighters with unnerving accuracy. They collapsed to the ground.

More mana bullets flew out of the spell formations, gathering around Erik, whizzing off to hunt down targets.

Erik raised his hand. A healing dagger appeared next to Tully, stabbing into her with a jolt. Her wounds started to heal rapidly.

Roska led them to the left as fighters started to flee.

"Break into five-man teams and clean up this mess." A spell lit up. Erik raised a barrier just in time to stop it.

Erik felt the strain of energy as other spells rained down on his barrier. A group of mages behind a short wall hurled spells at him.

Spell formations appeared above them and fired down to meet a mana barrier.

Spells struck Yuli. Her barrier was torn apart, and her mount died nearly instantly.

Erik felt his chest tighten as he hurled out healing daggers. She crashed into the ground, rolling to a bloody stop as he threw out a revival needle. It shot out like a bullet, striking Yuli in the chest and delivering its payload.

She breathed on the ground almost in a convulsion, her armor in tatters.

Erik hurled attack after attack down on the mana barrier, making it near impossible to see out of or in as Yao's half team and Erik wheeled to the left, centering on the mana barrier, charging.

They readied their spells and went through the small barrier.

Jurumba's spells were all around the front of his mount and went off like a claymore, tearing through the ranks of fighters as he wielded a halberd with devastating effect.

He cut down on the mana barrier, tearing the formation apart.

Tian Cui and Jamie, who were on either side, cut a bloody path along the edges of the enemy formation. Erik and the rest threw in attacks at the rear at those who had escaped the first three.

"Eleven o'clock!" Yao Meng yelled.

An explosion went off next to Jamie, throwing him from his mount. Spells wrapped around him to protect him as mana barriers snapped up around him. The sect's attacks were dashed across the barrier, coloring the sky and ground holding steady against the barrage.

Erik traced the spells back to their origin and fired upon the fighters. The special team opened up with him. The fighters broke under the fire.

Erik threw heals into Jamie who was moving on the ground, and a stack formation and a healing mana barrier enveloped Yuli and Jamie.

The special team didn't let the enemy fighters have time to recover, keeping them pinned down or on the run. The Undead legions ran across the open ground, smashing through buildings and jumping into the midst of the sect fighters.

The remaining forces broke or were too focused on surviving to attack the special teams.

"Yao Meng's people on me. Roska's roaming patrol, clean up anyone that's left behind. Storbon, check in with command." Erik turned Gilly toward Jamie and Yuli. "I've got Jamie; Sang, get Yuli!"

Erik set to work, using healing spells to stabilize Jamie.

"I need stretcher-bearers!" Erik yelled as Jamie's stamina bottomed out.

Erik pulled off Jamie's armor, pulled out a revival needle, and stabbed. The potion went in and spread. Jamie's heart had stopped. Erik started compressions as he heard feet on gravel sliding next to him. "I've got no heartbeat or breathing!"

Lucinda pulled out a breather and affixed it to Jamie's face, pumping in air.

Erik stopped his compressions to check if Jamie was able to do it himself.

Nothing. Shit.

He glanced at Jamie. He'd seen it enough before to recognise the *look.*

"No, you fucking don't!" Erik pulled out another revival needle and stabbed it into Jamie and did his compressions. He pulled out a third needle as Lucinda reached out and caught his hand.

He stared at her as she silently shook her head.

Erik felt his body go limp as he looked at Jamie.

Two undead ran across to Erik. One pulled a stretcher off the other and they held it out next to Jamie.

Erik gritted his teeth and moved to his feet. Lucinda grabbed his shoulders. They put him on the stretcher. "Go!"

The undead ran off with Jamie.

Erik checked on Sang.

Tian Cui was with him, watching Yuli taken away. Sang patted Tian Cui's shoulder. She nodded numbly, and they headed for their waiting mounts.

Shit.

"Erik?"

"I'm sorry, Yao. There wasn't anything…" Erik hung his head.

"I understand. We've got to keep moving." Yao Meng's voice strained.

"Yeah," Erik and Lucinda mounted up. "Storbon, how are we looking?" Erik forced out through his tight throat.

"Command has two more possible teleportation formations in the area. Nearest one is northeast."

"Sit rep?"

"Mana recovering. No issues. Good stamina. Mounts good. All okay," Roska reported.

"Mana recovering. No issues. Good stamina. One mount wounded, will recover. All okay," Tully reported.

"Mana recovering. No issues. Good stamina. One mount killed, two wounded, will recover. One KIA," Storbon said.

"Mana recovering. No issues. Good stamina. One mount down, one KIA," Yao Meng said.

Erik pulled his thoughts together. "Storbon, you take point. Yao Meng, follow behind. Roska, Tully, have your half teams move in the parallel streets back from Team Four."

"Yes, Boss!"

The teams orientated off Storbon, who moved through what was the battlefield, away from the destroyed buildings.

"Command has ordered us out to hunt the teleportation formations," Niemm yelled in Rugrat's ear.

"Got it!" Rugrat swiveled his dual repeaters and fired. A line of blue tracers arced through the sky ahead of his target like an inevitable fate. Tracer and target intersected, the target trying to escape their fate. The rider's barrier flared for a few seconds before disappearing, dropping the rider and mount into the city below.

"Gunner!"

A man ran over.

"Locked and loaded. No issues. Make sure you lead them," Rugrat said.

"Yes, sir." The man grabbed the dual repeaters and started checking it.

"Let's go."

Rugrat and Niemm walked into the tower and ran down the stairs.

"Team Three is prepping at their tower. Here are the suspected landing areas for teleportation formations." Niemm showed Rugrat his wrist map.

Rugrat's map was continuously populating with new markers. He checked the locations. "We'll head here." Rugrat grabbed Niemm's wrist and pointed to a marker.

"Okay, I'll relay to Gong Jin."

"We'll sneak in as close as possible and hit the formation with stuff powerful enough to destroy it."

They reached the bottom. People ran into the tunnels of the under city. The special team checked gear as they waited on their mounts.

Rugrat jumped up onto George's back scanning his people and the area. "We're all here; let's push out!" He led them out to the gates of the tower. They opened to the fighting beyond. A spell glanced off the tower's barrier, crashing into the street and tearing through several buildings.

Come on, boy! Time to earn our pay. Oorah!

George leapt forward. The entire team built up their speed. They were galloping when they left the tower's mana barrier.

"Deni and I will jump off here. Keep moving down the street and into the buildings in partners." Rugrat rolled off George, who shrunk to the size of a large dog.

"Yes, sir."

Rugrat checked his repeater and looked at Deni. "Good to go."

He took point, moving between two empty stores. He went up the stairs back and forth, up several floors, and past apartments. He stacked up on the door, ready to breach. Deni hit him, signalling those behind were ready.

He used mana blades, cutting the lock on the door and throwing it open as he rushed in, moving to the right with his rifle, but there was nothing. "Clear."

"Clear," Deni repeated back. They checked the other two rooms, finding an empty bedroom and bathroom.

Rugrat moved to the bedroom window that overlooked the rear of the building. He moved the curtains slowly.

Just a curtain moving in the breeze.

He peered through his section of window. Two streets over, several buildings showed signs of fighting. The teleportation formation had landed in the street between buildings. Undead skeletons crashed through buildings and ran through alleyways and streets to reach the sects that had been unable to gain a foothold.

Rugrat checked their positioning against his own. "Fire Support Control, this is Viper One-One. I have a target for you, over."

"Viper One-One, this is Fire Support Control. Do you have grid, over?"

"Fire Support Control, grid two-three-two-zero, one-zero-one-three. Confirm?"

"Viper One-One, Fire Support Control confirms grid two-three-two-zero, one-zero-one-three?"

"Fire Control, confirmed."

"Viper One-One, be prepared for incoming rounds. Mortars should be with you momentarily."

Rugrat switched channels. "Mortars coming in on target momentarily."

They waited several seconds before a whistle filled the air.

Rumbling explosions covered the area where the sects' fighters were.

Smoke started to clear, illuminated by the broken light of the formation activating. More fighters poured out in a flash to be met with undead that had survived the mortar strike. They had no time to react, fighting before they cleared the teleportation pad.

"Spell scroll," Gong Jin said.

A spell formation appeared under the formation plate. The formation plate sank into the ground.

"That works." Rugrat looked at the undead who finished off the sect fighters and started moving through the area. Some grouped up and patrolled. Others pulled their fellows together who were regenerating and recovering.

"Okay, and we're moving." Rugrat glanced at the fight happening in the skies above.

We need to cut off these teleportation formations as fast as possible.

"They're going for the workshops!" Santos yelled.

"Command, we have a breakaway group heading for the crafter district!" Captain Wazny yelled. He leveled off and fired his repeaters among the rider's spells that buffeted his sparrow who strained against each near-miss.

"Understood, kestrels moving in support."

A trio of kestrels dove in from their holding positions. Their gunners cut blue trails through the sky. Aerial mounts spun away, crashing into the city below.

Spells erupted along the aerial group, taking one dozen more.

They banked over the Battle Arena district and over the smithies that bordered the area. A beam spell hit a kestrel, throwing out wood as it punched into the cabin.

Wazny dropped another aerial beast. His sparrow dove and yanked back up in erratic movements.

The kestrel tried to right itself when other beams hit it. The aerial rider's mages tore spell scrolls, forcing the Alva Air Force to go on the defensive.

They went over a park as Wazny saw several riders bank. Formations dropped from their storage rings into the park.

"Command, we have teleportation formations in the Solitude Park!" Wazny felt he noticed something weird.

Focus!

"Understood, teams will be sent. Target if you can."

The aerial forces were hurling out spell scrolls, making it hard to get close. They came in close to the inner wall.

The wounded kestrel dropped out of the sky, taking a fatal blow. Escape formations were activated, destroying the cabin and hurling the crew free.

Undead mages blasted at the aerial forces, working with the air force.

The group broke apart and fled, using their buffing spells on their mounts.

Wazny broke off. Whatever he had seen, it kept pulling at his mind.

He looked over at the southern mountain range that bordered Vuzgal's rear valleys. Then he saw them moving low. "Command, we have enemy coming low along the southern mountain range, right in the rear of the city."

"Understood."

Wazny looked back to the park. "Santos, you up for some remodelling?" A formation up on its side activated as fighters fell out on the ground.

"Yes, Boss. Bombs?"

"Yeah, follow me in."

Wazny banked, targeting the formation plates.

"Release!" He and Santos dropped a stream of bombs that left a path of explosions through the park, tearing up dirt and trees. The fighters hadn't had time to put up a barrier the bombs detonated among them. Wazny surveyed it all with a cold gaze, using his handles to change his direction, climbing higher to find his next target.

He passed a street where a close protection detail massed with undead fighters. He was low enough to see one of the detail punching his repeater into the air in salute.

Wazny banked again, Santos trailing as they went back, doing another run on the plates they'd missed.

They were setting up for their third mission when Wazny got new orders.

"All sparrows on this channel, group up at mana barrier tower one-nine-zero-nine. I say again, all sparrow pilots hearing this, break off and regroup at mana barrier tower one-nine-zero-nine. Suspected force coming in from the southern mountain range."

"Our aerial forces are experiencing heavy losses. Some of them are refusing to fly anymore," Leonia reported to Marco.

"How bad is it?"

"Three in four do not return."

"I didn't think that their aerial force would be so strong." Marco held his chin.

"Our teleportation formations have allowed us entry, but they are bombing them once they hit the ground. The footholds we had are gone," Marino said.

"Tell Onam and Feng Dan to use their spell scrolls."

"They have only made it halfway through the metal forest."

"We need to breach Vuzgal now. If we do not, they will gain superiority in the air and hammer our infantry and deny us access with our teleportation formations inside the city. Their forces focusing on removing the formations will reinforce those in the defensive bunkers and there are plenty of bunkers that have not been active. Either they don't have the people to staff them—which I doubt, seeing as the enemy must be ten times larger than what we thought—or they are still holding back. The spell scrolls will keep their attention on the front of Vuzgal and allow our aerial forces to enter the dungeon valley and into the castle district."

"I will pass on the message," Marino said.

55 Breach

"About damn time," Onam muttered under his personal barrier. Explosive bolts passed through the area where the main barrier had been. A cascading light showed as its formations burned up and its protection evaporated. Whistling weapons rained down among the metal bushes, filling the air with metal and stone that would tear a man apart without a barrier.

Mana cannons targeted barriers, bursting them for the other weapon systems to reap the lives of those underneath.

Trap spells the mages had missed went off here and there, wounding the clearing parties.

A barrier failed as mana cannons punched through the formation of soldiers. The explosions of the whistling weapons and repeaters covered them.

Won't make it out of that.

Onam pulled out a spell scroll. The mana in the area fluctuated wildly. Onam's breath shuddered. It felt like his mana system had been gripped by the scroll. He felt both excited and awed. With a grunt, he tore the scroll apart.

Runes burned free of the pages, expanding and drawing on the sparse mana available. The wind picked up. Lines of mana burned into the world, giving the runes structure and shape.

He winced as mana being drawn into the ground leaked away from the spell scroll, weakening its power and giving it to the enemy.

Explosive bolts were pulled off target and the storm clouds above the battlefield behind Onam were dragged away.

Metal bushes shook against one another as the world dimmed, the elements and mana of the world channeled into the spell scroll.

This is the power of a scroll from a mage at the peak of the Seventh Realm.

Like a hungry beast, the spell drew in anything and everything from the surroundings.

The world seemed to grow silent for a second. Onam shook, releasing the twisted energies, they spiralled, shredding everything in the path bursting against Vuzgal's barrier. It *flexed* with the impact and darkened rapidly, and *broke.*

The noise made Onam duck, the elemental spirals' shaotic power of their combination burned through the defenses beyond and disappeared, clearing a ten-meter-wide path to the front of Vuzgal's walls.

"Push forward!" Onam yelled.

The army charged with renewed vigor, passing Onam. He hung back, seeking the protection of numbers, watching for other traps that might lie ahead.

The sects, seeing their opportunity, pushed ahead. The low buildings that had attacked them without any way to fight back were now in reach.

"Goddamn," Domonos hissed, looking at the updated map. He moved to a console and removed the covering. A siren blared through Vuzgal as everyone braced themselves.

Domonos waited for the three blasts and turned the formation.

Power flooded him as all the conqueror's armor across the entire city linked together, buffing everyone to twice their original power.

Second Lieutenant Acosta looked at Vuzgal's renovations. "Shit."

She heard the siren. "Brace yourselves and remember your training." She used the wide channel to everyone.

The flood of power was heady as Acosta moved from side to side. The people in the command center shifted around, testing out their new abilities as their armor activated.

The sects freed their mounts and charged forward, capitalizing on their progress.

The mortars and repeaters hit harder. The spells used on them had a multiplicative effect.

"Check mana barriers!" Acosta barked as the enemy reached the edge of Scarecrow's Hill and passed through Vuzgal's main mana barrier.

"Barrier shifting to position two!"

The barrier receded through the bunkers, stopping at the external wall behind them.

Spells struck out at the bunkers, flaring barriers across the line as they returned the attacks.

A titanic amount of mana gathered.

Another one?

Runes flew into the air, forming a formation as it drew in the surrounding mana.

"Brace!"

The formations completed, turning the world white. Sounds and sight were removed as Acosta yelled, unable to hear herself as she stumbled backward.

"Neumann, take the periscope. I can't see." The ground shook, forcing her to her knees before the first smashed into the ground.

The power running the formations fluctuated. The world was still a mass of white as she tried to heal it away.

The last of the strikes ran through the ground.

"Neumann? You okay?"

"I'm good, Ma'am. Are you okay?"

"I can't see shit. You?"

"I can still see." She heard shuffling and felt his hands on her. She batted him away and felt for a chair or wall to support herself.

"Don't worry about me. Our spotters will be blinded. Give the teams bearings and corrections. Report what happened to command."

Acosta used healing spells on herself.

"Shit," Neumann hissed. "Command, this is Dragon one-alpha-one-four actual. We've been hit with some kind of artillery spell. It targeted the bunker line. Broke through in several locations. Trying to reinforce, but they're coming in close."

"Understood."

Neumann changed to the unit's channel. "All right, listen up, everyone. Target is fire zone breakpoint. I say again, target is fire zone breakpoint!"

The whites dulled into greys and blacks. It faded faster as Acosta found her feet.

"How bad is it, Neumann?" she asked.

He was bent over his map, checking with his range finders and tools—uploading what he was seeing to the other linked Alvan maps. "Some of the bunkers are gone. Smashed right through their barriers before they had time to recover. The barriers are back up now. Teams are going to check on them." His voice was grim. Anything that made it through the barriers and the bunker wasn't bound to be nice to those inside.

Acosta looked at Neumann, seeing his outline. "Shit," she said.

"Yes, ma'am."

Wazny saw a wave of dazzling light-filled snowballs along the bunker line before they slammed into the ground like dandelions and exploded.

He saw the light through his arm and his eyelids before the rush of heat and the roar of sheer energy, like a house of glass shattering all at once and rolling through the ground and sky.

"Keep your heads in the game!" Captain Ishii growled.

Wazny looked forward. They were perched on the towers that rose out from the inner wall, supporting the city's massive mana barrier. He teared up as his eyes were already starting to repair his stomach in his chest.

"One minute to launch! All our stats just got boosted. Make sure you're used to the power and get ready."

Wazny felt the power coursing through his veins as he checked the spell casting formation plate that was part of his cabin. "Everyone good?" Wazny asked his third sparrow wing. There was only Bell, Santos, and Xia. The others were fighting in other places, wounded or dead. There was no way to know.

"Yeah, ready to rock," Bell said.

"Good," Xia said.

"Ready here," Santos said.

"Okay, stick together and we'll give them a nasty surprise." Wazny moved around in his cockpit, patting his mount, who gave him a happy chirrup.

"Launch!"

The first teams leapt from the tower. The others followed afterward.

Wazny saw the opening get bigger and then the drop as his sparrow dove, catching the air and banked, following the stream of the other sparrows.

They spread out into their incomplete formations as they went northeast.

The enemy dove, entering Vuzgal's barrier. The inner-city towers opened on them, thinning their ranks as they poured on the power, heading for the castle district.

Wazny glanced to the west, where another stream of aerial fighters rushed in. He turned back to his target. The enemy had a nearly four to one advantage, but they couldn't allow them free entry to the city.

Four to one, bad ratio for them.

Wazny heard a noise that wasn't like the sparrows nearby. He checked on the rest of his people. Santos was on his left behind him, Bell and Xia on his right.

"What the hell is that noise?" Wazny asked.

"Erik."

A dragon rose into view. The panthers trailing behind it seemed to run on the air itself, white wind gathering right before they pressed into it.

Wazny's hair stood on end at the power rolling off the group.

"Looks like the special team has come up to play," Bell quipped.

Wazny looked to the west, seeing a trace of fire in the skies.

Rugrat and George.

Wazny focused on his task.

Spells went off in the enemy aerial forces who were weaving around in the air, broken up into their different groups so they wouldn't all be caught in one attack. Spells appeared ahead of the sparrow and special teams formation.

"Break into wings!"

The groups devolved and spread apart but maintained their heading.

"Prepare wind spells!"

Wazny gathered his mana, feeling the power of the formation resonating with him. "Fire!"

The spotty spells from the aerial forces were washed out by the blue arrows that shot out from the air force.

It ran through the aerial forces ranks, cutting them down and tearing apart the buildings below.

Then they were both in range.

The aerial forces shot their spells back. The exchange was a series of brilliant lights and reactions as blues, reds, whites, greens all ignited the very air, coming faster and faster.

Blue and brown drowned out the world as Gilly used her breath.

Erik raised his hand and the city responded. Hundreds of stone spears shot into the sky and exploded among the aerial forces. The elements circled him, creating a cloud as he charged in. Then the forces crossed one another. Wazny was just a pilot now, in knife fighting range and dancing with the devil.

He dove, feeling the crackling power of a near miss, hurling his own in response. The fireball was the size of a beach ball instead of a tennis ball as it exploded, catching the mount and rider.

Wazny barrelled away as arrows shot down at him. Santos was there, his repeaters connecting with the attacker. Santos dove past Wazny, who leveled out and tried to gain height. He hurled out a lightning spell that struck an armored aerial knight, then jumped between several armored warriors and mages in his group, dropping them to the ground.

Wazny felt a rush of wind and banked away.

Gilly passed overhead. The special teams were a force of nature. Desolation lay before them as they cut through the enemy formation. They had banked and were now flying up the tail of the formation.

Mana gathered in Erik's hands; the sky crackled with power. His body started to glow, the power too much for mere mortals to handle.

Erik reached out as lightning extended from his hands. Claws of lightning fifty meters long swiped through the air. Dozens of aerial fighters were removed from the sky.

Spells of massive power cut through the enemy. The aerial forces were no longer a silent attacker. They were rabbits fleeing from the wolves into whose den they'd just walked. Spells that missed crushed buildings and tore through streets.

Barriers were of little consequence. "Check in!"

"Santos here."

"Xia here. Bell, he didn't… He didn't make it. No spell scroll."

"Shit." Wazny checked on Santos. "We're going back in. Erik smashed them apart, but there are aerial forces all over the place."

Domonos started at the ever-changing symbols across his map as aides called out reports.

"The eastern and western aerial forces passed over the castle district. They released formations. The undead destroyed them before they could activate."

"The enemy is attacking the bunkers, looking to force entry."

"Empty the first layer of bunkers and arm their defenses," Domonos barked.

"Second Division and Tiger Regiment are in the Fourth Realm."

"I need them in place as soon as possible," Domonos yelled. The balance was tilting. He needed to slam the gate shut in the face of the Sects now.

"I have reports that fighters are coming through the cities supporting the Willful Institute's army and going right through the teleportation formations. They'll have reinforcements soon," Elan said.

Domonos glanced at his father and back. "We have all the teleportation formations inside the city sealed off?"

"Yes, the kestrels are moving to bomb the formations that were placed by the last aerial forces. Undead have been mobilized."

Domonos looked at the glaring hole through his bunker defensive line. "If they get into a bunker, blow it. We cannot give them a position in cover to put down their teleportation formations or access to our underground lines." He glanced over to Hall, the man's clenched fists and straining jaw. Those bunkers contained his men and women.

He quickly composed himself and nodded as if to say it was behind him and he was ready to carry out his duties.

"Release Level Three weapons. Once we've cleared our skies, I want the kestrels on long range spells. Sparrows are to meet up with undead flying mages and do diving attacks through their mana barriers. Have the Undead Legion move to reinforce the front line. Get them on the outer wall *only* if we can confirm that there are no other teleportation formations and the aerial forces are not going to be coming back."

"Yes, sir. Some of the bunkers have been cut off. Their formations are broken or their defenses opened up."

"Have them switch to operable bunkers or assist others. We don't have anything else for them. Cancel the weather and bring the undead mages up to the walls."

"Lieutenant Colonel Zukal wishes to speak to you, sir," an aide said.

Domonos opened a sound transmission channel as Tan Xue, Qin, and other teachers from the academy entered the command center, looking at the map and the glaring path of destruction throughout the city.

"Silaz, go."

"Our allies are gathering and preparing at satellite locations and are ready to attack. The barriers are going to be an issue and we need to hold the enemy here."

Domonos' eyed the craters and pockmarked roads, broken houses, gardens, and fountains around the Castle District.

"Level Three weapons have been released. That should help, and the special teams will be ready."

"You sure?"

"You think we can stop those two?"

"No."

"Coordinate directly with our people. The fuckers not only stockpiled barrier formations, they're chaining them together so we can't get to their formations. They're pushing the bunkers."

"We have a breach!" an aide yelled in a panic.

"Blow it!" Hall barked.

A bunker disappeared as an angry red tumor ballooned, spreading from their breach point. The bunkers had been moved by the mages to cover the road. The enemy had taken heavy losses, but they soaked them up as even more of them streamed from their teleportation formations.

They're not consumable items but they're using them like they are. They stockpiled everything before attempting this attack.

"How long?" Domonos asked.

"Within the hour."

"Shit, tell them I'm not sure if I can give them an hour before we have to use everything."

"Yes, sir."

Domonos cut the call. "Go to fire plan Delta! Have the bunkers cover one another. Get the kestrels in the area doing runs. Hammer them with spell scrolls. And get those artillery cannons online!" Domonos yelled.

An aide ran up. "Sir, the Vuzgal academy's staff and their students are asking permission to help with repairs."

"What?" *They can get some of those bunkers back into action.*

He had everyone fighting that he could. There were as many crafters in the bunkers as there was military trying to keep them together, healing and helping however they could.

Qin stepped forward. "We aren't fighters, but we can help repair Vuzgal and keep you in the fight."

Domonos looked at Tan Xue. "Do it."

"Thank you, Colonel."

Qin's fierce expression softened as she hugged Domonos and their father. "See you later." She turned and left the command center with the other volunteers.

Domonos and Elan shared a look and returned to the chaos around them.

56
Closing the Vise

"Level four weapons are authorized! I say again, level four weapons are authorized!"

Acosta looked over to the massive artillery cannon that dominated two-thirds of the room. "Open the blast doors!"

Neumann turned a formation on the wall. Lights blinked as massive gears turned. Light streamed in, glancing off the gun's formation-covered barrel.

Acosta put her eyes to her periscope and aimed at the leading edge of the united army charging through the outer wall.

The weapon operated just like the mana cannon but was slaved to her periscope and fired actual rounds instead of just spells, requiring an ammunition bearer.

She reached out and turned a formation on the wall beside her. The platform that the cannon was on rotated, as did the gears controlling the elevation of the barrel.

Neumann worked other controls. A powerful pulley system activated as the cannon's barrel pushed forward between the square gap in the inner and outer armor shells. He ran to the rear of the gun. There was an ammunition cradle and formation arm ready below the open breach.

"Ready to load!" Neumann yelled.

"Barrier Penetrator round."

Neumann dropped the round from his storage ring and pressed a formation. The rammer pushed the round forward. The breach closed and locked itself.

He pushed off to the side. "Ready to fire!"

Acosta looked over as the cannon, for the first time ever, poked out of its shields. It was primed and ready; her formations glowed dangerously.

She checked her aim and activated the palm control. She felt the roar in her chest as the cannon barrel recoiled. Its downward momentum shifted into backward motion as its formations dimmed.

The automatic systems kicked in, tossing out the empty casing in a blow of gas. Gas extractor formations powered up as the cannon moved forward.

"Splash!" The round tore through a large-scale barrier of incoming reinforcements, ripping away their cover.

The shell dropped downward, hitting secondary barriers covering the smaller units and went off in a wave of light.

Several units disappeared in the blast, their secondary barriers torn apart by the secondary blast.

Acosta shifted her vision as the cannon moved back into the ready position. The forward enemy units were moving among the bunkers, attacking up the hill. Their barriers gave them cover to get close to the bunkers.

Grenades were tossed down the hill, taking out the fighters.

The soldiers evacuated bunkers before the fighters reached them. The bunkers went up in a spray of stone and metal, killing the would-be attackers.

Artillery cannons got into the action. Their rounds hit the barriers like a soldering iron driven into plastic before they exploded, reaping lives.

Mana barriers started collapsing. Mana cannons fired as fast as they could reload, showing their true ability.

The beast woke up.

Kestrels dove from above, dropping bombs on the broken barriers.

The United Sect Army still poured in hundreds of thousands of fighters.

"Loaded!" Neumann yelled.

Acosta changed her point of aim. The cannon rotated on its gears, the shield moving with it as Vuzgal's artillery cannons bellowed in a flare of power. They tore through barriers and detonated, rarely taking more than one shot to do so.

Marco let the viewing glasses slip from his numb fingers.

Master Teacher Marino looked at his pale face. "Did we have no information on this?"

"We knew they were hiding secrets, but those weapons..." Marco dragged his fingers through his hair.

"They're tearing our barriers apart. The aerial forces have just thirty percent of their original numbers and not one teleportation formation in the city to show for it." Eva Marino turned to the map table, leaning heavily on it.

"We have no more of those scrolls and have yet to engage people in person, other than inside the city. We have no idea of their numbers or condition. Master Teacher Feng Dan and Hae Woo Sung are dead. Onam is still at the front, but he's badly wounded. They're using weapons we didn't even know existed. If we lose our foothold ..."

Silence hung in the room.

"We need to do what is best for the sect," she said.

Marco pulled himself together. "If we can get past their walls, then we have a chance. If we're stuck fighting the bunkers, we have nothing."

"Can we only attack?" Marino asked.

"If we don't, the other sects will turn on us. We can't be the first to back out. We have reinforcements coming. Get Onam to direct them forward. We don't need to take out all the bunkers, just drive forward into the wall and the city beyond."

"What about the city lords? They tore through our aerial units. Their personal guards are so strong."

"Enough spells will take out anything. We need reinforcements to secure the city. Hold back our own people. It will take a lot of losses to take the city and they could flee. No wonder Vuzgal challenged our sect." Marco snarled. His easy victory was coming apart at the seams. "We must push on, or else the Wilful Institute will fall, and we will never get this opportunity again."

The under-city was in chaos. People moved underground from one bunker and up into another. Wounded were carried away by newer undead as medics worked to stabilize them before they were teleported to the hospitals.

Qin and Tan Xue ran through the tunnels, through the cutbacks and up to the front bunkers that had taken hits from high level spell scrolls and needed repairs. Qin started up the stairs, then froze. A solider coming down was carrying another covered in blood.

"It's gonna be all right, Phil. You hear me? Just gonna take you to medical!"

"Get moving." Tan Xue pushed Qin.

She swallowed, allowing Tan Xue to push her.

They reached the bunker, opening the metal door.

"Get some, you mother fuckers!" Weapons fire rang through the other side.

Qin walked into what had once been a bunker.

The left section of wall had been torn away to reveal open sky. There were two bodies on the ground. Three soldiers were covered in dust, one in blood; each manned machine guns as they fired.

"Fuck, reloading!"

One grabbed an ammunition box, looking at them both. "Barrier's fucked. Blinked out and Detriech got hit!"

He used his chin to indicate to the corner. The armored housing around the mana barrier was dented and leaking power.

Qin looked back, but the soldier was focusing on his weapon.

"Come on, Qin," Tan Xue said. She summoned mana blades and guided them around the mana barrier's housing.

Qin checked the tools on her belt and the vest she had been given. The helmet felt strange on her head like a kid playing dress-up.

Tan Xue grabbed the half-foot thick iron housing and pulled, shifting it out of the way. Qin moved to the gap that formed as Tan Xue kept pulling.

The mana barrier formation was a stack formation about a meter tall and a half meter wide. This one had been bent, throwing everything out of alignment.

"Tan Xue! I need you to reform this metal!" Qin laid out materials and checked the stack numbers running down the side. She pulled out replacement plates for the ones that looked too far gone.

"On it," Tan Xue said.

The sound of shooting changed as the bunker shook.

"Eleven o'clock! Spell scroll user!"

Tan Xue knelt beside Qin. Flames appeared around her hands and around the struts of the stack.

It shifted, moving back into position.

"Good," Tan Xue said.

The bunker shook again.

"Don't mean to worry you, but our barrier is now out!" a gunner yelled.

Qin pulled out the section of plate and grabbed the rest with mana, drawing it out. She took the new plate and shoved it into place.

The stack bloomed.

"We're back up!"

Qin eyed the other plates. She didn't have the time to take them out, work on them and put them back in. She switched out broken formations as fast as possible. Qin drew out her tools and cleaned up the carvings on the struts, causing the power to level out.

Tan Xue had fixed the structure and used a spell, speeding up the drying and sealing process.

"Good to go," Qin shouted.

Qin and Tan Xue pushed the iron covering into place. Tan Xue used a spell to repair the covering enough to hold it in place.

"Reloading! Thank you, ladies!"

The gunners kept at their tasks as they slipped out of the room.

"Buffing formation for mages is out nearby." Tan Xue started to run.

"Okay," Qin said.

"You did good work. Replacing is faster than repairing when people's lives are on the line. We can't take the time to repair everything." Tan Xue held her shoulder as they kept jogging.

"Thank you."

Tan Xue nodded and led the way.

They arrived at another bunker and went through the hatch.

Five mages stood in the room on formation plates with periscopes overlooking the battlefield.

One looked over.

"Hey, Tanya, what's your issue?" Tan Xue asked.

"Formations are out. Power connection issue, I think!" Tanya turned back to the fight. Her Doberman was sitting off to the side, alert and watching.

Qin felt the gathering of power, bending the natural world to the mages will and attacking others with its sheer power. The conqueror's armor gave them a new level of fighting ability.

Qin reached down to a formation plate and peeled back a layer of the housing. Formations linked into the power runes below. They ran like veins all the way back to the dungeon core.

"There's an issue up here. Raw mana must've got into the runes and blown out the ones here. Tan Xue, at the stairs where we came up, go left down the hall to the broken section. It'll need to be repaired to fix this."

"Okay, I'll head back down."

Tan Xue ran back out of the room.

A mage staggered as he released his spell, grabbing the railing around his formation as he pulled out a mana recovery potion and chugged it.

Qin could smell how powerful the potion was, but the man treated it like water. All the mages were covered in sweat as they chanted or twisted their hands, bending the elements to their will.

Light flashed in the bunker.

"Fuckers," a mage spat as the group gathered their strength, drawing from their own power.

"Make sure to conserve! Use external mana to supplement your own!" Tanya barked. She pressed her hand forward, completing a spell as a thunderous roar echoed through the bunker.

Qin reached the buffing formation panel of the bunker.

She opened it and got a shock of raw mana through her mana system. The formations had melted from the overload and the runes were smoking.

Qin ran to another panel amid the light display going on throughout the bunker. She opened the panel and pulled out her tools, carving into the formations; power fluctuated in the room.

The formations looked worse for her tampering, but power surged through the buffing formations.

"You're jacked into the main power! No breaker between you and the main power lines now. Just a temporary fix!"

"I'll take it!" Tanya yelled as she gathered her power.

The mana responded as it flooded toward her. The mages glowed with the power running through their bodies, drawn in through their mana gates.

Qin returned to the main breaker panel and pulled out the broken sections. She repaired what she could and pulled out new pieces of plate, cutting them to fit and writing into the metal, her brush strokes leaving runes behind.

She slammed them into place as the bunker shook violently.

"Looks like they found us, teacher!" a mage yelled.

"All they have are spell scrolls. Not one real mage among them!" Tanya yelled.

Qin looked out of the slit at the front of the trench. The mana barrier was shaking fiercely, coloring as attack after attack rained down upon them.

"Qin, get the hell out of here!"

"I have a job to do!" Qin yelled, working on the panel still.

Sound rushed into the bunker.

"Barrier is gone!"

Qin was thrown against the panel she was working on. She rolled on the ground. Part of the bunker had been carved away. Mages near the broken wall groaned, having been hit with the rocks. The other mages stood back up and cast their spells.

Tanya glowed with power as she formed a mana barrier, taking several hits from spell scrolls. A section of roof collapsed under a spell, covering the mages.

"Get the hell out of here now!" Tanya yelled.

Mages grabbed the wounded and one grabbed Qin, pulling her away.

"No, what are you doing?" Qin tried to push the mage off. He threw her over his shoulder as she punched and kicked him.

Tetsu enlarged to his full size as the bunker started to come apart, nearly reaching the ceiling as he sat next to Tanya.

"Get out of here, you big idiot!" Qin could tell Tanya was crying as she grunted and dropped to her knee under the weight of the attacks and the drain of power on her body.

Qin was thrown to the side. Rocks hit her as she fell to the ground. Darkness found her as she looked around. Why was she on the ground and not on that man's shoulders? And where was Tanya?

She pushed some rocks aside to see a whole section had collapsed. Tanya was on the ground under Tetsu, who had covered her from the attack and taken the impact of the roof.

Qin coughed in the dust as another spell struck the bunker. Her legs were trapped under some broken section of stone.

"Qin!" Tan Xue yelled as she ran into the bunker.

Qin tried to speak but got a mouthful of dust. Tan Xue grabbed the mage that had been carrying Qin out and pulled him to his feet.

"Over here!" Qin used a mana manipulation spell to toss the stone off her. She grunted at the pain that ran through her legs.

"Get her out of here! I'll get Tanya!" Tan Xue yelled.

Tan Xue ran through the collapsing bunker, grabbing onto Tanya and pulling her free. Qin bit into her lip as the mage grabbed her pulled her free.

He picked her up in his arms and ran down the stairs.

An explosion went off behind them, dust and smoke filling the air in a rush.

"Tan Xue! Tanya!" she yelled as the mage gritted his teeth. Medics rushed past them, taking the stairs two at a time as the mage continued down.

"We need to help them!" she yelled grabbing onto the man's shirt and trying to leverage herself over his shoulder. Her grip was like iron.

"Put her down on the stretcher."

He lowered her down, but she tried to fight him, to get her feet under her. She growled in pain from her legs touching the ground as she was laid down on the stretcher.

"Help them!" Qin felt tourniquets pinch her legs, making her groan. A needle pricked her skin as the pain dissolved and she tried to sit up. Medics worked over her as the mage looked up the stairs. The mages moved down the stairs with one person.

They looked at the mage and Qin, shaking their heads.

"No, noo!" Qin yelled. Tears rolled down her dust-covered face as the medic held her in place.

"You have to let me go! She needs me, I can't leave her up there."

The bearer waved something under her nose. Qin coughed. Her limbs weakened and her head felt fuzzy.

The lights shuddered with the near explosion.

"She's good to move! Go!" A medic told two bearers at either end of the stretcher.

Qin cried as the lights passed overhead, dust falling from the explosions above.

"Tanya. Tan Xue…"

The medic got another to assist, putting her onto a stretcher held by two undead and affixed a tag to her vest. "Take her to the hospital."

The ceiling moved past quickly and Qin saw lights passing as her vision faded.

57
Double Down

Head Asadi read the latest report from Vuzgal. "To think that a small city state has that much power," he growled.

Cai Bo stood there, waiting.

"Regular soldiers as strong as people in the Seventh and their lords' power unknown! How did we not know of this?" His eyes weighed down on Cai Bo.

She didn't say anything. It would only draw greater ire.

Head Asadi threw the report down. "They have the power to contend with us here. The power to reach into the Seventh Realm, but they maintain a city in the Fourth Realm. We attacked a fat pig thinking it would solve our problems. Instead, it was a tiger in disguise! If we do not win, they will swallow us all. If not them, then the sects that we have taken cities from in the last month and our *allies* will seek repayment and look to avert Vuzgal's anger. No, we must win this!"

Asadi looked back and forth, trying to think of a solution.

"What about the students in the Seventh Realm?"

Asadi grimaced. "They are pillars of our sect. If we were to lose them, our connection to the higher realms would be severed. We would have to recover them all over again. They will demand a great price from us to intervene."

Rugrat cursed as his machine gun stopped firing. "Goddamn double-feeding piece of shit!"

"They let you come out and play as well?" Erik yelled as he crouched, running with his special teams. He came to a halt near Rugrat. "This looks like a good spot! Even has a resident redneck for entertainment!"

The special teams checked their gear, laying out ammunition boxes, mounts, and formation plates.

"Are we going to spontaneously fucking combust being so close?" Rugrat yelled, clearing his gun.

"They're pushing for the wall. Best place for us to be!" Erik was toting a grenade launcher as he rose over the wall. Picking out targets, he raised the launcher skyward, casting explosive shot, and fired.

The grenades looked like red meteors with the spell Erik had laid on them.

"Fucking belt feed is all fucked on this!" Rugrat slapped in the belt feed and pulled the cocking handle, firing a burst into the swarm below.

Erik reloaded his grenade launcher. The other members of the special teams used spell scrolls, grenade launchers, and machine guns.

"Close Protection Detail coming up!" a voice called out.

"¡*Ocupado*! Check down east and west!" Erik yelled.

"Well, shit! I was hoping for room service and folded sheets!" the second lieutenant who appeared grinned.

"We'll head east!"

"Good luck!" Erik yelled.

"Fuck you, you pricks!" Rugrat swiveled and fired on new targets as George appeared above the wall, sending out a beam of flames.

Gilly followed, flapping her wings into a hover as she released a beam of water from her mouth, rubble rose around her, collapsing into spikes that rained upon the attackers.

Erik finished reloading and looked over the wall. Spells rained down on bunkers. A barrier failed, the bunker getting torn apart under the weight of fire.

Artillery cannons tore up mana barriers, peppering those beneath with their explosive payload.

Mana cannons fired off time with one another, tearing up barriers and people as mortar whistles were drowned out in the fighting.

Tracers from machine gun bunkers left lines across mana barriers and cut through enemy fighters as their explosive shot went off.

Enemy fighters charged forward, but it was a fucking meat grinder.

Erik aimed and fired his grenade launcher nearly straight up as he heard the whizz and felt a rush of air as Gilly released her spikes. They hammered barriers, crashed into the ground, and went through fighters, adding to the toll.

"Fuck," Erik muttered as he ducked and started to reload.

"Reloading!" Rugrat yelled as he ducked, changing out ammunition cans.

More of the close protection details moved from the towers to the wall and into the bunkers to support the frontline forces that were getting hammered.

Erik stood up and fired his grenade launcher again.

Gregor stomped into the tower acting as a command center for the rabble outside.

"This is the commander of the sect forces, Marco Tolentino." Petros waved to a younger man standing in front of the other sect leaders.

An offering. Gregor snorted at the thought. The sects didn't seem to change no matter the realm one was in.

Some time had passed since Petros had reported the possible connection between the Sha clan and the fourth realm to Commander Stassov, his investigations had led him to Vuzgal. Petros was confident that Esther had met the city lords of Vuzgal. Considering the mess the United Sect Armies were making of attacking the city, it seemed his suspicions were right. There was far more to Vuzgal than was immediately obvious. *At least they've softened up the Vuzgalians some.*

Gregor knew that there was little sects from the lower realms could do about the Sha firearms.

Marco averted his eyes and bowed deeply. "Lords and ladies, I am honored by your presence, but sad that I greet you in such a situation."

"This city… Tell me its history before it was taken," Gregor asked. He could feel the trepidation and confusion in the room.

"The city was abandoned. The dead had claimed it. No one went to the city because the undead were strong enough to hurt most forces and those that had died on the battlefield would turn."

"Were there powerful dungeons in the past? What kept the undead spell running?" Gregor talked over Marco.

"There was a powerful dungeon, Bala Dungeon. I do not know what was used to power the spell."

"How long did the undead last for?"

"Centuries." Marco sounded unsure.

"Did the area that the undead occupied increase?"

"I don't know." Marco opened his arms and pressed his lips together.

Gregor looked in the direction of the city.

"Petros, what can you tell me?"

"They have weapons similar to the Sha's firearms, but they're different. They don't have the skill of the Sha gunsmiths, but they make up for it in numbers."

"You think the two are related?"

"I do," Petros said.

Gregor chewed on his words for several minutes. "I need to take a closer look."

"Do you think there is something special about this city?" Marco asked.

"Ready my aerial mount. Do you have a mount, boy?"

"Yes, sir."

"Good, you will come."

Gregor left the room not waiting to see if he had caught up. He walked to the peak of the command tower, blasting out a section of the roof and withdrawing his mount, his guards and Petros did the same with Marco quickly behind.

Gregor jumped onto his mount who climbed into the sky with a screech. The others grouped around him before he led them toward the city. He paused to use his interface, and then pushed forward again, his frown deepening.

They got closer to the city and passed over the trenches.

"Tell the clan that I have found a dungeon core of the high earth grade, possibly Sky grade. I believe it might be a hidden Sha location." Gregor grimaced. They would have to move quickly to break the city and tear out the dungeon core from its heart.

Two guards turned and shot flew toward the main camp.

"Dungeon lords?" Marco asked.

"Dungeon lords," Gregor confirmed but didn't expand on it as he looked at the city. "You have brought me a great prize, Marco. My clan will be pleased. Petros, you will be rewarded."

Petros bowed his head. "Getting back to the seventh realm will be a welcome relief from this sparse mana."

Gregor smiled and nodded. *It is so thin, like watered wine.*

"I am honored, Lord Gregor, though I'm not sure how I've helped you," Marco said, bowing atop his mount.

Gregor gave him a hungry smile. "My clan will take this city for ourselves and we will not accept others encroaching upon it. These other sects…" Gregor sneered and waved his hand. "They would have to be one hundred times stronger to think they could take anything from the Black Phoenix Clan."

"You want to take the city? A city in the Fourth Realm?" Marco asked.

"I do not care for the city, but for what is underneath it."

"What do you mean?" Marco asked. They were off to the side of the command center.

"I mean that the Black Phoenix Clan has claimed this city. There is nothing we can do!" Marino hissed.

"They're another sect, right?"

"A sect that controls *warships,* Marco! Pull back your people into the cities. It is the only thing we can do. Put the blame on the Black Phoenix Clan."

Marco gritted his teeth. He didn't like being on the other end of a sect telling him what to do.

"Dammit." He stared through the windows at Vuzgal beyond.

He had known that there was something special about the city ever since they'd been engaged in the mountains. He had hoped to crack open their secrets and find out just what else they had been hiding and now it was all gone in an instant.

Those in the room looked at him as he breathed out, standing back up and regaining his composure. A good upbringing had its perks.

"Withdraw our forces from the battlefield as quickly as possible and start evacuating. I doubt that the Black Phoenix Clan will care enough to not hurt our people if they get in the way."

"Look, they're breaking!" someone called out.

Erik looked over the wall to see the flow of fighters reverse toward the teleportation formations.

They pressed onto the formations and threw down any extra they had.

Everyone kept attacking, harassing them as they sped away. In no time, they seemed to have all disappeared except for the field of dead and the destroyed bunkers.

"Is it just me, or is that fucking weird?" Rugrat said.

"Something strange about it, yeah."

"You see that group on strong mounts up in the sky? I've got a feeling they're not from around here. Haven't felt that kind of power before. Lower cultivation, but I'd guess they're a higher level than us," Rugrat said.

"Domonos, this is West."

"Go."

"We've got some people from what might be from the Eighth Realm hanging out in the sky and the sects just retreated. I don't think *we* broke them."

"What are you thinking?"

"I'm thinking something else is coming. We need to hit those camps as soon as possible. Evacuate the wounded and non-essential down to Alva or the backups."

"Understood."

58
In the Clouds

The bridge of the Black Phoenix Clan *Eternus* shook, the scrying screens showing the outside world.

The skies ahead gathered in a violent sandstorm. The sand would condense, creating boulders the size of a house, a city tower, or a man's fist, and fall apart just as quickly.

They sparked on the frigate's barrier as it calmly flew through the elemental storm.

Some of the boulders dropped toward the ground, only to slam into the volcano range below. The sudden introduction of the boulders caused the volcanoes to erupt, lighting up the earth element cloud the color of the dying sun.

Captain Stassov tapped the arm of her command chair, colored by the thin pillar of refined mana. She looked around the command bridge. Cultivators moved between different workstations as they navigated the earth element storm.

Above her, a phoenix of sculpted flame spread its wings. Runes traced down the phoenix, focused on the talons that grasped the dungeon core. Formations were carved into the floor and roof, perfectly framing the phoenix's outstretched talon.

Through these formations the dungeon core controlled the entire ship.

Stassov rose from her chair, moving toward the command table. It showed an overlay of the *Eternus,* which was cigar shaped with a flat top and angled sides filled with mana cannons.

The man in dark red-and-black armor turned from the table and bowed.

"Update." She turned a formation and a map of the area appeared.

"Commander Ranko is in reserve with his air forces. Commander Bela is ready with her ground forces."

"Seems suitable to use flying ground forces in this place." Stassov sneered at the screens across the bridge, showing the turmoil of the elemental storm. "Rise, Gregor." She turned to the mages standing around seer tables to the side. "Have we picked up any signs of other airships?"

"No, Captain."

Stassov looked back at Gregor. "Dungeon leader."

He closed his eyes, and she felt the pulse, the gift she had given him.

"I do not detect any other dungeon cores."

"Good, raise the conversion nodes, and increase speed. Mana stones won't make themselves."

The armored plates of the ship opened. Crystal and metal rune-covered pillars pushed skyward, sprouting across the ship and locked into place, turning the ship into a crystal spiked hedgehog. The airship's speed increased.

"All conversion nodes are extended!"

Power was drawn toward the forward conversion nodes. They began glowing. Flashes of lightning sparked between them as they were activated.

Runes across the bridge lit up, reaching out to the twin formation circles on the floor and the roof. Like a dam opening its locks, brown element-heavy mana shot out from the twin formations and met in the middle of the air. Gregor and the guards were jostled with the rush of power.

The pillars of power struck the dungeon core, sending out a clear pillar behind the bridge into a third formation on the wall behind the commander's chair. Runes along the frigate lit up and power ran through the phoenix before it descended through the walls and wrapped around her chair.

She so wanted to jump back in and start cultivating, but many captains had lost a ship focused on cultivation over safety.

"Conversion at eighty percent," one cultivator said.

Stassov checked the projections. "Increase our speed and keep up the sweep. We don't want to remain in one place for too long."

The ship shuddered as boulders dropped from the skies, striking the barriers. The majority of the dungeon's purified mana was sent into mana-storing formations, creating mana stones that the crew then harvested.

"Eighty-seven percent and holding. This area hasn't been harvested in a long time. The element density is incredibly high," a seer reported.

"That will be good for the dungeon core to expand. Continue our course," Stassov said.

"Bela, Ranko, go to standby. I'll use my dungeon sense to make sure that there are no other airships," Gregor said.

"Understood," Ranko said.

"I was hoping there'd be more Sha around," Bela grumbled. "I was looking forward to trashing a few of their ships."

"You'll get your opportunity. The war with the Sha isn't going anywhere," Gregor said.

"I hope so."

Stassov had a grim look on her face she turned toward the forward windows.

A messenger bowed deeply. "I am sorry for overstepping, Captain. A large fight has happened in the lower realms. A group using weapons similar to the Sha have appeared. A boy there discovered a dungeon core. A *Sky* grade dungeon core."

"Is he sure?" Stassov opened the scroll, reading it.

With a Sky grade dungeon core, they could create another frigate and grow the fleet. The contribution to the Clan would be immense.

"Has this information been passed to the other families?" she asked in a low voice.

"No, Captain. Only through our family."

Stassov's eyes flicked to the dungeon core suspended in the phoenix's talons. It was only of the Earth grade. With a sky grade dungeon core, one could build a destroyer around it. "Prepare for realm transit. I want that dungeon core." Her mana infused voice reached everyone on the bridge. "Gregor, make sure that the ground and air leaders are ready."

"Yes, Captain."

"What is the city called?"

Gregor looked to the messenger who bowed as deep as possible.

"Vuzgal, Captain."

"Seems that we are the first to discover the Sha's hidden base. We must act before they have time to retreat."

"Yes, Captain."

Esther Leblanc's boots rang out on the marble floors. Old Jia whistled a joyful ditty behind her. He held his hands behind his back and took the time to look at the different paintings, suits of armor and weapons that were displayed along the walls of her uncle's manor.

"Old Jia," she said, seeing he had fallen behind again, staring at a painting of two ships on water with sails. Billowing clouds of gun smoke rolled from their decks.

"So many interesting trinkets." Jia laughed and caught up with her as they reached a finely carved door with golden accents.

"The admirals are in a meeting," the guard said.

"It is an emergency."

They looked at one another and opened the doors, revealing a room of men and women in red and blue uniforms. Those with less gold on their uniforms stood off to the side; those with more gold and with medals on their chests were closer to the table.

They all turned to look at the doorway as Esther walked in. Eccentric Old Jia trailed after her with a wide, simple smile, peering at the map table.

Her uncle was wearing his uniform of blues, reds and golds, a golden sash across his chest and a sword at his side.

"Miss Leblanc?" he said, every part the Marshall. She could see the twinkle in his eye as she caught the eye of her father standing nearby.

"Lord Marshall." She bowed. "I come with news. A group of scouts in the Earth Cloud Valley were keeping tabs on the frigate *Eternus* when its realm transferred."

There was a stir in the room.

"Did other ships transfer?" the Marshall asked, his dark eyes unwavering.

"No, we have no reports of any other Black Phoenix Clan ships transferring. The power signature was so strong, it could only be to another realm."

"Do we know where they might have gone?"

"The lower realms, specifically the Fourth Realm," Esther said.

"The Fourth Realm? We have some cities down there, but nothing to interest the Black Phoenix Clan. They only care about making more ships, harvesting mana stones, and increasing their cultivation." The Marshal frowned. "Wouldn't it be better for them to send raiders and corvettes? They require less mana. A frigate will burn through mana stones at a precipitous rate in such a low mana density realm."

"We should tell our people in the Fourth Realm to be on high alert," an admiral suggested.

"Already done," Esther said. "What is even stranger is that the frigate was harvesting the mana of the Earth Valley when it disappeared."

"How much did they draw?" another admiral asked.

"Not much; they only spent a few hours in the valley."

"I say that we take this opportunity and send our ships into the valley," one admiral suggested.

"It could be a trap," another said.

"It could be, but there have only been corvettes and smaller craft patrolling that area in the past. Without anything in the skies, how will they know we're there? This is a chance to deplete one of their tightly held areas. Could your scouts set up a transfer beacon?" The admiral looked at Esther.

"They have the equipment."

"Lord Marshall, we should not let this opportunity go. If we move the Third Fleet, into the Earth Cloud Valley, we can suck the valley dry. If they return or send someone else to the valley, we can ambush them."

The Lord Marshall studied the maps, the different regions that butted up against one another, and the known fleets and ships across the lands.

"Head back to your ships. First Fleet will head to the Earth Cloud Valley and empty it of power so the Black Phoenix Sect has no way to mine mana stones there for the next five years. Esther, find out where that frigate went and what they are doing in the Fourth Realm. I feel that something is wrong."

"Yes, Lord Marshall."

Esther turned and left the room as the admirals exited the war room.

She looked out of the windows of the Marshall's manor, over the manicured gardens that shifted in the light breeze. Clouds extended to the horizon as the manor started to lower, sinking into the airship.

"Ah, once again to battle," Old Jia said. He'd stopped at a window, looking up as metal extended above the manor, cocooning it.

"Old Jia, come on. We have work to do. Why did the Black Phoenix Sect go to the Fourth Realm? They must know something to take an airship down there. They're just burning mana stones otherwise. Not even the Associations would do so; at least not without a reason, a damn good one at that."

"Well, what else is interesting in the Fourth Realm other than our cities?"

Jia looked over, his expression placid.

"You think?" Esther paused and frowned.

"Vuzgal?"

Jia shrugged.

"They have weapons similar to our own. I will give them that. But they are not on the same level as ours."

"Yet, they might be in the future. And they have a great number of secrets." Jia released his hands from his back, holding his elbow and chin with opposite hands.

"You think they will attack them to make sure that another force like ours will not be able to rise? They are years away from achieving that."

"Didn't we say that they should come and find us when they reached the Seventh Realm?"

"That will take them decades."

"What if it doesn't?" Jia asked.

"They are a Fourth Realm group." Esther fell quiet before shaking her head.

"They are up against a Black Phoenix frigate with thousands of aerial and ground forces on it. Just one squad of fighters would be enough to bring a city in the Fourth Realm to its knees."

Esther dismissed the thoughts with a wave. "Come, we have work to do."

59
Turning the Tables

"Did you order a complete retreat?" Marco demanded. The command center's people were clearing out every piece of information, stripping it away before his eyes. The camps were being dismantled. Tents and supplies had been tossed into storage devices as supply wagons were hitched to mounts and loaded with supplies.

"*We* need to evacuate *now*," Marino said.

"The Black Phoenix Clan is coming. It is not the end."

"Marco!" Marino yelled, rising to her full height. "The Black Phoenix Clan holds an unwavering position in the Eighth Realm. The Associations have to show them respect. This is no longer our battle. We can only get our people out of here. I have never heard of the Black Phoenix coming down to a realm lower than the Sixth. When one of their clan was slighted, they destroyed an entire city. They are a small group, but the power they wield is massive."

Marco ground his teeth.

Marino ignored him and turned to her guards. "Send word for all the camps to evacuate."

"New target!" Acosta yelled as she moved her periscope and looked at the main camp. The artillery cannon shifted with her aim, elevating itself.

Across Vuzgal, weapons adjusted their aim.

"Load high explosive!"

"Yes, ma'am!" Neumann sounded only too pleased to do so. He dropped the round into the cradle as it tilted back with the artillery cannon. The gears clicked before its final adjustments were complete.

"Load!"

Neumann hit the rammer formation as the shell was pushed up into the cannon and the breach sealed.

"Ready!" Acosta waited and listened to her sound transmission device, putting her hand to the side.

Bai Ping crouched, holding his fist up. The rest of the squad crouched with him. He heard the rustle of plants on either side settle down. The skirmish line was hidden in the forest, at the edge of the trees, looking at the camps.

He checked the time. Just three minutes to go.

"Hold, hold, hold," Colonel Yui's voice rang in his ears.

"Hold, hold, hold," Bai Ping passed to his squad, they gave him a questioning look.

Bai shrugged and tapped the side of his helmet.

"Gunny, you won't believe this. The camp, they're running, just leaving their shit and leaving through the teleportation formations." Baines used his sound transmission device.

"They broke?"

"I don't know, maybe. I thought they'd have put up more of a fight."

Event
You have successfully defended Vuzgal.
Rewards:
801,200,000EXP +10% defensive bonus to Vuzgal defenders.

Blaze swatted the notifications away. Being outside the walls of Vuzgal, the bonuses wouldn't affect him or his people.

"I don't like this," Blaze said to Yui, Domonos, Elan, Erik and Rugrat through his sound transmission device.

"That group is still hanging out in the sky. They showed up and the sects started running. They're not even taking all their shit. I think they're scared," Rugrat said.

"Do we attack them or hold and wait?" Domonos asked.

"They're running like the Devil is chasing them. I'm getting teleportation pads laid down for immediate transfer. I say we regroup and see what the hell is going on," Yui said. "Else we'll stick our foot into something we don't have the slightest idea about."

"The teleportation formations are a mangled mess. Extend the barrier back out, recover our dead and wounded," Erik said.

"Nothing to do but shut up and wait."

"Move the damn skeleton up here. We might need him," Rugrat said.

"Egbert?" Domonos asked.

"If this shit scares the sects, then I'd like to have some extra firepower on our side."

"Doesn't hurt," Erik agreed.

"Our spies heard people saying something about the Black Phoenix Clan showing up. That's why they're all running. That's who that group is."

"That one group of people broke the United Sect Alliance?" Blaze asked.

"They're from the Seventh Realm. To them we're nothing but annoying bugs," Elan said, bouncing between sound transmission devices.

"Contact Glosil. I want him and Egbert up here now," Rugrat said.

"I think that we should consolidate our forces, get them all into Vuzgal," Yui said.

"Makes sense to me," Domonos agreed.

"I don't like the idea of sitting out here in the forest all afternoon," Blaze agreed.

Erik badly wanted to hit the rear of the United Sect Alliance, but something felt *wrong*. There were too many unknowns.

"Get everything out of Vuzgal we don't need and anyone that is not military or vitally important. Pull the dungeon cores in the crafting and training dungeons. Leave just the dungeon core for the under-city. Rugrat, and I will talk to the Associations. They might know more."

"You do not know what it took for me to get these," Elise said as Egbert inspected the four *sky* grade mana cornerstones.

Egbert waved his hand, pulling them from their boxes and rotating them. They glistened, drawing in the surrounding mana. "Very good! These will help finish off my preparations!"

He shot up into the air, appearing among the mana stones that grew across the Alva dungeon ceiling. He moved toward the pillar of power that struck the mana storing formation and spread out through to the mana cornerstones.

Egbert reached out, plucking cornerstones from their fittings. The threads of power diverted to cornerstones farther away.

He pushed the sky grade cornerstones into place, fittings molding to them. As they connected, the further reaches the formations died down. All the power was being consumed by just one of the sky grade cornerstones.

The mana would be sucked up by the sky grade cornerstones before reaching the hundreds of earth grade cornerstones that filled in the other fittings across the roof of the dungeon.

Egbert dropped down to Elise.

"That should double the amount of mana Alva can handle."

"I heard you added mana storing formations to every floor and mana dispersion formations?"

"Yes, the storing formations will gather as much power as possible and bleed it off. The dispersion is if we cannot hold all the mana released. Then it will spread it out over a larger area, so we don't have a spike. The mana gathering formations will draw that power back in, creating a cycle. We can choose to release some, increasing the mana density of the Beast Mountain Range slowly. It is a massive area so it will suffice."

"When do we kick off the drill?"

"We can start it anytime we want now. I'd like more sky grade cornerstones." Egbert shrugged.

"Egbert, I need you to go to Vuzgal," Glosil's voice rang through Egbert's head.

"Right now? When we are ready to start the drill?"

"Right now. Something is happening and no one likes it. A sect, the Black Phoenix Clan, has shown up. They might have dungeon hunters or dungeon lords in their ranks. You and I are heading up there."

"Great, I was hoping we wouldn't need to use the box," Egbert muttered.

"What's that?" Elise asked.

"Going to the Fourth Realm. See you in a bit." Egbert took off, flying toward the totem.

He checked the formations and the dungeon quickly, calling out to Davin and Delilah.

"Delilah, I am heading to Vuzgal. You have control over the drill now. I am starting it."

The dungeon dimmed as formations switched and altered. The power that had been rising to the mana storing formation reversed as the power was drawn down through the floors. The dungeon brightened again, running off the cornerstones without there ever being a spike in power as the energy pouring into the mana drill increased in power slowly.

"You're going?"

"Yes, I'm needed. Look after yourself and I'll be back soon!"

"Good luck, Egbert."

"Thank you, little Delilah."

Egbert sensed Glosil riding up to the totem with his staff. People appeared and disappeared around the totem at an increased rate.

The teleportation formation flashed as he brought Davin from the Fire Floor.

He zipped over to the totem and was waiting there as Egbert landed and Glosil rode in.

"Where're we going? Will there be treats?" Davin asked.

"Vuzgal."

"They have so many treats!"

"Well, maybe not for much longer. A clan from the seventh realm has shown up to attack it."

"They want to destroy my treat city?" Davin's power lashed out as Egbert created a barrier around him so he wouldn't melt the ground.

He pulled out two square boxes covered in runes glowing with power.

"Ready?" Glosil asked, not dismounting.

"Yes. Davin." Egbert indicated to a box and threw in a pie.

Davin zipped into the box that closed on him.

Egbert handed him to Glosil, who passed him to a member of his staff and tossed the other box up. Egbert collapsed his bones, piling himself into the box.

"This will sustain me for several days. If I have to exit without a connection to a greater power source, or in a higher mana density area, or have to use spells, then that time will be cut down considerably."

"I understand," Glosil said gravely.

"Been a few centuries since I left Alva." Egbert sounded uneasy as he floated his box over to Glosil, who put him under a blanket in front of himself.

"Well, as Momma Rodriguez says, best to rip off the Band-Aid quickly."

In a flash, they disappeared from Alva and appeared in a city.

"Welcome to Vuzgal." Glosil's voice was grim as he surveyed the damage.

"Come on, to the command center." Glosil took them down a path into the under city.

"How can we still use the totem? Aren't we under attack here?"

"The sects fled. It released the city from its restrictions."

Wounded streamed past through the totem.

Davin was released from his box. He flew around, licking his lips. The pie was mysteriously missing from his box.

60
Black Phoenix's Frigate

Rugrat jogged out of the headquarters.

George noticed it first, making Rugrat look up.

A massive black ship hovered over the soup where before, there had been nothing but sky. It looked like it was from the age of sail, but without the sails and angular sides down to the keel.

"Guys, you seeing this?" he asked the command chat.

"Warship floating in the *sky*, yeah. Why did we have to come to some magical realm? Why couldn't it be a planet covered in beaches, beer, and women?" Erik growled.

"And steak and food," Rugrat added.

"Well, this is rather disappointing," Egbert said.

"You all set up?" Glosil asked.

"Yes, I am linked to the dungeon core. I'm in the main tower. That is a powerful looking ship. I think the exterior is made of stone. Rugrat, could you use your dungeon sense?"

Rugrat activated his ability. It spread out, telling him of the dungeon core blazing underneath the tower and the empty valley where the three dungeon cores had been recovered.

Then it passed through the ship.

"Shit. That warship is a flying dungeon. There's a big ass dungeon core inside it. Well, it's tiny, but strong. A little weaker than the one under us."

"Well, commander, plans?" Erik asked.

"We take out whatever is keeping that thing in the air, then we assault it," Glosil said.

"The ship seems to be charging up. It must take a lot of power to move something that size. I think we have some time before they attack," Egbert said.

"Dungeon Lords West and Rodriguez, I am Captain Stassov of the Black Phoenix Clan. You have ten minutes to turn over the dungeon core you control and submit to our rule as vassals of our clan, or we will wipe out your city and take the dungeon core."

Everyone fell silent at her proclamation.

Rugrat used a spell to throw his voice. "What makes you think we have a core thing?"

"You are not the only people with Dungeon Sense."

Rugrat canceled the spell. "Well then." He got onto George's back, the rest of special teams one and three mounting up. "Those artillery cannons, can they hit that thing?"

"Yes," Domonos said.

"I'm increasing the Conqueror's armor to two hundred percent. Anyone below level forty is to be evacuated. Mortar teams withdraw to secondary positions within the city." Glosil's words were punctuated by the rising wail of a siren over Vuzgal.

"The forces out in the field?" Rugrat asked.

"I'm ordering the forces under Blaze and Yui to withdraw immediately," Glosil said.

"A retreat?" Rugrat felt anger spark in his chest.

"If we must." Erik's words made Rugrat pause.

"Everything that is not necessary and is useful, evacuate it now. If we need to retreat, we need to be ready for it."

"Erik," Rugrat said.

"This might be our city, but we have another. Our people are our strength, not the walls."

It felt wrong to Rugrat, but he knew Erik was right. "Damn, all right."

"I listen and obey," Glosil confirmed.

Gregor landed on the ship's deck, sliding off his mount with practised ease. Guards saluted as he passed. The doors down into the airship opened.

The rippling wind that pulled at him and his personal guards' clothes disappeared.

They passed stables where fighters of the clan were mounting up. Seeing Gregor, they saluted and stepped against the walls, moving out of his path.

Gregor had nothing to say as they moved past cannon batteries and went deeper into the ship. They walked along a walkway of glass and polished wood instead of the metal and stone of the upper decks.

A park lay in the center of the ship with trees that rose several stories. It looked idyllic with a Chinese-influenced tower in the middle, and walkways of glass and wood connecting it to different decks.

Guards checked their medallions on the bridge, then again at the entrance to the tower.

They entered a ringed walkway that went around the tower. They passed another checkpoint, and Gregor led him up a set of stairs. Men and women with the severe look of those on a mission nodded to Gregor and kept going, giving room but not stopping their actions.

They reached the top of the stairs, the command tower surveying the surrounding park.

The room was laid out like an octagon. At the front, three walls were pure glass tilting up and away to allow one to peer down at the park below.

Projections covered the windows, showing the exterior of the airship as if they were at the front of the ship instead of in its heart.

People worked at consoles that were laid out according to the shape of the room. In the center, a crystal-clear map pulsed as greater detail was added.

At the table, a man wearing an emblem with a blue backing was talking to a woman with a green backing.

Ranko looked older. There were streaks of grey in his black hair. His green eyes were pale and almost washed out. His eyes and mana channels glowed with power. His casting hood was down. Golden lines had been tattooed into a formation at the back of his skull, running down his spine and across his face, making him appear regal and aloof. They framed his aged years instead of being garish.

His armor was lighter than Gregor's and he had white cloth robes that shimmered with sewn formations.

The woman, Bela, looked younger, or she took better care of herself. She wore similar clothes. Power washed out her eyes as well, making them both look ethereal, as if they were spirits only visiting this plane. She had brown and black lines tattooed on her skin. Her blond hair was pulled back in a severe braid without a piece out of place.

The white of Gregor's emblem denoted him as part of the Dungeon Recovery team; green for ground forces, blue for aerial.

Captain Stassov sat in the back of the room on a great throne.

Her emblem backing was made of the finest crystal that shone with prismatic light.

"Captain Stassov." Gregor knelt as he bowed his head and cupped his hands.

"Rise." She walked past him and to the map, Gregor trailing behind to join the aerial and ground force commanders, Ranko and Bela.

Stassov looked at the map. "Have they shown any signs of surrender?"

"Not yet, commander." Ranko traced the golden line through his goatee.

"Are your aerial forces ready?"

"They are on the flight deck and ready to advance as needed." Ranko bowed his head.

"Bela, your ground forces?"

"We are just waiting for the first wave of attacks, my lady."

"Gregor?" Stassov sounded amused as she looked at the man.

Gregor grinned, showing his teeth as he cupped his fist toward her. "The Dungeon team stands ready!"

Captain Stassov moved her fingers through the light that made up Vuzgal like rippling water before she closed her hand.

An aide saluted. "There is a group flying toward the *Eternus* from the sect's camps."

Stassov's hand stilled.

"That should be the one I asked to be collected, the one who led the attack against the city," Gregor said.

"Gregor, it's best to tell me these things earlier. If any of those other sects try to come up here…" Stassov's eyes lay on the aide, who started sweating and shaking. "The main cannon will take another five minutes to charge. Then we will begin." She turned and walked back to her seat.

Ranko, Bela, and Gregor bowed to her back. She flicked her cloak out of her way as she sat back down. Formations appeared in a pillar in front of her, around the dungeon core.

"Deploy the main cannon."

Those at the consoles picked up their pace as they input commands to the airship.

61 Shattered

Erik pushed off the castle district wall he'd been leaning on. "That thing has to be charging up," he said. Power was being drawn from the area, from the sky and land. Pillars extended from the ship-mana gathering formations, drawing the mana into the core-ship.

"I think we're about to find out what for." Roska pointed.

Sections of the ship pushed out and moved as the lower section of the ship slid away from the sides that extended out.

The blue light of mana appeared between the sections as they parted, allowing them to see right through the ship.

Egbert landed next to them wearing his casting robes.

"Well, that doesn't look good. Looks like a big cannon right through the ship."

"Egbert, put our barriers to full power. Activate all secondary barriers."

Barriers rose from the inner barrier towers. Power glowed over the different bases and camps. Other barriers rose around the castle and powered up.

"You think we can beat that thing?" Storbon asked.

"Best to try." Erik's sound transmission device vibrated.

"Erik, Rugrat, this is Glosil. I'm moving all personnel below level fifty out of the city. That's most of the reserve divisions and the Adventurer's

Guild. Both of you will hold in the castle district. Your goal is to protect the dungeon core. If they breach the dungeon core, I will instruct the special teams to evacuate both of you, even if they have to knock you out and drag you away. Those needing medical assistance will be teleported to back up dungeons."

"Got it," Rugrat said.

"Copy," Erik said.

"I've sent word to Alva. Evacuation from all secondary sites is underway," Elan said.

"What are you thinking about the Wandering Inn, Sky Reaching Restaurants and such?"

"I've passed it onto the council."

Erik hadn't faced a fight where they were preparing to lose before it had even started. Looking at the ship, which had stopped its transformation, carved formations hung between the sections of ship like ribs. Looking through them, one would find a perfectly circular path.

"Heading down." Erik ran down the stairs from the wall, heading to the castle.

They jogged across the castle grounds as the shadows of the city shifted.

Erik threw up a mana barrier, as did Egbert, as the Frigate's main cannon fired.

The mana from the ship and its surrounding area was sucked in, creating a spear of energy before it shot through the crackling formations.

The spear tore through the outer mana barrier, then the inner mana barrier, through the castle compound barrier, and darkened the castle barrier. Wind collapsed buildings and the destructive energies tore apart the castle wall and gardens, destroying the parks, stables, training areas, and wrecking the Vuzgal Academy. It lost a considerable amount of its strength at each barrier, but the discharge of forces still cleared out blocks of buildings and tore apart the ground.

Any aerial beasts in the air nearby were hurled away by the force.

The special team's barriers protected them from the wash of the cannon's impact.

The cannons along the sides of the Frigate glowed and then fired again, raking Vuzgal with attacks.

Someone caught the back of Erik's vest and pushed him toward the castle.

Erik grabbed at Egbert, catching his arm.

"Egbert." He looked into his blue flames. "Do whatever you can to take out that ship!"

"And what will you do?"

Event
The city of Vuzgal is under attack!
Role: City Lord You have picked to Defend Vuzgal

Erik swiped the notification away and gritted his teeth. "I'll head to the rear and lend my support."

Egbert put a skeletal hand on Erik's shoulder and squeezed. "Be safe."

"And you." Erik clasped his shoulder.

They released one another. Erik turned and ran with the special team toward the dungeon core. The heat at the back of his neck spread across his face, burning as he turned his back. Duty was a heavy word when lives hung in the balance.

Acosta hit her fire panel; the artillery cannon activated, and spell formations appeared down its length, revealing its full capabilities.

The pre-sighted artillery and mana cannons rippled as they fired on the ship.

A massive mana barrier enveloped the ship. Their repeated hits were flares of sparks against the ship's background.

The ship's cannons fired again, pummeling the ground, and causing the bunker's smaller mana barriers to darken as they fought to protect the basic mana cannon bunkers beneath.

"Reload!" Acosta yelled.

Vuzgal's main barrier crumbled like a soap bubble popping in slow motion.

"Loaded!" Nuemann yelled.

Acosta triggered the cannon again. The wave of force hit her as she stared at the barrier. She shook herself and focused on her task.

"Reload!" Acosta growled, watching for anything, *something,* to tell her they were having an effect.

Three hits registered on the barrier, causing it to flare violently.

"Damn you, beautiful rail cannons!"

She picked a new point of aim, right where the rail cannons had hit. The cannon rotated with the periscope as the next round was loaded in.

"Firing!" The cannon bucked as the darkened section of barrier, like a tumor, started to grow, the other artillery cannons locking onto it.

"Reload!"

"Loade—" Acosta was thrown to the side, smashing into the bunker wall. She felt something snap in her right arm. Her helmet saved her head as rocks fell on her.

Another hit struck the bunker, dropping a section of roof. Acosta raised a barrier around herself, taking the impact of the roof.

Hits rang out around her as she lay on her back looking up at the section of wall. She put force into her right arm and pushed. The section of wall was thrown off.

"Two hundred percent power," Acosta muttered, wincing at her right arm as it hung limply by her side. Minor wounds covered the rest of her body.

"Neumann! Neumann! Where are you?"

She used a detect life spell. The wave of power spread through the room, but it didn't find anything.

"Shit. I don't remember having skylights." The formations were dead, no longer connected to the power runes. The cannon's runners were broken, and the cannon now rested on the inner and outer shields, pointing into the sky.

"Neumann!"

She moved to the other side of the cannon; rubble shifted under her feet.

"Fuck sakes." She growled, looking up as she gritted her teeth, ignoring her arm. She looked at where Neumann should have been.

She grabbed onto the stone with mana and threw it to the side.

"Ah, fuck." She stumbled. Neumann was flat on his back, staring opened-eyed at the roof. "Dammit." She forced her eyes away from his lower torso. There was nothing below his ribs.

She moved closer, grabbing his dog tags from around his neck, fumbling with them to pull off the one she needed. She closed his eyes and stored him in her storage ring, then hobbled toward the rear of the bunker.

"Must've fucked my knee up too." She grunted and used the back of the cannon to pull herself over a pile of bunker.

She looked at the closed breach. She looked up the barrel of the cannon. It was still pointed at the ship. "One last shot, huh, girl?" Acosta patted the barrel as she got down on the other side. She only needed enough power to loop the formations into the fire controls. There would be a secondary manual fire control somewhere. She looked around the breach of the gun and found a hook.

She pulled out mana stones, using them to power the formations. They flickered to life as she took a piece of string and hooked it onto the manual firing pin. She hobbled to the rear of the bunker.

She cleared out a path and checked her string.

"Fuck you, pricks!"

She pulled on the string. The cannon fired and rocked backward, the formations dying around it as it tilted and fell off its carriage.

Dust flew everywhere as Acosta coughed. She looked through the bunker skylights at the ship. A cannon round had made it through the barrier and struck the side of the ship, exploding and making some formations stutter and fail More hits opened up on the barrier.

Acosta hobbled out of the bunker and down the stairs.

She opened what looked like a fire alarm, pulled the lever, turned it, and pressed it down.

Explosions rang through the artillery cannon bunker as she hobble-ran through Vuzgal's tunnels.

Egbert stood in the air. Sections of the castle compound's manicured grounds shuddered as rail and artillery cannons' armored coverings opened. The cannons fired, their barrels releasing gouts of flame and mana discharge skyward, their constant thundering peeling through the city.

Rounds crossed over the different defensive zones, striking the heart of the United Sect Army Camps. The railguns and artillery cannons lit up the sect's mana barriers. They held for several seconds before collapsing.

The command towers at the center of the camps were the first victims. The towers shattered, spraying destruction through the camps. Releasing shockwaves blew apart the roughly built structures. Sprays of flaming embers dotted the ground, setting the miniature cities aflame.

The retreating sect forces were caught up in the artillery's fire, tearing apart the camp.

Fighters ran for the forests. Anything to get away from the two behemoths crashing into one another.

The crews changed from their pre-set targets. Their smoking barrels tilted toward the frigate, the formations along the barrels gathering power.

The first cannon reached its peak, pausing and shuddering with thunderous intent. If Egbert had breath to hold, it would have been torn from him in the wave of pressure.

The second cannon reached its targeted height, paused, and fired. Artillery crews, tired from days of fighting, worked their guns.

Egbert felt stronger than he had ever felt before as the guns locked onto their target. A series of batteries fired, devolving into a constant stream of attacks that pock-marked the ship's mana barrier.

The frigate's advance slowed; its cannons changed their point of aim, targeting the artillery cannons with a vengeance. Bunker barriers collapsed and bunkers were torn apart. The frigate's mana barrier was starting to spot in places. The artillery crews zeroed in their attacks to the same areas.

The first few artillery rounds passed through. Mana barriers popped up around the ship, a second layer of defense that was smaller, more focused.

"Now?" Davin asked.

"Wait," Egbert drew in more mana. He looked over to the castle as a window was smashed open. Rugrat shoved a desk against the window, using it as a rest for his railgun.

The airship's outer barrier collapsed as the frigate shifted to spread the fire over its mana barrier instead of just one location.

Formation enchanted plates dropped from the bottom of the ship, carrying ground forces. The formations flared as they neared the ground, coming to rest on the ground at a sedate pace.

Black Phoenix riders on aerial beasts dropped from the ship and charged the artillery positions. Machine guns opened up with their stream of tracers.

Egbert felt the heat rising in his bones, the crackling of power that channeled through his body. Even if they took *Vuzgal, they wouldn't defeat them. You won't break Alva. And you'll have to pay a price.*

Egbert turned back to the airship as a round punched through the mana barrier and struck the side of the ship.

"Now?"

Egbert drew power directly from the mana storing formations, channeling it through himself into the spell formation in front of him. "Now!"

The ground shook, and the wind was beaten into submission as Egbert glowed with power. He reached into the heart of the mana and turned it to his will. Five formations appeared around him, one green, one blue, one black, one red, and one yellow.

Buildings shook and collapsed as elements were torn from the ground, powering the rotating formations. Egbert's bones burned away as he pushed his hands forward. The runes throughout his body flaked off under the sheer power channeling through them.

Several formations appeared behind and through the five rotating formations.

"Take my drill!" Egbert yelled at the ship.

The five elemental formations ignited with mana. Beams of elemental energy hit the spell formation pillar.

The pillar directed and added power to the spell.

Vuzgal fired a beam of elemental energy through the sky and into the weakening barrier. It punched a hole through it and smashed into the ship. The force was enough to lift the ship, carving a line into the ship's side and under-decks.

Davin raised his arms. Flames came from his hands, forming into dragons of hardened flame half the size of Gilly. They roared and rushed toward the airship.

The first spell faded. Egbert's body started to recover.

He dipped from where he had been flying.

"You good?" Rugrat yelled from his window.

"A little weak. That was a third of our power reserves." Egbert glowed with power once again. "And for my next move, an oldie but a goodie. Meteor shower!"

Rugrat looked at the rail cannons. "I have an idea! Don't use all the power!" Rugrat ran deeper into the castle, using his sound transmission device. Egbert traced him jumping into the basement and running to the railgun cannons.

"Here come the sailors," Davin said.

Egbert looked at the aerial beasts that had rushed into the air. Formation-covered platforms dropped from the bottom of the ship while the cannon through the middle of the ship powered down. The ship covered it up, taking impacts along its side.

He looked at the front of Vuzgal and projected his voice into the Vuzgal command center. "Commander Glosil, the bunkers have been lost.

The enemy is sending out their aerial and ground forces."

"Thank you, Egbert. Nice spell."

"I think it surprised them." Egbert gathered in more power. "I need some time before I can cast another spell on that scale, else I will burn out my bones."

"Get to cover. Let me know when you can use another spell."

"In the meantime, I can control the undead and the mana cannons."

"Do so. I'm pulling back my people to the inner city. The outer defenses are lost." Glosil forced the words out. The combined sects hadn't been able to breach their outer barrier after weeks of trying and had paid a heavy price to attack their barriers directly.

"There is always someone stronger in the realms." Egbert's eyes glowed brighter as he gnashed his teeth and stopped projecting into the command center.

"Davin come with me."

Gregor felt the ship shift following the hit before settling down once again.

The staff looked in shock as the trees in the park beyond shed their leaves.

"Launch our forces. Cover the core cannon." Captain Stassov's words cracked through the room "Gregor, bring the old commander of the sects here."

"Yes, Captain!"

Gregor turned and ran, his people following him as the frigate shook with impacts. He found the boy where he had left him. Grabbing him by the arm, he hauled him back the way he had come. "Captain!"

He caught the look on Marco's face, trying to take in everything as Stassov looked over.

Marco had the presence of mind to bow to the commander. "I am Marco Tolentino. How may I serve?"

"This Vuzgal, what are their capabilities?"

Marco didn't dare to hold anything back. Her commanders were stronger than his father who was one of the strongest men in the entire Willful Institute. "Their people are stronger than their level. They have much higher cultivation than we first realized." He clenched his fists into tight white balls. "They have weapons I have not seen before. Like mana cannons, but they shoot out solid projectiles covered in formations. They do not rely on their own power. Instead, they rely on the power of their weapons."

Stassov gave Gregor a pointed look. "Sha weapons," she snarled. "You did not know who you were messing with." Stassov snorted and walked to the map. "They took their time building this city. They didn't flaunt their power. They kept it hidden. They were thorough in their preparations, which means they are smart. Many show off their strength and we deal with them before they are a threat."

"Who are they?" Marco asked. He paled at Stassov's glare, lowering his head, but seemed determined to find an answer.

She relented and looked away. "They are the Sha's lackeys. A hidden group that must have been working on something for them. Why did you attack them?"

"They attacked our elder."

"The real reason, sect rat." Stassov's aura pressed Marco to the ground.

"They had trade routes, crafters flocked here, and they had a powerful crafting dungeon and the protection of the Associations. They have a Battle Arena, crafter workshops that span their city and training facilities that are rare in the Sixth Realm."

"Dammit," She hit the table in front of her. "Those sneaky French bastards. They've been working to build a fleet right under our noses—right here."

"Do you think that they were able to finish any ships?" Gregor asked.

"I don't know. They might have been making parts and sending them to the seventh realm." Stassov growled, turning her eyes on Marco with a tooth filled smile. "You pulled the tiger's tail. Good thing for us. I would have never let you get to the city's defenses. Just their modified mana cannons would have been enough to keep your sects at bay. They didn't want to show their power and draw attention." Stassov's breath hissed through her teeth.

"This Vuzgal, where did they come from?"

"It was owned by an empire from the time when other races walked the realms. The humans fought the lizard folk. The emperor used a powerful spell and turned people into undead. They remained that way, killing one another, and any animals or people that came this way.

"The city lords took the city a few years ago. Shortly afterward, they saved the Associations from being killed by a sect. They gained their help and built up the city. The lords are powerful crafters as well as fighters. Some people think that they are from the higher realms."

"What do you think?"

"They are not pure warriors like people in this realm. They are strong crafters, possibly at the high journeyman level. They have strong mana cultivation and at least some body cultivation. They are not like people from the Fourth Realm."

"You are smarter than you look." Stassov turned him around, inspecting him. "What else?"

"That is all I know. We attacked the Adventurer's Guild inside their city. They killed a cousin and an uncle of mine and the sect had to reclaim our honor. The Guild attacked us across different realms and now they have disappeared. They could be allied." Marco's voice strained against the ropes of mana that appeared around him.

"Strength of their forces?"

"We have not fought them in close range. We used spells and spell scrolls to attack them." Marco's voice relaxed as the ropes loosened.

Stassov closed her eyes then checked the map, looking at Marco. "You say that there are three dungeons, but I only sense one." Stassov raised her hand.

"There are three dungeons in the valley behind the city! The city was made to control entry to the dungeons!" Marco was sweating as he spat the words out.

Stassov lowered her hand. "So, they are dungeon lords indeed. They must have combined the dungeon cores to increase their power."

"Mana spike above the ship!" a controller yelled.

"What is our barrier status?" Stassov turned, letting her hand curl around her back.

Marco dropped to the ground with barely a grunt.

"They cut through several cannon decks and overloaded the mana stone supplies. The ship is working to recover but, with this Earth grade mana, power output and work is slow."

Stassov threw out her hand. Mana stones piled between the formations. They cracked and fell apart and the power was devoured by the dungeon core. The formations looked like they were made from glass instead of vapor as the phoenix holding the dungeon core glowed with power.

"Focus on strengthening our barriers!"

The ship shuddered violently.

"What was that?"

"A mana relay was hit. It blew throughout the ship and took out some stabilization formations!"

"Two dragons, made from mana, are approaching."

"Have the cannons focus on the ground. Get the mages to focus on the dragon spells."

Chains with links as large as a man shot through the park and reached for the dungeon core.

Stassov stretched her hand out. Several blades of air appeared beyond the tower, cutting through the chains. They dropped to the ground and faded.

"What was that?"

"An enchanted arrow covered in a powerful spell from their large weapons! It made it through a gap barely wider than the arrow." The aide looked at the information not understanding it.

"Our cannon?"

Gregor looked around as clan members attacked the chains that had punched through the park, tearing up trees and grass.

"It is inoperable."

Stassov hit the table, breaking off part of it. "Mana barrier around the tower!"

The chains were like giant tree roots as they tore through the ship, weakening the inside.

Gregor steadily regained his feet when everything seemed to explode at once. He ducked away, relieved to be alive, and looked through the tower windows.

Light projection formations sparked with chaotic mana and smoked, cutting off and leaving them blind.

"Get my barriers back online and take out that fucking dungeon lord!"

Rugrat circulated his mana, drawing in more, reaching out to his connection to the dungeon core. The torrent of energy contained there was as terrifying as it was seductive.

One can be a god with that much power.

He was operating scan constantly, seeing through the stairs of the bunkers, up through the sandwiched plates of metal and compressed stone. He watched the men and women operating the rail cannon as it fired, shaking the bunker itself.

Mana congealed and opened the door ahead of him as he walked in. "I need that gun," Rugrat said. his voice rumbled through the room. He no longer contained his aura and drew upon all his mana gates.

The team looked at him.

"Going to need a mana blast round, jack it up with the most mana you can get."

"Get loading," Gong Jin yelled from behind Rugrat.

Rugrat moved to the rail cannon, scanning it with his domain.

"Hey there, sexy!" He patted the gun and looked down the barrel, adjusting for distance, for wind, for changes in air pressure from the attacks outside the different barriers.

"Ready!" the ammunition loader said as the breach was secured.

Rugrat did some last alterations according to the round's weight and powder ratios as he walked to the casting plate. "Well, never tried this before. Might want to step back a bit," Rugrat said.

The people moved.

"Quickly now! Trying to blow up a dungeon ship here!" Power *leaked* through skin tracing through his body. He reached out and placed his right hand on the enhancement pad. It looked the same as the pad on the mana cannons.

The formation under his feet lit up as he braced himself, reaching out his left hand backward toward the castle.

"All right, let's see what this does."

> Do you wish to draw power from the Dungeon core and revert mana storing formations?
>
> *YES/NO*

Egbert or the Gnomes must have kept this in mind when they came up with it.

"Hell, yeah!"

The mana in the area surged toward Rugrat. He opened his mana gates as the wind tore at the people inside the bunker.

"Come on, come *on!*" His voice commanded mana itself, tearing it from its bonds. Mana redirected from the dungeon core and the mana storing formation was unleashed. It came in like a beam, passing through the walls without affecting them. It *slammed* into Rugrat's open hand, breaking on his left wrist mana gate.

Rugrat gritted his teeth, closing his eyes and looking up as his body shuddered.

"More!" He stared at the beam as if seeing through the dirt, stone, and metal to the dungeon core entombed within.

Streams of power like ribbons of light split from the beam, dragged into his other mana gates, through the crown of his head and the base of his skull, through his elbows, his back and sternum, his lower stomach, the base of his spine, upper legs and his feet.

A thicker beam travelled down the first and crashed against his hand, thickening the spreading beams.

A whirling noise came from within Rugrat's body as he compressed and guided the mana through his body. His mana channels lit up in brilliant blue light like electrical veins illuminating him from within. Smoke started to rise from his body. His skin darkened and blackened around the mana that thrummed in his veins. A loud *whomp, whomp, whomp,* came from his body, increasing in volume as the others in the room fought against the wind.

He created hands of mana, turning the traversing and elevation gears.

"Chains of mana." Rugrat's words gave direction to power, creation to energy. Power surged from his body as spell formations appeared around his hand and the pad.

The power from the dungeon core shut off.

The formation plate under his feet poured more mana into the spell as he released it. It traced through the pad, down into the floor, and up the side of the rail cannon into the breach.

The power of the spell transmitted into the heart of the round.

"*Bon voyage.*" Rugrat grinned and reached out and hit the activation formation.

The rail cannon's formations lit up in sequence as the primer was struck, throwing the covered Sabot into the heart of the railgun, accelerating faster and faster. Its sheath came off as Rugrat stabbed a needle in his gut, depressed the plunger and staggered to the barrel. He took it out and leaned on the barrel, looking along her length, seeing the thin blue lines as the frigate closed her maw.

"Too slow, bitch." Rugrat laughed as his features returned to normal.

A few sparks showed on the closing stone of the frigate as the blue lines disappeared.

Rugrat's body was smoking as Gong Jin forced a potion into his hand.

He drank as an act of reaction over conscious thought.

"Fucking-A, sir." Gong Jin whistled, looking at the ship

"That should have fucked something up." Rugrat looked along the barrel of the rail cannon.

"Right about, *now.*"

The frigate staggered in the air. Rugrat grinned.

"What was that?"

"That was the round hitting and the spell expanding. *Explode.*" Power once again filled his voice, commanding momentous mana.

Formations died on the ship's surface and explosions rocked it as it dropped several feet. Barriers were thrown up haphazardly, showing openings in its shields.

"That was me detonating it. Come on, Erik, you slow army bastard."

Erik yelled as power coursed from the dungeon core, burning through his body and into the rail cannon.

The world bloomed with fierce light from the mana discharge. A second rail cannon bucked, the round hurtling through the sky.

Erik watched as it struck the side of the frigate, carving a silver scar in its blackened sides. An explosion tossed the ship to the side.

Erik panted; his mana channels were burning. He could feel the limits of his body.

The ship listed to the side. The impact made the multi-ton behemoth shudder.

He heard the auto loader loading the next round.

Just one more round should take them out of the sky and bring them down to our level.

He braced himself against the gun, gritting his teeth with the pain, ready to take on the full power of the dungeon core to enhance the round again.

He was aware of the state of his body, the state of his mana channels. It wouldn't take much more to break them, to break him.

His thoughts turned to Alva, and to the mana drill.

His breath caught as he swallowed sharply, thinking thoughts he didn't want, feeling his bone-deep fatigue.

I can't. And he knew it to be true. He could power up another round, buff it to do some massive damage, possibly strike a critical blow, but he could die in the attempt and he couldn't—wouldn't—let that happen. If he and Rugrat weren't around, Alva could fall apart. *Look at what happened with the dungeon and the drill. At all of this. If we die, Alva will die too.*

He cursed, releasing the cannon's barrel. He balled his fist, wanting to punch it but grunted and turned away. His duty lay with Alva. Dying here, trying to take out the ship, maybe taking it out… If he was just a soldier, he would do it. But he was a Lord of Alva and Alva needed him.

His life was not his own to throw away and that burned something fierce. He wanted to rage against it but deep down he believed that Alva, while they had developed, had not yet grown.

"Sir?"

Erik smacked the barrel with an open palm. "We'll support the withdrawal. I want to make sure *all* Alvans return home."

Commander Glosil assessed the situation. Attacks were raining down a lot closer now. Black Phoenix's aerial beasts, birds of red and black, breathed fire while their riders cast destructive spells.

There were thousands of them, while only tens of the kestrel's and sparrows remained, bringing a trail of undead mages with them. Having fought for the whole day, they were being torn apart.

"We can't hold on for much longer," Kanoa said.

"I need ten more minutes. Let our people get into cover and organized, then pull back your sparrows and kestrels," Glosil said and opened a channel to Kanoa, Domonos, and Yui.

"Yui, once the bunkers have collapsed, pull back to the inner wall. Peel back those in the towers with you. Domonos, defend the castle compound walls. Kanoa, organize the evacuation. Push people to the backup dungeons. Those with the lowest levels first—Adventurer's Guild and reservists. Then the air forces, then the ground forces."

"Sir," Yui started but Glosil talked over him.

"We will not be able to hold Vuzgal, but we will do everything we can to make sure that the enemy pays to take it. I will not let our people die for a city filled only with our own fighters. Our people are gone. I am preparing plan Sunken City."

"Yes, sir," the others reported.

"We must buy time for our people to retreat. Every minute we hold means one more person we can get to safety."

Glosil cut the channel and opened four new ones.

"Pull the lords out to the backup dungeons."

"Yes, sir," the special team leaders reported.

Rugrat looked over the sandbags that made a wall inside the castle's side doors. Covered walkways reached out to different sections of the wall.

"Let's move." He sprinted with the special team and ran under the covering toward the walls. Spells hit the ground around the barriers, throwing up sprays of dirt and stone.

"Missed, prick!" Rugrat yelled as they ran to the wall. Rugrat slowed as he reached the bottom of the stairs, breathing heavily. He coughed, grabbed onto the railing, and hauled himself up the stairs with a yell.

He got to the third floor. Dragon Regiment was setting up across the wall. Machine guns were fired from the roof and others were shooting in the hallway. Rugrat moved to a firing slit and looked at Vuzgal.

Towers fired into the sky with their machine guns. Blue airshot spells cris-crossed, taking a heavy toll from the Black Phoenix Clan, but the tower's mana barriers were rapidly darkening.

The Undead Legions moved to the rooftops or flew on their aerial beasts into the maelstrom, casting spells, hurling spears, and firing bows, or throwing debris.

Rugrat looked at the map on the inside of his arm. The enemy was landing among the bunkers and in the city.

"Shit, they're going to cut off our front lines."

"Sir, you need to come with us," Gong Jin said.

Rugrat kept checking his map as Gong Jin guided him down the stairs. "Shit, we have no support. If they all go into the under city, the enemy will follow them down. And we don't have the teleportation formations to move an entire regiment in one move."

Rugrat grabbed a potion and drank it. His strength was still coming back as his body healed from the stresses he had placed upon it.

Thank shit I only used a few percent of the power stored in the mana storing formation. If I'd gone a little higher, I'd be popcorn.

"Sir, we need to get you out of here," Gong Jin said.

"Wait, *what?*" Rugrat stopped, pulling up Gong Jin short as he asserted some power.

"Sir, you are the dungeon lord," Niemm said. "We need to evacuate you."

Rugrat glared at them both. "And you think I'm going to fucking abandon my people?" His voice grew deeper as the power in his mana channels gathered. His domain stabilized around them all as the two team leaders looked at one another and Rugrat.

"Maybe you forgot, boys, but there is a plan if Erik or I die. I hate this dungeon lord this, city lord that," Rugrat snarled and pulled his arm from around Gong Jin's shoulders.

He started toward the downstairs.

"Sir, what are you doing?" Gong Jin asked, raising his voice.

"My fucking job!" Rugrat pulled out his rail gun, staggering slightly. He stabbed out his foot to support himself. His hands moved faster than his brain, checking the modified rail gun before he slung it and kept walking. He made it to the bottom floor as spells still struck around the covering.

George jumped from his shoulders and expanded.

"Sir, Alva needs you!" Niemm yelled.

"Alva has the council. My fucking troops need me. Erik and I are your nukes. Well, I say it's about time we have a fucking atomic winter! These motherfuckers and their shiny fucking ship!" Rugrat's face twisted, his teeth clenched as he pulled on his helmet activating his linked sound transmission device.

"Doc!"

"What?" Erik said.

"'Bout time we got into this motherfucker, you think?"

"Yeah, yeah. I think you're right. What you thinking?"

"Draw a line in the sand and hold it."

"See you in the air."

Rugrat jumped on George's back and looked back at the special teams. "Now, you going to baby me like some green fucking recruit, or are you going to get on your mother fucking mounts and do your fucking job?"

The team members behind Gong Jin and Niemm pulled out their mounts and got on.

Gong Jin and Niemm did likewise.

"Anymore of that shit and I'll shove you through a teleportation formation myself. Am I understood, Captains?"

"Yes, Sergeant Major," Gong Jin and Niemm repeated.

"You with me?"

"Until the end," Gong Jin said.

"I'm not one for waiting in the rear. These fuckers knocked on our front door. We best give them an answer," Niemm said.

"All right, we're going through the air to the outer wall. Keep it tight. Arrowhead formation. Make sure you have your railgun ready and check your spell scrolls. What's our rule?"

"Use your rounds, not your spells!"

"Too fucking right!"

"Fuck me." Santos' laugh was hollow.

"Yeah." Wazny's throat was dry as he looked out from the secondary mana barrier tower on the inner wall.

It was just Santos, Xia and Wazny now. The sparrow and kestrel wings had been dispersed over the towers so if one tower were knocked out, it wouldn't take out all of Alva's air force.

"Not much for it," Xia said.

"No." Wazny blinked, holding his eyes together to wet them. "How are you looking?"

"Formations charged, bird fed. Armor at two hundred percent. Railguns are in and loaded," Xia said.

"Same here," Santos confirmed.

"Good to go here. Did you get resupp on spell scrolls?"

"Yeah, got a full spread," Santos said.

"Barrier, buffs, and attacks," Xia said.

Wazny looked over to Xia, seeing her look through the different spell scrolls and pull tabs arranged around her cockpit as her sparrow moved around, scratching his wing.

Wazny looked to the other side. Santos held beads in his hand, silently moving them between his fingers.

"We all need some prayers right now," Wazny muttered.

"What was that, Cap?" Xia asked.

"Time to do the day job." Wazny's mount moved forward to the flight line. Formations lined the walls, ceiling, and floor, humming with power that flickered randomly.

"Looks like the rain is rather heavy." Santos gave a tired laugh.

Wazny looked out over the flight line and the formations. Aerial mounts rode the wind down in a wave of blacks and reds. Platforms dropped from the bottom of the ship. Alvan mana cannons and machine guns fired on them, striking mana barriers around each platform.

Formations flared, throwing up mud and igniting spell traps in the ruined Scarecrow's hill. Then they hit the ground; mounted fighters charged toward the bunkers.

Spells darkened the mana barriers as attacks cut into the landing forces. They fell under the withering red fire of explosive shot, unable to use their barriers in the chaotic environment.

More platforms dropped around the bunkers, offloading their forces, splitting the bunker's fire.

The towers opened up with their airshot as the Phoenix aerial forces got into range. Barriers took the impacts, and the riders responded with their own spells. The barriers flared.

"Another round of who has the stronger weapons and the better barriers. Fuck," Xia's voice broke.

"You good?"

"Yeah, I'm good, Cap. Let's get in this. Our people need us."

Wazny looked at Xia and then over to Santos. "It's a fucking honor to lead you into battle."

"Same here, sir," Santos said.

"Wouldn't trade it for anything," Xia said.

Wazny connected to the command channel. "Sparrow wing Alpha Three launching."

His mount ran forward, flapping her wings. She caught the formation, Santos and Xia right behind him. Undead aerial mounts and their mages unfolded from their standby positions and rushed out after them.

Wazny checked Xia and Santos on his wings. "Okay, long range them with railguns and spell scrolls. Keep them from attacking the towers. Don't try to get tangled. They have numbers and the towers can't shoot."

"Copy."

"Understood."

Wazny took a breath. "Okay, target the group at our ten o'clock with spell scrolls. Santos, target left. Xia, right. Undead, attack after we use our spell scrolls. Only ranged attacks."

"Talkative group!" Santos said.

"Follow me." Wazny altered his heading. The group moved with him.

He saw other groups of sparrows and kestrels shooting out from the airfields and inner barrier towers.

"Targeting." Wazny grabbed a pull tab. The area of effect appeared in front of him over a tower that the Black Phoenix aerial forces were strafing, then banking away and attacking again.

"Watch for spell scroll."

Wazny ripped the pull tab. A spell formation snapped into existence right in the path of the Black Phoenix aerial forces. They couldn't stop themselves as air blades flew out of the spell formation.

Their barrier took a few hits before it passed over the formation and the spell was inside, right in the Phoenix's beaks.

Xia and Santos activated their spell scrolls. As the Phoenixes broke to the sides to get out of the path of the air blades, they ran right into their spells.

The force was torn to ribbons. Their barrier carrier must have been killed as it disappeared.

The tower and undead mages exacted vengeance on the remainder of the group.

"Follow me, new—" Spells hit around Wazny.

"Barrier! Barrier! Barrier!" He pulled a tab, and a barrier covered him and the others. They pulled their own spell scrolls. The barriers didn't activate being under his own.

The spells went wide but the undead mages were targeting and returning attacks.

"Where the hell are the undead shooting?" Wazny looked for where their spells were going.

"High and left! Good tracers."

Wazny saw what Santos saw; a group was diving toward them.

"Break to the left and spell scroll them!"

Wazny banked to the left and targeted the other group. Spells appeared in what would have been Wazny's path. His spell skimmed over the top of their covering barrier as they changed their flight path.

"Break! Break! Break!"

Their formation came apart as Santos, Xia, and Wazny went in different directions. The undead broke, following each of them.

Impacts dotted Wazny's spell scroll barrier as he fought back with his spell scrolls. Santos raked their barrier with his rail guns, stitching lines up its side as Xia's spell scroll missed.

The Black Phoenixes dove in formation. They were slower, running right into Wazny's forming spell as it exploded in a fireball.

Burning birds and people were tossed out of the burst barrier, falling to the ground.

"Okay, let's head to the east!"

Spells hit Santos. He dove to get away from them but one of his unprotected mages was hit.

Their mount staggered, but they returned the attacks.

Xia returned fire with her railguns. The group was unprotected, and her air shot rounds tore through several as the others dispersed. The undead mages targeted them, raking them with spells as they tried to flee.

Their barriers fell away.

"Barrier up! Don't hold back. You run out of barrier spell scrolls RTB." Wazny pulled on a barrier spell scroll.

"Yes, sir."

"Copy!"

Wazny saw a flight of kestrels get hit with spells as they fought through, the gunners firing off spells and their repeaters in every direction.

"Bank to the left. Moving in support!"

They turned toward the kestrels, piling on the power. Wazny tore spell scrolls, getting it in the general area of the three aerial groups.

Their spell scrolls hit the Black Phoenix aerial forces. They peeled away. Two of the kestrels were in a bad way; the third had lucked out. They were all turning and dropping back toward the nearest airbase.

Spells overshot Wazny's group.

"High and right!"

"Break away. They have the altitude!" Wazny yelled. They dove toward the city, coming in low over the buildings, and through the undead that dotted the roofs. The undead attacked those up high and below the towers, sending hundreds of blue tracers skyward.

Spells hit the buildings around Wazny, the blast shaking his barrier.

"Circle the tower!" Wazny yelled.

A spell smashed into Santos's barrier.

"Shi—" He slammed into a building.

His aerial mages kept attacking the Black Phoenix group that was harassing them, turning to follow Wazny and Xia.

Wazny tightened his jaw as his sparrow jinked side to side, diving low into a street and then taking the air up and over a building.

He banked with Xia around the tower.

The gunners switched their aim, firing on their hangers.

"Buff scroll!"

Wazny tore the tab. The buff enveloped himself and his sparrow as his speed surged. "What about Santos?"

"Command will send undead to check."

"We can't leave him!"

"Second Lieutenant!" Wazny snapped.

"Sir," Xia said tersely.

"We need to gain altitude and—" Spells once again passed Wazny and Xia. Their mages responded to the attacks, hitting the enemy and making them break away.

Wazny glanced at the chaos. "Push higher. We need to take some of the weight off the towers."

"Yes, sir." Xia didn't sound angry, just accepting.

They pushed for higher altitude to get back into the fight.

Corporal Landrith ducked as a spell hit before his machine gun, sending a spray of dirt through his bunker's barrier and all over him.

He didn't have time to care about the dirt in his clothes as he aimed and fired.

"Platform left, close!" Private Zhan yelled.

"Stay on target!" Sergeant Cao yelled. "Let the cannons break their barrier then we switch fire!"

Landrith watched his explosive shot trace land among the Black Phoenix fighters that ran forward.

"Looks like they never learned about machine guns!" Private Basheer sneered as she switched targets.

The enemy were bunched up and running forward, perfect targets for machine guns.

Landrith didn't duck anymore as spells crashed through a bunker barrier.

It was a signal to all the Black Phoenix mages as they attacked the bunker with spell after spell.

The bunker went up with a surge of mana, blowing apart.

The lights in Landrith's bunker flickered.

"Mother fuckers!" Zhan spat.

Impacts struck the ground, cannon fire from the frigate.

Two barriers and bunkers nearby were torn apart.

Their own bunker shook.

"Barrier is out! Get out!" Cao yelled and pulled on a spell scroll that threw up a temporary barrier.

Landrith felt the first impact and the second as his squad ran to the door at the rear of the bunker. He was picked up and hurled across the room before light filled his vision.

"Shit," Staff Sergeant Yi cursed and changed his point of aim.

Bai finished reloading his machine gun, looking down over the outer wall where the Tiger Regiment had reinforced.

Two bunkers went up, and a third lost its barrier. Several more mana cannon rounds pounded each of the bunker locations, destroying the third and turning the first and second into glowing craters.

Bai fired down over the bunkers.

"Platforms behind the wall!" someone yelled on the command channel. Bai looked up and over his shoulder.

"All frontline forces, this is Colonel Yui. Bunker forces pull back to the inner wall. Tiger Regiment CPD's, contain the platforms landing in the outer city. Those on the outer wall, cover the bunker force's retreat and prepare to retreat to the inner wall once they are clear!"

Bai looked over to see Colonel Yui on the wall. He grabbed a conjured spear of light and hurled it. The spear smashed into a Black Phoenix mana barrier and broke it. Machine gunners altered their aim and fired.

Light came from above Bai.

"Fuckers are targeting the mana barrier now," Baines muttered.

"Keep the reservists together. Make sure you get a solid count on them. We need to fall back in order. This can fall into a rout too easily." Bai scanned the wall, looking at the faces of the reservists still under his command.

One of them was fighting to get his machine gun running.

"Donner, run through your IA!"

Donner looked over, grimaced, and nodded, remembering his training.

Bai aimed, casting his explosive shot and fired down into the enemy. With all the buffs, each round was as powerful as a grenade from back on

Earth.

"Tough fuckers!" Bai gritted his teeth.

The Black Phoenix members took multiple hits to kill.

"How? How!" a reservist yelled, turning into a scream. "Just die!" They went limp, sobbing as they dropped to the ground, holding their helmet in their hands.

"Pull your head out, Alvarez!"

"They don't die even with all of our buffs!" Alvarez yelled back, covered in snot and tears.

Bai moved down and grabbed the man, picking him up into standing by his vest. "I don't give a god damned fuck! You are a fucking Alvan soldier! You will do as you are fucking ordered, or you will be the reason we fucking die! If those Eighth Realm fucks want our city, they have a bill to pay!"

Bai turned him around and pushed him toward his gun. "Get on your gun and get shooting!" Bai hit him on the back of his helmet.

Bai walked back to his own gun.

Alvarez yelled and fired, venting his frustrations through his weapon.

Bai aimed and fired, the barrier lighting up his face as platforms rained down all around. The Black Phoenix's fighters engaged Alva's fighters.

"Aerial!" someone yelled as shadows passed.

Spells struck the back of the wall, running through the soldiers.

Bai un-mounted his machine gun, pointed it high, and braced as he cast airshot and fired ahead of the aerial mounts.

As a level fifty soldier, with Body Like Iron, a formed mana core, all fourteen open mana gates, buffed to twice his original strength and armed with a machine gun and the knowledge of a mage squad commander, Bai's rounds tore into the mana barrier, opening it up as he led his blue airshot rounds. They ripped through the enemy, slaughtering the aerial mounts.

"Odd squads turn and face the inner city!" Colonel Yui ordered.

Bai lowered his machine gun and grabbed the ammunition box attached to his ammunition feeder.

He used a battlement to rest his machine gun on.

"And that is why we are using machine guns and not just hurling out spells. Spells drain a lot of power and we can hit harder casting stronger spells on our weapons!" Bai yelled. "Now shoot me some of those crow bastards!"

"My people can't hold on for much longer." Kanoa pressed his lips together, looking at Glosil.

"We need the air cover. If we don't, then their aerial forces will rake our towers and the walls. We are still evacuating the people from the bunkers. Egbert is using the dungeon core to fire the mana cannons. They took out our forward artillery cannons as fast as they could. Tiger Regiment is manning the outer wall. The frigate is firing on their position. I need cover or we're going to lose people. Domonos is organizing our forces at the castle compound."

"I thought we were holding at the inner wall?"

"We don't have the people. We'll be too spread out and we need to evacuate everyone."

Kanoa looked at the map with heavy eyes. "Fuck. Yui is cut off on the surface. How is he going to get his people down into the Under City and back to the castle compound?"

"We..." Glosil's eyes latched onto two symbols moving rapidly across the map. "Captain Roska, what the hell are you doing? You were supposed to get the lords out of here!"

"Glosil, this is Major West. We are rendering assistance and acting as a Quick Reaction Force. You promised me you could deal with us as soldiers, so deal with us like soldiers. Sir."

Glosil gritted his teeth, his hands balling into fists. "Major West, I need a distraction, something to take the pressure off of Tiger Regiment on the wall. They're getting hit from both sides and in the air. Our air force is getting hammered."

"Yes, sir. We'll cover their retreat." Erik's voice was level, holding a hint of warning as he closed the channel.

"Egbert! How is that spell coming?" Glosil yelled into the ceiling.

"I need another seven minutes."

"Let me know the second you can cast it. Send orders to the towers. As soon as the Tiger Regiment is past them, they are to evacuate. Kanoa, once the towers are evacuated, leave the undead to fight and break off your people."

"No more platforms or aerial beasts are leaving the ship," an aide reported.

"How many do they have in the air and on the ground?" Glosil asked.

"There are about thirty thousand on the ground and twenty thousand in the air," Egbert reported.

Glosil grunted. "We have an advantage with our weapons. Advise all leaders to not engage in close combat."

Explosions rippled over the city as sparrows and kestrels did bombing runs on the Black Phoenix ground forces.

A sparrow was struck with multiple spells, spinning away into the ground.

Rugrat locked onto the group of Black Phoenix fliers and closed his fist. The air responded, turning into air blades that tore through the group. George released a breath of fire, crashing into another group's barrier. Gong Jin and his team brought the barrier under fire, tearing it apart as they rode across the skies.

Gilly shot out a beam of water from her mouth while Erik waved his hand. A building collapsed like it was sand, the debris smashing into a group of Black Phoenix ground forces.

Roska's team dropped bombs on the stalled group, tearing apart the surrounding buildings and the group. Storbon's group raked a platform with spells. Its barrier failed, then its formations as it tumbled, dropping its fighters nearly a hundred meters to the ground before the platform smashed into a Sky Reaching Restaurant.

They were wreathed in spells, stirring up the mana around them as they carved a path through the air.

"I see the platforms!" Rugrat grabbed his rifle and aimed.

The Black Phoenix ground forces were rushing through the streets on mounts, half heading to the inner wall, half to the outer wall the Tiger Regiment was pinned down on.

He fired. The rounds cut through his targets and struck the ground. Chains bloomed out from the ground, stabbing and grabbing at others passing by.

They blossomed in explosions, cutting through the nearby fighters.

Rugrat's domain twitched as he looked up and fired into a reinforced group of aerial fighters.

Chains grabbed onto the mounts, causing them to plummet and spin away before exploding.

Erik drew out a grenade launcher. His eyes shone, black, red, and green flecks under his striking blue eyes. Veins of black and red ran down his hand

and into the weapon before he fired. The grenade had new veins running through it. Erik sent a command through his linking mana. The grenade exploded above the ground forces, cutting them down in droves.

They flew over the battlefield.

The enemy forces charged into machine gun fire from the outer wall, taking hits on the mana barriers that were covering their rear. The main barrier arching high over them was showing spotting as attack after attack hammered it. Ground forces on both sides were pushing the outer wall, a strip of stone between a sea of black fighters and red tracers.

Close protection details were behind the outer wall in positions they'd pulled together, shooting down the streets.

"Break!" Erik yelled.

Rugrat and teams One and Three went right as Erik and teams Two and Four went left, washing over the outer wall.

Rugrat dropped bombs from his storage ring, enhancing them as George roared; a spell formation released. Flaming feathers raked the buildings and ground.

The two teams released bombs as their mounts attacked the ground.

The first bombs hit, leveling buildings and throwing dust in every direction, clearing out dead ground beyond the wall.

Rugrat led them into the sky and banked. He fired on the aerial forces before they had time to react.

"Gong Jin, cover the skies. Niemm, cover the ground!" Rugrat said.

Gong Jin's team blasted spells into the heavens.

"These bastards are tough, shit!" Gong Jin missed one and kept hurling out fireballs. Angry red veins traced through his body the color of lava, burning from the inside out.

They were all pushing their limits, no longer hiding their strength.

"Here we go again!"

They went back over the buildings. Attacks came up from the ground, striking their mana barrier as they laid down a carpet of bombs, cutting back into the city.

"Yui is evacuating his people to the inner wall," Erik said through the sound transmission device. "Once they're out of the fight, we're moving to the towers."

Rugrats' group went over an open area. Spells shot out, striking the barrier and breaking it. They were nearly out of range at the same time it collapsed.

"Status!" Rugrat yelled.

"Just a graze," Niemm grunted.

"I'll be fine; just need a heal or two." Han Wu coughed.

Rugrat saw the man applying first aid as Setsuko activated a new stack barrier formation, the barrier enveloping them.

"Fuck, don't get comfortable! We're going back around." The words were as much for the others as it was for himself.

62
Lords and Hunters

Gregor, Ranko and Bela studied the city below upon their mounts. Their guards flanked them, staying back a respectful distance.

"The Sha are working with *them*?" Bela sneered.

"The Sha are using them for something. They have similar weapons, and where would they get that dungeon core from otherwise?" Gregor said.

"They are stronger than I thought. Their tactics are different. They do not try to engage us in close combat and use weapons similar to the Sha." Ranko considered the fighting as if it were happening on another planet.

"It seems that they are connected. Your people are getting torn apart." Gregor pointed out Bela's forces.

Bela shot him a glare before directing it below, shifting with her mount's wings.

"The mana here is—" Ranko grimaced as he rubbed his fingers together. "—useless. We trained to fight in the seventh realm, not some fourth realm backwater. Our mana reserves can't regenerate fast enough down here without density enhancing formations." His eyes dropped to the formation on Gregor's hip.

Gregor grimaced, adjusting it. "The formations, how much will it affect us?"

Ranko took a moment to consider the city below. "Thirty to forty percent decreased power for the lowest level fighters. For us, fifty to sixty percent."

"Why will it affect us more?" Bela asked.

"Mana density," Gregor supplied, not looking away. He tensed his hand, feeling the power of his body cultivation.

"Should you not be recovering their dungeon core?" Bela pulled him out of his thoughts with her impetuous question.

"Patience, Bela. Cousin Gregor has his own task and we have ours."

"Commanders." One of Gregor's people pointed downward.

A group surged over the city. Most rode on panthers that ran across the sky. A man sat atop a dragon breathing water and leaving a wake of stone spears jutting out from the ground and buildings below. Another rode a winged wolf breathing flame.

The group raked those below, the Clan's forces unable to hold them as they rushed toward the outer wall.

Gregor pulled his spear from his storage ring and looked at the guards behind him.

"Cousins Ranko and Bela, if you excuse me, I think that the hunt has begun."

"You think you can take them on your own?" Bela smirked.

Gregor shifted the spear in his grip, using his sensing spells on the two groups. He couldn't get a clear understanding of their cultivation. With their debuffs, they could be people from the sixth realm. *As long as they are unaffected or even buffed, then it would make sense.*

"You think they are wearing masking formations?" Gregor asked.

"We do," Ranko said.

Gregor rolled his spear in his fingers. He sniffed at the thin mana in the air, grimacing. These people were showing ability. If they were not dealt with, they would cut down too many of their people and weaken morale. He needed Ranko and Bela's forces to help capture the dungeon core. Gregor clenched his jaw, tightening his grip on his spear with a smile. "Splitting the spoils three ways is a fine idea! What is family for if we do not all benefit? Killing off their elites should make it easier!"

"You would fit in well with a sect for your fake smiles alone, Cousin." Bela clicked her tongue and her mount dove forward. Her guards dropped away, following her, their green robes flapping from under their armor.

"Let the hunt begin!" Gregor roared. Lines of power traced their mana and element-gathering tattoos, bringing the surrounding mana and elements into sharp focus.

Gregor and Ranko dove. Their guards followed.

"Iron Rain!" The spell formation appeared in front of Bela as she channeled mana into it. Iron bolts howled through the air toward the group below.

Gregor felt like a balloon being squeezed as he entered the mana gathering formation's range.

The group cried out and split into two; one group around the fire wolf, the other around the Dragon. Their mana barriers flared with the iron rain before tearing through the street and buildings in a plume of dust.

Rubble from the collapsing buildings formed together into tens of spears and was hurled skyward.

"Meteor rain." Flares of fire appeared, growing and shooting down to crash into the stone spears.

"Iron Wall!" Bela called her defense in a panic. Her guards hurled out their own mana barriers to protect her like layered bubbles.

The air exploded around her, causing the barriers to shudder.

Gregor laughed. He and his group slashed out with their spears, greeting dozens of spells to meet them head-on.

Ranko's tattoos glowed as he drew in the surrounding mana. He closed his eyes, condensing mana into a shimmering sphere around himself. When he opened his eyes, light spilled out.

Gone was the tired elder. Now, a lord of mana sat atop his mount.

"Mana spears." A surge of power exited his body. Spears of mana pushed out from the sphere and dropped toward the ground like shimmering glass tears.

The spears dodged around Bela, picking up speed as they raced toward the groups below.

Several spears were destroyed in the skyward attacks. Ranko shifted his hands. The spears shattered into several copies.

Several somethings struck Ranko's sphere, causing it to indent and push him to the side.

Two of Bela's guards' mana barriers shattered, torn apart in a stream of light.

Gregor's eyes traced where the broken line of light came from. *The second group.*

"Water Spears!" He thrust forward with his sphere, rotating spell formations condensed and ejected water spears, catching the midday sun as they cried across the sky.

"You deal with the Dragon team. I'll deal with the fire wolf group!"

Gregor didn't give them time to argue as he dove away.

Streams of light impacted his personal mana barrier as he weaved. His dungeon hunter squad moved erratically in the sky, their weapons freed as they hurled attacks at the group below, changing their own movements and exchanging attacks.

"Barriers!" Erik yelled. The teams came to a halt as he drew his hands together, tearing the stone, steel, and dirt from the surrounding buildings into a shell over the street.

The sky darkened as the shell started to form.

The mana spears exploded against the shell, shattering it as it fought to repair, build, and cover the group underneath.

Erik gritted his teeth, trying to maintain the shell for the meager cover it offered. He saw and felt the explosions around him, smacking his barrier and sending him and Gilly back and forth through the sky as her strong wings fought for control.

Each member was bounced around like a boat upon an ocean of chaos.

He saw a barrier fail and a team member drop toward the ground.

Erik grunted under the pressure of holding up the shell. His left hand flared with power, drawing the shell together as a spell formation appeared on his right hand. "Healing dagger!"

The dagger of green glass weaved between the team members, pouring their mana out in their defenses. Their barriers shuddered against impacts and nearby explosions.

The healing dagger struck the falling member, Yang Zan.

Green healing power drove through his body, forcing him to recover. With a yell of pain mixed with determination, Yang Zan reached out, grabbing onto the mana around him and slowing his descent until he landed on a roof, panting.

"They're coming!"

Erik sensed the mana boiling off each attacker. He clapped his hands together; the shell came apart. He pushed his hands forward, and the sections shot into the sky, smacking into the advancing enemy.

Metal shards wrestled from this control, smashing into the other debris. The pitted iron wall opened, revealing a woman covered in glowing tattoos.

Railguns fired. Streams of different spell-enhanced rounds struck her and her riders in an extended V, tearing apart the split metal wall and striking the force's mana barriers.

Erik scanned the area, looking for a place with terrain to help them.

The woman wasn't without her tricks. With a yell, she threw her scarred metal shield. It tore apart into twisted metal birds that rushed forward into Erik and his teams.

Flames appeared around Erik. The strain on his mana channels was like tensing his entire body under weight as they burst into blue flamed beasts. Using his flame technique, they crashed with the metal birds in a flash of sparks and melted metal.

"Team One, focus on the woman. Team Four, the man! Watch the guards!" Erik ordered.

"Lightning!" Storbon yelled.

The woman's gathered power and lightning split the heavens, dashing between the metal shards, turning into a drill of white that shot outward.

She lifted her head, smirking down at them.

Erik's eyes widened as the lightning splashed outward between the metal among his people. Sang, Lucinda, Tian Cui, and Deni fell from the sky.

Erik reached up and called the lightning toward his hand. His skin turned translucent as he grunted with the power he had consumed. Burn marks appeared on his skin as the woman's eyes widened.

Erik redirected the lightning upwards.

The second group, led by the man in his physical domain of mana, pushed forward. Their attacks met the lightning head-on, forced backward as they split the tree-trunk of lightning a dozen meters tall.

An off spark of the lightning struck the ground, exploding close to Yang Zan and peppering him with stones.

Yao Meng's mount was killed as he leapt free of the body, shooting as he fell toward the ground.

Gilly turned with Erik's thoughts as he rapid-cast. "Ranged heal! Healing dagger! Yang Zan!"

The four falling toward the ground were covered in a green haze as the heals took effect. Four green glass daggers ignored their armor, injecting healing power into their bodies.

"I saw a square to the northeast! Roska, we fight there!"

"Sir!"

Gilly breathed life into a water attack, consuming the enemy's concentration as they grouped together under the rail-gun fire, dodging through the sky, slowing their descent.

The special teams were withdrawing from the buildings to the northeast.

"Team one! Pull back on my signal and use your spell scrolls! Ready! Now!"

Erik pulled the rip tab for all the spell scrolls on his right. Dozens of spell scrolls burned, turning into gossamer formations brimming with power as they unleashed their attacks.

Deal with that!

Erik spared a glance in the direction Rugrat had taken. Attacks sparked in the air above the park.

Erik checked on the wounded. Yang Zan jumped, holding his beast storage crate. Imani grabbed his hand in mid air, pulling him up behind her as they raced to the open square.

Erik aimed and fired on the group in the sky. Two guards had been killed in the spell and rail gun onslaught.

Another dropped from a well-placed shot.

Seventeen more and their leaders to go.

"Team Four, prepare to fall back!" Erik said as the spells started to dissipate.

Attacks rained down through the spell scrolls.

"Use them!" Erik yelled.

He tore his remaining spell scrolls.

Four more guards died, and the groups had to fight for their lives.

"Go!" Erik ordered. He drew upon the power of the elements. Silver, yellow, and red flecks of light circulated in his eyes as he seemed to grow. A faint silver sheen appeared on his skin as his veins glowed like red magma and his skin took on the appearance of stone. His senses expanded as he let out a breath in his helmet and smacked the enhancing spell formation in his chest, activating it.

He felt as if the world was under his domain. His power surged again, buffed by the city, his conquerors armor, and drawing upon the elements.

He channeled his power into his railgun and fired on the group between the spells. Gilly pulled on a strap under her harness, activating her own armor.

Erik cut down a guard lining up an attack. He depressed the trigger, firing at the golden tattooed man with a mana domain stretched around his body.

The man's guards used their domain to cover him.

"You ant!" the golden man yelled, a blade of mana coming from the side.

Gilly flapped a wing. A building to the side shifted like a wave of water. Stone separated from the building and clashed with the mana blade, stone raining down on the city below as she breathed water.

"Reloading!" Erik dumped his magazine and grabbed another from his vest, smacking it into place.

The pillar of water struck the green and silver tattooed woman. She scowled, stabbing her sword forward.

Green and silver energies combined and struck the water pillar.

Gilly dodged to the side and the silver and green energies passed under her wing, striking a building and twisting through it, cutting a hole from the roof through several stories and deep into the earth.

"Think you can take us both?" the man's voice boomed as his power surged, parting as a mana spear shot out.

Erik yelled, mana swelling through his body as he flexed his muscles in connection with one another. Red, black, and yellow traced down his arms. The sounds of dragons and tigers filled the air as mana surged through his arm and Erik reached out his finger.

A point of compressed power shot out from his finger. It tore through the sky, destroying the spear.

The glowing man dodged to the side as a line of power shot past him. He frowned at Erik below. The spear shattered, but the residual power struck Erik. The woman hurled lightning at him.

Erik reached out toward the lightning. It crashed into his hand and ran through his body. Erik laughed, his body drinking in the power, speeding up his recovery.

The man and woman's eyes widened, taking a half-step backward. Erik drew upon his own power. The sky became thick with static energy as he opened his left hand. The lightning's power redoubled as it streamed out of his body, throwing the sun into shadow. It wasn't aimed at the duo, but at the guards flanking around the left side.

Pure lightning raged through their ranks, tearing up their covering barrier and striking three.

Two were killed instantly. The third fell from his mount and smashed through a building.

The golden man let out a "*hmmpf.*"

The air turned into a weapon. It struck out against Erik, catching him unaware as the blast of force, like a cannonball, struck Erik and Gilly.

Erik felt his armor break from the impact. He and Gilly were hurled backward, separating from one another. Erik smashed into the ground, skipping and crashing through the stone fountain in the middle of the square. He rolled to a stop.

A barrier flashed above him.

"Mana barrier!" Shimmering light grew from his hands. His helmet had come off at some point. He spat out blood, his cut-up face healing as he grunted to his feet. Gilly had landed on the side of a building. Flared to her full size, she dominated the four-story building.

Her body shook with a roar. The building came apart. Stone shards flew over Yang Zan and the wounded.

Erik stabbed a stack formation into the ground, protecting and healing the wounded at his back as he and those that could had their rifles out shooting.

He followed the tracers and tide of stone to the Black Phoenix Clan.

The Special teams lined out across the square from north to east using barriers of mana, stone, and what had been trader's stalls as cover.

The Black Phoenix Clan man and woman rushed toward the ground with their guards. The mana user released a mana bolt the size of a man.

Erik yelled as he threw out his fist. Stone shifted and shattered around him, the elements running through his arm reflected in the fist and arm that rose from the square.

Storbon fired at the mana blast, weakening it under enhanced rounds that wreathed it in smoke.

Erik's stone fist and the mana bolt clashed, annihilating one another as elemental energies and mana intermixed. They created a distorting light that burnt shadows into the square. The mana blast and fist came apart in an explosion of force, buffeting the forces in the air and tearing apart trader stalls and storefronts, exploding a cross-section of the living quarters above and stores below.

Stone was carved away and cracked under the force.

The team's barriers left the ground around them unmarred.

"Blank." Roska's spell made Erik shake his head, hurting.

The beasts of the Black Phoenix Clan folded their wings and dropped suddenly.

Their riders jumped free.

"Kill the mounts!" Roska growled, mana distorting around her as her eyes shone with power.

The team members shot the beasts. Roska's spell kept them unresponsive as they dropped with tombstones above them.

Lightning crackled from the pale-eyed woman. It split on Roska's barrier.

The woman dove and raced toward Erik. The Guards threw up barriers as they dropped toward the ground.

The Special team's weapons sparked across the barriers, breaking several.

Someone was trying to reach Erik through his sound transmission device, but he ignored it.

"Concentrate on the guards, Team Four!" Storbon yelled.

Two fell from the sky, crashing into buildings and showing tombstones. The guards broke away, flying over the building.

"Shoot that glowing fucker, Team Two!" Roska barked. The heat-dissipating blocks on the railguns popped up with each shot. They were shooting close to the limit of the weapons' capabilities. They tore up the glowing man's barrier, hitting him several times. He disappeared from view among the buildings.

"Think we got the bastard!"

"Incoming!" Storbon yelled.

The woman crashed into the ground, having jumped from her mount. She sent out a stream of lighting into the teams. Erik was unaffected, but Xi was thrown backward, crashing against a storefront, a tombstone above his head.

Erik flicked his railgun's power output. He fired at her. She drew mana into a barrier.

He aimed and fired controlled shots at her.

She yelled, throwing lightning and mana back. Flames took the shape of beasts, crashing into the attacks, reducing their effect. The power of her attacks overwhelmed his resistances, cutting bloody lines along his arms.

He kept on shooting and advancing. Driving her back, he unclipped his rifle and charged the woman. He switched to auto; his rounds ate through the stone she threw up and struck her barrier.

His weapon clicked empty as he gathered his power. Fire exploded at his back as his speed skyrocketed. His skin darkened, turning a glossy black.

Magma traced down his veins, while grey stone appeared along his knuckles. Lightning crackled across his body as the air shimmered with heat.

Erik's fist shattered the remaining rock, striking her barrier, blowing it apart. The sheer concussive force of his punch sent her flying backward,, and she struck another building.

Attacks rained down from above. Erik raised his arm as the ground rose to protect him when the special teams opened fire. Their tracers cut into the guards as Erik punched upwards. The shell of stone turned into projectiles that exploded among the guards.

The woman hit Erik in the side. Her skin had hardened and turned into a mix of black and grey color.

"Pillar!" It erupted under his feet.

Erik jumped backward, sensing a mana spear from the left. The golden man walked out of a street. His robes were in disarray and there was blood on his face, but his attacks were no weaker.

"Explosion!"

Erik's fire spell threw him to the side and singed his clothes as the mana spear struck a building, tearing through it.

"Pillar."

"Lightning strike!"

The spells hit Erik in the back and threw him forward. The woman drew out a sword of lightning from the air. The air crackled as dust shot up as she charged Erik.

Erik roared as the world seemed to slow. Using all of his reaction speed, he reached out.

The woman coughed blood as her momentum stopped in an instant. She stared at Erik in horror. Lightning ran through his body as his hands clamped around her blade like a vice.

A wave of force ran through the ground behind Erik, causing a building to crack in the distance.

She stabbed out with her real sword. Green and silver swirled as mana spears appeared above Erik and stabbed down.

He pushed back on the woman, sending her stumbling backward, but found his feet were stuck. He partially dislodged one foot as he raised his arm.

Erik screamed as the mana spears stabbed into his arm and exploded, breaking him free of the ground and tossing him backward. He pushed to his feet, raising his armor plates to meet mana blade, his left sleeve flapping in the wind.

Four mana blades struck Erik's front, tearing up his armor.

"Kill his guards!" the golden man said. He fired mana blasts at the teams, the guards pushing forward to clash with the teams head-on.

Erik saw tombstones as he raised his arm. Lightning tore from his hand, striking the golden man. He was tossed backward, his barrier rippling and distorting, but not breaking.

Erik ran forward, fire at his back speeding him up as the woman charged him.

"Water's might!" Her body became almost translucent. Throwing her hand forward, a spear of water grew in her hand, becoming larger as it cut through the air.

Gilly let out a screech. *Master, down!*

Erik saw what she wanted and threw himself down. A pillar of water passed over him, tearing apart the spear and striking the woman. She was pushed back, but remained largely unharmed.

Erik smacked his hand on the ground. Throwing himself up, he landed on his feet. He felt the flush of energy welling up within him, ready to be called forth. He could kill them both, here, now. If he just detonated his mana core.

If I fall, then Alva will.

The golden man, stained with blood, grinned at him, standing.

Erik was within his domain. Mana spears shot out of the ground and hit.

"Shit!" Erik yelled as flames poured out from his body, turning into beasts that crashed into the mana spears, tearing them apart in mutual destruction.

The golden man yelled in frustration, detonating the spears.

The force threw Erik backward.

"Lightning speed!" The woman, covered in lightning, shot around to Erik's right side. She struck out.

"Explosion!" Erik used the force to push himself out of her range just as her blow passed his head, close enough he could feel the wind through his hair.

"Focused Heal!"

Erik drew on the power of his body that he had been halting. Bone regrew down his arm. Muscle and tendon wrapped around it. Veins and fat snaked down as skin followed. Green veins shot through his elementally enhanced arm as he reached forward, his fingers clad in flesh as his hand covered her face. Green smoke poured from between the spaces in his hand, forcing its way into her mouth and nose.

"Poison!" the man yelled, firing mana blasts at Erik.

Erik dodged, driving his foot into the ground that pushed back on him, shooting him forward as he drove his feet into the ground. Flames were at his back as he veered toward the restaurant.

Erik threw out potions and needles. His mana wrapped them up, stabbing them into his body as his power grew.

He punched a guard in the side that was fighting Storbon, crushing his ribs and sending him flying away.

"Spike!" Erik raised his hand. A spike of stone shot up through another guard. "Strike!" Lightning appeared in mid-air and hit another guard.

The golden man prepared to attack, but he messed up the casting, coughing blood and staggering.

The woman was coughing green smoke as she threw her head back and drank potions.

Yao Meng kicked a guard back. Tian Cui's blades cut through the back of his knee as Yao Meng strung and released an arrow, shooting the guard through his neck.

Erik jumped. Stone rose to greet him as he bent his legs. Shattering the stone, he took off like a cannonball toward four mages that were attacking the restaurant.

Erik grabbed one mage by the arm and punched him in the head. He dropped the corpse as two spells hit him.

The hits made Erik cough blood, halting his momentum. He punched the ground. Two streams of rock rippled to the mages before magma exploded underneath them, burning through them.

The woman threw out wild, aggressive attacks, hitting Erik with a blast of lightning and slamming him into a building, smashing him through several walls.

Mana was drawn toward the golden man as Jurumba roared, hacking into the last guard, his armor holding his blade there.

Others fired on the golden man gathering his mana.

He formed a barrier that shook with impacts.

Erik climbed out of a shattered wall only to be sliced by the woman's blade of water.

Erik's armor took the first blow. The second cut his left arm, while the third cut his legs. He had no time to hiss in pain as blood welled from the new wounds, his silver bones showing through his skin.

There was a wild look in her eyes. Green veins traced around her head, distorting the clean tattooed lines. Mana and elements surged under her command as her power increased. The formation on her hip glowed as if it would spark into flames at any moment.

Erik's punches were met with blades as they sped up, their attacks becoming blurs as the building they were in came apart under the force of their attacks. Erik used falling blocks as spikes to attack her from the rear.

She jumped clear and pulled the building down, collapsing it upon Erik.

Erik smashed out, leaving a trail of dust.

She was there in an instant, attacking him with her violent, direct attacks.

Erik fended her off as she leapt backward and pulled out twin blades, one black, the other brown.

"You are stronger than I thought you would be. Then again, you are a dungeon lord, but just one from the Earth Realms."

Their attacks struck out at one another. Erik was thrown backward; she took the opening.

Mana vapor emanated from her mana channels and eyes as she stabbed forward. Lightning hit him straight on, burning through his eyes as it hit him in the side.

Erik gasped in pain as he struck the ground, rolling away. He pressed a healing spell into the wound as he pushed away from the ground. Spikes shot from where he had been lying.

A path of lightning forged through the ground, melting it.

Erik was breathing heavily as he pulled out his rifle and fired.

Her blades snapped out. Lightning ran through the path of rounds, causing them to explode. Erik was peppered with shrapnel as she flicked her swords and shot toward him. Her blow sent him flying out of the building, back into the plaza.

"He forced you to use your mana formation, Bela." The golden man was standing behind his half mana barrier. He threw a potion bottle to the side, wiping his face.

Erik stood up and charged the woman. She struck out as he halted his movement and unleashed a mana drill into her front.

A shocked expression formed on her face as her medallions cracked and the drill surged through her body.

"Bela!" the man roared as the world seemed to compress around Erik.

Erik was hit with mana blasts and mana spears. His leg was blown away as he was tossed backward. Another blast threw him forward. Attacks rained down on him as a spear drilled into his arm.

Gilly's attack on the golden man threw him to the side.

"You beast!" The man pulled in power, consuming his shield as a pillar of mana struck Gilly.

"No!" Erik yelled as blood blossomed and Gilly smashed through the building she had protected the wounded from.

He didn't care about surviving to lead Alva anymore, nor did he consider the long-distance ramification of his survival. He should have destroyed his core from the start and taken them both with him!

Power rippled out from him as he grew. Fire, earth, metal, and wood. The elements circled him. Wind tore through the square as he extended his domain. He blinked to the side, a cracked line in the ground where a spear of water crashed into the ground.

He used finger beats fist on the attacks coming from above. A ragtag group of four guards and the man in red armor rained attacks down on Erik.

Erik roared, taking a hit to his left arm in exchange for killing one of the guards.

"Ranko, I cannot hold him for long!" the man yelled.

"No, you don't!" Erik turned and hurled spells at the golden man.

The man tore a spell scroll. A red and blue light embraced him and hurled him into the sky away from Erik's attacks.

Erik drew on the power of the area. The buildings came apart, forcing the special teams to run for cover as Erik used finger beats fist.

A chaotic light of green, red, silver, and yellow cut the sky. The golden man's sphere transformed into a barrier, expending the last of his power.

Erik's attack colored the barrier and caused it to waver and then break before it struck Ranko in the side. The energies spread through the wound and the man, wreaking havoc.

Attacks rained down around Erik. He raised a barrier against them, feeling his energies dissipating. He'd stressed his body way beyond its limits.

The attack volume died down, revealing the weapons fire from the railguns.

The teams drove off the armored man, who chased after Ranko on his mount with two guards.

"Gilly!" a voice thundered from above before something slammed into the ground, throwing wind through the area. Erik was unable to see as he poured power into his body to fight.

Two more impacts shook the ground. He looked over to see a familiar figure.

"William?" Erik was feeling weak from the stamina and mana fatigue as he sped up the healing of his body.

William roared as rain suddenly poured from the skies above, rushing toward the building Gilly had been thrown through.

Erik felt his connection to her; it was weak, so weak. He pushed himself to his knee, using his good leg and arm as the other two regrew. He clambered toward the restaurant.

Special team members were being pulled out. The rain washed the dust away as the sky started to clear.

Roska was coordinating a defense, ignoring her broken right arm. Others rushed to help Yang Zan with the wounded.

Yao Meng stabbed a revival needle into what looked like Tian Cui.

Erik pushed on, picking up speed. Gilly had smashed through several walls. She lay on her back. From her neck down to her abdomen, mana still burned. Her wounds were horrific as she keened against the stone.

A man with long hair was patting her chest.

"There, there little one." His voice was choking up.

It was Fred. He turned, looking at Erik with tears in his eyes.

Erik pushed away from William, hopping forward and reaching out to Gilly. "Oh, Gilly, girl."

He pulled out a revival needle and used organic scan. As he drove his hand forward, the man held his hand. Erik turned to yell at him, seeing Elder Fred's tear-stained face.

"There's nothing that even you can do, Erik."

Erik wanted to argue, but his organic scan told him the truth.

Gilly nuzzled him.

He fell to the ground, letting her put her head on his lap. He took out another needle and pressed it to her neck and injected it. Her body relaxed as the pain killer took effect.

I do good, master?

"You did great, Gilly. You saved me." Erik ran his hand down her head.

She had a pleased expression on her face as she got comfortable in his lap and closed her eyes.

A few seconds later a tombstone appeared over her body.

He lay down Gilly's head gently and scratched her favourite spot. Something raw and rough reached into him, twisting his guts and heart. He looked down at his ruined body. He slammed a revival needle into his leg and took a sudden breath, letting out a shuddering sigh. "I need to check on my people."

Fred nodded, moving to where Erik had sat.

Erik hobbled on his regrowing leg into the square. He didn't see Fred buckle to his knees as he leaned his head over Gilly's still form.

There were more wounded than healthy. Everyone sported injuries of different kinds.

Roska, Yang Zan, Yao Meng and Rajkovic worked on those needing critical care. They were laid out in the street. Jurumba and Tully put another body on the opposite side of the wounded.

Three bodies lay there. They moved to help the others.

Erik joined them.

"Pri Alpha, Bravo, Charlie," Roska pointed at the different groups she'd created. "Erik on Alpha, you two on Bravos."

They bent to work.

"Roska, find out what the situation is. We need to get moving before we have more people on our asses," Erik said.

"Yes, sir," Roska said in a terse voice and stepped to the side to use her sound transmission device.

Rugrat saw the attacks raining down on Erik and his teams in the distance. "On me!"

They banked and turned, picking up speed as the sky darkened.

"Barrier!" Rugrat yelled as he felt a surge of mana.

Water spears crashed into the barrier, just short of breaking it.

"Get low, between the buildings! They have the altitude!"

Rugrat led them down into the streets. They blew up dust as they flew between the buildings just above the street.

"Where the fuck did these guys come from?" Niemm yelled.

"They're strong!" Gong Jin grunted.

Water spears rained down ahead of the group. They hammered their barrier as they drove through.

Rugrat conjured fireballs that shot out, striking the water spears, and shattering the ones that would have hit his people. He raised his hand, firing a fireball into the houses at the end of the street. The houses exploded, creating a new pathway for the teams to squeeze through.

"Shit, there's a park up ahead!" Niemm yelled.

"We need to pass it to get to the others!" Rugrat cast a speed buff over them all. Their speed increased, and they surged over the large park. It was pockmarked with signs of fighting, formation plates, and undead skeletons. The sect's ground fighters and aerial forces that had broken through here were only corpses.

"Incoming!" he shouted. George and the other mounts slowed as a group of fighters raced past them and rode over the ground. They dismounted easily and landed in the park as their mounts flew away.

Spells appeared above Rugrat and his teams.

"They're forcing us to land!" Gong Jin hissed.

"Do it!"

They stored their mounts and dropped to the ground. Rugrat took the impact with his legs, his rifle up and ready. He fired at the man he could sense the least about, but who was drawing in the most mana.

The man's barrier stopped his round, stunning Rugrat.

"Break into two. Take his guards. I'll deal with the dungeon lord!"

The teams fired as the guards and their leader charged.

Their barriers sparked with impacts or deflected the rounds into the ground.

Niemm, Deni, and Setsuko fired grenade launchers.

The explosions sowed destruction among the eight guards, but four of them still stood.

A tombstone appeared over one guard. Two others hit the ground on their feet and kept running. The fourth was stumbling, barely remaining upright.

Rugrat fired on full auto. His heating blocks shot up as his explosive shots covered the leader's barrier.

His barrier broke just five meters from Rugrat.

"Rugrat, what's your situation?" Erik's voice rang in Rugrat's ears.

Spells rained down on the teams as Team Three dropped two more fighters.

A spear shot out at Rugrat as the leader took a round to the chest. His armor stopped it from getting any farther. His wild eyes and grin scared Rugrat more.

Rugrat hit the ground and threw himself back up. He attacked the man with mana blades.

"Melee!" Niemm yelled.

They stored their rifles and pulled out their blades as the guards tore into the special teams.

The spear-using leader lashed out at the mana blades that attacked him, using his armor to take the hits.

Rugrat fired at his feet. The man jumped and used the resulting explosion to propel himself forward.

Rugrat created a fireball and hurled it at the man. He cut it away with a flick of his spear and landed on the ground, shifting his spear to the ready.

Rugrat could see the fighting behind the spear leader. An Alvan was cut down and another hit with a spell that sent them flying backward.

The teams were strong. The fact they could stand up against these fighters was a testament to their ability.

Rugrat cast chains under the feet of one of the guards. Chains captured him as Deni separated his head from his shoulders.

The spear leader charged forward, using the distraction of his guard's death.

Chains of elemental mana tore free of the ground, trying to capture the man. The field of chains grabbed his right arm, pulling him to the side.

Rugrat aimed and fired in one fluid motion. The man twisted and jumped, and the rounds struck his leg armor. His leg below the knee disappeared.

The group of guards fighting Team Three broke their formation and all the remaining fighters joined in on the fight. They were a whirlwind of attacks. Only the special teams' coordination kept them alive.

"Simms, left!"

"Tyrone!"

"Now Jackie!

"Deni, duck!

One mistake, one pause, could mean dying.

The spear user struck the ground and his domain surged outward, clearing the spells around him.

Rugrat changed his magazine as the other man's leg regrew at a visible speed.

"Interesting weapon you have there. You'll have to teach me how you use it!"

There were still five guards, unleashing techniques on the team members, pinning them into place. Simms was thrown backward with an attack, crashing and rolling on the ground.

"Simms!" Han Wu yelled, still fighting. They didn't have time to help the wounded.

The spear leader launched his attack. Mana blades attacked the man, but he wove through them, his spear stabbed into Rugrat's shoulder.

Rugrat felt his mana being drained from him.

The spear user had a cruel expression on his face.

"Not the first time I've not had mana, fuck head."

Rugrat wrapped his teeth around a pull tab inside his helmet and yanked on it. Chains of air coiled around the spear user, locking him in place. Rugrat raised his rifle.

The armored man held out his hand, creating a barrier. Rugrat fired. The piercing round hurled the man backward. All the railgun's heat blocks popped and smoked as one.

The man tore his spear from Rugrat as he landed. Rugrat stumbled. Mana flowed back into his body. He yelled, turning it into a roar as the ground shook. His domain expanded to its limit.

Chains exploded from the ground, their bladed ends seeking Black Phoenix Clan members.

The guards were captured, distracted, and killed. The spear user fought on with only five guards left of his fifteen.

"To *Eternus*!" the red-armored spear user yelled.

He jumped into the sky, pulling out a mount. His guards rushed to follow him into the sky. One mount was caught by a chain, exploding and killing the guard that had pulled it out.

Another guard dodged a chain attack as Han Wu punched him in the chest, throwing him backward.

The man stumbled as the explosive Han Wu put on his chest went off.

Gong Jin's war hammer smashed another guard to the side, and he fell to the ground. Deni shot him with her railgun.

The team fired on the fleeing group, spell scroll barriers protecting them.

Rugrat lowered his rifle, withdrawing his domain. "Report!"

"One dead, three wounded!" Gong Jin yelled.

"Two wounded!" Niemm said.

"All right, get them stabilized. Niemm, stay here. Gong Jin, and whoever you can spare, we're moving for the other teams."

"Father's gone over there to support them." Racquel's voice came from above.

"What the hell?" Rugrat lowered his rifle, waving to the others.

"We came when we heard you were under attack. We got into contact with Commander Glosil and assisted Colonel Yui's people on the outer wall. He couldn't raise any of you, so he sent us to assist.

"Colonel Yui, this is Rugrat. Report."

"We got the teleportation pads back online. We're pulling back. What's your situation?"

"We dealt with the threat." Rugrat watched as Simms' body was gathered into Gong Jin's storage ring.

"Yeah, you should watch out. The groups that were attacking us shifted away."

"Got it. Meet you back at the castle compound." Rugrat cut the channel and felt a wash of fatigue. "Fuck me, operating at two hundred percent is a bitch." He pulled out a stamina potion and drank it.

"So, hello?" he said to Dromm, Racquel, and Elizabeth.

"We heard things weren't going so well. The ship wasn't part of what we heard," Racquel clarified.

"A new addition." Rugrat's voice was sickly sweet as he turned and jogged to the teams.

"We're linking up with the others. They've dealt with their threat. We'll head into the under city and run for the castle compound. That ship is fucking up our teleportation abilities, so we have to move quickly. Good to go?"

"Good, sir." Gong Jin nodded.

"Yes, sir," Niemm agreed.

"We're going to Lagola Plaza. Let's pick up the pace."

63
Best Laid Plans

Commander Glosil's brows pulled together as he studied the map of Vuzgal.

"Colonel Yui has gotten into contact with the special teams. They're heading toward the compound through the under city," Major Hall reported.

"Has the enemy gained access?"

"No. We collapsed any section of the city where they tried to get into the under city."

"Good." Glosil watched the markers of their forces retreating to the castle compound. "The Rail cannons?"

"They are being disassembled as we speak, and all materials of the Vuzgal Academy have already been removed," Hall said.

"Good. Without supporting weaponry, the railguns wouldn't be able to do anything. We may need them in the future. I don't like how that frigate is getting closer, but at least they're not rushing in. Egbert!"

"Yes, Commander?" A voice rang through the command center.

"Meeting room." Glosil turned from the map table and headed to a private meeting room. A few people looked at one another with unspoken questions, but Glosil didn't deem to answer any of them.

He closed the door behind himself. "Is this room secure?"

"Yes, Commander. Nothing will be heard outside. I still cannot cast another large spell. I could lose control and hit the wrong target."

"That's not what I want to talk to you about. I wanted to ask..." Glosil gathered himself. "Could you recreate the spell the Emperor of Vuzgal used to create the undead?"

"We can already create undead," Egbert said.

"We can create undead that follow orders. We don't create undead that follow a will."

Egbert paused. "Do you know what you're asking?"

"I think I do."

"Creating undead is not hard. They're just dungeon creatures that require materials. But true undead, those that will follow a person's will, they will passively increase in power over time and carry out their caster's will. They are powerful beasts, not automatons. They are guided with a will they will carry out their tasks forever unless the spell is broken, and their power lost." Egbert's voice rose in indignation.

"Yes."

"Do you know what the cost is, Glosil? The caster's life! Whoever gives the undead their will, their life will be consumed! This is why necromancers are liches, as they cannot die from these kinds of spells."

Glosil nodded. "I thought so."

"You thought so?" Egbert yelled.

"Can you recreate the spell?"

"Recreate it!"

"Egbert," Glosil's voice hardened. "My duty is to Alva, to protect it until the end of my days. To train men and women to take up that mantle."

Egbert was silent.

"So, I will ask you again, can you recreate the spell?"

"Yes, sir, I can. But you would—"

"Will you require much of the dungeon core to maintain it?" Glosil held Egbert with a stern gaze.

"No, I can use the formations in place. I will leave part of the power stored and use it to increase the range. It will reach from Bala Dungeon to where the main road splits east and west."

"Good, and don't worry about another big spell to hit the ship with. Work to cover our people's retreat."

"Yes, sir."

Glosil walked out of the meeting room, seeing Blaze. "How are things?"

"I have most of my people away." Blaze shook his head. "I never thought—"

"How were we to know that a group of dungeon hunters would come for us? How are things up above?"

"Domonos and Yui are on the walls with their strongest fighters. The enemy is massing for a charge. They're strong; each of the enemy fighters can fight five of my people."

Blaze had a faraway look that seemed to relive something that would haunt him for decades to come.

"Move out with your people. We need to evacuate as fast as possible."

"What about the lords?"

"They encountered the enemy and took casualties but they're returning to the compound."

"Are we really going to abandon Vuzgal?" Blaze demanded.

"Can we fight *them*?" Glosil pointed upwards.

"We—"

"Will be slaughtered! Our forces are buffed to twice their regular power. Their bodies are falling apart against these forces, despite them being debuffed by our city formations. We can fight them at a distance with railguns, but up close… They have the fighting techniques, the gear, and the weapons."

Blaze bit his lip, the energy draining from him.

"Blaze, Alva will need you in the coming days. We have gained great victories and struggled, yes. But our greatest struggle is coming. We will either collapse into nothing or grit our teeth and do things the Alvan way."

Glosil patted the older man—the man who had made him guard captain of Alva village all those years ago, who he had learned how to command from. "Go, we must save everyone that we can."

Blaze nodded and hugged Glosil, who returned the gesture.

"See you on the other side," Blaze said.

"Yes, on the other side." Glosil patted his back.

Yui checked the castle compound defenses. The ring wall had been improved and upgraded since they took the city. He watched as the wall grew out of the ground. Dirt fell from its freshly raised sides in a clear, dark line.

The wall stopped growing. Dirt was shaken free as sergeants and officers yelled to their men swarming up the exterior stairs.

"We predict that they can jump at least twenty meters with their estimated power. I'm more worried about breaching spell scrolls." Lieutenant Colonel Carvallo rested one hand on the handgrip of her railgun.

Formations in the wall glowed with power, spreading across and up the walls.

"I agree, the fight for the walls is just the start." Yui looked back at the castle. The ground cracked and fell away as bunkers grew from the ground.

Mages hardened dirt between them into mortar positions for mortar squads to push into.

"We just need to buy time. What's the situation with the teleportation formations?"

"The weaker or smaller versions have been knocked out. All teleportation formations outside of the compound have been destroyed. Commander Glosil believes that the ship has something that messes with the formations. It is slowing down the evacuation. The defenders around the valley have used their teleportation facilities to get out. The air force is only mini—"

"Incoming above!"

"Get to cover!" Yui barked.

Machine gun positions in the castle and the tower opened up. Blue spell tracers exploded in the air as spells rained down from above. Yui and Carvallo ran for an entrance in the wall that soldiers were piling into.

"Push through! Move to firing positions inside the wall!" Yui yelled as he used his sound transmission device.

"Domonos! We're under attack—" A spell hit the ground nearby, heat washing through an arrow slit in the wall followed by dirt.

Shit.

The mortar positions collapsed as the aerial forces targeted them and the castle.

"On the northeast."

He grabbed Carvallo to yell in her ear, the wall shaking with impacts. "Get the bunkers to extend their barriers to cover our mortar positions!"

"Sir!"

They pushed up the stairs inside the wall, people racing to set up their firing positions.

"We're extending our barriers out from the bunkers to offer protection to our mortars or we're going to lose our mortar cover here."

"Good idea." Domonos was quiet for a few seconds. "I've passed orders to the same effect. The northwest is under attack as well. I have reports of the ground forces pushing up using the aerial forces to soften us."

Carvallo grabbed onto Yui and moved her lips to his ear as she made sure he didn't run into anyone. "Command reports the frigate is accelerating."

"Domonos, frigate is moving. Looks like this is it."

"Yui, what's the status of the special teams?"

"The last I heard they were humping it through the under-city; they don't have teleportation formations to hop forward on. Should be here soon. Our biggest problem is our teleportation bottleneck."

"Dragon Regiment will hold the left."

"And Tiger will hold the right." Yui passed machine gunners setting up behind modified arrow slits.

The channel was cut off as Yui pulled Carvallo close. "What about our charges?"

"They're set, sir." Her voice was coldly professional.

"Good." *Can't tell the troops we're standing on top of a massive bomb.*

Captain Stassov stood in the open space between the formations around the dungeon core and the glowing city of Vuzgal.

These Vuzgalians are not how they appear on the outside. They damaged my frigate!

"What of our progress into the dungeon under the city?"

"Every access point has been destroyed, killing or wounding our people and blocking entry," an aide of the ground forces said.

"Keep trying. They will mess up eventually." Stassov manipulated the mana around her with a thought. Marco landed on the ground to her side. He hissed but held it in, knowing his position in all of this. *A sect rat, but this one shows some promise.*

Stassov smiled and turned to the pillar of formations around the dungeon core.

The mana density within the ship was sucked away as she diverted the power to repairs on the teleportation formations.

"Make sure all wounded are evacuated from the ground. Hold back two-thirds of our force in reserve. They're cornered; we should be wary of what they may do."

She was starting to think of these Vuzgalians as a force on the same level as the clan. *Amusing.*

Several men and women with tattoos and formations that passively increased the mana density around them appeared in the command center and dropped to their knees, waiting.

"Report."

"Bela has been killed. Gregor and Ranko are healing rapidly. They engaged with the Lords of Vuzgal."

She quickly hid her surprise.

"Increase the attacks on the dungeon. Hammer their mana barriers. We *must* take that dungeon core."

Rugrat turned and checked the rear. He was tail-end Charlie, making sure that no one ran up on them.

The under-city was quiet now. Facilities had been abandoned. The food fields still grew, but there were no dungeon monsters or farmers to tend to them. All the entrances to the different buildings had been cut off.

Buildings had been smashed open to make the removal of gear faster. All the training facilities were gone, as well as the answering statues. *Nothing but a skeleton city.*

The shaking rumble of buildings collapsing followed muffled explosions.

"What is that?" Racquel asked. Since she had appeared, she hadn't left his side.

"Glosil is blowing sections of the city where the enemy is trying to gain access to the under-city."

Rugrat turned around and ran up toward the rest of the group. George ran beside him.

Erik was working on the wounded. Yawen assisted him. The stretcher-bearers ran as fast as possible. Gong Jin was up at the front, Niemm's and Roska's teams with the wounded, carrying, healing, and protecting.

Rugrat was in the rear with the residents of Bala Dungeon and Storbon's team. Yao Meng was commanding with Rajkovic, Foster and Jurumba supporting. The rest of their team were either dead or on the stretchers.

Everyone was switched on. Chatter had been cut out.

Rugrat pulled his eyes from Erik.

Fuck.

He knew a part of what Erik was going through losing Gilly.

Erik was visibly pulling himself together. They'd lost many good people today.

Rugrat turned and checked the rear again.

"Aerial fighters are flying through the castle compound barriers and attacking the defensive positions. We need to pass off the wounded to the medics and support the castle compound. We'll be stationed in the castle."

"What are the Black Phoenix ground forces doing?" Niemm asked.

"Playing it safe. They're weakening our defenses and moving their ground forces into position," Erik said.

"Gonna be a tough fight," Yao Meng said.

"They thought they could roll over us when they got here. Once bitten, twice shy," Rugrat said.

They continued forward. The wounded groaned and hissed as they were jostled. The healers went between them, checking on the IVs that were carabinered to one of the stretcher-bearers.

They passed the training centers and the gates, through the wall that marked the inner city. It opened for them as they ran through the under-wall that extended all the way up into the ceiling.

Units were running full out. Carts had been used to carry wounded, medics working on people as sections of the ceiling collapsed. Mages blasted them away. Soldiers carried wounded on their shoulders, covered in dirt, grime and blood.

Rugrat saw movement within the walls. The flood of defenders compressed down as they entered the gates.

Medics took on the wounded to casualty points. Soldiers were organized into squads and put to task.

As they arrived, a medic and an officer stepped forward.

"They're all stable. Got them morph'd up. Just need to get them into hospitals for their injuries. Feeding them stamina potions and letting their bodies do the work." Erik briefed the medics on his batch of wounded as Rugrat and the rear security moved into the gates, watching for anything that might follow them.

"Pull back!" Niemm ordered. The soldiers and his team peeled back into the gate that closed behind them, leaving the under city empty as mana powered down.

People were formed up into squads, moving forward at a quick pace.

Lieutenant Colonel Zukal ran out into the path through the squads. Rugrat waved him down as Niemm and Yao Meng grouped together. Erik was still briefing the medics as the stretchers came to a halt. New bearers took over.

"How is it?" Rugrat asked

Zukal tore his eyes away from the wounded. "We have four teleportation pads operating. Formation masters are working to bring two more back online. The frigate is getting closer. We've got three thousand defenders up there. Another two thousand down here to get out, not including all the ones that are coming through the under city."

"How many can the pads support?" Niemm asked.

"Forty to fifty at a time." Zukal grimaced.

"Shit." Rugrat shook his head. His eyes fell on a soldier in a troop formation moving toward the teleportation formations.

Armor.

"Hey, troop, I need six sets of armor, two female!" Rugrat yelled.

"What for?" Roska asked as she jogged up.

"They're *fucking* powerful." Rugrat used a thumb to point at Fred and his people. "How strong do you think they'll be with conqueror armor?"

A few soldiers stripped out of their armor, pulling out their carriers and adjusting their formation sockets. "Your teams all have commander version, right?" Rugrat asked.

"Most of the pieces," Yao Meng said.

"Go scrounge gear and ammo if you need it. Make sure you get plenty of grenades."

They fell quiet, looking at him. *You think they'll get that close?* Rugrat could read the question in their eyes. "Get to it."

They moved into the ranks and exchanged gear with others.

Rugrat got a set of armor and took it to Fred, who was next to Erik.

"Put this on."

"I have armor." Fred touched his robes.

"Does it double your overall strength?" Rugrat pushed the boots, vest, and helmet into his arms and turned to Erik. "You good?"

"Not in the fucking slightest, but I can fight," Erik said.

Rugrat tapped his shoulder, pressing his lips together as his guts twisted. "Yeah, that you can definitely do. No stupid shit though."

"You know me."

"Yeah, let's do this, brother. How're you for ammo?"

"Good, going to need some more grenades though." Erik turned to people filing into the formations.

"Who has grenades?"

"New pants, shirt and gloves too," Rugrat mentioned.

Erik looked at his gear. His limbs had regrown, but not his clothing. All the blood had been removed with his clean spells.

"I was feeling lopsided." Erik pulled off his slung rifle and held it out.

"Got it." Rugrat held the rifle as Erik pulled out an old armored plate. It came apart in several sections once free of his carrier.

"Shit," They shared a look, wondering just how the hell did he'd survived that. Erik shrugged and pulled out fresh plates, replacing them. He grabbed a new set of pants, shirt, and boots to replace what he'd lost.

"All right this is the situation…" Rugrat quickly filled Erik in as he got dressed and armored up, trying to forget the plate and their mortality.

Fred and his people geared up, putting on the new armor, boots, and helmets as well.

Everyone checked their gear again as Rugrat passed the rifle back to Erik. He took out a needle and stabbed it into Erik's arm.

"What's that? Eurgh!" Erik breathed in as he blinked.

"You still look like shit, but that should keep you going."

"Fuck." Erik rolled his shoulders as the potent stamina potion flooded his system. "A bit of warning next time?"

"Takes all the fun out of it."

Erik barked a laugh. "Thank you, Brother."

"Anytime, stupid."

"Tell Davin I need another fly by!" Yui barked before a shadow passed over his position. Soldiers fired up at the aerial beasts through the gun slits in the wall.

Behind the wall, several bunkers were smoking craters. The mortar squads gritted their teeth and fired as fast as they could load their mortars, dialed into the enemy advances.

"Here they come!" Carvallo was down the wall, spread out so that command could be passed faster.

Yui pushed to the other side of the wall.

The prominent clan houses that had stood on the other side of the large road that ringed the outer walls had been turned into rubble, clearing two hundred meters of open ground.

Mortars exploded at the edge of the rubble, shattering buildings as fighters moved between them to the edge of the open ground.

The Phoenix Clan raised walls for cover. Machine guns fired into them, pockmarking their surfaces and breaking them down. Gunners fired around the edges of the walls, their explosive shots going off to either side.

The Clan continued to create cover to cross the open ground as fighters flowed forward. Like a river crashing against the rocks, they pushed forward to the different walls.

Spell impacts rang out in the castle compound.

"Fucking aerial," Yui muttered and switched to his leadership channel. "Hit those fucking walls with grenades. Keep firing at the edges with explosive shot!"

"Yes, sir!"

He heard a buzz and switched channels.

"Yui here. Go."

"Special teams are heading toward your position," Zukal said.

Fireballs rained down from the sky as Davin made his appearance. The little imp had body armor and a helmet on, looking like a kid playing dress-up. His attacks were anything but.

The aerial beasts shied away, their instincts overriding their training.

He trailed destruction and then shot off toward Domonos' position to support them there.

"Good! We're going to need them."

"Cannon!"

Yui ran toward the man that had yelled. "Where?"

He pointed to the position. Yui put his head next to the man's and looked down his arm, seeing the mana cannon.

The cannon glowed and bellowed.

The spell hit the barrier, and smoke filled the area ahead of the wall.

"Ah, fuck!" He flicked channels. "Commander, Colonel, they're shooting me up with smoke."

"I've got cannons over here doing it too," Domonos said.

"Pull back to the castle. We get stuck in melee range, we're going to lose a lot more people and this gives us cover."

"Do it. We have just under two thousand people remaining in the under city and one of the modified teleportation formations is up and working. Push another three hundred from both of your units down into the under city. If you are getting cramped, move more people lower. Once the enemy reaches the wall, I'm hoping to give them a surprise."

"Sir," the Silaz brothers repeated at the same time.

"We getting any support from Egbert?" Domonos asked.

"He's working on something for me. He should be done soon," Glosil said.

"Yes, sir."

Yui changed channels. "All right, we're going to pull back to the castle since the enemy gave us some cover! Major Quan, your Fourth Company will pull back first, followed by the Third and then the Second. Major Sun, First Company has the short straw. You will pull back last. When you reach the castle, shed your riflemen units, and send them below. We'll be working our way up the ranks. Riflemen, then artillery, then support, then CPD. That gives us our strongest fighting units last."

"Sir, we're really giving up Vuzgal?" Major Long asked.

"It's just a place on a map. Our soldiers are the sword and shield of Alva; the people are our lifeblood. Today we faced the armies of dozens of sects and we defeated them. Now we face a force from the highest reaches of the Eighth Realm. We have made them pay for every meter and we will make them bleed for every other meter they take this day! The Alva army has fought with honor, with discipline. You have shown your ability and proven yourselves. No other city in the Fourth Realm would have lasted as long as we have. We may lose this city, but it is not our true home! We will be back, and we will come for payment for the blood spilled."

"Yes, sir." their voices were stronger than before.

"Now, let's do our jobs and get our people out of here. This is not our final battle!"

Erik was feeling better after the shot Rugrat had given him. He locked away the losses, promising to deal with it later. He gritted his teeth, taking four stairs at a time.

"Fuck these stairs!" Gong Jin yelled.

"Too used to the teleportation formations," Roska said.

The special teams reached another landing with defensive walls and a barrier covering it.

The stairs created a funnel down into the under-city.

Rifle squads ran down the stairs, past them and through the defenses, down toward the teleportation formations.

"We're withdrawing to the castle. The enemy is using smoke spells to cover their advance," Zukal reported as they reached the top of the stairs.

They were between several armories filled with lockers in disarray. More soldiers streamed past them. They ran down the corridor and up another set of stairs, arriving on the castle's main floor.

The roof shook with impacts as a window was blown out with a spray of glass. Someone screamed.

A soldier ran over through the glass. "I've got you. I've got you! Stretcher-bearers!" She threw her rifle to the side and secured it with a tie, grabbing the man's medical kit and tearing it free.

"Zukal, you head off to your regiment. We're going to head to the fourth-floor offices." Erik kept running down the hallway.

"Sir!"

They passed a doorway. Outside, soldiers were spread out, streaming from the wall down the spell-struck road to the castle, trying to not group up to present a good target.

Machine gunners were set up in the doorway and the nearby windows, covering them as they shot up at the aerial fighters trying to cast their spells.

A fireball struck the ground between two soldiers, throwing them into the air.

No!

Erik slowed his pace, ready to run out. The two men clambered to their feet.

"Baines, you good?"

"Yeah, get going, sir!"

Erik recognized Bai Ping and his staff sergeant. They were covered in dirt. Bai grabbed onto Baines and hauled him to his feet. They ran for the doorway.

Erik increased his speed, making it to the bottom of the stairs. "Clear a path!" he yelled at the people coming down.

He launched himself up the stairs.

"What you thinking for positions?" Rugrat asked.

"Our office faces east. Team One and Two, with me on the offices to the left facing northwest. You, Team Three and Four take the offices northeast!"

"Got it."

Erik opened a channel to Commander Glosil's aides. "Command, this is West, message over."

"West, send message."

"Command, can we get an engineer to place explosives on the castle floors to make a way for our people to drop down to the main floor instead of taking the stairs?"

"West, understood will pass on."

"Command, understood, out."

Fuck the stairs.

They reached the fourth floor and ran for the offices.

Rugrat and his group peeled off as they ran past the northeast offices. They kicked open doors and pushed in.

Erik looked into his office. Three grenade launcher teams were prepping their weapons as they watched the grounds. "We've got a grenade launcher crew in the office. Rugrat make sure you knuckle onto them."

"You got it, West."

Erik turned to the group around him. "Okay, Niemm, I want you on my left. Roska on my right."

"Got it. Team Two, start pushing in. Um ..." Roska cleared her throat. "Tully, I want you up against the boss' offices Everyone take a window."

They rolled down the hallway, crashing through office doors and clearing a path to the windows.

Erik shoulder checked through a door. His feet crunched on glass as he moved through the area of cubicles. The windows went from hip height to just under his chin.

Erik looked through the different windows, searching for the best spot.

Smoke billowed up along the wall as people streamed across the three hundred meters of open ground toward the castle. Guns on the different floors opened up on the aerial forces, mages applying their spells to the rounds, reinforcing the other's power.

The aerial beasts, black birds with red markings, raced by.

The castle's barrier shook with impacts.

Good thing it's the strongest barrier we have.

He picked a window and stuck his barrel along the frame and ran it around the side, clearing out the remaining glass.

He turned off the lights in the room, cloaking it in darkness. He secured his rifle to the side with a tie and flipped a desk, pushing it into place against the window.

Erik drew on his power. Stone from the walls and floor acted like mud as it flowed over the desk, using it as a form. It thickened as Erik released the spell. He staggered, feeling the drain upon his body as his new leg shook.

Still needs time to heal.

Erik grabbed a chair and put it behind his barrier. He unlimbered his railgun and checked the wall, sitting down heavily on the chair.

He made to rub his face, but hit his mask instead. "Come on, work to do." He laid out magazines in reach.

He pulled out a stamina needle and stabbed it into his left leg.

"That's the good shit. Better than coffee sludge."

Smoke shot inwards with a flash of light.

"They've breached the outer wall!" Domonos reported.

Erik aimed at the breach. The walls were already starting to rebuild-pumped full of mana.

Soldiers dropped to the ground, watching the breach. Others ran past as fast as possible.

Good luck. This is the heart of our domain.

Another flash opened a hole in the wall. Several others expanded as the smoke pushed through.

"Mages, get some air spells into that shit," Yui ordered.

Air spells met the smoke, rolling it back to the wall and pushing through.

Erik saw movement between the walls and fired. The movement stopped, and the smoke kept rolling back.

Aerial attacks hit the barrier.

Erik ducked as spells ran down his length of wall. Wind ran over him.

That was close. He looked at the nearest breach again.

The smoke rolled back past the breach.

"Fire!" Erik said, shooting at the human forms climbing over the remains of the wall.

Tracers shot down into the breaches as grenade launchers fired past them. Sections of wall exploded with the Black Phoenix's attacks. The aerial forces were coming in hot and heavy now.

Fuck off!

Erik fired at passing aerial mounts. His rounds exploded, spraying shards of metal through the sky, tearing them apart.

He aimed back at his breach. The remaining bunkers were opening up on them now.

Spells activated right in the enemy's teeth, cutting through their ranks.

Then the rate of fire went down as there weren't any more targets. Even the aerial force backed off.

Erik looked for the frigate. He sighed when he saw it was still a distance away and its cannon was sealed.

"Anyone else get the feeling they're testing us," Yao Meng asked.

"It's what I'd do," Erik replied. He frowned, feeling like he was missing something. "Rugrat, check our flanks!"

"Shit! Yeah, they're moving around to the east and west."

The leadership channel flared to life. "Dragon Regiment, link up with the groups facing north and create an all-round defense along the west to the south. Tiger, do the same for the east. Send your mortar teams down. Prepare secondary fallback positions within the castle. We will activate Sunken City once they commit. We're making a central space for personnel to drop through to the main floor. Once Sunken City is activated, all forces from the higher floors are to fall back to the secondary defenses. Command out!" Glosil closed the channel as Erik looked out over Vuzgal. Towers had collapsed, smashing apart homes and businesses. Buildings were no more than piles of broken stone and belongings strewn across the streets.

Night was coming in.

Sky Reaching Restaurants' glass had been shattered, leaving them as skeletal pyres, their glass catching the red rays of sunlight.

Some lights flared to life; others flickered weakly.

Light formations came on around the castle. The academy lit up, the gardens and park lights giving off a low light as the creeping darkness hid the tombstones, divots and craters.

Erik opened up a channel to Rugrat.

"What's up?"

"Just, you know." Erik surveyed the destruction. "Wish we weren't leaving it how we found it."

"Yeah." Rugrat's voice softened. "How you holding up?"

"New limbs are a pain, but I'm working through it, and my stamina potions."

"Gotcha."

Erik breathed in through his nose and released it through his mouth. He stood to the crack of glass and scraping noise of pebbles under his boot against stone.

"I'm going to check on the teams here."

"You sure? I can do a walk around."

"You do your people; I'll do my side. Don't need us holding their hands, just us telling them when to shoot or hold their fire." Erik walked to the busted-up door and pushed it aside, part of the wood clattering on the floor.

"Got it," Rugrat grunted, shaking his legs.

"Them knees?" He had a tired grin on his face.

"Always the knees, brother." Rugrat laughed. "Shit, even with all the healing, they creak like a mother."

Erik snorted half-heartedly. The events of the day were too fresh and raw. "Get me that sitrep. I feel that this might be a long one."

"On it."

Erik walked down the hall. The lights were off, the ones down the stairs or in the stairwells spilled out into hallways filled with dust and pieces of stone.

"Housekeeping," Erik said as he pushed through a door.

"Sir." Roska got up from where she was crouching next to the window. She had her magazines laid out with a few spell scrolls.

"Just checking in."

"Good on ammo and supplies," she said.

"Good to hear. Why you right next to me instead of in the middle of your team?"

"In case your stubborn streak shows and we have to drag you from this position." Roska shrugged.

"Ah, so I should expect Niemm on my left?"

"Yup."

Erik snorted. "I'll try not to make your job too hard. I'm gonna check on everyone before I head back."

"Yes, sir. I'll let Niemm know."

"Ah, shit, yeah. Sorry. forgot."

"Been a day." Roska's words were heavy.

She squatted, leaning against the side of the window, holding her railgun. Her eyes kept scanning the wall.

Defending yet another wall.

"We just need a few more hours and we can get everyone out of here."

"Yes, sir."

"Well, I'm off to do my rounds. Let me know if anything shows up."

"Will do."

64
Abandon Vuzgal

Egbert looked at the formation carved into the ground. He stored his supplies in a finger bone.

The whole room was covered in mana stone dust. More dust floated down from the mana stones being consumed by the mana storing formation above. It fell on a fresh formation plate laid upon the carved formation surrounding the dungeon core that was feeding power into the mana gathering formation in a pillar of pure mana.

Egbert locked onto Glosil in the command center and projected his voice. "Preparations are complete. Permission to rejoin the battle?"

"Head to the castle main floor," Glosil said without pause. "You will be covering our people's retreat."

Egbert opened his jaw and then closed it. "Yes, sir."

He ran from where the dungeon core was housed and through the formation-covered entrances that activated as he passed.

Soldiers marched onto teleportation formations and disappeared in a flash of light. The next group waited for the formation to clear and stepped forward. Vuzgal was quickly being evacuated.

Formation masters from the engineering platoons were working on the formations that were getting deformed from repeated activations and heat accumulation.

Egbert stopped on the stairs. "Commander, permission to assist the teleportation formation masters!"

He saw through the walls as Glosil looked up. "Can you?"

"Sir, I did help build Alva."

Glosil grimaced and hit his forehead. "Help them and destroy any formations we can't use."

"You think they will try to trace where we went?" Egbert asked.

"They're from the upper realms. I'm not leaving anything to chance."

"Understood. I'll get to work."

Egbert dropped toward the teleportation room. Four formations were laid out in front of two lines. As one formation cleared, groups of ten soldiers moved onto the formation as quickly as possible.

Egbert could sense how hot the formations were from repeated activation. It was slowing down how fast they could be used.

"Qin, I've been sent to help." He didn't look down at her missing legs. A quick healing spell would fix them, but it'd knock her out. She wore awkward-fitting armor and a helmet. She looked well past the point of exhaustion. A human automaton.

"Egbert, good. We can use some help. Carve runes under the formation plates to dissipate heat. This is the formation design that's working." She spun in her wheelchair, waving at the formation. It took him a second to see through the design.

Her legs were broken, a quick fuse and a wheelchair, and she was commanding the teleportation formations. She flat out refused to leave before she got everyone out.

He accessed the dungeon core, inputting changes. The ground started to depress, revealing lines and runes cut into the stone surface behind the four teleportation formations. "We need to fill in those formations, but that should dissipate the heat nicely. I'll get working on the new teleportation formations, as well. They won't be as strong, and the dungeon core will need to fix them constantly, but they'll help."

Qin lowered her voice. "Make sure they work for the last group. If they don't get out, they'll be stuck here."

Egbert looked at her face. Her eyes were sunken and dull. She was exhausted, both mentally and physically.

"Don't worry, I will be part of the rear guard and I'll make sure they all get out," Egbert promised.

"Just, don't die. Too many—" Qin choked and then sniffed. There were no more tears left to cry. It was only now Egbert could see the lines through the dust under her eyes.

"I did that once before and I don't plan on doing it again." Egbert patted her on the back.

Qin hugged him, shocking him slightly. "Tan Xue. Tanya. I-I… I couldn't—"

Egbert held her and patted her back. *I may have no heart, but it hurts all the same.*

Qin sniffed and pulled herself together.

"Later, later." Egbert didn't know if he said it for him or to her.

"We have work to do."

"That we do, Miss Silaz."

Erik had walked up and down through the teams. Now he sat on his perch eating a high stamina regeneration bar.

Darkness had crept in as the enemy reorganized.

Machine guns fired in the west as they pressed the walls and castle.

Erik cast eagle eyes and scanned his section of wall.

"They're fond of that smoke spell," he said around his food bar and lowered his rifle, holding it one-handed on his leg, quickly checking the linked map on the inside of his forearm.

The door to his office area fell apart.

"I think you need to call maintenance," Rugrat said.

Erik grunted and finished checking his map, resting his right hand on his rifle and grabbing the bar with his left, taking another bite.

"What flavour?"

"Blueberry, I think?" Erik looked at the bar and shrugged. "Ah shit, where are Fred and his people?"

"I got them squared away. They're roaming around the floor, supporting people. They're as strong as us, if not stronger. Certainly got more spells. Gives Davin a break."

"He's done well. Been running around laying down fire since he arrived."

"Yeah, he's been running on fumes. Got him drinking mana potions on a mana regeneration formation. Should be good to go soon." Rugrat pushed some papers and things off a desk and sat on it, resting his rail gun across his legs.

"This is going to be the last one here." Erik tore off another piece of the bar as he turned his chair so he could look sideways through the window and see Rugrat.

"I think so too. Sunken City should give us the time we need to pull everyone out. Artillery platoons are evacuating now. Egbert is supporting the engineers with the teleportation formations."

"Good shit." Erik finished off his bar and rubbed his fingers on his pants before grabbing his canteen. He drank from it and held it out to Rugrat.

Rugrat opened his hands, and Erik closed the canteen and tossed it. Rugrat opened it and tilted it back.

"Incoming up high!" someone yelled as the night sky lit up with machine guns and blue tracers.

"I'm off!" Rugrat grabbed his rifle in one hand and stored Erik's canteen.

"Make sure I get my canteen back!" Erik yelled. He grabbed his metal mask and cast a fuse spell as he put it over his face, sealing it up. "Odd team leaders watch the ground. Even team leaders watch the skies!"

The aerial forces had come in down low and dangerous, creeping right up to the edge of the broken buildings across from what remained of the castle walls. Barriers flashed and failed over the aerial forces as their mounted beasts covered the open ground, closing with the walls in seconds.

Erik fired, leading his trace across the aerial beasts. They passed through the castle compound's barrier and opened up.

Prepared spells and spell scrolls activated.

The elements seemed to rebel as spells crashed against the castle walls. Stone struck Erik's faceplate as he kept firing on the aerial beasts.

The soldier manning the grenade launcher perched in his old office was firing air shot spelled grenades, turning it into a massive shotgun, tearing up the aerial forces.

A spell crashed into the wall.

That's my office. Shit. Clear as day, the thought slammed into his head.

"Tully, status!"

"I'm good. Fucking wall blew out. Fuck, the launcher team didn't make it. The aerial forces are pushing through the breach!"

Erik watched an aerial forces group head for the hole in the castle. They were determined to close with the Alvans.

"Ground forces are pushing!" Gong Jin yelled.

"Sunken City. I say again, Sunken City!" Glosil ordered.

Erik barely heard the explosions behind him as he tore out his magazine and slammed in a new one.

"Roska. Gong Jin. Control that entry point."

"Sir!"

Other hits struck the wall. The bunkers opened up on the ground forces pushing forward; spell traps and formation traps went off. Undead mages and archers added in their attacks.

The aerial forces weaved through lines of tracers, forcing the ground forces to fight for every inch.

"Get ready to pull back!" Erik said, waiting for the signal.

Rippling explosions that reminded Erik of building demolition charges shot dust into the air, spreading out from the castle compound.

There she goes.

Erik tossed his empty magazine and loaded a new one. He nailed a group of aerial riders who were staring at the explosions and kept running.

Captain Stassov was sitting back in her command chair. She drank a mana elixir, causing her body to relax in the low mana environment.

Someone gasped. Her eyes flickered over as the map changed suddenly. "What?"

She stood up, forgetting her drink. Explosions ripped through the city as everything from around the castle walls and beyond dropped in sections.

This must be their plan. Those explosions and sections are too uniform.

"They must have been preparing this for years," one aide hissed.

Stassov gritted her teeth, her thoughts in line with the aide's.

"Have our aerial forces continue the assault. Gather our ground forces and push through the dungeon underneath. Have them ready to deal with any dungeon creatures."

The aerial forces regained control as they redoubled their attacks and pressed the breaches they'd created in the castle walls.

That should be your last trick, right?

"Slow our forward speed and bring the cannons to bear," Stassov ordered.

"Mother fucker!" Rugrat ducked as what was once a stone wall was blown into his side. He kept running as the stone struck him. He scanned behind the doorway ahead of him. There was a gaping hole in the floor where soldiers were jumping down.

"Team Three, watch that side." Rugrat threw his hand out to the hallway to his front. "Team Four, watch the way we came!"

The teams raised barriers of stone from the ground, creating a skirmish line through the corridor.

Soldiers streamed past and into the doorway Rugrat held. They leapt down the hole.

A group of aerial riders without their mounts blasted spells down the hallway, chasing a group of soldiers who were leapfrogging backward, stopping, turning, and shooting to cover one another.

"Contact!" Gong Jin's people held their fire; they were excellent shots.

But it raised the hairs on the back of Rugrat's head, thinking of a blue on blue.

Rugrat aimed at the ceiling, past his retreating soldiers. "Mana chains."

He cast the spell and fired blue-coated rounds. Chains of mana exploded out of the ceiling. An aerial rider screamed as the chains stabbed through his body and exploded.

The chains tried to attack and grab the other riders.

Explode.

The spell twisted and the mana making up the chains detonated. The ceiling collapsed, raining down on the aerial force.

"Move it, troops!" Rugrat barked.

The retreating force got up and ran, threading through the walls, protecting Gong Jin.

"Fire!" Gong Jin and his team opened fire. Their rounds cut through the aerial force, tearing them apart in a few moments.

"Cease fire!"

The officer patted Rugrat and yelled in his ear. "Last man."

Rugrat raised a thumb; the officer ran on.

"Yao, how things looking on your side?"

"Got one group lagging. They have wounded."

"Push out and cover them." Rugrat changed channels. "Good on this side, just pulling in a wounded group." Rugrat raised his voice as a spell went through a wall and an office blew out into the hallway, spreading dust.

"Han Wu, Tyrone, cover that hole!" Gong Jin yelled.

"We're ready to pull back," Rugrat said.

"Got it. Fifth floor has collapsed." Erik paused as a spell went off on the floor above.

"Seems they've found our traps. Rugrat, we'll meet at the armory stairs. Team One and Four will go first. Two and Three will be with us. We are the rear guard."

"Yes, sir!"

Yao Meng and his people pulled back behind their defenses as the squad carrying wounded passed and headed for the hole.

"Just cleared our wounded."

Erik was silent. Rugat knew he was doing one last life detect scan.

"Activating formation traps. Get moving."

Rugrat saw the flashes of mana as simple-looking tiles activated their secondary hidden purpose.

I had hoped we were just being paranoid fucks.

"Pull back. Team Four, drop down and cover us on the ground. Team Three, second!"

Gong Jin's team split into two, manning the defenses as Yao's team ran for the hole and jumped, disappearing.

"Contact!" Han Wu yelled as he fired.

Rugrat threw his rifle to the side, securing it with a tie, and pulled out a ready grenade launcher.

Spells hit their stone defenses, exploding and tossing Tyrone and Jackie backward.

Rugrat could tell as soon as they were thrown that there was no saving them.

Explosive Shot.

He fired into where the spells came from, silencing them.

"Gong Jin, grab them." New spells tore down the corridor.

Rugrat's left arm blazed in pain as it was tossed backward.

He aimed and fired his grenade launcher one-handed into the new spell's location.

He took a second, a piece of shrapnel embedded in his forearm.

"Move it!" Rugrat yelled as his body lit up with power, tearing out the shrapnel. He breathed in the world, drawing in the surrounding mana. His domain stretched out as chains of mana tore out from the outer reaches of his domain, hunting down the aerial forces.

Gong Jin grabbed Tyrone and Jackie, hitting them with revival needles and tossing them in his beast storage crate.

He rushed past Rugrat as Rugrat waved his hand. Chains of mana tore through a section of offices, tearing apart anything in his path: walls, desks, beasts and people.

"Rugrat!" Gong Jin yelled.

Rugrat turned back, his eyes glowing orbs. He detonated the chains as the power was ripped from his body. Rugrat coughed as he struggled forward, his head hurting. It felt like his mana channels were shrinking.

He stored his grenade launcher and reached Gong Jin. Gong Jin grabbed him and jumped. They fell four stories. Gong Jin took the impact with a crouch.

Rugrat hit the ground with his feet and rolled. He pulled out a mana and stamina potion, pulling off the tab and sucked it back.

"Armory stairs!" Rugrat grabbed his rifle's pistol grip and made to move his left arm to undo the tie.

Pain flared through his arm as he winced, letting out a hissing breath. He let his left arm lay limp and called mana into his hand.

They ran out of the dust and rubble-filled room and through a series of rooms that had been smashed through to create a direct path to the armory.

"Covering fire!" Yao Meng yelled.

He stepped out of a broken wall and fired down the hallway.

The group of soldiers carrying their wounded rushed across the hallway with half of Yao Meng's team. They kept running as Rajkovic and Foster took up position.

"Covering!"

"Go, Gong Jin! Rugrat!" Yao yelled.

"Alpha move!" Gong Jin yelled.

Rugrat and half of Gong Jin's team spread out, running down the hallway.

"Asaka, Otus, help them!" Gong Jin yelled.

Rugrat grabbed his medical kit and pulled out a healing needle from his butt pouch. He stabbed the needle around the wound that went through his bicep and tricep, injecting the potion.

He blinked and forced his eyes open, the stamina fatigue hit him at full force, and he bit the inside of his cheek so hard he tasted iron. He tossed away the empty needle and grabbed his rifle. His left arm and hand were still arguing with him as he undid the tie around his rifle and checked the window on his magazine.

Gong Jin pulled out Tyrone and Jackie. He hit them with another revival needle. The two were blackened husks covered in red cuts of fresh meat.

Rugrat gritted his teeth and changed his magazine out as Yao Meng and his people made it across.

Asaka and Otus stood back and reloaded as Rajkovic and Foster stepped into their position, giving covering fire.

It seemed the attackers stopped caring about the covering fire as Han Wu and his Bravo team's spells landed around them. Rajkovic and Foster altered their aim, silencing the spells as Han Wu and his people made it to the other side, somehow untouched.

"Good to go!" Han Wu's voice was shaky as Asaka and Otus threw grenades down the hallway.

Gong Jin secured the wounded as Yao Meng put a hand on Rugrat's shoulder. "You good?"

"I can fight." Rugrat stood up from his crouch.

"Yao, on point. Gong Jin then Han Wu. Let's move!" Rugrat said.

The teams pushed forward. Han Wu and his people threw out trap formations and more grenades.

Explosions and a rush of air told Rugrat that the ceiling had collapsed behind them.

They slowed upon reaching open areas. They passed two more without issue. The third they saw and heard spells and tracers being traded back and forth.

"Do not bring out any dead or those without vital signs!" Glosil ordered.

"What the hell is he doing?" Rugrat asked no one as Yao reached the end of their path. They came out of an arch. To their left were two arched entrances into the area. Halfway down the length, there were stairs leading up to the second floor.

On the right, there was a set of stairs that disappeared below to the armories and past them into the under city.

CPD teams manned walls that had been pulled from the ground, firing down the hall that was littered with stone walls, which had been torn apart in the crossfire.

The enemy flitted between the walls and cast spells. Some ran in with barriers, not understanding the power of the railguns. They were cut down. Tombstones showed the bloody cost of the aerial forces to reach this far.

"This is where we hold!" Rugrat yelled through the reduced noise of his helmet.

Erik reached the other archway and nodded across the hall. "You move first. We'll cover, then you cover us."

"Got it!" Rugrat switched back to his teams.

"We're moving first; get ready. The other teams will cover us, and we'll take up position. Go to general teams channel."

Rugrat boosted his volume. "CPD, we're moving in. Give us cover!"

"You got it!" one yelled back from the defenses.

Rugrat and the others readied themselves for the run, moving back from the doorway. It was only a few meters, but it was out in the open.

"Covering!" Erik yelled as he and the rest of his team fired. The CPD added in their own fire.

Their rounds tore up sections of the enemy walls and took out the central space between the two pillars, dropping a section of the ceiling and wall, creating a rubble pile between the two broken arches.

Rugrat and the others slid into cover. He pushed back on his ass with his feet. His left arm was still mostly useless. He turned, got his legs under him, aimed, and rose in a crouch.

"Covering!" He added in his fire with the rest of his teams.

Erik and his teams ran out, dropping down into cover.

Rugrat was jittery, scanning for threats as the fire dropped down. The CPD started to reload.

An aerial fighter scrambled over the rubble toward them. Several rounds created a tombstone as the man's body slid to the bottom of the pile.

"Okay, CPD leaders, prepare to pull your people back," Erik said in the lull of shooting.

Rugrat kept scanning as he flexed his hand. It was hurting less, but there was still a dull throb when he raised it.

"Rugrat and your group, watch twelve to ten. My group will cover twelve to three."

"Got it!" Rugrat yelled out with the rest of the teams.

Rugrat used the wall to aim down the arches to his left, still working his hand, hoping to get it functioning faster.

A CPD member grabbed his medical kit and opened it.

"What are you doing?" Rugrat growled.

"Shut up and aim," the first sergeant shot back as he used a clean formation on Rugrat, cleared his wound and started work on his arm.

Rugrat relaxed. "Thanks."

"No problem." The man didn't look at Rugrat as he kept working. "You good for mags?"

"Got any extra railguns?"

"Sure thing. Rothman, you got some extras?"

"Yeah." Rothman kept aiming, grabbing, and dropping magazines from his storage ring.

A spell blew through a wall down near the arches on the right side, raining down dust and stone.

Roska returned with the dull thump of a grenade launcher.

Rugrat spotted someone looking over the left arch's' rubble and fired. They disappeared from view, scared or dead.

The first sergeant tied off the bandage on Rugrat's arm, making him grunt.

"You'll be fine." He hit Rugrat with a stamina needle then tapped Rugrats mags, changing out the half empties with full ones before he pulled out a spare medical kit and hooked it to the back of his carrier.

"Well, it was good bandaging you up—" He wiped Rugrat's back where his name was markered. "—Rugrat!" The man's voice rose.

Spells shot out from the arches and another section of wall opened as the enemy pushed forward.

Their spells struck the mana barrier covering the fighters above the armory stairs.

Rugrat aimed and fired. He was on semi-auto, leaving bodies in his wake.

The attack calmed down again.

"It's just a name. What's yours?"

The first sergeant chewed on the question before sighing. "Chang."

"Thanks for putting my broken ass back together, Chang. Now get ready to pull back. Alva needs people like you and Rothman more than ever."

"Dragon details, prepare to move!" Domonos called out.

"Yes, sir," Chang said.

"Move!"

Chang moved with the detail, threading through the walls to the rear, and ran down the stairs.

The hall exploded with spells and the front half disappeared. Mana cannons fired through them, striking the mana barrier.

"Fuck me!" Rugrat muttered as he shot back, trading fire with the mana cannons. His shots hit with the power of a mana cannon. He drained a mag, breaking the barrier. The rest of his spells exploded around the cannon, killing the gun's crew. Mages with barriers stood outside the hall and cast spells. Tracers and spells mixed with one another with the blast of mana cannon.

"Tiger details, move!" Yui ordered.

"Nice sharing a wall with you, sir!" Rothman said as he turned and moved to the rear.

"See you in Alva, smartass!" Rugrat ejected his magazine, picked up one Chang had laid out for him, slammed it home, and kept firing.

Glosil stood in the command center. Most of the viewing displays were dead, and there were only a handful of people remaining. The map had been zoomed in, showing the fierce change of positions within the castle compound.

Colonel Domonos ran in. "We need to get you moving, sir!"

"I need to head to the dungeon core."

"Understood. I'll be at the teleportation formations."

Glosil jogged out of the command center and to the dungeon core. Egbert was there.

"Are you sure about this, Commander?" Egbert asked. The room was growing darker now that most of the mana stones had been cleared out. Runes flickered, trying to connect with the rest of their formation but finding nothing.

"This is the only way we can deny the enemy access to the city."

Glosil stepped forward and froze. He grunted against the mana wrapped around his body. "Egbert!"

"There have been enough Alvan deaths today." Egbert said privately before he raised his voice to include others. "Hey Erik, Rugrat, permission to raise the undead, destroy all traces of Alva, and attack our guests?"

"Do it!" the two voices yelled.

Egbert interlaced his finger bones and stretched them out ahead of himself as he stepped on the formation around the dungeon core.

"Let's see what these old bones can do." Egbert *smiled* as he looked at Glosil. "We'll switch the mana gathering formations back on and set the dungeon to use all but fifteen percent of our remaining power so we can raise the undead. We'll start with those at the outer reaches, with orders to gather closer to the dungeon core." Egbert raised his hands. Golems rose from the ground, covered in runic lines.

"I don't have much building materials, but these golems are moving formations. All that metal and reactive materials, a few changes and they'll turn back into a formation. Now, if I command the golem—" Beads formed around the dungeon core, separated out, and shot into the five golems. "—I control where the dungeons are placed. Oh, high and mighty, Ten Realms, will you allow me to create a dungeon that falls under your rules?"

A golden glow appeared around the dungeon cores.

"And now the dungeon cores are activated, free of our control."

The golems ran off toward the under city.

"What are you doing!" Glosil shouted.

"Saving your ass and putting your *modified* plan into action. The dungeon cores will create small dungeons around them. The golems will carry them to spread out over the city. Then they will create formations, increasing their range of effect.

"The dungeon cores will bury themselves in the ground and keep the undead roaming as dungeon monsters. That way, we cover more ground with lower grade dungeon cores.

"Our dungeon core is raising the undead. Once we leave, the mana stones and mana gathering formation won't matter. Might as well use that power. We can reach really far right now. We pull all the bodies of the sects into the city, flip the switch, put them under the Ten Realms dungeons and we get the hell out of here."

"You'll turn all of Vuzgal into a series of dungeons?"

"Correctu-mon-do! Which allows me to do things like use the dungeon core to track all the gear in Vuzgal and destroy it. One second; it is a pain to split my head that far."

"Why didn't you tell me this?"

"Working!"

Glosil's bonds released as mana flashed around Egbert. Glosil heard rumblings in the distance, large and small.

It took Egbert several minutes before he moved again.

"Okay, well, it doesn't look like much down here, but I activated every destruction formation that we had in our weapons and magazines, and liberally sanitized everything. The dungeon cores will be located in areas of the most fighting. They'll consume everything as building materials to create their dungeon so that should mess up everything else. Erik and Rugrat are pulling back on the armory stairs. We have just four hundred people to go."

Egbert turned to Glosil. "I know you had good intentions, but I came up with a better plan. Alva needs its commander. Go to the teleportation formations. I'll follow with Erik and Rugrat. Just want to give these people one last middle finger."

The tombstones around the dead faded as their bodies shuddered, then started to rise. They attacked the nearest Black Phoenix members in the hall, startling them and cutting them up.

"Group one, pull back!" Erik said.

Rugrat and his people turned and ran down the stairs into the armory, disappearing.

"Spell scrolls!" Erik pulled on the scroll tab. Spells shot out across their front. "Go!"

Erik and his group turned and sped toward the armory stairs. Yawen missed the steps and hit the ground rolling. Roska grabbed him, hauling him to his feet as the special team slammed into the wall at the end of the stairs.

They turned left and ran down the hall, past Rugrat and his group, who were at the corridor entrance, watching the stairs.

Han Wu was covered by Rugrat, Yao and Jurumba as he threw out trap formations.

Erik turned out of the line and looked at the rear. Niemm smacked Rugrat on the shoulder.

"Last man!"

Erik nodded to him.

"Don't wait too long!" Erik yelled as he raised his rifle and kept running. He ran past the armories, threading through the lockers that had been thrown in the hallway and covered in stone. He slid to a stop behind one and aimed down the hallway.

Rugrat and his people turned and ran down the hall, passing the locker blockade and ran through a locker room at the end of the hall. The floor and wall opened to show the passage into the under city.

"Covering!"

Erik's group peeled back from the front like a wave. He heard the trap formations going off on the first set of stairs as he passed the other group and ran down the stairs.

A close protection detail was waiting there with Yui.

"We've got this stairwell prepped to blow. Keep going!" Yui yelled.

They threaded their way to the lines going through the teleportation formations. Rugrat and his group filed in behind them.

"You go first," Erik yelled. "You have wounded,"

"Go!" Rugrat yelled as an explosion went off, followed by the rush of air and dust.

Colonel Yui appeared.

"Get out of here!" Erik yelled. "Egbert, how are things on your end?"

"Good to go, heading to you—"

An explosion rocked the remaining sections of the under-city. Erik ducked, acutely aware of the hundreds of meters of rock, castle, and tower above him.

"Now!"

"What the hell was that?"

"Just a little present I left behind. We really must be going!"

You have lost command of the Dungeon: Vuzgal

"Go," Erik yelled to the special team members. They were now the only people remaining.

"Not without you, sir." Roska grabbed Erik and Niemm grabbed onto Rugrat.

Egbert appeared in a spray of rocks as he came right through a wall. More rocks fell from the ceiling.

"We're leaving!" Egbert grabbed all of them, picking them off their feet as they flew to the teleportation formation.

"Keep your asses in the formation and suck your guts in!"

The remaining special team members jumped on the teleportation formations.

Egbert opened his mouth as grenades fell out of his molar storage ring, falling among the teleportation formations.

There was a flash, and the darkness and flickering lights were gone, replaced with metal walls and machine guns watching the teleportation formations. They had arrived at a backup site.

"No Alvans are in Vuzgal anymore," Egbert reported. A messenger disappeared through another teleportation formation.

Erik felt the strength leaving his body. Egbert's words were driving home as he walked off the teleportation formation numbly.

He heard the cries of the wounded through the gates.

Soldiers drew their swords and cut the transportation formation apart, passing it to mages and smiths who melted the metal down.

Erik watched them as he passed.

"They are making sure that we cannot be traced through the formations or that someone else can force their way through," Egbert said.

Erik nodded, letting his rifle hang from his sling. He undid his helmet and pulled it off, feeling the air on his sweaty face and hair. He stored his helmet as they walked through the defenses. Soldiers opened and closed the doors. The last one revealed the dungeon.

A field hospital had been set up outside the teleportation defenses. Medics were moving between people, performing surgery on stretchers as needed.

Erik unslung his rifle and put it away. Using a clean spell, he pushed his fatigue away, accepted it, lived in it.

"Where can I help?" he asked a medic checking people.

"Sir."

"As you were. Where?"

"Surgery is this end, Pri Alpha closer to the defenses. Not as bad the farther down you go."

"Okay," Erik looked around. There were so many wounded.

He extended his domain, his senses reaching out to assess them as fast as possible so he could get to the people that didn't have much time left.

"Fighting is fierce in the lower levels of the castle. The ground forces report that there are no weapons or enemy bodies left behind. They are all evacuating."

"Well, get in there and finish them off," Stassov said.

"Commander, we have dungeon cores on the move!"

"The hell is happening?" She stood and walked quickly to the map table. One dungeon core light split into one medium light and five tiny ones flying apart.

"Mana fluctuations around the city." The aide bent to their console, trying to make sense of the changes. Shaking his head.

"Undead creation!" An aide to the ground forces shouted. "Our dead are attacking our own people and the dead in the city's defenses are grabbing other dead and hauling them into the city."

"We have lightning striking across the city!" The aide that had been studying her console stood up, words tumbling out. "Mana change!"

Stassov looked up. Her windows showed the castle compound; the barrier evaporated, power diverting down the tower, gaining speed and becoming brighter as mana from across the battlefield was dragged in like water breaking a dam.

"What are they ...?" an aide started to ask.

"Pull out our forces now!" Stassov yelled, reaching out her hand as *Eternus'* shields grew brighter and the ship slammed backward with emergency power.

Vuzgal Castle ballooned, rising on a mushroom of dirt. Blue light shone from underneath, becoming brighter for a second.

The castle exploded with the tower, hurling itself in every direction.

Stassov stood there, the color draining from her features and the power from her limbs as she held onto the map table for support. Winds buffeted *Eternus* but the silent crew didn't notice, looking at the city as smaller explosions tore through.

The defensive towers, the Battle Arenas, entire *districts* turned into nothing more than rubble.

I underestimated how far they would go.

"Get me casualty reports! And get our people out of that city. We do not know if they left any other traps."

An aide bowed deeply as she looked away.

"The dungeon cores, where are they now?" Stassov asked, drawing power back into her body, forcing herself forward.

"They're spread out through the city. They're ... They're active."

"Don't lose them. Once the situation has stabilized, recover them."

Stassov turned from the table and moved toward her throne. She dismissed formations around her dungeon core and sat back down. A servant came up with a mana elixir.

She sipped it while looking at the room. She had to think quickly. She had believed she could claim an easy victory, crush a group associated with the Sha, and steal their dungeon core. Accolades and position would have been hers.

This was not at all what she had feared in her darkest thoughts. She glanced at the broken city before her once again, closing her eyes and breathing deeply.

65
Rise and Fall

Delilah stared out of the dungeon headquarters balcony. She could see the towers in the distance that broke up Alva's skyline reaching toward the mana gathering formation across the ceiling.

People were holding one another, subdued. Tears stained more than one set of cheeks; hope and pain filled their eyes and hearts.

Alva was scared. Her people reeled in pain, at loss, unsure of the future, and it was her job to reassure them, to bolster their hope and focus their efforts.

A small but calloused hand took hers in their own. Momma Rodriguez smiled up at her. "You'll do fine." She patted Delilah's hand.

Delilah gave her a tight smile and exhaled. Some of the tension between her shoulders loosened. Momma Rodriguez released her hand.

Delilah glanced at the others around her; Jia Feng, Elise, and Arenson. They nodded or smiled at her.

She glanced back out at the balcony.

Come on, this is the job.

Delilah walked out. People filled the street around the dungeon headquarters. They spread down the streets, hanging off balconies.

More Alvans in Alva than ever before.

The mutterings and chatter died down.

"A few hours ago, I got a report. Vuzgal has fallen." The people erupted into chatter. "*This--*" She raised her voice and eyebrow as the street became quiet. "--was planned. Our forces have spread out to their backup dungeons. No movement will be allowed in or out of Alva for the next four days. After that, we will review the situation.

"Many were wounded, and the medics are working hard to save their lives. I am sorry—" Delilah sighed, closing her eyes as she pulled herself together. "—but there will be no communication between the dungeons." Noise rose as she plowed on. "We have the casualty lists as they stand, but until the dungeons contact us again, we will remain in the dark. I know this will not be easy; it definitely will not be for me or my family."

The noise from the crowd grew in volume.

Delilah smacked the banister, the noise amplified by the medallion at her neck.

"This is Alva! We stand together; we stand united! Now is not the time to fall apart. Now is the time to train, to regroup! Training will continue for the army! We will continue to produce weapons, spell scrolls, ammunition, raise beasts, and grow food! We will consolidate our gains in the Beast Mountain Range and prepare to receive our loved ones."

The streets once again grew quiet.

"We have been tested. Now…" Delilah looked at the people in the streets, and on the balconies. "Show me, show one another, but most importantly, show yourselves what Alvans are truly made of!"

People stood straighter as they stared at Delilah and the council at her back.

"We have work to do. Let's start."

Delilah looked at them once again and turned, heading back into the dungeon headquarters. She wished Rugrat or Erik had been there. She squirmed, and a small smile appeared on her face, thinking of Rugrat before she shivered and banished the thought.

The dungeon had been turned into a hospital. Row upon row of wounded lay on beds and cots.

Egbert had carved massive stamina regeneration formations under the beds. Anyone that was medically qualified was helping. Soldiers that weren't gave blood, moved people, or ran supplies. The rest were patrolling, cleaning weapons, repairing gear, or getting forty minutes of sleep in the mana tempering beds.

"Need some help here!" A CPD member yelled as he worked on a patient.

Erik drew his mana out of the patient's throat, causing them to cough. He used flames to burn away the blood suspended in mid-air.

"Should be easier for him to breathe now. I patched his lung, but he still has internal bleeding." The man gulped down air as Erik pulled out a needle and catheter. He put the catheter in the man's chest. Wet air expelled from the man's chest and his breathing calmed. Erik secured the catheter with tape. "You're gonna be good." Erik patted the man on the shoulder, looking him in the eye before he ran over to the CPD member, casting a clean spell on himself out of habit. "What's the problem?"

"She's in shock!" The medic yelled in a panic.

The patient was missing both legs and had shrapnel wounds across her body.

"I'm giving her an infusion! Add new tourniquets to her legs and left arm. Do a tracheotomy," Erik yelled to the medic working on her.

"A what?"

"Put a hole in her neck and put a breathing tube down it!"

Erik grabbed scissors from his carrier and cut through the patient's sleeve up to the shoulder and neck. He pulled out an IO band and drill. Using his domain, he saw into her shoulder.

He placed the IO and drilled into her shoulder. Feeling it give way slightly, he stopped, put the drill away, and grabbed a bag of his blood.

"Come on, girl!" Erik hooked up the bag and squeezed.

The CPD member secured the left arm.

"Do a femoral IV."

Another medic came up. "Where do you need me?"

"Revival needle in the heart."

The medic pulled out the needle and pressed the patient's chest, using their Medical Scan. She stabbed into the chest and depressed the plunger steadily.

"IV in!" The CPD member had an IV going into the patient's inner thigh as Erik put a bag of stamina potion on the patient's stomach.

The CPD member hooked it up to the IV and squeezed.

"Heartbeat is leveling out." Erik sent some surges of Focused Heal into the woman's worst injuries, stopping her from losing more blood. "I hit her with some healing. Need her to get her stamina back before we can work on her some more." Erik sighed and raised the blood bag, hooking it to one of the wires that ran above the beds.

"You stay with her," Erik told the medic who had run up to them.

"Yes, sir."

"Help over here!" a medic called out.

"You go," Erik said to the CPD member.

He took off running.

Erik spread out his domain, looking for the ones that were flying under the radar. He ran over to a man shaking on his cot.

He turned the man over. The cot was covered in blood, dripping on the floor. Erik tore off the man's carrier and opened his shirt with his scissors. There was a small hole in the man's back.

Erik grabbed gauze from his leg pouch. Tearing it open, he applied it to the man's back and rolled him back over.

"Sorry, I'm sorry," the man said, nearly in tears.

Erik grabbed the man's shoulder and met his eyes. "You ain't got nothing to be sorry about, troop, so shut the hell up and heal your ass!"

Could've done self-aid.

Erik pulled a blanket out from his storage ring and put it over the man.

The man relaxed.

"You falling asleep there, troop?" Erik barked.

The soldier jolted as Erik pulled out a balm and smeared it on the man's upper lip.

He coughed with the pungent smell.

"That'll keep you alert. Don't overtax your stamina. Heal if you can. Understood?"

"Yes, sir."

"Say it back to me."

"Stay awake. Heal myself. Don't use all my stamina, sir!"

"Good shit!" Erik smacked his shoulder and stood.

"Make sure *all* body armor is removed! Runners, do blood checks. Wipe your hands over the patient. If there's blood on your hand, note where it is and inform a medic!" Erik yelled.

There are some healing formations, but that's only to keep them stabilized and get them here.

Erik looked at the stack formations among the patients, buffing their stamina stats to two hundred percent.

"Help over here! Cardiac arrest!" a medic yelled.

Erik ran over to them, instinctively casting a clean spell.

"And they took Marco with them?" Head Asadi asked Leonia Tolentino. The girl, still covered in the signs of battle, bowed as she stood in Head Asadi's office. Elder Cai Bo stood off to the side.

"Yes. I came to report to you immediately."

After you talked to your father. Cai Bo didn't feel amused knowing before of the Head. Instead, she had a hard time not biting her bottom lip. This had all gone so *wrong.*

Asadi's eyes shot back and forth, organizing his thoughts. "Did he know if the Black Phoenix Clan made any declarations?"

"No."

"Of course they wouldn't. They're a power of the Seventh Realm, like royalty!" Asadi threw up his arms and started pacing.

"Shall we press forward with our other attacks?" Cai Bo asked.

"That is what I am trying to figure out!" he snarled, veins popping out along his neck and head.

She waited for him to calm, taking a conspiratorial tone. "If the Black Phoenix Clan wishes to destroy us, they will. If we continue the attacks in the lower realms, it will at least look like we have the support of the Black Phoenix Clan."

She saw the light catch in his eyes.

"Why would we not be worried!?" Asadi asked, taking a neutral tone as he stared at Cai Bo.

"If we attack, we are confident. People might think we have their support."

Head Asadi grew silent as he stared at the floor. "That could work. What of Vuzgal?" he asked Leonia.

"The city ..." Her voice shook. "There's nothing left."

"The other sects won't be happy. They spent blood to take that city," Asadi hissed, running a hand through the thin sheen of hair. They'd want loot and winnings. All they had so far were bodies.

"There ... there are dungeons located there now, filled with undead."

"What do you mean?" Asadi asked.

"It has dungeons in it, spread right across the city," Leonia said.

"So maybe not all is lost. Undead dungeons. Are they large?"

"They cover a large area. The bodies are from the sects and the Black Phoenix Clan. They were sending people down into the dungeons. They did something and stopped them working I was told."

Asadi let out a sharp breath and shook his head.

"We all need a win to save face and to show others that we are not to be looked down on," Cai Bo directed Asadi.

"They must have been claiming the dungeon cores," Asadi muttered. "Cai Bo, continue the attacks across the realms. Reclaim our cities, assure our people. Get the head of the Tolentino clan to come here. Pull together gifts to sway the other sect leaders."

He said it as if it was almost his idea. Cai Bo didn't care. With this latest mess, her plans were on unstable ground. *But I could use this to get close to the Phoenix clan.*

"Yes, Sect Head." Cai Bo bowed and indicated for the girl to follow her out of the room.

They exited, and Cai Bo grabbed Leonia's shoulder and spun her around. "What was it like?"

"What?" Leonia seemed shocked and bobbed her head as she bowed to Cai Bo.

"What was it like fighting the people of Vuzgal?"

Leonia's brow wrinkled. "They toyed with us. We thought there was a chance we could win, but they hadn't even used half of their strength to deal with us. Their weapons hit the frigate with ease. Our camps were always within the range of their weapons. Every day they could have used their large metal tubes to attack us. They tore through our barriers while theirs stood unshakable."

"What of the Black Phoenix forces, what happened?" Cai Bo snapped as the girl smiled and shook her head, her eyes unfocused.

"They ran into the real Vuzgal. They broke their wall and defenses in a matter of hours. They lost a third of their riders, half of their aerial mounts and they were still figuring out how many of the ground troops died." Leonia's eyes focused. "There was a rumor that one of the commanders died—people who are honored in the Seventh Realm, and they killed Seventh Realm fighters in the hundreds."

She could see fear and incomprehension in Leonia's eyes. She felt a chill that they'd poked such a power. A single city that could fight a force from the seventh realm and then simply disappear.

Just how much experience had they earned?

She frowned and clapped Leonia on the shoulder. "Get some rest. You may need it in the coming weeks."

Leonia gave her a weak smile and walked away. As she left, Cai Bo was already planning. If she could use the Black Phoenix Clan's honor, the loss of face that was sure to come with losing a fight so many realms below their power base. At the very least, it could give her another opening, a path of higher expansion.

What is the Willful Institute compared to the Black Phoenix Clan?

She smiled to herself, excited as she sent messages to those in her faction.

Blaze sat down across from Domonos, sliding him a stamina tea across the table.

Domonos nodded in thanks, working on the papers that lie around him.

Blaze stepped over the picnic table style bench and sat down, leaning forward on his elbows. He twisted and turned his cup, staring at the black tea, feeling the steam on his face, watching the granules move at the bottom of the cup.

He breathed deeply, clearing his nose, and grabbed his cup, barely feeling the scalding, bitter tea. He forced it down over his tight, swollen throat. The acidic liquid hit his gut, but the sensation quickly dulled.

He dropped his head on his left hand, sighing and rubbing his eyes. Groups of soldiers sat around them, looking numb as they ate, or talking in hushed voices.

Tension hung in the air with people drooping over their food or drinks, consuming them mechanically.

They had lost Vuzgal. *Vuzgal,* a city full of hopes and dreams, a jewel of the fourth realm, a place where Alvans walked freely with few secrets.

Blaze's gaze fell to his cup again, remembering the guild hall they'd had there. He remembered standing in the upper balcony, smiling as he drank a beer with Lin Lei, watching the revelry in the Guild Tavern as a group of their members banded together to play some bawdy tune; the beer flowed and there was dancing and laughter.

Blaze closed his eyes to the memory. He pictured the flash of the frigate's main cannon as it fired on Vuzgal. The cracking of the barrier was like a punch to his gut as he'd stood there with his people, powerless to do anything but watch. The emptiness in the pit of his stomach turned hard as the hairs rose on the back of his neck and the wave of noise that had struck them before the breeze crossed the battlefield, shaking the trees around the reserves and the Adventurer's Guild. Time was a blur. But he remembered Glosil's orders.

"Pull back your forces *immediately.*"

"The Sects?" Blaze had answered, confused.

"They are no longer our concern. You and your forces are out in the open. If they find you, they'll cut you down. Get moving. Now, Blaze!"

The pages shifted and Domonos dragged the metal cup across the wooden table, lifting it and taking another gulp.

The tea had grown cold, the bitterness coating his tongue.

Domonos stretched his neck. His aid took the papers he had finished with to a table behind them that had turned into a command table.

They worked quietly, subdued.

Blaze watched Domonos as he finished stretching.

The lines of command had worn into his features, adding several years, and giving him an aged and authoritative edge. *So young, and with so much weight resting upon his shoulders.* Blaze's chest grew heavy. *How many young men and women, who never knew the love of another, had laid down their lives in Vuzgal? How many would never see their children again, or leave a hole in their parents', their friends' hearts? War should be an old man's sacrifice, not rain in the blood of the young.*

Blaze shook his head, playing with his cup without seeing it.

"We'll make it past this," Domonos said.

Blaze took a deep breath, regaining clarity as he straightened his back and looked at Domonos. "Morale is at an all-time low. We *lost* Vuzgal." Blaze still choked on that word. "We have hundreds of wounded. The sects and this new force, the Black Phoenix Clan, will be searching for us. Who the hell are they, anyway?"

"We don't know, my—" Domonos cleared his throat. "Director Elan is looking into it. Right now, we need to recover as fast as possible. We'll lie low for a few days, let things settle. Then we'll begin sending our people back to Alva and the backup dungeons in the lower realms. We're stronger there. With the reduced mana, their power will be a fraction of what it is up here."

"And that airship will have to burn through mana stones to stay aloft."

"Yes."

Blaze nodded. "So, retreat to the lower realms, bide our time, find out who our enemy is and train?"

"The greatest asset we have is time—time to increase our cultivation, make more weapons and improve them, to train people."

Domonos fell silent. Blaze took another drink of his cold tea and grimaced.

"I wish there had been something we could do. All that training, preparation, teleporting up to the fourth realm without being discovered... We were right *there*."

"You don't think I know that? We bled them for months on those walls. They paid with their lives for every fucking inch." Domonos hit the table. His cup jumped and spilled tea as he glared at Blaze.

Blaze's stomach twisted. "Domonos..." Blaze raised a placating hand, tilting it palm up.

Domonos' snarl died on his lips and he crumpled, a lost look on his face as his eyes drifted to the tea staining the wooden table.

"I'm sorry Blaze. I just—"

Blaze reached out and patted his arm. "We're in this together." He gripped his forearm, then pulled his hand back.

"Four days and we head to the lower realms. And we will train and cultivate. When we meet the sects or that clan again, we'll show them the true strength of a nation. Of Alva."

Domonos sat up straighter with iron in his bones and eyes. "We might falter, but Alva will not fall."

"Not as long as we draw breath. We may lose ten times, a hundred times, but we are Alvans. We will work together, and we will learn and grow stronger *together*. These sects are nothing but individuals fighting for benefits. We fight for one another."

Blaze held up his hand, grounding his elbow on the table.

"Together," Domonos agreed. His elbow rested on the stain on the table as the two men clasped hands.

Author's Note

Thank you for your support and taking the time to read **The Seventh Realm.**

The Ten Realms will continue in **The Eighth Realm**

As a self-published author I live for reviews! If you've enjoyed The Seventh Realm, please leave a **review**!

Do you want to join a community of fans that love talking about Michael's books?

We've created this Facebook group for you to discuss the books, hear from Michael, participate in contests and enjoy the worlds that Michael has created. You can join using the QR code below.

Thank you for your continued support. You can check out my other books, what I'm working on, and upcoming releases with the QR code below.

Don't forget to leave a review if you enjoyed the book.

Thanks again for reading ☺